They had asked her

who were the ler players of the game Zan? What was the significance of the Game? Were the players free of other obligations, save self-support?

She had felt chill dread at these questions, and hoped that her projected innocence had convinced them. Ah, indeed there was a rich area in herself for them to mine. They were closer to it than they realized; and not to solving petty vandalisms either. It was partially fortune that they did not press her there. But it disturbed her.

The other players needed to know this line of inquiry, the Shadow needed to know . . . and there was no way for her to tell anyone. For once set in motion, the forerunners would not ever come to a complete problem halt until they had followed every line out. Yes, they were great completers, but after all that was the true meaning of intelligence: following through.

She was ler, but she had no contempt for humans. To the contrary.

THE
GAMEPLAYERS
OF ZAN

M. A. Foster

DAW BOOKS, INC.
DONALD A. WOLLHEIM, PUBLISHER

1301 Avenue of the Americas
New York, N. Y. 10019

"God hath given you the stars to be your guides
in the dark both by land and sea."
—Mohammed, the Koran, Sura 6.

"He whose roof is heaven and over whom the
stars continually rise and set in one and the same
course makes the beginnings of his affairs and
his knowledge of time depend upon them."
—Al-Biruni

FIRST PRINTING, APRIL 1977

1 2 3 4 5 6 7 8 9

PRINTED IN U.S.A.

THE
GAMEPLAYERS
OF ZAN

BOOK ONE

Instar Cellae Sylvestris

ONE

NOVEMBER 1, 2550

> *Processes have uses; it is also important to re-*
> *alize that fascination with a process can grow,*
> *there being no automatic check against this, un-*
> *til the bemusement obscures the intended results*
> *of the original procedure. This is the easiest*
> *trait of all to observe in others and the hardest*
> *to see and act upon in ourselves. We shall speak*
> *of obsessions with results upon another day.*
> —*The Game Texts*

One always makes an identification of self in terms of a matrix of otherness, never saying simply "there am I," but always with the implicit definition "there am I in relation to all others I can know." And so now alone as she could not imagine anyone ever being, there was only herself. She could no longer measure who she was; only refer to a what-she-had-been, which she suspected either was no longer valid, or else was now based on distorted memories. There was herself, the memory, the whole of her life and all the things she had seen and done. There was also imagination, projections of fantasies of hopes and fears, the projections of her mind into all the places and circumstances she could never be in actuality. She balanced delicately between that which was and that which might have been. The impossible now. There was nothing else.

The present is never still, but a moving line between two points; in moving there is direction, source, destination. But with all references removed, by which one can measure motion, there was no longer any sense at all of the bridge of motion in time connecting the past with the future. They existed, of course: her memory and imagination reassured her of that; it was that she could no longer imagine quite how she related to those quantities. She was adrift in her own mind.

She could review the circumstances easily enough; in fact, she had already done so a number of times, perhaps several hundred times, seeking an alternative, a flaw, a slip, some error she could at least feel guilty about, or blame on someone else. But it was all as impervious as armor plate, there was no chink anywhere in the fearsome blankness of existentials. She imagined she felt like someone who had stepped into an elevator at exactly the moment when all of its safety devices failed: accidents happen which are in fact not the fault of their victim. She had been caught near the scene of the mission for which she had been sent. For which she had volunteered. It now seemed in hindsight that her life had always been a series of closing doors, not opening ones, of narrowing passages and shrinking rooms. And this was the last door and the last room. There was no passage. It ended here, wherever *here* was.

Near the Museum of Ancient Technologies, yes. There was nothing that could link her to the apparent vandalism that had destroyed beyond repair two obscure instruments left behind from the age of petroleum exploitation. Left behind, like astrolabes left behind from a rude era of ships powered by the wind they caught in their sails; left behind as the waves left shells, relics of life, on the beach. Artifacts of a vanished art, for there was no oil worth exploring for anymore. Yet of all those who might have been there, nearby, only she had been *ler*, deep into human lands beyond the reservation, and she had not had, even for herself, a convincing explanation for what she had been doing there. It was natural that they connect her with the damaged instruments. Her only remaining defense had been to remain quiet and somewhat passive, giving them nothing, not a name, not a reason.

They had conveyed her to their headquarters; others, in their turn, had taken her farther, to a large urban area, to a building, to a room within the building. Everything seemed unmemorable, bland; there had been no way to memorize directions or landmarks. Everything was featureless, or nearly so, as much so as could be managed. Then came the interrogators. They had been insistent, but considerate and subtle, masters of their arts. They had been firm, not especially unpleasant, and above all persuasive. She had said nothing. Only repeated in her soft voice that they should notify the Shuren Braid—hostel-keepers by the main entry into the reservation, close under the Institute—that they had picked up a lost girl. They had agreed to do so immediately, and were very polite. She knew they hadn't. No one came for her.

There had been a lack of overt threats, and there had never been any mention of anything like torture. She had not been fooled. She was too wise in her own ways not to know that people who hold all the cards have all the strengths and none of the weaknesses, and that they do not need to rant, rave, shout, pace up and down making histrionic gestures, parading about to turn suddenly, shouting bombast and threats. Or interrupting the silences with harangues and hectoring. No. They had no need to intimidate: these are acts that characterize an interrogator who is more interested in fondling the power he holds than in digging out the information he is paid to get.

Her story had been transparently flimsy, but she had repeated it anyway. She had been lost, she said, after a little exploration, and had been trying to get back by dead reckoning. She had never been in the Museum. She was sure they saw through that, but she stayed with it, however skillfully they tried to steer her into other areas. She thought that it had been easy to resist the gentle but constant, tidelike pressure, compared with other experiences in which she could draw analogs. But under her own sense of self-confidence, she could see that her visitors were in fact extraordinarily skillful among their own kind, others of the humans, the forerunners. One untrained would have broken in hours under them, and all without a single raised angry voice, a single twinge of pain. She couldn't really determine exactly how long it had gone on. There had been frosted windows, but the light shining through them was gray and never changed; she never knew if she was seeing filtered light, or some artificial light. It grew dark through those windows regularly, and there had been conspicuous clocks in the room with her, but she suspected that in a subtle world the obvious was mutable. She knew the rates of things; that had been part of her skill, her training, and she could sense subtle fluctuations of rate. But they had allowed her to sleep when she had been tired, eat when she had been hungry, wash when she had felt dirty. She learned nothing from those experiences—the noise levels were precisely uniform whatever her position.

She maintained her silence and her evasion as long as she could. After all, there had been some other close calls, and always before she had been able to bluff her way out. But perhaps those had not been so skillful as these, who seemed to sense the presence of deeper secrets in her silences, a presence that teased them, kept them at it. So despite the easy manners, the almost-pleasant sessions, the easy, relaxed interrogations, they smelled a secret. They didn't know if it had anything to do with the original issue or not—they were not, she could see, not that perceptive. That had ceased to matter. . . . The girl has secrets and will not talk: dig them out and we'll see.

Their closeness to the truth terrified her, their knowledge of the basic relational needs of people, ler and human alike (after all, they were not all that different), shook her to her foundations, and their physical presence overpowered her. To her eyes, no matter how often she had seen them before, humans were harsh, angular, hairy creatures whose tempers were at best uncertain. She herself was almost to her full bodily growth, but they were all larger than her, taller, heavier. She imagined that the larger ones must weigh almost twostone. They were wild, primitive beings who, in her view, were not yet tamed, although the logical, factual part of her mind knew well enough that most of them thought of themselves as rather effete and overcivilized. And now she was in the very midst of them, completely in their power, separated from her own intricate and carefully structured environment. One step closer to the ancient and unforgiving wild, to the primal chaos, to the world, left long ago, of tooth and claw, sinew and strength.

Here, in the city, the tooth was covered and the claw was sheathed, but neither had been removed, nor had been the will that had animated them. So, in the end, they had finally tired of her and their little game, and politely, always politely, suggested that she take a little rest, that she refresh herself, in the box. The box! Everything they did in their world revolved around a box, as it was called in the slang of the day. The box was a simulator. A training device with a controlled environment. Some were crude and simple. Others were so fearfully complex they were fully capable of denying the evidence of one's senses. So did one have a job to learn? In the box! Bad habits and antisocial traits? In the box. Criminals? Eliminate them or put them in the box. And likewise with odd suspects who are obviously covering up something, who refuse for days to answer the most simple questions. In the box. Behavior changed by the classical methodology of the cult of behaviorism, orthodox as the dawn. They never questioned ends, and why should they when they had a means that worked so well and so consistently? In the box. They could transform by their simulator alchemy a misanthrope into a philanthropist, an artist into a salesman who won prizes, a satyr or nymphomaniac into a celibate philosopher, and an autistic child into a faith healer. Those who had never been able to cope were transformed into veritable paragons of efficiency. And for those who held to their silences, there was the remedy of total isolation.

They shot her from behind with a dart; that alone, in itself, filled her with a sense of evil: they used a weapon that left the hand! The dart contained a drug that paralyzed her but left her conscious. She felt a bee sting at the back of her neck. Then, nothing. She could neither move nor feel. This part of her memory was clear and bright. Then they had gently placed her onto a little wheeled cart and rolled her down a hall into some other room, a larger one, although she could see little of its details. Her eyes could see only in the direction they were pointed. She had trained peripheral vision, as did the others of her craft, but against the bland background even that could pick up little. She sensed, rather than saw, meters, dials, instruments, switchboards. The room possessed a different odor, one that suggested machinery, electricity, not people. Then they had undressed her and looked over her body, which, judging from their expressions, seemed to them to be underdeveloped sexually; smooth and subtle of contour, hairless save some almost-invisible fine down which was all over her, undeniably female. In the eyes of one she saw the distorted longings of the child molester, but the implied assault within their imaginations did not disturb her. She did not object to nudity per se, and as for their longings, she had given a bravado mental shrug: she had given away more than all of them could take.

And after that, after they had looked enough, they had carefully and tenderly placed her within some enclosure: from its smell she thought it was a machine, but with a human fear-scent veneered over it as well, a dark place that

disturbed her. She heard them refer to it as a sensory deprivation unit. She heard some more talk as they set the machine
up, and fitted her into its bowels, so that she could deduce
what the machine was. The unit was a life-support system that
maintained a constant temperature and controlled all the in-
puts and outputs of the body. And some extra things: it
caused total anesthesia of the sensory and motor systems, and
what functions it didn't control, it monitored. It could speed
or slow her heartbeat. It created and maintained a sensory environment of exactly and precisely zero.

Her universe now. Dark, odorless, weightless, sensationless.
She felt nothing, was a disembodied mind. If the absence of
discomfort could be said to be comfortable, then it was comfortable. There was no sensation whatsoever. She could
remember being placed in it, but afterward had come the
darkness and the silence. An unknowable span of time had
passed since then. Sometimes she thought that it had been
only minutes since then, or at best perhaps an hour or so.
Other times, she felt weary and thought of years, of growing
old, of reaching elderhood in the box, or else being prolonged
as an adolescent-phase infertile ler forever, as the monitoring
sensors either disregarded or suppressed the hormone chemistry of her reproductive system, which she knew to be different from the human. She suspected the machine thought she
had some disorder and was trying to cure her! But the time.
Minutes or years. She didn't know the difference anymore.
The reality of the now expanded to enormous distances, gulfs
she could not imagine.

So now she could not avoid the realization that in the end
it had not mattered how effective or ineffective her passive
defiance had been. She had been confident at first, although
she admitted to some fright and self-concern; yet she must
face the fact that, to this point, she was losing this one, and
that she was facing a path with only one way to go, no exit,
and no place in which to turn around.

At first, the box had been easy, almost pleasant. She
couldn't believe this was a threat: after all, all it did was allow one to be lazy and to daydream, which people wanted to
do anyway, but somehow never found the time. She had a
number of open-ended practices which were primarily cerebral in nature, and which served admirably here, in the box.
So at first she renewed her sense of defiance; it had served
her well before she had been caught, and so it would serve
her now. After her initial adjustments to the new environ-

ment had been made, she started out by spending her waking times playing the *Zan*, a game of large scope and interesting subtleties. At first she left all the virtuoso play to herself, her side, but later this seemed too easy, no matter how complex she made the play, so she began to elaborate and embroider the antagonist side as well, carrying both sides simultaneously. This had been some challenge, for she had played before primarily in the protagonist team role; in any event, it kept her occupied.

She also tried her hand at dramatization, making up or recalling tales she had heard before. This was more challenging, as the ler did not produce plays on the stage, but either read them or listened to a storyteller, the practice of which was considered one of the ler social graces. She admitted to a deficiency at the telling end, but she had always listened well, and now the habit initially served her well. They favored tragedy, borrowing freely from human sources and presenting them as they were, or else changing the names of all the characters to ler names and proceeding from there; they also made up dramas of their own according to a complicated set of storytelling rules, and these could occur in various cultural matrices. So it was that she made up and remembered, perfecting her powers of visualization. She recalled great dramas whose roots were openly acknowledged to be from the forerunners: *Trephetas and Casilda*, essentially a tale of lust thwarted by rigid social conventions. She liked that one, for it reminded her, at a certain remove, of a situation which applied somewhat to herself. She also recalled *Thurso*, with its violet-eyed female antagonist, which always made an audience of ler listeners gasp with horror; ler eyes were invariably lightly and subtly colored, definitive colors almost never being seen, such traits indicating a force of will which could not be borne without tragic consequence to all around the possessor. *Tamar Cauldwell* and *The Women of Point Sur* pleased her with their studied intricacies and soaring flights of emotion. There was a famous ler version of *Tamar*, changed somewhat in details, called *Tamvardir the Insibling*, which in some ways was an improvement over the original.

She moved from realistic, if highly emotional tragedies, to more fantastic dramas, *Ericord the Tyrant*, the scary *Siege of Kark*, and the wierdly beautiful *The King of Shent*. And then the pure ler dramas, some of which had been adapted from human legends and tales: *The Revenge of the Hifzer Vlandimlar*, *Hunsimber the Beast*, *Schaf Meth Vor*, better known perhaps as *Science and Revolution*, and *Damvidhlan, Baeth-shevban, and Hurthayyan*, the last of which she found herself recoiling from somewhat, as she tended now to identify herself with the victim Hurthayyan.

Being ler, she possessed almost total recall; therefore she could also replay at her leisure pleasurable experiences, moments of beauty or sweetness in her past life. She could also project daydreams, imagined and desired scenes about herself, in the future or the past. With the memory, she could remember far back, virtually to infancy, but back of that was a feared region in which the smoothly cycling lines of memory became tangled and confused, and further back knotted, and further, blurred. The infant did not remember the womb because it had not been awake. Now, here, in this dark place—this box, this sensory deprivation unit—the lines of time had once more become confused and blurred, and she sensed that another womb had been imposed upon her. The lines were uncertain. She slept. She dreamed.

Like the rest of the lermen, her memory had always been a resource to her, a close friend, a reference. She knew that the farther up the evolutionary ladder a creature had climbed, the more it projected itself into the awareness of time. People, the natural humans and the forced ler alike, had been a giant step forward in this dimension. Yet now and here in the unmeasurable and unknowable time of the box, her memory, from overuse, had come to resemble some ancient recording—full of the noises of boredom and weariness. Scratchy and worn. The fidelity of reproduction was slipping and random noise was gradually swamping coherences. Information theory and the brain. Memory in living creatures was not a static thing, fixed in specific sites, like some mechanical computer, but a dynamic, living, moving quantity, a flying body of abstraction moving through the billions of cells and synapses exactly as a bird in the medium of air, dependent on the motion to define it in its function. Holistic.

But it was also like a recording in this way as well: in replaying the good parts so often, she had allowed herself the habit of skipping to the best scenes. This was fine, but after so much use, the scenes, extracted more or less from the matrix of reference which had made them meaningful, had become progressively more shallow and, in the end, less good. Some of them had become almost tiresome. She would find herself saying as she reviewed them, "Yes, and so what?"

As for the daydreams, the imaginings, the fantasies, she

had found that it had become steadily more dangerous to allow herself to do this. *Berlethon*, she called them in her own language, paradreams. Her dreams and paradreams were becoming stronger and steadily more clear, all the while her realities were growing weaker. As her memories of the real which had been were slowly sinking into a morass, a quagmire of noise, the projections were becoming more clear and even reasonable.

At first the projected paradreams had been like dreams; the individual scenes had been highly detailed, but the scenes had permutated one into another with disregard for the laws of causality and consequence. That, after all, was what distinguished them from realities. Now, however, in the box, it was the memories of the real which had become the anticausal phantoms with the illogical shifts, while the projections had become the logical ones, vibrant and electric. Reality had become faded and meaningless. In the normal environment, dreams were the mind's algorithm for sorting and placing experiences in an orderly and accessible manner in the flying holistic patterns of memory. All well and good; but there was no provision made in the program of a living brain for a zero environment. So the process of filing and sorting went on unimpeded, using that which had already been placed as an arbitrary input, feeding on images which had already been sorted and placed, resorting and refiling. At each transfer the images lost both fidelity and coherence. At every transfer noise gained on coherent content.

From the first she had encouraged visions which had been erotic in content; in her own cultural reference as it applied to her own phase, adolescence, such activities, their recollections, and their projections, were neither considered reprehensible nor undesirable, but rather encouraged by all, part of growing up. Affairs, trysts, meetings, rendezvous of variable duration, and the gatherings, where participation was not limited to a single pair, were all part of an elaborate process that instructed one in care for one's fellow creatures, intimacy, consideration. Knowledge came later; it was important to learn to relate with others and to learn to tolerate others, in view of the conditions which would come with parent phase.

So she had naturally thought of these adventures; they were pleasurable in a direct bodily manner and helped greatly to pass the time. But now, of course, they had become the worst offenders against the rule of reality. They ran away with her. In these, so great had become the confusion that she had been forced to invent an elaborate mental procedure to segregate the real and the unreal, a complication that added further waves of its own, further elaborations. Just as there was no ultimate end to the definition of meaning, and no final fraction of a transcendental number, so there was no real limit to the process of elaboration. None whatsoever. And so now she was in very deep water, being carried away from the shore by the undertow at an alarming and increasing rate. Had there ever been a shore? Had there ever been such a thing as a shore? The very projections that in the beginning of her dark journey had helped save her mind, where a lesser one would have broken, were now the very elements contaminating it.

The forerunners who had remanded her to this place and into the box knew little or nothing. They certainly did not know who she was, or else she suspected they would not have been so polite. They would not then have waited for the box to work its terrible magic on her. No, more direct methods would have been used. But their questions had reassured her of that; that they knew nothing. They did not know the right questions to ask. But they were suspicious, and of more than just the incident of the Museum. Somewhere there were other things that bothered them; there had been noises in the night, and they knew not the source, nor why. Or had it been just the settling of the house, the wind in the trees, a natural event? Obviously she had some connection with the vandalism in the Museum; at the least, she appeared to be the only suspect they had. And why those particular devices? But those questions did not bother her; she expected them. At another point, however, they had pursued other topics. For example, they had asked, quite casually, who were the ler players of the game *Zan*? What was the significance of the Game? Were the players free of other obligations, save self-support? Apparently they had several lines of inquiry going, and since she had been close to hand, they had tried a few at her. She had felt chill dread at these questions, and hoped that her projected ignorance had convinced them. Ah, indeed there was a rich area in herself for them to mine. They were closer ot it than they realized; and not to solving little vandalisms, either. It was partially fortune that they did not press her there. But it disturbed her, even now. The other players needed to know this line of inquiry, the Shadow needed to know ... and there was no way for her to tell anyone. For once set in motion, the forerunners would not ever come to a complete problem halt until they had followed every line out. Yes, they were great completers, but after all that was the true meaning of intelligence: following through. She was ler, but she had no contempt for humans. To the contrary.

Her mind wandered. After a fashion, they had been kind enough with her. They did not believe they were causing her particular harm by placing her in this sensory deprivation unit. Almost casually, yet they had no idea of the effects of it on her. Perhaps among their own kind they were pleasant enough persons. At home, or in some warm tavern, with friends, or lovers. She had heard that they did not have lovers, at least openly. And did they have taverns? She now realized that for all her previous trips outside she knew in actuality very little about how they lived, what their dreams were.

So as the interrogation had continued, she had begun to see into the basic surface smoothness of her interrogators, just as a glassy surface of water meant deeper channels; there were things they wanted to know, they had her, and she knew. Indeed did she know. And that, no matter what the cost, not a word of it could be told. The worth of it was simply too high: it was easily worth *perzhan**, one hundred and ninety-six, of her lives. It really was not even worth arguing about, even with herself, even in the box. However it went. She thought, with a certain irony, that the people who talked the most about sacrifice were always the ones who knew they would never have to make that decision. She did not particularly worry about pain, for she knew from the box that they had more sophisticated methodology at their disposal, once they had an idea who she was. That was more important than the business at the Museum. And once put into use, she was sure that these methods would leave more permanent scars on her, figuratively, than flesh would hold: they would be inside. So she kept the silence.

At times like this, when she had to reaffirm basic quantities to herself, she allowed herself the luxury of recalling the secret, as she had come to call it. It was her only remaining source of comfort, but she only allowed herself to recall it in full when her mind felt clear, for she had no way of knowing if she was talking or not. She took great comfort in seeing how successful it would be, now that it was almost complete, how much it meant for all the people. Just a few more years.

---

* One times fourteen to the second power. Ler counted with a fourteen-base number system.

She saw the part she had played in it, more minor than it should have been, but who after all could have foreseen the exact circumstances, ridiculous as they were, and who could argue intelligently against the Great Rule, even though somewhat disadvantaged by it? But what of that? She had used the traditions herself back against the problem, and aided by a rare stroke of good fortune, had come close to regaining her place, which should have been hers by right, unquestioned. She had almost made it back ... and now, in the box in an alien city, it pained her to know, as she had known all along, that she was not to make the contribution she knew she was capable of. They had planned things to a nicety, the elders who had guided it from the Beginning, but reality had slipped them a cruel twist. But they could not have foreseen this situation, with its ironies of the best and the worst misplaced. She thought bravely, *But I have kept the faith where no one else was ever tried.* Of course, it wasn't consolation. She recalled the drama *Damvidhlan, Baethshevban, and Hurthayyan** again. Yes, she was sure of it; the plight and fate of Hurthayyan had indeed analogously applied to her, to include a match for the identity of *Hofklandor* Damvidhlan. But who or what did Baethshevban equate with? She could not be entirely certain, for it did not match a person, but rather a diffuse something, an emotion from many directed to one. And coveted, now seized. *Zakhvathelosi.*

She could easily recall the image in her memory of the human interrogator, and his superior. The interrogator had been as bland and featureless as his surroundings, distinctly unremarkable, but the superior had been another matter; he had been tall and rather bony, and his face was angular enough to deserve the term "hatchet-faced" without further explanation. His ears protruded after the fashion of jug handles and his jaw was long and equine. His hair was sandy-colored with reddish overtones, cut brushy short and springing out in odd little tufts at unexpected places. In her eyes, more accustomed to the smoother and softer lines of the ler face (which correspondingly appeared childish in the human frame of reference), he had been primitive, raw, rough-cut, homely, in

---

* The drama referred to was a ler adaptation of the tale of *David and Bathsheba*, with the names changed to ler names. Hurthayyan was Uriah the Hittite. She could from this identification find the equal of David/Damvidhlan, but in her case, Bathsheba was not a person but rather a sense of regard or admiration.

fact, as an oak post. But she remembered him with dread and fear, homely as he had been, for she knew that when they came back for her, after they judged she had had enough time in the box, he'd come with them and she'd talk to him in the mode of intimacy, just to have contact with someone, some stimulus. Citizen Eykor, they had called him. She would start talking and would not be able to stop. Something would slip in her relief and the tale would start, and it would never end. She suspected she could not survive the box; she *knew* she couldn't keep the silence if they took her out and started questioning her again. A spasm of fear passed through her, gripping her momentarily; perhaps she would love him, just for talking to her after the box. Yes, that was possible. He would reassure her, probably reaching to touch her shoulder, not realizing the overtly sexual connotations of the gesture in her reference . . . and this could not be, must not be; it must not even be allowed to approach the potential to be. There was nothing she could share with Citizen Eykor, and less she could allow herself to say to him.

They must not know, not one word of it, she thought. The wave had felt the first intimations of the bottom underfoot and was beginning to steepen, after a fetch of miles and years. Centuries, really, so long had it been in motion. Yes. Let it happen in its time. Then it won't matter what they know; in fact, we could even drop them off a copy of the Histories; let them try to duplicate it and follow them into the night. Then it won't matter. But now? It would neither be fiting nor sufficient for her to return, broken, to the Mountain of Madness, the Holy Place, and say, to the Shadow, "I held out as long as I could, but I broke in the end. Yes, I spoke of it, and they know. They will be coming tomorrow or the next day, they will take it for themselves, and for us it will be gone forever." *And with our low birth rate and unstable genes we will be the wards of the forerunners forever, tied to old Earth with them. Intolerable.*

She stopped that line of thought, for it led to hard choices. Choices whose solutions were all too obvious. She returned once more to the present. The zero noplace nowhen, a universe in which she was the sole inhabitant. She and her memory. She was quite nude, but she could no longer perceive any sensation whatsoever; what little the box had left her had quickly disappeared, dropped as recurring items of no consequence by her own mind, just as one ceased to hear a familiar clock, and began to wonder if it still ran. Hard to catch even in normal circumstances, in the box these reports from oneself simply vanished, leaving no ripples to mark the spot where they had gone under. She returned to her nudity, tried to sense it in some way. She couldn't. There was no body there! She thought in anger, *I may not be able to feel it now, but I can remember it. You can't take that away from me. It's my body and it's my mind, you* hifzer dranloons*! She returned. Nude, yes, it was pleasant to be clothesless, with someone exciting ... something more than just pleasant, a thrill. With a body-friend, a lover. Much better a deeplover. As an adolescent ler, she did not perceive a rigid line of distinction between friends and lovers. Sex with friends of the opposite sex was just part of the relationship. However, she did differentiate between sex and affection. They might complement one another, or reinforce one another, in a relationship, but in the matter of degrees of each they operated independent of one another. Why not? One expressed one quantity, and the other something entirely different. Where a specific person was involved, one perceived degrees of intimacy, of both personal functions, elaborated by certain cultural reinforcements—for example, as the use of parts of one's name with persons with whom one had such a relationship. The definitions were both complex and dynamic, possessing many variables simultaneously, and so one spent much of one's adolescence learning the definitions. Many grew restive and questioned the elaborate distinctions, the subtlety, the hedging. But she knew very well what the use of it portended. Relationships among elders were highly structured, and so after the Braid years one remembered the definitions of one's youth, and used an analog of them to enter the elder custom.

It was as a spectrum of many colors, each shading into the next, and no line anywhere which could be said to cause a definite distinction. It was, in fact, a smooth continuum which went from childish games in the woods to couples who lived together in emotional entanglements so interpenetrating that they lay somewhere along the very borders of sanity. *I have been there. Having been to the place, with him, where the real and the unreal are segregated. I have no respect for those who imagine that the distinction is a casual one.* Him. Was all; she had long since ceased to think of him-her-last as a name. One simply disregarded it. There had been two presences in the world. Herself and him. She felt a sudden

---

* Literally, "illegitimate trash"; *loonh* is an intensifier.

constriction somewhere undefinable in her chest, gone before she could be sure if she had felt it at all. Whisked away by the box. She thought she could detect a trace of moisture in her eyes, open in the darkness. But the sensations were gone. Had they ever been?

Nude. Yes, that. She returned to the memory, a composite of many experiences, from which she could select the specific image she wanted. The sharp thrill of slipping out of her light summer *pleth**, pulling it over her head, when their relationship had been new, turning to him smiling. Or awaking softly in the night, knowing warm breath along her neck, feeling warmth along her flank, weight . . . a wisp of memory drifted by; they had gone together down to a place they had made deep in the forests of the northeast reservation, a place where he had . . . what? It had slipped away, not forgotten, but mislaid, tangled in a thousand phantom alternatives, real and unreal, thrown up by her mind, running free. She made an effort of will: yes, down in the woods, far to the northeast, in a part of the reservation where hardly anyone made their home. This memory was a recent one, the summer just past, early in the season; the sensations came back, now vividly, now vague and evanescent, threatening to vanish in the next instant. She held on to them by a great effort of will. The rich odors of the damp forest earth, vines, and green leaves, the warm air heavy with the scent of flowers; the sunlight played in the shadows of the new foliage, the wind was in the crowns of the trees, and, listening carefully, one could hear the sound of running water. Together they had slipped their light summer pleths off over their heads, feeling the sudden rush of body feeling at the touch of cooler air, and the quick flash of goose-pimples which had disappeared as fast as it had come. He had looked deeply at her body, and she at his; he was thin, pale, and smooth, worked all over with a delicate tracery of muscle and sinew. They had laughed, and she had made him chase her running through the trees and vines and tangles, the flower scent strong in the air. The memory steadied, held firm, ran true.

There was a small treehouse, with a sun-warmed platform all around it, and when they had both climbed the rope ladder leading up to the platform, she had let him catch her and wrestle her to the warm wood; touching and kissing each

* An "overshirt." This was an ankle-length garment superficially resembling a long shirt, but whose neck opening never extended down past the navel. A garment of general use.

other lightly, childishly, like making leafprints in the fall.
And then a sudden, hard embrace, and she had relaxed back
on the rough wood, melting, heart pounding ... was it
pounding now?

She couldn't be sure, feeling the memory slip a little. Had
the body-now responded to the memory? Had replaying it
caused even a small sympathetic echo? Had indeed her heartbeat just now sped up, before the box could respond and
damp it down again? She lost the image momentarily. Had it
ever really happened? She went back, straining, and grasped
the thread at the point she had left off, and remembered; just
like it was happening now, she felt the wild surge of runaway
loosed emotions, the whispers of skin on skin, the wet shoul-
der-kisses, the sudden warmths and hot flashes, little
peaks of anticipation and the first touch *there;* then an awkward moment, followed by oneness. In the now she felt herself moving with the memory, flowing, an energy building
within her greater than the box, and then she lost it, the sequence slipped away from her and swirled away quickly in
the currents of her mind, fading into other erotic images, of
lovers she had had, and paradreams of lovers she would like
to have had. She did not know if these latter were real or
imaginary. Now they were rock-hard and clear, now insub-
stantial and changeable as smoke, fading into other
lineaments. Other images intruded as well; him again, afterward. She had let her mind go blank and had been idly following the motion of a leaf above, seen over his shoulder,
and marveling at how the eye could follow and track such
random motion, a leaf high in the sunlight, the strong light
making it translucent and showing the pattern of veins inside.

It whipped away, pushed and pulled by the press of other
images, real and unreal. Yes, that one: once in an orchard, a
walled garden, the Krudhen's. There had been a rough wall,
stone, unmortared, higher than their heads, and they had, after the invitations of each other's eyes, casually stepped
around into the garden, not even bothering to remove their
overshirts, but pulling them up about their waists and joining
their bodies while leaning against the rough, bumpy surface
of the wall. Some people had passed meanwhile along the
path outside the wall, but they knew that the passersby did
not care, even if they had noticed anything. It was doubtful
they did, for they had been subtle and quiet, making a game
of it. That had not been him, but another, earlier, when she
had been younger, and more reckless. ... That one vanished,

replaced by another: this boy dark-haired and dark-skinned as herself. They had been swimming in the river, the muddy Hvarrif, the rich summer water leaving a sweet summer scent on their skins as they sat on the banks in the sun and air-dried. He had been so shy and tentative, younger than herself, touching her thigh accidentally, brushing against her. Sudden cool touch of skin, warmth beneath; the moment became expectant, tense, the exterior details of the instant overwhelming in their clarity. Everything registered, the sun, the still air, the heat, the clangor of the July-flies in the trees, and she had reached for the younger boy, smiling. . . .

And it vanished, leaving behind the bitter little backlash that revealed its true nature, that particular image; it had been a paradream, a projection, a hope, a fantasy, not real. She didn't know if she had imagined it earlier, or had made it up in the box. It didn't matter. It wasn't real. She savored the memory of an unreal memory and smiled mentally to herself; knowing herself as well as she did, she knew why the last one had not been real, although the one by the wall in the orchard had been. She had never been so aloof and teasing, nor had her body-friends and lovers been so innocent or shy. That was a refinement she had added herself, internally, to satisfy some deeper fantasy. Unreal, unreal. She experienced a weird emotion composed of angry chagrin and wistful sadness. There would be no more embraces by the orchard wall, no more treehouses, even no more dreams of quiet seductions along the Hvarrif banks.

That last incident broke the chain of emotional and erotic memories. She felt as if she had been on tiptoe, straining. She tried to flex her leg. No good. She couldn't feel it. With no distraction, she began to drift back from the sense of sexual anticipation she had been on, aimless, frustrated. Regretfully. She had greatly enjoyed the few moments she had had in her life, particularly the last ten years, of the adolescent phase. *And there would have been ten more of them, but for this,* she caught herself thinking. There had been fewer such events for her than for most ler girls, for during all the time, she had been busy at many other things, too serious, too bound up in the Great Work. *Now,* she thought. *Now it is time to make that decision. Time to commit oneself, time to end hesitating, time to cease waiting for a rescue that will never come because they will never know where I am. I'm getting lost in my own memory; it is a home no longer, but a labyrinth with neither way out nor way in.*

She approached the point she had been dreading; and now she was at it. Earlier, she had imagined what it would be like when she faced it: a mental image of a major forking in the path, a most remarkable intersection, a singular location at which choice, with all its terrors, was exercised. Perhaps symbolically, within this image, there would also be emblems of arresting significance: flashing lights, great illuminated signboards. Something resembling the forerunner motorways. But now that she was actually at the place, she saw with her imagination that the reality was nothing like that at all; her mind provided a symbolic image which fit better: not an intersection at all. The image was of a broad smooth road on level ground in undifferentiated country. There was not a landmark, not a reference, not even a post along the side of the road to mark the point. She was, she realized with a wistful sense of resignation, already past it and the choice had been made long ago. *The solution was obvious.* And in the middle distances, the road and the surrounding country alike ended, not with a change of conditions, but in an undefined yet total foggy nothingness. She had been on this path a long time; her life led here.

I will not speak of it, I will not talk with them, I will not even wait for them to come for me again. I am . . . She groped frantically, trying to find the name she had mislaid, burying it under tons of hopelessly tangled data, real and unreal. There were hundreds of names, and she couldn't decide which was hers; an impossible situation. Yes, apples. Something about apples. And this almost-recognition set off another train of memories and associations: apples. She could feel vividly the hard firm flesh of an apple, crisp, cool; biting the fruit, the juice had been sweet and acid on her lips. An autumn sunset, smoky orange somewhere, somewhen . . . she had been the chief player, the Center, and her team had won. And her opponent. The opponent had no identity, it was blanked into a dark shadow, a fog, a presence whose outlines gave no clue to its identity, but at the same time, she knew she could rip the curtain aside and see her antagonist in fell open brightness; she could, but she recoiled from it, for she knew her opponent, in truth, better than she knew any other person, ler or forerunner, on Earth. Here an odd chuckling thought intruded, flashing by almost before she could catch it: *On Earth or off it. Why was that significant?* But before she could pursue it further, her wildly precessing mind threw out another image: *And there was metal, wood, artifice, there was a sense of a construct all around her, a sense of being-in-side, a great, powerful machine, a device, a Daimon, perhaps. Yet neither machine nor Daimon, but something greater and different than either, something whose operation closely paralleled life rather than mechanics or electronics.* Vanished, replaced: And once she had made bread at home with her insibling, and the warm air had been filled with the scent of dough and yeast. Another: Her first sexual experience, the first clumsy, awkward embraces (her partner had been as ignorant as she); they had felt like younger children trying to assemble some intricate toy, neither knowing where to begin nor imagining the results, but faithfully believing that if they could somehow accomplish it, they were sure to be astounded and amazed. Strange, vivid, sharply etched in her mind. And indeed they had been. *We had breathed so hard, so hotly upon each other's shoulders.* A sensation like climbing a steepening hill, ever harder, then over the top by surprise and a swift ballistic ride down, spinning, slowing. The odd, salty taste of another's mouth, the oily-sharp scent of sun-warmed skin.

Stop! She shouted into nothing, the furry all-embracing darkness that surrounded her. She could almost fleetingly feel her lips trying to verbalize the word in her own speech: *muduraile!* But the half-sensation was gone instantly, as in a nightmare when one tries to call for help, or to cry out to break the slow-motion spell, and nothing came out but incoherent, clotted throaty sounds. Croaks and gurgles. She returned to the dark. *Very well, then.* She formed letters of fire in the dark, sending them forth, changing their colors as they flew away into the night. The letters faded, leaving green afterimages which pervolved into an iridescent violet. She made the triple negative: *Dheni, dheno, dhena.* No, more no, most no. Her mind slowly responded to her Herculean efforts to bring it under control, giving in, tossing out one last image weakly: Metal, a machine, immense shifting fields of power. Metal, plastic, cloth, leather, wood. She almost had it, she could operate it and feel the control and the mastery, it had almost been hers, so close . . . and the Game. And the image was gone.

She thought clearly. She had always had, all along, one escape. But it was a drastic, irrevocable one. With total recall, the ler mind had by compensation also gained the ability to trueforget, erase data, remove it. The one balanced the other. It was something rather more than forgetting in the old sense, as the forerunners referred to it. That, in truth, was merely mislaying data. But autoforgetting was erasure. It was easy and simple to start the process—one knew instinctively how to do that, like knowing how to imagine: it was so easy and natural that one had to teach the growing child to attend to reality. But that referred only to starting the process of autoforgetting. Stopping it was only for the experienced and the learned, enormously difficult. One could master that only after one had reached deep into elder phase, the end of one's third span*. Elders, she had heard, could do partials, forget certain sections of their memories, condense and resymbolize, making room for more raw experience . . . but she was not an elder; she was *didhosi*, adolescent, she had just celebrated her twentieth birthday this past summer. And so for her it could be only everything or nothing. She had heard that it was easy, fearless, painless. Like going to sleep. That one simply picked some point in any valid memory and undid the image, like picking a thread out of a weave: it then unraveled.

And then the ego, the persona, would be gone, vanished, as if it had never been, save for the existential traces left behind on the lives of others, on the enduring physical pieces of the world. Yes, the ego would be gone, but the body would live on, protected by its autonomic responses. The protection of secrets had not been the intent of autoforgetting, but it was of a fact one of its by-products. An ultimate protection. And afterward, her human interrogators would return and discover that all they had was an infant in a twenty-year-old's body. Hopefully, not knowing what to do with such a one, they would then return her to the people, where she would be cared for properly, washed, fed, and carefully raised to a functional persona again in the ten years remaining before she would become fertile, adult. So by then she would be conscious again, functional, a person able to breed, to be woven, to carry on the next generation as was the obligation of everyone. She felt a small pleasure in the midst of fear. And in the clear knowledge of what she had to do, there was also a confusion. She thought hard, bearing down on it. *And I will come again in this body, this sweet flesh which has given me and others so much pleasure. . . . I? No, not I, I know*

---

* Span is a period of twenty-four years. Spans (age, pure time) and phases (body development) were not synchronized, but their interplay determined key events in one's life. Adolescents 24–30 were considered "provisional addlts," even though yet adolescent in body, infertile.

*that. It will not be me that inhabits this skin. No, another,
one who does not exist now and who will not be borne of
Tlanh and Srith. She will have another name. Not mine.
I take my name with me into whatever place forgetties go.
Yes, another. She will be childish and absentminded, but she
will function; knowing what she is, the others will love her
and help her. By the time the children weave, she will be
virtually complete.*

She laughed to herself in her mind, wryly, suddenly seeing
it clearly, without apprehension. *Me, a forgetty. One who has
autoforgotten:* Lel Ankrenamosi. She had thought in the past
of autoforgetting with dread and fear, feeling something un-
clean and wretched about being a forgetty. But there was
something worse, a whole universe of somethings-worse. She
balanced her distaste of the condition against what in her
weakness she could reveal and therefore cause. Hobson's
choice it might have been, but it was still clear: *I will be true
to my oaths. Now!*

Without hesitation, she reached deep in her mind, to the
very keystone of her being, her *Klanh* role, the pivot point of
all that she knew, had lived. She strained, reaching, seeking
the unraveling-place deep within the complex of mnemonic
tangles, found it, a knot, a nexus, pulled, felt it loosen, and
unhooked it. There was a sharp, piercing pain, an acute spike
of intense energy, unbearable, over before it had really began. She instantly forgot that it had hurt. Stunned and
now not knowing why, she reached again for the particular
memory, which had been the time of her initiation. Initiation
into what? She couldn't remember. It was gone. There were
only odd little pieces left, and they were fading. At the center
of her mind there was an expanding blank void of un-
knowledge; almost like what they called an image-reversed
Game, in which one played absences, not presences. A void,
expanding. Already she had to ask, most curiously, *What
Game? What had been the Game?* It had been important to
her, once. A puzzle, and something crucial was missing, the
piece which could explain this odd lapse of memory. What
was it? She stopped trying to remember and began to work
on logic, working from the outside, filling in the center, and
thus to recapture what it should have been. She could do it,
but she found that as she did, the eradication process seemed
to work faster than she could fill it back in; it was eroding
her memory faster than she could fill it in at maximum effort.
Useless to fight it; hopeless. Her awareness had been like a

sphere, filled from the center, always expanding outward into
the emptiness of ignorance and not-knowing, ordering. But
she sensed now that she was different from everyone else in
the world: she had an emptiness inside the sphere as well.
And the void inside was growing, forcing her awareness first
into a hollow ball, then a toroidal shape. *There's no stopping
it now*, she thought; *I know what is doing this, but I no longer know how to start it*. After a moment, she added, wryly,
And I damn sure can't stop it.

She had no knowledge concerning how long the process
would require to erase her mind. Nobody knew. Or if they
did, they did not speak. Forgetties did not remember that
they had forgotten. She felt tense, internally, and did not
know why. Now she relaxed, letting the process play over
awareness, like summer sunlight over one's bare body, something from long ago. *Now I will remember everything I can;
all the sweet moments of my life*. She scanned quickly
through what remained of her memories, noting what was
there, the good and the bad, the pleasant and the unpleasant.
There was much of both; she had had her moments, but she
had also known bitter disappointments, cruel reverses which
had not been her fault, but existential, circumstantial. But not
accident. She settled for a sample: Name fourteen* of the
most wonderful things that had happened to you. That was
easy. Then, one at a time, she began to relive each of them
through the magic of total recall, reseeing, reknowing, redis-
covering. Under them, though, she sensed the presence of
something which had not been there before: a growing void
of darkness, part of her, yet not part of her either. She could
not remember now why this curious condition existed. She
would have to speak to someone about it.

Mornings were nicer. She had always loved the morning-
time, and of them all, she would always be the first of the
children to wake up, seeing the firstlight turning the translucent panes of the windows of the *yos* deep violet. She would
untangle herself from the others, for in cooler weather they
all slept in a pile for warmth, and would then climb down
out of the children's compartment, into the hearthroom.
There had been four of them. Two boys, two girls. An ideal
ler Braidschildren. But somehow something was wrong, there;
she could no longer recall why. Now the hearthroom would
be dim and dark, the hearthfire ashes dead or almost so. In

---

* This would have the same significance as ten to a decimal user.

her nightshift she would tiptoe barefooted through the *yos*, their home, and pass through the double entryway, pushing the doorflaps aside as she went. She would step gingerly out on the landing. The air would be cool, even in summer, and would bite at her skin through the thin nightshift, the skin beneath still sleep-warm and child-fragrant. This memory: it was winter and there was frost on the ground. Crystals of frost-heave at the bare patch by the creek. The creek by the house muttered quietly to itself, its sounds clean, precise, and clipped. The speech-of-winter. It always sounded like that in winter. In summertime its voice was rounder, looser, more flowing. She imagined that it spoke a language. No, someone had told her that. Recently. Who had it been? But the creek spoke: a running commentary on the nature of things, ground-water state, humus, moles, earthworms, new-fallen leaves of the season releasing their nutrient material to add to the rich forest soil. A sense of almost-freezing. The things water knew. She looked up. Farther down the creek she could make out the dim shape of the neighboring *yos* through the winter-bare brush, briars, and vine-tangles. In summer, it would have been completely hidden. And farther on, visible through a gap in the trees, was the lake, still and cold and deep blue in this early light.

She scanned again, sensing that she was losing ground more quickly than she had imagined she would. *No time for fourteen. Have time for one more replay. So let it be with him. That one will I hold, even to the end. Let it be last, and then nothingness. Even if now it is just a figment of my memory, never to be again.* Suddenly, the phantoms were gone.

The process continued inexorably, returning her mind to its entropic ground state, but as it moved, it caused ripples of pseudoknowledge to form in the central void, a logiclike action that seemed to her to be sudden flashes of insight. These momentary new forms were diverse as their origins: some were obviously invalid, others incomprehensible and alien. And some had the ring of truth. She did not know how she knew this. These last she tried to hold on to. One in particular, a towering edifice, permutating wildly. For an instant, she saw: and relief flooded through her, for she had seen the future. No fantasy, no paradream, no pseudoknowledge. Real. And that future was both true and good: There would be sorrows, caused by the very thing she had just done but not her fault, her blame, but another's. And they would succeed in the Great Work. It would be. She saw and was happy, but she did not understand, nor did she know why the thought had pleased her. Then it was gone. And also gone was the memory that something had pleased her.

She fixed on his image. Him. Her deepest. Cool and distant at first, there had been something about him which she had not liked . . . or disapproved of. She couldn't remember. It had soon ceased to matter. And then she had discovered that he could do something she did, something . . . that was gone too. No matter. The memory of him as he had been was clear and uncluttered. If anything, the clarity of the image had been increased by the removal of the background in which they had met, and the growth of the emotional tangle which had sprung up between them, and soon tied them together. She could see him clearly: slender, wiry, almost delicate; but strong and quick. Precise movements, no wasted motions or mannerisms. A little younger than herself, but by less than a year. His hair, cut in the relaxed bowl cut common to all adolescents, was much lighter in color than hers. In a distant way, he reminded her of . . . whom? A younger child, related to her, but she couldn't remember whom. Thin, precise facial lines; tense, but not overbearing. No, not that. He had been the most tender of creatures. She knew.

She sank deeper into the memory, feeling in it a wholesome refuge from a growing dark emptiness outside it. Everything beyond this memory seemed dim, obscure, fading. That was her spatial orientation. In time, it was no better: it began with a blank and ended with one. Now she could not remember anything except the last time they had been together.

They had gone down eastward into the deep woods, in the autumn, recently. To their own secret place they had built, a treehouse. It had grown too intense between them, and they did not want others (or were afraid of them?). It had been their last time, just before she had somehow arrived in this nonplace. They had been lovers, more than that, they had touched and kissed each other's bodies, clasped one another closely with their limbs. She thought she felt a pain in her heart, wetness in her eyes. Were they real? Something oppressive was preventing her from feeling what she knew she must feel. *All gone soon. Was real? Will hold this until it is all gone. So good then. Did it in a beam of sunlight, we did. Thought my heart would burst.* She fell utterly into the memory, letting it take her, merging with the recent past, dimly sensing that somewhere she possessed a now-body which was at last beginning to respond to the then-body, as the difference between the two evaporated to her consciousness, the strength of the impulse now so strong that it was beginning to override whatever it was that had prevented her before. *It had not been designed for this.* Felt the yearning take her; she let it flow, unresisting, the undertow of the intense single-mindedness of desire, and the memory took over; in the now, in the box, she responded as one with it, synchronized with the memory, reaching, reaching, one last fractional effort and *now* the focus passed through her and for one single burning instant everything was crystal clear, gestalten, the sum of the universe and all its parts, playing over her, fire and light. She flew. Body centered, her hands wielded power. Then there was no desire, no need. She had one last thought in coherent forms, in wordlike concepts, then the words fell away. She had lost that. There were only pictorial images: She had a vision. *As from outside herself, she saw herself floating in space, looking back at her. The figure met her gaze, looking down on her from slightly above; it was wearing her own special pleth, the one to be used only for high ceremonies, with an abstract design embroidered down the front panel, odd little dots arranged in a mysterious but sensible pattern. The figure was barefooted. The sleeves dropped loosely halfway between elbow and wrist. All around outside the figure a bluish space seemed to enclose her, a cruciform shape but with an additional arm to the front and the back, precisely delineated, and everywhere with ninety-degree angles. Made up of eight cubes. The figure had extended its arms into the cubical spaces by the shoulders. And behind it, dimly in the background, there was something else, a curved screen, a large panel, immense, its true size distorted by perspective. She could not tell how far away it was. Patterns similar to the design on the pleth, but infinitely more involuted and complex, filled the screen, living, moving, changing in a way that wrenched at her mind. The girl was herself, that she knew. And now, the self she watched, who had been gazing sorrowfully back at her, turned her head slowly to the right, as if to look back just once at the design in the background. The face turned away. The pattern stopped moving, and a deadly stillness filled her mind. The vision was now lifeless, fixed forever. It lost contrast, then color, then winked out. There was only darkness absolute.*

She let it go, knowing almost nothing now. She had seen, but she had not understood. She felt fatigue, exhaustion, but completed, satisfied. She was sleepy. She had no more desires, no needs. The darkness was close, but she did not fear it; it was a friend, something she had called for. She had now forgotten a lot, and there were no more confusing images. Only some random percolating fragments. She ignored them. She had no interest in those fragments at all. She was sleepier than she had ever known, heavy, sinking. It was like swimming in a shallow summer pond at night, under an overcast sky. The warmth waited. All she had to do was kick off and flow. It was so easy. There was no longer any time, no more duration. Now that was gone, too. She was free. The universe collapsed to a point, one point, undimensional. She no longer knew who she had been. There was no past, there was nothing, and what fragments remained seemed to make little difference either way.

Either way.

Either.

Clane Oeschone, medical technician of the fourth grade, abbreviated MT4, had been working his first midnight shift of the new cycle in the Nondestructive Evaluation Facility appended to Building 8905; this was a new assignment for him, one which could be regarded as a tentative promotion. But so far his assigned duties had been absurdly simple: he was merely to attend to certain laboratory equipment, which appeared to be various Instructional Environment Enclosures. His responsibilities were limited and clearly specified, befitting to a technician of the fourth grade, although rather more than what might have been expected of the ordinary fourth. Indeed, as Oeschone thought. There was, after all, something to the acceptance of a programmed name. He had casually forgotten his old name. That person no longer existed. So one accepted, and became a cut above the average earner. It opened the doors to special assignments, and in his own case, out of the Sectional Palliatory.

However it had come to pass, his present task was simplicity itself: all he had to do was monitor the manual override panel, be alert for alarms, and tend the recording instruments, changing the paper as required, adjusting the current flow to the electrostatic needles as indicated by technical orders, and other related functions. Oeschone had received a thorough briefing on his duties here in 8905 from the evening-shift technician, including a description of patterns to watch for on the multiencephalograph, normal patterns as well as some abnormal ones. He also had, close to hand for reference, an operating manual with hundreds of conditions and responses listed, which he was also at liberty to use. He had glanced through it; it was a heavy tome of several hundred pages. To be absolutely candid, he had not memorized all that he had seen therein; but he had noted the section dealing with emergency procedures, particularly those pages dealing with specific patterns on the graph paper: these conditions called for the standby medtech. Those called for the duty medic.

Oeschone glanced idly at the machine. It was the only one in the room he had been assigned to. Before him, needles scratched with a faint but annoyingly repetitious sound, regular as clockwork. The paper was fixed on a huge drum easy of access. It passed under the needles, and thence to an equally bulky collection reel. Oeschone made a gesture of attentiveness to the markings being made on the graph paper, although he was quick to admit privately to himself that of the data they were recording, he could interpret only the most simple and primitive portion. However his limitations, the knowledge of them did not disturb him, for Oeschone was a modest man, sure now of his career progress to come. He had no burning ambitions which could be vitalized in his day-to-day routines. He also knew that it never counted what one actually did, but rather how it was perceived. And here, a programmed name was a coin that spent well.

He bent and looked more closely, trying to see if he could read this one. He looked again; the patterns on the paper moving beneath the needles were by no means standard curves. He estimated that he could at least determine that the subject was conscious, but it appeared to be an extremely relaxed state of consciousness, almost an Alpha wave pattern. But not quite. He looked again. Yes, it was clear; he understood. He could read it: it was yet conscious, but there was a strong phi factor. That was one he had learned. It indicated hallucinations. Momentary, not yet of the obsessive variety. Oeschone felt uneasy, and consulted his operating instructions just to be certain. After a time, after reading the text and consulting the graph again, he relaxed. No action was called for. Abnormal, but not out of tolerances. He returned to his chair and settled himself comfortably.

So it was hallucinating, was it? Well, that was nothing to him. He did catch himself wondering briefly, without particu-

lar concern, why this one, whoever it was, had been put in
the box, obviously on isolation. But after all, there was simply no telling, no telling at all. Isolation . . . Oeschone looked
away from the box. This was an easy shift; nothing to it.

Even hallucinating as it obviously was, that one in the box
could last for days more, weeks, before the symptoms became
serious, or one of the alarms went off, and the medtech came
to break open the box, carefully, of course, taking all the
notes, warnings, cautions, and expansions of the operating
manual in mind. But it was always the same whenever they
opened up an isolation box: they invariably found an emotional beggar who would say anything, reveal any secret, no
matter how trivial, just for an instant of personal contact. It
was the ultimate fear, the fear of having to face the inescapable evidence of one's unique loneliness, and they had exploited it further than any previous ruling order had exploited
any fear. It was physically painless and left no marks. Outside. And one who had been in the box was completely trust-
worthy, perhaps more so than the higher grades, if rather
meek. Oeschone had heard tales . . . that after isolation, many
would beg for a little light torture, just for the stimulus. For
reality, however degrading.

Pitiful, such persons. Why did they allow themselves to
came to such a sorry pass? Oeschone was certain that he did
not know. Or if he did, he did not want to. It all worked the
same in the end. But they knew the rules, they did, the order
and the consequences. And after they had done whatever it
was such people did, it all ended up the same way: in the
box. Oeschone looked at the box. A dark gray structure
somewhat higher than his height, occupying the end of the
room, large enough to be a small jitney bus, almost. Silent,
motionless, clean, powerful. Oeschone turned and went to his
chair, sat. He pulled the narrative scanner on its telescoping
mountings toward him, turned it on. He did not look back to
the isolator again for a long time. . . .

Some hours later, when he had become bored with the repetitious events being depicted on the scanner programs,
Oeschone looked up, rather sheepishly, wondering what the
time was and thinking about a cup of coffee. He stood up,
stretched, looked about the room, more to rest his eyes than
anything else. The room was silent, save for the whispering of
air in the circulation vents, and the faint scratching of the
needles on the graph paper. That reminded him of something,
after a time. He thought guiltily that he should have been

checking the readout every fifteen minutes. But he wasn't particularly disturbed; it was simply a matter of adjusting his duty logs. He was sure nothing had happened worthy of note; nothing ever did. Oeschone walked over to the recording device, looked cursorily at the graph, straightened, nodding to himself. Nothing had changed.

He looked again, some subliminal cue tugging at his dimmed consciousness. He could not, however well he rationalized it, avoid the suspicion that something subtle, but not the less drastic for all that, had occurred while he had been looking at the entertainment-scanner. Oeschone looked closely, now, at the pattern still unrolling before him. There was something there, he was certain. Now he had to find it.

Each of the needles was tracing a unique pattern, and it seemed to be just as before. Just as before he had gone to his chair. Oeschone looked again, feeling that sinking feeling. No, it was not just like before. Now all of the wave-forms were perfectly regular, with no variation whatsoever being overlaid on whatever pure frequency they tapped. All of them. Regular wave-forms, as if they were being generated by a computer. He bent over the collection reel and began to unroll it frantically, looking desperately for the section in which the regular wave-forms had started. His heart leaped; then sagged again, in disappointment; he couldn't find it. Oeschone reached for the alarm button, the one which would summon the duty medic. He would know what to do.

The unexplained, unmodulated wave-forms continued without any change or deviation until the duty medic arrived, some forty minutes later. A sizable group accompanied the medic, apparently standby personnel he had called out. Oeschone tried to make himself as inconspicuous as possible.

Once he had taken stock of the general situation, the medic took charge of things in a stern manner at variance with his youthful appearance. That, at the least, did not surprise Oeschone; duty medics were a surly lot at best, and he had not yet heard of one who enjoyed being called out during his shift. It was widely believed that they napped on their shifts, and of course if they were awakened too quickly, they growled like bears. But, growling or not, Oeschone was secretly glad to have the medic here; the matter and the responsibility was now out of his hands. Perhaps there would be other circumstances as well to muddy the water and divert attention from himself.

The medic appeared to ignore Oeschone; an assistant dug

into a voluminous carpetbag and extracted a weighty blue text, from which he read cryptic instructions and rejoinders, to which the medic either nodded assent or performed some action, such as turning a potentiometer, reading a meter, or flipping a toggle. They performed with an efficiency that bespoke both knowledge of the subject matter and considerable training. At several points in the sequence of actions, the medic would consult the multiencephalograph. At these occasions, he would also review Oeschone's duty log, here turning to leer knowingly at Oeschone. But he said nothing. After considerable time had been spent on the preliminaries, they began to disassemble the box, proceeding carefully in accordance with instructions so as not to disturb out of sequence the delicate life-support mechanisms. Having completed most of his preparatory actions, the duty medic then climbed up onto the box, using cleverly concealed hand- and footholds. At the top, he opened a small inspection plate, and shining a small pocket flashlamp into the opening, looked inside intently.

Oeschone knew the routine, although he had never personally observed an emergence; the medic would now climb down from the box, take a few more actions, and then stand back, grumbling, while his crew completed disassembly. But Oeschone began to feel uneasy, for it did not proceed after that fashion. The medic, instead, remained atop the box, staring intently into the opening for what seemed to be an overly long time. Then he shifted his position, and looked into the opening from several differing angles. At last, shaking his head, he climbed down from the box, very deliberately and calmly, and walked slowly over to Oeschone's console. His face looked congested, angry, although controlled.

"You have an outside line?" Indeed there was something more than irritated inconvenience in the tone of the medic's voice.

"Of course, Medic Venle," Oeschone replied, remembering to read the man's nametag so he could use the name. This always helped to allay hostility; even more so in this circumstance, since the medic was also the holder of a programmed name. Oeschone hoped that the medic would appreciate the gesture and recall that, after all, he and Oeschone alike were fellow-members of a privileged group. Oeschone also added, "Is there some problem?"

"Just get the line," answered the medic impatiently.

Oeschone complied with his request. Shortly afterward, Venle was seated at the console, looking belligerently into the viewer. The other members of the recovery team looked expectantly at Venle, as if they expected further instructions, but he waved them off, signifying they were to wait for further instructions. At the console, the Operate light flashed on.

A voice spoke from a speaker. "Operator PZ. Go ahead."

"I am Journeyman Medic Domar Venle, ranking four step C. I desire a priority conference be set up, connecting this terminal with those of, respectively, Acumen-Medic Slegele and Overgrade Eykor, the Chief of Regional Security. Precedence is flash, Authority Section B."

"Medic Venle, I understand and will comply, but the time is oh-five-three-oh local. The officials you have enumerated are, in all probability, yet sleeping. They are, of course, both dayshifters."

Venle said, calmly and deliberately, "Asleep, are they? Well, then, arouse them." Then he added, maliciously, "Wake the bastards up." While the operator hesitated, he added further, "I accept responsibility. Indeed, I demand it."

There was a pause while the operator complied with Venle's instructions and rang both mentioned parties. There was some further delay while the called parties awoke and tried to assemble some official dignity before coming on the conference call. But finally the screen before Venle divided and two faces appeared side by side. Venle spoke first. "Operator, record this."

"Recording."

"Noted. First, Acumen-Medic Slegele: Are you aware of the nature of the subject remanded to the sensory deprivation unit located in room seven-thirty-five, Building eight-nine-oh-five?"

Venle knew very well the acumen-medic did not. It was merely an opening question to put the senior man off balance. And it did. Slegele answered, "Of course I don't know at five in the morning. I don't keep rosters in my quarters. Is this why you get me out of bed at this hour?"

Venle said, "Well, let me be the first to tell you. You have a quote live unquote ler in your magic box, that's what."

The puffy face in the viewer moved, registering several emotions at once. Slegele said, "But, Venle, that's impossible. I recall the circumstance, and remember seeing the forms on info when they went through; you must be making some mistake. That particular unit holds an unknown female subject, I believe a suspect of vandalism or something similar."

"Somebody lied," Venle said sternly, not bothering to

conceal his elation at confirming something he had long suspected: that Acumen-Medic Slegele was a mere paper-stamper who knew nothing about what was going on in his departments. "Yes, indeed. The forms were in error. It's a female, true enough; I looked. But not human. With them, I'd have to guess the age . . . she appears to be about middle-adolescence, over fifteen, under twenty-five. Small breasts, well-formed, no pubic hair. Second thumb on the outside of both hands. That sounds like a ler to me. And you know the terms of the Compact as well as I: No imprisonment or experimentation. All suspects are to be conveyed immediately to the Institute. You and I, we'll fry for this. How long has she been on isolation?"

Eykor broke in, his composure recovering. He was a horse-faced man with a shock of unkempt reddish hair. But despite his rude appearance, he was both suave and controlled. "There is no problem, Venle. We listed that one in that manner on the invoices. All of the extant records were paperwhipped by my people. What's the problem? More specifically, how did you come to be over there?"

"I believe I can state the reason briefly: I was called on a blankout alarm which your cretin watchman sent out six hours late. The subject, as you refer to her, has somehow managed to dismind herself. Zero. You've got a live warm body, Interrogator, but that is all you have. Apply your methodology on that. She has virtually no responses whatsoever. I should estimate early newborn, if anything."

Slegele began stammering, "But, but . . ."

Eykor interrupted Slegele. "This conference will be classified secret under the provisions of Code four-oh-one-five, section B amended, and is hereby confiscated, all recording thereof to be forwarded to this office, Organization S. Operator?"

"Noted, sir."

"Venle, complete your procedures and await me. I'll be over there immediately."

"Very well."

"And, operator, arrange an appointment for me with Chairman Parleau. Naturally, the discreet person would specify that such a meeting be at his convenience, but as early as possible."

"That is noted. It will be as you say. Shall I inform your office facilities? The Regional Chairman's unit will not be open for an hour or so yet."

"Notify me in person at room seven-thirty-five, Building eight-nine-oh-five. Venle?"

"Present."

"You verge upon insubordination."

"Others have noted that tendency, sir. But I must add that where I err in one regulation, it might be said that your office has erred in another, perhaps one with more serious consequences. I must stand upon my right to advise of error, freely and without reprisal, however subtle." Venle was quoting.

"Oh, your rights have been noted in full. Proceed with your function. Break." Eykor's half of the viewer winked out. Slegele's puffy face filled the screen. Venle was indeed sorry he had dragged the acumen-medic into this. The man simply wasn't prepared. . . .

To Slegele he said, "We'll recover her, well enough. It was fortuitous I thought to bring my own crew over here. But I will still require some assistance; can you send over the Central Palliatory and have them send me some, ah . . . pediatrics assistants?"

Slegele stammered, "Of course, if you need them. But why pediatrics? I don't understand. . . ."

Venle said, patiently, "Apparently the girl, whoever she is, now has nothing but the infant responses she was born with. She breathes, she has a strong heartbeat, all the vital signs. As far as I can determine now, her blood chemistry is good, although I'll have to refer to some other manuals. But infant responses! She'll have to be cared for: she's an infant with a full set of teeth. She'll bite her tongue off before she discovers what those little pearlies are used for. And what do we tell her people when they come for her, as they surely must? That we're bloody sorry? She's obviously an adolescent. Not bred yet. They'll ransack the place when they find out." Venle mused for a moment, then added, "A shame about all this, too; she's quite attractive, if a bit childish for my tastes. . . ."

Slegele, waking up, interrupted Venle's train of thought. "How could they know she was missing? And knowing, how would they know to come here looking for her?"

"I should imagine someone will find her absence curious. They are close people, you know. And it won't take a genius to discover Building eight-nine-oh-five. Of course, we can always deny the whole thing, but that means we have to dispose of the body, also. That means that many more who know something about it. You see what I'm trying to hint at?"

"Yes ... I think so. We could always say she did it to herself, couldn't we? We can't be held responsible for that."

"I suppose it's worth trying. But I'll say this: you and I have more to fear from our own people than from them. Get it?"

"You're cynical."

"Realistic is the terminology I prefer ... I know that people who set events like this one in motion never pay for it. They arrange that someone else foots the bill. I'm not in danger, but you could be. Cover yourself. I'll do what I can for you."

"Let us both hope it doesn't come to that. But at any rate I appreciate the gesture."

Venle signed off disgustedly and went back to work on the occupant of the box, ignoring Oeschone entirely, save in his private thoughts, which were malevolent ones; Venle took his work more seriously than he did his status, and one of his private hates included those who applied for programmed names and then expected to ride free for the rest of their days. Careerists, he grumbled under his breath, inaudibly. There were entirely too many of them these days, and no real way to get at them, either.

Not so very long afterward, the girl was carefully lifted out of the box and almost tenderly laid on the waiting stretcher. She was, as Venle had observed earlier, lovely. Out of the box, in the open light, she was something more than that. Her hair was a lustrous dense deep brown, almost black, worn in the fashion affected by ler adolescents, a simple short style resembling a tapered bowl cut, in human eyes boyish. The face was delicate and soft at the same time, oval-triangular, rising from a small but not weak chin to large, deeply set eyes, which were an odd light brown color. She had a small nose, very straight, and her lips were pursed rather than full. There were no lines on the face whatsoever, but it was a strong face filled with myriad adult determinations, and something else as well: a sadness, something wistful, other-worldly, deeply emotional. From the head, a slender, fine neck led to a taut, athletic body, smoothly curved and completely feminine, whose skin tone was a ripe faded honey-olive. Venle looked at her long, sighing. There was only one thing out of place; she could have been human, save for the hands. The hands were narrow, three-fingered, with an opposable thumb on each side, both thumbs being narrower than the human thumb. In addition, her hands were powerful and angular, a bit at variance from the rest of her.

Venle looked back at the face, now relaxed. There was a faint shadow of a smile set along the lines and softened planes of the girl's face, something ineffably subtle, something about the set of the eyes and mouth; save for that, the face was empty of expression in the present. No one present with Venle could quite place where they had seen a smile like that before, if indeed they ever had before.

TWO

> *The appearance of the quality of randomness is often the most reliable indication of high and subtle systems of order.*

> *We learn from simple analysis of the Zan (Life Game) that time is asymmetrical, one-way. To try to work time in reverse brings one immediately into the principle of uncertainty. Things may be mysterious, incomprehensible, or ineluctable, but nothing in the universe is uncertain. This is basic to understanding higher-order phenomena.*

> —*The Game Texts*

Fellirian* was explaining, "The Four Determinants of a person are these: Aspect, Phase, Class, Position." She added fastidiously, "Gender is not a determinant. So, then; if one of us knows all four determinants of another person, we are thereby able to predict, with reasonable accuracy, what that person will do in various circumstances."

Fellirian was an adult female ler of many roles and relationships. In the present case, she was serving as resident

---

* Ler names in this story will be given untranslated, except for special cases.

sociologist, Visitors Bureau, at the Institute for Applied Inter-
relationships, a problem-solving organization which was the
primary organ of human and ler interaction. Once a week,
Fellirian traveled down to the Institute from her home deep
inside the ler reservation, and explained an alien culture to
visitors, both humble and distinguished. This particular audience appeared to be of the more humble variety, and it was
close to the end of the day, and Fellirian was bored.

"Aspect," she continued, "is distantly related to your own
concept of astrological sign, save that it is much simplified.
We use only four: Fire, Air, Earth, Water. These correspond
to the four seasons."

It was autumn, on Earth, the year 2550. Fellirian lived
partially in two worlds, and in the human world she visited,
even the little taste she got of it at the Institute, her presence
generated paperwork echoes of herself. On various rosters,
lists, collations, and assorted personnel summaries, she was
listed as "one each Fellirian Deren, female, ler, reservation
resident, age 45, married (local custom), three offspring, two
male, one female. Position: Instructor of Customs. Branch:
Visitors Bureau. Supervisor: W. Vance, Director. Fertility
Board Index: (not applicable).

She could, had she pondered overly long on the matter,
have produced a much longer "full-name" in her own field of
reference, with an even longer list of titles and identities. Her
full-name, in her own environment, was Kanh Srith Fel Lir-
yan Klan'Deren Klandormadh; which translated, more or
less, to the following: Earth-Aspect's the Lady Starry Sedge-
Field of the Counters Clan, Head-of-Family Foremother. But
she never translated the name, as was the case with all of
them. Names were names, meant to suggest in their meanings, not to describe. To friends, adult relations occasionally
in the formal mode, and humans, she was simply Fellirian.
That sufficed. There wasn't another; ler names never repeated
that of a living person, and inasmuch as was possible, one
who had ever been, although they admitted that this last
would become unfeasible with time.

To her fellow Braid-members at home, in the mode of intimacy, she was Eliya, and to the Braidschildren Madheliya.
Foremother Eliya. She was never called Fellir anymore, for
that was an adolescent love-name. Morlenden, her insibling
and co-spouse, sometimes called her Fel, the child-name, but
more often he called her by an embarrassing pet name,
Benon, which meant "freckles." The matter was embarrassing

because the freckles were on her shoulders, which led to connotations she did not care to recall now at her age and phase.

Fellirian's phase was Kanh, the mode of the power of Earth. Her season was spring. She was saying to her audience, "Now, Phase: this is approximately how old you are. *Hazh* is a child, up to about ten years. *Didh* is adolescent: ten to twenty-nine. *Rodh* is parent, and *starh* is elder. We are *rodhosi* until age sixty, and then are *starosi*, although this last is somewhat arbitrary. Technically, are only actually *rodhosi* until the end of the fertile period."

Fellirian had children, and yet lived at home, her children not yet being of weavable age; therefore she was Parent Phase. In gender, female, but sexually neuter. So it went with all after last-fertility, the so-called *hanh-dhain**.

Fellirian, being of the Earth mode, was a child born in the spring. Without being overtly obvious about it, she did in part live up to the theoretical attributes of a person of that mode, although none could consider her the prey of erratic aspectual compulsions. Spring was her preferred season as well; like her own manner, it was a direct season, things proceeding toward their due ripening, earthy, direct, practical. She did not care so much for the present season of autumn, with its *tanh* air-aspect moodiness, its constantly shifting weather, off and on again, now looking back into summer, now anticipating winter.

"There are, in theory, four social classes: Servant, Worker, Journeyman, and Grower, from the lowest to the highest; but in practice now we only use the top three, and this is of less weight than the other determinants."

One of the visitors inquired, "And what class do you belong to?"

"Worker. My Braid is part of the ler government. My family and I are, in the eyes of our peers, rather low-class, although I feel no sense of either pride or envy therefrom. Class, odd as this may sound, is only applicable to persons who are within a Braid, or family. Once you are elder and leave home, you are classless. Elders have no class. Utterly none."

---

* Difficult to translate. *Hanh* means last, and *dhain* (pronounced "thine") is a word describing the sex act, but utterly without the connotations of vulgarity or hostility common to such terminology in English. It is purely descriptive. "Fun" might be closer to its real meaning than any other word we might use here.

She saw some expressions in the audience she did not care for. She said, "Lest you mistake me, I must define things here, although it is somewhat off the path we go upon. I am not in the government because my family and I are worker-class. It is the other way around. I derive class and status from my occupation, so to speak." She waited for a rejoinder, but there was none. Good.

She continued, "Last, and perhaps most important, is the determinant of position. What we refer to here is what place you occupied within the Braid when you were a child." Here she gestured to a chart beside her that diagrammed the intricate family relationships of the ler cultural surround. They had used it earlier. "We can be one of five different positions, with some subcategorization, of course. This measure, like class, also runs from low to high, thus: *hifzer, Zerh, Thes, Nerh, Toorh.* You would say, Bastard, Extra, Younger Outsibling, Elder Outsibling, and highest, Insibling. These stay with you forever. They are basic identities. I was *Toorh,* and I shall always be perceived as one, no matter my age. Also this is not a smooth scale. A *Nerh* is almost equal to a *Toorh,* and a *Thes* is closer to a *Zerh.* Families do not, by definition, have *Hifzers.*"

At this last, the group immediately began an argument among themselves, one faction in particular taking some exception to the concept of position being more weighty a determinant than social class. Fellirian did not know why they were arguing over this, for it did not affect them one way or another; but she did not enter the argument on either side. She felt as if she had somehow espoused a doctrine held or shared by one faction and above all she did not wish to be identified with one human faction or another. As the sides became more defined and the visitors began to polarize among themselves, she withdrew and walked slowly to the side, to the window ledge, where she settled and looked outside, leaning on one hand and half sitting on the broad metal sill.

She looked out the window, through the rain-streaked polarized glass, through the damp and rainy November airs to the wet land beyond, now taking on a bluish tint with the approach of evening. From her viewpoint, looking somewhat northeast, she could see in the land itself the clear delineation of the two cultures, human and ler. On the left, the reservation, a 4,200-square-mile forest preserve in which the ler were now allowed to pursue their own ends, whatever those ends were; and on the right, the end product of several thousand years of human culture. Both were on the same planet, Earth, the same year—2550.

To the left, the land appeared unkempt, empty, overgrown with trees and brush. To the right, as far as she could see through the light rain and foggy haze, everything was neat, orderly, trimmed, laid out, controlled. Far to the right at the edge of visibility, a manufacturing operation dominated the landscape: it appeared to be a low, rather featureless building of square ground-plan, betraying its inner activity only by the action of small vents along the roof, some of which emitted pastel clouds of vapor, while others trailed away into the rainy darkening air wisps of smoke which soon vanished. It looked dormant, inactive; but she knew this to be an illusion. Inside, unseen, it was as busy as an anthill, madly producing still more of the perishable artifacts on which their society seemed to exist. There was little traffic in or out of it; transit-ways underground handled the material flows, and the employees lived in air-conditioned cubicles in the basement. Bosses and bossed alike; it cost less to totalize their entire environment than it did to provide transportation and housing for them elsewhere.

Farther to the right, the remainder of the view through the Institute window took in agricultural fields, some smaller buildings and miscellaneous sheds, a light grid of access roads and hoverways. There was nothing but a sense of neatness and order in all that she saw, a tincture of everything calculated to a nicety; she could not help but admire it to a point. Still, a part of her insisted on another, more chaotic view: that the fine sense of order and regulation concealed something perilous. The higher the degree of apparent order, the finer the line that divided the arbitrary order from the merciless down-drag of entropy. *Nature only appears random to the unobservant,* she thought. It was one of the basic ler maxims. In reality, there was a deep and subtle order in the changes of nature, its wavelike progressions, its cycles of time.

Even so, she thought further, *eruptions are few and far between. Give them that credit.* The forerunners accepted the regimented, managed life forced upon them by overpopulation and had even managed to reduce their increase-rate to a niggling, infinitesimal amount. But they were all conscious decendants of an age, not so very far away in the historic sense of time, which was still vividly recalled by Earth's billions as The Black Hand of Malthus. The Days of the Hand.

They had reduced its visibility, but never its presence: the Black Hand still awaited the unwary, offstage in the wings.

Facing to the right as she sat in the window, she had to look back over her left shoulder to see what little was visible of her own country, the sole home on Earth, or in the whole universe, for that matter, of the New Humans, *Metahomo Novalis*. There was a fence around the reservation, an ordinary chain-link barrier about eight feet high. It served no purpose save to mark a boundary, for few there were on either side of it who wished to cross to the other side. Near the fence, the land inside seemed to be empty, abandoned, allowed to be feral, half-wild, scrubby; but farther back, the forest started, here tall dark pines that concealed the inner lands. It looked ancient, a remnant of the great forests which had once covered most of the continent; but in reality most of the forest growth in the reservation was recent in terms of nature. Second-growth. The eastern sections of the reservation, in particular, where newer growth gradually extended out of the older sections farther west. It had been a forest preserve that few knew about until they had asked for it. Fellirian sighed deeply. She felt a sudden longing to be back inside, back within her own identity, in her natural surround. This room in this overbuilt Institute building was too hot, too dry, and it smelled of plastic, an odor she never found especially unpleasant, but nonetheless one she had never got used to. . . .

Chronologically, Fellirian was forty-five. Parent phase. In appearance, however, she struck most of the human visitors who met with her to be somewhere in a vague adulthood, late twenties, perhaps early thirties. A smallish, but not petite, slightly built woman with the traditional subtle figure of the ler. Somewhere along the way, she had collected an almost invisible network of fine lines along the planes of her face, lines that helped and accented the subtle beauty of the plain, almost elfin face. Fellirian was not a beauty, neither by her standards nor those of the humans, but her appearance reassured. Being relaxed and at peace with herself, she projected a reassurance that included others as well.

In her own view, her appearance fit her age, more or less; she did not ponder on the matter overly. She was not vain. She knew how others reacted to her, always had. She was satisfied; she had lived a reasonably full life, in many ways better and more fortunate than some.

Forty-five. *Almost through the second span.* Then another

of the many transitions they used to mark the stages of their
lives in time. Sexually, she was now, and had been for some
five years, effectively neuter, although she retained her personal sense of gender unchanged. No, not unchanged. If anything, it had increased. She had been one of the minority of
ler females to have a third fertile period after the second. She
had been pleased with their *Zerh,* the boy Stheflannai. Third
fertilities and fraternal twins were the only way the ler ever
got ahead of the merciless algorithms of population increase.
And before that, she mused, *it had been Kevlendos, one of
our insiblings, who will weave in his season with the child of
our others who is called Pentandrun-Toorh. And of course
our firstborn Pethmirvin, a slender, fragile girl who resembles
none of us.* Ages five, ten, fifteen. Twenty years hence,
Kevlendos and Pentandrun would weave to become the then-
Derens. And for her, Fellirian? They would then be the Der-
enklan; the name, the work, the family holdings—all would
be theirs. She would be just herself, free. Fellirian Srith. Lady
Fellirian. A new life. She could live by herself, solitary, a
lonely *mnathman**, or remain with her former Braidmates,
although they would have to find another place to live. They
could not stay in the old Braid holding—that went to the
children. Or perhaps she could join one of the lodges, communes into which most elders eventually moved. The ler analog of marriage was like the human model in that it had a
beginning; it was utterly unlike it in that it had a predeter-
mined end as well. It was also unlike the human model in that
it was neither desirable nor optional, but mandatory. . . .

Fellirian rarely delivered her lectures, or occasional harangues, alone. Much of the time the Director of the Institute
was in and out, visiting with the strangers, hobnobbing with
the tourists who had come to be amazed and astounded, and
have their suspicions allayed. But for all that he did with
the visitors, Walter Vance admitted candidly that his primary
purpose in attending the meetings was to spend a rare moment with Fellirian, who had been his friend, associate, and
confidante for the more than twenty years he had been associated with the Institute. Their relationship had, like all close
relationships, probably raised more questions than it answered, but at the least it satisfied a basic orientation shared
by both of them in equal measure: they preferred to deal
with real, though flawed in various degrees, creatures of flesh

* Literally, "wise person," but in actuality a hermit.

and blood and the moment, rather than a set of lifeless abstractions borrowed from a carelessly written programmed text.

With trust and a genuine fondness for each other, they could explore aspects of otherness with little fear of giving or taking offense; this was not a little thing, for the cultural gap between ler and human was an order of magnitude greater than the genetic differences, and it was growing yearly. When Vance had persuaded Fellirian to spend a little time with the Institute they had not one single ler assigned to expound on their values; all was done by humans, mostly well-intentioned but who had little direct knowledge of their subject material. They spoke skillfully, they adhered to rigorous scholarship, but they missed the feel of their subjects. Conversely, ler labored under much the same system in their view of humans. Painfully aware of their vulnerability of slow population growth, they withdrew into their reservation and further into their own identities. Vance and Fellirian could not arrest or greatly change the course of the drift of several centuries, but what little they had done they regarded as being of a value considerably above zero.

Vance now sat in a chair to one side, bored with the endless tailspin semantic arguments of the visitors among themselves, a process of which he had to endure entirely too much within his own organization. Above and below. While he waited for them to return to reality and finish the day, he watched Fellirian as she sat on the windowsill and looked into the depths of November, overcast and rain-spattered.

His perception of her was subjective, colored by memory, subtly distorted by many emotions, some of which had sources that remained concealed from him, no matter how hard he tried to dig at them. Paradoxically, he had found Fellirian to have more objective perceptions than he had, even where accustomed and familiar matters were considered. He had imagined that having total recall would muddy the image of the present even more, but, to the contrary, he had found that for them it made the present clearer. The images were distinct.

In the light of the room, and the soft overcast daylight coming in through the windows, he saw a graceful ler woman of indeterminate age sitting in the windowsill, wearing the typical general-purpose garment of males and females alike, in its winter variation, the zimpleth. This was, in essence, something resembling a loose, informally cut shirt with a very long tail that reached to the ankles. It flowed loosely around the contours of her body, terminating along her arms in wide sleeves which did not quite reach to her wrists. There was nothing under the zimpleth save Fellirian, but somehow it managed completely to conceal the shape within its lines. She was barefooted, but for the moment little showed, as she had folded her legs beneath her. He saw in her profile that she yet had the visage he knew of old, a tomboy, impudent, mischievous face, with a strong nose just slightly too large for the face, and a wide, generous soft mouth inclined to secret laughters. Her skin was light in color, even so slightly shadowed by a darker tone. The hair was a neutral dark brown, very fine and straight, tied at her neck into a single braid which fell to the middle of her back.

Vance had met Fellirian when he had come to the Institute; they were approximately the same age in years. During the time he had known her, he had seen many aspects of her; as an adolescent, in his eyes then promiscuous and oversexed. But also as a *rodhosi*, of parent phase, serious and practical, and as head-of-clan completely absorbed in the management and continuity of its affairs. Now, on the edge of true elderness. Ler lifespans reached to one hundred and twenty and beyond; half their lives spent in the first three phases, and the rest in the last phase. They held that one did not become oneself until elderhood, when, as they put it, the distractions fell away, and essences were revealed. In Fellirian, some creature within herself, more individual and unique than he cared to imagine, was beginning to emerge.

Twenty years. They had worked well together, learned from each other. They had become close friends and grown to enjoy one another's company as few such pairs had in the history of the Institute. Nothing had passed between them deeper than friendship, nor more intimate than a handshake, which always felt odd and unreal to Vance. One could convince oneself that ler were just other humans of small stature and almost childish appearance until one saw and felt the hand. The inner thumb was smaller and more delicate than the human thumb, and the outer opposable thumb, derived from the little finger, was stronger than its original. This change made the ler hand seem too long and narrow, and it felt *wrong*. Moreover, they seemed to lack the concept of "handedness" entirely. Ler wrote with either hand equally well, holding the writing instrument with either thumb. Still, after twenty years, it disturbed Vance's perceptions to watch

Fellirian writing some office memorandum, holding the pen with an outer thumb and pulling it along the direction of writing.

If the hand had become a symbol for the alien quality, the one thing which stood out above the many ambiguities, then the reality had been more directly evoked when he had met her insibling and (then) co-parent to be. This bothered Vance, too, in some unconscious manner he could not quite fathom; the insiblings did not have common biological parents, yet they were raised together. They were always close in age, separations of more than a year being so rare as to be not worth mentioning. In some ways, closer than brother and sister in the human analog. Indeed closer, since the ler had no incest-taboo. This circumstance took the ancient argument of nature versus nurture, genetics against culture, and brought it head-on into direct opposition. The insiblings were alike, and different, all at the same time.

So Morlenden: rather alike, and totally dissimilar. In some subtle way beyond Vance's perceptions, he was most like Fellirian, in expressions, turns of speech, gestures. But he did not look like her at all. Against Fellirian's soft features, Morlenden had crisp, almost chiseled features. There was the tiniest possible suggestion of an epicanthic fold in the corners of his eyes, and his glance was direct and disturbingly contemplative. But he was neither dour of disposition nor abrupt of manner, but rather easy and sometimes inclined to elaborate pranks. His skin was darker than Fellirian's, of a tone that suggested American Indian rather than Oriental. Seeing them apart was to see reflections of the other in the one at hand. Vance had come to understand that it was similar with all insiblings. Vance could not conceive of sleeping with the same person for forty-five years, growing up together, occasionally taking one another after the casual manner of ler adolescents, and then making the transition into dual heads-of-family. Humans for the most part lived in dormitories and kept the sexes separate. Nothing else had worked.

Like all poignant experiences, meeting Morlenden had caused Vance to reassess his perceptions, both of Fellirian and of the female; in both secondary sex characteristics and culture, there was almost no sex differentiation among them. Dressed, the differences almost vanished to the human eye. He thought this quality was what disturbed humans most; an internal drive. *We do not lust for the opposite sex, but for youth and innocence.* The thought formed before he had time to cut it off at the source. He refused to follow it, even to prove it false; it led into a whole world, a universe, of heresies and forbidden speculations ... forbidden, at any rate, to a member of a culture which had been forced to become puritan, not out of religious mania but of necessity. Of all methods of contraception, only abstinence had the combination of one-hundred-percent effectiveness and zero-rate side effects. Zero? Not quite zero. There were obvious consequences, even if they were in the mind and not especially located in the body. Vance shut that one down, too. His mind was wandering in disturbing tangents today; perhaps the moody autumnal *tanh* weather. . . .

The omnipresent low buzz of conversation among the visitors had become faded and quiet in the last few moments. Vance now noticed it; Fellirian, for all her apparent inattention, had also noted it and climbed down off the windowsill, using a flowing, graceful motion Vance had always noticed in her. She went over to the chair she sometimes used, but now she did not sit in it, but stood, quietly, and nodded to the group to indicate that she was again ready to proceed.

A member of the visitors' group, a nervously aggressive woman of indeterminate middle age, wearing the heavy pleated and folded clothing of the day with indifference, and still retaining rubber covers over her heavy shoes, stood up, clearing her throat.

The woman began, "I am somewhat awkward here. I do not know how I should address you, directly." She had seen the same data as the others during her tour, and she could visualize the ler family structure as well as any of them present; yet she felt ill at ease in the presence of an active member of such a family organization. The family was now a rarity in human society. The voice which had made the tentative overture was heavy with the linguistic woodsmoke of the Balkans.

Fellirian smiled and chuckled, trying to set the woman at some ease. "Well, not Mrs. Deren, whatever you do. I suppose the nearest I could come to that would be to call myself the female half of an entity that corresponds to a Mr. Deren. I am an insibling. I retain the Braid surname. But here and for now, 'Fellirian' will be fine. It is the way we would address one another." Her voice was pleasant and clear, alto in intonation, projecting the Modanglic of the day without recognizable regional accent or mannerism. Still, there was some fleeting suggestion in the way she chose her words and enunciated them that Modanglic was a foreign language to her, however well she spoke it. It was.

The woman sighed and said, after an appreciable pause, "Very well then. So. That sounds easy enough, although I have never accustomed myself to addressing people by their first names. But I understand. The way you would use it in your own environment, I imagine it would be formal enough."

Fellirian agreed, pleasantly. "Indeed. We have a great deal of formality among ourselves, little distinctions that sometimes reflect kinship groups, or relative social status. Never fear! We make mistakes, too."

"These matters are the cause of much misunderstanding, I agree. So, then, to matters at hand. Fellirian, here you represent your people for us as people, so perhaps this is inappropriate to ask. But in my own Region* we have little contact with your people. Virtually none, as a matter of fact. And of course one hears tales. Our office has to deal with recurring questions relating to this."

Fellirian felt uncomfortable. It was a long preamble. She nodded, saying, "Please continue."

"I am very confused by what I have seen here. Out in the world, it is common belief that you are somehow superior to us, that you have an ... ah ... evolutionary edge on us. In short, you are greatly feared. Yet here I see a tribal, agricultural society, apparently disliking both aggressiveness and technology. Not to mention surrounded and outnumbered. In short, you do not appear to be competing with us. No competition, no threat. Can you shed any light on this ... contradiction?"

Fellirian saw something that made her wary. At the start of her question, the woman had been tentative and embarrassed, projecting the image of a bureaucrat of some rural Region about the tatters of Europe. Yet as she had come to phrase her question, her confidence had risen noticeably, and in fact she had almost answered it herself. Somewhere in the back of Fellirian's mind, a relay clicked. She felt a sudden oppression. There was subtlety here: the woman was bait. Someone was waiting for her reaction. Her answer. She was not certain, of course. Intuition, only.

She began, tentatively, "If you wish me to take the Aristo-

* Current political subdivision, equivalent to a large province. Regions might be geographic or ethnic in organizational basis.

telian path and say yes or no, I must, on the balance, say no."

"No? Not superior?"

"I know from my history that such was the aim of those who manipulated human genetic material to bring us into being. True. They were after the Superman, sure enough. It is an old dream. We have not been immune to it. But they did not have then fine control. Not then and not now. They could not, for example, read the message of the genetic code and then change exact parts of it to order. They could shock or juggle or graft larger segments and then screen for viables. As you may know, mutation means only change. I cannot stress that too much. It is not a matter of one set being inferior or superior. Just different. In nature, a highly structured feedback system with the environment and with others, and in higher forms, with culture, tends to stabilize organic forms and fine-tune them. Out of their program of artifice, several forms actually appeared, all of which were equally viable, more or less. They took us because we looked the least alien. It's that simple. I am afraid that when our firstborn grew into adults, they were more than a little disappointed in us. When they discovered that no offspring results from a human–ler mating, they were double disappointed."

"None whatsoever? I had not known that."

"We are different, that's a fact. Conception occurs, but the female aborts within forty-eight hours. Either way you try it. We are, in a sense, a door into another possibility; but it is a door that is not open to you. Or to us. But in many ways we complement one another, so we endure. We are strong in the intuitive patterns of thought, but you outclass us in deduction. I might point out that you are physically stronger and able to endure a wider range of climatic conditions. Whereas we seem to take crowding a little better. Did you know that? Much of human aggression arises not from any genetic predisposition, but from simple overcrowding. Not recently, I mean to say. You reached that point early in your prehistory. Ten thousand years ago."

"You appear to be very knowledgeable about our history."

Fellirian answered, diplomatically, "We hoped to learn from your experiences. You are the forerunners. We have no other example to hand."

Without evoking confrontation, Fellirian had boxed the woman in, if indeed she were a provocateur for someone else.

She could not rebuff her answer without making the background obvious.

"There are other differences?"

"People make much of our memory. It is a total-recall system. It sounds like an advance, I agree, but it has drawbacks. For example, we do not have a structure like your subconscious. In you, that serves as a buffer for contradictory experiences. We have to deal with the same events directly. There is a high degree of skill required, since we are now discussing basic sanity. All do not, of course, attain the preferred skill level. People envy us now for our low rate of reproduction, but it cannot be other than a serious disadvantage. And not only short, but an estrous periodic cycle as well. Twice, rarely three times, and it's over*. That basically gives us a one-to-one ratio, which is zero population growth from the beginning."

"May I ask your rate now?"

"One-to-one-point-oh-five or one-to-one-point-oh-six. Doubling every six hundred years. It was held artificially higher at first, but in the last two centuries it has been stable near that figure. Our marriage custom tends to diffuse exceptionally fertile types, so the increase is well-spread."

Fellirian paused. There was no comment. She continued: "This now means, on the average, that one Braid in six has an extra child. We cut the rate down to that. Our society is complex and delicate, and at a rate of one-to-one-point-two-five every Braid has one extra. You cannot imagine the dislocations such breeding causes. I admit that much of the problem comes from our own ordering of things. For if you have four children of the right ages, pairs five years apart, then they must go into a Braid to mate. If one does not exist, then one must be made for them. Braids have traditional basic occupations, and once set, cannot be changed, within the life of the Braid. It imposes a rate of social change upon us greater than our society has mechanism to adjust to it. We could stand an even lower rate, in my opinion."

"You said earlier that you were parent phase. You have procreated?"

Fellirian winced, internally, she hoped, at the phrasing of the question. Still, she understood it. Not many humans these

---

*Ler Braids ideally produced four children. Fifth children occurred in one Braid in five or six, from third-fertilities (80%) or fraternal-twinning (20%). Identical twins (clones) do not occur.

days "procreated," as the woman had put it. And the strictures of the Fertility Board were by far the most exasperating regulations of all. She replied, "Yes. My Braid is one of the one-in-six five-child Braids. I had a third fertility. I have had three children, all normal and live. Their ages are fifteen, ten, and five. A girl and two boys in that order. Their names are Pethmirvin, Kevlendos, and Stheflannai, in the same order. But rest assured. My days in brood are over."

She now paused to allow the idea to sink in. It was one thing to discuss such concepts in the abstract, quite another to accept such a thing personally, or in the sense of a personal interaction taking place now in the time of the real. She waited. Fellirian was patient. She knew humans well from her long association with them, and looked at none with contempt. They were always full of surprises, the inner person not always matching the outer. *Still,* she mused, *we are not so different in that,* either. . . . She also knew very well that the words of a single-channel language were also great illusions; not matching the realities they symbolized, and varying considerably in degree of variance, words tended to persuade the slow that they were one with the swift, and equally, the swift slowed to a crawl.

The woman pondered, drifted, hesitated, took another tack. "You told us about the ler family earlier, but not so much why such a structure. Is there some genetic reason for it?"

"Antigenetic, if anything. We have a small population and a high mutation rate; therefore we want a homogeneous population. We also noted that across time the family tends to become longer, more structured, more important. What we have now mixes us reasonably well, provides social stability and makes change controllable, and is the best compromise so far with our peculiar assets and liabilities. I might add here that an unforeseen consequence of the timing criteria of Braids also tends to bring, over the years, one Braid into resonance with another, and after that such groups form what we call 'partial superfamilies,' until terminated by the ending of one of the Braids involved, or the insertion of a vendetta into affairs. My own Braid is so resonant with Klanh Moren: The *Thes* of one becomes the afterparent of the other."

"You do not use human terminology to describe your relationships in a family?"

"No. Nor the concepts."

"Then the effect of resonance must be to reduce variability.

It increases order, rather than continuing the randomizing you seem to value."

"This is true. We are aware of the problem. In fact, there has been consideration of declaring such a pattern to be not desirable, and prohibiting it. It is not at this time. One of the reasons why the practice continues is that with such a small population as we have we are all rather close relations anyway. In your terms, we are all not less than sixth-cousins or something very close to that. Right now, superfamily resonance with a Braid-pair has no appreciable effect. A triplet, of course, maintained over several generations, would, and is not permitted. Now, later, when our numbers are much greater, hundreds of thousands, I think resonance of any sort will be prohibited. It is, as you say, a producer of more order. But you have to realize that our oldest Braids are just now only at generation fourteen in the adults-to-be, who are now yet adolescent."

The woman seemed to be at a loss. She hesitated, as if waiting for something, moving her weight from one foot to another, a motion which produced transient heavy wrinkles to appear and fade in her garments, which were made of some heavy, stiff dark material, somewhat shiny or lustrous, which seemed more intended to use in furniture or draperies than in clothing. Additionally, the style was full of pleats, folds, tucks, darts, and gave the impression of adding bulk. The women wore skirts that fell gracelessly below the knees, while the men wore in their place heavy oversized pantaloons. The upper garments, composed of several layers of undershirts, shirts, vests, jackets, and various accessories, were similar to one another and continued the style. Fellirian watched the woman closely, sensing the others out of the corners of her eyes. The woman seemed to be waiting for some cue, to go on.

A man not far from the woman cleared his throat and asked, politely, "Fourteen? Is that all?"

The woman resumed her seat, seemingly in great relief. Fellirian answered, "Just so, fourteen. My own generation of the Derens is only generation eleven. Of the old families, we are relative newcomers."

"Let me think," the man mused, half to himself. "That would, at thirty-five years per generation, put the firstborn of the oldest generation back to, say, about 2050 or 2060. But didn't Braid family structure date from a later date, in the twenty-second century?"

Fellirian's sense of oppression increased. "True. But the two items are not contradictory. Braids were tried first on a limited scale by those who believed in them. They were adopted somewhat later by the whole of the people."

"Are those Braids still in existence now?"

"Yes. The two Player Braids, the Perklarens and the Terklarens. They were not, at the time, Players, you understand, but in fact members of a peculiar religious order, if I have my history straight. Now, I believe, the Perklarens are at *Ghen Disosi*, generation fourteen. The Terklarens are at thirteen, although due to disresonance between them individual members of equivalent ages are about ten years older."

"And fourteen has much of the same nonnumerical symbolic significance to you that ten would have, say, to us."

"Yes . . . there is a similarity, an equivalence."

"Odd, that. I have heard of a book, called *The Wisdom of the Prophets*, in which mention is made to 'marvels and wonders in the house of the last single generation.' "

Fellirian let herself drift from affirmation into ambiguity. "I have heard also of the work you mention. However, you must bear in mind that its origin has been questioned. It has not ever been accepted as cult dogma by any theosophical society of our people in my knowledge. And, of course, prophecy is always somewhat equivocal."

"You do not agree with the content of *Wisdom*?"

"I read a copy here at the Institute when I was adolescent. I found the concepts therein rather repugnant. It heavily stresses the concept of serial evolution, which is erroneous, and it injects a competitive aspect into affairs between the inhabitants of Earth which does not ring true." Fellirian felt threatened by the circumstances of the questions. Never had she faced such a situation. All her intuitions warned her; she could not resist, however, letting go one last sally, just to make matters clear. "You are, sir, doubtless familiar with a similar work, I believe called *Protocols of the Elders of Zion*? I personally place *Wisdom* in the same category. Indeed, in *Wisdom* I felt an alien mind at work, one not compatible with myself."

"You don't think *Wisdom* is of ler origin?"

"I know not the number of thumbs on the hand of he who wrote. I speak of the ideals of the author, which is of the domain of the mind. And, at any rate, I know of no marvels. The Player Braids are both rather withdrawn and uncommunicative. They keep to their own affairs, which I imagine is

Gameplaying. And also I am not a follower of the Game, so they could very well perform a marvel and I would be unaware of it." *Now let this one make something out of that*, she thought.

He said, "Excellent, excellent. You have clarified the matter beyond any possible doubt for me. I am doubly reassured. I do have some more questions, but they are inconsequential."

"Not at all. I am here to answer them."

"In many ways, to us, you maintain a primitive style of living. I mean no judgment of relativity here, but merely describe. You have no method of temperature control in your houses save the family hearth, and that is useful only in the winter, for example. You virtually ignore vehicular transport, when a number of sophisticated mechanisms are located only no more than fifty miles from the heart of the reservation. To the observer, if I may put it politely, you assume primitive modes by choice. May I ask why? It is a curious matter."

Fellirian paused, then began: "The first lived among you and shared your manners and styles. But they soon came to believe two things: that your culture reflects your needs, not the needs of all creatures, hence us also. And that in many instances, you had inserted the widespread use of artifacts without considering the consequences of such introductions. The classic study in this area, concerning the automobile, concentrates not on what it did to your previous value system, but in the measurable increase it caused in the size of your cities, an increase and a lowering of density which had profound, unseen effects on your society for years. These things, by the way, most conclusively did not result from increases in population. Indeed, we still feel echoes of the period in this century. It was apparent, then, that artifacts had enormous influence on culture, having the power to change many parts of it. The prediction of such effects is an arcane discipline, and in some cases not greatly more reliable than the reading of tea leaves. Therefore we had seen and were wary. We are accused of conservatism. Not so. We are merely cautious. We desire change and improvement, but we also desire that we, the objects of such change, have some willed control over the rate of change. Is this not reasonable? Therefore we moved into the woods and eschewed central heating. And vehicles. They expand the requirement for space greatly. Now we have the space to live and breathe. Why trade it for momentary and selfish conveniences?"

"You sound critical."

"Not so. You were not aware of the principle of consequence. We would not have been either, had we not seen your example and been warned. But there is more, of course. We wish to see things develop to reflect us, not a copy of you. We had to go far back, into primitiveness, if you will, to find it."

"Have you found it?"

"It is not expected for many spans."

"How long?"

"Not in my lifetime, nor that of my children's children."

The man nodded, as if he understood, and sat back in his seat. Another took his place. The latest one was rather younger than the first two, and more polished, almost offhand. Fellirian felt as if the focus of a terrible, concentrated attention suddenly had been removed from her. Not withdrawn, but no longer weighing and measuring her. Yes, that was the word. Weighing. What was the source? She glanced about the room covertly. There was no indication of anything amiss.

Vance breathed deeply, relieved also. Although the two visitors had not exceeded the lines of general propriety, they had overplayed it, he thought. Now this next fellow: probably was a regular fellow. He certainly appeared to be, although it was not out of the realm of possibility that he too was part of the act of the previous two. Two to provoke, and one to lend controlled and measured relaxation phase. It was, after all, one of the techniques of the men of history. This one seemed to be some very minor careerist out on a boondoggle, traveling around. Vance privately knew such trips to be a waste; he had seen so much even in his limited travels. Earth, at least about ninety-five percent of it, was as homogeneous as variations in climate allowed. What had been Bulgaria did not now differ appreciably from what had once been New Jersey; Vance caught himself wondering if it ever had. Surely places differed? The light was different, the odors, the constituents of the soil? Vance thought further: few now ever saw the open sky, and when they did they disregarded it to the extent possible. The rest of objective experience was similarly shifted from the natural. Vance thought of Fellirian and what he knew of her; her perceptions were honed so fine that she could claim her nearest neighbors, the resonant-in-time Morens, actually lived in another country, one whose strangeness always amazed her. The Morens lived slightly

more than a mile away. Such microprovincialization was
common among them; in fact, it was a minor art form and
diligently pursued, although with recognition that one of its
limitations was that the "provinces" tended to grow rapidly
the farther they were away from the viewer. The object of
the art form was ultimately to bring everybody's perceptions
into agreement and divide their whole world up into micro-
provinces, purely as an exercise in perception.

Vance glanced at the roster of the visitors, to see if he
could catch a hint of where the questioners had originated.
He looked in vain; the whole list was comprised of programmed names, which of course gave no hint whatsoever of
national or ethnic origin. Vance also felt some irritation. He
was the only human in the room not having a programmed
name. The visitors probably secretly regarded him as one of
the obstructionists.

The most recent questioner seemed friendly, even apolo-
getic for taking their time. He asked, "You must excuse my
curiosity, but I have found today's tour fascinating. There is
only one question I cannot lay to rest: what do you do for
entertainment? I can imagine sleeping out of doors now and
again, but after a time I should imagine becoming stifled by
nothing to see but woods and nothing to do but survive."

It was tactlessly put and poorly phrased, but Fellirian
thought she understood what the young man was getting at.
She looked away for a moment, through the window into the
deepening evening. She felt a wave of fatigue pass over her
and wished to be on her way home. She turned back, her
voice on the edge of a companionable chuckle: "You would
be astounded to learn how much time is spent in the process
of being primitive." She laughed her laugh again. "The children have to be instructed, there is the *Klanh* profession, the
work of supporting the household, cleaning, washing, tending
the garden and the stock. Our individual competences.
Hauling water. This last is the reason for the tradition of
building each *yos* close to running water. Entertainment? By
the time I reach home tonight I won't need any." She became
more serious. "Please don't take us for an assemblage of dour
work-lovers, drudges of yard and kitchen. We have our own
humors and games and pastimes, some of them subtle and intricate. And there are many other things; we tell tales to one
another, sing, dance. Cultivate friendships, and enemyhoods,
too. There is a whole cycle in itself on that last alone. I come
here often, so I feel more at home in your house, but even

so, I find myself bewildered by the entertainments you have. I would fall asleep trying to sample even a few of them."

"You don't sound bored."

"No. We have tried to order things so that ennui is at least one enemy we do not have to face. Boredom leads to revolutionary desires, not oppression, there. And change-of-boredom never improves. It gets worse. No, speaking for myself and those I know, I want no change. Only my own life."

Fellirian intended to say more, but something checked her, and she stopped. As it was, she felt naggingly that perhaps she had said more than she had intended to. *Well, too late. The words were now birds in flight.* But she thought she knew the source of the oppressive feelings during the meeting: yes, she was certain, although she could not prove it. She had been monitored. The questioners had been bait for someone else, offstage, listening, recording. She nodded to the last questioner, the young man, as if to indicate she was finished. Expressing his gratitude, he resumed his seat. Fellirian looked over the rest. They had lost interest in today's matters, and in the ler and the Institute. Now they were anxious to depart. It was an emotion she could appreciate, even share. She was anxious to leave as well. So now they had seen the famous New Humans. Well, they weren't so special after all, were they? The only thing they had really been interested in, although they went to some pains to conceal it, had been in adolescent sexual behavior and mores, which, to their minds, seemed indistinguishable from simple promiscuity. And of course that which they wanted most to see, Fellirian was unable to deliver for them.

Vance, watching the clock, was noticing that it had arrived at the proper time for the visitors to leave; in fact, several of them had also been watching the clock, as Vance had observed. They noticed him in turn, and began to busy themselves with preparations for departure, scraping chairs, arranging their coats and overcoats, retrieving rubber overshoes to put on. After a few perfunctory good-byes and appreciatory remarks, some awkward, the members of the visitors' party one by one put themselves together and filed out of the room. The last one out made some polite comment to Director Vance, and closed the door behind him as he left. The meeting room returned to silence.

Fellirian stood by her chair, Vance by the door, doing nothing, Vance remembered, turned, and turned down and then out the overhead lights. This was in deference to Fel-

lirian who always felt uncomfortable in varying degree in any
illumination other than natural light or the yellow glow of oil
lamps and candles. Now she appreciated this little gallantry.
The soft blue light of late November replaced the hard-emis-
sion spectrum of the overheads, flowed into the meeting
room, softening it with its bluish rainy light. Outside, distant
lamps began to come on, getting a headstart on piercing the
darkness. Fellirian moved her chair over closer to the windows, sat.

By the door, Vance hesitated for a moment, uncertain.
Then, abruptly, he called down to the canteen through the in-
tercom for two mugs of hot tea. That done, he turned back
to Fellirian, who was now rummaging through her belt
pouch, retrieved from where she had laid her other things.
From it, she removed a small, shallow smoking pipe, which
she packed with a light brown tobacco. Vance approached,
produced a lighter, held it for her, stood back to watch her
get the fire up in the bowl. Started to her satisfaction, she sat
back, rested an arm along the windowsill, and blew a large,
roiling cloud of blue smoke at the ceiling.

"I know, I know," she said. "It will dirty up your ventilator
system."

"No, no, go ahead. I don't care. Let them get dirty. Most
of the visitors were dying to smoke as well but they were too
shy to ask."

"Not too shy to press me closely." She paused. "But never
mind." She turned to the window for a moment, looking at
nothing in particular out there in the deepening blue of evening, now approaching a violet in tone. After a time, she
turned back. Vance had pulled a chair over to her place, and
was waiting.

Fellirian sighed deeply, as if still phrasing the words she
wished to say. She began, "Walter, you have contacts there,
in the real world. I mean, at Region Central. What are the
changes? There is something odd in our visitors, something
orchestrated that has not been there before; the last few parties of visitors and trainees have been a spooky lot, more nervous than the usual lot of sightseers we get. They seem full of
odd sets of contradictions, repressed things, all under the surface, nothing out in the open. As if they suspect something,
but are afraid to even inquire into it. I could feel the hostility
of this last group, the looks, the attention they gave my remarks, the questions they asked. There was purpose there;
someone was feeling me out. But for what? They know, those

repulsive Security people, that they could ask directly and I would speak freely. I am no plotter, no member of secret covens."

Vance noted her indignation, but did not comment on it. Instead, he said, "There have been some changes recently, at Region, but I have not been able to gauge the full impact or direction of them all yet." He paused. "And of course you already know the feelings of the mass of the people. Those feelings range from outright paranoia through envy to exasperation. They say most often that you are 'a gang of oversexed mutants who refuse to save the world. . . .' "

Fellirian interrupted. "Oh, oversexed! Would that it were so, now! But it's gone . . . we were fortunate with the third child, but . . . Well, it's just gone, the way it is for all of us. Surely they know that side of us as well."

"It is your infertile adolescence that nags at them. At us," he added. "We don't have anything like it. And in this century, bastardy is a capital crime, you know. More than that, it's two for one. . . ."

"Both parents depersonified. I know. But we are no less severe with those who would outbraid mate and conceive, in our terms. But the rest is just as much nonsense. They should see me chopping wood, or Morlenden walking through the woods to the remotest districts to keep up with things. Or Kaldherman and Cannialin and Pethmirvin up to all hours out in the shed, bringing in another batch of paper for our written records; or writing entries, cross-referencing. I don't feel like *Ubermensch*; I feel like an overworked bureaucrat in one of your own vast civil service hierarchies."

The tea arrived, carried upward to the conference room by an automatic dumbwaiter set in an alcove in the wall. Vance went over, collected the cups. They were still steaming. Returning, he said, "Yes, I sense some of the change that you have. I know of others . . . but so far I have not been able to tie any of it to anything concrete, like a change of policy. I write it off as just a periodic mood-shift. Thrills and adventure, something to get excited about. It's the pressure, you know. We need relief. We grind away, knowing that all our best efforts are just something temporary to keep us afloat until next month, or next year. One crisis succeeds another, one shortage another. You can keep it going, but it wears hard. Even here, secluded as we are, I feel that every day."

Fellirian looked toward the window, as if looking for some hint in the darkened sky, the rain, the night-fading vistas of lights and shiny streets. She turned back, asking, "And you have heard nothing?"

"Absolutely nothing. As you know, I used to have good contacts at Region Central. Old Vaymonde, they say, wasn't much of a chairman; no charisma. But he kept the infrastructure up, he did. Always talked with the Division heads. He was liked, not tolerated."

"I remember him well. One of the few to die in office."

"Right. At his post to the end. You know, there is a vulgar story to the effect that . . . Never mind. But when Denver installed this new chairman, this Parleau, my sources dried up, one by one. Retired, replaced, shifted, reassigned. All gone. Nothing sinister; he just wants his own people. But I keep a close eye on him, this Parleau. They say that he's one of their favorites, from somewhere out west, Mojave Region, or Sonora, or even Baja. One of those desert places—solar power and mining. He's a no-nonsense type: action, long hours, clean desk, business before pleasure, the needs of society, all that. And they say at Central these days that a new broom . . ."

". . . Sweeps clean. Ugh. Tell me no more tales of brooms. That one is worn to death." She sipped her tea, nodded. "Yes. I can see that. And I also know that it has been getting harder to get off the reservation, too. More papers, forms, registrations, passports. All amply justified, of course: that's the very soul of a bureaucracy—everything has its reasons. Of course, I could say that the real reasons are never stated, and sometimes even unknown to the official; many would be offended to know them. But even so, enough. I am overly sensitive to these things because of my own role—the permitting of weavings, the allowance of names, the registration of children. Nearness breeds suspicions."

She stopped for a moment, sipped at her tea, turned and gazed once more into the distance through the windows. She turned back, saying, "Besides, it's hardly worth the trouble. We have little enough outside the reservation. And I've heard tales I'd not care to test firsthand. We've had some disappearances. . . ."

Vance looked sharply at the head of Braid Deren. "You hadn't mentioned that before. . . ."

"No."

"Who were they?"

"Not so many. No one I know personally. Elders, by the talk of it. And all very vague, you know. It's all fourth-hand stuff. So far it has apparently been only elders, who could disappear for any number of reasons. The Final Cure Cult believes in natural death, alone in the woods. No one sees *them* again. Now, if something like this were to involve someone of brood phase, or adolescent, people would be more interested."

"How interested?"

"I couldn't say, right now. If it were deliberate, and some human agency were involved, I'm sure there would be some reaction. *What*, is the question. I cannot imagine how we could threaten you; we have neither the power nor the weapons, and if we had them, I don't know the way of their use. You know the Command of Demirel—not to use that as weapon which leaves the hand. No guns, no numbers."

"But you have butter, which could be withdrawn."

"The input, through the Institute? Oh, it would have to be very serious, then. I do not wish such a confrontation."

"Nor I, Fellirian. We have learned much from you."

"Not enough, if you don't put it into practice."

"Give us time. Institutions die hard."

"You've had time: four hundred years with your backs to the wall. Twenty billion humans! I don't know what I'd do with so many bodies. The very idea gives me nightmares; we'd run out of allowable names!"

"That's your worry?"

"That's the Deren part of me speaking. The county clerk, the registrar. Just think of the awful names people would have to use: we'd use up the good ones right away. Then there would be a girl named Gallflanger and a boy named H'wilvsordwekh."

"Only one Fellirian at a time."

"Only one. As long as I live no one may have that name, no matter what aspect. But one Braid couldn't cope with that level of work, nor would the people; instead, there would be First-derens, Second-derens, Third-derens ... not for me, such multiples. I like being unique, even if what we do is not the most desirable role in the community."

Vance returned to an older topic: "So then, you sense some hostility?"

"We always sense some. It's not a matter of none and some; it's some, and then some more. Always greater than zero."

"Do you know anything on your side that might be fueling the present feedback you are getting?"

"No. That is what makes this time so troublesome. Mind, I do not say that nothing is going on; just that I know of nothing. But I know a lot. And we can look again. Morlenden is due back late tonight or tomorrow. I'll ask him. He moves about and hears more than the rest of us. He has the bad job, you know. And you. You must have a snoop planted around Center as well. Why don't we compare notes next time I see you?"

"Probably nothing going on that some sunshine wouldn't cure."

"Indeed, it could be the season. I am moody in the rainy autumn as well. It is not my season." Fellirian finished, and sipped once more at her tea. It was gone. She returned to her pipe. It had gone out. She looked up. It was time to leave.

Vance saw the cue, and said, "Well, let it be. Don't worry about it. I know of no reason either, right now. Will you be coming next week?"

"I would like to miss next week if I can. If it's just the same with you. Why don't you see if you can get someone else to fill in for me here with the visitors. For instance, that Maellenkleth Srith Perklaren. Or the Shuren girl, Linbelleth. . . . They're both young, but they have done this before. I am far behind in Braid work, and I wish to get caught up a bit. That is also why Morlenden has been out so much lately in the field; we all have been catching up with everything that happened this summer. There is more to the role than you realize. And we were irresponsible this summer, we lazed around and played with the children, worked the garden. We got behind. So Morlenden has been out weeks at a time. I have actually begun to miss him."

"Didn't you before? I thought you were always close. . . ."

"So we have been. But you also know"—and here she slipped into her own speech, Singlespeech—"*Toli len Tooron Mamnatheno Kurgandrozhas*: Only the insiblings know the way of incest. We are too close. We take each other for granted. It's the way. We always fought a lot when we were little; we competed. But under that, we always knew what was coming for us, so after the fights we always buried the hatchet. We never had the luxury of being able to say, 'Well, fly off, Turkey-wattle, that's the last I'll see of you.' No. We always knew that whatever happened, what had been with friends and lovers, in the end the fertility would be ours, the *Klanh*-holding ours . . . and so it's been forty-five years for us, sleeping in a pile together most of the time. A little while out for the inweaving of the afterparents. So we always took the future for granted, too; when the time came, we'd go along our own paths, as we'd waited for so long. But after Kaldherman and Cannialin, and my own third fertility . . . it changed. We found that we actually felt more right together, somehow. So now we have been talking of remaining together when the Braid unravels. This causes another problem: where do we go?"

"Of all the things you can't make up your mind about . . ."

"Morlenden wants to join an elder lodge that, as he says, has some 'rigor' to it. One which does what you would call speculating into the nature of things. Or even Beechwood Lodge, the geneticists. For myself, I'd be pleased to go off somewhere, tend a garden, eat and drink, and tell made-up adventure stories by the fire in the communal hearthroom. But he's Fire, and I'm Earth. Aspect conflict. But also I think perhaps Olede-Kadh is just kidding. When all's said and done, he's nowhere as rigorous as he'd like people to think."

"I'm sure you'll make up your minds by the time—after all, you've got twenty years. It isn't like it was tomorrow. At any rate, your future is either decided or decidable. As for my own . . ."

"The Fertility Board has not answered your request yet?"

"Not yet."

"What can I offer but my regrets. I should like to see you with a family as you have seen me these years."

"So should I. But time is passing."

"That it is. I have heard they only approve the best. . . ."

"Were it so there I choose to believe I should have children older than your Pethmirvin, but they choose the visible. It works out to the worst sort, by and large, of toadies and arse-kissers. My records and achievements are second to none. But this job at the Institute never has had much favor . . . and there's the matter of my turning down a programmed name back when I was a trainee. It's been no secret, but I knew then I was taking my chances. . . ."

"You know, Walter, if you had taken one of those awful random-generated tags, no better than a number, you'd not have stayed here, and that's been worth something to many of us. Many of us now work willingly here, where before we did it only out of a sense of obligation, a debt. There is a difference in the input and a measurable one in the output. They should mark that one for you."

"You'd be surprised what they dig up to hold against you,

when the time comes. You know what they say over in Inspection Directorate, and in Standardization? That no matter who it is, no matter how good they look, they can always find a way to Unsat* them. It's just how far they want to go."

Fellirian looked away from Vance for a moment, something flickering across her plain, open face, too quick to be seen, something, an emotion, close to annoyance. Vance's remarks were in themselves not wrong, so much as was the emphasis he put upon them, here, now. A wave of uneasiness moved in the back of her mind, then subsided. They all knew about bureaucratic systems, and they both knew that any system applied to classifying people which advertised objectivity drifted toward the worst and most crass forms of subjectivity. They? It was common knowledge along both sides of the fence.

She commented, as neutrally as she could, "I still hope for the best for you, nevertheless." After she spoke, she turned again to the window, now rising from her chair. She looked pensively outside for a long time, and then turned and went to a recessed alcove by the door, retrieving her outer clothing. Drawing the winter overcloak about her shoulders, she stepped into her winter boots, soft, supple leather, lined with a fiber material.

"It's time to go. The mono is in and waiting for latecomers such as I."

"Of course, Fellirian. I understand about the other two, the ones you mentioned. No problem. I'll see you in a few weeks, then. Come again, and we'll visit some more over some tea."

"Oh, I'll be back. I like to study the visitors as much as they like to study me." Here she paused, as if phrasing some difficult thought into bearable language. "But you know I need to refresh myself in my own surround. You and I, we are old friends. But because of that we overlook the fact that we are really very alien to one another, that we have different perceptions. Even so, I . . . but never mind. Next time, then?"

"Next time. I shall wait."

Fellirian turned and passed through the sliding doorway, which closed behind her, leaving Director Walter Vance alone in the meeting room. For considerable time, he sat quietly alone in the dimming evening light, now close to darkness, thinking of nothing in particular, forcing no specific pattern of coherent thoughts. He walked over to the window

---

* Unsat: To give someone an unsatisfactory rating.

and looked out into the same evening landscape Fellirian had
been watching not long before. The light was now a deep
sourceless violet-blue, the end of another rainy November
day, deep in what as a child he had thought of as the bottom
of the year. Bare, dripping branches. Shiny pavements, reflecting a silvery light. Shallow puddles ruffled by a light, variable wind, their reflections broken into shards by fitful gusts of
raindrops. The monorail which ran into the far reaches of the
reservation was yet standing in the station, waiting. Vance
watched as a hooded and cloaked figure, rather more slight in
stature than a human would appear at this distance, walked
over to the mono along the platform, unhurriedly. The figure
slid a door back, entered a coach, and vanished from his line
of sight. The pale, pastel coaches sat immobile, breathing
tremulous, tentative wisps of steam from the heaters into the
damp and chilly air.

Then he noticed that the mono was moving, had been
moving, and it had started so subtly he had missed it. Its
speed increased, and it glided effortlessly along its single, flattened concrete track, silently. It curved away to the northwest, passing through a grove of pine trees. For a time he
could follow its motion behind the trees, watching the lights,
but at last it vanished from view entirely, fading behind the
shoulder of a low rise. Vance looked away from the window,
walked back to the dumbwaiter panel, and ordered more tea.
Then he returned to his seat and waited. He knew what
would come.

The room was almost dark. It grew fractionally more dim,
almost night-dark, and the night advanced still another incre-
ment. Vance waited. He did not wait because he was a patient man, or because he had learned the fine art of time-
watching from Fellirian. Or because he was placid of disposition; rather he waited because he expected a certain specific
event to occur. For a time there was no indication of any
event to come. But at last a tiny sound broke the after-hours
stillness of the building. It was a small noise from the ceiling,
an indeterminate click whose precise location could not be
pinpointed. Vance heard it. He did not look up.

He said, seemingly into empty air, in a tired voice, "To
whom do I speak today?"

The voice replied with perfect fidelity, just as if it were is-
suing from the mouth and throat of a person physically
present in the room here with him, the mechanisms transmit-

ting even the most subtle inflections of personal mannerism which reproducers usually missed. The voice was a breathy one, a little scratchy, a voice with a bubble of confidence in it. A smug voice. A voice belonging to someone having all the high cards.

It said, "Very sly, there. As if you had known before, and so I should follow the habit. Smooth, Director. But you know that the identity is never given; against the rules, so it is. And after all, what does it matter? We all say the same things."

Vance replied, "As usual you are right. I just wondered if I would draw an inexperienced one of you, just once."

The voice chuckled, genuine humor which it deigned to share. "Hardly that, sir. We don't work that way. You wouldn't believe the training we get, the evaluations we must pass. Rigorous is simply not the proper word! We even have a simulator to reproduce this kind of environment, to prepare us for fielding these little questions, these sly feints. But, Director, I assure you, we deal with some real masters; sly indeed they are, sneakier than an agency head in budget-cutting time. But enough of the poor Controller's job, yes? We want to get to business. So I must congratulate you on an exceptionally fine performance tonight and this evening, yes, all of it. The remarks about the new staff at Region Central, the new chairman. He'll be pleased, he will, and if I may reveal a confidence, he's pleased as a rule with little enough. No nonsense, him. Why, with a bit of training I believe you could make an agent provocateur. A provoc. Or were you sincere? Impossible. But yes, indeed, they'll like all this. The chairman likes a little hostility, controlled, of course. He says that it gives his directors that cutting edge."

"I'm sure."

"So I must regretfully inform you that we shall probably stop this circuit now."

"And so you have agreed with what I first told you."

"Yes, yes, of course. This was not doubt of your word, Director Vance, just routine verification. What we derived today has already gone upchannel to Timely Analysis Branch. Real-time forwarding, or almost so, at any rate. They concur, but their concurrence returns when they send it; they have to mull things over up there, not like us front-liners down here on the killing floor, so to speak. So they agree, as did we, you and I, if I may use the pronoun loosely. There's no ore in this Fellirian for processing, neither a dram nor a scruple. Her stress index appears rather high today, but it was steady; no jumps when special tagged subject matter is introduced. We quite agree with her that she knows of no conspiracy."

"So much for what she and I know. Is there one?"

"Aha! Questions from the answerer! You'll be a Controller yet. But conspiracies? I couldn't say at this point in time. There are anomalies, peculiarities. You have no need to know them now."

"Oh."

"So this circuit will be terminated. Deactivated. If you care to forward an evaluation of the proceedings as they have occurred, please utilize form eight-four-four-A, address attention F-six-three-two. I can use index points as well as you, as everyone in this competitive world."

"Speaking of points, when do mine get registered?"

"They have already been credited with the Bonus Section. You'll get a come-back copy soon. Congratulations on your sixer."

"Six? I was told it would be twenty!"

"Who was it told you that? I . . . well, you almost never see much over a deuce for this kind of work. After all, one can demonstrate negatives all day, can't one?"

Vance had no answer. The voice paused, then added, "Do you have any final comments before I break the circuit? It's my break time now."

Vance felt, almost like a pain, a sudden surge of pure rage, of frustration, of anger, growing rapidly, a spike of clean emotion, now; but it passed, and his system of internal modulations took over without too conscious a thought, leaving behind only a bitter aftertaste. Vance, like everyone else of the day, was expert at controlling his own emotions. He had done so for years, with the system, and with individuals, such as Fellirian. He said to the bodiless voice, "Perhaps this might be considered overly bold, but I must say that spying upon one's oldest friends is a degrading act requiring great compensation. I hope you have no more of these cooperations."

"Freely said, freely taken." There was a pause. Then the voice began again, "Analysis says you get one bonus point for honesty, minus two for too great an attachment to an imaginary peer-group value." The voice hardened. "And you're too soft in that area, you know. We do. Still, you end up with a fiver for today's work. Over average. Keep working at it."

"Thank you, I will."

"I have a last word of advice. Guidelines, if you will. The first is this: if one will sell, his price can be driven down to its true value. We could have run this operation without your cooperation, entirely. But then you would have got nothing. Perhaps a minus, who knows. Consider yourself lucky that we asked first. You know the rules; we don't have to. The second thing is this: you believed the ler lady's innocence of conspiracy. So it has turned out to be no little thing to assist Control in a little surveillance when one's friends are indeed innocent. What harm does it do? We work by eliminations, by isolation of most-improbables. So now, by a little work, your friend has been eliminated as an active suspect. So states the report. That should relieve you. And then this third thing: you are director of Interface Institute, and the New People, the ler as they call themselves, are most interesting. But to us who must manage the dangerous world, they represent a greater danger than the Cro-Magnon men did to the poor Neanderthals. We never found the aliens in deep space, Director; we made them here at home—and those people are stranger than anything we could expect to find out in the stars. Fins, fur, hands, paws, flippers; air-breathers, water-filterers, ammonia processors. Those kinds of aliens we could handle. These we can't. And these we take no chances with."

"They are much like us. Almost the same, really. Could it be that we don't really understand ourselves?"

"One problem area at a time. Control doesn't work Research."

"Certainly, but . . ."

"Good evening, Director."

"Good evening." Vance never heard any audible indication that the circuit had indeed been broken. After the last parting remarks by the unnamed Controller, there passed only silence. Vance could not be sure at what moment they turned it off. If they turned it off. He got up from his chair and walked tiredly to the dumbwaiter. The tea was cold.

They were disembodied voices in the night; where they were didn't matter, couldn't matter. They could be anywhere; they were everywhere, seemingly. In the place where they were, it was always night, the lighting artificial. There were no windows. Shift relieved shift. Incoming members reviewed instructions, read notices, signed forms. Outgoing members also signed forms. Shift relieved shift. And the voices had passed and echoed through the circuits so many times that when repairmen went into the cable tunnels, they sometimes found unexplained traffic still going on what were supposed to be deactivated lines. They called these fading voices "copper ghosts," the imprints of gone and forgotten Controllers still wandering through the circuits. Voices in an eternal night.

"Sector Ten. Go ahead, there."

"Two-Alpha Control. A hard copy record format follows my voice report. Going now, there, depress your acknowledge."

"Got it there, Two-Alpha."

There was a pause, but the line remained open and live.

"And Ten here."

"Two-Alpha. Go ahead."

"Re your hard copy, noted and concur. Eval says Vance to be reassigned to a more innocuous position at the first discreet opportunity. Negative haste. Promotion category Delta. He's getting unreliable. Too specialized. Needs more generalist work. We also recommend that there be no more passives like this, permissive, you know, for not less than thirty days, as per Schedule twenty-nine, column twenty, line fifteen."

"Charlie your instructions. Have it right here. We'll set up the involuntaries, and forward tell the take to your house."

"Right that. According to schedule, there. Ten out, break."

And for a time, along a certain channel of communications, along wires, over laser beams in evacuated pipes, along wave-guides in which nothing passed save microwaves, there was silence. The line was dead. But there was not, at the ends of such channels, inaction.

THREE

The teacher instructs the student; just so the master with the novice. It is the final measure of both instructorship and masterhood how much the instructor learns from the student. We can further state that the greater the distance-of-

> *relationship between the two, the more apparent
> this becomes, so that with a very young child, the
> best teacher actually learns more than the child
> in the process of instruction.*
>
> *—The Game Texts*

The Reservation Monorail was their sole concession to modernity; for the rest of the space enclosed by the boundary fence, the only modes of travel available were walking, riding a pony, or driving a cart pulled either by oxen or the heavy, solid horses the ler preferred. Its track plan covered most of the reservation in a skewed figure eight, the north loop leaned sharply over into the northwest corner, and the south loop broadened and spread out to the southeast. There were two trains, which ran in the same direction twelve hours apart, each drifting around the whole of the route more or less in the course of a day.

On the days when Fellirian worked at the Institute, she had to spend almost all of the previous day traveling, spending the night at the Institute hostel (operated by Braid Shuren). Then, the next day, she would board the mono for the ride back. But where before the way of motion had been against her, so that she had to ride all the way around to get to the southeast where the Institute was located, the way back, to the contrary, was short and almost direct, straight into the center of the reservation, where lay her Braid holding.

It would be late when she arrived at last, after a long ride, a long day, and a long walk as well; and in the cold and damp season of the year. Still, for her, it was better than spending another night out. It would be near midnight when she finally got home, but that was fine enough—they would save some supper for her, and some would stay up late to share some talk. She did not care so much for travel, as did her insibling and co-spouse Morlenden, who did most of the Braid's field work. That was the drudgery, the visits, the ceremonies. But Morlenden never complained, aside from some grousing which they all knew was not serious. Her work down at the Institute was tiresome; but it was a window on the outside, one of the few maintained of which she was aware. Her evaluations of that narrow view were all part of a grist constantly being fed to the lineal ruling Braid, the Revens. Pellandrey Reven, Insibling and *Klandorh* . . . the feelings and the thoughts which went with them trailed off.

Boarding the mono, which was operated by the Gruzen

Braid, she could see yet, even in the deep evening light, the modest monument the people had erected for the enlightenment of the visitors; it reassured her. An inlaid woodcarving with an overlay of subtle color wash, it was supposed to be a visual image of the central doctrine of ler self-image.

Circular in outline, the bas-relief of the Emblem was divided internally into four quarters, as aligned with the four points of the compass; within each was depicted a person, highly suggestive in symbolism. The upper quarter showed a ler elder, with the long double braids characteristic of the class, wreathed in clouds bordered with lightning in the sky and flame along the base. The heraldic figure was reaching out of the clouds with its right hand toward the center of the Emblem, while its left hand, upraised, held some of the lightnings. The expression along the planes of the face appeared stern, judicial, abstract, emotionless. It was, so far as the human visitors could determine, utterly undifferentiated by sexual characteristics.

The figure depicted in the right-hand panel seemed to be a military figure, drawn with great subtlety and respect. This figure seemed mature, rather than elder; the single braid of hair falling to the middle of the back reinforced this impression. And where the elder in the upper panel had been clothed in a simple pleth, a utility garment, this one was depicted wearing a kiltlike garment about the hips and thighs, while the upper torso was covered by a light sleeveless vest or jacket. The kilt or skirt seemed to suggest leather, the vest a coarse weave, or perhaps chain mail. On the head was a light leather helmet with a stiffened ridge along the top. The Warrior, as it was known, held a short, leaf-bladed sword in its left hand, the one nearest the viewer. The point was held down, deliberately, not simply drooping. And with its right hand, it reached also for the center of the Emblem.

On the opposing left side, the figure depicted appeared to be similar in age and class to the military figure on the right, but it was dressed in a long, flowing gown, with a hood attached to the garment, but folded back. This one was shown in the act of emerging from a garden through a simple arched masonry gate, carrying a basket filled with various fruits and vegetables, some recognizable, others enigmatic. It carried the basket in the right hand, toward the viewer, and reached into the center with its left. This figure suggested a feminine nature, to the same degree that the figure to the right suggested masculinity. Subtly. One imagined, but was not quite sure.

The figure in the bottom quarter panel seemed the most striking of all: unlike the others, which were colored in a direct and naturalistic manner, she was almost completely painted in tones of blue, as were her surroundings in the panel. She: the image was of a young girl dressed in a filmy homespun shift that suggested almost every detail of the supple body beneath; and she was shown reaching upward, yearning, with both arms and hands upraised, her young and innocently lovely face also turned upward, filled with an expression of rapture. She was shown emerging from a pool of water around which water plants grew profusely. . . .

Riding along the track of the mono, Fellirian now saw full night through the windows of the coach she was riding; and little else. The mono made its deliberate and unhurried way through the nighted country of the reservation. She looked through the windows more closely; while she could not make out much of the passing unlit details, she could make out the forest silhouette of the treetops, outlined against the weak sky-glow which was always present, no matter what part of the reservation one happened to be in. There were no lights within the reservation to cause this; rather, they were all outside its borders, the signs of the industrial civilization which surrounded it on all sides. It was stronger in the west and north, but the glow was never invisible, not even in the center.

There was hardly a place on the entire planet, on the waters as well as along the lands, where it was not possible to read a newsgram from the public information agency by available light in the hours of darkness. Human society worked around the clock, in total disregard of local time. On their calendar, they still showed the ancient days of the week, but the number of people who actually used them for their schedules was very small, almost nonexistent. For the rest, the vast mass of twenty billion, they oriented themselves to their particular shift cycle. There were four of these shifts, interlaced so that each person within a shift worked, in succession, five evenings, one off, five midnights, one off, five days, followed by five days off. Four shifts, each with an identity of its own.

Fellirian continued to meditate, relaxing, letting the thoughts lead where they would. Shifter Society, they called it;

its emblem was a cube with a staring brown eye upon each of its visible faces. Fellirian thought it peculiar, unnecessary. They didn't need to put the whole planet on shifts for a war footing against some invader, not for production reasons, for it took as much to sustain a twenty-four-hour-a-day operation as they gained from it. But she thought she knew. There seemed to be two main reasons; one was that by having shifts one could use space more efficiently, and hedge against the panic brought by overcrowding. It also gave the millions idled by arbitrary changes something to do while they were being reoriented.

As each man's work had become steadily more piecemeal and meaningless, so had establishments interlocked into one another and pressed into private lives. One by one, the nations had grown into one another; governments did not protect their people, but protected themselves. Some radicals hoped and strove for the day when people would wake up. But if they ever had, there had been no sign of it; the conscious decisions were no improvement over the half-asleep ones. Of course, at the very end of the old period, pre-shift, there had been some frictions, bickerings, adjustments. That had been the days of the Attitude Patrols, volunteers who did not monitor performance, but intangibles such as feelings and motivations. The end of the first population crisis had seen Shift Society emerge triumphant. And so afterward public buildings were multipurpose, used full-time, all year, every day. There was no wasted space. Every square foot which did not contain working space, contained the minuscle living quarters allotted to all. Everything left over was either power production or agriculture.

But they forgot, by will, design, or accident, that once buildings had been made to serve men, whatever perverse uses they had put them to, however seldom. The more logical and reasonable life came to be ordered, the more illogical and confusing it became; now people existed to fill buildings to maximum efficiency, just as customers in a queue existed to give the bored clerk something to do. Once buildings had been inspirational; now they were four sides and a top, functional, and reusable. Each one lasted, on the average, less than a person's lifetime. As with the buildings, so it was with everything else. If one quarter of Earth's population was at work at a given minute, so it was also true that almost another quarter were deep in their cups, drunk as lords. And if there were no more armies, there were vast numbers of police in their place so that the actual number of armed men was greater by percentage than in the worst of previous periods of world war.

Over the shifts were the members of the hierarchy, most of whose numbers were stabilized on permanent day-shifts, although certain of their order worked other fixed shifts: midnights, eves. Recruited from the upward-striving shifters who had already demonstrated their allegiance, few had other than programmed names, and fewer still had any recognizable family ties. The organization was all.

They called this system civilization, and considered it the best of all possible circumstances; considering the chaos which it obviously held at bay, perhaps it was an excellent compromise. But to Fellirian, it suggested nature at its rawest. And the ancient dynamics of nature, the uncontrolled fears out of the past, had not been eliminated at all, but painted over with a set of new colors. There were strains and tensions everywhere, growing slowly and insidiously daily, monthly, yearly. Man's runaway population growth had been slowly braked to an agonized halt, but the price had been the complete loss of everything else. And the sad thing to her was that the people of today knew no better life, remembered no wildlife, no freedom, no open-ended self-checked ecology; they thought the ler quaint and eccentric, impractical and superstitious. . . .

The darkened coach moved on through the night. She felt at last the letdown after a full day of work, on her feet, tense with fielding question after question. The motion lulled her, and she became first relaxed, then drowsy. She began to drift in and out of a light half-sleep; there were others in the coach with her, seated away from her, in the far end, and they seemed to be absorbed in their own affairs, or perhaps also just drowsing . . . she thought she saw one of the seated figures rising, surrealistically slow, as if under water, or it might have been a dream, a daydream. She felt her head nod, and her eyelids felt heavy. Was someone now taking the seat beside her?

"Fellirian?"

She came awake instantly and the fog cleared out of her mind. She turned to her left and looked at the person who had joined her. The voice had been male, but the person was hooded. She thought that odd, for the coach was not cold. In fact, the coach was almost too warm. "Yes," she said. "I am

Fellirian Deren. And who is it who speaks from within a hooded pleth in the overheated mono coach?"

The low voice from within the hood said, almost inaudibly, "One whom you once knew well."

She leaned forward to peer into the hood, caught a quick glimpse of a face, one she indeed knew well. Had known well. It had been some time since they had spoken. Her mouth started to form syllables of a name, but a finger was placed across her mouth. Within the hood was motion, a negation.

He leaned closer, saying, "And so it was, just as now. By the love I have had for you and your house, have I come this way to bring a warning to you."

She shook her head, as if unbelieving. He noted it, and continued, "One will come to your *yos*, asking a service which only your house can provide. You must neither delay, nor refuse it. Negotiate as you will, but let it not be in doubt between us now."

She answered, without hesitation, "It will be according to that you have spoken. But . . ."

"Ask no questions. They will all be answered in time. And not all the answers will be satisfying to you. Indeed, they will trouble you in your heart. I would not have had it so, but events press us, and they belong to one among the Powers. The Air element lies heavy upon us, and only Will counters it. But with this I also warn you to take care in all things relating to yourself from henceforth, and most especially to what you will do for this task, for there will be danger. It is for these reasons that I wear a hood, and ask that you not speak my name aloud. The mono is no place for such dialogue; I have risked much to come as far as I have."

"You could have met me elsewhere."

"Not so much as you imagine. I am watched. So are you, although not so much now. But do you not feel a change in the Institute, a shifting of balances?"

"Yes. Yes, I have, this last time. I was disturbed, but there was nothing I could see. What is it?"

"Times change always. There is nothing fixed; only varying degrees of the skill by which the riders ride the wave of the present. We enter different waters now, and the waves change. An accident, perhaps more malice than we anticipated, and perhaps something more—these things have made turbulence at a critical time when we do not need it. And now questions are being asked, sensors are being activated, old thoughts being rethought." He gestured at the outside, at the sky-glow visible beyond the treetops. "There, they are stirring again. Something bad has happened. We cannot make it as it was, but we can find out of it what we must, so that we may know how much has befallen us."

"What has happened?"

"I will not speak of it; to tell what I know, and to add what I suspect, is to describe something which may not be spoken of openly here, even between such as you and me. Not even hints will I give; you do not know it now: you will have to unravel it as you go along. I want no preconceptions. But you must do it, when you are asked, and you must be careful." The last word was emphasized so strongly it came out almost a hiss. Fellirian drew back.

She paused, and said, "You speak in riddles."

"I speak as only I may, now. I fear in the end of it you will know what I do. I would have spared you the weight of it." Now the hooded shape moved, as if looking away from her, to the front of the coach. "Your stop will be soon; how say you of this?"

"It will be as you have said. We shall, we Derens. I only ask why there was haste."

"Because the one who will ask of you is either approaching your *yos* now as we speak, or is already there." He added in a suppressed half-chuckle which spoke much of some private joke, "I came to use my influence and ensure your response."

Fellirian looked to the front, and glimpsed familiar landmarks passing by. She felt the mono slowing for the halt. She stood, and the hooded figure moved to allow her to pass into the aisle. She turned to him and said, "So it will be as you have asked. I wish only that we might have met more openly. We parted so."

"We will meet again, I think. And after that, who may know the future? But however the past was, we know that it is only shadows in our minds now. Pleasurable they were, but not to be repeated. We have lived other lives. And hard decisions lie ahead for me. For you. I will not trouble your heart with them now; when the time comes you will face them better with an innocent heart."

The mono stopped, fairly smoothly, but fast enough to cause Fellirian to sway slightly. He said, "And now, your stop."

"You will come with me along the long path?"

"I cannot. There are others yet to see this night, along this way, and in the north where lies my *yos*."

The coach doors opened. Outside it was so quiet the dripping of rainwater could be heard. Fellirian said quietly, "I have kept the tradition of the *vayyon*."

"As have I. But in time all secrets may have to go overboard. But think not of the past, and prepare to wrestle the future."

She nodded. "Just so . . . it was good to see you again."

"And you. I do not forget. And may it be with your *Toorh* as with you."

"And so with yours as well." She turned to depart the coach.

The doors opened, and Fellirian focused on the immediate now, where she was. Her memory had distracted her, disoriented her, reinforced by the voice of the man who had spoken. She stepped down out of the coach into the cold dampness. There was fog now; the rain had stopped, yet only recently, for all things dripped. It was almost noisy after the muffled quiet of the coach, her attention single-mindedly riveted. It was an elevated platform made of wood, shingled, charmingly rustic. To her left was the waiting-shed, open on the side facing the track; a sign, weather-beaten and stained, displayed the name of the stop: Wolgurdur, it said in the plain shapes of the Singlespeech alphabet. Flint Mountain Halt. The cold air touched her, and she shivered, adjusting from the warmth of the coach. Then she took a deep breath, clearing her head, and started slowly for the stairway which wound down to the forest floor.

At the head of the stairs she turned back to see if she could still see inside the coach. The doorway was open, and within it was the same figure, his face obscured in the shadows of his hood. She raised her voice and called to him, in a clear but still quiet voice, "Never fear! I will do it for you."

The figure answered, "Not for me, but for us all. You will see." Then he looked to his left, into the shed, back to her. "Is someone waiting there, in the shed?"

Fellirian turned back. She could not see around the corner, so she walked over to the edge of the shed, looked within. Sure enough, there was a person there, wrapped against the night damp, huddled over, apparently asleep. Fellirian shook her head, chuckling to herself. Here was some night-wanderer who had come the long walk down to Flint Mountain to await the mono, and, tired from the exertion, had taken a catnap in the corner; now not even awakened by the arrival of the train, nor their talking across the platform. The mono was waiting. Fellirian approached, and gently shook the traveler's shoulder, an adolescent by the feel of it. The person awoke, and looked up with the blankness of one awakened suddenly, undoing the hood of her overcloak.

Fellirian smiled, then laughed aloud. She said, half to herself, "Well, well, well! Whoever should I happen upon in the mono halt waiting-shed, but my own *Nerh*, Peth-child." She turned and waved to the train, that they should depart, and turned back again to Pethmirvin. "Whatever are you doing down here in the very bowels of the night?"

While Pethmirvin collected her wits, the mono began to move. The coach in which Fellirian had been riding moved past, slowly accelerating. In a moment, it was gone. Pethmirvin, the elder outsibling of the Derens, Fellirian's firstborn and her secret favorite, looked up at her foremother blankly for a long moment, and then away, averting her eyes, deeply embarrassed to have been caught thus dozing in the shelter. Fellirian's child and favorite she might have been, but the girl resembled neither her mother nor her forefather, Morlenden. Peth was another quality. She was slender, thin as a reed, awkward, self-conscious. Her hair was a pale, washed-out light brown. She was tall already for a ler, and very pale in color. But in the summer, her hair bloomed into a warm, rich golden color, and her skin turned the color of lightly browned toast. In her face, there were faint reminders of Fellirian, in the large, expressive eyes and the broad, generous mouth; yet there was a crispness there, too, something which subtly echoed Morlenden: the long face, with its suggestions of boniness, the hard chin. Pethmirvin was variable as quicksilver: lovely one moment, homely the next.

The girl tried to speak, but since she was not yet completely awake, the words came all tumbling out, like a badly wrapped parcel suddenly coming undone, then falling completely apart. But one way or another, it somehow all got out. "Madheliya, here. I was supposed to meet you here. Am supposed. Here I am. When did you come?"

"Just now, sleepyhead."

"Oh, I'm sorry, really I am."

Fellirian reached into the hood, ruffling the girl's hair gently. "No sorries, Peth. Although you would have felt

funny had you missed me, and waited all night down here."
Fellirian laughed warmly. "But why have you come all the
way down here, and in the cold, too? Was it to fetch me
home? It's not as if I didn't know the way. Nor am I afraid
of the dark. And, inasmuch as time has treated me somewhat
cruelly, no lovers to make rendezvous with along the way."

Pethmirvin stood up, a little stiffly, and stretched, shivering
in the damp night air, even though she was dressed quite
warmly, as if she had been out for some time, and knew she
was going to be. When she stretched, she was taller than Fellirian.

Fellirian watched her, thinking to herself. *Fifteen and already she's taller than me. Prettier, too, in her own way. And
cast into the outsibling's lot. I worry about her, poor thing;
she hasn't the temper for it.*

Pethmirvin continued, "Kadh'olede* is supposed to be at
the *yos* by now; he had not yet come when I left, but he was
expected at any moment. One of the Morens had seen him in
a tavern by the old ferry crossing on the Hvar. They sent me
down to tell you to hurry along, and not to stop along the
way for tea at the Morens, nor visit with Berlargir and Dar-
bendrath†, because we have guests, important guests, and
they won't talk until all the parent phase Derens are present."

Fellirian had been half listening. Morlenden seen in a tavern! Of course they saw him in a tavern! She had been hearing that kind of tale for many years now. But the words
about important guests brought her to full attention, remembering what he in the mono had said. She interrupted Pethmirvin. "*Kel'ka Arnef*? Who was it?"

Pethmirvin replied, "An elder, the Perwathwiy Srith, accompanied by a didh-Srith, a bit older than me. Sanjirmil
Srith Terklaren."

Fellirian leaned back. "The Perwathwiy, indeed! At our
yos. I wonder what would bring her there."

"Madheliya, neither she nor Sanjirmil would speak of it.
And you know elders; wouldn't set a foot in the *yos*. But that
Sanjirmil thing did, though. Came right in and helped herself
to my supper she did."

"Peth, you know the way of the hospitable. We must share
with the stranger. Sanjirmil would expect supper. And as for

---

* Short form—"Forefather Morlenden."
† Insiblings of the previous generation of Derens. Specifically,
Forefather and Foremother of both Morlenden and Fellirian.

the Perwathwiy, I'd expect the full rigor of discipline from her."

"Do you know her?"

"Only by repute. Not personally. She was a Terklaren herself, first born insibling and Klandormadh in her day . . . many years ago, of course; she is the foremother of Sanjirmil's foremother. If she's a day, she's *perh meth sen-dis* years.*"

"Yes, that's her. She's all gray. She stood outside in the rain until Kaldherman went out and unlocked the shed." Pethmirvin giggled. "He said, so Sanjirmil wouldn't hear, that if she wouldn't come in, the old bat could stand all night in rain for all he cared."

"Pethmirvin Srith Deren!"

"That's what he said, Madheliya, not me! But Cannialin told him that the old woman would put a curse on him if he didn't give her some shelter. And that if she did, that she, Cannialin, would probably help her."

"Peth, you know an elder's not supposed to enter a *yos;* that's one of the Basic Arbitrations. When one's insibling children complete the weaving ceremony and the initiation, then one leaves the *yos* forever. Not just your own, anyone's!"

"I know. But a lot of them do it anyway, on the sly. And besides, it was cold and rainy."

"Doesn't matter. She would stand there anyway. But good for Ayali. So now, my sleepy girl-child; come along then. We won't get home standing here in the mono shelter and talking the night away." Fellirian put her arm around the younger girl's slender shoulders, giving her a quick hug; and so together they descended the worn, unpainted staircase to the ground, wet and quaking from the rain which had ended. They said no more, but set out directly under the bare dripping trees, northward, into the central provinces. Fellirian reflected as they began the walk homeward that in most circumstances she would have been irritated to find Peth out so late at night; yet this night she felt comforted by the girl's presence. Perhaps it was just the cold and dampness. Or more likely disturbing impressions, augmented by the cryptic rejoinder she had received riding the mono. No doubt about it: the future had become a troubled and uncertain one, and it was measurably easier to face such an uncertain future when your future could walk along for a time with you.

---

* Literally, one and seven fourteens of years, in the fourteen-base number system. In decimals, ninety-nine.

And her thoughts insisted, *The Perwathwiy Srith is then she of whom he spoke; she would ask something of us. Perwathwiy and her own Toorh's Toorh, Sanjirmil.* Her mind raced, seeking data: Perwathwiy was hetman of Dragonfly Lodge, the elder commune reserved for the Gameplayer Braids. And Sanjirmil? Fellirian had no knowledge of the girl directly. She recalled images of Braid Linebooks, reference logs, registered births, deaths, weaving ceremonies. There: she had it. Sanjirmil Srith Terklaren. Eldest *Toorh* and *Klandorh*-to-be of the Secondplayer Braid. Age, one and two fourteens, almost mature. Was there a connection? And was there a connection with the events in the Institute? She could see none. But that failed to comfort her, for she could see no reason why the Perwathwiy should come to her *yos,* and that what she would ask be agreed to beforehand. Fellirian shivered, and not entirely from the cold.

The path soon narrowed as they walked upward out of the valley in which the mono ran; had it been dry, it would have been wide enough for the two of them to walk abreast, but with the rain, the worn path was too slippery along the edges, so they walked single file, silently, Pethmirvin leading with her long-legged stride. Apparently the girl was taking her instructions seriously, for she wasted no time and set a steady pace. Fellirian, used to walking many miles, found that she needed her breath for the walk.

The path wound gently upward, meandering here and there, following lines of passage through the old forest that had been made long before Fellirian and Pethmirvin; indeed, before the ler had assembled and moved to this place. Game trails, the trails of humans who had lived here long ago, remnants of old logging roads. It crossed others, some broader, some equally broad, others hardly visible, mere pressed-down places that trailed off to either side. The path they followed led northward from the mono line into the heart of the reservation, the Wolguron, the Flint Mountains. The name was somewhat of a misnomer, for the range consisted of low hills of no great elevation, and no particular distinction, save that they were higher and steeper than the rolling country which surrounded them. But it was an old range, and it once had been high and proud, although no person had seen it so; now it was the gnawed and eroded wrinkle-remnants of the creases and folds made aeons ago in the collision of two great continents, North America and Africa. It had been eroded many times. Some argued that the range had never been high and great; but to the ler who now lived under its shadow this was no great matter. The Flint Mountains endured. They survived.

The rain had stopped, but under the many bare branches of November the icy water still dripped, and the creeks and streams were busy with the newly fallen water. The night was filled with water-sounds, drips, gurgles, rushing blurred sounds deeper in the woods. It was pleasant to hear, and it drowned out the distant sounds one heard when the woods were silent: the muted rumble of the civilization behind the lights. They found as they walked that they could see the path well enough, even with the overcast darkness and the weakness of the ler eye at night*, because of this very sky-glow. But they also had something more, for the night is never dark to those who allow their eyes time to adjust to it.

From time to time, they could sense they were passing either near some solitary *yos*, far off deep in the trees, or by some small elder lodge. Both of them knew the way well enough, so much of their knowledge was what they called unbidden memory. But there were other hints: woodsmoke, odors of cut wood; barnyard odors, stables, compost piles. Someone lived nearby. In this area there were few elder lodges, and all of the ones that were hereabouts were small, hardly larger than family Braid groups. Members of such lodges felt more like a contained Braid than a commune, where the Braid identities were quickly submerged. Indeed, Fellirian's own forefather and foremother lived in such a lodge; she saw them seldom now, but tried to drop in and visit from time to time on her way back from the Institute. From these visits, extended by Fellirian's talkative forefather Berlargir until nearly dawn, had come the phrase, "visiting at Berlargir's," which meant being away for an indefinite period of time.

The path passed close by one of the elder lodges, not the lodge of the former Derens, close enough that they would have been able to see it had it been daylight. Tonight they could not make out the buildings deeper down in a hollow, but before the entryway they could see flickering the ghostly blue of a spirit-lamp, a small paper lamp illuminated from

---

* The ler retina was more sensitive to color than the human, but it was deficient in rod cells. Their night-vision was poor.

within by a single tiny candle. It was a sign of mourning for the dead.

They passed by no other dwellings. Ler did not build their homes, whatever phase they were, close to path or roadway, but always at the end of dead-end paths which terminated at running water. Custom and ritual, just as there was only one doorway into a *yos*. They saw no other lights. The hour was late, now near midnight, and all the folk who lived along this creek, Thendirmon's Rivulet, had long since tumbled into sleep. Ler retired early.

"A rainy night," they would say, "and good for sleeping and dreaming under the rounded roofs while the raindrops fall from the branches overhead." And acorns would also drop in the autumn, shaken loose by a sudden gust of wind, resounding hollowly as they struck. Fellirian found herself thinking just these thoughts as she and her *nerhsrith* walked silently as ghosts through the dark, damp woods. And after they arrived? To come into the hearthroom, eat and talk a while, and then climb into the broodroom, removing clothing and wriggling a cold, tired body into a warm down-filled comforter, close to someone and the kind of warmth only a well-known, long-time close body can provide. Yes. She remembered: back when they all had been in their fertile period, the second for herself and Morlenden, first for Canni-alin and Kaldherman, as they had paired off with their two new co-spouses; at night they had hung a light print curtain across their common sleeping compartment, dividing it. Not for prudery, nor for jealousy, but for politeness and privacy. A rare privacy. They had all as a matter of course lived adolescences of active sexuality, with little hidden. But that was what one wanted to do. Fertility was different; compulsive, driven, almost a kind of desperate madness. The intensity of desire was of a different order entirely. Then they wanted seclusion, aloneness. It was as if children who had played games of war had suddenly found themselves in the manic violence, confusion, and panic of real war in all its horror. The playing and the fun were over: the real thing had begun. Thus, the curtain. Now it was down, packed away for the next generation. Fertility and desire had come and gone. Not their regard for one another. "Only a Braid after fertility," went the proverb, and indeed it was true.

She let her memory dig deeper into itself as they walked. Far back in their past, Morlenden—Olede whom Fellirian-Eliya could not remember not-knowing—had himself suspected that after the birth of Pethmirvin, Fellirian would bring to him for second-weaving the girl Cannialin, the *Thes*, younger outsibling of the Morens, the next Braid down the rivulet. Their ages were right, five years apart, and the Morens and the Derens always, rules permitting, exchanged younger outsiblings. Their own Kaentarier Srith had already so gone to the Morens. No surprise there, and indeed they had dallied off and on for years. But Fellirian had no idea who Morlenden would bring to her second-weaving. She had expected to be surprised, but not as astounded as she had been; she had never let the image of that day slip from the forefront of her memory.

. . . She had been feeling the first twinges of returning fertility, and this aspect of herself had begun to elicit subtle responses from Morlenden and Cannialin, although at this particular time the Moren girl had not yet moved in with them. But it had been a day late in the spring, with heavy, wet, sagging dark clouds presaging a storm, and she had been hoeing in the garden, all the while playing with Peth. And Morlenden had come strolling up the path from the *yos*, with a stranger in tow, and Fellirian, deeply embarrassed by the dust and sweat that streaked her, caught first sight of her co-spouse-to-be. Her immediate impression had been one of a truculent roughneck with a hard, severe face, rusty hair with more than a hint of curl in it, and almost a swagger to his walk. No doubt a bargeman from the River Yadh terraces.

Now at this time Fellirian had just started going down to the Institute regularly, although she had been making sporadic visits since she had been about twenty. And as a result of her travels, she had gained a spattering of romantic ideals somewhat at variance with traditional ler visions of practicality. So in her imaginings she had wished Morlenden to bring her a poet, a dreamer, a gentle charmer. She had received, to Morlenden's apparent vast mirth, what appeared to be a hewer of timbers and a piler of stones, showing along his limbs the visible corded muscles of a wrestler. She learned later that indeed he did hold a local championship for just that. But his home was far to the northwest, and she did not know him. More, as she found out later, he was *Nerh* in his own Braid, and much accustomed to having his own way among his contemporaries. And to add insult to injury, he was already full fertile. As they were introduced, and Fellirian made the ritual responses, she could already feel her own body responding to the exaggerated maleness of him. Deep in his time, as they would say.

Later, she had abused Morlenden as she never had before, and then run away into the forest, in tears and complete exasperation. But Olede had followed, patient as he always was, and after a time explained that his choice—undeniable for her as hers had been for him, except for narrowly specified reasons which almost no one used—had been intended as a rare and subtle gift, a most high token of the regard in which he held his insibling, as she would find out, if she just would. As she did. Alone in the woods, she had stopped by a quiet pool of water, and had looked long at herself, seeing more therein than the outline and shaping of a face; and she had begun to see. And as usual, Morlenden-Olede had been right. The hints were there; for Kaldherman, Adhema she now called him, was a rare gift, indeed; for he had been as tender and giving in the reality as his apparent roughness had repulsed her at the first. Fellirian also knew herself to be no notable beauty, like, for example, the heartless flirt Cannialin; she was instead simple, direct, plain, and straightforward. But to Kaldherman, she had cast a dazzling light, Fellirian-the-wise, who walked among humans without fear, in their vast cities, levels of organization to which the ler possessed no parallel. He seemed to consider himself among the most fortunate of all outsibling *Tlanhmanon*; he had woven into a Braid containing Fellirian, a prize beyond words, and in addition the urbane Morlenden and the exotic Cannialin. And already with Pethmirvin, then a child of five, it also seemed that he would be the best of all four of them with the children.

And so it had been all these years, she thought, returning to the present. Fellirian realized with a start that she had been daydreaming, and that they had come far while her mind had been elsewhere; they had been trudging steadily through the nighted, rain-wet forest. For an instant she felt disoriented, vertiginous, lost. She looked about for a landmark, some subtle reminder; she sensed they were near home. Yes. They were already past the forking in the path which led to the *yos* of the Morens, almost at the one that led to their own, far down the steep, root-strewn path. They rounded a curve in the main path, and Pethmirvin lengthened her stride, anticipating.

They came to the place where the path divided along a slight rise; from here, in daylight, one could catch a quick glimpse of the entire holding, the *yos* by the rivulet under a feathery canopy of ironwood, the sheds and outbuildings, the garden, the animal pens and yards, stone walls carefully laid. Now it was night and ahead of them were only suggestions of shapes, some dim lights showing in the translucent windows of the *yos*. The memory filled in what the eye did not actually see, and they felt a release, a happiness; they had arrived.

Fellirian paused for a moment at the foot of the stairs to the entryway—the hearthroom section of the *yos* looming above them like the high stern of some strange ship, its elliptical shape distorted by perspective—not climbing the narrow wooden stairs, but instead turning, reluctantly, to the washtrough to her right, closer to the rivulet. She looked long into the dark water gurgling into the trough from a large clay pipe communicating with the rivulet, in her mind already feeling the bite of the water on her skin.

Pethmirvin did not enter either, but remained, waiting just by the foot of the stairs. Fellirian turned, not looking at the girl, and said, "Peth, dear, you don't have to wait for me; go on in and tell the rest that we've come at last."

The girl hesitated, cleared her throat. "Can't right now, Madheliya. I must take the ritual washing, too, much as I would wish not to." Already Pethmirvin's voice seemed to have the chatter of her teeth in it.

For a long moment, they stood silently in the dark and looked at one another. They both knew the rituals and traditions and obeyed them with little hesitation. Indeed, Fellirian sometimes stressed orthodoxy, as she felt she had an example to set. Morlenden avoided the trough as much as he possible, although he was fastidious and would soak for hours in a huge washtub out back while Pentandrun and Kevlendos ran relays of hot water from the hearth. But there was the wash-custom, even in winter when it was a feat of daring to address oneself to the water. Fellirian knew that she would need to wet herself with the cold creekwater before she could properly enter her own house; she had been outside. Here the purpose was not cleanliness, for any excuse would do for a bath; rather, here was ritual, magic. Fellirian had been exposed to strangeness, alien values, and the wash invoked the cleansing power of the Water elemental to remove the dross of the outside. The pollen of the strange.

Now as for Pethmirvin, she could have incurred the water obligation for any number of reasons; but Fellirian also remembered her own adolescence, and the occasions when she herself had stood before this very trough, trembling with fear of the cold water. She thought she knew the reason, although she was mildly surprised by the season and time of occurrence. Night and winter?

Fellirian addressed Peth with mock severity, "Nerh'Emivi, by some accident did you meet a *dhainman** along the way to the mono?"

The girl answered shyly, looking at the ground as she did. "In the shed by the mono line, Madheliya. Farlendur Tlanh Dalen. He walked with me when I came down to fetch you." For a moment Pethmirvin looked up and held Fellirian's eyes in her own gaze, unflinching. Then she looked down at the ground, shy again.

Fellirian threw back the hood of her overcloak, and opening the upper part of her outer garment, retrieved the long single braid of her hair from behind her and began studiously to unfasten it. She smiled at Peth.

"Well enough, for the *didhosi*. Nevertheless, I see you at least know your custom: a wash before the *yos* for each flower-fight outside it. Careful, Peth-Emivi†, that you don't grow gills from all your dunkings!"

Pethmirvin giggled, hiding her face, which was now blushing furiously. "Well enough, indeed. But now you must go first. You are *Klandorh* and Madh. You have the right of age, and besides, you've been outside."

"And warm the water for you? Certainly not! I waive my precedences and rights: into the trough with you! And by the way, was your tussling fun? This was never my season, although I never stinted in the warmer days. . . ."

Peth shifted her stance from one foot to another, saying breathlessly, "Oh, yes, except that it was too cold and we had to . . ."

Fellirian broke into the beginnings of what promised to be a long story whose purpose was to delay entry into the trough. "Never mind the details, please. If you must relate the entire circumstances, tell them to your *toorhsrith* Pentandrun. She has seemed a bit slow catching on. And for now, into the trough!"

"Oh, Madh."

"Oh, Madh, nothing. You can go to bed and sleep. I will

---

* In this context, a casual lover, emotional relationship not specified.

† Child-name plus body-name is an address of endearment.

have to stay up, probably all night, and talk nonsense with the Perwathwiy. Go on, hurry up! Waiting won't make the water any warmer."

Pethmirvin removed her outer overcloak reluctantly, stepping out of her boots and wincing at the cold touch of the wet wooden platform against her bare feet. She took a deep breath and quickly flipped off her overshift, undershift, and all with it, over her head, ruffling up the short, adolescent-cut hair, and stepped resolutely up to the trough, getting her courage up. The water in the wash-trough was nothing less than icy. Fellirian looked at the bare pale body before her. Pethmirvin was slender, graceful as a young sapling, sleek as a young squirrel. She had been well-named: Willowwand Windswaying was the sense of it, in the aspect of the Water elemental. Fellirian appreciated the young girl's grace, her small breasts, hardly more than buds, her delicate pale ribs, flat belly, lean, strong thighs. Her skin was goose-pimpled with the cold.

With no warning, Pethmirvin suddenly leaped into the wash-trough and began splashing madly, scattering water everywhere. Underneath the noise she made, Fellirian could hear the quick hissing of the girl's breath. While Peth splashed about, spilling much of the water, Fellirian began removing her own clothing; Outercloak, overshirt, winter undershift. And then she stood nude, feeling the bite of the cold now in earnest, looking down at her own bare body, almost as pale and spare as Peth's, but more compact, shorter in stature, and accented with the riper curvings and lines of a longer life, of bearing children. Three, no less. Pethmirvin, Kevlendos, Stheflannai. *Not bad,* she mused. *And so I still have most of the shape of my body left to me. Not that it does me any good, as it once did, except to know that there's a lot of endurance remaining in it, a long life. But once I met lovers in the night, just as she does now, and Pentandrun will soon. Once, in the spring of my life, twenty years gone and more, boys chased me through the woods and called "Fellir" after me, as they now call "Pethmir" after her.*

Peth finished her splashing and thrashing and ran gasping from the trough, gathering her clothes hurriedly as she ran.

Fellirian, startled from her recollection, said, "Tell them I'll be along. . . ." She stopped. Pethmirvin had already ran up the stairs and disppeared into the *yos.*

Fellirian shook her head, resigned. *Peth could do this in haste, for what she rinses away is nothing more than a little sly fun. The water reminds her that fun is fun, a little thrill, but that tonight, she must leave this one, this Farlendur, at the door. The mystery of the stranger. Our ties in Braid are closer than blood and genetics. But what I wash away is something more subtle, a corrosive worry about which I have seen, after all, only the tiniest part. That Vance, as long as we have known each other and been associated, could allow himself and me with him to be recorded, investigated, observed, and, well, spied upon, without a protest, a word of warning! Yes, I know. He imagined to conceal it, when his body-language shouted truth. But an obscenity. To invade the awareness is no different than to invade the home, the body.* Fellirian took a deep breath, releasing it in a long, controlled sigh, listening to the gurgling of the water in the wash-trough, allowing the random noise, the pleasant sound, to blank her mind of everything except the now, the razor-thin present, the edge between eternities. A last turbulent wave roiled the calming surface of her thought. *We live in many ways an idyllic, slow-paced life, insulated from pressure. I who see the outside know these things that I cannot tell to the others. We have pursued the silence too long, set ourselves against one temptation, one pressure, for too many summers. I sense a shift of balances, different forces. We are not now an agile people to move with them; indeed, having sought the primitive, we have attained it in all its fragility; and the world always changes. I know fear.*

When at last she felt the stillness inside, when she could hear the silences within herself, she repeated subvocally the invocation to Water, her lips moving silently, almost invisibly. Then it was time. She stepped calmly into the water, feeling the bite of its cold on her legs and feet, then her thighs as she kneeled, and then the full shock of it as she slowly, deliberately immersed herself into the water, coming to rest facedown, completely covered. *A deep fear, a corrosive worry, a mindless anger; take it all, trough-water, take it to the sea.* From the first it was painful, an assault upon the entire body, all at once, a sensory explosion blanking her mind. There was an urge to panic. She resisted, and lay still, gently thinking nonthoughts, letting the cold grip her in its teeth of iron, clamping her firmly in its clammy jaws. When she could stand it no longer, she got to her feet slowly, carefully, standing, releasing the pent breath she had been holding. Then she swiftly rubbed herself down with her hands, using the back-scrubber hanging on a peg nearby to reach her back. The air now felt warm.

She was finished with the rite of Water. Still, despite the numbing cold, Fellirian forced herself to be slow, measured, deliberate. *Nothing is any good in a hurry, and rituals least of all. I must wait for the water to become still before I leave it. That is respect for what it is.* She waited, wrung out her hair, and stepped out of the trough. Then she gathered up her clothes, picked up her boots, and Pethmirvin's as well, for in her haste to get into the *yos* and warmth, Peth had left hers behind. *That scatterbrain,* Fellirian thought warmly. Only when she was completely finished did she look back to the water. It was still again, rippling only from the fresh water falling into it from the pipe. Fellirian turned away, her skin goose-pimpling violently, climbing with measured steps up the stairs to the entryway.

She brushed aside the heavy outer winter-curtain and stepped inside over the sill. As she put her old clothes down, she saw in the half-light spilling through the inner curtain that someone had left out her favorite autumn kif, a loose wraparound with wide, deep sleeves. By the light she could make out its pattern, a plain brownish hue with a pattern of cherry leaves ticked subtly throughout it. Wrapping her hair in a soft cloth, she took the kif up, putting her arms into the sleeves, wrapping it around her body, luxuriating in the feel along her skin of the smooth inner lining, already feeling it warm her. Then the wide sash belt to fasten it together, and she brushed the inner curtain aside, entering.

Inside the hearth, the others awaited her, Morlenden, Cannialin, Kaldherman. Not the children; they had all gone to bed, even Sanjirmil. Fellirian suddenly felt as if she had been gone for years, instead of the two days it had been in reality, and she looked long at them, and around the hearth, as if she wanted to reassure herself with its familiar contours. She saw its spacious roundness, the dome of the ceiling, its outlet vent blackened around the lip by the hearth-smoke of generations of Derens. To her left was the hearth proper and table, and to the other hand a cushioned shelf for sitting, all the way around the compartment. In the back, three curtained crawlways led off to other compartments, left for adults, center to the workrooms and recordium, right to the children's sleeper. Tapestries arranged behind the sitting-shelf illustrated the Salt-pilgrimage and stages along the Way. Every *yos* except the very poorest thus displayed some symbolic reminder of something great the Braid had done. Theirs was old and somewhat faded. Still, it was theirs, and this was home. It smelled of woodsmoke, clean, familiar bodies, onions.

They had kept a fire on the raised hearth, and there was a pot of stew still on it, steaming away. Nearby was the ever-present teapot. Fellirian went to her place* and sat. Morlenden ladled out a bowl of the stew, Kaldherman cut some bread from a loaf, and Cannialin stood behind her and began to braid her hair.

Fellirian, realizing how hungry she was, began to eat immediately, blowing on the spoonfuls of hot stew to cool it down. Kaldherman replaced the loaf on its shelf, sat back in his place, and leaned back expansively.

"No need to hurry, Eliya. We've bedded them all down for the night: the *starsrith* in the shed, and the little fox with the rest of the children."

"Did the Perwathwiy not wish to talk, then? Peth said she had come to talk this very night." Fellirian spoke between mouthfuls.

Cannialin answered from behind her, a soft, pleasantly hoarse throaty voice in her ear. "Oh, no. She wanted to talk, sure enough, but we convinced her it would be better to wait for daylight. One could not know when our *Klandorh* was coming home, and she did insist that you be there. I do admit we used the argument of her convenience, although it mostly is ours. But since she had to wait for morning light, she could wait to drop her secret then."

"Did she drop any hint of what it was that she wanted?" Fellirian paused, almost saying something else, then changing it. "I cannot imagine what would bring her all the way down here at night."

"And in the rain, no less," Kaldherman said. "But she never said. Although she's in a hurry, whatever, it is, and an elder in a hurry is a remarkable thing—especially out of Dragonfly *Zlos*."

"Indeed, so it is." Fellirian turned to Morlenden. "When did you arrive, Olede?"

"Not so very long before you."

"Are you tired?"

"Tired isn't the word for it. Mind, I don't mind walking in the rain all day; I'm used to that. What inconveniences one is

* Adults always sat around the hearth in a specific order.

that last evening I had to attend a weaving-party, and woke up this morn not in the best of humors."

Fellirian chuckled. "Serves you right. You're supposed to officiate at those parties, not join in them."

"Ah, who can say no to a host in his cups?" Morlenden smiled back at her. Morlenden was somewhat heavier in build than Fellirian, indeed, than any of them, and his hair was fractionally darker, now beginning to show some hints of gray. His face was more sharply drawn, full of planes, defined lines, demarcations. It was a harsh face in certain lights, but for the most part it was also a face animated beneath by poise, confidence, general good humor. He continued, "Well, I suppose it would have been nice enough, except for the fact, denied with vehemence and zeal by all parties concerned, that the *Toorh* were already full-fertile and obviously had no use for anybody besides themselves. Had them dressed up all in white, they did, when I, a stranger, could tell they'd been doing it a month at least. I think the girl was pregnant already, carrying the *Nerh*. And of course the potables were the vilest sort of stuff you can imagine. Homebrew! Peach brandy, they had the nerve to call it. May as well call a squeal the whole hog to be consistent. It was, so I discovered, raw corn whiskey, not even cooled decently, with some peach-pits in the bottom of the crock, or I'm a human."

Here Kaldherman interjected, "Nothing wrong with that. Just good, honest folk. Why put on airs?"

Morlenden leered askance at Kaldherman. "Even up your way they don't go so far. But this was really remote. And you know how it goes in the most distant districts; too much ag-ri-cul-ture." He drawled the last word out bawdily, making a lewd face to go with it, suggesting some yokel gaping in astonishment after the barnyard antics of bull and cow.

Fellirian laughed, waving her empty bowl. "Where was this?"

"Beshmazen's."

"You walked all the way from there?"

"Oh, indeed, all the way from the far side of the Hvar. Cleared my head, it did."

"And then you waited up for me, well knowing that the Perwathwiy would wait for the morrow?"

All of them nodded agreement.

Fellirian said, "Well, then, I am grateful to you all." She turned the teacup up, draining it. "Now you can all come to the sleeper with me and warm my body to sleep. I'm freezing!"

Fellirian arose from the hearth, placing her bowl with the others in the soak-tub by the fire, and went directly to the sleeper, pushing aside the curtain and climbing in. Morlenden and Cannialin followed her, while Kaldherman remained behind momentarily, banking the hearthfire and blowing out lamps. One by one, they all climbed into the adult sleeper compartment, at a higher level than the rest of the *yos*, reached by a short ladder. Inside, they carefully removed their kifs and overshirts, folded them up, and placed them on shelves that ran all around the circular wall of the compartment. Here, they did not make lights; it was a smaller compartment than the main hearth, and they all knew every inch of it, especially Morlenden and Fellirian. She reached upward to a shelf for something she knew would be there: a large double comforter, which she retrieved and with Morlenden's help spread out and buttoned the edges together. Finished, they spread it out, just so, and slid into it, moving close together for warmth, feeling the familiar bumps, angles, and contours of each other as they moved, making tiny adjustments in position until the fit was exactly right, just as they had been doing on winter nights for the greatest part of their lives. Across the compartment they could hear Cannialin and Kaldherman doing exactly likewise, rustling the comforter, arranging themselves, seeking out the most comfortable and warm position; for while the material of which the *yos* was traditionally built was a good insulator, it was also unheated inside except for what warmth from the hearth took the edge off the chill.

Fellirian moved closer to Morlenden; she was still chilled thoroughly, more than she had thought, from the long walk up from the mono line and the Water Rite as well. She felt the body next to her own; the skin was cool, but underneath he was warm. She stretched, tensing and releasing every muscle, feeling Morlenden curl around her. Across the sleeper, Cannialin whispered good night in her quiet shy voice into the darkness and the quiet, broken only by an occasional drip on the roof, and then by deep, even breathing. Kaldherman, like an animal, fell asleep instantly.

When she was sure that the others were asleep, she nudged her insibling. Morlenden nudged back. She whispered, under the covers, barely audibly, "Do you have any idea what is going on? Why the Perwathwiy, and Sanjirmil?"

"I know no more than you, Eliya. They told me naught save that it was a Braidish thing—that all of us would have to hear and judge, and agree. Sanjirmil said nothing. At any rate, when I came home she was too busy eating Peth's supper to say anything."

"Did she really?"

"Thus she did. But Peth did all well enough, I think. She wanted to go out anyway—I suspect a young buck hidden away in the brush outside."

"She had one, so it was."

"Might have known; comes from her foremother. You used to do that."

"Never mind the things I used to do. You used to bring them home, you rooster. Where you ever found such bedraggled things I'll never know. Did you scour the whole reservation looking for the poorest girls?"

"Well, as I have often averred, the wealthy give luxury, but from the destitute comes speed."

"Speed, was it? It was never speed that kept the rest of us awake half the night with your whispers and giggles under the window. And after I had spent most of the evening record-keeping so at least one of us would do it right after weaving."

"Ah, Fel, you always were too serious for your own good."

"Serious or not, what do you think of the Perwathwiy walking down here from Garkaeszlos in the rain?"

"I like it not. Nor the fact she wouldn't talk, either. It can't be a good thing, can it?"

"I see no way it could go thus."

"And you are tense, too. Something else? You spent too long in the water for things to be normal, even for a zealot like you. Have a bad time of it down there among the *Hauthpir**?"

"No, not that way. No different from other times. The same, more or less, and the same tired old provocs in the crowd. But I realized something I'd been stupid enough to overlook for some time. I really can't be sure how long it's been going on, but Vance has been having me monitored during the meetings, and after the visitors leave, when we sit and chat a bit. He hasn't been pushy, just a little more leading and curious than normal. At first I thought it was just him—

---

* "Ancestral Primates." A derogatory epithet. Morlenden had little contact with the human world, and distrusted it greatly.

he is a little erratic in behavior. But when I saw it, it was clear. I tell you, something's afoot, something's going to happen, something bad. Maybe already. But I don't know to whom, or why."

"Maybe it's already happened."

"No. If it has, that's not what we're looking for."

"That's not like Vance. He's an old friend."

"So he has been. He's been a good channel for us—working both ways. Keeps the worst of them away from us, and lets us have a freer hand than we might have had. And I know him well enough, or so I thought. . . . He wouldn't without good reason."

"Perhaps. But we don't know those reasons, even assuming what you say is true."

"Mor, I think there's some connection between this visit and the change at the Institute."

"Nothing we can do tonight. Unless you wish to walk out to the shed and wake the Perwathwiy."

"No. I want to sleep. By the way, did Sanjirmil say anything at all?"

Morlenden was silent for a time. Fellirian could hear only his regular breathing. She prodded him. "Morlenden?"

"Hm? Sanjirmil? No, she said nothing. Nothing at all. She was here when I arrived, but she kept her own counsel. A few pleasantries, politeness . . . no, nothing."

"Were you not as much past the Change as I, I'd suspect you of distraction."

"Distraction? Hmph. Hardly. Although you have to admit that Sanjirmil certainly possesses more erotic quality than the average girl."

"Bah. A primitive, that's all."

"Just so, just so. . . ." He mused. "And a waste too, for one hears along the road that she's a bit of a zealot, a *Zan* fanatic."

"All those players are odd, you know? Well, so be it. I leave them to their *Zan* Game, however they will. Good night."

"And you, Eliya. On the morrow."

FOUR

The more dimensions in a Game, the more complex become the factors in the surround that influence the state of a given cell. This becomes significant when we recall that only two things determine what a cell's state will be: what it was in the last temporal frame, and what the surround is. Now if we imagine that our familiar universe of three dimensions is instead a three-dimensional projection of an n-dimensional Game, then the task before us of first importance is to determine the dimensional matrix. Is this not obvious?

—The Game Texts

Fellirian seemed to drop into sleep instantly, as soon as she had moved a little, finding just the right position she wanted. Her breathing became deep, slow, and regular. Morlenden did not fall asleep. No less tired than Fellirian, something deep in his mind itched, something basically wrong. Wrong? That was not quite the proper word. Un-right might have been better. He could not place the source of these feelings. For a time, he probed at it, but he could not find the unraveling-place, so gradually he left it. He reflected on his past, keyed by the events of this night, and the visitors who had come to their holding. Perwathwiy. Sanjirmil. Yes, Sanjirmil. Morlenden reflected on his past. His, and Sanjirmil's.

It had been long ago. Two and a fourteen years ago. In 2534, in the human calendar. In the early autumn. He had been one and two fourteens, twenty-nine, and she thirteen. At this time had occurred the interplay of two separate customs, or traditions, in a most curious way he had never put away in his mind.

The first had been the Canon of Permissibility: the rules governing sexual activity among ler adolescents were few, and of those that existed fewer still were the ones restricting it. Thus, it was said that among persons of adolescent phase age of itself would be no bar, provided that all acted according to their own desires and wills. In practice, one most usually paired off with partners near one's own age, but exceptions did occur, and one was neither praised nor defamed, either way.

The other tradition was more restrictive, for it pertained only to insiblings. Normally avoiding one another somewhat as they grew up through adolescence, as fertility drew near, insiblings gradually spent more time with each other. But at the same time, the rivalries and tensions accumulated during their long childhood and adolescence began to simmer and come to the surface. Knowing how tense this period could be, and was, and knowing how important it was that the insiblings remain together, the ler had inserted a period of relief into the very last part of adolescence, so that a hostile relationship would not unravel Braid lines carefully nurtured over hundreds of years. It was custom, then, that sometime in the last year of adolescence, the insibling was allowed a *vayyon*, a walkabout, an idle wandering-off, a last adventure, a great affair. It went without saying that these walkabouts were undertaken more or less specifically for the purpose of having one last fling, something to remember and cherish for the rest of one's life.

Autumn, 2534. Fellirian had already had her adventure, her *vayyon*; in the spring of that year, in accordance with the custom, she had simply wandered off one rainy day. Three months later, in summer, she had returned, saying nothing to anyone, dropping no hints, revealing no confidences. She had been tense before, uncharacteristically sharp-tongued and acrid of remark. Now she seemed settled, placid, relaxed, at home again within herself, most of the earlier late-adolescent fidgets gone, her perplexities resolved. Or were they? Morlenden did not know. He had never known. She had never spoken of it, what she had done or with whom, if indeed anyone. That, too, was the custom: what one did on the *vayyon* was forever a secret. And so Fellirian had returned, calm as still water, silent, enigmatic.

All this time Morlenden had felt the urge to the unknown building in him, and had found the environs of the Deren Braid holding increasingly bland, unsatisfying. Fellirian had been not only *Klandorh*-to-be, but she was also eldest insibling, so it was her right to go first. But within a few days of her return, Morlenden gathered a few things and also left, as silently as had his insibling. On the way out to Main Path, they had passed, wordless. There was nothing she could say to him. One found one's own truth, and no other's words could tell it.

At first, in the first days, it had been tremendously exciting; he had never known such a sense of freedom, such a feeling of total irresponsibility. Morlenden wandered first northward, then northwestward, sleeping in the open, feeling the chill of night which was now in the air, doing an occasional odd job in exchange for a meal and a bath, or perhaps some small change, at someone's *yos*, or again, sometimes an elder lodge, where the silent inhabitants gave him knowing leers, but said nothing, made no disparagements. Those who had been insiblings in a former life had known the *vayyon*. They knew.

The great affair had not materialized. Morlenden could not put into words exactly what it was he was looking for, but whatever it had been, there seemed to be an ever-receding chance of finding it. It was not that there were no girls; there were girls in plenty, and his days and nights were not, by and large, totally devoid of dalliance, teasings, flower-fights. But somehow the connection he wanted seemed to be absent. This one was busy, house-bound, and would not wander off, though she had possibilities. One who would readily go off with him was less than hopeless; Fellirian at her worst appeared preferable, even as a companion. Others he only caught glimpses of. In earlier days, Morlenden had delighted in the busy interplay of eye and gesture, of suggestive word. Now that he was free, really free, that whole universe seemed to have dropped away and vanished; what irony—now that he was available, no one was interested. Prospects were few, and he always seemed to be arriving at the wrong place at the wrong time, too early, too late. He began drifting from place to place, becoming bored and dissatisfied, frustrated and full of an ambience he could not put a name to. More than once he had caught himself doubting that this was really the great adventure. Was it all to be summed up in the end as nothing more than the value of a long walk? An unfulfilled expectation? Was it the surrounding matrices of routine life which made momentary exceptions to it exciting? Indeed, was it rarity that gave value? And was the lesson of the *vayyon* that the adventure wasn't there, had never been, never could be, but was entangled in the slower growths and procedures of the ordinary life of managing one's holding, raising the children? To be sure, he sensed that these were basic testings of reality which all have had to learn, individually, over and over again, human and ler alike, but like everyone else he was surprised at the pain of losing many of his favorite illusions.

For a time, Morlenden grew uncaring, diffident, even a little hostile; his sight seemed to grow crystal-clear, piercing, powerful, solvent. He saw things from a distance, but in his mind the distance grew greater; he saw those ler of parent phase, *rodhosi*, at their works, in field and shop; younger adolescents, *didhosi*, learning, pursuing their affairs. And after all that, the elders, retired to their secretive lodges, deep in their own matters. He had waited all his life to be free of that endless cycle, but now free, he found little enough to stay for. The real life was there, not here.

These were bitter thoughts; Morlenden spent more time along the empty paths of the forest, lost interest in eating, let his weight drop. He became, over the weeks, rather gaunt and hungry-looking; his sharp and somewhat chiseled features became honed and sharper. At one time he tried fasting for a vision, a practice he had heard of. But there was no result there either; he grew tired of it. Either he lacked some innate sense of awe requisite to the religious experience, or perhaps he lacked some basic competence of discipline necessary to make the vision work. At any rate, one never came. He simply grew fractionally thinner, and a lot hungrier.

He returned to his old ways and returned, tentatively, to the routines of working and eating. His weight began to return. And he thought ruefully to himself that he had indeed learned the last lesson. And it was then that he turned back to the south and began his journey homeward. He tried to imagine how it would be, when he did return: Fellirian would wonder what he had done, and he would smile knowingly at her and let her draw her own conclusions, make up her own imaginings. Perhaps he could drop a cryptic remark from time to time, faintly suggesting, never saying directly, never declaiming forthrightly. It would serve her right. She had probably seen herself the same emptiness he had discovered, whose core was within himself, the basic loneliness that lies at the heart of all sapient creatures in the universe. He knew now that all of them who had been privileged to the *vayyon* were sharers of this secret.

He returned slowly. There was no hurry now. He had covered much of the distance, leaving only a few more days of leisurely travel and work, when he happened to pass close by a place called Lamkleth, meaning "resin-scented," which was

a combination of many things: faded resort, hostel, elder
lodge for a lodge organization which seemed to have been
forgotten by most elders. It carried the name of a settled
place, or town, but it seemed to be no more than a random
collection of cabins, rambling wooden apartments built to a
high-gabled, eccentric style, rambling worksheds, and seedy
pavilions along the lake, all half hidden and subtly blended
into and among the conifers of the forest. The site was a
gloomy defile, a rocky, narrow valley which opened up suddenly into a wide lowland. At the mouth of the valley was a
still, enigmatic lake, bordered by a mixed sand and rock
beach on the east, the valley side, and on the west by a
watery, tree-choked swamp. The area all around the defile
and the lake was dense with pine and cedar, swamp fir and
arborvitae, deodar and chamaephyte, ground yew and ret-
inispora. A pungent, resinous odor hung in the air, and the
smoke of the fires was rich and fragrant. A moody place,
which was doubtless much of the reason why it had never
been popular.

Nevertheless, Lamkleth was known for one thing; adolescents gathered there, with the force of tradition behind them,
to meet like-minded others, to seduce and be seduced, to
dance in the night under the colored party lanterns, to sing
and listen to the last heart-songs of yearning before the halter
was finally put on them. Personally, Morlenden had never
cared very much for the place, and as a fact, although he had
passed it often, had never stopped or visited before. But this
time—passing Lamkleth on the ridgeline above the valley and
the lake, the dark water, the deep shadows, and the bright
lanterns—he thought once again of last flings, of last oppor-
tunities. . . . He wandered slowly down into the settlement.
He caught in himself the last shreds of anticipation, that here
at last he would find the one, her, an insibling like himself,
also in the last of the *vayyon* and likewise illuminated. He
imagined. He projected images.

With the money he had accumulated, Morlenden secured
for himself a small but comfortable little cabin with an attached bath and woodstove. A pile of faggots had been con-
veniently deposited outside by the door. The cabin was not
close to the lakefront but was situated farther away, far up
the valley, under the ridge, half invisible under the trees,
buried in a grove of ancient arborvitae, their feathery fronds
hanging over the mossy roof. The odor of resin was in everything. The elder who accompanied him to the cabin said

little, noting only that the season was apparently over, and that most had already left. Remaining were only a scattered few latecomers and hangers-on. The nights were quite cool now, and this had apparently dissuaded most of the late summer visitors. Morlenden, thinking how gay and festive the lanterns and their reflections along the water had been, listened to this news with sinking heart.

Nonetheless, he was tired of walking, and a good rest here in a comfortable little cabin was an improvement over sleeping in the forest under a tree. So he bathed and dressed in the last dress-overshirt remaining to him, carefully removing it from his rucksack and pressing it out with his hands. It was his favorite, tastefully patterned with the heraldic emblem of his aspectual sign—Fire, the Salamander. It had been dusk when he had wandered down from the heights; it was fully dark when Morlenden left the cabin and wandered down the hill to the lakeshore. The path was smooth and well-tended, swept free of twig and pebble, groomed of roots and knots.

From a distance, it seemed as if the summer season were still in full swing: the lanterns still swung above the pavilions, sending brightly colored reflections dancing along the water. There was music in the air as well, floating from an unseen source, lending a further anticipation. But all these things were faded reflections and shadows; most of the painted tables were empty, the pergolas and gazebos abandoned, and the music, upon closer listening, seemed to be slow and reflective of mood rather than exciting and gay. Emerging from the pines and entering the pavilion along the shore, Morlenden was able to confirm his worst suspicions: the place was almost empty. Within sight, in an area which could easily hold a crowd of *terzhan** young adventurous bodies, there seemed to be only a handful, most of whom had already paired off for the night, or who sat quietly and rather disinterestedly looking out over the water into the darkness.

He also noted as he looked out over the whole of the pavilion that the ages of the remaining celebrants appeared to be wildly varied, as if the low density had made it more noticeable. Some were late-adolescents like himself, of comparable age. Others were obviously younger, still deep in their first span, country bumpkins down from the farm in the period between the end of the growing season and the beginning of the harvests. A scattered few were much younger, veritable

* Two times fourteen to the second power—196.

urchins, playing rowdy chase-and-tumble games among the
old whitewashed stands and under the trees; some of these
were barely adolescent, while a few were yet little children.
These he ignored.

For a time, Morlenden wandered up and down along the
pavilion, looking over the prospects, as it were, hoping that
certain among those he was looking at were harboring similar
thoughts. If they were, none of it showed. Everyone he saw
seemed to be immersed deeply in their own thoughts, their
own projections of the subtle manifestations of reality,
emerging from the end of summer about the precincts of a
faded resort. Failure and the ambience of second thoughts lay
in the lamplight like a tincture.

Morlenden, while savoring this air, was not daunted and
attempted to make the acquaintance of a pair of girls who
were diffidently lounging at one of the pavilion tables over
glasses of mulled wine. The first was convincingly uninterested, and the second hardly less so, although she did give her
name, Meydhellin. She also mentioned a certain young man
with whom she would conduct a rendezvous presently. Morlenden excused himself, after a tactful and strategic pause,
and wandered some distance away to a table of his own,
where he seated himself and brooded, watching the scanty
crowd evaporate into even lower densities as individual members of the vacationers and pleasure-seekers drifted away one
by one. The noise of the urchins behind him faded. After a
time, he observed that at the least the girl Meydhellin had
been truthful; a boy appeared and joined her at the table.
The other girl uttered something rendered enigmatic by the
distance, and departed. Meydhellin and her friend greeted
one another with a reluctant formality. Morlenden grew disinterested.

From the cookhouse nearby and behind him, an elder approached Morlenden, informing him discreetly that the
cookhouse was on the verge of closing for the night, and that
perhaps the discerning young gentleman would like to order
some of the remainders, at reduced stipend. Morlenden
nodded enthusiastically, for he was suddenly aware that he
hadn't eaten all day and was ravenously hungry. He inquired
into the bill of fare; unfortunately, nothing remained but
some dner, a preparation made by arranging paper-thin slices
of various meats along a vertical skewer, roasting it along the
outside by rotating it past the grates of a vertical charcoal
burner, and then slicing off slivers of it. It was a heavy, over-

rich dinner, and Morlenden ordered it without great enthusiasm, selecting to wash it down a small jug of the local wine,
Shrav Bel-lamosi, tart and resinous. Presently, with no great
ceremony, the meal arrived, along with a tray of local wild
greens. Morlenden ate, because he was still hungry, but it was
with no great sense of culinary relish. He thought, *Indeed,
this is the very end of it. Tomorrow I'll go home.*

Gradually, the wine and his somber musings led him to
disregard his immediate surroundings and he ignored the
comings and goings of the few patrons and proprietors remaining. They all receded into a common background. He no
longer heard the noises of the urchins.

As Morlenden ate, thinking random and somewhat moody
thoughts, he slowly came to suspect that he was being observed closely by someone, someone nearby; in fact, someone
who was standing by his own table, cautiously positioned to
his right and just out of his field of vision to the rear. Morlenden stopped, fork halfway between plate and mouth, and
looked.

It appeared to be one of the children he had noted earlier,
one of the nondescript gaggle of noisy urchins playing tag
and grab-'ems along the shadow line under the trees beyond.
This one, he thought, seemed to be female*, and perhaps
even adolescent, dressed in little more than a ragged pleth
which had seen better and cleaner days. He looked at the girl
again; there was immediately apparent a certain dashing
quality about her, a piquancy of expression, an adventurous
quality, a recklessness. Morlenden thought that she would
have made a very good approximation of a bandit, but a bandit constantly poor from careless expenses. Indeed, almost a
desperate look about her. A brat for sure. An urchin of dark
skin, large eyes, sharp, predatory features.

Her eyes caught his glance immediately: they did not move
about, looking at this or that, but seemed to stare glassily, unfocused yet intent at the same time. The set of her face
showed that she missed nothing. Morlenden looked more
closely at the startling expression in her eyes. He saw movement in the spaces framed by the angular face. She seemed
not to regard directly, but to scan in a regular pattern, using

---

* Secondary sexual characteristics in the ler were subtle where they
existed at all. Sometimes it could be difficult even for a ler to determine the apparent gender of another.

her peripheral vision. This lent her expression a dualistic quality, glassy yet deeply animated as well.

Morlenden had quite forgotten his fork. The girl observed Morlenden's notice. She said, in a flat tone with a hint of nasality, "Enjoying yourself?"

Morlenden thought the question boorish. He recalled the fork, thoughtfully took a mouthful of dner, and answered, equally boorishly, "As a fact, no."

"How does one call you?"

"I have responded in my time to endearments and curses, anonymous hoots and hoarse whispers. I have been known to reply to 'you, there,' although I deplore the practice. I am called Morlenden Tlanh Deren."

"I am Sanjirmil Srith Terklaren. I, too, respond to other addresses."

Morlenden thought, hearing the form of her name, *Aha! An adolescent after all, however scruffy and abrasive.*

She added, "What do you here in Lamkleth?"

"Going home," he said, trying to ignore her, hoping she would receive his intent and depart. A brat.

"Can I have some of that Bel-lamosi?"

"Are you old enough to drink fermented spirits?" he asked, aggressively.

"Fourteen less one and *didhosi*? Of course! Old enough for other *didhosi* things, too."

"I can imagine . . . well, here. Drink the wine." He offered her the jug, which she took, shyly for all her previous belligerence, and turned up, drinking deeply. He looked closely at the girl, Sanjirmil. On a second inspection, perhaps she didn't appear quite so childish as he first thought. Her shape, under the ill-fitting overshirt she wore, was already full and ripe; no, not childish at all. She was dark of complexion, an olive skin and coarse black tousled hair which fell carelessly about a face of planes and angles, a face that could be harsh and peremptory, yet a face of a certain beauty as well. The strange eyes were of an indeterminate color, dark and brooding, and her nose was delicate and fine. The mouth was thin-lipped and determined, the chin set, but there was also an intriguing pouty set to her lips as well. In the poor lighting of the pavilion, her skin seemed dark enough so that there was little contrast between lips and face; it gave her face an odd expressiveness. You had to watch the shadows. This Sanjirmil could very well be just the unwashed and underage brat she seemed. But there was also about her an unknown quantity of something more.

He asked, as she set the jug back on the table, "Have you eaten?"

"No."

"The cookhouse is closed now."

"I know."

"My serving was overlarge. They were cleaning up for the night. You may have what you wish of it. And what would one be doing out adventuring without money, begging for a supper? Or do you sing as well?"

Sanjirmil took the proffered food shyly, but she could not conceal her hunger and ate quickly in swift, catlike bites. In between mouthfuls, she haltingly said, "No sing, no dance. Had some money, but it ran out. Was going to go home tomorrow . . . maybe tonight, if I had felt like it. You know of the Terklarens?"

"The Second-players? Of course I know of them. But I had never met one."

"Northwest. Day and a half."

"A long walk. You're a young one to be so far out in the forest."

"No, not us. We're adventurous . . . besides, we never take the *vayyon* as you are doing."

"How would you know what I might be doing?"

"Watched you, I did. *Mavayyonamoni*, they're always the same, looking for something and not finding it. I guessed; and I was right. I come here a lot, at least this year."

"Meet a lot of friends?"

"Some. Not always the ones I want. When do you weave?"

"Soon, this year. I think sometime around the winter solsticeday. My own *Toorh* has already done hers and returned. We have felt the tension at home."

"Hm. And I am free for a time yet . . as little good as it will do me. So: if you are on-*vayyon*, then you are *Toorh* also."

"Just so; Fire aspect. And you, Sanjirmil?"

"I also—both, just as you. That is very good."

"Not so necessarily for you. You're too young."

"Indeed? For what? What did you have in mind?"

Morlenden looked away from the intense, eager face for a moment. All the time he had been on his pilgrimage, he had turned every possibility, looking for the flow, the current, the onrush of the one single magic meeting. Now he felt the un-

dertow, the pull of a powerful current indeed; and both of
them of Fire aspect, strong in will. He could interpret this
drift and flow only one way: that they both were working
powerfully for what was to come, whether they would admit
it to themselves or not. He glanced at her again, out of the
corner of his eye, seeing the warm honey color of her skin,
the streaks and shadows where her muscles ran under it. She
was thin, but wiry, angular and strong; he could not deny her
beauty, her sense of earthy, pungent sexuality; there was
something wild in her, something desperate. The rumpled, un-
repaired overshirt. Contrary to this, he also thought that this
Sanjirmil was not exactly what he had walked all over half
the reservation for. He wryly added to himself that if it had
come to molesting thirteen-year-olds, there were several much
closer to home he perhaps would have preferred. Those were
second-thoughts. There were third-thoughts as well. Morlenden told himself that she wasn't really his type, that he preferred amorous adventures with girls who wove flowers in
their hair for their meetings, who were softer and rounder ...
and he didn't really know how he could tactfully disengage
himself from the piquant, earnest face before him.

"No," he said, "I didn't have anything in particular in
mind; except going home tomorrow myself. As you have
doubtless guessed, the *vayyon* leads us to few of the great adventures it seems to promise. You may see that later; or perhaps you are precocious there as well."

Now she looked away, sadly, he thought, as if she were reviewing some painful interior knowledge. Then she turned
back to him, fixing him once again with that odd, sightless
yet penetrating gaze. She said, "No ... it's not precocious.
But I do know it. That's why we don't go on it; none of the
Players. There are things we have to give up. The *vayyon* is
one of them. So we get our little dash of freedom earlier,
Morlenden."

"And later?"

"We are the Players of the Great Life Game; we do things
that others do not even dream of ... even now, I can already
do some of them...." She trailed off, making odd fingering
motions with her hands. She grew self-conscious, rubbing her
hands nervously, almost as if she were on the verge of saying
too much.

Morlenden knew well enough that there were two Braids
of the famous Gameplayers in the ler world, and that their
line had been maintained from the beginning with a focused

sense of purpose which defied all reason, for the Players did nothing to integrate themselves into the elaborate structured relationships of ler society, except barter some occasional garden produce. All they did was play the Game with their rival Braid. They were curious and secretive, and did not answer questions. Most put them out of their minds, for the Game was cerebral and difficult and had few partisans. Suddenly he felt very much out of his depth.

Sanjirmil continued, "Yes, and we . . ." She stopped, biting her lower lip. "Yes, just so. Indeed we do. But I may not speak of them with you. Please understand, it is not you yourself; you are not one of the elect, and you are not of the Shadow. I may not speak of it with you. But personally . . . I think I like you. For instance," she added cheerfully and matter-of-factly, with disarming candor, "I should rather sleep with you tonight than spend the darkness in the freehouse."

Morlenden looked at the harsh, determined face, the thin mouth with the faintest trembling hint of a smile trying to form on it. After a time, he said, "I hadn't really thought so far ahead. . . ."

"I know."

"Very well, then. As you have seen, I am free and without commitment. I shall invite you to repair to my cabin, which I have taken yonder in the grove." Having taken the step, he suddenly felt awkward, uncertain as to how brash he could be. He added, "I hardly know you, no more than just now, and I wouldn't have you take offense."

"I saw, before, and I knew it would be so. I watched you; that is why I came to you."

Morlenden pushed his chair back. "You will come with me, then?"

"I will, later. I have to go wash first. I have been running a lot and should not come to you as I am."

"Never mind that. I took a special place, one with a fine bath. You can wash there." He paused, and then added impulsively, now swimming full in the current he had released himself into, "As a fact, if you will, I'll wash you myself."

"Oh, very good! What girl could resist such an invitation in the least. Indeed so I will come."

"Do you need to gather your things?"

She gestured at herself. She said, "These are my things." The gesture took in a rather bedraggled, rumpled girl, barefooted, whose sole visible possession seemed to be a smallish waist-pouch slung carelessly over one hip.

All the time they had been talking, the girl had remained standing; now Morlenden arose from his chair uncertainly. He hesitated, then offerred his hand to her shyly. She took it into hers with an exaggerated gesture of gallantry, almost as if she were playacting. Morlenden looked about to see if anyone might be watching. But there was no one; the pavilion was now deserted. Far down the lakefront, one of the elders was blowing lamps out, carefully tending the colored paper lanterns that hung along the beach and cast their reflections out into the lake surface and the night. One by one, the lanterns were going out, and the dying sense of summer gaiety as well. Soon there would be nothing save some boarded-up sheds and cabins, and the winter darkness. He listened, and heard a wind rising back in the pines and arborvitae, rushing along the sharp needles and sprays of delicately scaled branchlets. There was a sudden spatter of cold rain, gone in an instant. He turned and set out in the direction of the cabin, the girl following, grasping his hand tightly.

Along the way, they kept silent, saying nothing more to each other. Morlenden listened to the wind, now alive all around them up in the trees; there was a chill in pungent, resinous air. Impulsively, he placed his arm about Sanjirmil's shoulders. She was shivering, ever so slightly.

Once inside the rented cabin, Morlenden set about getting a fire started in both fireplace and water-heater, while Sanjirmil brought in armfuls of wood. They did not talk, waiting for the water to heat, but sat quietly looking into the fire. Once, perhaps twice, Sanjirmil looked at him shyly from under her eyebrows, a faint, tentative smile forming in her face in the moving, dancing firelight. This touched Morlenden; for he had expected once that his great adventure would be with a brilliant conversationalist, one who would engage him completely, as they savored the last fling to the very end; but here they sat, and said nothing, save what their eyes said in quick little glances. That was everything. Yes. He was beginning to enjoy the idea.

The water began to groan in its tank, and testing it, Morlenden pronounced it hot enough and began filling the tub, a huge round wooden tub on a low stand. Sanjirmil stood, stretched, removed her waist-pouch and carefully laid it on the rough platform where the sleeping-bags were. Then she slipped her pleth upward, over her shoulders; her motion was graceful, but fatigued as well. She tossed it into the water, and feeling as she went, followed it into the tub.

The only light in the cabin came from the fire in the stove, and in this weak light, even weaker to his eyes, Morlenden looked at the body of the girl who was going to spend the night with him. Her body was muscular and hard, but thin, a little paler than the sun-browned face, but still a deep olive color, streaked and shadowed in the firelight, where the muscles and tendons showed; Sanjirmil was thin and wiry, yet she was also smooth and supple and utterly feminine. She sat slowly, gingerly into the hot water, wincing from the heat of it. As she finally settled completely into the water, Morlenden pushed his sleeves back, soaped his hands, and began scrubbing her back. Sanjirmil leaned back against the pressure of his hands and turned her face to the dark ceiling, her eyes closed.

And after a longer time, and many scrubbings, when her skin had become rosy, she finally said, very softly, "You should know that I told you a little lie back there at the pavilion; I did not want you to think I was such a little beggar. The truth is that my little bit of adventuring-money ran out several days ago. But I kept on staying, as long as I could, longer, grubbing, borrowing, stealing a little ... because ... because when I go back there, there will be no more holidays for me, no more adventuring. I'm almost fourteen, and that is when the insiblings of the Terklarens are initiated. This autumn. I know some things already; you can imagine it if you watch closely ... there really isn't any other way it could be, or so I think. But after initiation, the real work starts and one must learn, learn, learn, master it, control it, impose oneself upon it. One fourteen and two years to become a master of the Game, and a fourteen more before the next crop of brats. And then you teach and guide and end up in the Shadow, a Past Master. People think we are idle, that we do nothing, but it isn't like that. It is the hardest Braid-role of all. Already I can feel it drawing me to it. And so our time for adventuring is very short and we usually do not get so very much of it. And I want it all, both the Game and the Life; yes, the power but also the lovers and the dreams that all the others I see have. I hoped you would want me."

"I didn't, at first. I thought you were just another of the urchins; but there is a likeness between us now, and I see through the years that separate us."

"Say no more of separating; I would have you speak of joinings and meetings."

"So then I will: ours now-tonight." He stood up from his place by the washtub and offered Sanjirmil his hand.

She stood, wet and dripping, now soft and flowing curves and firelight shining along planes of wet skin. She said, almost in a whisper, "You are more loving-kind and giving than you know; I hope that you have fortified yourself for a long night."

"Indeed I have done marvels in the way of abstinence in the last few weeks." While he searched for a towel, Sanjirmil retrieved the much-abused overshirt, and wrung it out. Morlenden brought her the towel, and she dabbled absentmindedly at her body with it. She swayed a little, balancing on one foot, and Morlenden reached to steady her.

Sanjirmil laughed, turning to him. "you should remove that fine heirloom of the Derens that you wear, for I shall surely dampen it if you leave it on."

He slipped his overshirt off over his head and laid it aside, and stood bare in the firelight and resin-scented air just as she had before; she looked at him as he had looked at her. Morlenden felt a curious distortion of time from the intensity of their upwelling emotions, as if the whole of his past, or most of it, had occurred within this cabin, the water and the tub and Sanjirmil's bare, wiry body before him, and his future only extended as far as the next few moments. This sense of distortion was not static, fixed, but a growing, dynamic process, happening now, still working its alchemy upon his perception; there was a tense silence in which he could hear his own heartbeats. He reached forward, palms out, and stroked Sanjirmil's shoulders softly, following along the angular line of her collarbone to her neck, following with his eyes the soft shine of her skin in the dim light. She stepped out of the tub unsteadily and to him, touching him all at once, lips, limbs, body. Morlenden felt the bath-hot, strong, vital body touching him, the smooth skin, and knew madness in his heart, wildfire, and time collapsed into a dimensionless present moving forward at the speed of light. The salty taste of her mouth, the childlike, musky scent of her person close about him. She moved her body, pressing hard against him. Her legs moved.

Her mouth moved to his ear, and she said, almost so softly that he missed it under the roaring in his ears, "Now."

"Yes, Sanjir, now," he said, brushing his face in her coarse, dark hair, moving, half carrying the girl to the sleeping-bag, half falling to the platform, never quite disengaging them-

selves enough to retrieve the covers, while they performed
that which made one where two had been before. The fire
sank and the air in the little cabin cooled before they became
aware of it. . . .

And some time later, with the fire now diminished to a bed
of glowing coals, they moved under the covers for warmth,
side by side, yet engaged still, touching their noses. Morlenden felt completed, perfected, arrived at last; but in this
completion and ending he sensed beginnings, too. Many beginnings. He sensed above all that he and Sanjirmil were not finished with each other, and would not be when their time in
the now ran out. By him, she breathed deeply, evenly, seemingly relaxed, yet he also knew that she was not asleep.

He said, "Truly, you are Sanjir to me now."

She answered, "Would that we were Ajimi and Olede, if
you will. We are something more than casual lovers coupling
on the path."

Morlenden lay quietly, feeling their legs rub together, a
distant warmth, a rustling sound in the quiet dimness, a hard
foot. He tested the feel of the girl's body-name in his mind,
projecting, wondering if it had gone that far. He could not
say; at once, he felt that they had not come to that, and that
they had gone far beyond it. Yes, that was the great secret
here—they had gone beyond it and were in a region of desire
where there were no guides and no landmarks save those
monuments they chose to erect.

"Ajimi . . ." he mused aloud, "and yet we have known each
other but hours, and we are being taken away by currents in
time that cannot be denied."

"And gathered by the same," Sanjirmil added. "I know.
And consider—are we not both Fire aspect? Were we not
here for the same thing? And are we both not soon to
change?"

"My life passes through its progressions more or less in the
traditional manner, prescribed by the rote of orthodox ways.
My individual variations are my own, but no one else will do
them, I think . . . you know that well enough, well enough to
know me. But I know nothing of what you will do."

"It is simple enough, as much as I can say here to you: we
got to the Magic Mountain and master the subtleties of the
Game, expand its scope, delve deeper into it. It has no end,
no limits, you know."

"No. I know nothing of it."

"It is something I would have us share besides what we already have, but even what little I know I cannot give you, even though I shall call you Olede and always think of you so. At initiation, I know that I will not be able to face the foremother of my foremother if I do, when she will ask me if I have spoken of the Game to others who are not of the Shadow."

Morlenden chuckled at her sudden seriousness. "You could lie."

She put her fingers over his lips, abruptly. "No, no, we must not even talk about such a thing! She will be able to read that in my face, my every move. She is the great Past Master: she reads truth from the traces and ripples that acts leave behind them. You and I, even such as we, we can read the guilty face immediately after the sin, the worry after the crime, can we not? But she can read faces and see—literally see, with the eye of projection, things as they happened long ago. And so tonight by love I shall tell you what I know to keep you, and sixteen years hence I will stand before her in the smoky lodge of the elders of the Game and hear her denounce me and describe how we lay together."

"What would be so vile about that, Ajimi? This is sweet beyond my wildest dreams."

"You do not understand. There are others there, too, who have power over the non-Game parts of our lives. Not only do I lose the Game; I lose place, Braid. As strangers are made honorary insiblings, *shartoorh*, by arbitration, so are made *sharhifzeron*, 'those to be designated out-Braid bastards.' I could, if so judged, lose my life. We Players know well the saying, 'and Tarneysmith spoke aloud of the Game in the market, and what person now remembers Tarneysmith? It* did that which caused its* name to be stricken from the lineages and records and totems. Where one smile was of opened knowledge, now there are two."

"Ajimi, you lose me. I don't understand."

Sanjirmil took a deep breath, and shuddered. "In plain *perdeskris†*, so I am led to believe, one called Tarneysmith, whom no one knows now as Tlanh or Srith, spoke of the Game openly, or carelessly perhaps, or displayed knowledge to impress others—who knows? They cut its throat. Then they expunged all the records and made everyone forget.

---

* Singlespeech also uses an asexual, genderless personal pronoun.
† "Singlespeech" itself.

There is left only the name as a reminder. To die is bad, but to be erased is a horror."

"And your fear is real."

"My fear is real."

"Then I am endangered as well. I have bedded down . . ."

She interrupted him. "No, say it not! Not true! For I have not told you secrets. The danger is to me and all the others of the Players. What we have is a thing to be desired over all things, even love. But we see others as yourself and envy your lives, you who have all your *didhosi* years to have lovers and dreams, to make liaisons, to absorb the ordinary things of life. But for us the fun ends at fourteen. And I want something sweet to remember."

Morlenden felt a warm arm laid over his, pressing his back. He searched for Sanjirmil's thin mouth, kissed her lightly. "Yes, and I, too."

Sanjirmil moved her body, her limbs, pressing herself closer still. Muscles moved invisibly beneath warm skin. Morlenden, who had been lazing in post-love contentment, suddenly felt something awaken in him, deep down, illogical, apersonal, animal. And she felt it as well. He felt sharp white teeth along his neck, shoulders, and heard her whisper, "Again, yes?"

They moved slowly, deliberately, again knowing the rushing surge of anticipation. He whispered back, "Slowly, slowly. We have time. And what we have not we can make, for a little."

She replied, distantly, as if from miles away: "You do not know how much we have to make in what little time."

"But we do not have to go our ways tomorrow, either, Ajimi."

And Sanjirmil did not answer him immediately, but moved closer to Morlenden, if that were possible, embracing him yet more tightly. And she said, "No, Olede. But someday soon."

"And until then . . ."

Then their senses were fully awake, and for that night at least they talked no more. At any rate, they said little more of explanations and histories and legend.

They stayed on at Lamkleth a few days, sleeping, eating, dashing into the cooling lake water for quick wild splashing dips, and making love when the mood fell upon them, sometimes lazily and contemplatively, students of an art each would shortly lose in one fashion or another; at other times they would suddenly fall upon one another in wild bursts of passion and desire, as if each moment were to be their last. Until the little store of money which Morlenden had laboriously built up during his travels had begun to come to its end.

In the meantime, Morlenden, one not given over to fits of brooding self-inspection, mused over the odd circumstances of his meeting with the younger girl. He had soon lost sight of their differences, as had she, and both of them had begun to see each other as contemporaries, at least in the days of their futures to come. True to her age, Sanjirmil was somewhat abrupt, erratic, and irresponsible; but she also carried in her head a whole cargo of insights far in advance of her years, and he learned to feel at ease with her peculiarites. It even came to seem as if most of her odd behavior came not from her youth, relative to him, but from an innate nature common to all the Players. At any rate, there was less a gulf between them than the years might have suggested, for after all they were both still adolescents, and in the highly structured environment they lived in their behavior was more similar than different.

They decided to remain together for a time longer, and left Lamkleth, to wander fom one Braid holding to another, from village to village, from elder lodge to elder lodge, helping with odd jobs and the harvest, which was just now beginning. They walked along paths in the forest, along the edges of fields, cultivated and fallow alike; and when the weather permitted, slept outside, wrapped tightly together for warmth. After the first night together in the cabin, they talked little, and when they did, their words were only of little things, insignificant things, things which they could see immediately in front of them. As long as it was possible for them to do so, they set aside time and lived in the present, from moment to moment, making love when they found the time and place and ambience right, sitting quietly together when they did not.

But all things end which have a beginning, some sooner than others; and after some time, Morlenden and Sanjirmil became aware, as if they had been bemused, of the passage of weeks into months. The nights grew steadily cooler, and then cold, and then some days did not really warm up, even in the sun. The canopies of the forest began to open up, and washes of bright color flowed over the face of the mornings. They spent fewer nights in the open. And gradually they be-

gan to admit time between them once again; they spoke of
the lives behind them and before them, of changes; Morlenden of the role coming to him of parent, of holdingsman.
Sanjirmil spoke of the Players and their insular, abstracted yet
passionate lives. She spoke no more of the Game itself. He
did not ask. They did not really listen to the words, though
they listened close enough, for it wasn't what they said
in words, in Singlespeech or Multispeech, but rather what
the unspoken words under the spoken words said of their
inner uneasiness, and their knowledge of ends. For now
Morlenden was beginning to feel change stirring within himself, an odd set of unfamiliar new sensations, as if the prolonged liaison with Sanjirmil had stimulated the onset of his
fertility. He knew it was not yet. But it would be soon. Very
soon. The ancient, cultured pair-bond of the Braid between
himself and Fellirian began to reassert itself, driving his orientation toward the odd, wiry hoydenish Sanjirmil away from
the flesh and more into the heart.

And she, in her turn, began to grow apprehensive about
her return, which was now long overdue. The Players, so it
seemed, did not care so much for long visits out of their own
environment. Certain elders, whom she would not name,
would be angry with her for staying so long. There were punishments, of which she would not speak.

They allowed their wanderings to carry them around, drifting to the northwest again, more in the direction of Sanjirmil's home territories, by unspoken agreement. And they
spent their last night together in the ruins of an ancient,
pre-ler water-powered gristmill somewhere deep in the upper
waters of the River Hvar, in a place where the old stone
and brick buildings were overgrown with creepervine,
trumpetflower, and kudzu, and where enormous aged beech
trees hung over the mirrored surface of the millpond behind
the piled-stone dam and shed their yellow leaves into the
muddy water. It was rainy and miserable on the night they
found the mill, but the morning was bright and clear, cold
and windy.

A variable, willful breeze played in the leaves and ruffled
wavelets over the shallow pond. They did not speak of it, of
ends and departures, but stood by the dam for a long time,
standing close together, hands interlocked. Sanjirmil looked at
Morlenden once, with the disturbing blind, fixed gaze of hers,
the scanning motion of her eyes readily apparent from so
close. And after that, she turned abruptly and walked swiftly

away across the dam, deftly skipping over driftwood which had piled up over the years along the upstream side of it. It was only when she was completely across, off the stonework dam, on the far side under the trees, that she looked back. Morlenden watched her for a moment, seeing the wind teasing her short, coarse black hair, ruffling her overshirt, the same much-mended one she had met him in, and he waved, as casually as possible. Sanjirmil waved back. Morlenden looked away; and when he could look back, Sanjirmil was gone. The woods on the farther shore were empty.

He returned homeward directly, seeking no further adventures or idle wanderings, taking shortcuts, wasting no time. It took all of that day until far after dark, but he made it all in one day. And when he had at last come into his own *yos*, the old, homey, weather-stained ellipsoids of the Derens, after a long, thoughtful soak in the icy water of the wash-trough outside, he found Fellirian waiting for him in the hearthroom.

She looked questioningly at him for a moment, but said nothing beyond an offhand greeting, as if he had just now stepped outside to fetch a pail of water from the creek. And although he found that he was actually deeply happy to see his insibling again, he said no more than as if he actually had done just that: gone outside for water an instant ago. He found that his earlier desire to make a clever allusion to his great adventure had vanished completely; what had happened to him could not be told. And he knew a deeper secret about the *vayyon*: that below the level of the first revelation, that there was no great adventure, was a second, more cryptic level of the heart—that it was perhaps better not to find that for which one searched. He wondered if she had seen that as well.

They did not speak of such things. But that night, sitting together, sharing a bowl of stew, they made the small talk of members of the family, neighborhood gossip. Who had done what, with which, and to whom. Births. Deaths. It was only as they were banking the hearthfire for the night and blowing out the lamps that Fellirian told him that she had become fertile in the last few days.

"I'm not suprised, Eliya," Morlenden answered from across the hearthroom, not looking at her. "I've felt some twinges myself. I don't think I am right now, but it will be soon, now that you've come in."

"Kadh'Elagi and Madh'Abedra have set a date for the weaving."

"When?"

"Winter Solsticeday. And they've already made arrangements with a lodge."

"So soon?"

"Yes. We wondered what had become of you, if you would be back in time. . . ."

"I was unavoidably detained, ah, by the harvest."

"Indeed. They do say that it has been a good one this year. Did you work hard?"

"Yes. It was good for me."

"So it appears . . . you look somewhat the better for it. And more, too: from the look of you, you'll be fertile yourself by Solsticeday."

"Such are my suspicions as well." Morlenden and Fellirian paused by the curtained port into the children's sleeper, sharing an odd conspiratorial look. "Well, Eliya, after you."

"All right, I'll go first. But we won't be in here much longer, you know."

Fellirian climbed into the sleeper. As she disappeared behind the curtain, Morlenden reached up and patted her rump affectionately. When he had himself pushed the curtain aside, Fellirian met him, whispering fiercely "You randy *hifzer* buck! You know you shouldn't touch me now. You don't know what it's like yet." She quieted a little. "Really, it's no fun. Not like wanting *dhainaz* at all. I fear it. And I fear even more going long without doing what we must."

"I'll stay away, if you want."

"No, I don't want that either. . . . Did you have a good time, Olede?"

"I learned a great deal—the last few weeks, months . . . has it been months? Someday I'll tell you some of it."

Fellirian was spreading out one large double comforter on the soft floor of the sleeper. Morlenden was folding his kif, feeling around for the proper shelf. He asked, "And where's mine?"

Fellirian slid her kif off her shoulders and let it fall to the floor. She gestured to the comforter she had spread. Morlenden nodded. She was fertile, and nothing mattered now. He could not refuse her, even had he wanted to refuse.

She said softly, "It has to be us now . . . I have laid aside all mine of the past. You must do likewise, and comfort me."

The light in the sleeper was dim, but there was enough to

make out the smooth shape across the comforter from him. Familiar, as everyday as an arm or a leg. Fellirian . . . she was smooth and subtle of shape, inviting. He bent over her, touched her face, lightly. Her scent had changed, was no longer the tart, flowery, slightly pungent scent of an adolescent girl, but something warmer, richer, riper. It had an odd and immediate effect on him, and the speed of it surprised Morlenden greatly. He began to learn about the compulsions of fertility.

At last the sequence ended and Morlenden returned to the present, now sleepy. Beside him, he heard Fellirian's deep, even breathing, felt the familiar warmth of her body. *All those years,* he thought. *And us with a girl-child a year or more older than Sanjir was then . . . amazing!*

He had not spoken to Fellirian about his adventure, just as she had never spoken of hers. And in the intervening years, he had not been able to follow Sanjirmil very well; the Derens had led a busy life, and Morlenden had been doing most of the field work, and of course all the Players, of both Braids, kept very much to themselves. Rarely, he and Sanjir- mil had passed on some errand, but they had said nothing. He had once heard a distant tale, distortedly repeated by the tenth bearer of the tale, that something had happened to her, some drastic accident which she had survived somehow . . . here the tale had been unclear. And at any rate, he had seen her at a distance not long after that, a few weeks, and she had looked no different. There had been no injuries, no disfigure- ments.

But the disturbing tales continued, and they told that Sanjirmil had been changed in a way no bearer of tales could tell. But here again, he had never seen any evidence of change.

So now he lay awake in the dark, remembering, reliving it all again, his inner mind returning with abrasive insistence to the same questions he had asked before and found no answer to. Why was it that the Perwathwiy Srith, an elder, should walk in haste to the holding of the Derens; and why bring with her Sanjirmil, her own insibling descendant, two gener- ations removed? And the Perwathwiy had been, of course, a Terklaren herself, the *Klandorh* of the Terklarens, just as would be Sanjirmil in her turn. Next year. Maybe sooner.

Sanjirmil. Morlenden had enjoyed recalling the affair they had shared, with its strong sense of poignant emotions and extravagant eroticism; indeed, a piece of him was tied into that time forever, even though he had grown used to the knowledge over the years that their liaison was doomed from the start, made hopeless by the years that separated them. So one went one way, one another. A little ripple passed through him, something not quite laughter; soon she would look upon her own children with the same sense of astonishment that he did. It seemed to be forever coming, and then it was over. Yes, there were some regrets. But now . . . he did not care so much for the speculations, unanswered, that the visit suggested.

FIVE

The Game visually generates certain patterns which remain in one location and pervolve; others move over the playing field at various speeds, retaining various degrees of internal identity and coherence. Here, we have no difficulty whatsoever understanding that it is the Game and the parameters of a specific Game set which make such figures move. In the physical universe, however, we see similar motions and various conditions of identity and stability; and have thereon erected an incredible and erroneous set of "laws" to explain such conditions. When the laws fail to predict, add complications and subtleties, precisely as the Ptolemaic astronomers added epicycle after epicycle to their basically wrong model of planetary motion. So a better theory was devised. We speak of Copernicus, of Newton, of Kepler, of conic sections and conservations of angular momentum. Seen from the perspective of the Game, these things are hardly less wrong than Ptolemaics. We shall now discuss these things under their true names, understanding, of course, that they are expressions of a much better model.
—*The Game Texts*

In the earliest societies, the symbol of force replaces the force itself, and then symbols replace symbols, each becoming progessively more subtle: club, spear, knife, sword, pistol. They evolve to bearers of such things, mere suggestions to be sure, but not less in the importance put upon them by the observer. Or the owner. In the settled, civilized, mostly nonviolent bureaucratic state, these symbols become even more abstract: counters, desks, offices. The more massive the desk and the more empty the office, the greater the authority. The more insulated and invisible the office, the greater still. Klaneth Parleau, Chairman of the Board of Governors of Seaboard South Region, had such a desk, such an office. The office was excessively large, and would have been in any age, but in an age in which volume and space were at a premium and all buildings were designed with function and efficiency first in mind, it was particularly impressive. There were no windows; windows were conducive to distraction and daydreaming, and there was little time for that. Parleau, for one, could not imagine an age when there could have been time for it.

One who came into Parleau's office would first have to traverse the apparent vastness of the length of the room, and then face Parleau's desk, which was a massive cruciform shape made of a single casting of titanium, brushed and anodized to a dull, almost black finish. To increase the illusion of distance, the base of the T-shape of the desk was slightly narrower than the part nearest its occupant, which had the dual effect of making the occupant seem both farther away and at the same time larger than life. This neck of the T was used occasionally as a conference desk, and chairs were stored under it. They, too, were part of the effect, for as they increased their distance from the head of the desk, they grew smaller and more uncomfortable to sit in. And the occupant of the head of the desk could select, from a console blended into the working surface, which chair would be slid out for the visitor, varying status with circumstance. There wasn't a weapon within miles of this office, and it was doubtful if the chairman himself could have done violence to a starving orphan; yet within his office full in the powers of his position, he could reduce grown men to worms and they themselves would admit it first.

Seaboard South was not particularly more powerful than other, similar administrative units into which the whole habitable Earth was divided, save in one area: it possessed the

Charter of Overmanagement for both the Institute, which was the interface between the humans of Earth and their artificially mutated step-cousins, the ler, and the reservation in which the ler lived. This made it, in effect, the broker for the vast amounts of data which flowed into and out of the Institute, detailing every art and science of the planet.

In similar fashion, Chairman Parleau was not especially different from his theoretical equals, the chairmen of other regions near and far, except for this one area, and the Regional Chairman's consciousness of that fact. Parleau personally had as yet done very little in the way of direct manipulation of those powers. Yet. But the very idea that he could, should he choose, kept chairmen of the neighboring Regions closely attentive to events in Seaboard South.

Parleau himself was a large and heavy-boned but generally trim, balding individual of apparent early middle age: mature, securely settled in high office. No single facet of Klaneth Parleau would have distinguished him from a thousand other career administrative executives—other than a rather aggressive manner and a more closely cropped than normal hair-style (of what hair remained to him). When he moved he exhibited a crispness and a dynamism which somehow most of the others lacked.

In fact, Parleau was somewhat younger in years than his appearance suggested, and far from reaching a pinnacle, he was in fact being groomed carefully for higher advancement still; some thought to Co-directorate Staff, an anonymous coordination position. Others, no less well-informed, felt that it would be at the least to a post on Continental Secretariat, with a leg up to the Planetary Presidium somewhat later. Seaboard South had been his first regional chairmanship, and with its long association with the ler and the Institute, it was a key posting, selected by his peers. Historically, it had always been a make-or-break assignment, and the odds had been against most past chairmen. The majority, upon completion or replacement, had elected to move to positions of lesser ranking. But a few had made it into the rarefied upper levels, where they generally prospered.

The problem, as Parleau formulated it, was not that the New People were troublesome or unruly, but to the contrary. In fact, they were generally better behaved than their human neighbors. It was a fact that they seemed to react with less stress to crowding and personal restriction, but, he thought wryly, with the population density they had, they could hardly complain about a behavioral sink, however restricted they were to their reservation. More, the reservation did not impose a drain upon the resources of Seaboard South, as such a project might have been expected to do. No; together, the reservation and the Institute were both self-supporting, and their gross output net was larger than any conceivable alternate use to which the land could have been put.

No. The problem underlying everything seemed to be that humans knew no better now than in the beginning how do deal with the New People. In developing them out of their own mixed stock, the men of 2000 had been reaching for the goal long dreamed of—controlled mutation, and the transformation of man into superman. This would be the last victory of the flower of the old science, actually greater in significance then the as-yet-undiscovered faster-than-light drive. For they had cast aside the old myths about a mere physical specimen, a superman of body; they were reaching for the mind. And then they would have planned programmed men who would, under careful supervision, carry them to heights unreachable in the random, recursive, agonizingly slow processes of nature. They would, in short, not wait to grow into the garden of Earthly delights, nor would they countenance stumbling into it by accident, but would storm it by force, the force of the mind. But the program, starting innocently enough with experiments with lower life-forms, had progressed steadily through ever more complex forms; and when at last they had performed the final, half-magical reading and attempted programming of human DNA, they found that they had not constructed an avenue into the future but instead constructed a strange and mysterious door into an unknown and unknowable future. A door which only worked one way, and one that only the key of DNA would unlock. After a hundred years of "production," the door was finally sealed; and then destroyed.

Nothing was ever forgotten; it was rather that the whole discipline became discredited, then unprofitable, then unfunded. One thing technology never solved: it was frightfully expensive to alter DNA under controlled conditions in which results could be expected. And, paradoxically, unlike every other essentially technological process, the cost did not go down as it was repeated. The last ler brought into being artificially cost virtually the same as the first. In a time when a thousand projects were worthy of more attention, they beggared the planet to make something they couldn't use for themselves. Mankind wisely concluded, reinforcing the judgments of the theologians, that however thrilling it might have been to play God, it was also damned expensive. To do as well as the original might well be feasible, but it could not be paid for.

Physiologically, humans knew the ler easily enough, although the number who made such an area their interest steadily declined with time. But physiognomy was only the smallest part of reality, and the cultural gap widened yearly. Man opted for efficiency, the ler for harmony. Everyone had, rich and educated, ignorant and poor alike, anticipated the supermen: they would be large in size, strong, dominant of disposition, possessed of keen analytical minds, masters of technology at last, knowing all consequences in advance. There would be no haven for superstition and vanity.

But the New People—or ler as they decided to call themselves in their own developed language, meaning "new" but also "innocent"—were determinedly unherioc. On the average, they were smaller in overall size, lighter in weight, and slimmer in build than the average human. Moreover, they retained into adulthood what seemed to humans as an excess of human adolescent features. That this was the natural result of forced evolution, a process called neoteny, in which youthful stages were expanded at the expense of older mature stages, did not reassure those who insisted upon viewing them as children, something their adult members were not. And by the time a truly ler culture had begun to develop and take root, the specimens were increasingly wrapped in impenetrable veils of language, ritual, mysticism, and an eclectic, bucolic philosophy that seemed to deny every common-sense notion of progress. "How quaint," cried the harsh voices of the cult of expediency, entirely missing sight of the fact that ethic and ritual protect us from one another . . . .

And so Parleau spent each day in his office, hoping over the distraction of the other sides of Seaboard South, that there would never be a problem, which his contemporaries and peers might have referred to as "an opportunity to excel." And after dayshifter hours, which were his permanently by virtue of his high position, he would return to his set of cubicles alone* and hope, all the more fervently, that the next day would be quiet as well.

* Members of the high executive class did not have families.

The quiet had come to an end. Parleau knew and faced it matter-of-factly. It had been coming, of course. He could see as well as the next with hindsight, but he could also see, even without the Situational Analysis training the controllers got, that this situation could not remain stable and peaceful forever. Why should it? Nothing else in the known universe did. So at some point, the hostility would have to take an overt form. Then what? It appeared that the humans still held all the cards. But that was the weakness. It was a dependent and vulnerable command position. The Old People were in fact completely vulnerable to the output of the Institute, so much so that now, in this century, continued stability (they had long since ceased calling it progress) was tied directly into its steadily increasing output. There was no way out of it: the Institute tinkered with basic efficiencies, the very stuff of which a million lives a day hung in the balance, hung upon five hundredths of a percentage point of difference. Yes. Things were that tight. Had it been something so simple as some material shortage, Parleau felt that they could have coped, some way. Done without, maybe. Invented substitutes. But all those avenues had been explored already. The time had passed, several hundred years ago, when they could deal with simple shortages. The very idea. It was the hardest problem civilized man had ever faced, and Parleau did not expect to solve it himself in the course of an afternoon.

Consider mathematics and the classical three-body problem: even with computers to speed up the process of computation a millionfold, they still couldn't conceptualize it as it was, three-simultaneously, but ran it as a series of twos. Now blow that up, enlarge it, complicate it to a billion-body problem, crank in several theories of economics, five major schools of politics, including anarchy, add the now-semicontrolled ecology of the entire planet, and muddy it with an uncorrected human population which had continued unreduced, if slowed to virtual zero growth, at the unimaginable level of twenty billion. Yet, in a limited way, this was just what the Institute attempted to do, one question at a time. The human members posed narrow and specific questions, and the researchers disigned alternatives they called parametered solutions, series of *iffy* courses of actions whose basic trade-offs were known or strongly suspected. The questioners debated and made the value judgments.

It was painfully clear from this that the ler and their Institute had become indispensable, which was the utter horror of every leader and bureaucrat since Hammurabi. Indispensable man has a handle on you. Only when you can make all men and indeed all creatures immanently dispensable and interchangeable can this threat to the superstition of executive omnipotence be made to fade into insignificance. And the solution that came most often to mind—simply eliminate them and rationalize it afterward for the muddy thinkers—was in this case both ethically repugnant and obviously disastrous. They had long since assumed that to go it alone now without the ler partnership was possible, but all things considered, it wasn't desirable at all. There was a most delicate balance of tomorrows.

Now this thing, Parleau thought, suddenly too agitated to sit still behind his desk, the symbol for which he had worked so hard, and made so many resentful enemies along the way to it. A girl about whom almost nothing was known, save that she appeared to be circumstantially connected with some minor and unimportant vandalism. A simple incident, surely, but somehow along the way she managed to lose her bloody mind. Then responsible parties discovered that she was a ler adolescent. That they could see for themselves. Parleau stood by the corner of his desk, shuffling through the morning reports from the previous eve and mid-shifts; the quality control data, the indexes, the graphs. He was not interested in them, but only in the answer to the question, *Why me?*

The administrator in the outer office signaled that the visitors Parleau had called earlier were now assembled and waiting there. The time had come. Parleau cleared his throat, sighed deeply, and recomposed his expression from one of worry and concern to one of stern action. And they would not have to worry about interruptions, either. All other business save natural disasters and civil unrests had been tabled for the day. They had to know, here, now; that was for sure. This could prove to be either a nothing incident, forgettable and forgotten, or an invitation to conspicuous failure.

He depressed a button on the desk, signaling assent, and soon his visitors began to enter. They were all well-known figures, key personnel of the local regional upper administration, but at the same time Parleau recognized that he knew none of them well. They were all either holdovers from the previous regime or imports like himself, brought in from other parts of the world.

Edner Eykor entered first. He was one of those who had

come from somewhere else. Parleau had looked in the records, but had not assigned the facts any importance, and had consequently forgotten them. Like the other users of programmed names, Eykor's surname lent no clue as to place or origin. Where had it been? Europe, somewhere, Parleau thought. Eykor was a thin, nervous man who always seemed to be in a hurry, always on the verge of missing some item, at least in appearance. A bad sign, Parleau had thought more than once. Nervousness in an intelligence man. Not good at all. His opinion was that an intelligence man at the staff level should be as impassive as an idol. Eykor had sandy, non-descript thinning hair and a long, horselike countenance, upon which a set of rubbery lips ruminated aimlessly.

The second was Mandor Klyten, the Regional ler Expert. He was a curious one, for his post was almost totally unconnected with the Institute. Until Klyten had filled it, it had been little more than an academic post, a sinecure. Give Klyten credit: at least he had done much of his own field work, a notion unheard of for years, indeed if not generations. He studied and worked hard, and his advice regarding ler matters, while curiously unspecific, was always worth listening to. Outside the reservation, he was as well-informed as it was possible to be. Klyten was a short, plump, rather disorganized man of middle age; Parleau was not confused by the absentminded appearance. Under that thinning gray hair lurked a formidable and keen intelligence. Parleau did wonder at the turn of preferences that led such a one to scholasticism.

Aseph Plattsman was the last to enter. The analyst and Controller. In an earlier day, Plattsman might, from his general appearance, have been a musician, an artist. Today, a Controller. One who watched and monitored, who supervised, who managed. Who controlled. Odd, that, but again, not so odd. Parleau had heard more than once that the discipline of the Controllers, Situational Analysis, had become the last art form. And equally often, Parleau had also heard that the majority of Regional Chairmen were former Controllers. Not vast majority. Just majority. Plattsman was long and aesthetic, dark of complexion, having black, unruly hair and deep chocolate eyes that expressed little but observed everything. He moved without obvious gesture or mannerism, but with an effortless exactitude, as if every motion were exactly what he had intended it to be. Youngest by far on the staff, Plattsman could easily move to some Region as chairman someday. Slow and deliberate, when the pressure was on he could change into one of the most serious and stern of taskmasters. Parleau felt no particular threat from Plattsman, knowing it would be years yet; Plattsman had not been sent to replace him, but to learn. Parleau understood these things, and the loneliness of this path; after a time, nothing was worth any effort but the work and the power. Still, he felt the most empathy here, to Plattsman, and wished him continued success.

The three visitors waited by their accustomed places until Parleau gestured to them that they should be seated, lowering himself into his own chair as he did. He waved at them impatiently. "Good day, good day, daymen. Shall we leave the pleasantries and go to the matter at hand?"

They nodded, and began unpacking briefcases and untidy portfolios. Eykor, so it appeared, had the smallest pile, so by common consent he would be the first to speak.

He began "Why we are here relates to security, so I propose that we . . ."

Parleau interrupted. "Wait. I have read the résumés. Who reported the information and how far upchannel did it go?"

Plattsman answered, CenRegCon did, Chairman. The original B-twenty-seven report was on late mids. I have the pertinent duty logs. The first, capture, was routine and normal, so it went, eventually, all the way up. ConSec. No further, though. Not to my knowledge. The second one, of last night, was stopped here for comment or amendment before going on."

Parleau breathed deeply. Shorted out by the wily Controllers, just on suspicion, until it could be checked against the files. And it matched. And they held it. They could have let it go, and who could have taken clear reprisals against them? The Controllers were notoriously independent-minded; so they were saving him, but for what reasons? He would have to run that one later.

Plattsman produced several sheets of electroprint and read, from the forms; "Thirty-one Tenmonth two-three-four-five local hour . . . Item forty-six incident of suspected terrorism, Regional Museum of Technology and applications. Watchman reports certain instruments in the Petro section dismantled, destroyed by acid. . . . The next entry is . . . yes, Item sixty-two. A member, female, reported apprehended without papers or reasonable explanation near Museum, attempting to cross River Five on a methane pipeline from the composting dumps. Remanded to Interrogation."

He paused, shuffling the papers some more. "Then here's a follow-up. 'subject member refused to give name of number. Remanded back to Interrogation.' "

"And here . . . the last report, a follow-up, which we stopped. It looked wrong. By this time there's a case number on it. We were going to have a look into it anyway, but then this Medic Venle reports that Interro had somehow put a live female ler into a sensory deprivation chamber. While inside, something so far undetermined occurred to the subject, who we may now refer to as 'Item forty-six,' and Item forty-six upon recovery was observed to have no measurable mental processes beyond infant state; some kind of regression had taken place. One of the things that stood out was that this report was made in B format, but of course a B is not appropriate because as a ler, she never had an A submitted on her. It was kicked out of process control. When we cross checked, we found the references. That's all, Chairman."

Parleau said, "We will have to follow it up and finalize, because at Continental there's an open case file. Understand? But careful, now. Nothing on this goes out without my initials." He turned to Eykor. "Now. What's gone on there?"

"Chairman, it's all pretty much as in the reports. I was present part of the time, because the interrogators said that they could not crack her. We tried, but nothing. It was minor, of course, but the more we said, the tighter she became. We did not try drugs or stimuli, but total isolation seemed to be a good idea. At the time—we had no idea. . . ."

Klyten asked, "And what was her age?"

"She never said. We took tissue samples, along with the other routine identification procedures, but they read out too young using human data base. We didn't have the ler data and didn't want to ask for it, you understand, but fifteen certainly seemed too low."

Klyten commented, "You're right, there. It is too low. I might say a better guess would put her, say, about twenty. Yes, twenty, plus or minus a year. How long did you give her in the box?"

"Well, at the time she was taken out, about twenty-five days."

"Twenty-five days? I've heard that hard human cases break in ten!"

"Well, now, Klyten, that's more or less true, but we just assumed she'd react similarly."

"Judging from events, a poor assumption, something even a student adviser would have advised against. Or did you know then that they have the ability to autoforget, dump all the mnemonic data they have collected since birth?"

"No, we . . . well, hell, so we made an error. But all the same, we had enough evidence to connect her to the Museum job, and terrorism is a capital offense anyway, so . . ."

Parleau interrupted Eykor again. "Wait. Terrorism, is it? You must have a live victim to have terrorism."

"Chairman, we interpreted the destruction of valuable instruments and artifacts as a distinct crime against society, harming the people in general. After all, there were persons on duty about the Museum also."

Parleau looked off into space for a moment, then turned back to Eykor. "Eykor, all sorts of deeds, good and bad, have been done in human history, and they all carry the same reason: that they were done for the good of the people. Now I'm no moralist or ethicist, nor squeamish when it comes down to what must be done. Let it roll! But whatever we do here, please let us all use more rigor in our definitions that 'it's for the people.' That's just bullshit, and you and I alike know it. Now what were these valuable instruments?"

"Some ancient devices used in geodesy and petroleum exploration, to search out likely sites."

"Specifically, what?"

"A highly miniaturized Magnetic Anomaly Detector, apparently originally towed behind an aircraft. The other was a Gravity Field Sensor, likewise miniature. That was why the acid. This last measured the local field strength of gravity. The custodian informed us that both instruments were reputed to be very sensitive and capable of precise resolutions, say, on the order of a handsbreadth across."

Parleau said, "Curious, curious. What could possibly have been her motive?"

Eykor answered, "We have no idea."

Parleau looked at Klyten, who shrugged. Then at Plattsman. At first he shook his head, but began tapping on the metal desk surface with his long fingers. After a time, he said, hesitating, ". . . The instruments were used to find subsurface oil sites, you say?"

Parleau saw immediately. He exclaimed, "To prevent the

discovery of something, some mineral or petroleum on Reservation land!"

Plattsman stood. "Perhaps, Chairman. But I want to use your assistant's terminal. I need access to the Archives."

"Go ahead." Plattsman left, briskly. Parleau turned to Eykor. "Only one thing wrong, there. Oil has been out of use for several centuries. There's still some of it around, but just small pools, not exploited. Not worth it. Residuals, curiosities. Besides. I don't think the reservation area ever had a reputation for natural oils anyway."

"I could not comment on that one, Chairman."

Klyten asked, "Has anyone inquired why no mention was made that Item forty-six was a New People adolescent?"

Eykor replied, "No. It was unimportant. Is. We were interested in the crime itself."

"Unimportant? By Darwin's organs, that's the central fact of it, not what she wrecked. Why she wrecked it. If we worry about what she did, and forget who she was, or why she was there, we're chasing the bird with the broken wing. It's who she is, what she is. I agree with the medic, what's his name. This is serious. We are dealing here with large unknowns, perhaps dangerous for our welfare. We need to solve it."

Eykor, rebuked once again and told his own business, opened his mouth to put Klyten in his place, but at that moment, Plattsman chose to make his return.

Parleau asked, "Well?"

"There is no evidence of either oil or ore deposits about the whole region on either side of River Nine. In or near the reservation. No inquiries were underway, nor were any being considered. I also queried the use of instruments. the Magnetic Anomaly Detector was used in several ways, militarily, to detect undersea craft, and mines, and also, later, to locate high-density ferrous bodies, mascons. Meteorites, buried in the drift. The other was used to determine the exact shape of the Earth, and also in the search for mascons. But the recorded data indicates that there were no such anomalies in the reservation area."

"So we're no better off than before. Unless they were to hide something they found themselves. . . ."

Klyten observed, "We should not be so hasty there. We are reasonably sure that they are not, except in very specific and limited fields, technologists. So what could they discover and hide that our finest instruments could not perceive? I add to counter my own argument that we also know that their area

was never exploited. It was given to them because of that—
there seemed to be nothing worth while in the area."

Parleau mused aloud, "But even if they had oil, what
would they use it for? We have better and cheaper fuel and
the material stuff we get from synthetics the same. They have
no need for it, and they couldn't give it to us. . . ."

Eykor asked, "What about metals?"

Klyten said, "A better case, there, perhaps, but still tentative."

Eykor asked further, "But if so, why hide it? They know
the reservation's sovereign ground. There hasn't been a human actually inside it on the ground for a good two hundred
years, and I don't know of any case . . ."

Plattsman commented, "The previous government had in
its time also displaced aboriginal tribes and set aside inviolate
reservations. But for a long time, as soon as anything of
value was found or suspected on such lands, ways were
devised to circumvent or disregard such pacts. The ler are
aware of these facts, perhaps better than we. All they would
have to do would be to compare their own population density
against anywhere outside it. There, are, for example, more
humans living in Tierra Del Fuego. There is pressure from
that alone, and only by surplus production do they buy that
appetite off. Never mind any resource."

Eykor shrugged. "I know that as well. And I, for one,
would have to assign a lower probability to some resource.
But there are other possibilities; something hidden,
something made or built. The first thing to mind would be a
weapon of some sort."

Parleau exclaimed, "It's my turn to assign probabilities, and
that one is low indeed. Why, if they had a weapon to hide
that would do them any good, why haven't they used it?"

Klyten shook his head, agitatedly. "No, no, no. Anything
they could use would have to be powerful or of widespread
impact, which starts by violating their most cherished beliefs.
And it would have to be an artifact, probably quite large.
There are delivery systems to consider, aim, use, range."

"Wait, there," Parleau said thoughtfully. "Mind, I don't actually think it might be that, but . . . Eykor, did you run any
cross checks on this Item forty-six? Does she have a record?"

"No, we didn't. She seemed such an amateur. . . ."

Plattsman asked, "Can we run one now? I mean, not a full
scan, which would take days, but just a quick collation from

the Comparator. That will give us a quick glance over the continent. The matches, if any, should be along shortly."

"I have no objection."

Plattsman left, and returned shortly. "I referred to the record holos you took off her in Security Records. The Comparator will review all the Current Operations records of the stress checkpoints and see if there's a match."

Parleau asked Eykor, skeptically. "Are you sure you have gathered any evidence at all on this case?"

"Chairman, we had just started when this last event occurred. We were moving discreetly because of the sensitivity of the issue. There is another aspect to this, and we were trying to integrate the two. From our overflight series . . ."

"Overflights? Were they not prohibited?"

"We have been using gliders, launched across the reservation. Battery powered, inertial guided. Flown at night in the proper weather conditions, they are undetectable. They couldn't see one if they had radar."

"Go on."

"It's an old program. I didn't initiate it. And who will complain, when they can't see it, don't know it's there? At least, we assume they have never seen it, for there have been no complaints."

Parleau said, "Poor assumption. The one does not necessarily follow."

"Do you want it stopped?"

"Stopped . . . ? No. Continue it, of course, but supervise it closely. I realize many of us are new to these people, if they are that."

"Of course, and also we can . . ." And here Eykor launched into a detailed account of delaying, frustrating, obfuscative and annoying practices and examples of the same, which the Regional Government might have occasion to use. He continued at some length, until stopped by a signal from the outer office. Plattsman excused himself and left.

The group waited, expectantly. Plattsman was gone for longer than they thought, and they all began to grow restive. Presently he returned, animated.

"Incredible, actually incredible. Why we overlooked it is beyond me—more of these assumptions, in my branch as well as the next. There is simply no substitute for thoroughness, is there?"

Parleau said, "Well, on with it."

"The tentative match list was too large, and had to be narrowed. I had to cross-refer it with the chemosensors. When I did, I got this list." And Plattsman read: "Orlando, New Orleans, Huntsville; five discrete locations in Seaboard South; three more in the Oak Ridge area; once, Dayton; and twice on the West Coast, once in Sur and once in Bayarea. I requested pictures. And this is only in the last year!"

Klyten was first to speak. "She can't have walked to all those places clambering along methane pipes!"

Parleau said, "No, indeed not. She has moved freely among us, and for what purposes? I was not aware they could do this."

Eykor said. "They're not supposed to be able to. . . ."

Plattsman laughed. "And now it gets interesting. Not a vandal, but a spy. A real one! We haven't had one for centuries!"

And Parleau said, "Yes, very funny; one who risks her life to destroy instruments, and who faces the box and oblivion to conceal why. Plattsman! Have your people see if they can find some more of these instruments, somewhere, in working condition. And continue your check of the Comparator network. I want to know exactly where she's been, when. Stay out of the Institute until I say—she's probably left a dozen spider webs to trip over. Check her identity discreetly, open source stuff, for the present. We must know more. You, too, Eykor. And you were saying something about overflights . . . ?"

"Yes, I was, and this fits perfectly. There seems to be a pattern of activity that defies analysis, almost as if it were being purposely randomized, but we can draw conclusions from its growth and spread. We had made these tentative guesses—that there is a secret somewhere in the reservation, apparently unknown by most of the inhabitants, and that Game theory suggests a definite break with past patterns, in the near-future time-frame."

"What kind of time-frame?"

"Five to ten years."

"That's no better than an entrail-reader of ancient Rome could do. I could do as much with common sense."

Plattsman interjected, "Chairman, begging your pardon, but reading entrails is precisely what we do. We've substituted Data Terminal Printouts for the original bloody guts, but otherwise it's all the same—a little guessing, a little larceny, a little luck, and damn good obversation of the present."

Parleau smiled. "And so, Eykor, that was why your people were so anxious to get something out of her?"

"That is correct, Chairman. We needed a key, a tool to get at the larger problem. She offered a perfect chance. Unfortunately, we got nothing out of her directly."

"But the second chance, man! Now we can."

Klyten said mildly, "Maybe not. I must advise you that she would not do these things—if indeed it is her and not the error of an overzealous machine or that of a careless programmer somewhere along the line—completely on her own. They are a communal people and act together in all things and enterprises. The few who live alone become sedentary, fixed in place."

Eykor exclaimed, "As I suspected all along! A plot!"

"Yes," Kltyen continued. "And they are most fond of subtle ones. There are many possibilities here, and not the least of them is that she may have been dragged under our noses to prevent us from smelling something else, as the saying goes. I don't think they would sacrifice her willingly, that's not their way, but her capture could have been accidental. Or she could have been designed to cause us to precipitate certain events. I have long suspected forms of this type of manipulation—control by negative aversion. You see obvious forms of this in some of our own less sophisticated child-rearing practices, but as a management technique, it is capable of great refinement and control. There is the well-known study by Klei that shows grounds for suspecting that they encouraged and fomented the immanent racialism which suddenly terminated with their move into the reservation and their consolidation."

Eykor observed, "I see. Had they gathered themselves together of their own accord, it would have generated great suspicion, even in an environment of basically neutral feelings, but with a slight degree of encouraged race-fear, and proper stimuli ... but that's social control on a very large scale. Do they have that kind of control, and what are the margins for error?"

Klyten had their attention. He continued, "There is where we have not been able to reach the bottom of it. After all, as Controller Plattsman will doubtless agree, we have some fairly subtle methods ourselves, but there are operations we prefer to stay away from. So much so that there isn't enough data even to estimate how much control they have. We do note with relief that this sort of thing seems to have died out after the consolidation. I know this is rather far afield, but it supports the idea that we must consider this in our range of possibilities."

Parleau remained silent still, thinking hard, letting the others do the talking. But he knew Klyten's argument to be a valid one, and that they had many more options than simply the first one that had occurred to them. One simply could not know, now. There was need for more data, more caution. He had always figured in fudge factors throughout his career, and with the instinct of the careerist, he sensed the need for them now—large ones, in fact. To be caught off guard by them would be unfortunate, but not fatal. However, to make the wrong interpretation and then take the wrong course of action and precipitate undesirable events ... unthinkable. More was at stake here than his own merit report file at Continental.

He said, "Klyten, is part of our difficulty here the result of the way we perceive them? Or, I should ask, the way we respond?"

"I think so. The whole culture goes to great length to rationalize their apparent voluntary primitivism ... I think that many of them themselves are not aware of the dichotomy. I mean, you look at some of the solutions coming out of the Institute, and there's evidence of fine, educated technological minds at work, and then around seventeen-hundred or eighteen-hundred hours, the owners of these fine minds go home and chop wood, or draw water from a stream. We also see evidence in other ways that they are in fact not primitive at all ... their houses reflect chemical engineering and knowledge of geodesics, blended together, a field so far ahead of us that even with a sample of the material in front of us, we can't describe how it sets up and works. This branch of specialized technology is the monopoly of a single Braid, which cooks over a charcoal fire and bathes in an unheated stream. If this were occurring in the wilder sections of New Guinea or Borneo I could cite rapid change and incomplete assimilations, but here this is not the case; they turn away from the technology of personal convenience and then manage to master highly subtle alternates of essentially the same basic areas of knowledge."

Plattsman said, "Not necessarily suspicious in itself. Many of our people would do likewise if they had a reservation to live in and the low population density to get away with it."

Klyten concurred amiably, "True enough, I suppose. Still,

we must consider all possibilities, and in the light of other knowns, weigh it."

Parleau asked, "Then what is our best course here? Continue the investigation and try to get a vector downstream?" His use of the jargon of the Controllers and their pet discipline caused a faint smile to flow across Plattsman's face.

Plattsman provided the answer. "Yes, certainly. We do not have enough data even to identify the problem, much less work on alternates for solving it."

"Eykor, if we did actopt*, what kind of options do we have?"

"There's the graduated response system. For this, I should imagine Conops-two-twelve† would elaborate on the theme of trade-off and provide great flexibility. At the ultimate expression, where they were completely uncooperative and immovable, we could occupy the reservation complex, annex it, and remove the denizens to someplace like Sonora Region. Perhaps Low Baja, Mojave Inner. And we could segregate fertile populations."

"How far does that go?"

"As far as we have to, to get the idea across. I imagine that if two-twelve was implemented, it would come to that."

"It would." commented Klyten. "They have been known to take a drop in population in order to segregate obvious defectives. But there are serious objections to that, ethically. We are really dealing in unknowns, there. They would, of course, have become overtly hostile long before that, if we followed two-twelve to the letter."

Parleau said, "No worry about that. We haven't yet reached the point of two-twelve and as far as I'm concerned, it may not be used."

Eykor agreed, "Completely. More investigation is in order."

Plattsman offered, "You can have complete cooperation from Control."

Parleau now asked, "Will someone come for her? Or should we dispose the item . . . ?"

Klyten responded immediately. "No. Assume that someone will eventually come for her." He tried to ignore the knowing looks Eykor was displaying to all. "Somebody wants to know

---

* Bureaucratic jargon: means "to decide upon an active course."
† More jargon: Conops means "Concept of Operations. An arbitrary definition of projected reality in which to act."

what has happened to their favorite, and eventually they will come looking. Even though they will get nothing out of her, now, she is still worth saving, because with loving care and patience, a new personality can be grafted onto what is left. The end result is very similiar to severe retardation, but it is functional."

"Very good! We will dig further. Route everything through me and keep Denver off distribution for the time being. Stall."

Parleau stopped for a minute, thinking private thoughts and apprehensions. He said, "And, Eykor, send me up a copy of two-twelve. I'll want to be looking over it, just for information, you understand."

Eykor agreed. "And anything else, Chairman?"

"Yes. Find out, working with Control, who that girl is. Or as Klyten might have us put it, *was*."

Parleau stood, indicating to the others that, at least for the time, a solution had been started. That was something; still, he had to admit that there were far too many unresolved factors here. He had left out the issue of the propriety of Eykor's actions deliberately, and instead let random remarks carry the meaning of his displeasure. He wanted to see how far Eykor would go, and in which direction.

The members of this meeting departed without ceremony. Parleau watched them go, trying to resettle his mind to the other matters at hand, the thousand things he needed to look at. That long-overdue Letter of Agreement with Appalachian Region, for instance. He had hoped this latest proposal would keep them quiet for a while, but apparently the letter hadn't yet come up through channels. He sighed. Just impossible. He ran his hand through the thinning stubble of his hair, a gesture of impatience left over from the old days, when he had been a junior executive in Sonora Region. He was just getting into position to resume his seat behind the desk when the door to the office opened. It was Plattsman.

Parleau looked up, curious. "Yes?"

"Chairman, I was on my way over to Eykor's with something new and interesting. It occurred to me that you might also like to see it. It's just a suspicion, but . . ."

Parleau looked closely at the younger man. He could not be absolutely certain, but the Controller seemed a little worried, concerned. "Yes, I would be. Continue."

Plattsman came to the edge of the desk, producing from a portfolio a sheaf of photoprints. One he set aside, and the others he carefully held, indicating that Parleau should look for himself. Parleau bent closer.

Indicating the single print, Plattsman said, "Observe this print: this is the file image of the girl, as she appears now." He paused to let the image set in the chairman's mind. "Now this one," he said, adding one more from the pile, "was taken before she was put in the box. Standard surveillance stuff through one-way glass. Can you recognize her?"

Parleau nodded. "Yes. There are more differences than I would have imagined."

"Correct. This apparently is an effect of her regression. I should imagine from these alone that whatever happened to her, she lost everything, even the little quirks of personality that really lend us all identity. But the point is that you, not a trained observer, could still recognize her. Now let me show you these." With that, Plattsman spread out the remaining prints over the dull surface of the desk. He stood back.

Parleau looked at the prints, then to Plattsman. Plattsman pointed to the prints. Parleau looked again.

And again. He saw typical point-surveillance crowd images, much enlarged to center and to expand upon single persons, the pictures somewhat fuzzy along the edges from enlargement. At first he failed to see what Plattsman was obviously leading him to. He saw pictures of a girl, mostly dressed after the styles of the day, more rarely in ler clothing, the overshirt, short hair, dark complexion, although not as swarthy as Plattsman, intent expression which could have meant anything ... in some of the images, he could make out the shape of clean, strong limbs impressing their shape on the garments. He looked again. He had almost given up when something nagged at his mind's eye, caught it. And again. And then Parleau saw what had captured Plattsman's attention. The chairman made a choice, reached for two of the prints, removed them and set them aside.

He turned to the Controller and said, "Those two are not our girl, Item forty-six."

"No, Chairman, they are not. You and I have a greater depth of discrimination than the machine, no matter how sophisticated it gets. Especially where faces are concerned. Faces are more complex than retina patterns or fingerprints, but we are tuned to them by our own heritage of natural programming. You are correct. There are a couple more in question. We are analyzing the events."

"You didn't come back here to tell me your machine made a mistake."

Right, What we can tentatively project from the data we have—sensors, time of day matching, and the like—is that the second girl, whose face we can't make out so well, was involved in some way with the first one, Item forty-six. Same place, virtually same time, with the second passing the sensor after the first."

"Shadowing?"

"Seems so, although why is a mystery. Also, from the che-monitors, we know that both are ler, female, contemporary in age, more or less, and that the stress level of the second was always lower than the first, Moreover, Physiology informs me, again tentatively, that the kind of stress is different in the two. The first, Item forty-six, always has a fear-component. It may be with other emotional sets, or pure, but it is always one or another variety of fear."

"The second?"

"The second's emotions equate to nothing we can identify by analogy with humans. But whatever internal state it reveals in her, it is always seen pure, absolutely alone."

"I've heard something about the way you use those tracers. Something about mixed and pure sets . . . refresh my flagging memory."

"A pure chemtrace in a human almost invariably indicates a psychotic condition, usually a psychopath, I believe the ler system is similar enough for us to draw the same conclusion. I am presently having the idea verified."

"But think of it! Two of them! What is the connection?"

"We're going after it, Chairman. But it looks like nothing simple, that's a fact."

"Well, by all means pass that stuff on to Eykor. It will not make him feel any better, but he needs it all the same."

Plattsman nodded, gathered the prints, and left. And Parleau sat back in his chair and stared at a blank, random spot on the wall opposite him. He did not pick up his routine paperwork for a long time.

SIX

*What, they ask, is the Game? Most simply
put, it is a recursive sequence of changes in state,
which are varied by the Players according to
rules. It can be as simple as a sequence of digi-
tal data, or numbers; it can take more complex
forms in arrays of repeating cells deployed over
a two-dimensional surface; it can occur in three-
dimensional matrices, yea and more. It can be
played with blocks, on a checkerboard, inside
frameworks; it can be played on paper, or with a
computer, or, best of all, totally inside the mind.
Now they ask, what good is it? And we say that
through it we learn to understand consequences
and the recursive patterns of Life and the Universe. And through it we learn how much we do
not know.*

—The Game Texts

Morlenden awoke, making the transition from dead sleep
to awareness with no apparent symptom of change. Beside
him, he felt the warmth of Fellirian's body, and along his
neck the contrast of the night-chilled air of the *yos* in winter. There was light showing on the translucent ground-rock
panes of the narrow windows, a soft dawn peach light, but
also a light with a hard steel-blue undertone to it, a sense of
the clean air of winter, morning and clear sky. He moved
slowly, cautiously and experimentally feeling the air, testing
it, as it were, before committing himself to it. He stretched,
hearing soft creaks and pops, slowly and gently disentangling
himself from Fellirian without waking her. She moved, shifting position, but the rhythm of her breathing never varied.

Morlenden slid free of the comforter, listened: all he could
hear were the sounds of the forest in the beginning of winter.
Outside, the animals were already up and about in their pens
and barns, complaining, as usual, that no one had come out

to see them. On the other side of the *yos*, beyond the children's sleeper, the creek gurgled and bubbled contentedly . . . there was no rain-sound, not even a hint of a rain-drip from the trees overhead.

Now he was beginning to feel the bite of the cold; he took a deep breath, shivered violently, stood and began rummaging along the wall shelf for a fresh winter overshirt, estimating the cold. Not so bad, today, he thought, selecting a pleth of medium weight, slipping it over his head, and then retrieving his long single braid out of the back of it.

Rubbing his eyes, Morlenden climbed down out of the sleeper into the hearthroom, listening carefully to see if anyone besides himself was awake yet. There was no sound, save Kaldherman's light snoring from the sleeper. He must have moved, he thought. He wanted to knock over a pan, or something, so someone would wake up. He restrained himself: he did not wish to awaken Sanjirmil . . . but as much as he hated bad news, he wanted to get on with it and speak with the Perwathwiy. But no, there was no one up besides himself, not even the youngest, their little addition, Stheflannai, who was always the first to hear anything. Morlenden shrugged, and began rekindling the cookfire in the hearth; after a time, when he could see that something was coming back to life from the ashes and coals of the night before, he continued his way to the entryway to collect his boots, noting as he pulled them on that they were stiff and cold.

Stepping out on the platform, he paused to test the air, reading the morning, as they said. The sky was indeed clear, an astonishing clear, deep blue; in the east, the sun was rising out of the remnants of a shredded fogbank, shining through the spidery network of bare trunks and branches, starting to put some life back in the cold. It would be crisp, all day. Very fresh, as he was fond of saying, a phrase Fellirian always twitted him about when the weather was behaving at its worst. He went down the stairs, feeling better already, taking the turn in the paths across the yard leading toward the outhouse, reflecting upon the things that needed doing, as he always did. First would be the recording and cross-reference of all the material he had gathered on his last field trip; then properly entering it in the record ledgers, indexing, tagging. They would need to start a new batch of paper, too. Stock had been getting somewhat low, he recalled, and that was one of their Braid obligations—the paper concession. What a pain! Probably would need at least two weights unless Kal had

done up a batch of Number Three ordinary while he had
been out in the field. And, of course, meeting with the Perwathwiy, whatever it was she wanted. Perhaps that wouldn't
take so long, and they could get on with matters at hand.

He remembered to watch for the root, which he had
tripped over for several years on the way to the outhouse,
climbing the ridgelet behind the *yos*. He was barely in time;
he saw it, on the verge of tripping over it once more.

*Damned thing! I've tripped over that one root since I was
five years old, and, total recall or not, I still trip over it! And
every time, I threaten to cut it off, root and branch, the
whole damned tree. But I never have*, he thought reflectively.
*It's a sourwood, and they're rare . . . and what is it that Per-
wathwiy wants? Damn elders anyway! She could have sent
Sanjir down anyway, by herself; probably wants us to start
keeping all the records of membership of the lodges as well.
They've been after us for years to do it for them, as if we
weren't busy enough just keeping up with the Braids*. Now
he'd have to repeat the whole tiresome argument all over
again from the very beginnings. Yes, the whole argument. Perwathwiy wouldn't sit still for a simple negative. And even if it
was only her own lodge, Dragonfly, that wouldn't change
it: start keeping *their* records, and all of them would want the
same thing. Service. Balls on a goose! Let them keep their
own records! He reached the outhouse, a rustic little shanty
carefully hidden in the midst of overage Lilac bushes. . . .

Walking slowly back to the *yos*, coming over the ridgeline,
Morlenden could see now that a fine plume of smoke was rising from the largest ellipsoid, the one of the hearthroom. Nobody was visible, but the smoke was evidence enough; someone was up and about now; he guessed one of the children
had got up and was tending the fire, putting on a pot for an
infusion of root-tea, a pan of meal to boil, a couple of the
fine sausages from the locker that he and Kal had put up earlier this fall.

Higher up the hollow, toward the watershed, he saw the
elder, Perwathwiy, approaching him on the path, negotiating
the way in a measured, careful manner, but at the same time
not betraying any hinderance arising from her age. He had
not seen her the night before, or in years, nor ever well. But
he knew Perwathwiy well enough; she never changed. He
couldn't recall ever seeing her any different than she was
now, a stern, agile ancient with iron-gray hair and the sourest
disposition this side of the Green Sea, at the least. She was

known never to smile, and little children repeated the doggerel that she had been born just as she was now.

The *starsrith* approached, stopped, nodded politely. Morlenden returned the gesture, acknowledging her respect for the holding. So this was the Perwathwiy, "First Spirit of the Eagle-cry," as the name went in Fire aspect. Morlenden knew the data without having consciously to recall it. A lifetime of recordkeeping, ordinary full-memory (or was it the elder's overbearing sense of presence? A Fire trait to be sure), but there had always been something more than simply aspect to the Perwathwiy. Sanjirmil also seemed to have that trait. Perwathwiy was and had been for years the elected chief hetman of Dragonfly Lodge, certainly the most powerful of the elder lodges. There were rumors, too, of secret influences, but Morlenden had never given such theories much thought; Dragonfly was quite powerful enough in his mind without the additional reinforcements of sinister conspiracies conducted in stealth. But they were secretive, and also the most conscious of themselves: powerful, sure, almost arrogant people who veiled their comings and goings in mystery and arcane mannerisms.

The Perwathwiy was small in stature, thin, her skin wrinkled and darkened from decades of exposure and weathering. As befitted an elder, her hair was arrayed in two long braids that hung down neatly in front. The hair was absolutely gray, not a hint of color in it. Gray, not white. He could not recall ever hearing what color her hair had been. There were deep crow's-feet around the eyes, but the eyes themselves were bright, clear, birdlike, and of no particular color. Save perhaps rain-wet rock. Morlenden knew her age, and was surprised that the old woman was still in such good shape.

She spoke first, "I have been at my meditations. The letters are always clearer at dawn, as they say, but one must arise to see them, eh? You do not know the letters? The Godwrite of the ancient Hebrews, the cabalists: Hm. It is a defect you should remedy. I should have preferred to speak with all of you last night, Morlenden Deren, but savoring as I do the subtle essence of second-thoughts, I think the better of the morning. I might have said more than I intended. Yes. I was in haste, tired. One makes mistakes then, and in this matter there must be no more."

"The matter is . . . ?"

"To be revealed to you all. It is no light thing, but something all the adults among you must decide. It will seem like nothing at first, but I fear it will become a burden beyond bearing before you are done with it, if you agree to it. There are unsuspected depths in it, and once committed, your silence must be absolute. But for the now, let us return to the *yos* of the Derens and gather a good meal. I am hungry, and can lay to rest the horrid legend that elders subsist upon nothing more than a diet of boiled clabber, lentils, groats, and spurge."

Morlenden redundantly indicated the way she should go, and they went down the path to the *yos*. As they neared the stairwell on the downhill side of it, Kaldherman emerged, rubbing his eyes.

He looked at them sleepily and said, between yawns, "I see that you two are the early birds. The girls are, however, yet abed. Ayali is now snoring in a most girlish manner, but you don't have to say that I was the one who told you. They proved impossible to awaken. Peth and Sanjirmil have temporarily buried the knife and are busy at the hearth. I imagine we shall prove the poorer for it, but at the least we shall be well-fed."

From within the *yos*, they could hear a voice floating bodilessly, saying, "I'm coming, I'm coming, just this minute!"

Morlenden asked the Perwathwiy, "Where will you take yours?"

"You require an answer? On the stairs, here, of course. Finish yours and join me here, in the yard, without the children. Only Sanjirmil will witness for the *Zanklaron**."

Morlenden reflected a moment, then asked, 'Then you didn't come all the way down here to remonstrate with me about the Derens keeping elder records of enlistments and transitions."

"Hardly. On that I should approach Fellirian anyway. She is *Klandorh*, is she not? But on that subject, yes, I know I have hectored you for years, and I will doubtless continue. All of you Derens are stubborn, whether born to the role or woven to it. It is a most important matter, ever on our minds, but rest assured that I would not walk leagues in the rain to hector you some more. This, in fact, may change the requirements . . . but never mind. Go and see that all are fed. I have

---

* "Players of the Life Game," the manner in which both Player Braids were referred to collectively.

far yet to go, and one among you may indeed have to go farther."

And not long afterward, with everyone up and about and fed (as Kaldherman had predicted, with a stock of the sausages he and Morlenden had put up), the four Deren adults joined the elder Perwathwiy and Sanjirmil, who were waiting silently by the creek a little below the *yos*, out of earshot, so they hoped, of the curious adolescents required to stay behind.

As the Derens approached, the Perwathwiy continued to keep her silence, appearing to listen to the creek, as if meditating, choosing her words. The sound of the rushing water filled the cool air. Then Perwathwiy turned and stared at them pointedly, finally speaking.

"Dragonfly Lodge, with the cooperation and encouragement of Braids Reven, Perklaren, and Terklaren, has empowered me to request of our community registrars the finding of a person. This is to be regarded as a most important *thaydh**for which Klanderen will be compensated. *Mielhaltalon*† to determine the whereabouts, fate thereof, or confirmation of transition of this person, restoring aforementioned person to us, specifically Dragonfly Lodge, if alive. I may say no more than this. We are on very dangerous ground here, and since we have no police as such, decision was made and implemented to come to you. You know everyone, you trace relationships, and in addition are known to be adventurous and resourceful."

At this last remark, a fine description to be sure, everyone save Cannialin raised their eyebrows. Yes, save Cannialin. She lived entirely in the present, never anticipating, and thus was almost never surprised, neither at the things people said, nor what they did. It was all one.

Perwathwiy paused. Then she said, "Upon your concurrence, you will receive from myself a packet containing a name on a slip of paper. What say you?"

They did not answer. The hint of danger, the secrecy, all put them off; but the amount offered for the service was even more astounding than all of these, for nothing any of them

* Literally, a quest.
† Fourteen to the third power grams of gold. Approximately 2.75 kilos. Considering that most transactions were valued in fourteenths of a *tal*, such a sum was beyond counting.

could imagine could cost hardly more than a *tal* of gold, and here were offered, in decimals, 2,744 of them. Of the Derens, Fellirian was the most shocked, for she was accustomed in part to the standing-wave inflation of the human world and its corresponding devaluation of currency. In 2550, with such an amount in pure gold, Fellirian could have bought outright title to every building in Seaboard South Region. Even having so much to offer was unimaginable.

But she was first to find her voice. "And why us? Or perhaps I should ask, why not you yourself or the parties you represent?"

The Perwathwiy answered forthrightly: "Eventually, someone will have to trace these things out. You have all the records and, moreover, you are all used to meeting people, going among them, ferreting out relationships. You are known everywhere, trusted, and hence will be able to make discreet inquiries. Most importantly, you are now and initially ignorant of certain aspects of this affair, aspects which may well turn out to be matters of survival. Our survival. We think that eventually you will have to go outside, which Fellirian does weekly, and it will arouse no particular suspicion. And why not one of us? We do not wish it known that it is we who are interested in this person. We suspect foul play."

Kaldherman said, "Dangerous then, is it? To you, but not so to us?"

The Perwathwiy looked away, to the sun, now clearing the branches of the trees and casting a golden morning light into the yard below the *yos*. Then she looked back. "Of course there can be danger to you. Possible. But certain if, for example, I walk through the Institute gate into the outside. But then, there is danger in all things; even an innocent trip to the outhouse can be full of perils: witness the uncut root in the pathway of the Derens."

Fellirian said, "Come now. We ask specifics, and in return receive the parables of a hermetic philosopher, which in this case we all know as well as you. Especially the famous root, which is not the peril of the Derens so much as a pet of Morlenden's. Speak straightly or not at all: danger or not?"

She answered, "Yes." But her answer was framed in a quiet and suddenly respectful voice. Fellirian was a person of regard even in the circles in which the Perwathwiy moved, both for reasons widely known and for some not so well-known, and she well knew them both. "Yes, it is so. Very likely. The one whom you will seek was an adept, one of us.

You will have to be discreet ... indeed, secretive would not be the wrong wordings-way of it. And of what you uncover, you will speak of it to none, save in whispers among yourselves. And you will make your report to the Reven, who will correct you if you have gone astray too far. And you must start soon, for yesterday is almost too late. We have tarried overlong, and I admit the responsibility."

Morlenden sensed a sudden weakness, but he did not let her off, but pursued her, his hard, angular face becoming harsh, his voice keen and peremptory. "We are not armored knights as the humans of old, to set out on fearsome horses to the ends of the Earth. We know this little reservation to be a large place when one must cover it on foot, and look under every sparkleberry bush. And the outside?"

"Say I that the ends of the Earth may well not be limit enough. If we are too late, it could be to the ends of the universe. . . . But say it so now: will you do this thing? The price alone should convince you of our seriousness. It is the largest sum in our history ever paid for anything."

Fellirian asked shrewdly, "Will we be here to collect it? And having collected it, can we survive it?"

The Perwathwiy looked at her directly. "To the first, yes. To the second ... only you know the answer to that."

She said no more, and to emphasize the point, withdrew a little from the group, and turned away to contemplate the waters of the creek. Sanjirmil also turned away. The message of these gestures was not lost on them. As poor as the data was, now they had to decide based upon it. They moved back, instinctively, closer to the *yos,* and spoke in whispers among themselves.

At first, they defined basic positions each of them held, to begin the discussion. Cannialin was against it, calmly but openly apprehensive. Kaldherman was mocking and skeptical, openly hostile. They could refuse it, and he knew it. His vote was for sending the old woman back with a head ringing with vulgar instructions, most of which would be impossible for her to assume anyway. Fellirian was suspicious, but also carrying the reverse of the coin of suspicion, the obverse of curiosity. She sensed what difficulty it had been for one of the proud and distant Dragonfly Lodge to walk in humility halfway across the reservation, and start a sequence in motion which would certainly lead to the Derens being included in one of the arcane secrets of the Gameplayers. She did not know if she really wanted to know. But there was no denying the old woman's desperation. Nor the importance of the matter. One could not imagine what would bring them to offer so much—for the finding of a person. What had this person done? What had happened?

Morlenden, at first against it, shifted to favoring the proposal, and even argued for it. But he remained almost as hostile as Kaldherman, mentioning many reservations, so that they could all evaluate and decide cleanly. While they talked, he glanced in the direction of Sanjirmil and the Perwathwiy, trying to read something in their faces, derive some little hint of it. But the faces were blank and empty. Once Morlenden had seen pictures in a book, statues carved by humans on some empty and faraway isle. Easter Island. Their faces looked like that. Empty, fixed on the level horizon of the endless sea, terrifying in their impassivity. Rather, Perwathwiy's. Sanjirmil showed the same, but it was only a veneer, and underneath there was too much. Panic, desperation, fear? He could not guess. She would not meet his eyes, would give no sign, not even of recognition.

He knew that they knew. The Derens could refuse this, even though the Revens were involved, because in the language of the proposal, the word had been *thaydh* ... a quest, not a mission. A hope, not a command. But even if they had commanded, they had little enough power to enforce it without the support of the Derens, for outside pure physical punishments, the main penalty was disenfranchisement, and one could not disenfranchise the franchisers themselves. . . . He looked back to Sanjirmil. He saw only the haughty, arrogant face, with its sharp angles and thin lines. Strong and predatory. The dark olive of her skin, her deep eyes, framed in deep black hair, long for an adolescent, now considerably below ear level, with its bluish highlights in the sun. He turned his attention back to the group, where the tide had turned in favor of the proposal of Perwathwiy. They did not accept it gladly, or enthusiastically. But they agreed in the end to do it.

Fellirian left the group and walked to where the Perwathwiy was standing, apart, by the creek, formally, as befitted the head of Braid, speaking for the Braid. She said, "We will do it. *Rathaydhoya*. We will go questing." She had deliberately configured her assent as a verb of motion, transforming the noun *thaydh* thus so there would be no mistaking what she thought of it. Perwathwiy nodded, agreeing with Fellirian's selection of words. Verb of motion, indeed, it would be, before they were through with it.

There were no formalities, no speeches, and there was no particular change in the face of the elder. Indeed, if anything, there seemed to be regrets on the face of the Perwathwiy. Upon Sanjirmil's face, there appeared most briefly something too swift, a grimace, a shiver of revulsion, perhaps, but it was too swift to be sure. It was gone before any of them could read it. Morlenden, who had seen that face better and closer than any of them, saw nothing familiar in it, but something alien for a moment, then taken away.

Perwathwiy spoke. "Then, good, although it pains me. You will be paid in full upon completion. Delivery or report. Now I must return to Dragonfly and report to the Gathering, the Dark Council. Here is the packet. Good hunting."

She turned and began walking briskly toward the shed where she had left her meager parcel of worldly traveling goods. Sanjirmil broke and ran, suddenly, like a frightened animal, to the *yos* to gather her own things, racing up the stairs. Almost immediately she reappeared, ran breathlessly down the stairs, and took off after the Perwathwiy, who had already started out along the path upward. Catching up with the elder, the younger girl turned back only once, and fixed Morlenden with another odd expression on her face, an intent stare, blended with the odd scanning visage of her eyes, which the older Players seemed to lose. But whether it was an expression of sorrow, regret, or perhaps anger, he could not tell. They walked over the top of the path and behind the ridge, and then they were gone. . . .

Fellirian held the packet—containing what? She said thoughtfully, "You know, I got the idea they personally did not want us to take this. Especially that Sanjirmil."

Morlenden agreed. "I as well. All the more reason why we should take it," he added gruffly.

Fellirian said, "I think Mor and I should look at this and decide some things now, at least start the work. Do you all agree?"

Kaldherman said, "Fine with me." Cannialin nodded assent. And added mischievously, "Call me when Perwathwiy's danger shows up. I'll bring my chicken-splitting knife." This was not completely in jest, for she was fearsomely handy with the narrow blade with which she dispatched the Braid fowls. The two of them climbed the stairs and went into the *yos*.

Fellirian exhaled deeply, and opened the packet. Inside there was a slip of paper, bearing one word. A name; in

childish, almost rude capital letters: *MAELLENKLETH.*
That was all. Nothing else. No honorific, to determine sex; no
Braid name to determine family line. Fellirian muttered to
herself and handed the slip to Morlenden.

He took the slip from her and squinted at it owlishly for a
moment, as if expecting it to talk to him. He looked at Fellirian, then said, "Female, insibling, Braid Perklaren. Right,
Klandorh?" She nodded. "We'll check, of course. I want to
review everything about this one, but I believe that's the one.
Adolescent, as I recall."

Fellirian agreed. "About twenty. I know her, but not well.
She spent some time at the Institute, same as I. Somewhere
down in Research. I have no idea what she did. But we
should look up all the facts, make sure. I want to see if we
can . . . see what we're getting into."

"Agreed. Shall we start today?"

"You heard the Perwathwiy even as I. Are you up to it?"

"You bet. She was agitated enough. Let's see what we have
here."

The recordium was in a third sleeper built into the *yos* of
the Derens, being added on between the children's sleeper
and the one of the parent generation. It was not on a higher
level than the hearthroom, as were the real sleepers, but
lower, in fact mostly underground, reached by a short com-
panionway delving downward. It was also the only place in
the *yos* where there was a door. A locked one. Inside, there
were standing shelves of small and large ledgers, roll-racks
containing various scrolls, charts of Braidholds, flowery family
trees, all recorded more or less alike, according to what was
being recorded, but embellished by the individualisms of three
hundred years and more of Derens, each with different talent
and desires to apply to the problem. There Morlenden rummaged absentmindedly among the shelves and racks, humming an aimlesss song to himself, while Fellirian held the lan-
tern. There was a musty odor of old paper and dust in the
air.

"Hm . . . dum de dum de dum . . . m-hm! Yes. Here it
is! I think," he said, pulling out a large, rather new volume,
opening it, and leafing through the pages, stopping at last,
following down the page with his middle finger, still half talking to himself, which was a habit of his that infuriated Fellirian. He ruminated. ". . . May, Maen . . . yes, Mael. Mael
Len-Kleth, 'Apple-skin scent,' aspect *Sanh*, Water. Born in the

summer, yes, here it is, Human Calendar, 2530, July fifth. Let's see, the generation-totem is ... right, here it is, way over here." He looked aside at Fellirian. "Who did this record? Everything's out of place, all strewn over the page. Never mind, I can find it. Generation-totem is *Muth*, Condor. They all use birds for totems, eh? That is the last one shown."

Fellirian said, "Yes, that's the last one. And what's to prevent them from using birds for generation-totems? We use the names of the trees for the Derens and no one questions it."

"Nothing, nothing. But it just seems odd, that's all, especially since they stick to it so rigidly. Does that go all the way back?"

"I believe it does. The Terklarens, too. There is a letter of agreement in there somewhere, where they agree to use different sequences, so they won't have the same totem in use at the same time in both Braids."

"What I mean is why the symbolism of birds? We use the symbolism of trees because that's where we get paper from, from the plantation back over the hill. But what the hell do birds have to do with Gameplaying?"

"Well, how should I know, Morlenden? We don't have any say in it. They choose what they wish."

"I was just asking, was all. You said, 'last one.' What was that?"

"I remember now, there was something out of sorts with that generation. Like two female insiblings. The other one's name was Mev-something. It will be in the Braidbook. MevLarnan, perhaps. I'm not sure. I didn't make the entry. I heard Kadh'Elagi talking about it once, but I really wasn't listening to him."

Morenden replaced the ledger on its shelf, carefully. Then he turned to another shelf, bearing others, rummaged again for a time, but now not absentminded, instead rather more intent. He found the volume quickly. On the spine, the name *PERKLAREN* was labelled neatly. Per Klarh (Gh)en. Earth aspect, he assumed—thinking of the popular association of the name: the Gameplayers.

Of course, any root word in Singlespeech had at least four meanings, mostly according to aspect, and many had more than that. Something tugged at Morlenden's mind, the totem of birds that had bothered him a moment ago. The root *klarh-* was no different. "Play," as with some game, was only one if its meanings. Earth aspect. In Fire aspect, the root

meant "Fly," whence the association of birds. . . . Nothing
connected. Insects also flew, and bats as well, and, for the
matter, airships and the like, and they could have used those
as well. Odd people, those Players, all of them. Secretive and
eccentric. He let the speculation go. There was certainly more
to the Player Braids than wordplay on the meaning of names,
which few took seriously anymore, even those professionally
interested in it. And what did they do, anyway? They alone
had no functional relationship with anybody else—just with
each other, although they did some barter for various things.
All they had to do was play their Game in public, several
times a year, and contribute to an elaborate discipline called
Gamethink, which no one outside their environment knew or
cared anything about.

Morlenden supposed some took an interest in it, but he
never had. It was interesting enough, the Game, if somewhat
too abstract for Morlenden's tastes, and Fellirian's as well.
Cannialin he knew to be totally ignorant of it; on the other
hand, Kaldherman had been known to cast wagers upon
Game outcomes. But since weaving into the Deren household, he had kept his vice at bay, or concealed. And he was
sure that Kal knew no more about it than he did, however
well he had followed it in the past. That was just it—even
those who followed it knew little about it. They saw patterns
developing, upon a screen, controlled by some, while others
tried to disrupt the emerging pattern and its stable afterimages.

It was also generally known that at most times the Perklarens were favored to win, save in unusually bad years, but
the Terklarens seemed to collect the most spectator support.
They drew their strengths from the crowd, as it were, while
the Perklarens played from some unknown interior élan. Humans from outside sometimes attended the major tourneys,
but Morlenden suspected that they followed it no better than
the ler spectators.

He returned to the ledger he held in his hands. In the Perklaren Braidbook, he quickly located the most recent generation page, the last entries. The position of *Nerh*, elder
outsibling, of the adolescent generation, was filled by a
Klervondaf, Tlanh. The *Thes* was also Tlanh, listed as one
Taskellan. The insiblings were both Srith, so listed as Maellenkleth Srith and Mevlannen Srith. A large asterisk was
scrawled alongside their names in the margins, along with a
note, apparently in Berlargir's hand, to the effect that special

attention should be paid here, as if nothing intervened, these girls would be the last bearers of the Perklaren name.

Morlenden looked at the entry again, then turned and showed it to Fellirian. He said, "Now wait. This Maellenkleth we have to locate: She is a First-player insibling, but her Braid is terminating. And she also goes down to the Institute? How much of this does Vance know?"

"Hardly anything, I imagine. She only substituted for me once or twice. He would know that she worked in Research, when she came at all. She was never a regular. Remember, Vance is one of their pure management types: prefers not to get involved with the technicians, as they say. Now, Morlenden, don't look at me like I wasn't all here; that's the way they do things down there."

Morlenden's mind suddenly went off along another tangent, the manner of human management theory suddenly laid aside. "What was it she did in Research?"

"Its full name is Research and Development. Something to do with space flight, I think."

"What interest could she have in that? Unless it's all more of this traditional Player eccentricity. Or terminal generation lunacy. Now there is truly erratic behavior."

He placed the Perklaren ledger back on its shelf, abstracted and thoughtful. For a long time he remained in that position, one hand on the shelf, the other reflectively scratching his chin, his eyes focused off somewhere in empty space.

Finally he said, "I don't think we're going to find much of her inside. She's got to be outside somewhere. It makes it a lot harder: that's a big world out there if we have to do the looking. Do those folk have some sort of tracing system?"

"Well, yes, they do. A fearsome great thing, too. But it can be beaten, if one if willing to go to some trouble, and do without. I could beat it easily."

"You know it well. But how much could she know?"

"Why do you think outside?"

"If she was an everyday sort of a person, very much like you and I, she would remain inside, like the rest of us. What reason do we have? But she's missing, and for some time. Remember the Perwathwiy—'Yesterday may have been too late to start.' And they can't find her—which means they've looked inside, themselves, in the places where she might be expected to be. And they wasted a lot of time doing it, too, yes? But she's missing, and obviously important for such a price."

"Very well, I follow and agree so far. But someone still has to start inside."

"Oh, yes. If for nothing else than to find out something about her. I don't even know what she looks like."

"I can give you a Multispeech image of her, but it's not a good one, because as you know I am not that good at Multispeech, and also because I never saw her closely, or paid much attention to her. You have to get a good image. I suppose what I could transmit to you wouldn't distinguish her from Sanjirmil."

"Why Sanjirmil?"

"They don't really resemble one another, but there are enough basic similarities that in a vague-image it would confuse them in your mind."

"Hm. No, thank you, Fel, no Multispeech, if you please. If I have to put up with that, I want something good for the indignity. We'll want a good one, from someone who knew her well. Recently. We should start, I suppose, with the Perklarens, and then go on to her friends, lovers, and the like. . . . Fellir, I really do smell something unsavory here, and I want to talk to some of them first, to see if I can feel out what we are getting into. Danger, the Perwathwiy said, and hedged when it was referred to us."

"Indeed. I feel similarly. This could be a sticky business, one you and I really have no business in. And . . ."

"And?"

"I don't know why it should all be so mysterious. I mean, from Perwathwiy. And why not her own Braid, Morlenden?"

"Yes, go on."

"It's . . . deceptive. We haven't been told everything."

"We've been told damn near nothing."

"What's the word I'm looking for? It's something that draws attention, but it's not the real thing."

"Decoys," he said, after a pause. "So how do you call it?"

"I say start inside, soon, today, if you feel up to it. Tomorrow, for certain, no later. I'll await you and return to the Institute and see what I can find."

Morlenden groaned aloud. "Back on the road! What a beast you've become!"

"Don't complain so. I've got to go back, too, and but for the walking, you have the easy part."

"You always say that, Fel, but the mono never seems to go to the places I have to visit. At the least, you get to ride."

"You wouldn't like the environment. I've been outside, and I know. *I* don't like it."

"All right, then, settled." He paused for a moment, motioning to her to start leaving the recordium. As she turned and opened the door, he said, half to himself, "And if I get started, I can get there tonight."

Fellirian turned around. "Where?"

"The Perklarens, of course."

The two of them left the recordium and closed the door securely. Then, with the help of Kaldherman and Cannialin, they began to assemble the things Morlenden would need for a short-notice trip upcountry. Some food, extra clothing, an undershift for winter. His worn rucksack. Kaldherman accompanied him out into the yard, where the morning was wearing on into midday.

"You sure you don't need some help?"

"Not now, anyway. This shouldn't be anything but a brisk walk, some talk, some more walking. But never fear, Kal. Later on, this may require all of us."

"Strokes and blows, perhaps?"

"Eyes and ears and sharp wits, which you've as much of as fists and truncheons. Be ready! and I'll be back in a day or so."

"It will be as you say ... keep your eyes open, yourself, Mor. It would appear there's something afoot. There may be those who don't care for your questions."

"I'll do that." He waved at Kaldherman and set off.

SEVEN

The Game requires for definition five parameters that describe any conceivable individually specified game. These are: Dimension, Tesselation, States, Surround, and Transition-processes. There are two more supplementary parameters, nondefining, which are necessary to operate a given game. These two are Symbolism and Analysis.

Dimension sets the dimensional matrix in

which a Game occurs—within a linear sequence, upon a surface, throughout a solid, in and about an n-dimensional matrix. Tesselation defines how the dimension is subdivided. Linear sequences subdivide into bauds, which are the cellular units. Surfaces subdivide into familiar plane geometric figures, such as triangles, tetragons, pentagons, (never regular) and hexagons; but one should bear in mind that there can be many surfaces that are still two-dimensional. There are Euclidean surfaces, and also hyperbolic, parabolic, ellipsoidal, and spherical. Similar breakdowns also occur in volumes and n-dimensional matrices.

We have spoken of things that have either theoretical or practical limits. Now come parameters that have no limits of either kind. State refers to the number of conditions possible to a cell; it can be the most simple—as binary, on and off—or each cell can assume more states. In certain Games, different cells may even have differing states. Surround is that number of surrounding cells that influence and cause changes of state in a given reference cell. A Surround might be immediately adjacent to the reference cell; likewise, it also might be deployed some distance from the reference cell. It could also be asymmetrical, or changing.

Transition-processes are the rules that determine change. They may be as simple or as complex as one desires: simple summations with distributions of actions determined by decision-points on a probability curve of distributions. Or they might be instructional programs with hundreds of steps and subprocesses. Interweaving both summation of conditions in the surrounding cells with consideration of the position of these conditions.

Symbolism pertains to the system by which one orders one's perception of these parameters. Analysis is the study, comprehension, and prediction of whole-conditions within a Game. Symbolism and Analysis, considered in the abstract, define nothing; but without them, nothing

can become, in our minds, which is the only
theater of action.
—*Elementary Definitions*

Morlenden set out walking in the ground-covering stride he
used for distance walks to the more remote portions of the
reservation, reviewing in his mind as he went the things he
wanted to determine or, at the least, build a handle on. When
he had a complex problem to consider, he could become
quite oblivious to his surroundings, and this time was such an
occasion; he disregarded, and then ignored, all of the things
he usually looked for along his trips in the field: certain
angles of view across fields, patterns of sunlight into groves
of trees, hills and knolls of unique shape whose aspect had
not been noticed before. This was a common diversion
among the ler of all ages, and indeed, an elaborately structured art form was built upon this Aspectualism, as they
sometimes referred to it. Morlenden was no dedicated savant
of the art, nor of its near relative, the Practice of Subtle
Bowering; nevertheless he was fond of dabbling in Aspectualism, and always recalled especially fine places he had discovered along his many travels within the reservation.

He became so absorbed in the problem at hand that he
quite forgot in what direction he was heading, and the rate of
his progression, and before he could notice it, he had
progressed quite far northward and westward along the Main
Central Longitudinal Path, and had, in fact, began to angle
downward into the valley of the Hvar. Long, open vistas
across open fields began to replace the hill-and-dale views
that had been passing by him unnoticed. While this progress
pleased him greatly, as it was cutting down the time he
would have to be on the road, he recalled with a jerk, stopping suddenly in the middle of the path, that the Perwathwiy
and Sanjirmil had also departed northward along the same
pathway, and had only about two hours' start on him. Perwathwiy was a hardy old goat, he thought, but not all that
fast on the road. And he did not wish to meet either of them
again today, especially Sanjirmil. True, many years had passed,
and little contact had occurred between them, yet Morlenden also remembered vividly. And just as vividly remembered
the Sanjirmil of the last twenty-four hours, with her dour,
pinched, unreadable expression, and her brooding, withdrawn
silences . . . not the best of circumstances in which to sit to-

gether in a sunny glade along the path and reminisce about
the sweaty pleasures of the past, the soaring flights of emotion
they had known for the short time allotted to them, the
dreams and fantasies they had whiled away the days with.
He had always wanted to see her again; but today did not
seem appropriate. There had fallen an opaque screen between
them, and through it he could glimpse her shadow only
dimly. She had seemed to have the same problem seeing
him. . . .

Morlenden looked ahead, and across the lower country immediately to the west, falling away to the line of trees that
hid the watercourse of the Hvar. Today, now, everything
seemed empty and peaceful, devoid of throngs, bands, and
solitaries. The only sign of life he could see was some faint
smoke far to the west, a bluish, smudgy haze, as if someone
had a late smokehouse going. He reflected, looking about for
cues from the landscape. *Yes,* he thought, orienting himself
effortlessly out of the detailed mnemonic landscape built
upon total recall of thousands of trips. *This would be the
country of Velsozlun, where conjoined the Hvar and the Garvey. Just ahead. And the smoke would be most likely of the
forge of Braid Sidhen, the ironworkers, or the Kvemen, the
charcoaleers. Fine people, salt of the Earth. Ought to drop in
on the way back, just to say hello.*

But not today. He had a long way to go yet. Morlenden
started off, resuming his long stride, picking up speed slowly,
feeling the right pace set in, at last swiftly moving down
toward the joining of the rivers.

For a time some new-growth trees and the turnings of the
pathway obscured his distant view, but it was no matter; the
air was fine and crisp, the sky was clear, and the afternoon
slants of sunlight across the valley of the Hvar lent a subtle,
old-gold patina across the aspects of bare trunks and
branches, drifts of fallen leaves, quick flashes of hints of
openness, and a deepening of tone in the shadows and tree-
crowded forest, as if the whole were under water of the
most crystalline clarity. He began to feel expansive and ener-
getic, and confidently strode forward.

Ahead, the path lowered, curved, straightened for its plunge
across the Terbruz, the double bridges across the Hvar and
the Garvey, just above their confluence. Beyond, the pathway
turned to the left, changing its direction more to the west.
Morlenden stopped abruptly, peering ahead, all enjoyment
suddenly set aside. On the point between the rivers a figure

was standing, as if in contemplation, the recognition patterns of its stance and clothing broken up by a spattering of shadows from the liriodendrons across the Hvar, and the leaves on the ground, dropped by the winds. The person was not turned so that he or she could see him. Morlenden walked very slowly, as silently as he could, letting his drift take him toward cover as he moved closer to the Terbruz. Time began to slow, and his sense of progress with it. Sun, so still and fixed, began to crawl across the sky. The shadows lengthened. Morlenden crept as close as he dared. The still figure remained as if carved from an old deodar stump.

The afternoon wore on fractionally. Without anticipation, the person ahead suddenly moved, as if unfreezing, flexed itself, and looked about. Perwathwiy! The old woman looked about, as if reassuring herself that she had not been observed. What had she been doing? Meditating? Morlenden did not know. She set out confidently, if somewhat slowly and carefully, not across the bridges, but northward along a barely visible pathlet running between the rivers. Morlenden remained where he was, sure that she had not seen him, for her glance had been cursory, a quick scan across the directions, nothing more. He felt embarrassed, hiding fron an old woman. He watched the Perwathwiy fading into the distant jumble of undergrowth and tangled hillside, finally disappearing. He straightened. Not once had she looked back. He began moving forward, watching cautiously, listening. No. She was gone, out of sight. He resumed his walk, his gestalt perceptions shouting a fact at him. Sanjirmil had not been with the old woman.

Something about this nagged at his mind. He dismissed it. Why should she remain with the Perwathwiy? Her business was done—she had witnessed for the active Players, Perklaren and Terklaren alike, although Morlenden felt uncomfortable with that as well. Why should a rival witness for another Braid? For the moment, he dismissed this as another odd quirk of the eccentric Player Braids, and continued along his way into the golden light of the late afternoon west, passing under the great, tall boles of the riverside liriodendrons. True, this dismissal, he realized, was but provisional, but so was so much else in life, and he had miles yet to walk. He emerged into the open and increased his pace.

Perhaps, he thought, with a sly little chuckle, *Sanjir has found someone else who will whisper "Ajimi" softly in her caramel-colored ear.*

The sun drifted, settled, waddled along the horizon bristling with tree branches, reddened in the industrial haze out of the far west, and faded as one looked at it. Morlenden did not stop for supper, preferring to continue and go as far as he could. Twilight lingered, deepened. Night came and the stars came out. All vestiges of afterglow vanished from the west and north. It grew colder. The air, mostly calm all day, grew utterly still. Morlenden's hearing expanded in the crystalline darkness, reaching out into the passing country, evolving from fields and alternating forests to a country even more sparsely habited and partially returned to the wild. He thought he could glimpse, under the stars and the sky-glow along the horizon, the bulking of the ridgeline that terminated in the fabled Mountain of Madness, Grozgor. Morlenden shivered, not entirely from the cold, for he was walking along at a hard, driving pace, now. No, not the cold. They didn't venture along the slopes of Grozgor, none of them. There were tales, superstitions, legends. The whole reservation was riddled with ancient ghost stories learned from the last of the humans who had lived in the area, and passed on unforgotten and embellished for several hundred years. Of course he did not believe all of them. But neither did he care to cross Grozgor at night. It was reputed to be the haunt of Players taken by strange and fey moods—they came at night to restore their vision, whatever one could make of that.

The *yos* of the Braid Perklaren was located in the northwest of the reservation, close under the southern slope of Grozgor. Across the mountain, the ridgeline, lay the holding of the Terklarens. Not far away, north and east somewhere, was Dragonfly Lodge. More to the east was the holding of the Reven, the ruling Braid. Morlenden had never been to any of them before. This was called the lake country, although the arm of the lake that had once extended eastward from the Yadh to the west had long since silted up and been allowed to lower and dry out, forming a rich, though narrow plain, interrupted by ponds. Here the country was given over to pine cover, much of it of a variety of pine that formed, at maturity, dense, umbrellalike canopies high up at the top of the trunks. This cover lent the land a hushed, covered quality, deep in shade, the dense canopy overhead seldom permitting much light to enter. At night, the high fronds shut out all light, making a dense and impenetrable darkness in which Morlenden found some difficulty navigating.

Here, as in the rest of the reservation, they did not form towns, for at the heart of the ler way of life lay the canons of agricultural self-sufficiency. No matter what their role in the extended, low-density city that encompassed the entire society, each Braid and elder commune was expected to be in part a farmer, The solitaries became hunters and gatherers. Nevertheless, in certain areas, increases of density did occur. The lake country was one such area, as was Morlenden's own neighborhood, the Flint Mountain area.

Under the trees, then, he could catch an occasional flash of light, broken up by the habit of the locals of situating their dwellings in the middle of the densest groves of the oldest pines. But no more than those narrow, fleeting glimpses. Earlier, he had stopped and inquired of the location of the Perklarens, but now, in the dark, with landmarks gone, he wasn't so sure. And the still air was getting noticeably colder; there would be frost-heaves in the ground tomorrow. He passed a junction of the innumerable subtle pathways under the trees, an odd angle that seemed familiar, turned in the recommended direction. After an interminable stumbling walk, at last he arrived in the dooryard of someone's *yos;* whose, it would remain to be seen.

Morlenden stared ahead in the gloom under the trees; here the meshed umbrellalike canopy overhead was so dense he could see virtually nothing, save the rounded shapes of the *yos* directly ahead. According to his directions, the Perklarens had cultivated a privet-ligustrum as their ornamental yard-tree. If he could find that . . . yes, there was the pot. He moved closer, trying to make out the shape of it, looking for clues. And yes, sure enough, that was what it was, an ancient privet-ligustrum so large it could not be taken in at a glance, its semievergreen canopy spreading overhead and blending invisibly with the dark canopy. He turned toward the *yos* somewhat more confidently. Dark or not, he would go up and bang on the door-gong. Dense under here, he thought. Morlenden was as fond of his shade as the next during the hot, bright days of summer, but he also liked to have a window open on the sky; he sensed something oppressive and closed in, dark and brooding, here under the pines. He also reflected that the wind would sound much differently here. And in the *yos*? There were lights in the back, not so many in the front. Missing was that sense of suppertime business, coming and going, the sounds of voices; the *yos* seemed enveloped in an air of half-abandonment, despite the lights. In fact, it seemed almost as if no one were at home.

Morlenden climbed the stairs to the entryway and pulled upon the thong of the guest-bell, this one being a weighty and impressive terra-cotta affair suspended from a bracket that could have held up the whole *yos*. The bell rang with a deep, hollow, plangent reverberation that seemed to spread and die away, a soft, yet penetrating pulse of sound. The after-vibrations in the bell could not be heard, but they could be felt, and they continued, long after the original sound had faded away. He was about to ring it again, receiving no answer to the first, when at last a face appeared at the door-flap. It was a plain, very pale, rather awkwardly square face, framed in tousled, curly brown hair. The face peeped out farther. It was a girl, he thought.

"Yes?" she asked.

"Is this the *yos* of *Klanh* Perklaren?"

"Yes, it is," she admitted blandly. No more information was offered. The girl seemed to be slightly irritated with him for being there. In a similar fashion, Morlenden likewise began to feel a slight irritation beginning to rise in himself. Here, of all places, what should he meet but the most bland and literal-minded of evasiveness. This infuriating oblique girl could keep him standing outside in the night forever while he asked question after question.

He observed, "It is chilly tonight, is it not?"

"Oh, indeed it is."

"The traveler looks upon the house of a friend after a long journey as his own, and dreams of food, beds, and talk among those who would share experiences."

The girl nodded, agreeing most pleasantly.

"So now. Were you a Perklaren, I would ask to be admitted within."

At this, the girl seemed to lose the air of bland bemusement, and brightened a little. It was, Morlenden thought, an excellent transformation, for once animated, the girl's plain face became extraordinarily pretty. She exclaimed. "Me? A Perklaren? Oh, no. Not by a long way and a half. Did you think I was Mael? No? She doesn't live here anymore, I mean, she doesn't stay around here much. . . ." She stopped, as if she had perhaps said more than she had intended to. She continued, "But do come in. I think it would be all right." With that last remark, she vanished back into the *yos*, behind the door-flap.

Morlenden could hear her moving back into the other parts of the *yos,* calling to someone she named "Kler." Yes. This was the right place. That would be the *Nerh,* Klervondaf Tlanh Perklaren.

Morlenden pushed the door-flap aside and entered, pausing in the entryway to remove his boots. By the time he had finished taking off his outer walking clothes and entered the hearthroom proper, another person was climbing out of the children's compartment to meet him. Out of the children's compartment, that is, if they followed the same notions of left and right as did the Derens. The girl was peering around the edge of the compartment entryway, looking at him with undisguised curiosity.

Morlenden imagined the newcomer to be Klervondaf, the Perklaren elder outsibling; Klervondaf was a late adolescent of slender build, rather dark complexion, and a long, mobile face that suggested considerable flexibility of expression. Morlenden knew him to be approximately twenty-five or so, but in some ways he looked much older. He carried himself with a weary diffidence that suggested many things. This one, he thought, knows much, or has had to do much, a long way beyond what he expected. Klervondaf turned to face Morlenden, rearranging the front of his overshirt, looking at the visitor out of muddy brown eyes, a rarity among the ler.

He said, in a measured, careful manner, "I am Klervondaf Tlanh Perkleran, *Nerh,* and, for the moment, within the *yos,* responsible for Braid affairs. What was the matter you wished to discuss? If you are looking for the public house, you missed the turn back down on the main pathway; it is back down by the old dock."

Morlenden answered, "I am Morlenden Deren, Kadh and *Toorh.*"

"Aha! Of the Derens! I know of your Braid, sir. Have you come," Klervondaf asked saturninely, "with weaving offers for what remains of us?" In itself, the question was a curious one, certainly made not less so by the trace of sarcasm underlying the boy's voice.

Morlenden answered diplomatically, "No, it is hardly that. At any rate, we are not weaving-brokers, but rather registrars. I am aware, though, in general, of the plight of your insiblings, and have been on the lookout for suitable young men who are to be available. But for the moment, let us disregard that problem, for it is not for that I have come. I have something more immediate: Maellenkleth and Mevlannen."

"Mael and Mev? Oh?" His guard, invisible before, immediately became apparent. The boy added, "And what is it that a registrar would wish to know?"

Morlenden decided to proceed honestly. "In a word, everything you can offer me that would assist me in locating them, in particular Maellenkleth. She is now believed to be missing, and we Derens have been given a commission to find her. I do not think it possible unless I have some idea of her life."

For some reason, this seemed to allay Klervondaf's suspicions, and he relaxed somewhat. But not completely. "That will take some time, yes, some time. Maellenkleth ..." He stopped abruptly and made a nervous little motion. "You must excuse my impoliteness. You must be tired, if you walked all the way up here, and hungry as well. Please sit, make this dwelling your own, to enjoy at your pleasure. I will fix some things."

The boy turned from Morlenden and said, over his shoulder, "Plindes, I hate to ask, but can you leave for a little while? I need someone to go down to the Rhalens and tell them to send Tas home."

A voice, belonging to the girl, answered from deeper within the *yos*. "Oh I suppose so." After a time, the pale-faced girl Morlenden had seen earlier behind the door-flap reappeared, dressed now in an outer overshirt as well. What he could sense of the concealed body beneath the heavy winter garment would have been pale-skinned and slender, somewhat like Peth, but older and a little more rounded, fractionally closer to adulthood. Her hair was indeed a muddy, rich brown, still tousled, full of undisciplined curls. She hurried by, unspeaking, pausing only briefly by Klervondaf to brush his hand with hers. He returned the gesture shyly, and the girl departed the *yos*, pulling up the hood of her overshirt as she slipped through the inner curtain of the entryway. For another few moments, Morlenden could hear her rummaging about in the dark, finding her cloak and boots, but finally he heard her clatter down the stairs, and there was silence.

The boy waited, listening. Then he walked quietly to the entryway inner flap, looked sidelong through it, and then also outside, peering carefully through the outer flap. He returned momentarily and explained, "Plindestier and I are close enough, as doubtless you may see for yourself. But she is a most curious one and in this *yos* we do not speak overly loud of the doings of the Perklaren insiblings. I would not put it past her to eavesdrop."

Morlenden asked, to pass some small talk and set the boy more at ease, "Have you been lovers long?"

"Off and on," he said, noncommittally, and busied himself with the task of adding some more wood to the hearth fire. After a bit, he added, almost disarmingly and candidly, "Plindestier is excessively shy and I effectively have no Braid. We console one another." He checked the teapot to ensure there was enough water within to prepare an infusion, then turned back to Morlenden, who was sitting on a hassock, idly looking about the hearthroom.

Hearthrooms were, as a rule, laid out in much the same fashion no matter whose *yos*. But as Morlenden looked about this one, he could not escape the impression that there was something about this one that set it off. For instance, the decorations around the walls. It was considered traditional to clothe the bare walls of the hearthroom with antique geometric patterns, or at the least deviation from this, simple woven tapestries illustrating stereotyped religious images. Where this one differed was in two striking aspects. The first was that the walls displayed several excellent photographs, startlingly clear and beautifully mounted, of objects in the night sky. Morlenden knew that they were images of stars or starlike objects, but he recognized none of them; they were obviously greatly magnified. One appeared to depict a violent explosion somewhere in deep space, the tangled streamers of its detonation writhing outward into space, glowing with blues and violets. Others seemed to be large and small groups of stars, some of the assemblies globular in shape, others of loose, random associations, with tantalizing suggestions of an order that was, or might be yet to come.

The other difference was more subtle, for after all these were indeed woven wall-hangings. But unlike all others he had seen, these seemed to be representations of Game patterns. They were, one and all, strikingly suggestive, but Morlenden couldn't quite see through the symbolism into exactly what it was they suggested. Some were of a single color; others showed wild variation of hue and texture.

Klervondaf waited politely for Morlenden to finish looking. Finally, sensing an appropriate moment, he asked, "You wished to become knowledgeable about Maellenkleth and Mevlannen?"

"Yes, I did. Excuse my inattention. I was admiring the fine pictures."

"The photographs are the work of Mevlannen; she is a

photographer of some note as well as other things. On the other hand, the Game tapestries are Maellenkleth's."

"It is in both cases admirable work, I agree. But with the girls, where is it that we begin?"

"Best at the beginning, less some minor things you would not wish to burden yourself with. So, then. As you know as well as I, at the *vrentoordesh**, both insiblings turned out to be female. Had conditions been as in the expected norm, of course the insiblings would have commenced instruction in earnest at fifteen and would by now be deep in the Game, playing at least in the novice class in exhibitions and tournaments. But for many reasons, it was decided not to go this way with Mael and Mev."

"Curious, that. I am no enthusiast, I confess, but I have seen Games in which both centers were female. They could have played . . ."

"True, but only until weaving-time. And consider," he added with a minatory gesture of the hand, waving it didactically, "it surely would have done no one any good to become tournament level Players and then find themselves in, say, Braid Susen."

"I understand that a hog-farmer would probably have little use for the esoterica of Game enigmas."

"Exactly. And concurrently, decision was made to allow future Games to be conducted under the aegis of Klanh Terklaren, which will be renamed simply Klaren, as soon as Taskellan can be woven. After that, the Game is intended to come to an end, which will necessitate the reorientation of the Terklaren-Klarens. But that will be later; there are some final actions to be taken before termination of the program."

"Ended? Just like that?"

"The utility of it has, I understand, come to an end; perhaps more properly, I should say, will come to an end." Klervondaf stopped momentarily. "Understand, I am not the originator of these plans, nor was I included in any discussion of them. I relate to you such as I have been told."

Morlenden mused, "Since this will involve considerable manipulations of Braid-lines and -roles, I would imagine at that the Revens are deeply involved and fully knowledgeable."

After some hesitation, Klervondaf concurred. "Yes, of course. So in our case, the Perklarens, the parents picked up

* Literally, "Season of Insibling-birth." A time of great stress.

certain terminal commitments, and began spending most of their time with the Past Masters, developing the Game further. So they seldom sojourn here, but are busy with affairs. As you can imagine, as the carriers of the Perklaren traditions, they possess considerable lore, most of it carried solely in the minds of insiblings, to be passed on verbally and secretly in the initiation and weaving ceremonies. Much of this must be recorded, transcribed, analyzed, recorded for posterity."

"Strategy and tactics . . ."

"That which enabled us to keep the Terklarens in their place during most of the history of the Game."

"They are zealous and dedicated indeed, to so cleave to a dying Game and leave the four of you children to fend for yourselves."

"Zeal and dedication? Indeed. So are we all." He added the last vigorously, as if now expressing his own feelings. "And speaking for myself and Mael, I should wish it no other way, given what has been. Considering circumstances and plans, the configuration of eventing, what we have done has been generally for the best. Of course, they spent much more time with us all when we were younger; we were not abandoned, nor are we *hifzer* waifs, by any means. For the past several years, I have been in charge of Braid affairs outside-Game, and nominally over the two girls. And I have raised Taskellan."

"You said, 'nominally.' "

"Yes . . . Mevlannen is perhaps the easiest to explain. And if you require, easiest to find. Now let me explain: the Game is a game, true enough, but it is rather intricate and multiplex, and capable of truly bottomless subtleties. Therefore each who enters it comes to see different things in it. Some see music; others, language. Still others, life processes; and others, chemistry and the like. Mevlannen saw science and technology. And gradually, she drifted that way, into the life of a researcher, a technician, an engineer. We ler do not develop those modes save in certain elder lodges, so for fulfillment she would have had a long wait, and Mevlannen is not, may I say, particularly patient of nature. She made contacts through the Institute, entered, became knowledgeable in astrophysics and optics; other things, too. Two years ago she joined the human Trojan Project in those capacities, and so went to space. We hear from her still, occasionally, but ever more rarely. I do not know her intentions for weaving, which would occur in ten years, more or less; she has lived in the human world for some time and has naturally acquired some of their values."

"What is the Trojan Project?"

"As I understand it, the humans are building a large telescope system, multiband, in the trailing Trojan position, equidistant from Earth and the moon. They are not finished with it yet. It is, just the telescope proper, so large that it had to be sent up piecemeal and assembled in place. Mev was in charge of the optical systems ... in fact she developed the mirror material that would make such a large structure possible in the first place."

Morlenden expressed astonishment. "Mevlannen? An astronaut? Working in space?" He was truly incredulous.

"Indeed just so. Rest assured, we are not less astounded. She spends little enough time on the ground anymore ... her base is on the West Coast somewhere, close by the launch site and the fabricating works, and of course she spends most of her time there now."

"And what about Maellenkleth? Did she go also to the humans to learn the mongering of strange metals?"

"Into space? No, unless you could call where she went a kind of inner space, a truly unexplored region. Here I am facetious, for which I apologize. Mael, as a fact, despite all, stayed with the Game. She showed an unusual affinity for it at an early age, and was, well, something of a prodigy. We tried to discourage her, but of course she was never expressly forbidden, for we hated to lose such talent, you understand. We had hoped that when she was old enough to understand what had happened to us, she would abandon it on her own resolve as a lost cause. This was not the case. Maellenkleth is intensely competitive; she does not, in her own words, acknowledge the existence of odds. Her idea, which became over the years something of an obsession, was to become so good at the Game on her own that the Revens would be forced to weave her in-Game to retain the lore."

Morlenden interrupted Klervondaf here, saying, "Weave in-Game, you say? But since you and the Terklarens are out of phase in time, that could only mean that an outsider would have had to be brought into it. Or am I astray?"

"No. Distasteful as is this to speak of, that is exactly how matters were going. In the Game, she was considerably ahead of her plan, and had already won back much influence in support of her larger plan. But the choice she made for outsider.

Many spoke openly against her, saying they'd rather have a human than whom she wanted to bring."

Morlenden laughed aloud. "Now there's a one, for sure. Sounds just like my own *Toorh*, Fellirian. Really, I intend no offense; but I would have supposed that if he was acceptable to her, it wouldn't matter what his Braid."

Klervondaf spoke back proudly. "Had he but a Braid! But alas, he did not, but was a half-wild *hifzer* from the East-woods, scion of a defunct Braid line that went astray. Oh, it was a scandal, never fear. The shame of it stung us all to the core. They were deeply emotionally involved as well. Just imagine—Dirklarens, whose *shartoorh* was a *hifzer*."

Morlenden said mildly, "Well, I understand the objection, but of course we all were just such in the beginnings. All the original Braids had members whom now would be called *hifzer*."

Klervondaf obviously found the subject distasteful, and Morlenden's bland acceptance of it even more so. But he held whatever comments were in his mind, and proceeded with his story. "It was considered hopeless, and most wrote Mael off as simply gone mad. But things began to change; there were rumors, whisperings, shocked expressions. And I myself, as far from the Game as I am, have heard that there were some in the Council of the Past Masters who were now supporting her. And that the Reven, too . . ."

"Pellandrey Reven, himself?"

"Indeed. He implied he was like the rest, but took no action to stop it. And he had never approved it, either, but when the Terklarens formally petitioned him, neither would he forbid it, either. Perwathwiy examined Mael for truth and testified that Mael had not revealed the Inner Game to the *hifzer*."

Morlenden thought a moment, then said, "It would seem that she was slowly succeeding, against the odds, just as she felt she could. It would seem, then, to ignore odds would be the good course."

"You can ignore odds only if you are supremely good at what you do. I would not dream of doing such a thing. Even if I could stifle my repugnance at touching a *hifzer*."

"So, then, she was successful?"

"Who can measure success? But she had now made the possibility of Third-players real. And I do know that Mael-lenkleth was immeasurably better in the Game than Sanjirmil of the Terklarens, our rivals. But Sanjir is older—she and her

Toorh are within a year of weaving, something very close to that. I have heard some of the old Past Masters say that as a mature Player, Mael would have been the best in the history of the Game. Without question. Not even close to anyone of the Greats. I am not deep in the Game myself—no outsibling can be. But I have heard Mael explain aspects of it with insights I have not heard elsewhere, and of the living Greats, even Perwathwiy deigned to ask her opinion from time to time."

"Tell me more about this *hifzer*. Who is he?"

"He styles himself Krisshantem. He is a bit younger than Mael, but well within the tolerances. And recently, she never stayed here at home, but away with him. They were together all the time. They had built themselves a place to live together and work. A treehouse, not a *yos*. It is far east of here, in the forest. And besides the practical aspects of such a venture, them using one another to mutual advantage, they were deeplovers, and since meeting him, Mael did become somewhat more restrained. He is reputed to be something of a mystic; fey, strange, full of all sorts of knowledge of wild things."

"Did Maellenkleth sojourn here much before Krisshantem?"

Klervondaf paused before answering. He looked into the hearth fire for a long, reflective moment, and then back to Morlenden. "Maellenkleth was beautiful of face, graceful and desirable of body, passionate of disposition. She was one not greatly given over to excessive self-restraint. She was of the Water aspect, *Sanh:* she had in her life many lovers, many friends, many in-betweens . . . here, she was in and out, more or less, according to the season. But until she moved in with Krisshantem, she remained here."

"She was gone a lot."

"Yes, that. Gone. Rather more often than not, even before Krisshantem, and not always in the expected places, either. I know, because I had to go look for her. Then she'd show up. No one seemed to mind. Where was she? She would say, with so-and-so, or with the Past Masters. And other times she said nothing."

Klervondaf stopped now, as if he had said what must be said. He would offer no more for the time. Morlenden now reflected upon what he had heard; there was, concealed within the easy answers, almost glibly given, almost a kind of distraction from something else. There was something deeper here. This Klervondaf spoke, but he knew more, and suspected even more yet. But the answers helped to conceal, mislead, trap. Nevertheless there was truth in it, Morlenden could see. It hung together well enough, in loose fashion. He felt like the fox watching the bird with the obvious broken wing.

But it could have been just like that; the unweavable insiblings because of the same-sex rule, and then one of the girls turns out to be a prodigy for exactly the Game. One misfortune after another—it would disorient anyone. In a society that made the family more than a genetic unit, strengthened by the resonant occupation and interrelational ties to the rest, this ending of the Braid line would be catastrophic, especially to the younger members, within any Braid. But here, in the intense competitive atmosphere between the Player Braids, and in the elitism of their social status, it would have been more. Yet they acted strangely—rationally in one way, inexplicably in the other. They just give up and get irritated with the errant insibling who wants to keep going. The parents give up and apparently move out early, turning everything over to, of all people, the outsibling. Morlenden never credited himself with the penetrating powers of a *mnathman*, but he could see that here were many contradictions, many mysteries; whole areas opened up to question. But he was equally sure that they would not be answered here.

He could not let the whole of the idea go: considering that one would expect them all to be close and submissive. But not so—to the contrary. One even goes out and competes with the humans in their own pet project, and gets herself made a minor chief of it. And the other insibling, now missing, takes on the whole of ler society and its ostensible rulers, and her own *Klanh* chiefs, and with a *hifzer*, starts building a new Braid from scratch, counting on her verve and aggressiveness to carry it over. And seemed to be getting away with it. And the outsiblings cope. The enemies Maellenkleth must have made! Think of it—Sanjirmil's Braid petitioned! And were denied, what's the more.

His musings were interrupted by a noise in the entryway; Morlenden suspected that it would be the *Thes*, Taskellan. And it was; in a moment, a barely adolescent lad brushed aside the door curtain and entered. This one was small, full of swift, sharp movements, possessed of a deft, foxy face. Wary as a young squirrel; not gone bad yet, but definitely one to watch, Morlenden thought. So were they all, these Perklarens.

The younger boy glanced sidelong at Morlenden, a piercing, knife-stroke look, then said to his elder outsibling, "Kler, Plin said that you wanted me to come home. What do you want?"

Klervondaf looked up from his silence by the hearth, where he had been fiddling with the meal, and answered, "I wanted you home that you could get to bed and get an early start tomorrow morning. You will need to take this Ser Morlenden Deren down to the place where Kris and Mael built the treehouse."

Morlenden interjected, "Why can't we go tonight?"

Klervondaf answered, as if explaining to a child younger than Taskellan, "For one, it's a long walk, and so I hear, hard to find in the best daylight. But Tas knows the area—not so well he could find it in the dark, mind—and he can take you there. I hardly think you have such haste you would be willing to wander all over the old forest through most of a winter night."

Taskellan added, "Is that all? I could do it blind. We were just getting started down there. Let me go back!"

"Will you promise to be home early?"

"No later than the sun, Kler," said the boy, smirking.

Klervondaf ignored the provocation. "Oh, go ahead, go ahead. But be here and ready to go."

"Right!" he cried, and was halfway through the curtain.

"Hey!" Klervondaf called after him.

Taskellan stopped. A small, nagging voice said around the curtain, "Yes?"

"Where did Plindestier go?"

"She went home. Said she'd be along tomorrow."

"Very well, go!"

The younger boy clattered about the entryway and was gone. For a time they could hear his footfalls in the clear, cold air outside. Then it was silent. Klervondaf retrieved the pot from the fire, poured off a mug of tea, and handed it to Morlenden. He shook his head slowly.

"It's been a job, I will tell you that; raising Tas has been a piece of work for an elder outsibling ... mostly it has been just myself and Plindestier, although Maellenkleth helped. And it was easier when she was around; she had a way with Tas. He looked up to her. Then, too, when she was here, there seemed to be more people around, in and out, then. Tas is half wild, I don't know what will become of him."

"How many years has he? Fifteen? One and a fourteen?"

"Yes, that."

"How long ago did the older Perklarens leave ... or begin staying away most of the time? A year, two?"

"Ah, long before that ... although leaving is perhaps not the most proper word. They were just absent more and more. It was about the time Tas was born that things changed, I think. Yes, it's been a long time like this."

"It wasn't when Mevlannen and Maellenkleth were born?"

"Well, now that you mention it, I don't think so, no." The boy's voice faltered, as if he agreed with Morlenden, but at the same time he realized he had admitted the fact that the absence of the parent Perklarens—their strange, intermittent, almost permanent absence—had nothing to do with the same-sexing of the insiblings. And also, their absence could have little or nothing to do with Taskellan. That simply wouldn't fit. No. Something had happened about fifteen years ago, something out-Braid, perhaps even unrelated to it. Morlenden suddenly felt the boy's resistance go weak and soft; he thrust.

"Then there was an exterior event, eh?" The expression on Klervondaf's face told Morlenden that he had indeed got inside the boy's guard and was closing on it rapidly. He could sense it, something concealed, something hidden, coming into shape, almost tangible. . . . He reached, blindly, gambling. "And when Maellenkleth was known, known, I say, to be missing, why didn't her own Braid go looking for her—or at the least come direct to us, the Derens—instead of it being done by the Perwathwiy, a former Terklaren?"

It was the wrong stroke, and the missed target and the delay allowed Klervondaf to recover his composure by a supreme act of will. He breathed deeply, and answered, "So how should we know she was missing? She came and went as she pleased, and since she's been living off in the woods with this *hifzer*, she's hardly been home at all. Is that all so strange? All of us run off for a while, if nowhere but inside our heads! You, you are now Ser and Kadh so you had to be insibling when you were adolescent. Did you not walk away and have an adventure as well?"

Morlenden reflected an instant, and the earnest, strong, hard-defined face of Sanjirmil flashed across the window of his mind. He said, "I must admit that things have been much as you describe them." He felt the surety of the moment ago slipping away. And now again it was truce. Standoff. The two of them looked at one another, slightly belligerently, for a

moment. Morlenden added, "You haven't been completely
open with me, have you?"

"No," said Klervondaf, directing his glance downward to
the floor. "No, not completely, even though I believe you and
know you to be just what you say you are. And as much of
what I've said, that's truth. There are just some things of
which I am not permitted to speak, things that no nonplayer
may have the enlightenment of. No matter what." At last, he
looked up again directly into Morlenden's face with an expression of tentative, if unmistakable, defiance.

Morlenden tested his resolve. "What, then, was Maellenkleth really doing?"

"She was living with an adolescent *hifzer* calling himself
Krisshantem and planning to reconstitute another Player
Braid with the connivance of the *hifzer.*"

"That's all you'll say?"

"That's all I can say. Maellenkleth herself would tell you
no more. And besides what I won't tell you, there is much
that I would be unable to, if for no other reason than that I
only suspect, I do not *know.* I have been admitted to a level
of secrets appropriate to my position as *Nerh.* Of a matter of
course, Mael was much deeper in, parent-level or perhaps
deeper. She spent much time with Kris, and much time at the
Holy Mountain, or with the Past Masters. . . ."

"The Holy Mountain?"

"That which the nonplayers call Grozgor, the Mountain of
Madness. . . . But I also know that sometimes she was not in
any of those places. Where was she? No one has told me."

Morlenden slanted off, leaving the boy with his perilous integrity intact. He said, "I would know Maellenkleth's appearance, her *vidh.* My *Toorh* Fellirian said that she had seen her
and could do me a Multispeech visual, but I wanted a good
one, one from those who knew her well. Her own Braid."

Klervondaf smiled. "You should have taken it when it was
offered. I am unschooled in Multispeech, other than the pure
speech modes. I can't do visuals. Only in words, in *perdeskris.*"

"Tell me."

"She is small, but not tiny. A little under average, but
more muscular than most girls, most adolescents. Humans,
they'd say 'athletic.' She is dark-skinned, like myself, but not
so streaky-swarthy as Sanjirmil. Do you know that one?"

"Yes, I know her. Tell me more."

"Maellenkleth has heavy eyebrows, a triangular-oval face,

a little cheekbone show, hardly at all, a delicate and slender neck. Her lips are pursed full, as if she were on the verge of thinking of kissing someone. But her mouth is small. She's quite pretty, gentle-looking, abstracted, elsewhere: do you know? You don't see the determination and the fierceness until you get to know her better. She has dark eyes, deep-set, shaded. Intense. She and I share a Madh, but really, we don't look much alike, as much as Tas and Mevlannen. Tomorrow, ask the *hifze*r. Krisshantem can give you a visual. He's reputed to be good at it."

"What might a *hifzer* know about visual modes of Multi-speech?"

"I know not, but as a *hifzer* did he learn it. And Maellenkleth taught much more of it to him, the whole range, all modes, even Command. That was part of the training she was giving him. She could handle all modes, easily. Especially Command. All the Inner Game Players have to know it."

"Anything else?"

"She's very lean and spare. There's no extra on her—it's all muscle. Lean, but not thin. Her hands give her away; they're very long. And if she's not doing anything with them, they almost seem clumsy, bony, awkward. But when she uses them, they are strong and perfect."

Morlenden was going to follow some more of the intangible leads and half-starts about the person of Maellenkleth, when he was interrupted by another rustling at the door curtain. Both Morlenden and Klervondaf looked up, not expecting anyone. The entryway curtain parted before either of them could rise to meet it, to reveal Taskellan and the girl, Plindestier. Both were ruddy-faced and rosy-cheeked from the cold outside, which was, at this late hour, growing intense.

The girl said, "Klervon, by the time Tas got back to the Rhalens, they had all turned in for the night, so he came over to my *yos* and got me. I brought him back here, for he shouldn't be out and wandering in the cold."

The younger boy came into the hearthroom shyly, heading for the children's sleeper, but as he passed his elder outsibling, the older boy cuffed him affectionately across the back of his shoulders. Taskellan rolled with the mock punch and continued on toward the children's sleeper, slyly digging out of his overshirt part of a fresh loaf of bread.

Klervondaf said, "Well, Tas, you little thief, don't eat it all! Give some of it to Ser Morlenden. He's a guest, you little pig."

Taskellan turned back and began carefully dividing the loaf. The girl had remained by the entryway curtain. Klervondaf asked her, after Taskellan had shared the loaf and climbed into the sleeper, "Can you stay, Plindes?" His voice was hesitant, tentative.

She removed her heavy winter outercloak, sighing with visible relief. "I can always stay here, you know that." She turned to Morlenden. "Here, Ser and Kadh," she said, and handed him a small wedge of cheese. "I brought this from home. You may have part of it."

Morlenden took the cheese, broke off a piece, very informally, and passed the remainder to Klervondaf. The girl continued, as if musing aloud to herself, "I don't know what these two would do if I didn't look in on them every few days. Two outsiblings with a whole *yos* to themselves."

Morlenden watched Plindestier for a moment, until she grew self-conscious under his scrutiny. He thought that here was a fine situation indeed. More than a simple love affair was passing between these two adolescents; from her secure position in her own Braid, she was supporting these two. And why not? *We make no provisions for orphans; everyone has a Braid. Except Klervondaf and Taskellan.* He turned his attention back to the older boy.

"You are to weave in about five years; what will happen to Taskellan then? Is there a place for him around here?"

"I'll keep him with me until time comes to weave him."

"That's a hard job, maybe harder a one than the raising of him. You're talking about ten years yet after your weaving. And now, apparently, there's little enough you can offer in the way of weaving-price to an insibling, even if Taskellan were to become civilized enough to become interesting to one. I know the way of these things. You need influence. Now listen: would he come with me, come and live with the Derens? I have a *srithnerh*, his own age, and with the contacts we have it wouldn't be difficult at all for us to see he gets a good Braid to weave into somewhere. He needs the environment, the sense of Braidness, and we have room enough."

Klervondaf paused. "What would I do with the *yos?*"

"Close it up and turn it over to the Revens for transferral. Take what you wish and move in with someone else. You need it, too. Five years with someone is better than going it alone. You seem to have had to be too much the parent ahead of your time. I assume that wherever your elder Perklarens are, they won't come back for any length of time. . . ."

". . . They can't. You don't understand. I can reach them if I need, but they feel they cannot. We agreed."

"Surely someone in the community here . . ."

Plindestier offered, "Why not, Klervon? You could move in with us; we have the room, and it wouldn't make any difference to the rest. You and I are about the same age, and the *Toorh* are going to weave soon, so the elders of us will be gone." She added, turning to Morlenden, "I'm *Thessrith*."

The boy replied hesitantly, "I don't know, I'd have to talk to Taskellan, think it over, get permission from Kreszerdar. . . ."

Morlenden said, "Not to hurry it. Take your time. If and when you are ready, send him along downcountry to my place. We are easy enough to find; people come to us. I know not why this has gone on as it has, but I could not meet it and not make this offer, for it needs fixing. Your people have their reasons; even so think upon what I have said."

Morlenden finished and returned to his bread and cheese, withdrawing from the two adolescents, allowing them space to settle whatever uneasinesses lay between them. He refrained from asking any more questions about Maellenkleth, for the time being. He knew more now than he had when he had started out this morning, but he also realized that what he had learned was not yet to the degree at which he could begin to solve anything . . . perhaps even frame an intelligent question. He felt confusion, subtle, complex disorientations; the basic assumptions about his own people were that they had chosen simplicity, directness, orthodox transitions, and left subtlety and multiplexity to religion, language, philosophy, and art form. People themselves, so the proverb went, were plain as planks. Not so, not so . . . multiplex beyond belief. This Maellenkleth . . . A weak smile flickered across his face, as he recalled some inner vision. *And so are we all, in our own dirty little ways.*

Later, alone in the parent sleeper, settled in the heavy winter comforters, with an additional blanket wrapped around himself for double warmth, Morlenden lay, isolated in the silent *yos*, listening into the spare density of the night sounds of winter, which were even fewer here: somewhere off in the distance, he thought he could hear a dog barking, rather disinterestedly. The nearby creek whispered, almost silently, below the threshold. One had to listen hard for it, and even then, one could not be sure. Was it really the creek, or was that sound simply what one wished to hear? And the trees were silent—there was no wind to move among those overhanging pines and make the susurrous whispering. Whispering? Yes. There was whispering, and it was originating from inside the *yos*, not outside it, where there was no wind.

It was coming from the other sleeper, and judging from their timbre, the voices belonged to Plindestier and Klervondaf. He could not make out the words. It sounded like an argument, but with no words to hang the thread of it on, he could be wrong. He was not, suddenly, sleepy, even after the long walk upcountry; something would not settle. He began trying to relax himself, finding sets of tense muscles and loosening them, one at a time, He had never known this method to fail to put him to sleep. It always worked before you could finish. And while doing so, he tried to review the suspicions he had gained in the *yos* of the Perklarens.

Not very much, he had to conclude. A lot wrong, but they accepted it as right and due, some obligation.... And he thought again. Anomalies and enigmas casually strewn about as if their very multiplicity were intended to confuse, ensnare the mind, waylay. You could become so absorbed in figuring out *what* was wrong that you could walk right by the *why* of it. First there was this *hifzer* Krisshantem, influencing her as he was being influenced. And an insibling off working with the humans, a telescope builder, an astronaut, a photographer. Parents gone more or less for fifteen years. But at the least, he had the poor words of a verbal description to go on, although he could project several possible images of girls who could fit that description. And with Kris, at least he'd get a real image.

He was relaxing now. It would be soon. But his musings were interrupted by a soft whisper from the curtain leading down into the hearthroom. There was a movement. He looked, but could not distinguish who was there.

"Whoever is there, come along, if you've a mind."

A softer voice answered him. "It is I, Plindestier." The girl climbed into the compartment with Morlenden. He watched the shadow-on-shadow shape as it climbed in, bent, stooped, settled smoothly on its haunches. He could tell by the flowing of the motions and a soft, insistent fragrance of girl in the compartment, that Plindestier was quite naked. She bent close by his ear, to whisper.

"Klervon and I talked. We decided that you should know as well."

"Know what?"

"When I left, the first time, I felt as if someone were watching me, from nearby. He or she followed a little, then left me. Nothing I could see. That was why I hurried home; I was afraid. And when Tas and I came back, we were very quiet, like a couple of little sneaks, and we came back a different way. Tas has good wood-sense. And we saw someone by the entryway, someone who sensed us, and slipped away before we could get closer."

"Who was it?"

"Who? *What* as well, for I know neither. Not Tas, not I. It was formless and quick. It faded into the shadows. . . . We looked all about before we came in, but there were no traces."

"Then someone was outside listening to us. . . ."

"It must be so. I know that you were talking of Maellenkleth. Klervondaf will not discuss her around me; he says that we will all know about Mael someday, that she will be great among us, but he does not say how this will be. And around here, near the mountain, it's always a little wilder than in other places. There are lights, sometimes, and funny noises. Tremblings in the air. There are tales . . . well, people just don't stay out so much at night. But I had never seen anything until tonight. We agreed that I should tell you to be very careful and watch your backtrail as you go with Tas and from there."

"Be careful? Am I in danger?"

"Just take care, he said. Be alert. He will tell you no more than he already has, and that is too much. But despite that, he wishes you well on your quest. He thinks that something bad has happened to Maellenkleth, and that it could affect all our lives, if it has gone too far. Does that mean anything to you?"

"No. But I will keep my eyes open."

The girl rose from her haunches and flowed ghostlike out of the sleeper. For a moment, Morlenden could hear her moving through the *yos*, but then it became quiet. Her scent remained in the sleeper also for a time, about as long as the faint rustlings far off in the *yos*, and then it, too, faded, leaving behind it bittersweet afterimages in Morlenden's mind of things that had been once, long ago, now irretrievable forever. He felt a curious light-headedness; someone hiding under the curve of the *yos*, listening to their conversation in the middle of the night! What a thing to happen! But he now knew the questions: *Who was Maellenkleth? What was Maellenkleth?* They were the things in his mind that made him light-headed, for simple as they were, they demanded answers filled with voids and shifting, indeterminate vistas. Morlenden recalled his primary schooling, sitting in the yard at the feet of his own Kadh, Berlargir, and hearing about the human philosopher, Godel, and Godel's stunning discovery—that, ultimately, nothing was provable. Nothing was knowable.

Morlenden recalled that vividly and chuckled to himself in the darkness and silence of the *yos* of the Perklarens: Godel, indeed! And, Godel or not, he set it firmly in the innermost part of his resolve that he'd get to the bottom of it all and root it all up. That if he could even make an approximate answer to the two questions, the slippery *tervathon*, then he'd know where she was and what happened to her. And more yet, most likely. She would be illuminated, as would he. He was sure. He sighed, and fell into sleep without further thought.

BOOK TWO

Vicus Lusorum

EIGHT

DECEMBER 1, 2550

*You need some square-ruled graph paper,
some tracing paper, a pencil. Make a Surround-
template by cutting out a three-by-three square
from a strip of the graph paper, and set it aside.
. Now memorize these symbols: each square
on the graph paper is a cell. An empty cell is
symbolized by nothing inscribed in the cell,
while a full cell is symbolized by an inscribed
circle. These are the only conditions that exist.
Just two. Binary. Now there are two operations:
empty-becoming-full and full-becoming-empty.
The first is symbolized by a dot in the center of
the cell. The second becoming is symbolized by
an X over the cell.*

*Lay out a pattern of filled cells of your
choice on the graph paper, leaving plenty of
empty cells around the outside of the pattern.
Anything you want; but for beginners, keep it
simple: you'll see why. Now you have a playing
field. There are within it filled and empty cells.*

*Apply your Surround-template to every cell in
your pattern, ensuring you work all the way to
the outside of it on all sides, according to these
rules:*

*• If the center cell (of the three-by-three) is
empty-state, and exactly three of its eight adjacent cells are filled-state, mark this center cell
with a dot. This cell will be filled-state upon the*

next move. Any other number of filled-state neighbor cells will cause this cell to remain empty. Mark this condition with an X across the cell.

• If the center cell is filled-state, and two or three of its eight adjacent cells are filled-state, mark this cell with a dot inside the circle. This cell will remain filled on the next move. Any other number zero, one, four, or more, will cause this cell to become an empty on the next move. Mark this condition by crossing out the cell.

Copy the pattern of dots and transfer the pattern to a fresh section of grid paper. Move one is over and repeat over again for move two, the neighbor rules. You should continue this procedure until your playing field either becomes empty of filled cells or attains a stable or cycling condition.

The first thing you will notice is that your initial pattern will immediately undergo startling transformations. No doubt some of you will see your pattern vanish without a trace. Others will learn secrets.

Oh, yes. Don't use a computer. You miss the best parts of it. You are now a Gameplayer.

Apologies of the Author to Martin Gardner

There are simple games and complex ones, but the only ones worth playing are the multiplex ones in which all parameters are in a constant state of flux and change.

—*The Game Texts*

Vance sat back in his office chair, picking a sheaf of papers from the desk as he settled; he wasn't interested in their contents. It was simply and purely a gesture of defense. Vance wanted to put some distance between himself and the visitor his administrative assistant had announced. This Errat, whoever he was. A Controller. Vance did not wish this morning to talk to a Controller about anything, face to face, or via any alternate mode of communication one would care to imagine. He pretended to be vastly absorbed in the papers before his face, squinting owlishly at them and frowning. When he looked up again, he hoped that he would see this alleged Nightsider* just coming through the door. It was not to be so: Vance was surprised to see the man already in the room, standing before his desk in a posture suggesting painstaking neutrality. He had come into the office unnoticed in absolute silence.

Vance saw before himself a man of about his own age, late forties, perhaps early fifties, dressed in Nightsider navy blue pants and tunic and wearing on his right breast a Master Controller's Badge. Vance also observed that the badge was an old one, with decorative fringes and flourishes done in the style of roundels and curlettes in vogue some thirty years ago. Vance nudged his estimate of his visitor's age upward. After another reflection, he recalled that even a Nightsider was of higher status than any shiftworker, and that the badge was so obviously dated. Vance thought that in the condition Errat appeared to be, he must have been on gerries† for the past twenty years at least.

Now this Errat. Who was he? Vance had never heard of him. He may very well have been a Controller once, but he certainly had to be more than that now. Staff? Vance doubted that as far as Region Central went, even considering the newcomers who had come in with the investiture of Parleau. Continental Secretariat? Who could tell? Those people never went out in the field. In appearance, the visitor was tall, loose-limbed, erect, and alert; he managed to cast an impression of both great dignity and sinister decisiveness. Errat was dark enough of skin and curly enough of hair to have had more than a trace of black ancestry, although considering the intermingling that had gone on over the years, Vance knew instinctively that Errat was as far from a hypothetical ancestral African as Vance was from an equally hypothetical ancestral northeastern European. There were no more pure types left. Errat had a peppering of gray in his hair, and had over the years overlain the full, sensual mouth with a hard, compressed line of determination.

Vance also considered the name: Hando Errat. Programmed name. Those had arrived with the establishment of Shifter Society, and were simply no more than pattern-gener-

---

* In Shifter jargon, one who worked straight midnight shifts.
† Geriatric treatments, primarily but not exclusively drugs.

ated assemblies of phonemes and vocables, internationally
acceptable to all, with all traditional or meaningful or even
suggestive contructs deleted from the list. The original intent
of programmed names had been to offer persons an
opportunity to style themselves without reference to any
known national, ethnic, linguistic, or religious point of origin.
One had to have a name, but the name didn't have to mean
anything, other than a simple personal label. Name-changing
was nothing new; waves of it had often swept through new
movements, signaling new allegiances and new bindings. But
programmed names had come, and not gone. They had
endured. And even now, if anything at all, they signaled
allegiance only to cold efficiency, expediency, and the unifying
power of IPG, the Ideal of Planetary Government, which was
sought daily, but, according to releases, never quite attained.
Vance knew better. It may have been patchwork; but of one
piece it was now.

But now? For a long time, the bearers of programmed
names had seemed to have an edge on those who retained
their old names, with their taint of residues of older loyalties,
and virtually all of the key positions were held by such persons. But some decay had entered the system as well, for
Vance was sure that there were many careerist coat-riders
who took them merely to gain points in the Shifter Society
establishment.

Vance acknowledged his visitor. "Yes, Citizen Errat."

Errat responded politely. "Citizen Vance; I see that you
are at your work early in the day. Or is it late, as in my own
time-reference?" Errat's voice was deep and resonant, but
carefully neutral in tonation. And highly controlled; nothing
showing save that which Errat wished to be seen. Vance felt
some apprehensions—this one would be to no good for someone.

Vance replied, "It is early. As you see, I'm a Daysider."
Vance hoped his voice had come off as level as Errat's. Errat
was obviously playing with him, because he knew damn well
that Vance was a Daysider, from Vance's tan clothing. It was
nothing more than a status-game. Vance chose to ignore the
bait and engage in emotional arm-wrestling with Errat, to
demonstrate that even with a career going nowhere in particular, a traditionalist name, he was yet somebody to be reck-
oned with in the affairs of Seaboard South. A provocateur,
this Errat. That would have been exactly the reaction Errat
wanted, to provide the key into whatever he wished of Vance.

Vance knew field Controllers well enough. They were the same breed who had run the surveillance program against Fellirian. Or had that been a decoy for a target program upon himself? He would never know.

"Aha! Well, we Nightsiders are a misunderstood lot. Here I am finishing my duty day, just as you commence yours."

"Do you really like Nightsiding?"

"Never knew anything else; it would now be difficult for me to change. Circadian rhythms, you know. But regretfully, as I must say, to the matter at hand." Errat reached within the front of his tunic and extracted a thin, pliable envelope, from which in turn he produced a single, flexible transparency. He handed this across the desk to Vance. Vance took the proffered document, and looked at it.

While Vance was studying the flex, Errat commented, "The person in the flex is a New Human. She had been detained outside for questioning under, ah, I believe the word would be 'suspicious circumstances.' There has been some justification for the belief that some sort of shabby plot is afoot, within the reservation, possibly here at the Institute as well. The subject you see in the flex appeared to be useful for these inquiries, but she was ... uncooperative. Now we poor Controllers must not only pursue our normal onerous investigations and establish vectors of probability and consequence, but we must also turn aside and determine why she has been so reticent. I wish to ask your assistance in this, to help us to identify her and tie her to something."

"She looks familiar, like someone I've seen here. Why not ask the ler about the Institute?"

"We would not have them alerted. After all, the girl was outside, and seemed to know her way well. She had, we reasoned, to have left some traces in our world. Those are the threads we must pick up first."

"I have heard talk from others about suspicions about a plot. Is there anything to it?"

"The situation is by no means clear, and at the present it is a matter I would rather not comment upon, lest I express points which may prove to be wrong. We are also interested in any New Human attention to this girl, attempts to locate her, and the like. Naturally one observing such an interest would be motivated to report such persons."

Vance nodded. "Of course ... it will be as you say. Complete cooperation."

"You mentioned a familiarity ... do you know her?"

Vance glanced at the flex again. He looked back at Errat,
levelly, wondering what he was giving away. He said, "Well,
yes, I do know her face, now that I look at it closely, but not
very well at all. Her name slips me right now. I had used her
once to do the visitors' information-releases, as a replacement. I can tell you no more at this moment than the fact
that I remember her as cooperative and competent."

"I see. Could you recall more after some refreshing of
your memory?"

"Yes. It will be a moment. Can you wait?"

"It should not be required. . . . Take your time. We would
like to know everything you can find out about her, her activities. You will be contacted later. You may retain the flex."

"Thank you."

"Should you wish to make a report prior to contact, you
can reach me via ASTRA line, code BD, extension eight-
four-eight. Any time." Vance listened closely. There was absolutely no clue. An ASTRA line could be anywhere.

Vance asked, "I shall do so." He noted the reference on his
pad. "What's she done?"

"All in all, rather a small matter. But there live those who
wish to know why such a small offense should warrant such a
strong defense, or as much fear as there reportedly was in the
subject. We wish to know more about this curious person and
the even more curious circumstances surrounding her . . .
transition into her present status."

"Will you stay for some coffee?"

"No, no, I must be off, now; there are many minor affairs
to be concluded before shift-end. So, then, good day."

Errat turned and departed in the same silent and fluid
manner with which he had come.

Vance placed a call for Doctor Harkle to call him when
she came in, and sat back again, reflecting. What had been
the name of the girl in the flex? He couldn't remember. Had
it been Malverdedh? No, it wasn't that. But they wanted
more than a name, they wanted to see who came for her.
That sounded simple and effective, but erroneous as well.
Suppose the real conspirators sent someone who knew nothing. Send innocents after the girl. They could lose nothing.
Vance found himself wishing that Fellirian was here; she
would be able to make more sense out of this . . . or perhaps
not, for he could hardly tell her everything. But if there was
a trap here, she could spot it, he felt sure. *But who was the*

trap for? With Controllers you never could be sure. Was this another setup for Parleau's house-cleaning, setting himself, Vance, up for the emeritus executive treatment? Damn.

Vance would have worried more about it, but at that moment Doctor Harkle arrived, as usual, without announcement. She habitually forbade the clerks to say she was coming. She simply would not allow them to put her off. She was a severely dressed, somewhat portly woman of definite middle age, who retained, for those who in her estimation deserved it, great humor and warmth. With her she had brought two great steaming mugs of coffee.

She began, "Here, have some of this, Walter. We brew it up down in my shop, and it's a damn sight better than the stuff you have served up here, or in the buttery. That stuff is industrial strength cheese-dip."

Vance accepted the mug gratefully, for there was more than a grain of truth in the statement. He said, "I will take it; please take a chair, if you will. I asked them outside to call you because I needed my mind jogged." He handed her the flex.

Doctor Harkle looked at it momentarily, then back to Vance. He asked, "Isn't that one of the girls who works down in your place?"

"Yes. I remember her well, although my recollection of her is not the same as this image. What's the matter with her? She looks lifeless in this; perhaps catto, except that you can be sure that a catto is hiding something, and this one seems to have nothing to hide. Relaxed. Wait, I know a better word. Uninhibited. As if there's no personality here, not even a distorted one."

"I do not know the circumstances. What is her name?"

"Maellenkleth, I recall. Yes, Maellenkleth. Srith Perklaren."

"That's right! I remember. A First-player. What does she do for your people?"

"Primarily math, tensors, astrogation. She's quite gifted in the area, the whole thing, when you can get her attention. She goes at mathematics in an unorthodox way, but one can't argue with the results she obtains . . . she seems to run everything through an odd sort of iterative internal program; I should call it a topology filter, the best I can visualize."

"Get her attention? Was she absentminded? I have never seen one of them so."

"Well, yes, in a way, I would say absentminded. Or preoccupied. I have no idea what her people would call it, if they even noticed it. This, by the way, had been on the increase in the last year. She appeared to be working under some kind of pressure. When she worked, that is. Toward the last, her visits began dropping off. As a fact, I don't think I've seen her but once since we took the new kids up to the Museum on the field trip."

"Museum? Field trip? What is this?"

"Every so often I round up the newcomers, the ados who are drifting into the Insitute, and take them on several side trips out into the big, wide world. Actually, hardly farther than Region Central."

"Oh, a routine sort of thing."

"Well, not exactly routine, you know, but certainly recurring. I mean, when they do come down here to work steady, they will be dealing with essentially human problems, and I like them to get a look at the people they intend to go problem-solving for. . . . It was last spring. I had taken a group up to see the old Tech Museum at the old Research Triangle. They were all very excited, you know. I'm sure you recall the place—it's where they keep all those old worthless artifacts, in the old Tech Center. There was a university there in the old days. But they see so little of a genuine technological civilization that these old things are wonders to them—real eye-openers. Puts things in proper perspective. But this girl, Maellenkleth, reacted oddly. She was skeptical or contemptuous to begin with—I could not say which. But when we returned, she was morose and moody, much more than usual. As if something she'd seen had really shaken her somehow. I thought it might have been more of the usual stuff, intrinsically hers, but the more I thought on it, the more I was sure that it was something she saw or realized in the Museum. Then she got fidgety, couldn't wait to be gone. After that, I saw her only once, and then she wasn't working, but was visiting some friends down here."

"It certainly sounds odd, not at all like the usual ado we get down here." Vance was remembering Fellirian when he thought of the stereotype ler adolescent.

"Definitely, Director. No doubt of it at all. Now let me ask you one or two: why the sudden interest in Maellenkleth?"

"It would seem she's got into some kind of trouble and has been detained. One of these Controllers was here this morning asking about her. And of course, there are some other things, too, that I know. They seem to think there's some kind of plotting, conspiracy."

"Who suspects? Continental? Or Region? There's a difference in methodology you can measure."

"There's nothing I could pick that would tie him to Denver; on the other hand, he didn't resemble any of the Regionals I've dealt with in the past, either. There was definitely something high-level about him."

"Hm." Harkle snorted. Then she said, more reflectively, "You hardly ever see the Continentals stir themselves about anything, but just the same they seem to catch it all sooner or later. One thing for sure: if they're on to something, it could well get brisk. Very brisk."

"That's the trouble. I have no idea who he is after, beyond the girl herself."

"Worried? ... Oh, I understand. Well, if the fellow who came to you is a Continental, you needn't worry about double-blind setups and entrapments. They work direct. They suspect you, they call you in, ask you a few questions, and post you off to Rehab." Here Harkle looked about, conspiratorially. "Or they Adminterm*, They don't have to justify things the way the Regions do. They just do it."

"As a fact, Hark, now that you mention it, I would have to say he didn't seem like the Regionals at all."

"Fine, then, You have nothing to worry about. We can tell them what we know. It's little enough."

"Yes. Well, thank you for the information and the coffee. They were both welcome."

"And to you, Director. Call me any time. Now," and here she arose, straightened her clothing, "back to the cobalt mines."

Vance nodded absentmindedly, reaching again for his paperwork. Doctor Harkle left the office, leaving Vance alone for his next appointments. Eventually, he did get back to work, but it was not immediately. For a long time after the conversation with the Chief of Research and Development, Vance did exactly what she had told him he had no need of doing—worrying. Because even if what she had said were true, he couldn't avoid the feeling that a trap was closing slowly ... and that its jaws were going to close on innocents

---

* "Terminate via administrative procedures." In 2550, there was no legal death penalty. Nevertheless, certain people did disappear from time to time. Nobody asked where they went.

as well. He knew from Fellirian and his conversation with the Regional Controller that essentially there was no plot, no conspiracy. Then he thought again: or was there?

Simultaneously, some distance away, a person who had been passive up to this point moved from reflection into the domain of action, exemplifying, as the ler might have said, had they been aware of his presence or functions, the trait of Fire. He had been sitting in a smallish darkened room filled almost to the exclusion of everything else with racks of electronic devices, instruments, rows and banks of switches, indicator light panels, illuminated and darkened buttons (marked "press to test"). The only noticeable sound in the room was the whisper of cooling fluids through miles of heat sinks and the quiet movement of air through the ventilators. There were others in the room as well, seated in reclining chairs before the racks, all seriously intent upon matters at hand, oblivious to all the others.

The person arose from his position at one of the consoles, stood up attentively, and paused. He seemed to be listening to a headset he was wearing, a light arc of silver metal terminating in a tiny plastic earpiece. Then he removed the appliance. After consulting some notes he had made on a plain ruled pad at the console, he walked a short distance to another panel, set high up in one of the racks. Thereon were two matrices, one 3 x 3, the other 5 x 5. One contained numbers, the other letters. A set of zeros of various denominations bridged the two. Machine functions were displayed to the sides. The person played over the numbers and letters, both matrices, with one hand, deftly, occasionally manipulating the machine functions with his free hand. Almost instantly, dim letters began forming on an electroluminescent panel directly above the buttons. The letters said:

#330-12239 ANSWREP TO SUBKWERTASK A10/BT
GINIA SENDS/BT
SUB APPEL MAELLENKLETH SRITH PERKLAREN
RMK 1 ARRANG NAMEWAY INDIC ADOLESCENT
RMK 2 SURNAME NAMEWAY INDIC NH FAM GP
& OCCUPT/VOCAT EXHIB OF RITUAL GAME
& CF SUBJ/ACAD MATHEMATICS
& HUMAN REF FOLLOW:
1. VON NEUMANN

2. CONWAY, J. H.
3. GARDNER, M.
! 1950-2550 PERIOD/BT/BT

The person read the message, then depressed a button marked "INT-CL," and returned to his position at the consoles. He replaced his headset, adjusted his larynx pickup, and began speaking quietly as if musing aloud into thin air. The persons at the other consoles paid no attention to him. They never did.

He said, "For Plattsman, Ginia sends. Vance uncovered the name for us. Got a little more from Archives. Awaiting further query instructions. Taping relevants and forwarding. Acknowledge, now!"

He depressed a small extended button on his own console. Above it a small light lit red, changed to green, flashed red again and went out. He smiled. He waited a moment.

He pushed some more buttons, paused, said, "Operator, there was a break during the last transmission. Can you rebroadcast while I manual address?"

The operator apparently answered yes, for the person then set some switches on his panel. He also depressed some additional buttons, apparently another address group. These were not the same letters as the first. The acknowledge-light went red, then green, then a quick flicker of red again, and out. The person said, "Thank you. Seems to be working properly now. There will not be a requirement for further service or write-up of discrepancy."

Then, and only then, did the person settle back deeply in his chair, releasing a long, controlled sigh. He looked about quietly, but nobody was observing him. He sighed again. And after a moment he returned to his work, consulting some other logs. These were routine matters, for he went at their accomplishment with none of the vigor or decisiveness he had displayed earlier.

Plattsman was not in his office to receive this message. He was instead in the office of the chairman, Klaneth Parleau. Several subjects of general interest had already been discussed, and after those Parleau asked, "Well, what about those Comparator studies? Did they ever lead anywhere?"

"I have been waiting for you to ask! Indeed they did—to more of the same. Finally we were able to program the damn machine to discriminate, but the chemtrace of the emotion-sets still have us baffled. According to the medicos, that second girl shouldn't be able to walk about rationally, much less organize herself enough to carry out any program, but Klyten says to disregard that. Apparently they have an internal system for overriding chemical insanity, whatever the original cause. Very little is known about it, except that some selected higher functions of discrimination are temporarily lost, while the subject experiences the effect of heightened perceptions. I am told it is rather like alcohol intoxication minus the visual effects and the loss of motor coordination. Klyten is researching it now, and at our next meeting hopes to explore this further. This stuff is all buried, lost, mislaid. We know the original data exists, but it's hard to find."

"The second one is insane, then?"

"From the readings we have, yes. No other condition is possible. It's just too far out of balance with the rest. But we have to understand that ler insanity is unlike human . . . you know that it's said that if you think you're going crazy, it's the surest sign you aren't."

"I don't get it."

"Chairman, it's this way: if humans go crazy, they don't know it. Crazy people think they are sane. And contrarily, if you're sure you're going over the edge, that's the peak of your rationality. But with ler, it's the other way around: they know when they're insane, and they can compensate for it until someone else can effect a cure."

"In other words, functionally, insanity doesn't exist."

"Correct."

"So why is this one walking around loose unchanged? How long have we traced her now?"

"There are indications that some of the traces are four years old. We're digging."

"Four years?"

"Right. At about the same level, too. But mind, we still see much less of the second one than we do the first. But there's yet more, and the best yet."

Parleau groaned aloud, "Oh, no! Tell me no tales of a third!"

"There's a third, it's a fact, but the third one is a human, leaves no traces whatsoever on the chems, and in fact was only caught by accident. All the images are bad and we can't identify."

"Who is he following?"

"Crowd-scans so far have associated 'Human X' only with the first girl, but we are suspicious about some incidents . . . the trouble is that the only way we see the third man, so to speak, is through criteria that are worthless for addressing the crowd-scans for him alone. The data doesn't discriminate enough to pick him out alone."

"So, Plattsman, what you're telling me is that we have two ler girls who are agents and a human who is in league with them?"

"Such was my first impression, Chairman. We Controllers are prone to assemble things that way. But evidence suggests that is a wrongful vector; we are now exploring the possibility that we may be dealing with a whole family of plots, which may or may not be connected. But one thing we know for sure."

"And that is?"

"We ran some tests on the enlarged faces from the crowd-scans. To volunteers over at the medical school. Now you know that facial expressions are part of our infant programming and that we retain these residues all our lives, adding layers of subtlety as we go. So when we ran these images, with suitable controls, against the volunteers, we were able to statistically match the facial expressions on the three against known categories. . . . The first one is afraid and worried. The second is blank, and the third . . ."

"Yes?"

". . . is violently hostile."

"You can do this, and not identify them?"

"Recognition is one thing, of basic emotional sets. Picking individuals out of a hat quite another."

"Good work, Plattsman. Good work, indeed! This is better than I expected."

"I'm not so sure, Chairman."

"How so?"

"We are very uneasy about these multiplying coincidences. They are drawing our attention away from the original question. And as you may recall from the Control Functional briefing we give to all chairmen, the more diffused the question, the more useless the answer. None of these programs seem to be leading us to the questions we originally asked. We are not getting our vector of Karma."

"I understand muddy water hides many things. Still, you Controllers have information theory to help you extract data from noise."

"True, Chairman. But these things take time to run properly, and after that come the interpretations and the decisions. I want to return to the original penetration; pursue the first girl. We prepose bringing Klyten more into it."

"Very well. Until the next meeting, then?"

"Yes. And I hope we shall all have more to say than we did the last time. All we did there was allow ourselves to recognize that we had a problem."

"True enough ... and so far we don't know yet exactly what that problem is, do we?"

"I am happy that you agree with our interpretation!"

Plattsman turned and departed Parleau's office.

NINE

The finest tragedies are always on the story of some few houses that may have been involved as either agents or sufferers in some deed of horror.

—Aristotle, *Poetics*

The place where Maellenkleth and Krisshantem had established their workroom and ad hoc dwelling remained to Morlenden curiously vague in specific location, even though the boy Taskellan hardly talked of anything else during their long walk eastward through the naked winter forests of the wild northern provinces of the reservation. And during their walk together, Morlenden also learned the boy was something more than the simple rowdy he had first appeared. While it could not be denied that Taskellan was deficient in most of the approved social graces, it was also apparent that he held his two insiblings in almost worshipful regard, sharing, as it seemed, most of Maellenkleth's likes and dislikes. There were many: Maellenkleth was periously decisive in her opinions. But it was through such second-order reflections that Morlenden was able to begin to get to know the girl he was searching for. What impressed him far more, however, was the even greater regard the younger boy held for the *hifzer* Krisshantem. Morlenden half expected any minute to be informed that this Krisshantem was also proficient in faith-healing and dead-raising, among his other skills.

Morlenden was neither surprised nor amazed, even considering the exaggeration which Tas would have to be adding; a *hifzer* would learn fast to be quick or he would simply not survive. And this one did, apparently, survive rather well. He lived alone in the woods, far from any habitation, and seemingly prospered. But beyond the location of the tree-house, there seemed to be no way to determine in advance exactly where Kris was likely to be. It was as if the *hifzer* boy obeyed some internal variant of Heisenberg's principle—that one simply could not predict where he would be.

Krisshantem, so the story went, unraveling as they walked, was and had been a nomadic sort of hunter and gatherer, tied loosely by association to Braid Hulen, the potters. Kris ranged far and wide, uncovering various small deposits of clay and trading these locations with the Hulens for the few things he could not make for himself. By and large, the kinds of clays the Hulens used were few to begin with, spread all over in tiny nodes. But even they could not cover them all, and so Kris had moved in on the periphery. And there he remained, silent as the shadows of a wintered branch upon the new fallen snow. He wandered, seeking just the right beds of clay and mineral colorings, meeting rarely with one or another of the Hulens to exchange information.

Taskellan said, "The Hulens themselves are closemouthed, secretive. They are something of wanderers, themselves, and they drift in and out, saying very little. They go off in the woods to their special places and bring back loads of clays. They all might get together once a week, and they don't say much even then, or not so I could tell. They're all deep in Multispeech and use it among themselves more than anyone I ever saw, except perhaps the elders of Dragonfly Lodge. That is, when they talk at all. Mael got to know them well, through Kris, and came to like them after a bit. She was put off at first by their silences; she always did like to talk, argue, expound. But she told me that they listened a lot. Like this: that Kris could locate a good creek-bed for clay just by listening to the water flowing and tinkling, the way it sounded, the way the sound filled the places around its origin. 'Clay comes from peace in the water,' he said. 'Rest-peace, not stagnation. Once you learn to listen, water-wording is just like Multi-speech.' "

Morlenden commented, "We Derens are not such masters of Multispeech. We keep the records and Singlespeech will do for that. I can listen to it, but I don't like to give up to it and to its speaker* and I've never had what I'd call a successful transmission."

Tas disregarded Morlenden's disclaimer. "Mael knows it real good. I mean, she was good before, but since she met Kris, she's been able to do really wild things."

"For instance?"

"You know visual-mode? How you can send holistic pictures with it? These pictures seem like life, but aren't, because they're not movable. Or is that just stuff the elders tell the children?"

"As far as I know, it's true."

"Mael could make them move. Not so fast as real, slower, but they moved. I let her in once and she showed me."

"I had heard once that two or more elders who had worked long at it could do movers. I never saw one."

"I heard that your mind isn't ready for it until you can control autoforgetting." Morlenden winced at the boy's remark. Autoforgetting was a phenomenon they did not mention openly. Taskellan, for his part, caught a trace of Morlenden's discomfort and lapsed into silence, mumbling monotones when spoken to, or more rarely, subvocalizing, as if talking to himself. Morlenden followed behind, walking on through the frosted morning of the cold winter day.

Along the way from Yos-Perklaren, Morlenden had not once seen anything remotely resembling a *yos* or a dooryard, a bower, or even a widened place at the junction of paths where strangers might meet and speak without omen. They walked, seemingly, through a trackless, leaf-strewn hardwood forest, illuminated by a pearly, translucent sunlight filtering through a high deck or finely detailed altocumulus. Morlenden could remember hearing Fellirian call such a sky in some old human terms she had heard from an antiquarian. Mackerel sky, they called it, or sometimes buttermilk sky if the cloudlets were larger. They themselves in Singlespeech said *Palosi Pisklendir.* Pearl fish-scale sky. And the other they des-

---

* The reception of Multispeech demanded that the receiver allow his will to become passive. This relationship of individual submission to another's will had traditionally limited the use of this linguistic ability to certain Braids and elder communes, who included in their traditional regimens compensatory disciplines to handle this problem.

ignated *Hlavdir*—curd-sky. After all, they were much the same in either method of speech.

When they had started, the forest had been the artifically cultivated parasol pines, but out of the lake country, it soon reverted to nature and became a forest of oak and hickory, gallbarks, shagworts, mossycups with cupleaves, on the poorer soils and rocky outcrops. As the sun neared, attained, and began to pass the zenith, there was further change, and the trees appearing were beeches and ironwoods, wild-privets and planetree, sure signs they were in stream-dominated country. Not bottomland. There were still no paths. They walked on, in silence now, saving their breath, making only the small forest noises of rumpled leaves underfoot as they went. Shortly after what Morlenden thought was noon, they stopped, their breath steaming lightly in cold air as limpid and trembling-clear as spring water. Morlenden thought on it a moment, and realized with a start that he was hungry. He slid out from under his pack and retrieved the fine wayfood Plindestier and Klervondaf had thoughtfully provided—a small mesh bag of apples, sausages and bread.

Their lunching-place seemed little different from most of the lands they had been walking through all day, since firstlight. Save that here, of course, the forest was predominantly beech, and that they were in the shallow valley of a small stream, surrounded by the silvery naked trunks with their suggestions of the ropy strandings of muscles, broken only by the darker, more somber boles of ironwood, with its bluish bark color, or the deep, vibrant green of aborvitae. More rarely, there were scraggly junipers.

Despite the cold of the day, Morlenden was relaxing, wrapped well in his hard-winter pleth and traveling cloak, and full of a fine sausage as well. But Taskellen broke into his meditations. "We're likely to find Kris somewhere around here, if we find him at all." The boy waved his arm about freely, indicating the general area one could see through the network of smooth trunks and bare branches, some still holding a cluster of this year's browned leaves. "The treehouse is a lot farther, but it's on this creek, and the last time I saw him, he was working this area. We passed the way Kris usually goes over to the Hulens, but I saw no sign he'd been there."

"We could miss him easily in these pathless woods. Are you certain that this is the area?"

No doubts, no doubts at all, Ser Deren. We would find him

somewhere around here if for no other reason, than that he'd wait for Maellenkleth. She wouldn't wander all over the place with him. No! Not at all! She sat him down and told him to light in one place and stay there—and he did. After all, it was Kris who was being wooed, not the other way around. He was the one who had to learn the new role, not her! Ha! As if she would!"

Taskellan looked about, as if to reassure himself. He saw a forest floor covered with beech leaves, tree trunks, their numbers growing with distance until they formed a solid barrier and blocked out all sense of horizon. Tas looked back at Morlenden, not quite so sure. "This is where he'd be . . . but even if he was here, we could miss him if he didn't want us to see him . . . they say that he can disappear, just like that. Zip! He's there; and then he isn't. I came with Mael once and he showed me. He just got still, a minute, and then he was gone. No noise, no nothing."

"People can't just vanish. How does he do it? What's the trick?"

The boy shrugged. "Just his way . . . I don't know. Kris is strange. He and the Hulens alike are hunters and they eat a lot of meat, so they need to be sneaks, wood-crafters. They wander around in all kinds of weather and can't be bothered with carrying around a lot of provisions with them on their treks to the clay-pots."

Morlenden nodded, acknowledging what Tas said, but nevertheless, he was surprised. True hunters were rare in ler society, for several contributory reasons, not the least of which was their basic orientation toward farming, with its commitment to a fixed plot of land. They had long ago chosen this life. More, the restriction against the use of any weapon which left the hand weighed heavily against those who might have been so inclined. "Kill not with that which leaves the hand," went the stern injunction, reaffirmed by generations of Revens and their interpretations of the basic tradition. And so far as Morlenden knew, it was always obeyed, never broken. It was their most serious individual act of crime. To break it in any fashion made one outcast; against a person called for death by any means, fair or foul. . . . No doubt this made a hunting existence extremely difficult, or an interesting problem of discipline. He observed, after thinking it over for a moment, to Tas, "Then they and Kris must be very good at their hunting."

"You bet they are! Quick. They use hands and knives and

tengvaron*. Graigvaron, too, though I've never seen one. All kinds of animals, small and large, although they don't hunt the larger ones so much, unless they have time and feel like smoking it. But if Kris is anywhere around here, he knows we're here, probably what we came for as well. He's spooky; I think he can read minds."

"Road apples!" said Morlenden.

"That's what I heard!"

"So is Kris like the Hulens?"

"No. Much more so. I don't know what he was before he came here and started bartering with them, but he learned from them. And became something more than them . . . they're afraid of him now and avoid him, not for what he does, because he's very quiet and restrained, but for what he now knows. That's like him all over; I mean, I know Mael deep, a lot better than Kler, and I knew that he would have to be something special of himself for her to have anything to do with him, much less have *dhainaz* with him, even less integrate as they have done. . . . I don't think you'll get much out of him; he knows more than Kler and is a lot more secretive."

Morlenden asked casually, "Do you know what Maellenkleth was doing?"

"No. I don't *know*. I heard some stuff, but I always thought that it was all made-up, legends and fairy tales. It doesn't fit together so well and as for its *zvonh†* . . . it's just not."

---

* *Tengvar*, a light, elegant, half-meter machete. *Graigvar*, a delicate thrusting-spear. These were rare artifacts as they were weapons and used for nothing else. Since they were uncommon, considerable mythology was woven about them. For instance, each one possessed a name of its own, generated in the same three-root fashion as were the names of persons; each one possessed a complex, highly detailed history, which was learned rote by each bearer in turn and never committed to writing. "Gvarh" means weapon (and has no other meaning, being one of the few trans-aspectual roots).

† *Zvonh*: resonance. Ler set an extraordinary, in some cases, excessive valuation upon a logical concept called resonance or harmony. This was also called self-consistency. Nothing was unique or independent, but a part of some larger unit, which possessed purpose and meaning. To lack *zvonh* was to have contradictions, inequalities. Although a valuable logical tool, it was often popularly misused.

"Sometimes it's hard to separate lack of *zvonh* from a lack of more facts, or perhaps degree of subtlety."

"It's as you say, I know . . . but I never worried about it. Mael knew what she was doing and Mael trusted him and that was enough for me. And I know she took her oaths as a *Zanklar* seriously. She was a Player of the great Life Game, and would not betray guild secrets. But she had taken him far into it. They were in it deep."

Morlenden had been sitting with his legs folded under his body. He now unfolded and arose, stretching. "Well," he said, "we should go on a little farther, shouldn't we? At least to the treehouse. It's past noon already, and I don't care to sleep in the open in this wild country and the cold."

Stretching more, brushing leaves off his cloak, Morlenden bent over to pick up his traveling-bag, feeling different parts of his body readjusting to the new repose of his clothing, new patterns of warmth and cold. The day was cold, indeed. Cold and still and beginning to be damp, and though it was yet not far from midday, a bite lingered in the air of the beech forest. He looked along the shallow valley, upstream, trying to make some estimate of how far yet they had to walk to the treehouse. He could not. All he knew was that they had covered an impressive distance on foot in half a day, and that much more remained, in an empty forest without trail or path or blazon. He looked again, trying to get some better feel for the distances of the forests . . . and saw, standing not ten feet away, a person who very definitely had not been there before. It was not the exact way he had been facing, but likewise it had not been behind him either. Yet there he was. Morlenden stared at the silent figure, feeling an odd prickling along his backbone, and in the center of his fundament, a hollow tickling sensation. The person returned his gaze without expression or apparent comment, with all the impersonality of some natural object, a stone, a leaf, at tree trunk. The person appeared to be an adolescent, one of the people, a boy, very fair-haired, although not so pale of skin nor so gold of hair as Cannialin, he caught himself thinking. He was dressed in a patched and well-worn winter overcloak and felt boots, although the clothing was very clean and well cared for. He was hardly different from any other mop-head adolescent; slender and wiry, an angular, stony, serious face, muscular and hardened from years of exposure to the weather and the uncaring that had driven him here to the edge.

Morlenden spoke quietly, so as not to disturb the apparition. "Taskellan?"

The boy looked in the direction Morlenden was looking. He also got to his feet, and said, "I see. That's Kris. Come on, I'll acquaint you. And then I have to go back. Long way homeward, you know."

They gathered their things and moved slowly, cautiously, to the place where the other boy was standing, waiting for them; the still, silent figure nodded, virtually imperceptibly, now acknowledging their interest.

Taskellen said, "I present the worthy Krisshantem to a Ser and Kadh of the Braid of Counters, Morlenden Deren." All in the proper order. And as soon as he could estimate that the two strangers were measuring one another, he turned, abruptly, as if afraid this fragile meeting were going to suddenly evaporate, that one or both might bolt and run and return back the way they had come. The younger boy waved to Morlenden. In a moment, he was gone. In a few more moments, his scuffles in the winter-fallen leaves could be heard fading away. Then there was silence, at least to Morlenden's ear.

The two stood and watched one another. In the light falling through the clouds and branches, the impression was of being under water, a very cold and clear water. Morlenden watched the still, angular face before him with its sharp definitions, planes, and angles, and felt a tension, a wariness. Not danger. He was being weighed to an exquisite level of discrimination, and it was disturbing. He broke the silence of the forest. "And you, then, are indeed Krisshantem, who was the lover of the girl Maellenkleth Srith Perklaren?"

"Dhofter," the boy corrected. The correction was offered in a self-confident clear pleasant alto voice. The term *dhofter* surpised Morlenden somewhat, for the *dhof* was a specific category of personal relationship among lovers which went rather further than the usual pledges of undying desire that such persons were prone to utter in the salad days of their affairs. Far beyond the casual meetings, affairs, sharings, puppy-loves, however intense the sexual desire that went with them was. *Dhof* was a serious thing, neither done nor said lightly. There were obligations. . . .

Krisshantem asked, "Who sent you to me here?"

"The Perwathwiy Srith, hetman of Dragonfly Lodge, presented us with a commission to locate Maellenkleth or determine her fate. I went to her *yos.* Klervondaf recommended me to you." Morlenden added as tactfully as he could, "Although he was not overly fond of so doing."

The words seemed to make no impression on the stony face before him. "She is not here," Krisshantem said after a long pause.

Morlenden also paused, trying to synchronize somehow with the boy. He said, after a time, "Where is she?"

"Outside. Had you not guessed by now?"

"I suspected. Do you speak from knowledge?"

"Just so, no more."

"Will she return?"

"I think not . . . no."

Morlenden persisted. The replies were coming a little faster, now, reluctantly to be sure, but faster, as if the act of conversing were warming up some little-used mechanism somewhere deep within the boy. "Could you find her?"

". . . No. I do not know where to go, outside, in the human world. I do not know the texture of it. If I went, I would enmesh myself more deeply than was Maellenkleth. I do not think I could bring her back."

Morlenden breathed deeply. *What a mess to stumble through! The hetman says nothing. The outsibling evades. The younger outsibling worships. And the lover is stunned and withdrawn, waiting here in the deep forest for that which he knows will never come back. . . . Nothing.* Outside! The whole planet Earth, Manhome, teeming with billions, miles and miles of cities, labyrinths, procedural jungles of the mind of which they collectively knew nothing. She could be anywhere, and the closer he came to the flesh-and-blood body of the girl he sought, the more invisible she became. And the more crucial she seemed, but to what? *What was this thing, and why was everyone associated with her so much . . . such a . . .* Morlenden searched frantically for a word. *Yes. Basket-case.*

Krisshantem sensed some of Morlenden's exasperation, and volunteered, carefully neutral, "You intend to go out, then? For her?"

Morlenden felt some tentative stirrings of hope. He said, carefully, "Yes. We hold just such a commission. We will honor it. My word as *Toorh,* with that of my insibling and co-spouse Fellirian. But it is not an easy thing, and it promises to get harder, Krisshantem, for I have found so far in my studies that this simple girl, this didh-Srith, hardly older than the *Nerh* of my own children's Braid, is an enigma greater than the Braid of the Hulens or the passings of a certain outcast boy."

Krisshantem smiled faintly, but unmistakably. "I agree, Ser and Kadh Deren. Aelekle was full of destiny, as we have said, she and I. And others. Fate walked arm and arm with her and conversed with her daily. I do not know the substance of these conversations. But the Hulens? Myself? I am no mystery; I am as plain and obvious as weather. I live deep in the woods and partake of its essences."

"You are quieter in the day than a good thief in the night." Morlenden recalled the tale of Plindestier, of followers and silent listeners under the curve of the *yos* . . . someone woodswise and crafty. The thought submerged before it could emerge clearly. Morlenden thought, *No, not this one. He'd not sneak and lurk under* yos-*curves, listening at the doorway, and slipping off. No This one Plindestier would never have seen.*

"I can teach you tree-ness in a day; it is nothing."

"But the girl; I cannot know where to pick up her trail outside until I discover what she was. And no one will tell me."

The boy looked sharply away from Morlenden, now attending to the distances, into the background of naked beech-limbs, the tracery of branches and twigs, of curdling buttermilk skies, as if weighing, calculating something obtuse and difficult, amorphic and ineluctable. A truth, they might say, that could be approached only along a ladder of parables and enigmas and silent little explosions of enlightenments. He turned back and fixed Morlenden with a burning gaze that made Morlenden acutely uncomfortable. Something had shifted.

"What is it you wish to know, Ser Deren?"

"Everything you can tell me, will tell me. We must know what we are going into."

"Of course. Everything I can. And there is much. Some things I know, others . . . I know not. But all of them alike, one and all, you and I will explore and project from. We will listen to the voices of the night. Will you do thus with me in a treehouse far in the forest? Otherwise we shall have to seek shelter for you with the Hulen guesthouse, and it is far."

"I would not wish to walk so far, but I will sleep in a treehouse. I have not done so since I was a buck."

Krisshantem nodded, vigorously now. "Come along, then.

Follow me as you may." And Krisshantem turned and began walking up the stream-valley, silently, not looking back to see if Morlenden was coming along. They did not speak again until they had reached, much later, their destination.

TEN

Tragedy is intimately associated with freedom; we only find its depiction in art by people who experience it. Collectivists, when moved to emotion at all, prefer to substitute disasters and calamities, which invariably and inexorably "happen" to masses, multitudes, and other assemblies of crowds. Tragedies, on the other hand, are just as invariably caused by individuals, and so felt by other individuals.

Freedom is a most interesting subject; it must, in the bizarre systematology of basic ideas stretched to the breaking point, include the freedom to choose to be free of freedom.

To avoid the responsibility for complete study at the initiation of a plan guarantees that blame must be found for its unavoidable failure in the end.

—M. A. F., *Atropine*

It was considerably farther than Morlenden had anticipated to the treehouse; he walked, or trudged, now, along behind Krisshantem, growing weary as the distances unreeled behind them. The boy did not seem to hurry, but his progress was steady and covered ground at a rate Morlenden found somewhat exerting. He himself was no slouch at walking, and had made many a distance run himself, but here the effort was beginning to tell on him; he was, in a word, tired. And Krisshantem moved on through the seemingly endless forest of beech and ironwood silently and unhurrying, while the shadows softened and lengthened, and what blue remained in the sky deepened in color; the western sky, which was behind them, grew pastel bright and full of colored veils. The boy made no sound in the fallen leaves, crackled no twigs, left no mark at all of his passage. Morlenden was embarrassed, knowing that to Krisshantem's acute hearing, his own passage must sound like that of a wild bull, breaking through the leaves behind the boy. No wonder Kris never looked back— he could follow Morlenden's passage easily enough just by listening.

At last, they reached the treehouse, with evening close upon them, full night only moments away. Krisshantem did not hesitate, but went straight to the rope ladder extending out of the house and climbed within. Morlenden had been expecting something rude and unsubstantial, a shanty stuck willy-nilly in the crotch of a tree—but it was, as he watched Kris climb, an impressive, solid structure, built with an eye for endurance and resistance to stresses, carefully braced in an ancient, stolid beech. Far from appearing tacked on, it seemed to be so much an integral part of the tree and the surrounding forest that one could easily overlook it. He was sure that it was nearly invisible in the summer with the leaves to shield it and break its outlines.

They reached the inside by means of a crude rope ladder, which Morlenden found exacting and difficult to climb, something he had not the practice for. But once inside, any suspicion that the treehouse could have been crude vanished entirely. It was sparse inside, but comfortable and roomy. Rather like a combined hearthroom and sleeper, but instead of a hearth, there was an ancient iron stove, a wood-burner. A human artifact, from the days long ago. He assumed that they had found it nearby, for it seemed so heavy and massive that they couldn't have dragged it very far on muscle alone.

After lighting several lamps, Krisshantem reached into a locker and produced a couple of freshly killed squirrels, already gutted, dressed, ready for cooking. These he put into a pot, along with some potatoes and onions from another pantry, and threw in a couple of suspicious red peppers for good measure. Then he went to work on a fire, and within a short time, had a fire going, the stew cooking, and some of the edge began to come off the cold.

Now warming, they both removed their heavy winter overcloaks and sat on the floor silently, relaxing. Morlenden offered no words. The boy seemed tired and drawn as well, as if he had come a great distance, for the coldness of the treehouse suggested that it had been untenanted for something more than a day. Krisshantem offerred nothing, apparently deeply immersed in some private inner reverie whose boundaries only he knew. Morlenden did not interrupt him, and so they sat for a considerable time, in silence. But at last Krisshantem looked up, directly at Morlenden, with that same disturbingly intent gaze he had seen before. This time, the glance did not waver, but stayed; Morlenden found the sudden intense attention disconcerting.

"Ser Deren, you will wonder the reasons for my silence?"

"Yes."

The boy looked out the window, a real glass window, not one of the travertine panes they favored for *yos* windows, deep into the north and west. Only a hint of color remained in those skies, a deep far-violet; otherwise, it was night. "I was setting an image straight," he began, "making it just right in my mind, for a Multispeech transferral to you. Can you read such an image if I send in the visual-mode?"

"Indeed I can receive, and have the readiness for it. But tell me, where does one such as yourself learn the fine arts of Multispeech?" Morlenden felt apprehension over the voluntary submission in the will during reception of Multispeech, and wished to make the boy a little defensive before he gave up to him.

A light flared in the boy's eyes, then dimmed. But did not go out. "I learn well. Many things, from such as will instruct me. But it is good that you elect to receive and I to send, for thereby you will at least be able to say then that you know more than just a name."

Morlenden said, "Before I set out on this journey, my insibling said that she could send an image, but that it would be one weak and blurred. I had hoped to find a good one, with those who knew Maellenkleth well."

"And so it shall be, Ser Deren! You will see, as I did, with the eyes of my mind ... are you indeed prepared to see-in-*perdeskris?*"

Morlenden felt the intimidation behind the words, but nodded, tense, apprehensive, yet nonetheless determined to go ahead with this ... not without misgivings. Multispeech had many modes, many aspects. One was the direct transmission of an image direct from one mind to another, in which the medium of transmission was a kind of speech, voice, sound. But it was speech that far transcended the normal linear coding and sorting aspects of traditional language, language as the humans had known it, language as the simpler Single-speech was structured.

In single-channel language, the signal was broad-band, a fingerprint pattern of bands of harmonic tones, shifting frequency slightly, the whole pattern being broken from time to time by sharp clicks, drops, and hisses and combinations thereof: vowels and consonants, former and latter. But in Multispeech, the harmonic bands were individually controlled, and the breaks in tone came separately in each separate band; only with intense concentration would it normally work at all, for there was no instinct for it: it was all learned. And on the part of the receiver, total submission. This was the part of it Morlenden liked least, this sense of losing control, of giving in to another's will. In the past, he and Fellirian had played with it, experimented, but they were both unskilled, and in any event, uninterested in it. It was nice that the people had this ability, he had thought many times; still, they didn't need it in their *klanrolh* ... or did they? Well, in any event, there was as yet no suitable method of writing it. Or were they truly primitive ... and was Multispeech their true communicative way? And this one, this *hifzer* Krisshantem, was reputedly a master of it.

The boy sat across the room from Morlenden, hidden a bit in the patterns of shadow and lamplight, wrapped in his long overshirt, a plain but much-mended pleth without decoration. In his hand he held a small, pale stick or wand, and with this he began tapping regularly, slowly, on the platted flooring before himself; simultaneously beginning a slow rocking motion with his body. Morlenden shut his eyes, instinctively, to concentrate on the sound, even though he knew well enough that if they did establish contact, he would be blind while he was receiving; Multispeech in certain modes overrode and cut out the visual centers, programming routing from the ears into the visual cortex instead.

... He heard the night sounds of the forest and a nearby creek; he heard the rustling, blurry noises of a hardwood fire, the hiss and bubble of the pot. He heard the musing of a weak breeze outside which had come up, microturbulences as it flowed through the limbs and branches and branchlets and terminal twigs ... each tree had its own sound in the wind. Each individual tree as well ... there were those who had made an art of tree-listening and claimed to recognize individuals blindfolded. He heard the creaks and stress-shifts of the treehouse, as it moved in tune with the tree of which it had become a part. And he heard tapping, tapping, some-where far off, somewhere near.

He heard the tapping of the wand, and under it, a mo-notonous, repetitive humming, a droning, like the melody of a song such as a forgetty might make up, simplistic, iterative, recurved inward upon itself, simple, over and over again; yet when one tried to listen to it ... Morlenden found it full of sudden shifts and changes, permutations which had not been there before; unseen, unheard. Shifts in key, subtle changes in rhythm, damned subtle when he first noticed, and then get-ting harder to hear; he had to concentrate deeper on it, trying to anticipate, to find the key to the order of the changes. That was the way of it. Now listening very closely, Morlen-den observed, half aware of it, that he thought he could perceive not a tone, but a harmony now opening up; two melodies, perhaps more—yes, there were three, four, five and

THERE he had it, grasped it an instant, lost in as fast, but now he knew it was easier to pick up the thread, follow the changes, feel the coming shifts, and he always had more than one thread of it. The first step, the first linking between him-self and the boy Krisshantem. Odd, odd, it was like monocu-lar vision, or an ear blocked; something was trying to form in his visual center, vague, shapeless, a lump, a nothing, a blur, not-yet-ness. Morlenden began to hum the aimless tune along with the boy, tapping with his fingers, picking up the melody, the rhythm, the changes, the shifts, hoping the feedbacks would let Kris know he really was trying, despite his distaste of it, really trying to reach for it, and

NOW NOW NOW and the sensation of sound blew out like an impossible implosion and Morlenden felt himself grasped, in utter silence, by a monster raw will-force, pure as-pect stripped of its vehicle, the body-person, an enormity, a formless pulsing power that was reaching deeply into his in-nermost mind, imposing, dominating. He felt sudden panic, raw fear, madness, lust to break this web of Multispeech and run screaming out into the night. But it was too late. He had achieved empathy and synchronization with Krisshantem, via the aimless little forgetty song, and there was no escaping, no running, no avoiding. They were not completely separated in their minds, now.

Morlenden's memory flickered out, was gone, never had been. In its place was nothing. Immediately the vision started. At first it was dim and vague, but also somehow definite. In one moment, it had not been there; and the next it was there, as if it had always been there, clear as his own memory, and oddly offset. He could see it taking shape out of blurred nothingness, but as yet he could not "look" directly at it or any of its parts. Swiftly, now, the image, blurred and vague, began to brighten, to sharpen, to become detailed. Contrast improved. Blurs and shadows shaped themselves. The resolution improved. The holistic pattern of a Multispeech visual was working, forming like a hologram, the process making an image whole in two dimensions with the suggested dimensionality of parallax, just as Kris had seen originally, and remembered. The image was not built up of lines and dots; the time factor controlled how clear it became, as area worked in a hologram. The more Morlenden received, the clearer it became, and the more directly he could see it. The pressure increased from the will outside himself.

Now she was clear enough to see ... it was a girl, here, in this place, this treehouse, sitting in a beam of sunlight that had passed through the window ... smiling warmly, and almost nude, her legs folded to one side under her hips, toward him. She was wearing the dhwef, a long-taiiled, embroidered loinclothlike strip, held on her narrow hips by a belt of wooden beads. She was turned slightly, her left side toward him. It had been summer; something of the flat tone to the light falling on her body, the warm, tanned tone of her skin. The image brightened and clarified. So this was Maellenkleth, the First-player who was lost. She matched very well the words he had heard to describe her, but in this case, as with all the rest, the words had not matched the reality very well. She was lovely—Morlenden, now seeing with his own memory-eyes, felt his heartbeat speed a little, recalling the days of his own adolescence, how she would have seemed to him *then*, when he was a buck, how he would have responded to her. She was rare and exquisite, half in the perfect, taut body, lean and muscular, and half in the imperious will that animated it, filled those comely limbs with life and will.

Now Morlenden had a living memory of the girl, in this image of her identical with Krisshantem's own memory of her. It was so detailed, he could see-remember a tiny mole under her left breast, see-remember a light sheen of perspiration on her forehead, her collarbone, see-remember a soft youthful bloom along the skin of her ankles, a healed scratch on her knee. Her face narrowed down to a finely structured, delicate chin. Her nose was small, narrow, her lips soft, not quite full, slightly pursed. Her eyes were clear, not deep-set, open in their expression. There was determination and innocence in her every gesture, arrested here in midflight, but there was also a sweet, open smile forming on her mouth, too. Enchanting ... Morlenden felt himself both voyeur and burglar, despite that he was being given this, for he would always now carry the memory of that smile, its slight adolescent awkwardness and shy offering, and know that it had not been directed at him, though it seemed so. . . . Visuals were a cheat.

The image had long since ceased to become clearer, and now Morlenden felt at last that it was over. He relaxed, anticipating the moment when Krisshantem would release him and he would fall out of this reception-self. The pressure increased, became greater, painful, excruciating, making him wince, feel fear now, and the image faded, faded, became gray, blurred, indistinct, even though he could remember it well enough. It was what was being sent. That image faded, vanished. Nothing replaced it. There was darkness and void. Suddenly a series of ideas flashed directly across his imagination: *So you woven scum think a hifzer shouldn't learn your precious multispeech, do you? Then watch this elder-to-be, and learn how well one such as I learned his lessons.* The concepts were as if shouted by many Krisshantems, all at once, echoing and bouncing and multiplying, feeding back and forth across one another, feeding back upon themselves until Morlenden's whole mind reverberated with them. Then he went totally blank, aware only that something was being put into him, bypassing his conscious mind altogether—he would know-remember it later, but not now. Instruction-mode. Raw data. He knew something was happening to him, but he couldn't reach it.

Then he was aware that he was not receiving anymore, that time was passing again, that the presence had withdrawn, that the will which had gripped him with a force he could not have broken had faded away without notice. He was himself, sitting in a treehouse, now warm, smelling squirrel stew. He opened his eyes; Krisshantem was no longer sitting, tapping, humming the monotonous melody, but instead was casually stirring the stew with the wand. Morlenden did not know how much time had passed, nor how long the process had been stopped. He felt shaken, light-headed. Afraid to move. He remembered Maellenkleth, as if she had been his own then;

yet it was not then, in that summer, but was here, moments ago ... and something else; he remembered the Game. Morlenden touched the memory of the data, stuffed into his mind raw, without referent. Yes, it was all there, the Outer Game, what Krisshantem knew of it, stripped to essentials, his mind filled with strategy and tactics, millions of rules and configurations; one could wander there forever, bemused. He put it away. He wanted to inspect this curious new learning another time. He cleared his throat. Kris looked up at him, blandly, matter-of-factly, as if nothing at all had happened.

Kris asked casually, "Did you get it all?"

"Indeed I did; completely. . . ."

"I thought as much. I stopped augmenting the image of Maellenkleth when I sensed from your feedback that you had most of it. First it's slow, then it comes fast, then slow again ... it never quite reaches an exact copy. Not much good going on indefinitely, although I suppose one could. Pardon the intrusion, but I sensed doubt. You have doubtless realized that you are now as I in knowledge of the Game. That will save us much talk."

"I had no idea you would be able ... How much of that did Maellen teach you?"

"I knew some before. Not very much. Most of it came from her. I would have to know all modes to sit with her in the citadel of the Inner Game, which at present I know not. Nor you. I have some ideas on it, for one can always project from the data at hand, but, frankly, some of the conjectures I have imagined are so odd or perhaps outrageous that I have not pursued it far, thinking it had to be wrong."

"I remember it now, but I have not thought on what I have newly learned, whether I wished to know or not. How long was I under that?"

"There is, they say, no time in Multispeech ... I have no idea, but the stew is done. I have heard some elders say that the universe waits until one is finished. However, I remain skeptical there, for to the stew you may add the datum that there is no more light yonder westward. Perhaps the stars have more imagination than the average elder. Those are her words as well."

"You are too good at it. I think I shall not allow that again," Morlenden said without heat, stating a fact.

"I will not try again, although I must tell you that there is a variant of Command-mode which insibling Players must learn, Command-override, which does not require permission, or even knowledge of it on the part of the receiver. . . . Mael taught it to me, and it is a fearsome thing I will not use. But you may meet others not so restrained as I in your travels."

Morlenden was aghast. "But how can I protect myself?"

"No way. If you are of the people, you are susceptible. You can't even autoforget out of it, that is why they restrict its teaching . . . it's very hard to do right. I can't teach it to you. As I said, it's difficult. Mael taught me only part of it. I didn't use override on you. I am sorry I was angry; you chose not your position, as neither did I. But I suggest you get someone to teach it to you—you can at least strive with one who would use it."

"Who would try?"

"I don't know. But you get it all only in the Inner Game. But I am but a novice, one who sits at the feet of the great who deign to lend their arcane skills. I am not so good as you may think; instruction I can do; Maellen who was Aelekle to me and me alone I can easily do. . . . Obviously, for I knew her many ways. I knew her as a lover, and as a student of her wisdom. Random images are harder, abstract ones still more so. But should you wish another demonstration, I can now send you a picture of yourself, as I have seen you. . . ."

"Myself through another's eyes? Thank you, no. I must refuse. Please leave me my illusions and memories of the way things were. I should then no longer be able to imagine myself a buck like yourself. I know very well that I-now-Morlenden possess a potbelly from overindulgence at too many weaving-parties. Nevertheless I prefer to imagine myself a svelte youngster, lean and mean."

"Ha!" Krisshantem smiled at that. It was the first time Morlenden had seen him do so. And inside himself, he forgave the intrusion. He had in part asked for it. He was thankful this wild boy knew no more than he did.

During the meal—the stew turned out well despite Kris's heavy hand with the red pepper—they did not speak, but ate in silence, Morlenden was hungry, for he had walked far in two days and had eaten little, save pathway-food, cold meals packed to be eaten along the way. This was the first real honest meal he'd had since leaving home. Krisshantem, too, ate quietly, with a self-possession and attention to the present that surprised Morlenden. After all, it was beginning to be more than merely apparent that Kris had lost Maellen, to accident, not the usual cause of such separations, and he was only barely older than Morlenden and Fellirian's own Pethmirvin. But where Peth was still very much a child at fifteen, for all her busy sexuality, this boy was something more than the usual adult.

Finishing, Kris went to the pantry, returning by way of the stove, pausing, and producing along the way an infusion of the ubiquitous root-tea, then returning and settling back in his place, folding his legs under himself after the mannerism of a tailor, or perhaps a rug-maker.

Morlenden cleaned the remainder in his bowl with the last crust of bread, observing, "You cook well, indeed. I would become the fatted calf in your house."

Kris answered pleasantly, "Not so. When the cook is good, one uses him less . . . once a day or less."

Morlenden sipped his tea, looking at the boy from over the edge of his mug. The pleasantries were now over, and the introductions finished, the measures taken. He began, reaching with the words, "You are, so I have observed, a cool one for one who has been along the ways of *dhofterie*. . . . I should have thought you more, well, apprehensive about the whereabouts of Maellenkleth."

"My apprehensions are real enough, for all that I refrain from displaying them publicly like yesterday's unwashed laundry. They are, of course, much as you might suspect, perhaps more. But they do not, translated into the here and now, have much of an effect upon the nature and course of things. However strong they are." He looked away and did not meet Morlenden's glance.

"Have you thought of going after her yourself?" Gently, here.

"No. She told me specifically that not under any circumstance should I come after her should she fail to appear. She felt about her little expeditions that if she ever got herself into something that she couldn't handle, no one else would be able to do it for her, and it would be just throwing good people to waste after bad."

"We are edging into it. Shouldn't we start at the beginning?"

Kris answered, "Start at the beginning, start at the end, or in the middle; in a well-lived story it makes no difference. Does not everything lead to something else?"

Morlenden replied, "True, but for all the sophistry, the accipter flies not backward to present life out of its beak and talons to the Lagomorph."

"Hawk and hare . . . you are correct. I have been rude. You know that I do not wish to face this; that is the way of the words."

"I know these things and walk with you, though I may not now face them myself, in my own life. Once I had a lover. . . ."

Kris mused, "We never know what we will face and what we will not . . . let me caution you of that at least."

The remark rang oddly in Morlenden's mind. Not that its truth was in question, but that it sounded oddly prophetic after the manner of oracles; ambiguous, indefinable, unknowable as the dream-that-predicts. Until the moment came. What did this woodsman know?

Kris continued, "But, still, I would tell it my own way. Time clouds things, masks significances. You will want what I have, to add to what you already know or suspect."

Morlenden laughed. "Then say on as you will, for what I have is precious little enough." He sipped at the tea again. It was still almost too hot to drink properly.

"This time," he began hesitantly, "was to be her last venture outside. Yes, there were other ventures. Many of them. I do not know where she went, or what she did. But they were all short, never more than a few days. But she said that before we met there had been some longer ones . . . months, seasons."

"Maellenkleth was outside for a season? Three months?"

"Yes, among the forerunners the whole time, and they knew it not."

"Clandestinely? Where could she go for so long?"

"She would not speak of it any more than the others. Save once . . . she said in a mood of reminiscence, 'The humans said long ago that God created the universe in seven days, yet just now have I been to a place where the creation is still going on. And if that be true, perhaps their god still lives and works in that place.' I know not where it was, nor would she say, in the sense of how to get there. I saw, in *deskris*, as she sent, and she said that there would be a place like that for us someday. I said, 'Would we go there and live, us, out of our little land?' and she became suddenly sad and said no, not there, never. I saw it, but never *where* in relation to anywhere else: there was a dark sea, salt water, there were rocky beaches, cliffs, brown mountains, that ran in rippling waves above the waters and plunged into them at their northern ends. The sun set into the sea. No one lives there. It is free and open, but now empty. She said that once, long ago, they came there to be cured, to be healed, but that now no one will even walk in it, or pass near it."

"A human *sfanian*, a place of healing?"

"I would not have thought it, but I am blind to many of their ways."

"Just so am I. . . . But the last time she went outside: it was important?"

"Yes, very much so. She could refuse, but she would not. She could not let it go."

"Did she say what she was to do?"

"She was to break two machines no longer in use."

"Absurd! Perhaps if they were in use, but otherwise . . ."

"They—those with whom Mael spoke—were worried that if these things, still operable, were used, then the Forerunners would be able to see something they must not know before their time. That none of us could know until we were prepared. They could make more of these machines, but they wouldn't be so good, and by then it wouldn't make any difference."

"Did she not realize that destroying them would point a finger at the very thing she wished hidden?"

"I asked her the same question. She shook her head, saying that she knew. That all that had been considered, but she still had to go."

"I cannot imagine it. What was the secret?"

"Believe me when I say that I never learned it. I know the ways of trees, I listen to the speech of the waters, I have learned to watch the clouds move and permutate, I can slow time for myself until the sun whirls across the sky. I have mastered the silences. But I could neither get it from her, however else she gave freely, nor see it in her. Maellenkleth was indeed of the aspect of *Sanh*, the Water, but something in her was harder than the finest steel, and her mind was a mirror, as are those of all *Sanmanon*. She received instructions, and she obeyed them, whatever distaste she herself felt."

"The faithful soldier."

"I think that she liked some of it."

"Hm!" Morlenden snorted. "Instructions from whom? Perwathwiy and her elders of Dragonfly Lodge?"

"Oh, no. Not from those, or perhaps not directly. Mael

worked not for the elders, and in fact she held them in some contempt, for they were so willing to let the Perklarens go without a ripple. She took her instruction from Sanjirmil. Do you know such a one?"

Morlenden's mind stopped short, as if he had suddenly walked into a wall. "Sanjirmil? The Terklaren?"

"There can only be one, as custom allows." It was a pointed reproof. Morlenden of all people should know there could only be one living Sanjirmil. He looked away for a time, and said quietly, "I know her. Or thought I did." Morlenden thought deeply, unable to complete the import of it. Sanjirmil, who came in the night with the Perwathwiy. Sanjirmil who kept secrets at thirteen. Sanjirmil who was an arch-rival, and a co-plotter in something . . . and they were all operating something under the Game called the Inner Game. What had he walked or stumbled into? What devil's work were he and Fellirian doing, and in reality, for whom? And what cause was he taking up almost by accident, as he followed Maellenkleth's path, finishing her business? He left it. There was not enough yet.

He said, "Tell me about your weaving with her. How was that to be arranged?"

Kris answered, "We met and became lovers by accident. Indeed. I am Air aspect. It became more than casual, and she found that I could do certain things, things she gave value to. She offered to me, and I accepted. That is not so hard. Imagine, me becoming a *shartoorhosi* player of the great Game! But once I learned it, I felt it odd and . . . unfinished, and I thought of the flow of the life I have learned in the forest and visions of the sky. Very odd, those two."

"Odd? Why?"

"Because at first the two seem so different, but from a certain level of awareness they are much the same thing."

"I know. The wise say that there is only one reality, and that we catch only glimpses of it. The mad are so because they cannot turn away from it; but they also cannot live in it. They are pulled apart. And that categories are errors caused by the degree of imperfection; the more highly categorized, the greater the degree of imperfection. But the universe is one."

"Spoken like a Gameplayer, Ser Deren!" Krisshantem exclaimed. "But for all that," he continued soberly, "we imperfections must live on a workaday world, where there are, after all, categories, divisions, classifications."

"There is always, in any good list, a sort called 'other.' "

"Thus the Game as well. I had always thought of it, when I reflected on it, as a kind of manipulation, but as I learned more from Maellen-Aelekle, I saw that it was also a very curious way of looking at a process of perception, to perceive small detail and large overview simultaneously. Perception!"

"All games are that in part."

"But this one more so."

"I know that Maellen was a player of the First-players. A good one, indeed. Which came first—was it that she was to rebuild because she found you, or were you the last part of a larger plan?"

Kris answered without heat or offense, "We came first. She had thought of it before, but never seriously. She went for it long after we met. She did not use me, nor was there trade—legitimacy for becoming a Noble Player. In fact, she thought of taking the Inner Game by storm. It was rather impractical . . . the one we could have done in time, but the other would have been death for both of us; Maellen had many enemies."

"To start a new Braid would require the permission of the Revens. And I know that they do not grant that lightly, even to the simplest of farmer Braids. And to Gameplayers? When the community of the Players, past, present, and future, was allowing the Perklarens to end, just like that, without a whimper of protest—including the Perklaren parents themselves?"

"It sounded fantastic to me as well, when we talked and plotted of it, here, in this very place where sit you and I. But not impossible. I said she had enemies; she also had powerful friends. There was something about a check upon Sanjirmil, which both Pellandrey Reven and the Perwathwiy had come to. I think that they came to regret the decision to let the Perklarens go, after it was too late and they were committed. The others had a stake in it, and wanted things left as they had been committed to. Still, one must train for the real Game. That which I gave you in instruction-mode is nothing, just the basic foundation. It is not something most have any talent for. In fact, Maellenkleth was the only one anyone ever heard of who had a real talent for it. And, of course, the Terklarens were rather violently against it. They said that the work of two Player Braids was done," He paused, and then added cryptically, "Whatever that work really was."

"So, then; attend. You are now, for all intents, a Player, if somewhat unauthorized and unpermitted. Why would Pellandrey wish Sanjirmil counterweighted?"

"Hard to explain, Ser Deren. As a Player, now, I see things I could not realize before. There are many revelations therein. Now Sanjirmil, she's competent enough in the Game, I suppose, but there's no style to her. It's like swimming or dancing or making love or just good old *dhainaz* ... there's a sense of flow, motion, style. Dynamics. Maellenkleth's Inner Game names among the masters were Korh, crow, and Broḍh, otter. But Sanjirmil has no grace, no style. After all, she knows well enough that at fertility she'll be the Terklaren. Perhaps I should say the Klaren."

"I know. She is very strong-willed."

"I know not how you know her, but I know her in the Game; strong-willed is not the word. She is fierce and dominant. The masters call her Slansovh, Tiger-owl, and Hifshah, the Werewolf. She is Fire aspect. Her Braidmates, co-spouses, follow her implicitly. They are already woven."

"Woven?" Morlenden exclaimed. "Why, they aren't fertile yet, none of them!"

"None the less, it is so. She already has them trained. All four of them. The Revens know, the Perwathwiy knows. And had things gone as Maellen and I had hoped and dreamed, so would it have been with she and I and two others I do not know."

Morlenden sighed. "And we, the poor Derens who must register such things, are the last to be informed. I have never heard of such a thing, even among the Revens. Do they live together?"

"Indeed. The old Terklarens have already left, and joined Dragonfly Lodge; with the Perklarens. Once enemies, now uneasy allies."

Morlenden interjected, "Against two romantics."

Krisshantem said, with great dignity, "I assure you there was nothing of the sort in it. There I know Maellen well. There was more than desperation in her plan; rather, an urgent sense of necessity." He paused momentarily. "Maellen was very concerned about this preweaving of the younger Terklarens; for, despite the radical air which she may have projected, she was in fact very traditionalist-minded, very conservative. Her view of this was that it was stealing what you already possess, in the person of Sanjirmil, which is as you may know one of the omens not desirable to be seen. And so her idea was that with practice, and constant pressure on them, we could eventually win it all back and recover the rightful order of things. But however much she showed me of the Game, she always left something out; I sensed deeper purpose in it, but it remained behind the veil—within an inner adytum into which I was not yet permitted. And she did obey the Law of the Game, thus. I put together that there was to be an initiation in a cave somewhere near or on the Mountain of Madness, but only Pellandrey could permit it—or, in my case, perform it. And she said, 'not for love, not for *dhof,* not for all the sweetness we have shared, will I initiate you until they say I can. It is something more than I can give of my own desire.' "

"Even in *dhof?* She spoke exactly thus?"

"Aye, even in *dhof*, just so, Ser Deren."

"So now—what could it have been?"

"There I am lost, blind. Yes, with all that I can do of my own added to all that she gave me, it is still *ankavemosi,* that which is concealed. 'You cannot get there from here.' It is unprojectable; the knowledge of the Outer Game is both insufficient data and a program of misdirection as well. But now you are a Player just as I . . . everything varies in it, even the dimensional matrix. Those were the kind of games that Mael-lenkleth liked best. Because Sanjirmil falls upon her funda-ment within the higher-order Games. And Mael said, 'Present Sanjir-Dear with a matrix higher than four-dimen-sional and she can't tell her own arse from a knot-hole in a plank.' As unskilled as I was, I could see that from the plays I saw her make. But the lower-order Games she could handle well enough: crude, but very effective—her Game plans are heavy-handed, brute-force assaults. There is a feeling of de-struction about her maneuvering."

"I believe," said Morlenden.

"When she faces a problem, she burns her way out. Power, raw imposition of order. Maellen, of the other thumb, plays a delicate, laughing Game . . . artful, skillful, balanced. To fol-low her Games is to experience the wind and the water, to know sailing and flight and the surge and rush of the mount-ing wave of the sea."

"I have the idea," said Morlenden, "that much seems to be focused in these two . . . Braid traditions as well as what they may differ among themselves."

"Indeed, indeed, both. Their natures, their talents and abili-ties, the force of the traditions of both Braids. That was why

two Player Braids were established in the beginning—that
each should explore different aspects of approach to the
Game, substance and style. Another battle in the eternal war
between harmony and invention. We must have both elements. And you must not think that Sanjirmil was of necessity at a disadvantage for her lesser talent in the Game. She
had other abilities . . . the majority would follow her, within
the Game, and she has power under those closest to her; lust,
hope, and fear. She is dangerous."

"But they work together!"

"They have no choice. Sanjirmil is forbidden to leave the
reservation as the Master-Player-to-be; yet there is much, so
they say, to do outside. Sanjir is responsible for the work outside, and has only Maellen to send. And before Mael and I
met, she had little else to do, anyway. And in that aspect,
they do treat one another correctly, if somewhat coldly.
Sanjir has now the power, the authority, Maellen has much
valor. It has been so since Mevlannen determined to go out."

"Nevertheless, Maellenkleth sounds determined herself, to
go so far against the will of so many."

"Determined? Yes, she was so. But she was also gentle of
speech and manner in all things, save the subject of Sanjirmil,
about which she could surpass a bargeman in vulgarity. . . ."
And here Krisshantem looked abstracted a moment, as if recalling something, setting a tangled web of data straight,
things he had assembled piecemeal over the months. "They
made the decision to let the Perklarens terminate and unravel
when Mevlannen was born. She is younger-insibling. Sanjir
was about ten, then. And later, something like five years, I
don't know exactly, something happened to Sanjirmil . . .
something of the Inner Game that none will speak of save in
whispers. Not an accident, but as if something happened too
soon . . . there is something about timing of certain events in
the Inner Game. At any rate, from then Sanjir became ever
more ungovernable and wild. Fey, arrogant. And she became
conscious of what she had won, and that she had won it not
by valor or skill but default. The Terklarens had always been
the underlings. Now time was helping her, and all she had to
do was wait and her traditional enemies would be gone. But
it wasn't enough—she wanted to win it. She was hungry.
Some of the elders became regretful of their earlier
decision, but by the time enough had spoken for action, the

years had passed and Mevlannen had determined to go out. And when Mael and I had become lovers, she was spending most of her time inside in meditation, trying to free herself of the hold of it . . . because once you play the Game, there is nothing else that will satisfy you. Truly it is a most dangerous and addictive poison, even though it illuminates."

Kris continued and Morlenden listened to every word now, trying to pick up the threads of this tale. "We toyed with it, and I surprised her with my response to it; we traded. I taught her how I learn in the forest, from weather-watching, from trying to see the wind . . . you can, you know. It is hard, but one can. It flowed both ways. And she began to have hope again, and began to act again. We met Pellandrey once in the woods north of the Mountain of Madness and she spoke plainly of what she was doing. Then came interminable interrogations by the Past Masters. They called Mael names, they insulted her. Never mind what they said to me. But some were intrigued, captivated by this new situation, Pellandrey, Perwathwiy, even though she is of Sanjirmil's own line of the Terklaren Braid. Make no mistake: they are all afraid of Sanjirmil, even her supporters. Again the Inner Game and her strength and position in it."

For a moment, an inner fire, an enthusiasm, had risen in the boy's eyes and voice. Now it wavered, at the last, flickered, and went out. He resumed his demeanor of quiet resignation. He sighed deeply, and said, "But we knew however much help we had, it was a lost cause. Less than a year, and Sanjir has everything."

"Aside from her approaching fertility and investiture as senior Player, how so? I don't understand. Could Mael not challenge her later at her own fertility, with you as her *shartoorh* co-spouse."

"No. They let the Perklarens unravel—some say it was caused—because the Inner Game conceals something, and in the middle of Sanjirmil's generation, they will no longer need to conceal it. Whatever the Inner Game is, Sanjirmil will manifest it openly, to the astonishment of all, ler and human alike, and there will be no more Game."

"No more Game, but one Braid of Players remains!"

"Thus. And so that was why Maellen was desperate. It was her whole life, her special talent, and she could not bear to part with it; she would go against them all to keep it, even to

seek"—here Kris paused delicately—"*sharhifzergan.** She
would declare herself so and stay here. We would rebuild it
from scratch. Think: the only Player ever born with the in-
born gift for it, and by long love of it, she is far and above any
Player, living or dead, in skill, in knowledge of its range of
subtleties. All that, then, to waste, perhaps spent in the pursuit
of excellence in turnips. A Perklaren, who only held the Revens above them."

Morlenden asked, "The other, Mevlannen. What is she to
this?"

"They were insiblings without the sexual bond; yet they
have always been close, deep into one another. They always
met whenever they could, even after Mevlan's work took her
to the far places, space itself. There was more to it than two
standing together in the storm of troubles; Mevlan was a part
of it as well, what they were all doing, in the Inner Game,
and in the outside operation."

"I thought Mevlannen was with the humans, working on a
telescope in space ."

"True. But she also spends a lot of time on the ground.
Now when Maellenkleth went out this last time, it was to be
her last trip out; and after it there was to be a trip to meet
with Mevlan openly, to get something from her. They were
all elated, anticipating . . . things were to change. That is all I
know of it. I asked, and they all said, *Hvaszan*, Inner Game.
I had hoped to learn more. . . ."

Morlenden interrupted. "And so you may yet. Now listen
and attend: if Maellen is yet alive, we can get her back. Fellirian is working that end of it. But if she was as deep in
secrets as you say she was, and it is as touchy as her own
Braid acts, then there must be the possibility that what we will
find, if we find her, isn't Maellenkleth anymore."

"You suggest she autoforgot? *Sharhifzergan* she considered,
but autoforgetting . . ."

"I consider it possible, on the basis of what you have told
me, and what else I have seen with my own eyes. This last errand outside—if she was taken alive, she would have to protect what she knew . . . and if she would not tell it to you who
were her only hope of getting back, then autoforgetting cannot be ruled out. It is distinct."

---

* Perhaps, "honorary bastardhood." In the context of ler society,
such an event was considered impossible, the ultimate in undesir-
ability. Maellenkleth would be untouchable to untouchables.

"Then it would be a task indeed to bring her back, and in the end, nothing in it for me . . . for if she autoforgot, then she is a stranger, an alien. Not Maellenkleth. Her body was sweet and full of life, but that which I loved has gone forever."

"Painful as that is, so it is truth. And now I must ask, who can do a reconstruction in Multispeech, if we bring her? Neither Fellirian nor I have the skill."

Kris mused over the question, pondering imponderables. "A reconstruction? I don't know who does them . . . I can do it, although I never did it before. You can't practice it, you know—it's too dangerous. But I do know how, if only now in theory; it's rather like the Game, in fact it's related. But it's tricky . . . you need two others at minimum to do it. Mael told me how before she left. It was her last gift to me."

"As if she knew she might need it. But why that? She would have known if she autoforgot she wouldn't return. Just the body."

"I don't know."

"But you agree that we have to try to look, and if we find her, bring her back and try to reconstruct something; we owe that to her."

"I owe her more than that."

"So then, the reconstructors you need. How skilled must they be?"

"Only one need be skilled, and the other two only obey . . . are you volunteering?"

"Fellirian and I, yes. She will agree to it. And perhaps she can devise some way that we do it there, so we don't have to carry her back, if we find her. It will solve many problems if she can walk back under her own power. And you have invaded my mind once already; I suppose I can live with it again."

Krisshantem asked, tentatively, "Do you think there is a chance we could regain her?"

"I think that we must be prepared for that, so that we shall if we can. And there is no other place to look. Fellirian is looking into this, even now as we talk, perhaps walking into a trap now set for whoever comes looking for Maellenkleth. But it's worth trying—at least talking with Fellirian."

"Of course, yes."

"Can you come now?"

"Yes. I will. Not with you, but I can meet you at your *yos* on the next day. I had contracted with the Hulens and I must tell them I am not going to deliver."

"And afterward you will meet with us there."

"Yes, I will come. And along the way I will practice, as I walk alone in the forest where no one will hear the spells I cast in Multispeech."

"Are you sure the very rocks will not respond?"

"No, they will not."

"Good!" Morlenden reached across the low table and patted Krisshantem's suddenly tensed hand. "And perhaps we can find out what was going to or coming from Mevlannen Srith Perklaren. But first we find Mael; then bring her back. Then we find out."

"But from whom, Ser Deren? Perwathwiy?"

"I doubt from her," said Morlenden.

"From the Revens?" asked Kris hopefully.

"Perhaps yet from Maellenkleth herself." And Morlenden added, "She may have left something for us after all. I refuse to believe that a plot so intricate and impervious as this one seems to be would end in a nothing forgetty, a blank tablet."

ELEVEN

> *The things that really stand out in your memory of the past were, at the time you recorded them, so ordinary and unprepossessing that they were truly unmemorable. Yet the things which you imagined to be stunning and ever-memorable cannot be recalled save as vague blurs, phantoms, mergings, and rubbings. We admit to a problem here: we fail to learn what is significant until its significance and immanence serves no purpose save to haunt us.*
>
> —*The Game Texts*

Morlenden awoke as the sunlight was streaming in the window on the east-facing side of the treehouse, into an alcove in which a large and roomy bed-shelf had been fitted into the erratic, form-following structure. A patchwork counterpane, a

soft and downy bottom bag. Him between them. Coherence
returned slowly. This was the treehouse in the woods, of two
adolescents, Krisshantem and Maellenkleth, who had been
lovers. And something more ... allies in a war against an opponent who shifted from day to day and seemed to refuse to
be defined. Morlenden blinked and rubbed his eyes, as if that
would clear the fog in the inside. Perhaps the lack of definition was in him, not in the boy and girl. Better, perhaps they
were all suffering from perceptual problems. The human of
Chinese military history, a man whom the people studied often, Sun-tzu, had averred that if one knew his enemy and
knew himself, he could not lose. Maellenkleth appeared to
have lost; therefore ... The ler mind, strong in intuition,
made the jump for him: she had not known her enemy. And
this made his scalp prickle, for he did not know her enemy
either, and he himself seemed to be well-committed to a
course of making that enemy his enemy.

Their house, their bed. Not like a *yos* at all, with its sense
of being above the individual. The *yos* belonged to the standing wave of the Braid, belonged to time. When their time
came, they left it, never to set foot in it, or any other, again.
Objects were the artifacts left behind by forms of life. This
treehouse was another life-form's artifact ... something powerful and vital. Different. Alien. It gave him an eerie feeling,
like wearing someone else's clothing: they were clean and of
the proper size, more or less, but somehow they weren't *right*,
they weren't of a piece with one's self.

He and Kris had continued talking long into the night,
long past the time either of them usually went to bed. But
what they had said beween them had added little to what he
had already discovered, reasoned, put together. Just details,
color, the living texture of two lives which had somehow
been tangled together, and which had come undone, for reasons neither of them knew. Details. Morlenden knew that he
was the only person Kris had spoken with about Maellenkleth, since she had departed on her last errand, two months
ago now. His deep *hifzer* self-sufficiency had not served him
well in this at all; his silence and reticence had salved not at
all the loss of that which he prized above all things.

Morlenden pushed the counterpane down, stretched, groaning, and allowed the chill air to bite at him, nudging him
more awake, his hands behind his head, collecting thoughts.
Somewhere outside was a thirsty evil that drank the lives of
innocents whose only crime was an excess of zeal. Something

outside, in the human world of 2550, which had roots everywhere, within, around them. *She was a natural Player,* he thought, *and their only genuine prodigy born to it, reputed the best they had ever seen in the history of the Game. But she was also playing in another Game, several games, and in those she was just a novice, an amateur, a loser from the start. A Water-aspectual playing in the area of will and discipline. Playing in an area in which unknown persons bent others to their wills.* She went out, she was a spy for someone, perhaps an operative, for Sanjirmil surely, but for who else behind that one? But she didn't like it, she was terrified of it, and on this last mission she even suspected trouble, judging from the preparations she had made, the things she had told Kris. And still she went! *Fools!* Morlenden rolled over to one side, leaning on his elbow disgustedly, pondering innocence. Their innocence, his innocence.

That's the problem with her, me, Kris, he thought, *with us all; we lermen have not known evil. We have always had the luxury of attributing that to the humans. Aye, evil, vice, stupidity. Not for us! We were the New People, the mutants, the ler, we were as innocent as newly fallen snow, trackless and blameless. And what were your sins, Morlenden Deren? That once in your adolescence you refused a plain or homely girl's desire and injured her sensibilities? That you sometimes overcharged for your services as clerk and registrar? That you were sometimes overly fond of your tipple? You are stupid and know almost nothing of that which you have fallen into; into which you will assuredly fall more deeply if you pursue this Maellenkleth to the end.*

He felt apprehensions; yet he also was aware of a powerful current of wrongness, injustice, malice, something even more strange to him—that a person could be brought to nothing, by something no more involved than an idle procedure, or perhaps the blind machinations of a plot that didn't concern her at all. She was just in the way of others, who would not see what she was offering them. No, not that, either. There was malice in it. But from where? Whom? Morlenden looked for the manifestation of a power, an elemental, deep in his intuitive sense, but down there, there was only a sense of shimmering contradiction, a dichotomy. Wrong, wrong. He lacked data. He sat up on the bed-shelf. He had decided something. He felt uneasy about it, for an instant dizzy with fear, but he stuck to it, and presently the queasy feeling faded. It did not vanish, and he suspected that it would be with him for the rest of his life, but still it had subsided to a bearable level of intensity.

Kris had slept on the floor by the stove, offering Morlenden the bed-shelf. Obviously the boy could not have slept very soundly under that counterpane, full-remembering the emotions that had motivated the acts and encounters performed there, himself and Maellenkleth. Morlenden got up, pulling on his overshirt, and climbed down to the lower level of the treehouse where were the stove and the hearthroom, the room they had talked in. The treehouse was silent, empty. There was no sense of presence. Morlenden knew well enough that Krisshantem was a silent one, but not that silent. He looked about. Kris was gone. By the stove there were some hard-boiled eggs, some bread and cheese, and a note. He picked up the note and read what was written therein, lettered in a neat and precise hand.

> *Ser Deren, I kept you up far too late last night, still I had to be on my way. There are provisions for your return trip home. I will be there to meet you in a day or so. I did not tell you this last night, for I would not speak aloud of it, but be warned and full of care. Someone has been about, shadowing us, more likely you, although I do not know why this should be as it seems. I thought to hear traces of them in the night, but they know me, whoever they are, and they know my range and will not approach close enough for me to identify. At dawn I found a partial trace in the forest. But I still do not know who. I sense danger here, and know you have not the wood-sense of those of us who live here. So go straight to your own holding and do not tarry. I will catch you as fast as I can. Guard yourself as best as you are able.*

Morlenden read it through, and read it through again, wondering at the message and pondering over the odd, abrupt choppiness of style, so unlike the speech of Kris in person. Perhaps he really was apprehensive. So there were eavesdroppers in the night by the Perklarens, or rather what was left of them; and a watcher out of range by the treehouse in the woods, someone who by Kris's own admission was able to move with skill enough to neutralize his formidable perceptions. Indeed, it did appear as if someone were following him, watching him. Morlenden did not seriously consider that the two events were unconnected. Such skill was rare. He went to the window and looked through it into the forest, not really knowing what he expected to see. He saw nothing but the trees, the leaf-strewn forest floor, the bare boles and branches, the shadows of the morning, the sky filming over, hazy, vague. The light held a pearly, graying, fading quality.

He turned to the food, and, gathering it up into a bundle, arranged his clothing for the outside air and began to leave the treehouse, opening the trapdoor to let in the air. The air had warmed during the night; it was not nearly so cold as the day before. Rain coming, the kind that would go on for days—start as drizzle and end in a mud sticky from the slow soaking. He thought that he could make it back to the Deren *yos* before the rain started in earnest, though. He thought, somewhat ominously, that such would be the case, assuming that he didn't meet anyone along the way. On an impulse, he looked about for a weapon, something he could use, a knife, a bludgeon. There was nothing visible; and Morlenden had at this point much too great a respect for the inhabitants of this house to rifle through it, looking for a weapon. Which probably didn't exist in here anyway.

A weapon! Morlenden had walked alone all over the reservation, sleeping in the open when the weather permitted, and sometimes when it didn't, working with the rowdiest and the roughest, and unlike Fellirian, had never carried a weapon in his life. Fellirian did. But not him. He had never thought to need one. Nor for the matter, did Fellirian. But who could imagine him needing one? Fights he had had, in no shortage, knee and fist, foot and elbow, lost and won alike in equal measure. Still he carried no weapon. And now there wasn't anything. Morlenden turned to go, feeling uneasy, apprehensive. But also defiant: *So if my enemy is one of us, then let him close with me, face to face, blows on the front! I may be done with love but I can still fight, and I'll thrash his arse!* Morlenden knew that it was poor weaponry, those brash words, but all the same they made him feel better.

Before he left, out the trapdoor and down the ladder, he stepped out on a narrow landing, not large enough to be properly called a porch; just a place to recline on. At the far end, the corner, it widened into a shelf, a little balcony, a place on the west side to catch the setting sun; something he had seen before—but not before . . . he felt an odd sense of déjà vu. He remembered.

The image of Maellenkleth. There had been a pattern of light and shadow about her, and he had assumed it had been from the window, but of course it hadn't been; it had been sunlight falling through the summer foliage. Of course. The image now returned as clear as when Kris had sent it and he saw *her*, as alive as if he had seen her himself. And there was something about her he had not noticed before, dazzled by her youth and beauty.

Not the body or the pose, relaxed, at her ease, the lover's tentative smile-of-invitation playing along the planes of her face, welling out of her eyes; what was it about her eyes? The skin was a warm sun-browned tan-olive, the limbs still slightly awkward, unfinished, adolescent, the hands long and bony, just as Klervondaf had suggested. She had a high forehead, childishly hidden under the bangs she wore her dark hair in, in the front. And the eyes . . . the eyes! That was it! It had been in the eyes! Although the image had not moved, but had been a single instant's slice, still something about the eyes had been disturbingly familiar, and now he could see and integrate it. Morlenden had seen that same abstracted and vacant gaze long ago, in one who spent much of her time and life training herself to see primarily with peripheral vision, the eyes tracking in a pattern to be read out in the visual center, rather than concentrating upon and following a single object. Like Sanjirmil of sixteen years before, only here rather more pronounced. But it had not seemed a handicap at the time to Sanjirmil, nor did it seem so now to Maellenkleth. Of course, they were both Players of the Game *Zan*, and something they did in the Game gave them that peculiar gaze, that fixed, staring abstracted look. Morlenden reflected again: But Kris, taught as a Player, did not have it at all, and in his own inserted memories, he could not find anything that would give rise to it, that it would be so pronounced. It could be only a behavioral artifact of the Inner Game, something neither he nor Krisshantem had ever seen or known!

He turned into the treehouse, climbed through the trapdoor, and descended the ladder to the ground. Morlenden looked about, as best he could, and then set off southwestward, through the empty woods, guessing direction in the frosted, translucent shadowless gray light, carefully watching

for signs of company along his trail as he went. That he saw
no sign reassured him not at all. For when he and Taskellan
had found Krisshantem (or had it been the other way?), Kris
had materialized, so it seemed, out of nothing. Perhaps there
were others similarly skilled. At least enough to follow him
unawares, and stay away from Kris so that the follower could
not be identified.

By the afternoon, with the air turned cold again from a
wind out of the north with more than a hint of dampness in
it, Morlenden faced the conclusion that he was not going to
arrive at his own *yos*, or anywhere near it, on this day. By his
own internal system of dead reckoning, which he admitted to
be in error more often than not, total recall notwithstanding,
he thought he was located southeast of the lake district and
the Perklarens, and about a day's walk northeast of his home.
The area he was now traversing was nowhere as wild as the
far northeast, the country of the Hulens, Krisshantem, and
apparently few others, but it had still only recently begun to
be integrated into the holdings of the reservation Braids and
was rather underpopulated. Morlenden knew of few holds in
this part, and those which he could remember were nowhere
near here, wherever *here* was; he was not exactly sure. He
knew only that if he continued in the direction he had been
faring, he would eventually strike an area he was familiar
with.

The afternoon wore on, after the manner of land under the
influence of diffuse and slow-moving weather systems; soon
one could expect the rain to start, perhaps snow, and it would
continue for days. Now the light was failing, a late cloudy-
day light, weak and blue in overtones; the ler eye, with its
larger proportion of retinal cone cells, progressively lost
discriminatory ability at lower light levels, and in gray light
became particularly poor. Morlenden resigned himself to
being cold, and began casting about for suitable shelter for
the night. Unthinkable to walk on blind through the woods
and tangled new ground, cluttered with raw second-growth:
eventually, he would trip and fall over something.

It was while he was looking for some suitable natural shelter, an outcrop, a fallen tree, some ruins from the period
when this land had been under the humans, a barn or shed,
that he became gradually aware he was in a place showing

subtle signs of use: a fresh path, one used fairly recently by travelers. An odd clearing in the half-grown woodland, where a tree had been artfully removed. Rather unlike the work of a Braid, working the land for some product. They would be more careless, and also more specialized. So there was probably an elder lodge somewhere in the vicinity, most likely recently established. That could be anything: Morlenden had never concerned himself with the organizations of the elder class and in fact knew only of the more famous ones, where they were and how they lived. He listened carefully, unable to determine anything visually with any certainty in the distances, in the overcast pre-rain murk, shades of gray and violet. Nothing. A sluggish creek nearby. A dripping sound, very slow, somewhere off in the opposite direction. An expectancy, a waiting for rain. Yes, for sure there would be rain. He could feel it. No snow.

From far off, muffled by distance and the weather, and by the half-overgrown lands, Morlenden thought he heard the tolling of a bell, from across the overgrown fields. He listened again. Silence, for a long time. Then the sound: a bell's tolling, slowly, single deep pulses spreading like the slow ripples across a stagnant pond, tangled and choked with weeds and debris . . . again, pulse, followed by silence. Assuming that the first one he had heard had actually been the first, he counted them, as the almost inaudible pulses flowed deliberately through the wet air. The eighteenth hour. He did not know who might be ringing the evening in, but he turned in the direction the tolling had come from.

It was almost completely dark by the time he was sure, after much stumbling, that he was in fact coming to something; there was evidence of cultivated fields, cut-over brush, and an impression of neatness and order, almost parklike as he drew nearer. A light mist had begun to fall. Morlenden followed what seemed to be a well-used path. Something was ahead.

Walking along, half stumbing in the poor light, he almost walked into a figure standing in the pathway in an attitude of silent waiting. It wore a cowled winter pleth, dark in color, and stood, head bowed, even when Morlenden approached. Morlenden went around to the front of the figure, and peered within the dark hood. Within, a pair of calm eyes slowly moved their focus from the ground to Morlenden's face, fixing him with a steady, expressionless gaze.

Morlenden said, "I am a wayfarer, Morlenden Deren by name, homeward bound, caught out in the rain and the fall of night. Is there shelter nearby?"

The figure did not speak, but raised its arm and pointed along the path in the same direction Morlenden had been walking, inclining its head in that direction, once. Then the figure returned to its meditations, looking back to the earth as if it had been Morlenden who had been the apparition.

Morlenden inquired politely, "Do you not speak?"

The silent figure made no reply, and indeed made no further acknowledgment of Morlenden's presence.

Morlenden did not press the matter, concluding that perhaps he was already disturbing some delicate equilibrium; he turned from the figure and proceeded in the indicated direction. After passing through a few bends in the path, now bordered by tall and dense hedges of privet and pyracantha, he came upon a rustic wooden gate, and within that, a rambling compound of buildings, rough stone and half-timber stucco, some obviously pens for livestock, others worksheds. A few were larger, of two stories, apparently the living quarters. More of the cowled figures were about, proceeding on their errands with exaggerated slowness. One passed by Morlenden, paused, and pointed to one of the large buildings. Then it turned and continued on its progression, all in the profoundest of silences. One thing he knew now: this had to be an elder lodge. Which one?

Continuing to the indicated building, Morlenden found a door and entered. Inside there was a low counter, and behind that, a smallish and rather austere refectory. The counter was covered by a massive slab of blue glass, with a legend etched into its bottom in reversed letters, which read: *Granite Lodge*. In smaller letters, it was stated: CONTEMPLATION AND THE SILENCE. Morlenden found a neat little sign on a post which advised: *Distinguished visitors will share in our meditations. The buttery serves from the fifth hour until the eighteenth. Suitable accommodations in the floor above. The discerning guest will find the enumeration of specific tariffs unnecessary.* Morlenden understood; he dug into his waistpouch and retrieved several small coins, which he placed in a convenient depressed place in the glass surface. He looked about uncertainly. There seemed to be no one in the refectory. He sought stairs or a hallway to another part of the building; far to the right, a darkened hallway terminated in narrow stairs. Morlenden set off in that direction, and began laboriously climbing to the upper floors.

On the second floor, there was a narrow hallway, illuminated by fat, slow-burning candles mounted in sconces of black iron. Inside, the half-timber construction of the outside walls continued, broken by heavily timbered doors, which apparently led to sleeping-apartments throughout the floor. Morlenden went to the first door, tried it. It was locked. The second—located at an angle across the hallway, and a little farther on—was not; he entered.

Within, there were two beds, rather after the human mode, but very simple, mere frames for padded platforms. But they were piled high with plenty of coverlets and counterpanes. Morlenden opened his outer cloak and tested the air. Cold; he would need all those coverlets in this damp pile. At the far end of the room, a table and chair rested under a tiny window, which was set high up on the wall. There was a single large candle on the table, now unlit. Morlenden removed the candle and took it outside, where he presented it to one of the candles alight in their sconces, lit it, and returned to the room. Now illuminated with the warm yellow light from the candle, it did not seem quite so bare and stark. The woodwork was of the finest hand-craftsmanship, although with that suggestion of raw patina that signified new material, not yet seasoned by time. On the table was a large, heavy tome, accompanied by a sheaf of paper, a pen, and an inkstand. He looked more closely; the legend on the front of the book read: *Knun Vrazus*—The Doctrine of Opposites*. Morlenden smiled faintly and leafed idly through the book. Hand-inscribed, beautifully illuminated and lavishly illustrated with quaint drawings of mythological beasts and figures, demons, angels, metamorphs. He understood very well: one was intended to meditate here, in this little cell, and pass on one's

* A collection of anecdotes, told by obscure, unknown, or imaginary ler over the years. These always culminated in a dense parable, which might take the form of being too obvious, or else totally incomprehensible, at least until the reader realized the point. The work was considered open-ended and unfinished, and there was a large commentary and criticism attached to it. Humans of the era, where they were aware of it at all, considered it gross cynicism pushed to levels of perversity. It may be interesting to note here that Morlenden considered it boring.

thoughts and ruminations to the future inhabitants, as well as the denizens of Granite Lodge. He sighed dispiritedly: Morlenden would have preferred to visit the taproom for a dram or two, perhaps a draft, and a bit of conversation. He dug the remaining boiled egg out of his traveling-pack, and cracking it, ate it, sitting gingerly on the hard edge of the bed. As he ate, he listened to the noises of the place, noting nothing save the dripping of rainwater off the roof into puddles outside, and a light, sweet gurgling farther away, the running of water in a gutter or downspout. There was no sound of people at all.

Finishing his egg, and drinking water from a small pitcher that he uncovered in a tiny wall-cabinet, he looked about the small, bare room once more, shook his head, and began to undress, hanging his outer clothing on a peg on the wall. The rest he folded and placed on the desk, leaving on only his undershift. Morlenden set about making up the bed, grumbling to himself, chiefly about the nature of cold boiled eggs before bed. He was just about to blow out the candle when he heard footfalls on the stairs, then coming into the hall outside. *Another guest*, he thought. *May they attend the same party I did*. He listened. There was a faint rattle at the first door; just as he had done. Then the visitor tried his own door, which was now latched but not locked. It rattled once. There was a pause, and then the visitor knocked on the door. Raising his eyebrows, Morlenden took the candle and went to the door, and opened it: and found himself looking into the rain-wet face of Sanjirmil Srith Terklaren.

She was still dressed in a heavy winter overcloak with a hood that fell far over her forehead, the overcloak was turned water-repellent side out, and in the wavering candle-light, hundreds of sparkling points shimmered all over it, and along Sanjirmil herself where she was uncovered, her face and hands. Her dusky eyelashes; deep black with the same bluish overtones as her hair.

She spoke first, either recovering her composure or never having lost it, saying, "And you, here? May I join you?"

"Yes, yes, of course you may," he stumbled, waving the candle. "Yours is the first voice I have heard here; you will be welcome."

Sanjirmil entered the room shyly, avoided facing Morlenden directly, speaking as if to herself. "You have not visited here before? They are silent, these ones, true enough. Never have I heard them utter a single word." In the center of the room, she removed the outer overcloak, shook the rain off, and cast about for a peg on which to hang it. Finding it, the empty peg on the opposite side of the room, she hung the cloak, followed by a large bag that she had worn slung over one shoulder, which clanked dully as she let it rest against the wall.

Morlenden could see that the overcloak had not kept out all the rain, for there were damp patches along the shoulders and hem of her pleth. This she also removed unselfconsciously, draping it over the end of the unoccupied bed. All that was left was her undershift, which she left on. Morlenden noticed many things about her now, but the first thing that caught his eye was an embroidered design worked into the right shoulder of the undershift, similar to the patterns he had observed earlier in the *yos* of the Perklarens, but different in shape. Where the others had been simple geometric patterns, more or less symmetrical, the one on Sanjirmil's undershift had no obvious cellular reference and was asymmetrical—a line of blue dots, arranged in a curve at either end, the right end being larger than the left. He recalled the basic Player information Krisshantem had forced into him, looking into his new memories for the figure, and found it. It was one of the moving patterns from the beginner's Game, a figure that moved orthogonally along its base across the field in the direction of the larger curl. Like all persistent figures in the Game, this one had a name: *Prosianlodh*, which was to be rendered by an enigmatic idea—ship of the empty place. The name was not explained. Inner Game.

But he saw other things as well, things he had not troubled to see, or avoided, when the girl had accompanied the Perwathwiy Srith to the *yos* of the Derens before his trip upcountry. Sanjirmil was now hesitating on the edge of her own fertility, at the summit of adolescence, the end of it, trembling on that edge. He remembered in his mind's eye the hoyden, the ragamuffin of sixteen years before. Seen closely, as she was to him now, there were still large amounts of those same qualities present—the gestures, the hesitant impatience, the thin, pouty, determined mouth, the half-frown of concentration along the lines and planes of her face. But more, indeed, was there. Her hair was as dark and coarse and tousled as it had always been, but it was longer and fuller now, falling carelessly about her shoulders, almost ready to be braided into the single woven strand that was the mark of parent phase. Her body was fuller, also, mostly adult, but possessing something not quite lermanish in its rounder curvings, yet not human either, still subtle and muscular after their fashion. She took the candle from him and placed it upon the desk, moving with measured grace, as a young girl might before her lover, a flowing, dancing motional set, allowing the undershift to swirl about her, and standing afterward so that the light from the candle would shine through the undershift, suggesting much and revealing nothing. It was a classical move, only slightly less direct than a spoken invitation. Morlenden saw and appreciated all that she was displaying here for him, understanding the message completely. *She knows no less than I that my time for that is gone, past,* he thought. *So it is not so blatant as it appears. It is not invitation, but reminder. As if either of us could ever forget.*

He had not forgotten: Sanjir-Ajimi had been hot and sweaty, pungent as the scent of burning leaves, wet wood, and her skin had retained, even after washing, the faint taste of salt. He had caught her scent here as she had passed him: sharp and imperative, smoky as ever, more so. For the first time in his life he caught himself admitting to some regrets upon the course of things. Morlenden looked back over his life for a moment, quickly, and recognized Sanjirmil for what she had been to him: an ultimate, certainly of the domain of the body, of *dhainaz*. And of how many other things that he had missed? *What was it she was offering?*

Sanjirmil seated herself gently on the edge of what would be her bed, a little tiredly, stiff as if from a long walk. She asked, half-mockingly, "And what do you here, Ser Deren?" She leaned back on her elbows, allowing her undershift to fall more open about her throat, another classic ploy that Morlenden could not miss; and in the candlelight the yellow light fell along her dusky-olive skin, the shadows in the hollows of her collarbones, a place for kisses.

He answered cautiously, trying to maintain some semblance of neutrality, some little vestige of secrecy, a futile task, he knew, in the face of this arch-keeper of secrets. He said, "Little enough. I have been searching for an image of she who we must find, so that we would know the better to look and where. I was on my way home, caught in the rain, and happened on this lodge."

"You did not find her for whom you search."

"Hardly. We did not expect to. Just understand who she is, she is. Or rather, *was*. Fellirian is exploring down the

other way, about the Institute with her friends there. We
think she is still alive. At the least, we are proceeding as if
she were."

"You will go out for her?"

"Of course."

"Why? When you find where she is, you can report to the
Perwathwiy and that will be the end of that."

"Why? An honor thing, I suppose. We said that if we
could, we would find her and return her. There is much,
though, which we do not know yet. If she lives, her condition." He changed the subject, feeling an oppressive weight
about the subject of Maellenkleth. "And you, Sanjir, what do
you here, in this place of silences? Are you perhaps out of
the rain, as I?"

She did not answer immediately, but looked off into space
with the old blank gaze of hers, gradually turning it toward
Morlenden. Yes, the eyes, dark, heavy-lashed, wine-dark; they
still had that eerie scanning quality, but there was a controlled directness in them as well now, flashing with lightning
and fire when she concentrated upon something. But for now,
they were faraway, seeing something Morlenden did not
know. She said, after a time, "We met here, often, our group.
It is an excellent place to discuss secret plans, for they who
lodge here will not speak of what they hear or see. . . . Over
the years, I have grown fond of it, of this place, and come
alone betimes. And I was troubled, and so I came to seek solitude, peace. To learn peace, Morlen. I know I do not have it
in me, but would like to see it once, if but to refuse it."

She fell silent again, chewing the inside of her lower lip.
Tonight her lips were pale and colorless, lighter than her
face, which lent her an odd, ghostly quality. The lighter pink
of her mouth against the dark olive of her face. Then suddenly she turned to him and fixed him with an intense and
uncomfortable regard, saying, "You are thorough in this,
indeed. And why so? I know you well enough and know that
you never cared a whit for the Game or its Players. You
have been no Gamefollower, always at the exhibitions. . . .
You have no side, no color, no pennant to wave, neither a
red nor a blue."

"It is as you say . . . I am no Gamefollower, nor have I
supported one against another."

"But you must know of the rivalry between our Braids,
and that Maellenkleth and I were exemplars of that traditional rivalry?"

"Indeed. I knew that before you spoke of it."

"So why pursue this girl to the very end? You need only determine it and report."

"It would appear," he said after a moment's reflection, "that there are many intrigues about the house of Perklaren, some of which I must needs unravel as I go along. It appears extremely complex, just as does Maellenkleth."

"Maellenkleth was to the contrary; she was simple-minded and one-sided. I know her well, saw her often."

"So much have I learned. And that also she was reputed to be an excellent Player." Morlenden felt the necessity to be on his guard here, but he felt a greater need to needle Sanjirmil into revealing something more. He was right: she reacted immediately, although she covered it well.

She said, her voice unsteady, "Ah, who was it told you that? They also said, most likely, that she was a better Player than I. Well, I think not better—merely different. For my view Maellenkleth was overly concerned for matters of style, elegance, finesse, little internal codes. But I believe in results, that they tell the true story. And I get them, too." She added, "As a Player."

Morlenden felt reckless, and pursued the topic. "And I had also heard that she was possibly to be allowed to reenter the Game—the Inner Game, whatever it is—again as a *shartoorh* Dirklaren, of the first generation of Dirklarens."

Sanjirmil's face became darker, flushed, stormy. She responded immediately. "That was foolishness, stupidity, a nuisance! She—they, that out-Braid *hifzer*—hoped to change the inevitable by little hearthroom children's games and plots and scheming. But I tell you that it could not and did not have any effect upon me. For the law of the Game, arbitrated by Pellandrey himself, says that only a woven *Toorh* may be *Huszan*, master of the Game: I am woven, a *Toorh* and *Klandorh* to add to it, and the present parent Terklarens have already retired in my favor, voluntarily. Therefore by the law I am the master of the Game, to say who may and who nay. Perwathwiy and the others, they may advise, but likewise, the responsibility is mine and I may ignore. And I will be *Huszan* and *Klandorh* until our *Toorh* children weave in their turn. Now we are talking, Morlen, about another thirty years, more than a span." She repeated the number, emphasizing it: "Two fourteens and two! And the Revens may manufacture all the Braids they wish; in the end only I can admit her into it, her and her outsider. So what should I care about Dirklarens, Beshklarens, Nanklarens*?"

"Technically, you are not woven until, for example, I say that you are. I, or Fellirian, or Kaldherman, or Cannialin."

"But of course I am! I am fully initiated! Oh, yes, indeed, am I ever initiated!" And here, Sanjirmil laughed, involuntarily, as if at some irrepressible private joke.

"And you quote the law to keep Maellenkleth out of the Game, but you do not wish to hear the same law applied to you yourself." Morlenden allowed an edge to come into his voice, as if correcting a child. "There is no record; no Deren witnessed."

"Oh, but there was a ceremony. Even Mael attended. . . ."

"And carried flowers as well, I suppose?"

He did not wait to hear her answer, but continued, "And there was no notification to those who would legitimize your place and position. Not even a courtesy call, a letter by messenger." Here he also reminded her of their past, for it had been Sanjirmil who had so often insisted upon writing, but after the promises, had never done so. "But in the scale of all things, rights and wrongs, I suppose after all it doesn't really make any difference, either way. You need our approval: you have it, now, this minute. Write down the full-names of your Braid members, and I will enter them in the records. Done. I would not, in any event, obstruct what is obviously already accomplished. . . . I could only go to the Revens for arbitration, but I can gather from all that I have seen that they already know about it."

"Morlenden, you do not know all the reasons. . . ."

"Reasons, are they? The tyranny of reasons, so it is said; we can always find a *zhan* of them to explain things we shouldn't have done in the first place. And of course we can reasonably project that Maellenkleth is done for anyway."

"She was told of the danger long ago! Clearly, no tricks and nothing hidden! Still, she elected to soldier for us, we did not make her. She was of a valiant heart and could not be denied, but allowed to the very front of the battle, as it were. She pushed it that way . . . thus she gained obligations from those of us who could not go out, as I, even as I. That was not my issue to judge."

"And you say that you are *Huszan*, master of the Game, but *chlenzan*, too, prisoner of the Game."

* Third-players, Fifth-players, Nth-players.

"Prisoner, yes! So it is with all mastery! I am not so unique! And I do not regret what I have given up to get it, the trade of the one for the other. Any other. If you knew as I did, you would take it thus as well, and if it were within your grasp, you too would reach for it."

"I cannot speak of temptations I have not faced."

"But you could face them and gain thereby if you would but listen to me."

"How is it that I reach for that which has not been offered?"

"I have always offered it, just as long ago."

"To cleave to you as an elder when we could not otherwise? To make with our minds in the future that which we made with our bodies in the past?"

"Why not, then? I say of it that it was the best and sweetest of my life; and for one time, one only, I was free, just myself, and I forgot my name. I know it would be the same; you have reserves and perceptions you do not know. . . ."

"Even were I to agree to such a thing, so I would have to wait for you. . . ."

"As I have waited. But it is as nothing; something we of the longer sight see over, beyond. I never forget those days of the autumn. It is true that we all carry the obligation to the people, to the body, to bring forth and ever keep the line that was given us. Nevertheless the heart and mind know their needs as well."

"Neither have I forgotten. But we were skin-drunken, kiss-drugged, and it was done and left behind ages ago. You must have thought along the way that we were badly unsynchronized in time: we had our moment, but both of us have had to walk along unique ways."

"But I have heard that you do wish for something more to be in your free years. And they are free, yours to ask for. And have; that I can offer, that, and more."

"I remain skeptical. From what I have learned of the Game I am not so sure I would wish such an adventure. We are simple folk of field and forest, remember; accordingly we have essentially modest ambitions. Because I have spoken unguardedly of learning new things—for example, to swim—should not be taken to mean that I wish to swim the Green Sea all the way to the land Yevrofian. Do you offer the Game, or will you accept what elderhood I offer?"

"I am not offering the Game; for the one, I cannot. Maellenkleth did thus, for Krisshantem, but they were children. It is too late for that. Too much to learn, reflexes, Morlenden, reflexes. Knowledge of that is not enough. It's the speed you use them with, and it takes almost a full span to get them right. Action, decision, foresight, and the sense of timing. Too late, I must say."

"Then what is it you wish me to take?"

"Just myself. What more can I offer you?"

"I know only one part of you ... and even now, I cannot know how well I know even that part. Things change, and I know even less of what things have passed in your life."

Sanjirmil shook her head. "Little of that, to be sure. I have not known another with whom I would have my elderness. Could I speak plainer? You shame my essence evading me thus."

"It cannot be a thing I would say easily, or on the moment. At the least, I would like some time."

"Time, is it? The fifteen years until Pethmirvin weaves? The twenty until Pentandrun and Kevlendos are invested with the records of the Derens? We do not have twenty years! We do not have fifteen years!" She had allowed her voice to gain in volume and presence, but now it dropped abruptly to almost a whisper, as she added, "We do not have even five."

"Of course we do. We have until the end of time."

"We do not! Within the ..." Sanjirmil stopped. "I say we do not, and there I speak as *Huszan*, because I know it as *Huszan* of the Inner Game. Belive me."

"With no reasons for this unseemly haste, save 'believe me'?"

"You are as bullheaded as you ever were!"

"It is not bullheaded to ask why. You must tell me how it is you can be so sure of the time—so sure that you almost gave me a date. What is it and what is to happen?"

"I cannot. .... It is true that I read the law lightly, as you say, when it comes to my own actions, but even so, I could not initiate you until I was sure you were committed. To me."

"Those kinds of assurances do not come easy; the requirement is as difficult to satisfy as to fill a bottomless pit with stones. So, after all, this is just another case of Maellenkleth and Krisshantem? She would not initiate him either."

"So much you have heard of Kris? But he did not know Mael as well as he thought: so she told him she would not do it. But she told me that she would initiate him anyway, permitted or not! She promised, she did, although I should prefer the word 'threaten.'"

"Had she actually done that?"

"So she said. But we were at least spared that embarrassment by her departure on this last mission instead." (How convenient, Morlenden thought, if any of what she was saying was even half-true.) "It would have come, though, never fear."

Morlenden observed, coolly, "This Game and its Players grow more interesting with every Player I meet."

Her reply came in a low tone, and she peered at him from under her heavy eyebrows, so that the lower whites of her eyes showed. Although the words were mild, the effect was menacing, and Morlenden felt it was intended to be. "Be careful that you do not gain too great an interest before your time."

"I do only what we have been paid to do by the Perwathwiy, and Pellandrey Reven as well. Go to them for comfort; I will even go with you. But as soon as we are a little more knowledgeable, we are going for Maellenkleth, and whatever it takes to do it, knowledge or arts, rest assured we will attain it. Understand me: I would not pay so much as a thimbleful of the yield of our outhouse for one word of the Game or its Players, *in themselves*. But it is a matter of a missing girl who departed under the oddest of circumstances, and it needs uncovering. And to determine where she might be, we must learn what she was."

"If you find her, what will you do with what you find?"

"Bring her back, if she lives."

"And if she lives disminded?"

"As you know, she can be restored, slowly over the years, or quickly via Multispeech, each as circumstances warrant. She has intrinsic value in several ways, not the least of which is that she is a person. And as one of us who I think was caught in something quite beyond her; and as a future parent, who will have to bear the future with the rest of us. And the beauty and the spirit I have heard so much of? Surely it would be a waste to let it all go so casually, lose it without further thought. Not all of it was memory—some of it must reside as the cellular level, and thence to us through the children."

"But she has no family that can take care of her, that can take the time and trouble to rebuild her. You know that rebuilding a forgetty is much harder than raising the original child, for with a forgetty the instinctual cues and programming for learning readiness are gone."

"She is of such an age that if all else failed we Derens would take her in. Or perhaps the Hulens. I am not so sure that would be to Kris's liking, for he would still lose her, but even so . . ."

"Hulens? Ragamuffins, hooligans, wanderers, tramps, nomads!"

"I cannot speak of their methodology, but as much of it as they passed to Kris seemed to be effective enough. True, he is withdrawn and solitary, but he is competent and practiced in the basic social graces. He had to learn from someone, and with his tenuous contact with the Hulens, their way must have some values."

"Morlen, what have we lost that I cannot reach you now?"

"Now? We cannot lose what we never had, Sanjir. As for the rest, we lose no more than others have done, gracefully and tactfully, in somewhat similar circumstances. Do not misunderstand: I cherish the time when we were together. I can in truth compare that with no one else. But time has passed and conditions changed. You and I alike are *Toorh*, and we have debt to others, no matter what we feel. Not to mention other emotions that may have become operative in us. You for yours and likewise I for mine. Would you have me run off willy-nilly into the forest as some moon-child?"

"Then you will persist in this folly?"

"Even if I were disinterested and wholly mercenary I would proceed. Word is word. But there is far more. This Maellenkleth has obviously been ill-used by the very people who should have shielded her from the terrors of the wider world, whether she desired it or not. She was a child—she had no business being a spy. That is not the business of the young and zealous, but of the seasoned and calm. I know there are high stakes outside, worlds won and lost. Perhaps inside as well. But I have my own values, my own interests. And there seems to be much too much afoot to allow it to remain hidden for no other reason than that it may be sensitive cult-dogma! I owe the truth at least to myself, since now I apparently risk that person. And of course the Perwathwiy deserves what she paid for. So I would learn how Maellenkleth came to be where she is."

"Even though you *know* you are on the edge of things you may not be a witness to yet?"

"Indeed, there. Just so. But have no fears; I am discreet by nature and will retain any secrets I uncover."

"You expect to find them along the way, like stones in a path?"

"Of course! An excellent choice of words! I could not have put it better. For I have already, hardly looking, turned over several interesting stones of such a nature, things I imagine people would not have left casually strewn about."

"Morlenden, Morlenden, I urge restraint, I caution you! We are not a riddle to be solved, a puzzle for the curious to decipher . . ."

". . . but a mystery cult of which to stand in awe? While you stand serene and secure above the rest of us? Then explain it!"

"I cannot, I simply cannot. I would lose much, starting with you. You may see that in time, and why, although I wish with all my heart that you do not."

"Well enough," he said, almost grimly. "Well taken, all your warnings. But I continue."

"How far?"

"Until the end."

"I cannot be responsible, then. Not in your debt."

"For what?"

"For what may happen . . . it is suspected that Maellenkleth fell into a clever trap, the like of which has not been set before. It may be set even now for you, should you go to it."

"I will take that chance and rely upon ingenuity. She had hers and went, clean-eyed; I can do no less, with the less that I have to lose."

To this last, Sanjirmil had nothing to add, and so she sat, for a long time, saying nothing, her eyes totally reverted to the blind scanning, devoid of expression. At last she got up from the bed, wearily, as if she had been through some great internal struggle. She moved to the place where Morlenden was sitting on the edge of the bed, leaning forward. She took his face in her hands, which were hot and dry, and pressed his face to her abdomen, the muscles within taut as wires. She was trembling slightly, in the grip of some strong emotion.

She moved his face upward, pressing it to her breasts, then looking him directly in the eyes with a burning regard Morlenden did not know he could hold indefinitely, so intense was it. She said slowly, "I will not ask that you sleep with me; I still want you, the past is too well-remembered, and I know that you are beyond me now. But I will ask a last kiss."

"A last kiss?"

"A kiss before sleeping, that we may remember each other as once we were."

She bent farther and pressed her lips to his, childishly, her lips relaxed, making no attempt to shape them. As they touched, Morlenden felt the image of the past within his memory emerge, take over, become as one with the present. For all her aggressiveness and belligerence, he remembered vividly that Sanjirmil had been from the first a shy kisser, not teasingly falsely shy, but truly so, as if she were afraid to really give of herself, afraid to abandon herself even to a kiss, and much less what would come after. It was the same, exactly the same, the soft, relaxed mouth, barely parting the lips and not offering her tongue until he touched it with his. Morlenden remembered the past, their past, too well. But for the present, he felt nothing save some subtle, ephemeral emotions that had no form and no name, except in that they were related to a form of sadness, a form of regret. She breathed once, deeply, through her narrow nostrils, then broke, turned abruptly, and blew out the candle. Morlenden felt moisture on his cheeks; he did not need to taste its salt to know that it was tears, notwithstanding that he had neither felt nor heard a sob from her. It was blind-dark in the room now, and he could follow her only through the sound of her movements, the rustles of her undershift, the scuffling of her bare feet along the rough wooden floor, the touches and taps of her hands, and he heard the bed creak as it took her weight. Then silence matched the darkness, Morlenden turned under his own covers and began sinking into sleep almost immediately, one last thought surfacing in his mind like some great bulkhead behind the dam: *Yes, the bed creaked, but just this little once. We creaked, too, Sanjir and I, when we took the weight of each other's bodies; we still creak from it.*

In the morning, in the gray light of a rainy-day morning, Morlenden awoke and saw that Sanjirmil was still sleeping, breathing slowly and deeply. He slipped out of his bed carefully and quietly, gathering his things and dressing so as not to wake her. He wished no more of the laden conversation they had made the night before.

Taking one last look about to be sure he had left nothing, he paused, wishing to take one last look at Sanjirmil, Sanjir

whom he had met in the forest long ago, Ajimi with whom
he had been a lover, and also the new and disturbing Sanjirmil ... Terklaren, yes, adult, who spoke of traps and threats
and still more enigmas. Sanjirmil was on her side, lightly and
carelessly half covered, half curled, her lips slightly parted,
still deeply sleeping. He looked closer, remembering. Asleep,
her now-face lost much of its new harshness and seemed soft
and childish again, a ragamuffin, yes, but also a ragamuffin
who was very alone, very frightened of the uniqueness being
pressed upon her. The aquiline nose lost much of its predatory curve. Relaxed, it was a face of desires and passions and
something close to loveliness, ever so slightly slanted in the
angles of the eyes, this face delicate and strong-lined at once,
smooth and sleek as the face of some wild animal at peace.
He saw there was no mystery of how they had come to be together when they had met; Sanjir was indeed in a class all by
herself. Striking, commanding, she would have been excep-
tional even in the midst of girls of great beauty.

He moved yet closer, cautiously, so as not to awaken her,
peering closely at her eyes, which were still closed. He thought
to detect some movement under the lids, as if she were having a dream. He wondered idly what such a one would dream
about. Closer. Behind the closed eyelids, there was movement, but as he watched her, Morlenden could see that under
the soft black lustrous lashes the movement was not the erratic, looping motion of a normal person's dream, but a version of the same scanning pattern he had seen in her before.
The eyes scanned, rather than tracked, in a raster pattern: a
line across, then repeated, a little lower, until the bottom of
the field of vision, then repeating the cycle. It was slowed
now, and he could see the component motions he could not
see before. Odd, indeed, to be so impressed upon her that she
would even dream it that way. What was she dreaming?
The Inner Game? At the same time, he saw that her lips were
also moving, as if sleep-speaking, but he heard no sound. He
leaned closer, trying to hear, identify the mode, listening
closely, knowing that even if she were speaking Multispeech
he would be in little danger because there was no synchronization and no submission on his part. He could not be
caught in it.

It was there, and he caught a fragment of it, an odd form,
an unusual mode he couldn't quite identify, something similar
to the mode of one-to-many, but with an odd lilt, a catch, a
syncopation in the rhythms, almost as if she were somehow

controlling actions in another, others, three people. He began getting quick visuals. Visuals caught. And now receiving the full blast of what she was sending in her sleep, Morlenden was pinned in an iron net of command-override Multispeech, and he saw and performed, and did not understand what he was seeing and doing, but he did with great urgency, the persona being projected by Sanjirmil, because he could not help doing exactly as the instructions were passed to him. He did not have the option to disobey or reflect; and he did not hear, for through sound and modulation and the heritage of the people, Sanjirmil had somehow inserted her own persona directly into his mind and was manipulating Game skills he didn't know he had. A single will permeated everything, a force filled him with energy, with verve, with skill and power: hell and death flowed along his arms into his hands as they flew like manic butterflies along the controls of a Game keyboard that seemed to surround him, all around the domains of his reach. It was the Game, of course, and he could see it all above him; he was reclining, looking upward, scanning a ceiling the whole of which was a subtly curved Game display panel alive with patterns of light, color and darkness, the shapes and patterns permutating, evolving, shifting with terrible urgency, immediacy. Something was coming and they blanked it with some motion that caused the rest to tremble and shift and emit pieces of themselves. Waves of change, of destruction, and of reordering flowed across the field. There was more, and it continued, the intensity growing, but all he felt was confidence, exultation, the semblance of something coming into reality at last, of being victorious, of imposing some concept upon something else, and then there was a terrible stroke they all did together that made the multiple personality wince, flinch, shrink back with horror, but they could not reflect; they must move on. He felt and rejoiced in the exultation emanating from she-who-controlled: triumph, vindication, the utter joy of performing the ultimate crimes and atrocities upon one's most hated enemy, something hated and feared and not long ago hidden from. As stability returned slowly something was now being done that was incomprehensible to him. Energy long-stored, locked up in the prisons of cold matter, rigid, now leaped into freedom and fled shrieking at the skies; there was fire and carnage.

Morlenden knew he was feeding something back to the Control, the Will, but until now he had not attempted to insert himself. Now he did. It had gone on long enough. And he saw himself now as a sage, a governor, a steadying influence against excess, a stay against impulses even more wild than those he had glimpsed. Like oil on the waters he tried to steady what they were all doing, through feedback; after all, was he not Fire aspect, did he not have the Will also? There was conflict, here there could be only one Fire and *out*.

Shaken, he drew back from the sleeping girl, and he was now back in the real world. Or was it? He saw and did not understand. Now he remembered, and still he did not comprehend. He looked at Sanjirmil again. She was moving restlessly in her sleep, now muttering something unintelligible, the scanning in her eyes stopped. She had been acting out some dream only she knew, and Morlenden's hands trembled and tingled as if he had received some electric shock. It had been the Game, sure enough, but it had been in a form he had never seen, in a place he could not imagine. He tried to remember: the image was furred and distorted by being someone else's dream, but he could see it, crudely—he had been within a reclining couch, contoured to his body, slightly tilted, his hands at the ready arrayed along massive keyboard controls that lay all about him. But he had been scarcely conscious of all that, immersed in concentration upon the huge Game screen that curved all over him, over them all, dwarfing the tiny beings who manipulated the flying shapes that fled and changed over its surface. Morlenden could not imagine what it was he had seen, been within. The environment was abstract and alien. But there could be no mistaking the confidence, the arrogance, of the sender, the girl who lay before him, now relaxing again, drifting back into deeper sleep, almost pretty, exotic in coloring and shape, innocently dreaming in the gray early hours of a rainy winter morning. She moved slightly, adjusting her position, disturbing the covers, causing them to emit her scent, still that tart and sweet maddening odor of warm adolescent girl, gamy, all body. Morlenden shivered violently, shaken by the contrasts his senses and memories were making in him. He hurriedly fastened his overcloak, and slipped from the room as quickly and as quietly as he could. And as he carefully pulled the door to behind him, out in the cold and drafty corridor, he knew that however brave the words he had used, he was in fact very much afraid of this unknown, this imcomprehensible being concentrated in the sleek tawny body of Sanjirmil, who had been, upon a time, Ajimi.

He hurried down the corridor and then the stairs, empty as the night before, half-dark, feeling a pressing danger, a peril, a murderous threat, a panicky urge that inspired him to get out right now. The alternative to the search for Maellenkleth was to get out of it as fast as he could extricate himself and Fellirian. He suddenly did not wish to know how Maellenkleth got wherever she was; he wished to forget the whole thing, and return all the money to the Perwathwiy and all her henchmen.

But by the time he had reached the ground floor, he felt reason coming back to him, the old sense, familiar resolves and character, and the old curiosity and self-confidence. He entered the refectory and saw people again, and even if they were unspeaking, takers of vows of silence, it reassured him. He thought of Fellirian and her calmness, her steady pace, her quiet resolve to undergo this, she having many of the same misgivings as had he. The thought of his partner, insibling, co-spouse, mate, and rarely, lover, all sobered him. He suddenly found himself wishing to be free of the past, of memory. And of this suddenly uncertain future; to be resolved. He looked around and saw a few guests at their tables, all caught up in the rituals of silence in respect to the members of Granite Lodge, as well as the members themselves, a few of whom were-present. One was the cook, standing nonchalantly behind the serving counter and methodically frying sausages as if that were the most important task in the whole world. At that moment, Morlenden understood that it was just that, exactly and precisely.

He walked across the refectory and took up a position by the serving counter, holding a simple wooden bowl, wide and shallow. He also understood now that much speech was unnecessary; for to stand behind a counter with bowl in hand was as clear as speech; perhaps talk was what was unneeded, the idle rattling of acorns in a jar.

The cook piled his plate with a generous helping of sausages and flatcakes, nodding at the butter-jar close to hand, and proceeded on with his tasks. Morlenden helped himself, chose a table, and filled himself, knowing that he would have to walk all day on what he ate here. He reflected, as he sat and ate, that perhaps all the talk Sanjirmil had made about the members of Granite Lodge keeping secrets was indeed but an excuse, for the food was unsurpassingly excellent. That was a secret worth keeping. He looked again, and saw

that all within sight were well-fed, no doubt about it. He had
visions of great platters of roast dripping with gravy, tank-
ards of ale, and laughed inwardly to himself, thinking also of
what was expected of one in way of payment: meditation
upon the curious strictures of the Doctrine of Opposite. *Just
imagine*, he thought, *do that which you fear most; therein lies
freedom.* And then he thought again, and it did not seem so
curious after all. Perhaps he might yet have an entry to make
in the tomes of Granite Lodge. But however it went, he
resolved to bring the rest of them back here. At least for the
food. As for the rest, he was sure that only Cannialin would
actually like it. She loved quiet. Fellirian liked talk too much,
and Kal was hopeless.

Refreshed and mind more at ease, he left the table, setting
his bowl in a place set aside for them, and departed the refectory and the common-house, leaving behind some more coins
from his pouch on the way out. Yes, indeed, he thought. A
fine place to visit. And perhaps to live? He would have to
think on that. He loved talk no less than Fellirian.

Outside, the day was cold, overcast, and still drizzly. A vile
day for a long walk through the woods. But soon, he was on
his way again, covering the ground with his practiced pace
learned along many a path across the reservation. He followed paths now pressed into the fabric of the rainy damp
forest, the trees covered with a sparkling film of clear water,
dripping clear sweet droplets, the pines covered with silvery
luminescence.

He headed southwestward, and after not too long a time,
began to recognize familiar landmarks. Now, knowing a bit
better where he was, and being closer to home than he thought
he had been, he increased his pace as much as he could, considering the slipperiness of the path, now well-worn down to
bare earth. But throughout the gray day's passage, as he
walked through the empty woodlands and fields, the temporary sense of well-being he had gained gradually left him, to
be replaced by some of the uneasiness he had felt the night
before when he had been with Sanjirmil. Not the morning's
panic. No, not that. An uneasiness, and growing. But he began
to have some sense of apprehension, and by early afternoon
he was watching his back trail carefully, recalling the incidents
of the *yos* of the Perklarens and at the treehouse of Maellenkleth and Krisshantem. He saw nothing, heard nothing that he
could actually identify, detected no hard evidence whatsoever
of any follower lurking behind him or to the side, but he never

lost the feeling that he was being shadowed by someone expert at it, perhaps rivaling Kris in ability to track at a distance and still keep contact. Kris would not have exploited that talent; he would always approach directly, silently, but directly.

As he thought of it now, he realized that this intuition of being followed had begun not long after he had left Granite Lodge, and had continued, strengthening during the day. He began to keep closer to cover, attempting to conceal his location, trying to walk ever more silently. At first, these intentions had no measurable effect, but after a time the sensation of being followed did begin to decline a little. It neither eliminated it nor cured it, but merely reduced it; as if by being evasive he had broadened the area of probability about himself, and his shadow had withdrawn a bit, uncertain exactly where he was. Still, he felt followed.

The primary result of his efforts was direct and immediate; it made a long walk longer; and by the time he was truly back into what he considered his own territory, near the holding of the Derens, it was beginning to shade off toward darkness again. Late afternoon. The only consolation to him was that the rain and the intermittent drizzle had stopped. The ground was extremely slippery, here in the clay-and-hill flint country; red clay that stuck to one's boots when it was not threatening to trip one into a nasty fall. But the air was clear as spring water, washed, clean, sweet-smelling, and the overcast was breaking up. There were patches of luminous blue showing, and there was a lightning along the borders of the west, behind the Flint Mountains. It would be clear again by morning. And suddenly he noted that the sense of being followed had vanished as subtly as it had come, that it was gone, and had been for a considerable time. Fine, that. Perhaps it had been imagination after all, easily spooked by the incident of Sanjirmil's dream-speaking. Or perhaps he had lost his follower through all the detours he had taken. Ahead he saw—through the leatherleaf oaks, some still bearing browned leaves along their dark and twisted branches—his own outhouse, and beyond was the rise that hid the Deren *yos* from view from this direction. It made him feel a great deal more secure, although the logical part of his mind still persisted in reminding him that he was in reality no more secure here than he was anywhere else.

Morlenden detoured by the outhouse before turning down the hill to the *yos*, and, finished with his detour, was proceeding slowly down the slippery path, ruefully considering that after all he should indeed take the ritual wash down in the trough, and most assuredly it would be cold. He shivered at the thought of it. Perhaps he could lie to Fellirian, who would insist. No, that wouldn't work either; she'd spot that fast enough, call Kaldherman for help, and they'd pitch him in while Cannialin would stand to the side and laugh her laugh. But it was cold now. A freeze tonight for sure. Below, in the dooryard, beyond the pot holding the *yos*-tree, an over-age blackwillow, he caught sight of Fellirian and Pethmirvin walking slowly up to the *yos*, their breath steaming in the cold, damp air. Fellirian saw him, nudged Peth, and they both waved. Morlenden returned the wave, remembering to watch for his ancient enemy the root at the same time. There it was, and for once he had missed it, but in watching Fellirian and Pethmirvin, waving, and avoiding the root, he had misjudged his footing on the rain-slick path and the red clay, and began a ludicrous slip, now waving both arms wildly for balance. He thought in the midst of a most undignified escapade that he heard a sudden, sharp, woody noise close by, like a chop of an ax, but it was indeed a busy moment and he could not be sure. What was much more curious was the fact that he did not fall, but hung suspended, a strange happening indeed until he realized with a chill that he had been pinned to an oak by a large metal arrow, dully anodized into a vague greenish-brown color to make it blend into the background. Morlenden felt ice in his veins, for the arrow had passed through his clothing under one armpit and driven into the tree with such force that when Pethmirvin and Fellirian arrived, all three of them together could not pull it out. Morlenden worked free of it, and shortly afterward Kaldherman arrived. He returned to the shed behind the *yos*, retrieved a large machete they used against the always-encroaching brush about the *yos*, and immediately charged off into the brushy woods in the direction from which the arrow had come, following back along the shaft. That he found nothing, save some vague and scuffed tracks that shortly disappeared in the undergrowth, surprised no one.

TWELVE

. . . is there no place left for repentance, none for pardon left? None left but by submission; and that word disdain forbids me, and my dread of shame among the spirits beneath, whom I seduced with other promises and other vaunts than to submit, boasting I could subdue the omnipotent. Aye me! They little know how dearly I abide that boast so vain, under what torments inwardly I groan.

—Milton, *Paradise Lost*

They were all in Chairman Parleau's intimidating office, making small talk before the meeting got under way; Eykor was having one of his interminable low-grade arguments with Plattsman over the differences in functions between Security and Control, as well as the historical reasons for the rise of the latter at much of the expense of the former. Parleau took no active part in the argument, although from time to time he would goad one to make some audacious sally, which was immediately pounced upon by the other.

The heart of the discussion at this point lay in Eykor's accusation that over the years Control had actually usurped much of the best part of Security, namely, the prediction and anticipation of events warranting the use of deadly force. Plattsman was following the counterargument that the aim of Control, with its sophisticated statistical analyses, monitor stations, and status-reporting networks, was in fact to make the predictions so good and so accurate that corrective action was backed up from corrective, but coercive, force, to a "best trade-off" action taken this side of force. It might have been moot to say that the original object of the whole system of Control was to illuminate problems and cure them, a true bridge between managerial government and naked power politics.

Plattsman was saying, "Ultimately, we could not usurp Security, for we have, in plain fact, no troops."

"We are your troops, most of the time," replied Eykor.

257

"Symbiosis, then. Hands and eyes that work together. The ability of the hand to sense its field of action is limited to close field work—touch, heat detection. On the other hand, the eye sees and integrates, but can of itself take no action to implement its evaluations. It can't even evade a threat."

They could have continued much longer, and would have, but Parleau grew restive and waved them to a halt. He knew, of course, that Plattsman was basically correct in his analogy of hand and eye, but that he had left out several factors. One of these was that once Control had become firmly established, it began to evolve from an initial position of rather altruistic professionalism toward the self-perpetuations of the classical bureaucracy, thus lessening its true functional growth. Secondly, Control over the years had become vastly entangled in the manipulation of information for its own sake, and had, on several occasions, come perilously close to strangling itself on its own internal flow problems and turbulences. They had weathered these crises remarkably well, and their integrity was a watchword within the various regional departments. But Parleau was of the opinion that too much reliance was placed upon them; there had always been a requirement for "wetwork," as the jargon of the day put it. Parleau's own phrasing of it might have been, as he sometimes observed to his most trusted associates from the old days, "At the bottom line, you're always going to need some hard-faced bastard to kick the arses and take the names. There is simply no substitute for a good truncheon, a rubber hose, or perhaps a coat hanger, applied with a will and decided upon unhesitatingly." Security filled that requirement commendably, although it could often be denounced for excesses of zeal. And its requests for manpower were simply not to be believed!

Parleau motioned for them to begin. All those present shuffled papers, rearranged their notes, made their positions ready, moved restlessly in their seats, then fell quiet. Plattsman would be first, of course. He had the data they had been waiting for, or so they hoped and had been led to believe. Plattsman had sheaves and sheaves of machine-print reports and summaries, analyses and conclusions.

Plattsman began, "Well. Monitors in the office of one W. Vance, Institute Director, recorded a conversation between Vance and a Hando Errat, apparently of Continental, their subject being a representation of the girl who was picked up in the vandalism case."

Something stirred in Parleau's mind then, about Errat. He

had heard that name before, but he couldn't place it. Had it been at Continental? He tried to remember, but the expression on Eykor's face distracted him, and he lost it. No matter, they could follow it later. What interest did Continental have in this?

Plattsman paused slightly, to be sure he had their attention with his use of the word "vandalism" when Eykor had called it "terrorism" from the beginning. Then he continued, "Shortly thereafter, Vance solicited assistance from one Doctor Harkle, head of Research and Development. She recalled the girl immediately, and this data was reported upchannel. We also were able to capture a disprint of the repro, and it matches the girl."

Parleau interjected, "Was this recorded? Did you run a check on this Errat?"

Plattsman hesitated, then replied, "No, Chairman, no record was made. We had been overseeing Vance somewhat earlier, and the tap had been taken off. There was still sampling being conducted, but it was being run on a priority-five basis, which is 'no recorders.' We were extremely lucky to get this, as it was. Indeed, were it not for some quick thinking, with the disprint equipment, we wouldn't have been able to match the girl up. It was only uncovered for a few minutes."

"Naturally, no disprint of Errat."

"We didn't get one. By the time our monitor realized what was happening, Errat was gone. We did check with Continental Control, but they could not discuss the matter over an open line. Referred us to Section Q, Denver. We did not press the matter."

"I understand." Indeed Parleau did understand. People who asked questions of Section Q were asked questions by "the Q" and then faded away from sight.

Something was still nagging at Parleau's mind, but now Plattsman continued, "Pertinent data follows: the subject is one Maellenkleth Srith Perklaren, age twenty; sex, female. She was a part-time research assistant in the Math Department, then R and D. She was, according to evaluations we have been able to obtain, of a tendency to be somewhat abstracted and distant, but competent. She appears to have been shy and retiring, but withal, cooperative and pleasant. There was one uncorroborated entry about family problems, but we were unable to determine their nature. She is listed in the Institute personnel records as being an insibling in their family reference."

Plattsman stopped, and Parleau looked up, expecting more. This was what Plattsman called a meeting for? He asked Eykor, "Is that all? What does Security have?"

Eykor said, "We didn't think we'd find anything, because we don't get into reservation business. I would like to have chased down her family relationship, and all that crap, but we ran a routine check of our own stuff to see if there was any correlation. We found nothing on this one, but we did find in the records a reference, indeed a file, on another, who was listed only initially as Perklaren, M.S., in the space program, if you can believe that. We went further into it, actually physically dug out the fiche files. This one was called Mevlannen Srith Perklaren, and from the photo we determined that they are not the same person. The Perklaren that Security found is also a ler female, now has a security clearance of Level Four, Access type B, ratings excellent. Performance has been rated as 'outstanding and innovative.' Assigned to Team Trojan Eye. She is normally located about the West Coast Test Range, or actually in space. I cross-referred with Control and we were able to pinpoint her location as on the ground at present. Additionally, we were able to insert a request to keep her there for the time being. Distraction and excuses. We could bring her in easily enough."

"What does this Perklaren do?"

"Apprentice free-fall structural technician, and optics specialist."

Klyten laughed. "Now there's one for you! A ler in optics. Might as well find an amputee employed as a pavement-breaker, handling a chipperstripper!"

Everyone turned and stared at Klyten. He recovered his academic composure and explained, "They are rather notorious for having what we consider to be poor eyesight. The ler retina is almost totally comprised of cone cells. They have an extreme degree of color acuity, but less capability of resolution; and of course they are severely handicapped in light levels of semidarkness, where a human would see quite well, if primarily in monotone. They compensate for this by having more kinds of cone cells, and a broadened spectrum that includes, so I understand, two distinct 'colors' below what we call red and one in the near ultraviolet, but it doesn't help them much. So one working as an optician, building a telescope, is really something. You know, on the ground, here on Earth, they are reputed to have great difficulty seeing anything in the night sky below Magnitude three, rarely four. That's why I laughed: she's working under a severe handicap."

Parleau observed, "She must also be very good at what she does to work under it and still produce results. Is there any connection between her and the girl we caught?"

Klyten answered, "The custom in naming is that the names don't repeat. Each person carries a name that is unique and meaningful, if somewhat fanciful and exotic for my taste. They try to run seven generations before repeating a proper name. As for the surnames, they don't repeat either. Each surname of a family group relates to an occupation, and if they have more than one such group in an activity, they prefix a number to the name root. According to what I have in my files, the names 'Klaren' would equate to, well, 'Player.' But they have two such family groups, so the older is called Perklaren, 'First-player,' and the second, Terklaren, 'Second-player.' Now since neither name repeats, and we have two who are the same, then they are in the same group. Properly speaking, they don't use surnames once they graduate to elder status, so these would have to be in the same generation. Eykor, what was your girl's age?"

"Twenty."

"Then they are insiblings to one another. Hm. . . . But that would mean that their family group, or Braid, as they call it, has two insiblings of the same sex, unless there was a twinning we don't know about. This could be the source of the family problems."

Parleau said, "How so? I don't understand."

Klyten replied, "The tradition is that the insiblings marry, or weave, if you'd rather, each other."

"That would be incest," observed Parleau.

"Perhaps. Depends on your definitions. But it's not, genetically; the insiblings have different parents, completely, and are not related at all, as we would call it, even though they are raised together, if anything, more closely than the usual brother-sister relationship. But now, in this case, it would appear to follow the condition they call *Polhovemosi*: 'sexed-out.' If the insiblings are of the same sex, then the Braid ends and all must weave into other Braids in the outsibling position. They lose a lot: status, continuity with the past, tradition. These things are highly valued among them. To lose one's family-group role is one of the unkindest blows."

Eykor observed, "Well, I suppose that's interesting enough,

but not of very much use to us, here. Is there anything worth digging into in their surname?"

And Parleau added, as an afterthought, "And how about the connection between Maellenkleth the Player and Maellenkleth the vandal? If she resented her situation, as well it appars she might from what you say, then why didn't she vandalize something of her own people's? After all, we didn't make up their cultural strictures for them."

Eykor said, "It would appear that at least one of them harbored no resentments, at least visibly. Her ratings were impressive, and doubly so, when you consider Klyten's dissertation on ler eyesight."

Klyten answered, "It is true what you guess by instinct, that their family groups tend to be very homogenous in their value systems; that the one is an achiever probably doesn't mean that the other would be, but it does argue against her being a vandal.... But these are only probabilities, not oracles or predictions. What say you, Plattsman, for Control?"

"As always, that we need more data. Basically, I agree, but vandalism is an intricate structure, and I should like to know more about the girl, her matrix, internal values of the class of which she belongs. I don't know if we can project the human family structure or sexual values onto them with any accuracy either. Need some work, there, back in the vaults."

Klyten nodded, as if his suspicions had been confirmed, and began to feel his way into Eykor's question, which had almost been forgotten. What, indeed, was in the surname? He said, "I said that every Braid has a role or profession, which is indicated by the name. In the case of the two Player groups, that is what they do—play a Game. It is a very curious matter, just another of their oddities."

Up until this time, Parleau had been somewhat disengaged, aloof from the flow of the remarks, but now his interest deepened. "They play a Game?"

"Well, yes, it is peculiar, full of all kinds of anomalies; it seems that they have, included in their social order, two families whose role is exactly that, to play a Game in public exhibitions. But as we understand the term, professional sportsmen somehow seems inappropriate to this. You see, it happens to be the only organized sport they have, played with formal rules and organized teams. Without exception, all of the rest of their games are informal and very unstructured, more like traditional children's games than anything else,

What's more, it, this Game, is not played on a field or a court, but on a portable electronic display panel. This, mind, in a culture that almost never uses electric power or electronics."

Parleau raised his eyebrows, and opened his mouth to speak, but Plattsman contributed before he could, "We have also studied this game, in Control, and what Klyten says is true. Their board is both portable and durable, apparently has an independent power supply, and is extremely reliable. At the least, they have never had a breakdown during a public Game. We can deduce that a computer has been integrated into its structure, although we cannot as yet specifically locate its position within the machine."

Parleau leaned back in his chair, reflectively. He mused, aloud, "No breakdowns in public is not so hard to attain with good mechanics, engineers, and tight scheduling. And as for where the switching and logic and memory units would be— good, tight design could work it into almost any volume you could care to mention."

Plattsman replied, looking at the chairman's shiny forehead. "I understand, Chairman. That's all true. What Klyten is trying to point out, and I as well, is that this is occurring, over a period of generations, within a culture that suppresses technology, particularly electronic technology, as we know it."

Klyten put in, before Parleau could think of some rationalization, "*And* a formal Game with elaborate rules and rigid operations in a culture that plays unstructured children's games that occur spontaneously. Now consider this, too: this inside a conceptual Surround in which every family group has a functional occupation, a necessity to society. The Players do nothing, aside from some low-level self-support, except play the Game."

Parleau returned to a normal position, then leaned forward, his heavy arms and hands pressed flat on the surface on his desk. He said, "Every Braid supports and contributes to the whole, but the Players are, in effect, subsidized?"

"Exactly," said Klyten.

Plattsman added, "We don't have access to their macroeconomics, but by the models in the studies that have been done using offset simulations, it would appear that considerable cost is involved."

Klyten added more. "And that is verified by their whole value system. Marginal activities—for example, arts—exist in quantity, but only as sidelines. In fact, there is an extremely sophisticated management system integrated at the popular culture level that simply eliminates occupations that don't contribute, no matter how attractive they might be. And this management system is as hard to pin down as the location of the computer in their Game display board. We know that the function must exist, but no one yet has located it. There is also some consideration of the idea that the vast majority of the ler people themselves are unaware of this system. They fit into it so harmoniously. . . ."

Parleau knotted his brows. "This is hard for me to say, because I never believed that I'd ever find myself saying it. What you are saying by all your remarks, is that in fact these woods-bound rustics actually operate a . . . nation, with almost no visible government, at a greater efficiency and with less friction than we do."

Klyten answered, "So it appears. These facts have been known for years, of course, but it is so low-key that nobody ever assembled it before. This explains much—how they can operate the reservation at a profit, not counting what the Institute brings in, and it also explains the true source of the product of the Institute, and the data they feed us."

Parleau reflected, and said, "So they are, in effect, feeding us off the top of their system?"

Eykor interjected angrily, "Programming us, I'd call it!"

Parleau looked blandly and without rancor at the chief of Security. "There's no denying that if they are, it's been to the general welfare. I say, if it works, then let it be. Unless Control can project some nefarious purpose in these manipulations."

Plattsman said, "Control until this minute was unaware that we were being manipulated. And I hardly see evidence of detail work, the kind that would be necessary to bring us to some point desirable to them. But I'll certainly send this through Research, to see if we can prove it, and if so, find out where it's going." He spoke slowly, as if unwilling to believe the implications of what they had uncovered here: Control was totally unaware that a more subtle system was probably being applied to them all, a macrosystem involving—and here Plattsman's mind took a giant, risk-filled leap across normal deductive logic—yes, very likely the large-scale nudging and controlling of the whole damn planet! And for what purpose? As Parleau had most accurately put it, "to the general welfare." That could not be denied. He added, as an afterthought, "Yes, I'll have those crazies down in Games-Theory Branch get cracking on it right away."

Parleau nodded approval, and said, "I want to hear about that girl and this Game they play. How old is it?"

Klyten answered, "According to the annals, the Game appeared coincident with the move into the reservation. It seems to be tied up deeply in the popular religion, a kind of movable morality play. They have factions, rivalries, the whole thing. It is very Byzantine, and the fine points are shrouded in layers of allegorical nonsense."

Parleau observed, "So they sublimate aggression into sports? That's nothing new. We've done that, ourselves, for aeons."

Klyten persisted, "No, no, it's that there is an aggression present within the Game that isn't present anywhere else. Literally. And by no means does it reach all the people. In fact, on the whole, the people are rather uninterested in it. Less than half even bother with it in any degree and the number of real fans is probably less than ten percent, counting the Players themselves."

The data made no more sense to Parleau than it did to anyone else. He pondered on that for a moment, then asked, "Well, what in hell is this Game? We're talking about another of these things we can't see, or are we fishing in the dark there, too?" A sudden light had been illuminated in Parleau's mind. If he could but penetrate into this system, which he sensed was part of a larger, elaborate plan, then by opening it up, he would pave his way, beyond Denver. If he could only prod these blockheads to find the answers. Yes. Suddenly merely surviving his assignment to Seaboard South seemed petty, unvisioned, lacking scope.

Plattsman said, "It's a recursive system. . . ."

Klyten added, interrupting the Controller, "Yes, recursive. The Game itself, as we see it, appears to be very distantly related to chess, or checkers, but of course it is almost inconceivably more complex than either of those examples. It is manifestly difficult even to try to describe it. . . . They normally play on a two-dimensional field, which can be divided at will into one of several tiling arrays: triangles, squares, and hexagons, those being equilateral and regular, and also quite a number of irregular pentagons and hexagons. These divide the field up into cells. Inside the cell, one can have a number of conditions, ranging from binary on-off two-state on up. I don't think there is a limit to the number of states a cell can have, although obviously there are some practical limits. The Game begins with some simple, and I use this word guardedly in this context, patterns of states in cells . . . a move in the Game, or a time-component unit, is the sum of all the changes produced by considering each cell, serially, in relation to a surrounding number of cells, sometimes by raw sum, and sometimes by position of cells of different state arrayed about the referent cell. This neighborhood can also be varied, from close in to far away. Then they apply transition rules, some statistical, some arbitrary, and make the changes. When all the cells have been processed according to the program, then the whole changes and they start over again. The object of the Game appears to attain certain desirable configurations in shape and color and dynamics, while the opposing team tries to manipulate certain parts of the rules and other factors to prevent it; but they, too, operate under elaborate rules covering what they can do."

Plattsman contributed, "You have to understand recursive math to comprehend the Game."

Klyten added one more thought, "We think that this is why they evolved their cumbersome number system of variable-numbers with no permanent fixed base, as our decimal system. It makes it easier to understand the Game, when you have to or want to, in the case of the spectators."

Plattsman continued, "We in Control have tried to explore recursive systems also, because the concept is deeply tied up with decision-making, controlling functions, and programming. The concept was first worked out in the twentieth century, about the middle, if I have my history straight. There was an extensive literature on the subject well into the twenty-first century."

Klyten said, "They were playing random-start Games even then: just fill it up, more or less randomly, and watch it evolve."

Plattsman counterpointed, "But simple Games with unchanging rules and neighborhoods. Most people played on computers when they could get access, but a few fanatics were known to play it on graph paper, some of which they had to have specially printed for the purpose. Absolute maniacs!"

Parleau asked, "Why the difference?"

Plattsman answered, "The computer-players could see the motion and the patterns of change, and spot productive patterns faster, but the graph-paper players, while vastly slowed down by the need to run every single step in the program manually, were able to see farther into the scope of it, and the things it could lead to. Eventually, however, they were also forced into computers by the sheer volume of transactions, but they used the computers only as working aids. All ongoing work in the Game tended to originate from the minority Graphists, and what we know from the Archives indicates that the ler built upon one particularly active Graphist faction—one could almost call it a cult—that was active in the latter third of the twentieth century."

Parleau shook his head exaggeratedly from side to side. He sighed, looked at the ceiling, scratched his neck, and returned his attention to the group. "Tell me no more! I do not wish to become one of these Players—just relate this unknown girl to what she was doing and why, and why she insisted upon withdrawing into herself rather than answer a few simple questions. I will accept your description of things as provisionally accurate in substance, although I admit to imcomprehension. By what means do they control the display?"

Klyten said, "By a keyboard, something rather like an organ of the old days."

"I fail to see why they would devote so much energy to something that demonstrably produces no results. What *is* the use of it?"

Klyten observed, "We have been unable to determine that. Obviously it is of great importance to them, and nobody thinks that its sole purpose is entertainment. I mean, after all, the Players have a certain regard, an exclusiveness, but hardly are they lionized as popular figures."

Plattsman offered, "Chairman, we have some tapes of some Games material, if you would like to see them. It makes more sense if you can see it in action, perceive the motion in it."

"Yes, by all means," said Parleau. "I would like very much to see this Game. Perhaps we can all learn something from it. You have prepared recordings?"

Plattsman replied, "We have an extensive file of them, Chairman. Control has been studying the Game for many years. From that, we have selected what appears to be a typical, although short, round of a Game."

Klyten added, "This recording was made a few years ago, at their Solstice Tournaments. I have it on the good word of those who claim to be authoritative on such matters that this particular Game is a classic of its type, but is rather short in duration. The curtuosity here is after the manner of chamber music, rather than oratorios, symphonies, and grand operas. We mutually apologize, Plattsman and I, for the lack of sound, but none had been thought necessary, since the play is almost exclusively visual as medium."

Plattsman motioned to an unseen operator. The office dimmed, a section of the far wall opened, and the panels slid back into cleverly hidden recesses in the walls, revealing a softly glowing screen occupying most of the space between floor and ceiling. After an uncertain pause, the screen flickered, flashed bright momentarily, then went completely dark. Then gradually a moving series of images began to fade in, growing in brightness and contrast until it seemed natural to the viewers' dark-adapting eyesight.

The screen showed an open space in the forest, a pleasantly bucolic environment, a natural depression that had been subtly modified into an amphitheater. The show was in color, and though it appeared from the light within to be evening, there was no fading or overexposure; they saw as if they were there. They watched and became absorbed in it. It was a summer evening, deep evening shades and shadows in the small gathering-place of the Players and their audience; they sensed, rather than saw, that somewhere offscreen the sun was yet in the sky; nevertheless it was evening, not merely late afternoon. A subdued, middling crowd was present, all ler, at least as far as could be seen. Some wore summer clothing, light overshirts, loose robelike affairs, which were the everyday, general-purpose ler garment; others wore a garment suggesting a kimono, but with the belt or sash looped and hung loosely over one hip or the other. Many of the younger ones present wore only a saronglike wraparound about their lower bodies, leaving their chests and abdomens bare, while the ends of it fell to their ankles. Even then, with the identical haircuts, it was difficult at first glance to tell boy from girl, to Parleau's eye. You simply could not differentiate. . . . Only if he picked one and watched it for some time could he determine which sex it belonged to. It was as if the whole secret of defining lay in dynamics and motions, rather than in states-of-being, a disturbing notion indeed. He watched what he believed to be a boy, who was engaged in teasing, very subtly, what appeared to be a girl. What was it, the difference? She seemed softer, more delicate, smoother perhaps. He couldn't say just what it was. The way she moved, smiled? They were both trying to appear most serious

and attentive, but of course it was a summer evening, warm
and scented, and their minds were elsewhere, as well they
might have been, with the soft shadows falling across the
leafy little glade. The one who had recorded this little drama
unawares had not even been observing the boy and the girl,
for in the image they both were far off-center, and as Game
time came closer, he lost them entirely, expanding the image
and zooming closer to take in the display board and the Players.

The board itself was a large, square unit, supported on a
simple, broad base, completely unadorned. It looked simple,
but in no way did this display board suggest primitiveness, or
crudity; to the contrary, it seemed the product of a highly
professional technological civilization. Before it was a small,
desklike console, furnished with several rows of buttons,
while to either side were two larger consoles with imposing
multiplex keyboards, which resembled organ consoles more
than they did anything else. The Players were already in
place, the Reds to the right and the Blues to the left, two
Players by each console, and two more behind them. An announcer, was addressing the crowd, apparently in a most
relaxed, easygoing manner, as if he (or she—Parleau could
not tell) were among friends and acquaintances.

The announcer finished whatever remarks were required,
and then retired offstage with a flirty little flourish, to be replaced by a stern and imposing couple, elders by the look of
them and the twin long pigtails of iron-gray hair that hung
down the fronts of their garments. Their color was dark; Parleau thought black, although he could not be sure ... the
light of day was slowly fading in the recording. These would
be the referees. They made no speeches or gestures to the
spectators, but turned to the center console and one of them
made a chopping motion with his hand. And on the board,
immediately appeared a preliminary figure, a mildly complex
geometrical figure in five colors. It stayed in place a moment,
winked out, and then reappeared.

The whole board shimmered, came alive, changed to a
hexagonal cellular array, retaining the figure as well as it
could be accommodated into the new matrix; a series of inde-
cipherable symbols began flowing across the top of the
screen, and the figure began changing rapidly, evolving into
different shapes and densities as the initial moves of the
Game proceeded. Parleau watched in attentive astonishment,
riveted to his plush chair, as the figure first lost all its color,

becoming black against the illuminated background, and then abruptly began to change shape, colors flowing over it like firelight flickering over a wall, or perhaps summer lightning. The most basic color appeared to be green, and it seemed that the Reds were trying to control the figure and manipulate it into other shapes, desired configurations, while at the same time, the Blues, just as tenaciously, attempted to hinder this operation and tried to arrange things so that the developing figure would fly apart and dismember itself. The symbols flowing across the top of the screen changed constantly; scoring? A running commentary while the game was in progress?

At first, despite the interference of the Blues, the Reds seemed to be having the better of it; they manipulated the vibrating figure into a larger shape that seemed more impervious to attack, but this lasted only minutes. Soon, Blue attacked with increased zeal and dedication, their centers laboring mightily over the keyboards, arms and heads blurred in motion, moving faster than the scan rate of the recording device. Soon, the advances of the Reds were blunted, dissipated, brought to a halt. Parleau looked back to the Reds: they were playing, if anything, with even more vigor than the Blues, and as they occasionally turned, he could see that the expressions of intense concentration, indeed, they grimaced with effort.

Suddenly, a foul was called on Blue, and the referees engaged their controls; the Blues were forced to sit helpless for a measured time, their keyboard locked out, while the Reds advanced and rebuilt their figure into an impressively complex configuration. But when they returned, they reentered the Game furious with zeal, and by dint of extreme effort and a brilliant, virtuoso attack, forced the Reds to give up much they had gained, and in fact, as Parleau remembered, forced them to return to an earlier configuration. A foul was now called on Red, and now they also had to sit helplessly aside while Blue, with glee, dismembered the complex figure. But returning, they did not give up, were not routed, and hung on gamely. The Reds began to advance again, slower now than before, but inexorable, like the tide coming in. Blue sensed that there was nothing to be gained by further delay, and they changed the array to square cells, and after a moment, to the triangular lattice, all apparently in an effort to disorient Red and keep them off balance. At first, it seemed to succeed. Red seemed to lose momentum and drift, uncertain of what to do next. Parleau, now indeed caught up in the swirling patterns of the Game, sensed that this had been a reasonable course on the part of Blue, for Red had, he sensed, been gaining, if slowly. Perhaps this could lead to a stalemate, which would of course favor the defending Blues. But soon it became apparent that the maneuver was to be unsuccessful, for Red was still gaining. They had ridden with the attack, drifted with the changing current, and were now fully in possession of the field again. Blue riposted by a move of desperation, changing the field to a beautifully weird pentagonal tesselation, the cells irregular polygons, and after a moment, back to the square grid. But it appeared to be too late, this rearguard action; the audience was waving little red pennants, while partisans of the Blues stood about glumly, their heads lowered, expecting the worst.

It was not long in coming: in an amazing tour de force, Red finally manipulated the figure somehow into an astonishing and enigmatic shape, one which hung on the display board screen for a long time, emitting coherent sparks and particles that fled to the edges and vanished. Across the top of the board, the cryptic symbols flowed on for a moment, as if they had fallen behind the action, and then they stopped, abruptly, and without warning the board went blank, dimmed, and went out. Red partisans and their friends waved their pennants and applauded, rather restrainedly, while Blue fans began to walk away, dejected and expressionless. Some, however, despite their loss, also joined in the subdued approval, showing that they could appreciate a good Game, even if their team had lost. One of the centers of the Red team turned from the console and made a short speech. The view expanded, as if the operator had wished to take in more of the crowd; Parleau looked for the boy and girl he had noticed earlier, but they were almost conspicuously absent. The screen went blank. . . .

Parleau breathed deeply, once. The rest said and did nothing.

After a time, he asked, "Control, what can you tell us about that particular Game?"

"We can set up simplex sequences back in the labs; that is, Games with unchanging parameters. Now, this one you just saw," said Plattsman, "escapes detailed analysis. We think that this one was held to a minimum deliberately, probably varying between three-state and, say, fifteen-to-twenty-state for an upper limit. They use color to symbolize states; in some of the higher-order games, this can get serious, because they have greater color-discrimination than we do. The grid changes you saw yourself. By and large, most cellular arrays are pretty straightforward—equilateral triangles, squares, hexagons. But the pentagonal arrays are all irregular and have some tricky rules; the neighborhood can vary, even when it's at minimum closest to the reference cell. And the rules! Here is where we really are at sea! We think that none of those remained stable for more than a few moves, two to three. We have to deduce it by effect. They used to say, back in the old days, that one insurgent could tie down ten regulars; it's the same ratio here: to compute backward takes about ten times the number of computations, and without long time-strings of steady states of rules, that does us no good. The rules are never symmetrical with respect to time—they only work as rules one way. When you try to work them backward and figure back, you get an uncertainty factor. . . ."

Parleau exclaimed, "Jesus!" He reverted to ancient oaths, and they came easily, even though most people had forgotten the reason why they had been originally said. "Why hasn't someone been working on this longer, brought it up at Staff? All you have to do is look at that equipment and look at what they do with it. Those people are about as primitive as Buckminster Fuller!"

Plattsman said, "We had been trying to come to some conclusion about where the activity was leading . . . so far, it has defied all attempts to vector it."

"How long?" Parleau insisted.

"About . . . ah, since the Game appeared, Chairman."

"And nothing?"

"Nothing. It doesn't change in any manner we can measure. It appeared, and we took sample recordings, and attempted to analyze them. Inasmuch as we have been able to determine, the sole difference between a Game of say, last summer, and one of a hundred years ago, is the same as between any two Games out of the same cycle: individual variation and style of the moment, you know, personal variations."

"And you can't conclude from that?"

Plattsman answered shamefully, "No, sir, we haven't to date."

Parleau leaned forward, and added projection to his voice: "Well, I'm no Controller, but I can see of that remark that, if it is true, what you are seeing is a finished product, an artifact! Sports as we know them continuously evolve and shift, because they are responding to changing needs of the people who play and watch them. But your people, who are the masters of the science of change, can see no change in this Game, and you're stymied! That's the great secret! The Game doesn't change! You idiots, what does it conceal?"

Plattsman hesitated. "I don't understand. . . ."

"That's why I'm chairman and you're a Controller! An artifact doesn't change—*it's the end of the process*! They do something with it that has nothing to do with sports or entertainment or bleeding off aggression. Now what is it?"

Plattsman said, "We pursued that angle early, Chairman. That was the first thing we thought of, just as you did. Now this Game does have fine possibilities for a system of processing information, but it seems like an awful lot of elaboration, and a lot of calling attention to themselves when they could certainly be more secretive about it. I mean, it's like using a code—in some circumstances, that just alerts people to the fact that you have something to hide. Now a code can give you security, but you want the parameter of speed and reliability also in any information-flow system, and the use of codes lowers both, in some cases appreciably."

Klyten helped Plattsman. "The speed of the responses of the Players, and the actions they take, indicate that whatever messages are concealed in it apply to them. The crowds apparently see no more than we did, that one side or the other gains or loses control of the shape of the figure they are working."

Plattsman agreed, nodding his head vigorously, and Klyten continued, "And you have to remember that those Players are raised on a diet of that practically from birth. They get serious about it at around age fourteen, as I understand. By the time they are playing in tournaments, they've all had at least twenty years of it, more. Plus a lot of theory that we don't ever see; they release nothing about the Game or recursive mathematics through the Institute . . . they won't even acknowledge its existence."

Parleau's earlier attack seemed to lose direction now. He seemed stopped in his tracks by the fact that the Controllers had asked the same question he had, years before, and had seen nothing in it but an unchanging Game. . . . He said, "That's another aspect of this that bothers me; exactly that. The long time they spend learning it. How do they maintain motivation? Say what you will about training, about ability, about privilege, I can still see that that stuff doesn't come easy for them, no more than it would be for us. Those Players in the recording were working hard! How much exposure do they get?"

Klyten answered, "They have the great tournaments at the Summer Solstices. Lesser Games are played throughout the warm months. Technically, the Game runs from spring equinox to autumnal."

"And that's all they have to do?"

"That's correct, Chairman."

"Then they are only employed six months of the year? That's the damndest thing I ever heard!"

Klyten said, "Well, it's not entirely without precedent: their ruling Braid, the Revens, does almost nothing. Their role is to arbitrate disputes, but very little ever gets taken to them, so they *do* almost nothing. . . ."

"But they symbolize authority, nationhood, and all that, like the hereditary kings of old."

"Yes, Chairman, that's true, but you have to bear in mind that if they are following the royal-dynasty model, they are doing so without any of the traditional symbols of royalty; they have no ceremony, no 'court,' no deference. When he is not 'in his role,' as they say, the High Reven is a dirt farmer, just like the lowest."

Parleau said, "So this Mallenkleth . . ."

"*Mael*lenkleth," Klyten corrected, changing the broad, open *ah*-sound Parleau had used to a shorter, flatter sound, something intermediate between an "A" and an "E," but without the nasal quality of the North American Modanglic "ae."

"What's the difference?"

" 'Mal' means 'bad,' 'Mael' means 'Apple.' There's a difference."

"You're the expert. So, then, this insibling of a Braid of Gameplayers."

Plattsman and Eykor answered together, "Right!"

Parleau continued, "And a mathemetician with the Department of Research and Development at the Institute, and a captured 'vandal' who elects somehow to disappear inside herself rather than reveal one single word? And now she's gone and we can't ask her anything? Damn! I'd really like to know if there is any connection. So now we all know some things, but not which is relevant among them."

Klyten said, "We had hoped that these recordings of Game

phenomena would suggest something to you that none of us had seen before. We have all tried, in our way, beforetimes, but there was nothing. . . . No one ever paid much attention to the Game before, other than cursorily. And here, we got the criminal, as they say, red-handed at the scene of the crime. But no motive. A great anomaly. It's obvious that . . ."

Eykor interjected, "Obvious that they're up to something. Otherwise, all that we've heard still adds up to nothing. No other way! And now I must needs ask the learned doctor of the mysteries of the New Humans another question: what exactly is this stuff they call 'Multispeech,' anyway?"

Klyten looked about, sharply. "Why do you ask?"

"Our monitor facilities seem to be picking up a lot more of it now. Significant statistically."

Klyten said, "Little enough is known of it. They talk freely enough in their everyday language. Singlespeech. It's just another language, far as I know, if it is a bit more regular than most, and of course it has its difficult parts for one to learn. But now Multispeech . . . perhaps multichannel language would be a better term. It is something different, a new concept. Now we express ourselves multiplexually, too, but the media are different; ordinary voice, a broad, harmonic system. Then there is body-language. And there is the frequency-modulated fail-alarm system present in our voices all the time. It's just a tone that's always present in your voice, you never *hear* it. Nervous system to nervous system, direct. Until you have anxiety. Then the tone drops out and your voice flattens a bit to the ear. When you hear loss of safe-tone, you also lose safe-tone until you discover the source of the anxiety. Even infants respond to it. It has uses in verificiation interviews. Now, what has apparently happened in the ler brain is that they combine all three systems into one channel of communication, via sound waves modulated by the larynx, and their resonances are so arranged that they can control the individual harmonic bands of the sound, modulate them individually. We know they can communicate with it, but we don't know all that much of what they can do with it . . . we have some studies indicating that in Multispeech the data-rate drops. In other words, it takes longer to say the same thing. Quite a bit longer. So we can deduce that speed is not one of the reasons for using it."

Plattsman commented, "Wrong, there, Klyten, though I hate to say it. Communications systems are the heart of Controlling, and we know very well that we will gladly sacrifice speed for accuracy, because in a system that programs noise and semantic distortions out, the resultant lack of misunderstanding and the increase in clarity means an ultimate increase of speed in the end."

"That's no news! We already know that the principle applies to Singlespeech, which has a rather slower data rate than any modern, historic language. It's slower than Modanglic by far."

"Then why have they exploited the ability? It must be that much more accurate. And it may have other uses. Communications systems do more than pass words, you know."

"We know little about it. They tell us nothing more than that they can talk to three people at once, saying different things . . . we don't even know how different the texts are."

"Have you correlated Multispeech to specific activities?"

Klyten replied, "It is used extensively in playing the Games, but precisely what part it plays, we cannot determine."

Parleau snorted, "Hmpf! The further we go, the more we find that someone ought to have been looking into. What *have* you people been doing all these years? Writing evaluations of evaluations?"

Klyten said, thoughtfully, after a longish pause, "Perhaps, Chairman, these things we are just now turning up fit somehow into a picture that we were never supposed to see, and that this is the reason why the girl allowed herself to reach the condition she was found in, in the box."

Parleau answered, "That's possible. But in essence, we observe what people do and predict therefrom; not why they do it. After all, once you start asking why, all kinds of speculative Pandoras open up. . . . But if we assume that there was a plot, it can only be that others were in it; and if the girl allowed herself to be reduced to gibbering, slobbering idiocy to prevent us from making certain associations . . . then those associations must exist. I think we have parts of a picture now."

Plattsman interjected, "Or an unfinished map."

"Very perceptive, that difference," agreed Parleau. "But we are also in a bit of a bind ourselves in this. We cannot act precipitately. They keep a much closer rein on this Region than I ever saw at Mojave. We could move first, of course. I mean, execute a Two-twelve, full occupation, tomorrow. But we do not at this point know what we are looking for, or where to look for it. Hell, it could be nothing more tangible than an idea; and an ignorant execution of the occupation would in those circumstances amount to destruction or removal of any evidence or artifacts. For the labor we'd get nothing, and we'd spend the rest of our days explaining why we took the action to Section Q. So we can't act now, however attractive it might seem, working on no more than we have. Disconnected anomalies that's paranoia."

Eykor added, saturninely, "Sometimes even paranoids have flesh-and-blood enemies." He paused a moment, then said, "We in Security know that there is something to hide. Give me a little time, and I can document it, and possibly locate it."

Parleau stared at Eykor, as if he had not heard him. "So granted."

Plattsman interrupted. "Pardon me, but I am receiving a signal. May I retire for a moment?"

"Certainly," said Parleau.

He left the office hurriedly, but he was not gone from it for long. Plattsman returned, saying, "Well, news, of a sort. Not what we might have expected, but something."

"Go ahead."

"Our monitors report that Vance just entertained a group in his office. There was a reference there to an earlier conversation, which we must have missed; they could find no record of it. Probably was in a desensitized area. Anyway, this group claims to have taken a commission to locate a girl. Maellenkleth by name, and they asked for an introduction to Region Security, for assistance. Vance has forwarded them here, per request."

Eykor asked, "According to instructions?"

"Oh, indeed. Vance has become docile enough, and cooperates freely now."

Eykor chortled, "Wonderful, wonderful! A nibble at the bait, so it is, and soon, too. Great concern, within the plot. And who are our nibblers?"

"In the course of the conversation with Vance, they were identified, apparently he knew some of them personally. There are three: a Fellirian Deren, a Morlenden Deren, and the third was identified only as a Krisshantem. No surname. Vance did not know him."

Klyten said, "He gave no surname? None at all?"

Plattsman answered, "Well, I have only the report to go on, but none was listed. They are pretty thorough and if he had given one, it would have been forwarded."

"A curious matter, no surname. Everyone uses one, even elders, who style themselves with the surnames Tlanh or Srith as befits their gender, or rather former gender. We usually translate it 'lord' or 'lady,' as fits, but I suspect we miss something of the flavor. . . . Could be he didn't want anyone to know what it was."

Eykor said, "As if he were a Player. . . ."

Parleau asked, "What is the probability of Vance being in a plot with them, here?"

Plattsman replied, "Low. Lower than twenty percent correlation. As for the others, we are not so sure. The female Fellirian Deren was cleared previously; she is a long associate of Vance's in the Institute."

Klyten added, "By the names, the one called Morlenden is the familial co-spouse of Fellirian, although we can't see the exact relationship. If she is clear, he probably is also. But the other one, this Krisshantem. He could be anything. It certainly is possible that he could be, as Eykor suggests, a Player, or one of the plot, but it is also true that he could be in another relationship, either with the girl, or with the Derens, or something else, a specialist of some sort. We have no way of knowing, short of interrogation."

Parleau said, "I cannot permit that at this time, not after our loss of the girl."

Eykor commented, "Loss, perhaps, but look at what that loss has led us to."

Parleau answered, "Yes, I see what it has led us to: anomalies and more questions than we were asking at the start! So I direct that they be given the girl without obstruction. But not without the closest of observation. Have the medics state that we found her that way and have been conducting an investigation."

Eykor asked, "Is that entirely prudent, Chairman? After all, they may be able to learn something from her. And here we have three more . . ."

"No, no, no, don't take them. Unless they themselves show cause, and then handle subtly—we don't want three more of these basket-cases on our hands. However it occurs. Plattsman, can your people follow them?"

"Not easily, Chairman, but I believe we can work out something."

"Well, do your best. I want every move recorded and analyzed. As much as possible, Klyten, you go down to Control and work with them, interpret. And we will also want some reserves close to hand."

"No problem, there, Chairman. I can have a Tacsquad in parallel all the time."

"All right! So get to it and keep me informed."

Parleau waved them off, naggingly, hurriedly, as if he were shooing a group of schoolboys away from some valuable statue, or out of a tree they were not supposed to climb. The rest collected their portfolios and departed, leaving Parleau alone in the now silent office. He leaned back deeply in his chair, sighed thoughtfully, and at last, put his heavy feet upon the desk. At first, he placed his hands across his belly, but later, he folded them behind his head, thinking. He tried to fit the pieces together, but there were too many other pieces missing, and he could not make them fit. He reflected that Eykor had had the first crack at the girl, and had failed to extract anything; likewise, in turn, Control. Klyten admitted ignorance of reasons, but supplied considerable data, much of which disturbed him more than the original incident, the destruction of the instruments. That seemed very far away now, a niggling little problem not worthy of solution by him. Yes. There was much there, strands of coincidences . . . something was nagging, nibbling at the back of his mind. What was it? He tried to relax and free-associate. Yes, something to do with families. They certainly were strongly oriented to the family, maintaining their line with what seemed to Parleau to be a most artificial system, and keeping it going. Families. And those aristocratic Players, two family groups of them since the dawn of their time, doing something that had no function.

An alarm went off, silently, in his mind. Yes, he was on the track of it now. Yes, the Player families. And he sat back, mentally, as it occurred to him what they all had missed. It all fit, beautifully. They had control, they had management, even if no one could describe it and locate it. And they had an electronic Game in an anti-tech culture, a competition in a cooperative, primitive communist society. And a family, no, two, who were subsidized to do something that had no function but to entertain, in an economic environment that saw itself as severely practical. It all smelled. But not half so bad as the idea that was arriving sideways, as it were, deep in the recesses of Parleau's mind: that one of these Players was given away to the humans, and that the other was a spy, obviously out of the Game, and that the

Braid, the family group, was being allowed to end. And Klyten hadn't even seen it. Parleau felt a rush of pride: he had seen something their ler expert hadn't, even as he had been commenting on it. Sexed-out, he had said; they had to seek new identities. But the Game as he had seen it required two sides, and very soon, in a few years, there would be only one. They were going to let something go that they had carefully nurtured for three hundred years or more, without a comment! Parleau sat up abruptly, all semblance of relaxation gone. And from a recess in the desk, he retrieved a vocoder and began transcribing some ideas and instructions, as fast as he could consider them. Yes. It was all tied together somehow, and he was going to derive the answer, if he had to run all of them right into the ground.

THIRTEEN

In the Game, it is arbitrarily considered that the total number of operations on every cell in the pattern-area constitutes one unit of Game-time. How we do it is unimportant, serially or by parallel computation, or by scalar patterning; that is our limitation as finite creatures—but in reality it all occurs simultaneously, instantly, for that is the smallest unit into which time can be divided, an absolute.... And so across Game-time, we observe motion, as moving particles with varying degrees of coherence and self-identity; as ripples of unique wavelike patterns of presence and absence; as "invisible waves" that seem to transit empty cellular space and cause reactions in target portions of the developing pattern. There is no motion and there are no waves. Period. That is illusion. There is only the sequential and recursive interaction of the defined Surround with the associated Transition-rules and Paradigms. It is necessary to order our perceptions from the cellular unit outward, that we may fully comprehend higher-order

phenomena of appearances, and thereby not be
deceived, as one might easily be working from
the macrocosm to the microcosm.
                              —The Game Texts

To be attacked with malice in mind was, while relatively
rare enough, at the least understandable under certain conditions, Morlenden and Fellirian alike could vividly recall the
heyday of the Mask-Factory highwaymen of a span ago;
likewise they could also recall several inter-Braid feuds and
vendettas of greater or lesser importance. In particular, the
Khlefen—Termazen—Trithen triangular vendetta of the generation past could come to mind, even though in the present
it had been reduced in scale and severity to minor incidents
of mild disrespect, or perhaps contemptible behavior within
the precincts of neighborhood markets.

At any rate, they, the Derens, had no feuds at present with
anyone, and it was obvious that robbery was not the motive
for the attack on Morlenden. But whatever the intent, it had
come by arrow, certainly a weapon which could only be used
leaving the hand. On this basis, and after studying the arrow
itself, a deadly metal construction, they all reasoned that the
assailant had to have been human. But this raised more questions than it answered, for who could it be among the
forerunners who moved silently through the forest and brush,
in the middle of the reservation, and then vanished without a
trace? And then, more importantly, what human would wish
to injure Morlenden? Only a handful even knew of his existence.

Kaldherman, who was prone to eccentric ideas, had voiced
a suspicion that the assassin had been one of the people, a
concept which had disturbing overtones indeed. And to add
influence to this position, Morlenden had commented that
Sanjirmil had indeed expressed apprehension about his possible uncovering of Game secrets. But he did not tell all the
reasons why he could not bring himself to accuse her, and
the rest could see no reason why one elder Player would hire
them, and another try to prevent them.

Krisshantem was also suspected, if for no other reason
than his uncanny silence in the woods. And his status as
hifzer, who might be capable of anything; once the one set of
traditions went, who could say what others might follow? But
he had the least motive of all, and in fact later arrived to dis-
pel the notion in person, a day behind Morlenden, and in the

company of one Halyandhin, one of the elder Hulens, who completely verified his story and whereabouts. And the issue remained where it had been—unsolved. Krisshantem examined the place where the attack had come from, but he would say nothing of what he saw therein, if indeed anything. When pressed on the matter by Kaldherman to the edge of insult, he admitted ruefully that it seemed to him to be the work of a human of superior knowledge as a tracker, a notion he considered outrageous. There simply were none in the reservation at all.

So it was that with great apprehensions the party had departed the Deren *yos* and journeyed down to the Institute on the mono, and spoken with Director Vance; Morlenden, Fellirian, and Krisshantem. These were the ones Vance gave directions to. There were two more whom Vance did not see, and whose directions came from Fellirian: Kaldherman and Cannialin, who were to travel with them, but keeping a discreet distance, as if unconnected. Tourists, a young couple, out on a holiday.

Departing the tube-train at Region Central, the three ler appeared at some distinction from the humans who were using the underground terminal at that time of day. It was somewhat after the noon hour, so the terminal was relatively empty of the ebb and flow of shift changes; yet there was considerable traffic, incidental people on errands of unknown significance. Smaller in stature and lighter in build than the humans, they were also recognizable immediately by their clothing; the simple fall of overshirts, even heavy winter ones, was greatly different from the heavy folds, tucks, pleats, and stiff fabrics of their human co-travelers. They had thrown their hoods back; two had the long, single braid of hair that marked the adult and parent phase ler, while the third wore his in the anonymous bowl cut of the adolescent. To the casual eye, they suggested a family group on an outing, an air Fellirian had suggested that they cultivate, for the farther they were from the reservation, the less people would actually recall about ler Braid ordering, and would project their own images upon them. Kaldherman and Cannialin maintained contact, but also distance. They seemed to be only country yokels who gaped in astonishment at almost everything they saw. At least in part, for Kaldherman, this was not entirely playacting, for it was his first trip outside. He was astonished, in fact.

Standing in the station, pausing before further onward motion, the tube-train waited, making soft mechanical noises, while along its length, doors opened and closed, and in the terminal itself, along the platform, echoes moved in the air, up and down, seeking a quiet corner among the dull concrete facings in which to spin out and die. The underground terminal was a broad hall of indeterminate length—a smoky bluish haze obscured the distant ends where the tunnel dipped down into the earth again. One could sense that the end walls were there, not so very far away, but still vague and unmarked; there was nothing for the eye to fasten to, and the prevailing dimness, lit by weak lamps spotted along the low ceilings, stretched the capacity of their eyes to the utmost.

By the stairwell leading upward, a sweeperman absentmindedly poked with his pushbroom at an insignificant pile of trash, coughing randomly with no great urgency. At dimly lighted kiosks along the stained walls, patrons discussed apparently the prices of fares and the configurations of schedules. The answers, like the questions, were tentative, hedged, rationalized, qualified to a degree no ler could hope to understand, holding a melancholy air of perpetual indecision. As if, having nowhere to go, the indefinite wranglings over schedules and fares had become a peculiar free entertainment, a substitute for more meaningful communication and relationships. Over all hung an odor, extremely peculiar and noticeable to the ler sense of smell. It filled the clotted damp air: ozone, lubricating oils and greases, metals and metallic compounds, metalloceramic and plastic hybrids, stale clothing, cigarette smoke, humans of several degrees of hygiene.

Climbing the stairwell to the surface, Morlenden asked Fellirian if the humans, with all their vast technology, could not perhaps have installed a moving stairway, better lighting, as they were reputed to have done in some of their great cities.

Fellirian answered, smiling faintly as she climbed the stairwell to the upper world, "They have a phrase that describes that perfectly: they call it somewhere-else-ism. If you ask why anything isn't as it should be—social inequities, shift disparities, mechanical malfunctions, nonexistent conveniences, and loaded benefits—the responsible parties always cite some location, preferably rather far away, where things are just right. To your question about slideways, the local engineer would most likely say, 'Oh, they have just installed that system this very week in Tashkent Center.' And in Tash-

kent, or Zinder, or Coquilhatville, they are saying at the same
time to *their* complainants, 'In Old North America they have
all that stuff, and low taxes* as well.' And there's a time variation of it, too, not just of place: either they had it, and it
broke, or it's coming next summer. And they repair the hot-
water pipes in, you guessed it, the dead of winter, too. No,
Olede, I fear that very little of the technology leaks down to
the street level. In fact, these,"—and here Fellirian gestured
at random passersby with a slight motion of her head—"have
rather less, on the whole, than their foreparents did. Thus is
the way of all things like this, and why we pursue them with
greater caution."

They reached the top of the stairwell and emerged into the
more open air of a plaza, about which low, subtly-colored
buildings clustered. Before the stairwell opening, a painted
sign mounted on posts listed significant organizations nearby,
presumably of interest to the arriving traveler, identifying
their locations according to building numbers of the structures in which they were housed. Morlenden, not as familiar
with Modanglic as Fellirian, though there was something odd
about the sign, something he couldn't exactly place, until he
realized that several of the words on it were apparently misspelled, or so it seemed. One word was misspelled twice, in
two different ways. The errors cast a singular air of bland incompetence about the sign, and by inference, those who had
erected it, an impression reinforced by the shoddy repainting
the sign had received many times.

The air of the city was translucent, an effect compounded
of a light fog, overcast, steam from underground vents, and
various fumes; and as in the station platform belowground,
there was a similar vagueness, an indeterminacy, to the distances. A few forlorn trees filled elevated planters of concrete
sited at random intervals along the main plaza walkway, the
inhabitants now mostly bare of leaves and foliage and dripping with condensate.

Of the buildings they could see, as they paused to allow
Fellirian to orient herself, none appeared to be larger than
three or four stories, and none bore any indication relating to
their occupants or their functions; but they did, each build-

* To the ler, all permanent taxes, or standing taxes, were conceptually a horror; taxes were intended to be specific and unique.
Since Braid Deren collected such taxes as required, Fellirian could
speak with wry authority on the subject.

ing, bear enormous placards at their corners, which in turn displayed numbers, none of which seemed to have any relationship to any other displayed number. One announced, "3754." Another, immediately adjacent, said, just as definitively, "2071." The streets moved off in a square grid pattern, with regular ninety-degree corners, but it was the pattern of a maze, rather than thoroughfares; none of the streets appeared to go through to anywhere. Morlenden vulgarly observed aside to Krisshantem that it seemed the humans laid out their streets after the tile-joints on the floors of the public toilets at the Institute: the neat, ninety-degree lines went nowhere.

They knew where they needed to go—to Building 8905, as Vance had told them—but this building was not listed on the directory sign, nor could any of them locate it from their viewpoint on the plaza. Fellirian, more at home with humans than either Morlenden or Krisshantem, accosted a passerby and asked the location of Building 8905.

The man responded somewhat furtively, and hurried on his way, into the terminal, down the steps. Fellirian returned, and said, "That one said that eight-nine-oh-five is to our left, a few blocks over. Head left from the plaza, right at the first street beyond the end of three-seven-five-four over there, skip an alley, and then left and left at the very next streets. Left, right, skip, left and left."

Kris exclaimed under his breath, "Insane! None of these blocks is numbered in any order. Why number them in the first place?"

"I know," she answered. "It's an awful system. The original intent was a good one, I suppose; then there was order. But with rebuilding and changes, it got all mixed up. Now and again, some administrator tries to reorder his district, but when you change the number of a building, you also have to change all of the references to it, all of the records. All the directories. And people get confused. You should try to make a call through the public commnet as it is! Much worse! It takes, on the average, five or six calls to get the office or the person you need. Why, I know of one case where I called one number, and a person answered. It was not the man I was calling, so he gave me another number. I called it, and it rang; the same man answered the same instrument, and told me my party wasn't in! And the directory entries make no sense at all: supplies are carried under the section 'Logistics,' while the Logistics-Plans Offices are listed under 'Plans.' At first I thought that it was just me, that I was at fault for not learning the key to it all, but Vance told me it was the same with everybody; all of them carry around little personal directories, compiled over the years, listing the real numbers and offices and people. Some people actually have a side job on the sly as professional listers. Others sell personal directories for astounding sums."

Morlenden shook his head. "It certainly would seem that these numbers lend the appearance of greater order."

Krisshantem added, "I am surprised that they can have a working society at all on such a basis."

She answered, "Vance has a theory, to which I also subscribe, that there is a good reason for such tangles and why society chooses to work through them. He thinks that bureaucratic systems and number messes like this arise, not through carelessness, but through specific, if half-conscious, attempts to put distance between people, because the civilization has somehow compressed them closer to one another than they are capable of being naturally. They build a time delay into all their transactions, because, crowded in personal space, they must expand into time."

"They have traded frustration for satisfaction, no doubt," finished Morlenden as they started off to the left across the plaza toward 8905.

She said, "True! But that frustration with the time delay is a forebrain problem: one can rationalize it, which adds to its effectiveness. But body-space contact aggression is at a deeper level, more instinctual, and thus more difficult to control. No, trading time for space works."

He laughed. "And so we're building the very same thing! Look at us, you and I, Eliya; with all our records of births and deaths and transfers to elder lodges. Braid-line diagrams, Braidbooks, collations of names. Aren't we now preparing the groundbreaking for the same thing to come? I mean, in *miel* years, we could all come back and visit and see scores of little Perderens, Terderens, Zhanderens, all busy, scribbling away in their little offices, just like this, and instead of us visiting them, they will all be required to call us upon every minor little event."

Fellirian did not answer him, Krisshantem added, most cryptically, "Too, it is a way to slow or stop time. All events leave ripples, and these methods are sad attempts to make standing waves of those ripples. It gives the illusion of permanence and eminence to those who feel swept along in the general rate. But the events themselves are never prolonged beyond their time; they aren't even touched, for these things avoid them."

For some unaccountable reason, this remark left Morlenden with a dire sense of moody foreboding, some unspecified menace. Krisshantem was prone on occasion to utter oracular parables, statements whose true import even he did not understand completely on the conscious level. Nor did Morlenden. . . .

Now off the plaza, they had made their first turn and were proceeding along a narrow street between two buildings which seemed smaller than the general rule. The pastel, stained, or unpainted surfaces, the low cloud cover, the suggestion of winter fog, the pervasive mechanical smells, odors, tinctures, distillations, all combined in an alien gestalt to lend a sly, just-out-of-range-of-recognition melancholy to their journey. There was danger in this, indeed, so they all knew, great danger. But however near it might very well be, it also seemed remote, miniature, disinterested, accidental or blind policy if at all. All that remained was not excitement, but an odd sadness, a peculiar emotion they could not recall feeling before, though they had all known painful circumstances in their lives. It impelled one to lassitude and blind, wheel-spinning action for the sake of action at the same time. And passing humans seemed also to share it.

To ease the tension rising among them, they began to talk among themselves. The basic gray, the basic color behind the overcast gray day, changed and shifted, clotting suddenly, and then clearing again, only to close in again. Now it was yellowish, now blue and violet, and now again, pinkish. The cloud deck was thin, and as the clouds moved overhead in the spaces of sky between the buildings, above the faceless and nameless buildings, they changed the quality of light passing through their vague, unformed layers.

Krisshantem was the first to speak openly of it. "Why do we feel as we do? Is this city so alien to us?"

This time it was Morlenden who did not speak. Fellirian glanced about her once, muttering something uncatchable under her breath, adding, "They used to call it *sienon* . . . the blues. But few know the term anymore. They feel it, all the same. There is no natural law that says that men can't live in cities, or us, either. It's just that this kind of city isn't right for them. Or us. We feel the wrongness."

Krisshantem digested this in silence. Then he asked, "And

so you are sure that we will find Maellen here, in this pile, in this eight-nine-oh-five?"

She said, "So much Vance averred. But he also added that according to his informants there was something wrong with her. I have adjudged it was a good thing that we spent those extra days practicing recovering and reprogramming a forgetty."

"Now that we are here," Kris said, "I like that not at all. We should not even discuss such a thing in this place, much less assay to perform it here."

Morlenden agreed in part. "I'd also prefer to do it in a safer environment, but then there's the problem of carrying her back. . . . I also didn't want Kal to see us do it; he'll probably think it the vilest sort of black magic." Then he added, "But *rathers* don't count so much, do they?"

Fellirian laughed, deep down in her throat. "True, what you say . . . but I have a trick in mind, and for it to work, she will have to be self-propelled and ambulatory."

Morlenden continued, to Krisshantem, "So, then. You who have instructed us in the way of restoring forgetties; are you sure we won't get back any of the original Maellenkleth?"

Kris looked idly about himself, at the chipped and cracked facades, the blind windows, which were few enough, and those filmed over with dust and grime and the streaking added by the rain. He said, coldly, impersonally, "Completely sure. Nothing. Well, there may be fragments left, indeed, we can expect to see some, observing her over a few months, until the new persona digests and integrates them. Little odd pieces, flashes of partial mnemons, but the memory and the old persona? It's all gone. I have heard that forgetties say odd things, hints of the old, but they themselves don't know why they say them, and in time they stop."

Fellirian reached to the boy as they walked, touching him with an affectionate gesture, half a mother's reassurance, and half the consolation of one who has shared as co-equal. Krisshantem was a bit in both worlds. She said, "So this is doubly cruel, that she will most surely be a forgetty. You lose her, even as we are engaged in recovering her. What we will get back will be a stranger."

Kris responded, "That is how it will be, how it must be."

"I am sorry, sincerely sorry that we had to drag you into this. There were others, after all. . . ."

"It is no matter to regret, Fellirian Deren. I would not have it otherwise; it repays much of what she gave freely to me. Have no fears: I will do it right, lead you well. That sorrow has already been struck, and I do not moon over echoes."

And now they had made their last left turn, and stopped, looking about uncertainly. At last they discovered a small, grimy sign affixed to the side of an inconspicuous building, which read, 8905. After further searching about for a few more moments, they located the small and insignificant entry, passed through it, not without some misgivings, and were inside. And what had Vance told them? *In eight-nine-oh-five, do not sightsee or evidence any idle curiosity; ignore that which you see that is not specifically shown to you. Eight-nine-oh-five can be a house of lamentations for those who look too closely into it.* Inside, all seemed innocuous. A preoccupied, diffident reception clerk at a disorderly desk piled high with forms and worksheets directed them to a small anteroom, where they waited, sitting in plastic chairs that someone had, some time in a remote past, mistakenly assumed would be form-fitting.

After a wait of unknown duration, for it seemed that time was curiously exempted inside this building, a single human appeared, dressed in a plain, very dark blue tunic and pants, unadorned except for an odd heraldic device affixed to the upper left chest. This one was very dark in complexion, imposing and dignified, reticent yet vital, all at the same time. His face was immobile, but of a certainty not vacant. Fellirian, as she saw him, made an involuntary gesture, nervously brushing back her fine brown hair at her right temple; a nervous gesture. Morlenden had seen her make that gesture only rarely, and only when she met someone of considerably more *takh** than herself. He became very alert. This was the one.

The man spoke. "I am Hando Errat. I have been assigned to assist you, expedite any forms that may have to be completed. You are the persons assigned to take custody of the girl?"

Fellirian answered, rising to her feet, "Yes. We hold such a commission from her family. We are the keepers of the census records, the nearest thing we have to a civil service." Mor-

---

* Best translated, "force of personality," although a full explanation involves considerably more than just personality, delving far into concepts of aggression and projection.

lenden saw, as she stood to address Errat, how large the human really was: he topped Fellirian by almost two heads.

The immobile face did not change expression, but intoned solemnly, "There will be a small difficulty. She was apparently responsible for the destruction of some valuable instruments."

"We were not aware of this," she answered, carefully neutral.

"There will be no requirement for punishment. Compensation will be required for the value of the items. She has also received some custodial care in the interim since that time."

Fellirian said, "We have brought no currency for such a contingency. But in any matter concerning fees, I am certain that any agreement I sign will be honored in full by our sponsors. My word as head of Braid."

Morlenden asked, "What were the instruments?"

"Implements of no great account. A curious case; we have been unable to comprehend exactly why she did that. I believe the charges and surcharges will come to something near a thousand valuta," said Errat, disappointment showing subtly in the set of his face, his posture, the tone of his deep voice. Fellirian read him, and saw, relaxing herself, that he had weighed them and found them innocent. Controller-Interrogator, she thought, finally deciphering the badge. He would obviously have been box-trained to read minutae, derive volumes from the most careful evasions. And he paused, as if weighing imponderables, unseen quantities.

Then, "What will you do with the girl? She is now in a condition that I would term inoperable. I have been advised that it occurred under unknown causes."

Fellirian answered, "It is one of our liabilities. We were aware of the possibility of such an occurrence. We intend to return her to the community of the people, where there are methods available to restore her ... although not as before. She can never be as before; she has lost her entire memory."

"Amnesia?"

"No, something more. It's gone, that's all. We will rebuild a new personality in her, enough for her to function."

"You have such abilities?"

"She will relearn, after the manner of a newborn. All we do in accelerate the process somewhat. Personality and memory are timeless, dimensionless, a wave front. We will start another wave."

"You will reprogram her?" Errat was dangerously perceptive.

"In a word."

"We were not aware of this quality in the people."

"It is neither short nor easy—not on her, not on they who will build the new one."

"How is this done, may I ask?"

"By a process that has no analog in your people, and is useless to you; and of course, I would demean my honor by divulging what is in essence a highly religious ceremony."

There was an uncanny silence while Errat digested the import of what Fellirian had said. He felt that the small, diminutive New Human female was telling the truth, or at least most of it. Now, reprogramming! That was news! But it was also a distraction, for they would not offer it so readily otherwise. And it was a tacit admission that whatever the girl had been, whatever she had known, it was gone, for them as well. They wanted her back for religious reasons! Culture! What rubbish! But in the heart of Errat's certainty, he felt a tiny quiver of apprehension. There was perhaps a clever illusion here, but he couldn't quite grasp it; something just beyond. Well, she had said it would be so, but even so, instructions were clear enough, as was his own plan. *Let them have the room and see what they do with it. They are but simpletons pretending to be sophisticated, knowledgeable. But under it all, still just that: simpletons.* And another voice said, *Wrong, wrong. What was it about this?*

And he said, "Certainly, indeed. I would not dream of violating a trust. We have such as well as you. But, of course, any insights you could pass along, through the Institute, would be most gratefully appreciated by us all. Do you have contacts there? No doubt they would like to apply this kind of thinking to some of the problems we are facing. We have a considerable problem in this area ... people mislay and forget things, drift off into irresponsible reveries, start spending time daydreaming."

Fellirian shook her head. "Speaking with due attention to your goal, I see little we could add to help you. What we do does not aid memory, increase the span of attention, or energize people whose wits are slipping. But I will mention your needs to my friends in their departments; I am sure that they will be able to offer you some insights which will be useful to you." Standoff! Errat had been trying to lead Fellirian by negatives; let her deny enough areas of applicability, and he

could find the area and fill it in himself, with a little clever-
ness. But she had simply fed back his own categories to him,
and then shut down the conversation.

Errat nodded. He understood what had been said, as well
as that which had been implied. He stood back a bit and motioned to them to follow. "Well, come along, then. We can
release the girl if you're ready for her."

They followed Errat out of the anteroom, and Morlenden
watched closely, direct vision averted, warily, as they
proceeded by a most roundabout way through the viscera of
Building 8905; there were corridors with poor lighting and
many abrupt turns; short, dingy stairwells, lifts, walkways,
ramps. To his eye, 8905 was fey, alien, a structure embody-
ing concepts they hardly knew, much less cultivated. Its
strangeness, he felt instinctively, possessed a complexity that
concealed its essence from even its regular users. And he
could not escape the suspicion, arising just as instinctively,
that the way they were going was not the main route through
the building, but was a back way, a janitor's route, or a
watchman's patrolway. Or perhaps a secret route, known only
to initiates. Errat did not hesitate: he seemed to know exactly
where he was going. Along the way they met few people; all,
to a person, minded their own business and did not look, beyond a cursory inspection. And on they walked. Sometimes
up, sometimes down. The light from the frosted windows remained exactly the same, no matter how they found the windows, and the light did not change in quality. Morlenden
knew that they had walked farther than the outside of the
building could have contained. That, and the unchanging
light, convinced him that wherever they were, it was not inside the building they had seen from the outside. A cold chill
passed rapidly through him. *This whole neighborhood must
be eight-nine-oh-five, passaged like an anthill with connecting
tunnels and overwalks, and every single one of the windows is
blind to the outside, its lighting controlled artificially. What
shows on the outside is just a front, and located on a side alley
as well.*

He glanced covertly at the others who had come with him;
Fellirian, his insibling and co-spouse. She was not such a
stranger to the ways of the forerunners, and in this place,
seemed to be only slightly more alert than usual. It was obvious they were going to give them the girl and let them go.
What else they might have in mind, she felt they could
handle. But along her face, around her large, expressive eyes,

around the corners of her broad, full mouth, there were also infinitesimal little lines and tics revealing her concern for the condition in which they could expect to find Maellenkleth. Or, rather, she who had once been Maellenkleth. No more. She who was yet to be in this body they would call Schaeszendur, for though the body be the same, the persona would be different.

On the other hand, Krisshantem was tense and wary as a wild animal confronting the zoo for the first time. Every sense was alert, every perception was peaked at maximum receptivity. Morlenden had learned to trust the boy's perceptions, and he recalled that during their journey to this place, this anthill warren, he had not been so nervous, but moody and belligerent. Therefore he sensed something about this Building 8905. What was it he had seen, sensed, or inferred in these bland, sometimes cracked and stained walls, the substantial, heavy doors, the rare figures they passed who averted their eyes, and the silences? The silences? These, Morlenden knew, were not the quiet of absences, but a pressure of closeness, things carefully hidden.

At last they came to a section that revealed, in its better lighting, and a sharp, astringent scent in the air, it was devoted to medical purposes. In the odor-complex, there were also undertones of many other substances, mostly organic, some natural, some highly artificial. He could identify none of them. They passed through a brightly lit area that seemed to be the source of most of the odors, a laboratory, and onward into a suite of wards and rooms. Errat spoke briefly to an attendant who seemingly materialized out of thin air, and they entered one of the rooms. There was an inhabitant, tied lightly in a hospital bed. It was Maellenkleth.

To Morlenden, who could remember the mnemo-holistic image impressed into him by Krisshantem, the girl looked much the same in overall configuration and shape, although she was a bit thinner than he recalled in the image. But the expression in her face was neither that of a living adolescent, or of a person who had withdrawn within, but rather like an abandoned newborn: vacant, blank, uncoordinated. It was easy to see, but that difference said everything, even as one almost overlooked it and its simplicity. The personality, the persona, the undefinable, unboundable person that inhabited this body and acted in it was now gone, as if it had never been. This was not, strictly speaking, Maellenkleth, but an empty shell that had once responded to that name.

Morlenden had never seen a forgetty closely before in his life; and if it had not occurred to him before, it was brought home now to him with redoubled force that something had indeed been very, very wrong, to lead to this result. He did not know yet the secret Maellenkleth had been protecting, with her life, but knowing as much as he did, he was sure that this was no accident. Intuition: this did not happen. It was caused.

He watched Krisshantem closely. This time, above all others, must not be the one ruled by the power of Water. The emotions. Kris must not reveal to any watcher that he had any relationship with her whatsoever. What would he do? The boy did nothing. Krisshantem looked closely at the girl, dispassionately examining her as if she were just another specimen of these labs, and then turned back to Morlenden. The expression on the boy's face told Morlenden what he wanted to see: *This person is not the girl I knew, loved, slept with, made dhainaz with uncounted sweet moments we hoped would never end. Yes, it was her, once, but this one is a stranger. It deserves care and respect, this strange ksensrithman girl, but little more than that. And of revenges we shall speak later, when we know more. Much more.* It was a look of logic and duty. No more, save deep down under it there simmered fire.

Both Fellirian and Morlenden suddenly felt all their careful plans empty into a stagnant sump, dissipating. What could they do with her? She was helpless, and they could not in any way recover her here. Madness! They were at a loss for the proper action. Should they just go to the bed, and unceremoniously pick her up and cart her off, like a sack of potatoes? What could she do, or not do?

Errat, sensing their quandary, politely suggested, "To us, she appears to have no more responses than the average newborn, in fact, somewhat less than the human standard we have compared her with. She doesn't seem to learn as fast. At the first, it was necessary to restrain her, as she thrashed about uncontrollably; later she did gain enough control to avoid abrupt movements. Now she is generally quiet. She cannot turn herself over, nor sit up, nor care for herself in any way. It is a most odd condition. Is this a peculiar ler form of psychosis?"

Fellirian answered, "Most definitely not a psychosis."

"We have even had to exercise her, but I am sure there has

been considerable muscular atrophy.... What will you do with her?"

Morlenden volunteered, "We'll have to carry her back to our home. We'll need something to carry her in. I suppose a ... stretcher. Excuse me, but my Modanglic is strictly school level, and I don't know the exact terms."

Errat answered smoothly, "Yes. Of course. One can be obtained." He turned to an orderly, who exchanged words with him and then vanished. Errat made an impatient gesture. "Yes, easily. My man has gone for it even now. But even with the three of you, you'll need help."

Fellirian said, "We can manage."

Errat seemed to become fractionally more insistent. "It will be no trouble at all. In fact, the two who would accompany you are the very ones who have been working with her in therapy. They are both strong of arm and knowledgeable of mind."

"Oh, very well. We can certainly use the help," she said. As she spoke, Morlenden had the thought that he could indeed be certain that the orderlies would be strong and knowledgeable. Indeed. And a more accurate description of their role would be "agents."

Errat left the room for a moment. Fellirian started to speak, but Kris motioned her to silence. And shortly afterward, he returned with two large, muscular men, dressed in white uniforms, and they were pushing a low, wheeled stretcher. The two went to work immediately, gathering Maellenkleth and placing her into the apparatus. They did not appear all that expert in their work.

Errat said, as the attendants were completing their preparations, "We assumed that you would wish to return her to your own environment without further delay; the trip already has been a long one. So arrangements have been made; we have procured tickets on the southbound evening tube. If you leave now you can make it." He added, as an afterthought. "We had to settle for a local, so there will be more stops, but at the least, there will be private compartments."

Fellirian watched the two men bundling Maellenkleth clumsily onto the stretcher, and said, "Very well. We accept." She watched the two orderlies closely. "And what about the forms you mentioned earlier, the damage claims, the surcharges?"

Oddly, the question seemed to bother Errat no little bit. He looked about, almost apprehensively, saying quickly, "No problem there, at all. We can paperwhip it here and send the rest to the Institute later, through Vance. Yes, the forms will be routed through the Office of the Director. You may sign them at your leisure."

Fellirian nodded agreement, otherwise making no motion, no sign, but Morlenden saw a quick flicker in her gray eyes, a tiny brightening of expression, and then it was gone. Errat had not seen it, he had been turned away. And how would Errat have known to send it to Vance? He should know that paperwork routing and deliveries were the bane of civilization, and that one did not send valuable papers blind. Had they been followed all the way from the reservation, from before, even? How much did these people see?

The orderlies, having arranged the girl for transport, now began to wheel her off. They were fussy about their work, however inexpert they were at it. They did not, so it appeared, want any of the ler party to touch Maellenkleth in any way.

They indeed did depart 8905 through a different way than they had entered. Looking back once, Morlenden thought that the place where they left had the unmistakable look of a warehouse loading dock to it, rather than a regular door; and at that, one in not too much use. He also worried lest Cannialin and Kaldherman lose them through this labyrinthine game of evasion, but after a few turns, they were back on one of the main avenues debouching on the plaza, which the younger Derens had remained close to. Morlenden saw them pretending to admire a statuary group, all the time scanning the plaza entrances for them. They saw them, and across the distance, Morlenden could make out Cannialin whispering to Kal. And now they began moving off, as if to enter the terminal station from the other side.

The party escorting Maellenkleth boarded the tube without incident, although Morlenden, now carefully watching every move the orderlies made, observed that the orderlies were most careful to retain the tickets. Fortunately, they were separated into two compartments. He saw that Kaldherman and Cannialin also boarded the tube-train, taking a coach just ahead of them. And oddly enough, Fellirian had little trouble, once aboard, in convincing the orderlies that Maellenkleth would be better off in their compartment, with her people. It was as if the orderlies—agents—felt the train more secure. From what? Where could they go in the endless alternating urban centers and industrial suburbs of manworld? Escape was remote until they were at the Institute stop. Or was it secure from interference? Morlenden thought that if Fellirian had a plan, she had better use it fast. All had been smooth up to this point. Too smooth by far. It was not to have been so easy. That was the reason for including the others in it. And now?

Morlenden and Krisshantem moved into the compartment with the girl, while Fellirian remained behind momentarily, conversing confidentially with one of the agents, the one who seemed to be in charge. After a moment, she joined them also, closing the compartment door.

Motioning them to silence, she paused, and then began to speak in Multispeech, using the one-to-many speech-mode, but with the side channels suppressed. Morlenden was impressed; he would not have thought that she had learned the skill.

To any human that might have been listening, it sounded rather like nonsensical music, wordless, and with an odd, ringing purity of tone. Fellirian had told the agents that they would now perform a rite over the girl and that they would hear chanting. But to the ler ear, there was no music in it at all, indeed, as in most forms of Multispeech, there was no consciousness of *sound or ears* at all. It was just ideas, stripped to simplicity, somehow whispered directly into their minds.

She said, "Spy.two.they.now.here.speak.past.Eliya.tell.God-seek.for.her&thisspeak.noread.they@&!do.it.now.quick.yes??"

And Krisshantem answered in the same mode. "Two.here. know.parts.&&.same.now.Stop. + Two.here.make.base.line& three.make.her&lose.them(!)(!)."

Keeping the chant up, but now not sending anything in it, they moved quickly, carefully placing Maellenkleth on the floor between Morlenden and Fellirian. She was awake, but passive and unresisting. They arranged her as Krisshantem directed, and settled into position themselves, assuming a studied, rigorous posture with their legs folded under them, and sitting back on their turned heels. Krisshantem took up his position at the head of the girl, in the same posture. The process began.

Now Morlenden and Fellirian took up the chant, immediately shifting the mode, making it even more submelodic, exactly as Krisshantem had instructed them. Morlenden now felt his vision dim and fade, as the new mode took hold and blanked out his visual center, readying it for another purpose.

"Remember," Kris had admonished them with adolescent severity, "you must, you two, make the base line. The persona is four-dimensional, and the maker will erect the restored one upon that line. You must keep it steady; that is the hardest part of the whole thing—the steadying of the reference line. When I get fully into the rebuild pattern, if I get that far and residuals in her mind do not resist me, I can compensate for some dislocation, but if I get tied up in that follower sub-routine I will lose the growth pattern, and we all may be in danger of getting sucked into that forgetty program stored in her. Remember, no one ever shut it off. It is still the paramount instruction in her mind. That is why they couldn't do anything with her. Most of what she learns she erases immediately. And in the net, she can do it to us. Never forget this: this is dangerous to us. Also remember that I am no expert at this. I have never done it live before; only received instruction from Mael. So you *must be steady!*"

The theory, he had explained, was that the persona was a four-dimensional figure, a tesseract in space, the elementals Fire, Earth, Air, and Water permutating and pervolving upon themselves, making a cruciform (in three-space projection) figure of equal lines and ninety degree angles. For their part, Morlenden and Fellirian would make the reference line, which set orientation in space and the length determined how much would go into it. There was one such line, uniquely placed, for everyone, if one could but find it; here, they were making one from scratch. In Maellenkleth's case, they could, within limits, select any line they wished, for they were starting anew.

Holding the developing subject rigidly in the growing pattern, the maker reprogrammed the subject, nonverbally, inserting concepts directly into the appropriate parts of the brain. And to her, there was further risk: do it right, and they would end up with a retarded but functional Schaeszendur. And do it wrong, and a thousand disasters awaited them. They could kill her, for one choice. In another, she could become a dangerous maniac, beyond their abilities to subdue her, physically or multispecifically.

The Deren insiblings reached deep within themselves for calmness and strength, striving to make the base line, bring it into being, and hold it just so, at such a position in space. That was near what she had been before, Kris had advised, suggesting that orientation because she would be less likely to fight them. Yes, he had said. They had told each other what their lines had been. They had been *dhofters*, had they not?

At first the effort was just a song, but before long, Morlenden could see it in his mind's eye, slowly coming into being in the web of Multispeech, a bright, hard, sodium-yellow line, piercingly narrow, now varying in length and waving about in a rubbery, unstable, nonoriented manner, then slowing, stiffening, stabilizing in length, feeling the right angle of orientation, coming to rest now, but still as unstable as the opposing poles of two magnets, slippery, elsewhere wanting. And it came into hard focus, and all vagueness vanished. There was nothing else, a universe of utter black night. Night and darkness and the hard, burning yellow line. Morlenden, seeing it, tried to see through the vision and pick up something of the coach-sleeper, some outside sight. It was no use; he was completely blind, save to the vision being generated by Multispeech. He knew that Fellirian must also be equally blind now, completely into it.

The line steadied, and now, delicately touched and nudged by a third power in the net! Krisshantem. It drifted slowly, still moving in orientation, becoming steady. He let Morlenden and Fellirian hold it thus for a moment, to get the feel of it, measuring the chant he was entering and increasingly controlling. Holding the line was hard, hard. He heard, somewhere very far away, a subvocal moan from she who had been Maellenkleth and was about to be Schaeszendur. The line wavered with his attention, and he returned to it, increased the power, and nailed it down. And on the other end, he could feel the feedback from Fellirian, also clamping down, mastering the unstable yellow line. He remembered to take a deep breath, and concentrated, and

Now a third point in the furry darkness appeared from nowhere, and the line was a square, empty, hanging alone in space, still oddly and rigidly oriented. It hung a moment, a little uncertain. The Derens applied more pressure, more inner strength. It steadied. Morlenden could not now sense Krisshantem as a person, but as an intense force, somewhere offstage, who was manipulating their visions, their work. That was what it was. He could not imagine what Kris was seeing now. The same as they? And now Fellirian was fading as a person also, becoming the anchor at the far end of the line, holding it in space. He could not sense Maellenkleth-Schaeszendur at all: she was in the figure only. That was her, and they were making her now. But there were four here in the unity that three were controlling. They held the chant, held down the square in a vise of Will, and

Now the figure trembled off-center, making odd little perturbations, paused, and sprang into three dimensions, a stick-figure empty cube, now beginning to fight them, to resist, to know Will. It seemed to want to go back into its old square shape, but the Krisshantem would not allow it to, and in a sudden moment of weakness he had it and

Now it leaped into the shape of the tessaract and they saw it not as a projection in three dimensions, a cruciform shape with an extra cubical arm in the front and the back, but there was no time to contemplate it; the outlined, stick-figure tessaract suddenly became solid, instantly, without sense of transition, opaque, solid, tangible, hanging in the empty space of their minds, and the whole surface was covered, a living, scintillating mosaic of changing black and yellow tiny squares all over the surface, cells flickering, changing; patterns washed over the now solid surface in their minds, patterns that moved and lunged like the reflected light of flame along a wall, more so, the yellow *burned*, the bumblebee patterns reminding them too closely of the striking visual display one saw in a migraine attack. Like that, yes, and it went on and on, the deeper rhythms washing over the surfaces like the play of summer lightning. Morlenden grunted with effort. And at the far end of the now submerged base line, he could also feel Fellirian straining as well. And something was now actively resisting them, something inside the crawling figure in their minds. It took all their effort to hold it still, for now all of Krisshantem's attention was devoted to controlling the wild patterns flying over the surface of the tessaract.

The process continued, seemingly endless, inexorable, and they could see no apparent change in the patterns. They could not determine how long it was taking, for there was no subjective sense of time when that time had been integrated as a spatial dimension. To Morlenden, it seemed to go on and on beyond levels of endurance he thought he might have had; days, weeks, a whole span devoted to a sustained effort of raw Will, Fire-Elemental, *Panrus*. He ached in odd places in his body, places which in his mind's eye did not correspond to any known locations in his old familiar physical body.

Then there was change. The pattern on the surface of the enigmatic tessaract slowed, slowed, slowed some more, and changed to a regular, surging motion, rather like the slow and rhythmic beating of waves onto some low shore, calm, reflective, steady. The figure also relaxed something of its taut straining, and became easier to hold. A sense of time came back, into them from the edge of the universe, intruding a little, and they were able to hear, as from some immense distance, faint sounds from the everyday world. Everyday world; not the real world. This was the real world, and they were making it. The everyday world was now, seemed disheartening, disappointing; after all, the perceptual surround of a Multispeech reprogram was seductive and addictive. It was naked Power. And along the intruding edges they heard the voice of Krisshantem, speaking ordinary words, inserted into the stream of Multispeech, as if he could retain the present pattern by nudging it now and again.

The voice said hoarsely, "Worst over, the longest part. . . . Motor coordination, control, body . . . all in place, calibrated and tested. . . . Next will be verbals and pseudomemory, the repersona, Schaeszendur. Different . . . she'll fight us now . . . hold it down like never before . . . now, now, now," and

Now the voice vanished, blown out like a candle flame, as if it had never been, never could be. Darkness and the tessaract. The tiny cellular units seemed to randomize slightly, lose coherence momentarily, but in the cellular units, a new coherence was building, surging, coming in like the tide, like an approaching storm, powerful and inescapable. The sensation of waves rather than firelight became very pronounced, and Morlenden tasted a brassy, metallic flavor in his mouth, smelled an unknown, spicy and rotten odor; gone instantly. And this one was becoming much harder to hold. There was definitely another force now, opposing them, something whose location they could not determine, but which seemed to be emanating from deep within (?) the projected figure in their minds. It tried to move away, escape them, distort the shape of the tessaract. Morlenden reached deep, for reserves he was not sure existed; and there he found something that allowed him to hang on, clamp down some more, for a little longer. But the figure's resistance was also increasing. Yet now it was not so steady; it waxed and waned, now fighting them, now withdrawing, and oddly, sometimes catching the sense and rhythm of what they were doing and in quick flashes surging ahead of them, anticipating almost, very nearly helping.

Yes, it was harder than the first part, but it was not as long in duration. Already they could sense a weakening in the resistance, and as the resistance slackened, it became passive,

submissive, waiting. It was now much easier to hold, almost
no effort at all; and with the easing of their common tension,
now Morlenden began to feel fatigue for the first time, much
deeper than mere tiredness as he had felt before. He was
weary; releasing the figure felt like sinking into an ocean of
warm syrup. And the resistance faded even more, and now
they could definitely feel for the first time the actual presence
of a fourth in the web of Multispeech that had bound them
all together. This fourth was warm, engaging, friendly, like a
small child, of no great mind, but pleasant and without any
force whatsoever. They . . . he was on the verge of welcoming
her and

Now with no warning or anticipation the tessaract in their
minds everted, collapsed, and with it went the universal
night: and they were sitting on the floor in a compartment on
a tube-train, lit by ceiling fixtures that seemed too bright, and
they were back in the old, shabby world of reality, yes, as
shabby and subtle as it was. And in their midst, a girl named
Schaeszendur was sitting up, leaning on one arm, looking idly
and vacantly about, gazing passively over the compartment
with a dazed, uncomprehending expression on her pretty
face, the soft, pursed mouth.

Morlenden looked long at the girl, now-Schaeszendur, comparing the image of her with the memory of then-Maellen-
kleth, which he would never forget no matter what happened
to him. There was no doubt of it; there was a noticeable difference. This Schaeszendur was as pretty as the old Maellenkleth, perhaps more so, but there were lacks. This one lacked
the drive, the ambition, and the prodigy intelligence of the
old; she now was relaxed, at her ease, submissive and passive.
This was only a gentle, retarded creature who wanted but to
please, and to be happy and free of pain and sorrow. She
would be functional, she could look after herself. And if
cared for lovingly by people who knew what they were about,
in time, she would grow to be almost a full-person again. But
never the Maellenkleth who challenged the Gameplayers and
three hundred and more years of tradition, of course.

Morlenden tried to move out of the position he had been
holding himself in, but his muscles would not obey him, and
he more or less half fell over on one side, supported by one
arm. As he had fallen closer to Krisshantem, the boy felt the
motion and turned to him. Kris spoke slowly, as if recounting
a dream, as if trying to recapture the exact flavor it had.
"You felt her in the end, how first she fought us, and then

helped? There was a lot left of the original in her after she had disminded; also many of the mnemonic fragments did not subfractionate completely. She fought us, but she wanted to come back purified, too . . . that was not your imagination, for she really was there in the net with us. She was, unconsciously. Beforetimes, when she was Maellenkleth and whole, when we were together, we would speak Multispeech while we made *dhainaz*, the whole time, however long we took. That is like projecting mentally . . . mentally, that which your bodies do with muscle and flesh. There were echoes of that in this Schaeszendur."

Morlenden tried to speak, but his voice came out a croak. "Is . . . everything all right with her?"

"Yes. She is whole. It worked better than I imagined it would. We did a better job than I had hoped for, even better than she who taught me could imagine. But all the same, this Schaeszendur is a stranger. . . . And I know a secret, that the maker must want the new persona to come terribly. That would be common sense; but also the holders must want it almost as much. My motivations are clear enough, but what of yours and your insibling co-spouse's? How is it that you, a stranger to Maellenkleth-who-was, want this as I?"

Morlenden answered wearily: "I have not known a forgetty before. Had we done this as strangers who had just met for the purpose, upon an utter nobody, perhaps things would have been different. I . . . just felt that she needed this restoration to balance justice, that she had not, whatever she did, deserved to come to the forgetty fate. I learned to care very much about Maellenkleth, just as I suppose we should about everyone. . . . Fellirian told me it was the same with her, as she pursued memories and reflections and echoes down in the Institute. And neither of us would see anyone ill-used, no matter by whom."

Now Morlenden felt more control returning to his limbs; he got to his feet with effort, still somewhat dazed, and went to the girl, helping her to her feet. She stood unsteadily, blinking in the harsh artificial light. Morlenden hoped that the pseudomemories Kris had programmed into her mind were pleasant ones, of cool nights and warm hearthfires, of kindness and body-friends, and of love affairs that did not end out of phase with their owners' times. He took her hand and gently led her to one of the sleeping-bunks, and she came with him, unquestioning, trusting, accepting without doubt. Morlenden was of course now long past the days of his fertility, the springing erect seasons of desire, the sudden emotions, the tidelike urgings as it had been with Fellirian. But he had not forgotten the embraces of the girls he had known, nor the soft sounds they made in his ear, the unspeakable words they had said to one another, the sleek strong bodies; nor would he forget, let go the various thrills, anticipations, satisfactions, and, yes, dissatisfactions of which he had measured his portion. Even so, as he led the girl Schaeszendur to the small bunk, as he undressed her out of the voluminous palliatory coverall, as he laid her down, he felt something like an echo of what had been but was no more. And Schaeszendur who was Maellenkleth was slender, gracefully muscular without seeming angular or stringy, her skin a rich soft olive color with darker shades along the accent lines and creases; the tendons of her neck, the insides of her elbows; honey and olive and sandalwood. Similar to Sanjirmil, perhaps, but richer, more range, more degrees of contrast. Morlenden smiled at her, knowing what little else to do, hoping it would reassure her, tucking her in under the covers and kissing her forehead chastely, as if she were a very young child, which of course she now was, whatever the lovely, lean body shouted at one. And like a child, she fell asleep instantly, effortlessly, not fidgeting, playing, daydreaming or twisting and searching for just that right position to enter the Dark World. Her eyelids simply fell shut, and she was breathing deeply, her rosy mouth opened very slightly. . . .

He returned to Fellirian, who had not moved. She was still sitting on the floor, head bowed, breathing in lengthy deep sighs. Morlenden knelt behind her and began kneading the muscles of her back, neck, shoulders. He felt a shiver ripple across the spare, graceful frame he knew so well, better than anyone else, better almost than he knew himself. She sank forward to the floor and lay, facedown, groaning.

After a while, she turned her face to the side and said, "Once of that in a lifetime is enough. I feel as if I'd been beaten."

Morlenden lay down alongside her, turning his head to face her. "And I also."

"It's too close to childbirth to suit me. It's not fair, me going through that: my time was over long ago. Done. Even if this was all in the mind, not in the body."

"It is a birth, that's a fact."

"Except this is all at once, you don't have that year and a

half to get ready for it*.... What does she seem like to you? You put her to bed."

"Mixed, Eliya. Some ways, like a very young child. Other ways, like an adolescent, but with odd pieces left out."

Then they no longer spoke. They lay side by side for a long time, in a halfway state between sleep and wakefulness, conscious enough to be aware of the deep, regular breathing of the girl, and also to hear the faint but undeniable snoring of Krisshantem. They felt the motion of the vehicle carrying them at what unknown velocity through the bowels of the earth, through rock and dirt, far from the sky, the tube-train adjusting magnetically to tiny irregularities in its roadbed, a motion curiously alive and animal-like, more like careful walking than anything else.

After a time, Fellirian moved closer to Morlenden, whispering, "I hate to speak of it, but I think we should depart this machine at the stop before the Institute terminal."

"Why so? Errat seemed manifestly uninterested in Mael...."

"Only *seemed*. I am certain that we have been monitored in various ways since we left Vance's office; it's their way, but they're sloppy about it, so I doubt we've given anything away. They don't watch the tubes, they think they're secure enough if they control the entries. But I sensed planning in the way they tossed her off onto us; they expect us to make certain moves. It is my intent to confuse and muddy those predictions. But there's a problem."

Morlenden asked, "Which is?"

"The tickets they use are always coded magnetically for a specific destination. The numbers are integrated into the material; you can't see them. So if we just try to get off on our own at another stop, we'll set off an alarm and they'll spot us for sure."

"We're stuck with them, then."

"No, there may be a way ... yes. The ones who came with us, the agents. They would have to have some way to override the destination register."

"If they are in fact agents."

"They're agents, all right. Trust me in this."

"Do you know how they override it?"

"Yes, I remember. I heard Vance talking about it once,

---

* The ler period of gestation was eighteen months.

long ago, to someone else. I was very young. Before we
wove."

"So somehow we must get them to open the doors."

"Yes, exactly. And the stop before the Institute is a busy
one. Not for us, but for them. Big factory town. I know this
local will stop there, never fear."

"But they'll soon find out we're not where we are supposed.
to be."

"So let them. All we need is a little head start. I know the
way. We can cross into the reservation by climbing the fence,
in the northeast provinces. We'll have a hard walk, perhaps a
run, ahead of us, and what's more, after what we have just
done. And Schaeszendur out of condition as well, but there's
no cure for it. I know ever more surely that if we stay with
these two primates we'll never see the inside again. It's been
too easy. And I don't want them to see what we've done for
her, either, even if I did insist on building her as we rode. Do
you see why, now? She must be able to walk on her own. We
could not carry her all that way. And she would also have to
respond to simple instructions."

"Eliya, have you been planning it this way all the way
along?"

"Not completely. . . . It really didn't dawn on me completely until after we built her back up, since we received her
from that Errat . . . the whole situation smells like a trap set
to catch more victims, some who might talk, in place of one
who didn't."

"You think she did that on her own?"

"Absolutely. They don't have the facilities to cause it. She
was facing something she couldn't handle, and she made sure
the secret of the Inner Game never got out from her. Or that
no association be made between those instruments and any
living Gameplayer."

"So you say. But even now, you and I, we know in fact
very little."

"They don't know that. And we have suspicions, too."

"How much time do we have to get ready?"

"Not very much, dear. I lost track of time while we were
deep in it back there, and afterward . . . wait a moment."
Very quietly, Fellirian got to her feet, opened the compartment door, looked out, adjusting her overshirt. She left for a
moment, and did not return for some time.

But she did return, slipping into the compartment as quietly as she had left it. She bent close to Morlenden, whisper-

ing softly, "Not so much time as I thought we'd have. We'll have to wake Kris and Maellenkleth-Schaeszendur, get them ready. While I do that, you go up into the next car and collect Kaldherman and Cannialin; bring them here, quietly, quietly. Be a sneak for once. And you and I, too; you'll like this, Mor."

FOURTEEN

Everything you have ever done is training or the next moment.

—M.A.F., *Atropine*

Outside in the corridor, Morlenden and Fellirian waited and watched through the single window for the appearance. of the next underground station platform; they saw unrelieved darkness passing, a blurred blank wall, illuminated only by the dim running-light glow of the tube-train corridor, light leaking out through the few windows. There was not enough light to distinguish any details, and what few were there were blurred by the terrific speed with which they were hurtled through the tunnels in the earth.

They could not sense any change in elevation in the train, or increase or reduction of its unknown speed; if there was any it was too gradual to be distinguished. But apparently change was coming, for without warning, a series of bright lights flashed by the window, too fast for more than a glance. Whatever message the lights conveyed, it was not verbal, as the patterns did not form any letters Fellirian could recognize. And shortly after the lights, they began to feel the train slowing, as simultaneously a slight pressure told them that they were rising. The train slowed more, obvious now, and then the walls nearby fell away from the window, first into an empty blank void of darkness, and then into a more open space, dimly illuminated by fixtures set at intervals along the ceiling. The chamber was low-ceilinged, the fixtures long out of repair; many of them did not work at all. The train slowed now to a walking pace, and they could make out a large, dingy sign painted on the concrete underground wall, which red *CPX010*. And the tube-train stopped.

As Fellirian had anticipated, there was considerable coming and going all along the length of the train, in fact more than they had seen earlier in the day at Region Central. The activity suggested an air of busyness and relaxed conventions, but after a moment, this early impression corrected itself under closer observation; the procedure was formal, deliberately interrupted, highly formatted all around. Patrons who wished to depart the train walked up to the sliding doors, inserted their tickets in a convenient slot beside the doors, and waited for the doors to open. And when they did, and the waiting patron departed, they hurried over the doorsill, and the door closed smartly behind them, with enough force to injure one who was unlucky enough to be laggard in his motions. So one lurched through, a jerky, graceless motion, which they nevertheless performed with the expertise of those who made such motions through similar doorways often, daily.

Fellirian watched carefully, until most of the traffic in the underground terminal had died down. There were yet some people scattered along the platform, but they seemed either to be idlers, or else deeply engrossed in their own affairs. They were completely uninterested in the train, or any of its passengers. At a signal from Fellirian, all the members of the party assumed their positions: all save Morlenden and Fellirian hid themselves carefully in the compartment. They all paused, took deep breaths. Morlenden rapped loudly on the door of the agents' compartment. And, oddly, it took some time to get a response out of them; apparently both of their guards either had gone to sleep or had been dozing.

The older agent, most probably the senior man, appeared at the door, bearing an attitude composed of nine-tenths irritation and one-tenth suspicion. "Yes, yes, what is it, what is the problem?"

Morlenden hoped that he sounded panicky. He cried out, blurting, "It's the girl! She's gone! We finished with our rite and slept—everything seemed to be in order. But when the motion of the train at the stop here woke us, we saw that she was gone! Fellirian thought she heard the compartment door closing, but we had just awakened and could not be sure. It could have been some other noise."

"Gone? Where the hell could she go?" The irritation slid into apprehension, and the apprehension glissaded into stark panic. "Gone?" he repeated idiotically, as if she would reappear by magic and prove him wrong. "Gone? That's impossible! Someone would have had to . . . Shit! They did! Well, she can't get very far by herself, nor can anyone else carrying her." He turned aside, back to his own compartment, saying to his partner, "Bill! Here, get it up now!" A moan rewarded his efforts. He reiterated, "Come on, bones! The girl's gone and you know what that'll mean. Go and check it out, starting with their compartment, then we'll do the rest of the train. She may not be off it yet."

The second agent appeared, dull with rudely interrupted sleep. And Morlenden and Fellirian watched the pair very closely, while they let their plans mature.

The older one commanded, "You go to their compartment, I'll hold the train. Quick, they can't have got far, her and whoever's helping her. She'll have to have help. Look for at least two, most likely three!"

Now he turned to Morlenden. "There were three of you besides the girl; you two and the boy. Where's he now?"

Morlenden shrunk, diminishing his smaller stature even further, hoping to appear embarrassed. He said slowly, as if he hated or feared to admit it, "Well, I don't exactly know that. We haven't been able to find him either. I thought he might have wandered off down the way, looking for the public convenience, but he's not in this section, and I . . ."

The senior agent suddenly looked ugly. A flash of desperation rebounded across his already homely countenance.

Fellirian added, "They were lovers, beforetimes. He *has* been a bit unstable."

The agent interrupted her. "Where would they go?"

"I don't know. None of us know Complex Ten at all, and I know for a fact that those two don't."

Now the second agent appeared, arranging his clothing, and ill-concealing a yawn, still addled with heavy sleep. The senior agent hurried to the exit doors, removing a red ticket from within a little wallet inside his coat and inserting it in the slot. The doors opened, remained open, as he muttered to himself, "Damn it all, anyway! My last override spent on this goddamn wild-goose chase, and they're harder to get every day. Have to sign your life away now just for one, the chintzy bastards."

Meanwhile, the junior agent had pushed the door of the other compartment open and looked within, carefully enough for the brief time he had spent in looking. But he saw nothing. He turned to the senior, still standing in the doorway, and said, "Nobody here."

"All right. You stay here and watch this car." He looked menacingly at Morlenden and Fellirian, towering over them. "And you two also. I'll check outside, just to be sure. They won't get far in Ten, and that's a fact!"

He turned abruptly and hurried through the opened door. The second agent looked on for a moment uneasily and uncertainly, as if something were escaping him as he stood there, something nagging at his mind which he should have noticed, but had not. Fellirian made nervous little motions with her hands, breaking her tension, hoping that she looked worried and afraid enough to convince this one. The junior agent looked from one to the other, at Fellirian, at Morlenden, who was nervously watching the terminal outside the car; and back, tentatively, at the compartment. And at the compartment again. He turned suddenly and returned for one more look, this time actually walking into the compartment, the one vacated by the ler. They heard him start to say something, but what he might have said was never finished. "Oh, yeah, there's a b—!" There was a sudden silence, followed by faint rustling sounds, and presently the four from inside appeared: Kaldherman, Cannialin, Schaeszendur, Krisshantem. Kris was last, and he carefully locked the compartment door as he left, but retaining the key in his hand. He said, "How much time now?"

"No time!" she hissed. "Quick, now! Into the terminal!"

They all filed out into the terminal, quietly and sedately, into the concrete caverns. Sounds echoed along the concrete, faded into the dimmed distances. This place was smokier than Region Central. Fighting the urge to run, they walked almost disinterestedly to an empty kiosk along the wall, half in shadows, its own lighting disconnected. They could not all hide in it, but they concealed themselves as best they could, standing very still, just as Kris had showed them, still and silent as stones. And almost before they had had time to assume their positions, the senior agent returned, blundering down the grimy stairwell, leaving a trail of noisy footfalls they could all follow with their ears. He wore tiny metal taps on his shoes. He appeared, breathing hard, still in a half-run, and without looking either to the right or the left, still muttering to himself, he boarded the tube-train, flipped open the wallet containing the tickets, and inserted a green ticket into the door-slot. The door closed, and almost immediately, the train started moving, softly and slowly at first, but all the time accelerating rapidly. They could see him easily through the moving windows: he went into his own compartment without looking, slamming the door, making the plastic of the window bulge. The train began moving off into its tunneled darkness under the earth, at the end of the terminal platform. Outside, in the kiosk, they stood absolutely still. As the section in which they had been riding began to approach the tunnel mouth, far down the platform, they observed through another window how a figure suddenly burst out of a compartment, frantically looking up and down the corridor. He vanished, apparently into their compartment. As he went past the window, he looked out, sweeping the platform with his practiced agent's eye, a well-trained glance, yet his glance had been trained to record motion against a stilled background, contrast. And for human subjects, the stained gray concrete walls made a fine background against which to pick up nervous, jerky motions, people wearing dark clothing. That was exactly the intent ingrained into people, and the dark clothing the only kind available. But the six ler were still and quiet, although standing openly visible; but their winter overshirts and cloaks were gray, and to him they were virtually invisible, and would have been even if the train had been standing still in the station. He had not seen them, and it was apparent from his panic that he had found nothing in the upper world of Complex Ten, either.

The train glided onward, supported on magnetic fields, increasing its speed, sliding, and suddenly the last coach was disappearing into the dark mouth of the tunnel entrance. And it was gone. The tunnel gaped, empty. A butterfly valve doorway closed silently on the tunnel portal. Above the portal, an orange light remained illuminated a moment, then turned green, and then went out.

Morlenden, not yet daring to move, said, out of the side of his mouth to Fellirian, "As you said, a good trick. Yes, I liked it. Now how much time?"

"More. Maybe an hour. With some luck, which means mistakes on someone else's part, still more. These agents are now normally issued only one override ticket at a time. They were abusing the privilege, so they were made to sign for it; it was an awful issue a few years ago. But now that the train is moving, it must go on to the next local stop; it can't stop in closed sections of the tunnels, and it can't back up. Of course he can communicate, through his comment interconnect, but before he makes his report, he'll have to figure out what happened. By the way, the other one: you didn't kill him, did you?"

Kris answered, "No, although your Braid afterfather was frowning like a cat licking gravy off a hot basting brush, and your aftermother was fingering her chicken-slitting knife and leering. No, he'll sleep, with bad dreams, and feel the worse for it. And they may have a problem communicating, for I palmed the unit you are talking about, I think. The second one was carrying it."

Fellirian looked at Kris blankly, saying nothing. After a time, she said, "Well, I suppose we can make some use of it. We can listen to it, and it may give us some warning; then we are that much more ahead of them. So keep it, although I wish you hadn't taken it. And keep it out of sight, and whatever you do, whatever it does, don't touch anything on it."

Again she paused, as if she were thinking out something that was easy to conceive, but difficult to say properly. Fellirian had always been diplomatic and polite, sometimes even to a fault. At last she added, "And now let me offer some advice: were I to go adventuring in the deep forest in your company, Krisshantem, I would adhere to your guidance, obey your lead, for that is most properly your world. Just so, thus. And this world that we walk in now is, as much as it can be for one of us, mine. And this world is much more perilous than any of our reservation forests, our wild lands. This is for you *Beth Mershonnekh*, the house of the devil. If we meet any more forerunners, take nothing from them. Nothing. This is not the time for explanations, and I accept the error of faulty instruction. For the time."

Kris nodded.

"Now," she continued. "We must move. Walk briskly, as if you had somewhere to go, somewhere near, an affair to see to. No nonsense and no trotting or running. Schaeszendur, do you understand me?"

The girl answered distantly, passively, "Yes, fast enough."

Then, Fellirian leading the way, they emerged from the kiosk and climbed the grimy, littered dim stairwell to the open-air street level of the terminal.

Complex Ten was one of the more industrialized places in the Region; and whatever products were manufactured in this concentration, it required a lot of lighting in the streets, and produced considerable dust. It was much dirtier, by and large, than had been Region Central. There were other differences: most of the structures here were clearly devoted to industry, not administration, as had been the case in Central. More, the atmosphere, the ambience, was suggestive of a cruder, more expedient system of order than had seemed to prevail in the almost overfastidious Central. Here there were no plazas, no intersections with planters, no streets that artfully went nowhere. Here, the streets were broad, straight, and long, and the building numbers followed one another in careful order, sometimes affixing additive letters to signify relationships; 242 was succeeded by 243, and immediately adjacent lay 243a.

Fellirian, who seemed to have some basic familiarity with the layout of this strange and seemingly now empty city, led them along a swift path through streets and lanes and freight alleys, dodging drains and gutter-runs brimming with black water floating an iridescent scum on its surface. Nowhere did they see heavy traffic, although there was plenty of evidence that everywhere the trafficways knew heavy and prolonged use; the main routes were generally free of trash and dust, blown clean by the fans of hovercraft and burnished to a dull sheen by thousands of rollers, bladders, and pounding wheels. Only rarely did they see any sort of vehicle at all, and even less frequently passersby.

They passed through empty streets flanked by large, flattened buildings whose purpose could not be determined from their shapes. All were illuminated within in various degrees, and as they passed each one, they sensed different orders of additional evidence: heavy thudding pounding, or grating, rattling sounds. Odors of hot metal, plastic reek, burning rubber, ozone, and hot grease. Smaller buildings were arrayed at random among the larger edifices, some housing units, barracks, small retail outlets, kiosks, stands. An occasional store; more rarely, offices. In the damp, smoky air, there was in the heart of the city a sense of desolation, abandonment, which sat squarely at variance with the obvious busyness of the place. They crossed canals, where drains trickled limply, dark water steamed, and lusterless surfaces eddied flaccidly.

Walking briskly, they soon crossed the more industrialized area and moved into another—this one devoted to dwelling-blocks, barracks, dormitories, flats—beginning to alternate with open, vacant lots and small fields. Near one such unit, apparently a housing unit, they passed a straggling group of people who were standing by a vendor's kiosk, drinking steaming cups of some heated beverage. The patrons' faces were lit by the brighter lights of the stand, and there was a certain sense of reserved camaraderie among them. Two older men made earnest conversation with three women, while a younger man stood aloofly to one side, making a small contribution from time to time, largely ignored. Mostly he seemed to brood upon affairs known only to himself, keeping his nose in his cup. The patrons took little, if any, notice of the ler as they passed across the street. Morlenden tried to imagine the whole of the scene before him; conjectures rose easily in his mind, but none of them were of any impressive degree of verity. It was a static scene, extracted out of time and life, held poised in a moment of cryptic significance.

After they had gone well past the group, he asked Fellirian, "They didn't notice us?"

"No, not in Ten. Those are Midnighters, about to go to work, so I should guess; they are half asleep. If they thought anything at all, it would be that we are Midnighters just like themselves, going to work somewhere. And if they bothered to recognize us for what we are, the people, it probably would not bother them greatly. Some of the Institute ler sojourn here at times."

Farther back in line, shepherding Schaeszendur, Krisshantem could be heard, muttering, "A vile place, this! Worse than the other. What business could our people have here?"

Fellirian said, back over her shoulder, "A lot. Ten is a kind of test site, where things are tried out; that's why it looks so . . . transient, impermanent."

"Still, vile," Kris added, his distaste not to be denied, "You would not see many of us living in a place like this."

Fellirian agreed, "Not now, no. But when Earth held only a few millions of forerunners I doubt if they would have lived so by choice, either. . . . And I am not so sure that in the end we would arrive in any more style, even though we say now that we'd choose a different destination. . . ." For the moment, she fell silent.

Morlenden said, "I'll credit you with knowing them better than I, than most of us, their nature and history. You work with them. But we are conjecturing a very distant future."

She looked back, saying, "Yes, a far future. And you know the legend as well as I, that someday the people will leave Earth, crossing the oceans of space to make our own world somewhere. . . . I wonder about that future, though I will not see it; if we would be exiles there, too, though we were lords there, when here we were only poor relatives, cast-off and restricted. Here, at least, artifacts though we may be to some, we still share chemistry with the other creatures of Earth. I often try to imagine those strange skies, the different odors on the wind. Would the skies be blue? How will we react to that? Not us, Olede, of course."

Morlenden said nothing, preferring to let her mood take her where it would. She would return presently and become the practical Fellirian, Madheliya, once again, leading them as befitted head of Braid through a strange and dangerous world. A deep and brooding one, that Eliya, he thought. Always conjecturing serious things that at least for the moment were manifestly improbable, if not damned impossible. Ler living in factory towns! Crossing space to another planet in a spaceship! All that was legendary, true, but he had never pondered deeply upon it. Children's tales, they were ... tales to tell children under the stars of summer nights. But when he had looked back at the girl Schaeszendur when Fellirian had been talking about ships and journeys and futures, he had seen, just for a second, a trace, a print, an echo of an expression on her face which he could not identify, even as he had seen it. The remains of an odd little half-smile, and a lambent flicker in the dark eyes, a subtle tensing of that soft, full, pursed mouth, sweet as a ripe persimmon.

They walked on and on, now passing sections of cultivated fields, interspersed with fewer of the low, flat enigmatic buildings. The fields were empty, their crops harvested. And the air was changing, too; it was still every bit as heavy with the tinctures and essences of the city, but now there was also a fresher undertone in it. They approached and passed what seemed to be a warehouse, or processing depot, now vacant. Morlenden looked back at Schaeszendur again; she had begun to trail them a little.

They stopped and waited for her to catch up; when she had caught up with all of them, he asked her, affectionately, "How do you feel, Schaeszen?"

"Tired," she answered in a dull voice. "I hurt."

Fellirian went to her and began to stroke the girl's arms and shoulders, gently but firmly. She said, "I know. You haven't walked so far in a long time. You have been very ill."

"I have? Was I in the house of a healer?"

"You have been ill and those who looked after you acted as best they could according to their lights. Don't worry now. I don't want to force you to do more than you can, but we do have to go on as fast as we are able. I promise that when we get home, you can sleep as long as you want. We'll take care of you. Rest now, here, this little bit. Then we'll go on some more."

The girl said softly, "I'm cold, too."

Fellirian said, "Kris, warm her."

Krisshantem, who had been standing alongside uncertainly, sat down on the roadside on the curb beside Schaeszendur and put his arm around her shoulders, tentatively, shyly. She adjusted to his contours, fitting herself to him, smiling and glancing at the boy from under her eyebrows, half-expectantly. There was also, in her face, something of a flickering smile, very like the one Morlenden could still see vividly in the image he had of Maellenkleth. Krisshantem looked back at her, smiling also, but weakly, and then looked away, blank.

Damn, thought Morlenden to himself. *He's the first male this Schaeszendur has ever seen in her real life, save me, when I put her to bed, and of course she wants him already for a little casual flower-fight. And her body needs it. What an irony! Or could there be something left over from before, from Maellenkleth; could she be remembering flashes of that which she had done before with this one?* He moved close beside Fellirian, sitting, feeling the familiar contours and warmth of flank and thigh, buttock and shoulder, contours so ingrained in his own mind that he knew he could survive autoforgetting with them intact.

He whispered, so the younger couple would not hear, "Eliya, is there any way she could remember him from before?"

"I don't think so. . . . Here, put your arm around me as well; I'm cold, too . . . there. And Schaes, remember? No, no way, according to all that I've heard. To autoforget is final. And even if there were mnemons left, pieces, the rebuilding would obliterate many of them, substituting things in their places. I suppose that she would catch some glimpses, but they would be meaningless to her; she might feel some familiarity, as with certain dreams, but she wouldn't know why. Don't trouble her, you'll only disturb her. Poor thing, this Schaeszendur was only just born a couple of hours ago."

"I've heard much the same about this as have you, Eliya, but I've been watching her: there's something there."

"Perhaps. Remember, neither you nor I have known a forgetty before. You could be mistaking what you see."

Morlenden suddenly felt mulish, obstinate. He started to say, "True, true, but nevertheless I . . ." He had intended to continue in the infuriating manner he had often used to good purpose with Fellirian in their long days together, but he was interrupted by a sudden noise from Krisshantem's waist-pouch.

The boy hurriedly dug out the tiny electronic unit, small enough to fit comfortably in his hand. Commnet Interconnect, Fellirian had called it. Krisshantem looked dumbly at the unit, while a speaker somewhere in it made an eerie wailing noise, not particularly loud, but a sound that carried, a repeating sliding tone that shivered up and down a short scale, rapidly, oscillating.

Fellirian started violently, tensing her whole body. "Kris, give it to me!"

Staring at the wailing unit, he handed it over to her carefully, as if it were about to explode. As he did, the wailing stopped, replaced immediately by a tired, bored voice, male from the sound of it, speaking Modanglic.

"Green system test call, green system test call, test call in the green system, system green, I say again. All operatives initiate roll on my mark . . . mark!" A tiny red light illuminated at the top of the unit Fellirian was holding in her hand, both near and far thumbs gripping it so her knuckles were white.

She looked frantically over the unit, trying to see if she could discover the correct button to press. But nothing on the Commnet Interconnect was lettered or numbered. She looked at it again in the poor light. Even if she could press the right one, what if anything, was she supposed to say? Again she went over the unit carefully. Then she laid it carefully on the ground, getting to her feet. The red light began winking on and off, on and off.

The speaker said, still in the same, bored voice, "B-fifteen, depress your acknowledge button."

There was a long pause. Following Fellirian's example, all of them arose, anticipating.

The speaker now said, "B-fifteen, procedure two." This time an edge had crept into the voice.

There was another pause. Then the red light went out, to be replaced by two orange lights that flickered on and off, alternating in a hypnotic rhythm. The speaker said, with finality, "B-fifteen, ninety-eight Alpha Alpha, break, out." There was a pulse of static, a click, and the speaker went dead. The orange lights continued to alternate.

Fellirian began dusting herself off, scuffling the area where she and Morlenden had been sitting. "Get going, all of you. We have to move now, run if necessary. I don't know how to operate that model, but I can guess what it is doing: it's sending out a signal so they can locate it. So scuff your places well before we leave here; they'll bring infrared trackers and in this cold weather our body heat will leave ground-glow like hot irons. And come on, move! We've got to get away from here, now!"

Krisshantem helped Schaeszendur to her feet, with some difficulty, and even after that she stood unsteadily, swaying and shivering while the rest of the party scuffed up their places, and hers. As if by an afterthought, Fellirian picked up the Commnet Interconnect, looked at it stupidly for a moment, and then turned, and in one flowing movement threw it into a nearby field as far as she could. Then they began their journey anew; Fellirian leading, Morlenden helping the girl along, followed by Cannialin and Kaldherman, with Kris guarding their rear, alert and awake. They immediately left the road and began an erratic, zigzag course among the accessways in the fields, always trying to keep a shed, or a clump of brush, between themselves and the place where they had stopped and rested. Whenever she could do so without delaying them too much, Fellirian led them through brush, and close by sheds and warehouses. At first, she paced them at a brisk walk, but after they had warmed up to that pace, she increased their speed to almost a half-trot, something more than a fast walk.

Morlenden, and especially Krisshantem, had no difficulty at all keeping the pace that Fellirian set, nor did the others, but they could tell easily that Schaeszendur was tiring fast now; she had used up almost all her reserves just to get as far as they had come already. Still, she was trying mightily to keep up and not slow them all, neither crying nor complaining. But as Morlenden helped her along from time to time, he could see her mouth moving, as if she were talking to herself. He could not hear words, nor make out what it might have been, but all in all, he knew that she would not make much more distance on her own.

They made better progress toward their unknown destination than would have seemed possible on foot. Moving in and out of shadows, brushlicks, odd little copses, groves, clusters of sheds; they were now moving through land almost completely given over to agriculture, and were beginning to hit patches and plots not completely recovered from the wild, or else perhaps returning to it again. The sky-glow from the lighting of Complex Ten was growing fractionally dimmer, to something nearer the light level one could see at night inside the reservation. And with their gray winter overshirts and hoods and cloaks, they were close to being practically invisible, if their motion did not give them away.

And now that they were spread out somewhat, Krisshantem seemed at times to disappear, and reappear again, unless one watched him constantly, and with an effort of will. Morlenden looked back at the boy often, marveling at his facility; and also at the way Kaldherman and Cannialin were following his example; Krisshantem's motions were almost the exact opposite of that of the humans they had seen earlier in the terminals—the jerky, learned, deliberately difficult motions, deliberately designed to make the user stand out against a background, and become obvious to a trained observer, deep in the secrets of the perception of motion. Kris, on the other hand, moved in a manner that could only be called transinstinctual, the sinuous weaving, looping, graceful, sine-curve motions, half random, the minimum energy curve, the motions of a feral creature who had carefully cultivated the little bit of natural wildness remaining to him. To glance at him casually, one would have seen only a person walking, but on the second scan across the target, Kris would not break the background, by pattern or motion. He was grass in the wind, a tree, a leaf, a branch, a bird. And Cannialin and Kaldherman were imitating him, following his example.

After a hard, fast walk, they reached at last the edges of the cultivated areas and entered the boundary woods, which in this place were composed of young pine trees, more or less regularly spaced. They all stopped as soon as they had attained the dense, furry growth, now on rising ground, and looked back over the fields in the direction from which they had come. It was a good distance; they had done very well, all things considered. And there across the fields was the suggestion of activity, blurred by the distance and the darkness: movement and lights. Distant hummings and fainter throbbing sounds. For the moment, the activity seemed rather random, purposeless, and undirected, but it was nevertheless in the exact spot where they had stopped to rest. Morlenden watched and felt a curious duality of emotions: complete disassociation from the meaningless motion and activity in the far distance, and simultaneously a personal feeling of dread, a definite suspicion that the activity was, under the muddled surface, very purposeful and highly intelligent. A semiliving gestalt organism whose entire consciousness was becoming focused upon their group, its prey. Yes, it was a predator taking shape back there.

Fellirian stopped and let the rest gather to her side as they caught up, one by one; Morlenden shepherding Schaeszendur, Cannialin and Kaldherman, Krisshantem bringing up the rear. Schaeszendur they brought into their midst, closing their bodies tightly about the girl, shielding her from the sudden chill of their stopping in the cold air. They were all breathing hard, and Morlenden could see, in the sky-scatter from the city lights, that there was a fine sheen of sweat glazed over Fellirian's face. Her eyes were alert, but heavy-lidded and tired; she had been in no better shape for this than he.

She said, between breaths, "Now we can assume . . . that the agents have made . . . their reports . . . and that they have located . . . the Commnet Interconnect. Probably . . . seen some . . . witnesses in the city."

Morlenden suggested, "The group at the hot-drink kiosk."

"There, yes. Maybe others; we did walk openly. With what they know, they can easily anticipate that we will be coming this way, to the reservation boundary. And they will certainly be bringing tracking equipment."

Krisshantem asked, "Could we not now take another course, to throw them off?"

Fellirian, recovering her breath, answered kindly, "No, that would not work except to our disadvantage. Attend: we cannot push Schaeszen, which we must if we turn now. And we would lengthen our exposure in the forerunner world; it is not like your woods out here, Kris—away from this area, close upon the reservation fence, there is nowhere we could survive for very long. None of us, not me, not you, know their ways well enough to pass unseen and uncaught in their midst for long. No, no, we cannot; we must go as straight as we can and hope that they have difficulty in picking up our trail."

She stopped, suddenly attentive, listening. In the far distance, a change had come in the humming sound, and the throbbing increased; they looked back, to see a group of lights detach itself from the others and move upward, slowly. It continued to move about, without apparent purpose or goal, but they could also see that it was quartering over the fields about the place where they had rested.

Krisshantem observed, "That, at least, is no mystery. I know that: it is an aircraft, looking for tracks."

Fellirian said, "Yes, so it must be. We'll soon know whether to rest a bit more, or make the last run to the fence."

The random, quartering motion of the lights continued for a time, but apparently the aircraft did not sense any obvious tracks within its sensor search pattern, for after several sweeps over the search area, it returned to the cluster of lights on the ground, merged with them, and as it did, the humming noise faded. The sense of activity around the cluster of lights in the distance continued, and if anything, increased in motion.

Fellirian watched the activity closely, and when the aircraft had landed, she did not seem any more optimistic by that which she had seen. She sighed deeply, and said, "For now they have missed us on the first cast. From the sound and movement of it, it's a hovercraft, a platform on ducted fans. . . . They know the general direction we must come, though, so they will try again. And once they pick up a good trail, they'll let shock troops down on ropes. . . . We had better move on now. We have much less of a lead on them."

Fellirian now turned away from the group, facing the direction they must go; she saw only pine trees, densely packed together, an uphill slope, a suggestion of higher forest farther up the slope, a darker sky that had no lights under it. It was not physically far as distances went: no more than the same distance back to the place where they had rested. But the aircraft was very close now; on a good trail, the troops could be upon them in minutes, and they were all past their best now.

Krisshantem laid his hand on Fellirian's arm. "Wait. I have an idea; you say that I am not wise in the way of cities, and that is so . . . but are they not equally unwise in the open country? And you say that they track by body-heat? So would not a brighter target capture their attention better than a muted one?"

They had no flares with them, and it was too damp for fire . . . Fellirian's mind leaped ahead. "Krisshantem, I forbid . . ."

"Now let us not speak of forbiddings and permissions. Were I blind and deaf, I could evade such as those; I have watched the clouds change, measured the color of the sky, seen the green of the winter sky. I have watched day-shadow move. And they will see where I have been, they will hear echoes, but where they look, there I will not be."

The humming in the backrgound increased again, as if to emphasize Kris's point. He also listened, and then continued, "Now, listen. You start—you, Morlenden, Schaeszendur, Kaldherman and Cannialin will come with me. When you get to the fence, you will be near my old territory, and I can catch you there, never fear. But you are better at this than I would have imagined most townsmen to be, so you may get a bit ahead . . . but you cannot lose me. I will always know where you are. And we will lead them on a merry chase."

Fellirian stood still, saying nothing. Morlenden thought on it, considered. It would have to be that way. They could not now hope to get Schaeszendur across the fence to safety, back inside, unless someone decoyed the forces now arraying themselves against them, and distracted them away from the one moment they needed. He moved the girl, nudging her gently, to let her know that the rest was at an end. She moved sluggishly, as if under water, turning her face to Morlenden's, a blank, blind gaze of exhaustion.

Morlenden said, "Schaeszen can't run any more. I'll have to carry her. I agree with Kris's proposal." Close by, Kaldherman set his face into a grim expression and nodded assent. Cannialin looked upward, at the sky-glow, and let her mouth fall into a weird, beatific smile.

Morlenden thought, *Just such an abstracted smile I have seen on her pretty face when she was slaughtering a chicken, slitting its throat with that long knife of hers. . . .*

Reluctantly, Fellirian agreed. "Yes, I see. Very well, Mor, I'll find the best way for you; follow my sound, and I'll help you at the fence." She listened to the sound. Then she turned to look at the wood once more, and back for a moment, calculating, indecisive . . . then started off at a lope into the piny brushwood, resolutely negotiating a passage. Morlenden, helping the girl along, half carrying her, set out behind. Kris and the others remained where they were, staring after them.

Kris called out, as they disappeared into the dense and prickly underbrush, "Don't crash so, you dray-horse! They will hear you even over the motor noises!"

Deep in the brush, Morlenden paused and looked back. Through a small gap he could see the boy removing his felt boots, while Kal and Cannialin did the same: to leave heated footprints in the cold ground, while he and Fellirian and

Schaeszen left less obvious marks. And farther back, behind
them all, on the edge of the city, a cluster of lights was moving, not exactly toward them, but close enough. Then the
lights went out, but the humming and throbbing did not
change. And after a moment, Morlenden thought he could
sense, at the edge of perception, a darker spot, vague in
shape, moving against the background sky-scatter. He turned
and looked back up the hill: there the sky was darker, and
there was no sound, save the passing of Fellirian through the
pines, making as much noise as she could now. In that direction, there were no moving shapes in the sky.

Now he started out, helping the girl along as best he could,
partially supporting her, as she walked now only a little under her own power. He discovered that he could keep up with
Fellirian, ahead, as she moved back and forth, searching out
the easiest way for them. He hardly ever had sight of her, but
he could follow her by sound almost as easily, listening carefully. And behind them, the humming grew louder. Morlenden looked back, over his shoulder, and saw the dark patch
moving against the sky again, more clearly now, but still not
distinctly enough to make its shape truly. It had covered most
of the distance to the beginning of the woods, but seemed to
be drifting a bit to the south of his present position. There
was no indication that they who flew in the craft had actually seen anything, not yet. Morlenden increased his pace,
moving deeper into the woods.

Schaeszendur sobbed, and Morlenden felt her full weight
sag against his left arm; further progress had become impossible for her, even with assistance. She had reached the end
of her physical resources. Morlenden bent, and let her fall
across his shoulders, taking her full weight. She was lighter
than he expected her to be . . . Maellenkleth had been well-
formed, comely and strong, but this Schaeszendur was made
of fluff and bubbles, her flesh soft and stringy. She was, after
her long confinement, still her basic build, but much reduced
. . . and despite her weight, he made better progress, because
he did not have to half-drag her along.

Now he did not turn to watch the aircraft; he listened. He
heard the hum and throb of the motors change tone abruptly.
He tried to ignore it, but could not; swinging the load of the
girl slowly around on his shoulders, Morlenden turned clumsily about, to see. The darkness in the sky was almost abreast
of them now to the south, and it was falling, as an autumn
leaf might glide downward, but without the sudden turns and

swoops of the leaf. Lower, it stopped as if running into a wall
of feathers, the motors surging mightily, then falling in tone
again. The craft hovered, now stopped dead-still in the air,
and the lights came on again. Other lights came on with
them, searchlights directed against the ground. In their glare
he could see rope ladders falling, unrolling out of the craft,
and immediately, on them, figures climbing down, many with
bulky backpacks. Morlenden struggled with his burden and
lurched off in the direction he imagined Fellirian to be, trying
to move faster and more quietly. And behind him, he now
heard voices, faintly, muffled by the trees and the air, ghostly,
unsubstantial. The hovercraft powered up, rose sharply, turning as it did and withdrawing a little back toward the city.
He stopped, listening for Fellirian. Over the pounding of his
heart and the throb of the hovercraft motors, he could not
hear her. Morlenden listened again, carefully, all senses tense
and strained. The motor noise was fading. Otherwise, nothing.

And the voices faded also, fell silent. He now began to feel
a touch of fear . . . he half expected to hear, as he continued
slogging up the hill along what seemed to be the best way, a
sharp, peremptory command. Or perhaps nothing, a sudden
pain. His skin crawled. Where the hell was Fellirian?

There was no actual sign that he was being pursued. Everything seemed quiet nearby. Morlenden continued walking,
and noticed that the upward slope was beginning to level off
a little, and that the trees were larger, more mature; he knew
instinctively that they had to be near the fence, but as yet he
could not see it.

Behind him, now far down the gentle slope, Morlenden
heard a curious, half-muffled sound, more a prolonged puff or
whooshing than a report, of gunshot. He had never heard
anything like it before. After the sound died away, he also
heard calls, cries, hoarse exhortations, also distorted by distance and the intervening trees. Kris, Kal, Ayali. . . . He
heard more sounds, faraway crashing and tearing in the
brush, more calls, so it seemed, all in Modanglic. How many?
Three? Four? He had seen five or six men climb down from
the hovercraft. But from the noise they made, it sounded like
a small army. All the same, the continuing racket reassured
him; they would not be so loud, if they had caught any of the
decoy party. No, Kris would be teasing them, drawing them
off. That would be Kris's way; and then he'd just vanish

among the trees. The crashing and shouting moved farther off, more southerly, became fainter.

Morlenden stopped now, his head reeling, feeling the full weight of fatigue. He stooped over, and, as gently as he could, laid Schaeszendur down, resting her head on a pile of pine needles he had hastily scraped together. Kneeling beside her, he examined her closely; she seemed conscious, but she made no attempt to speak. Her eyes remained, open, but the expression in them was glassy, unfocused. Morlenden looked around himself. He saw nothing save darkness, the ever-present sky-scatter, the shapes of trees, black trunks looming. It was dense here, like the forests inside. He knew they were close, they had to be, but now the ground was level and he could not determine in which direction the fence lay. He could guess one way, for there was some thinning in the trees, a sense of openness. From that direction he heard faint scuffling in the carpet of fallen needles underfoot, glimpsed a suggestion of movement, a dark shape, becoming a gray winter overcloak; it was Fellirian. She was coming at a half-run.

Fellirian saw him, the girl on the ground, and called out, "It's not far now, just over there, where I came from. It's more open near the fence. Can you make it?"

Morlenden was still short of breath. "Have to. They drew them off to the south, I think. It's quiet again. But there are too many ifs. They know there is more than one of us, so they might catch on to the trick. And we are more visible here." He looked upward as he spoke, nodding toward the throbbing that now never faded entirely from hearing.

Fellirian reached them, knelt beside the girl, held the girl's eye open and looked closely. Then she looked in the same direction he had indicated, and nodded. Breath-steam wreathed her face and the overhanging cowl of her overshirt. She said, "I'll help you with her. Come on."

Together, they lifted the girl between them, and began moving forward again, supporting, half dragging Schaeszen between them, dodging around tree trunks, stumbling over fallen branches in their way, abandoning the pretense of stealth and quiet. They crossed a low rise, a swell in the ground, and stopped. Just ahead of them, Morlenden could see an old-fashioned chain-link fence, about twice his height. They stumbled forward to it in a last rush, reaching the fence and stopping, leaning against the links and mesh of cold metal. There were thin flakes of ice on some of the links.

Fellirian asked, "How do we get her over? I was counting

on her climbing herself. Now, I don't know; I don't think she can climb it on her own."

"I don't know. Let her rest a bit more; let me think." They tenderly laid the girl down again, propped against the fence, Morlenden kneeling partially supporting her. Fellirian stood over them, legs slightly apart, panting. Suddenly she turned her head, back, the way they had come up the hill.

She said urgently, softly, "Olede! Voices, there, speaking Modanglic! They're coming!"

"Sh! I hear them. Lights, too; see them? It has to be now, doesn't it, Eliya? Give me a hand with her, here."

Morlenden now leaned over Schaeszendur, shook her roughly, sharply, "Schaeszendur!" There was no response. She looked at him, but did nothing else. Her eyes were dull, lifeless. He shook her again. "Schaeszendur! Maellenkleth!" Some luster reappeared in her eyes. "Aezedu! Aelekle! Wake up! Listen to me!" The girl seemed to listen to him now. "Can you hold to me if I carry your weight?"

"Yes." The voice was flat and unaccented, but it was clear, steady.

"Then you must do this: hold to me, no matter what. Rest and sleep are not far now. Just one more effort and you're safe. Use all your strength and hold to me! We have to climb a fence!"

The same calm, distant measured voice answered him. "Yes, I understand, I must hold to you. I can. I will do it."

He stood and helped the girl to her feet, while Fellirian steadied her. She was very shaky on her feet, although she did now stand on her own. Her eyes were clear also, but somehow she did not seem to be aware of her surroundings. Morlenden turned to the fence, getting into position, reaching for and feeling the cold metal strands, experimentally feeling with his toe for a foothold. Fellirian helped the girl onto Morlenden's back, arranging her arms about his neck, placing the girl's hands so she would be steady, locked in position however Morlenden had to move on the fence.

She whispered in Shaeszendur-Maellenkleth's ear, "That's a good girl. Yes, just like this now, hold on, whatever happens; hold on to Morlenden."

Then to Morlenden, "We'll have to hurry, Olede, the lights are close now. I'll try to get them away from you." Her presence suddenly withdrew.

It was true. He could clearly hear the sounds of crashing in the brush back in the woods, not so far at all now. He took a deep breath, looked at the fence, tensed his muscles. *One more obstacle, and we're over. They won't dare touch us inside the fence.* He drew another deep breath, tightened his grasp on the cold metal, thrust. He could not look upward without moving the girl. He took his first step up, feeling the full weight of the girl settling on his back, shifting through his arms down to his hands, his fingers, pressing on the wire strands.

And behind him he heard footfalls in the ground-cover, sharp scufflings off to the left, in the direction Fellirian had taken. Then there were more from the same direction, but farther off. And now directly behind him, sudden crashing of brush, footfalls on the hard ground pounding, and an actinic light cast its glare upon his hands on the fence.

He heard a voice shouting in Modanglic, "There they are, two, on the fence!"

Another shouted hoarsely, "You! You, stop! Get down from there, *now!*"

Morlenden shook his head slightly, to himself, and took another step up. There was more commotion behind him, scuffling, hoarse exclamations, oaths, curses, and as someone cried out some unintelligible word, he heard at close hand the same odd sound he had heard earlier. A whooshing, a hiss, very close, especially loud. He felt Schaeszendur tense her whole supple body, sharply, heard her emit a short grunt, as with great effort. Her grip around his neck tightened convulsively, strongly, and she was choking him. She coughed, wetly, and the intense grip began to weaken. She was going to let go, she would fall; Morlenden let himself back down, and as he felt solid ground under his boots and bent to cushion her fall, she let go, relaxing completely, sliding off and slumping against the fence in much the same posture she had rested in only moments before. Morlenden turned around.

He felt a black, consuming rage rising, suffusing him, distorting his vision, altering his perceptions. He felt enlarged, he felt time slow, he expanded into something strange, fey, an evil released, clenching his hands convulsively, breathing in deep, steady breaths. Morlenden turned around, withdrawing his fish-knife from its baldric. He saw a confused blur of action.

They were all there—Fellirian, Krisshantem, Cannialin, Kaldherman—moving about a perimeter enclosing a small group of five humans, one of whom was struggling with an unwieldy piece of elongated equipment, gunlike in shape, but not exactly a gun, either, in the traditional sense. The remaining four seemed to be protecting that one. It seemed that none of them noticed Morlenden, so intent were they on the flashing, whirling figures approaching from outside their group. Morlenden tightened his grip on the long, thin knife, walking like an invulnerable sleepwalker. They did not see him, the invisible one, and he would deal among them like the angel of death. He felt like Kris, more so, invulnerable and invisible, charmed. The rest skirmished to the rear, opening up the gunner for him. The one with the odd, bulky gun was open, in front of him, still struggling with some adjustment; perhaps the weapon was jammed, broken. Morlenden walked calmly, quietly to him, almost reaching him before the man became aware of him. The man looked up, startled, raising the weapon, and as he did, Morlenden casually stepped inside the reach of the gun and calmly, still calmly, pushed the knife into the man's chest. There was a resistance, and blood flowed around the wound. He pushed harder, looking directly into the man's shocked eyes with a lover's intimacy. The weapon dropped from his hands and the man looked at Morlenden accusingly, incredulously, as if this could not be happening to him, him the weaponeer. And a darkness greater than the night passed over his vision, as he slumped to the cold ground.

The others now saw that their weaponeer was down, and they menaced the five ler with hand-pistols, while one among them struggled, panic-stricken, with a small device, something similar to the communications unit Krisshantem had taken off the agent. They seemed confident now, slowed, sure that none of the group facing them would use any kind of released weapon. They had been briefed. Before he could set the controls the way he intended to, Fellirian menaced him, her own knife drawn, before any of the others could bring a weapon to bear. The man danced backward, holding it high, out of reach, as the others tried to get into position for a shot. One went down immediately, as he suddenly met a Kris who wasn't supposed to be where he was, throat-chopped. Morlenden sliced at the hand holding the communicator, heard, as if under water, a harsh cry, and the communicator was on the ground. He stepped on it, breaking its delicate inner structure into a jumble of metal, now smoking and sparking as its power-pack shorted out. Cannialin dispatched that one, while he was trying to avoid Morlenden, with the crazed look in his eyes of a berserker, and Fellirian, who steadily advanced upon him, uttering terrible words in a language he did not understand. The last saw his position, and tried to run, but he met Kaldherman and Krisshantem and his journey, even in flight, was a short one.

And there was silence in the forest, marked only by hard breathing, and a distant hum and throb of motors from the hovercraft, quartering the distance, far away. Morlenden felt the rage abating, saw what they had done, saw that the others saw it, too. They did not speak, but dumbly walked about the scene of the battle, numb, astonished. Morlenden could see clearly again, and looking at Fellirian, saw streams of tears down her cheeks, although there was no change in the expression on her face. They all knew they had avenged something here, they had defeated armed men, with no more than their hand weapons. But something had snapped, and would never be the same again. There was blood on the ground, that had not been spilled in such a way before.

Krisshantem was the first to find his voice. He said slowly, "After a time, they began to realize what we were doing. They had tried a shot at us, to no good. While they shot at where they thought I was, Kal and Cannialin got one of them. But the rest saw, and knew we were not the ones they sought. So they retreated, turned back. They found your trail with that weapon, and followed it. They would not be diverted. We tried to intercept them, but they were then between us, and running hard. It was no good, no good, we couldn't prevent it. . . ."

Time was resuming its normal flow. Morlenden asked, distantly, "Eliya, what did they shoot her with?"

Her voice was flat, overcontrolled. "A filthy thing, a wire-guide. It launches a tiny rocket with an explosive head containing barbs. It's connected by a wire to the gun itself, which follows the flight with a computer, guides it. All you have to do is keep the target in the sights. They like to use it against fugitives. . . . Do you see? Once hit with that thing, the target cannot escape, even if it didn't have a mortal wound."

Morlenden said dryly, "Now I understand the weapon prohibition better. . . ."

"Yes," Fellirian said. "So do we all who were here. A weapon that leaves the hand magnifies the user too much, so much that often the original will that guided it is lost, expanded, diluted. Washed out. And that is why we fear much technology, why we labor to retain our innocence; other things magnify, too, just the same way, and we are not wise

enough yet to know if we really do want to see that magnified image of ourselves . . . until we have a better control of
ourselves. We are not restrained enough yet by half. Were it
so with them, too."

Morlenden said, "Innocence . . . I do not feel so innocent.
There is blood."

Cannialin interrupted. "Sh! Listen!"

At her command, they all stopped, in a circle, facing each
other, the five of them, and listened. Schaeszendur. The girl
was not yet dead. They could hear her in the silence after the
violence, by the fence, where she had fallen. She was talking
aimlessly, now protected by shock from the pain that would
have come. She was talking, but most of it was just babbling,
nonsense, not even words. The mortal wound she had received, the fatigue, the unstable implant persona, they were
all coming together now. They listened to the soft, hoarse
voice, childishly high in tone. Just babbling. Morlenden felt a
vast dull pain in his heart. And they turned from the place
where they had made murder, where they had fought in heat
with the men, the forerunners, and walked slowly to the
fence, to her.

They all knelt close around her. She was lying, partly
propped against the fence, as they had left her. Morlenden
cradled her head, feeling the soft, dark hair, the heated skin
along the back of her neck. He wiped her mouth; there had
been blood at one corner of it. And brushed the adolescent
hair off her forehead, out of her eyes. An odd frown creased
her forehead momentarily.

Her eyes had been open, but had been moving aimlessly,
sometimes independently of one another. She did not see, except some artificial interior scene Krisshantem had implanted
in her . . . some memory. But without warning, the expression
of dull shock and confusion in her face faded away quickly,
changing radically into something else. The contours of her
face began to shift, as if obeying instructions from a different
set of muscles, a different personality. The childlike roundness of face faded, vanished, and was replaced by a harder,
more adult set along the jaw, tense and concentrated around
the eyes. The eyes cleared, became focused, calm, then intense. Without moving her head, she looked hard at them all,
from face to face, pausing especially long when she came to
Kris. Morlenden recognized that look in her eyes at once: it
was the look of one who saw strangers and knew not how
they came there. Only Kris was familiar. He knew. Maellen-

kleth knew only Kris among them, while Schaeszendur had known them all alike. This was Maellenkleth, how, he didn't know, but Maellenkleth it undeniably was.

She took a deep breath, breaking something deep inside. They heard a rattling in her throat. She grasped Morlenden, who was closest to her, and with a capable, terrifyingly strong grip, pulled him down close to her, so that his face was by hers. All of Morlenden's senses were alive, tensed to ultimate receptivity, alert: he sensed all of her, how short her time-line was. She had only seconds to live. He smelled sweat, fear-scent, the reek of adrenaline, blood, musky, salty, all overlying the sweet fragrance of a young girl.

And he heard the harsh voice in his ear, ragged with shock and the leading edge of the wedge of pain. It was not the simplistic child's voice he had heard before, when it was Schaeszendur; this was different. Hoarse and wounded and dying it may have been, but it was also the voice of one almost adult, filled with knowledge and desires and incredible will for one born in the sign of the Water elemental. The grip tightened. And the voice rasped, "Mevlannen ... Mevlannen ... to Sanjirmil."

"What?" he asked.

The rasping whisper repeated again, "... Matrix .. from Mev ... from Elane ... get the matrix from Mev-Elane ... take to Sanjirmil. ..."

"What matrix, what for?"

"Get the matrix from Mevlannen ..." and then the voice trailed off into another series of nonsense words, drifting back into the childish intonations of the forgetty, Schaeszendur. Or was it? The face did not change, though the grip was now relaxing. The voice trailed off. She was yet breathing, but it was obvious that she had but a few instants left to live. Krisshantem stepped forward, and it was as if she was seeing him for the first time. Morlenden felt the hand holding his overshirt clench hard, almost as if she were going to try to rise to her feet. Then he saw her lips moving, trying to form words, and she found her voice, her eyes cleared completely, and she spoke, and

Now an immense Will suddenly grasped their minds and clamped down, hard, so intense it was painful. All five of them immediately lost the sensory input of the world around them. This was Maellenkleth, Maellenkleth the master Player, and she was sending an image in Multispeech. In visual Command-override, so powerful they could not move, or block it out of their minds. They all saw the same thing, and it would remain impressed on their minds, reverberating, forever. It was not a message, an instruction, a command, but a picture. A picture of Maellenkleth, not quite as any of them had ever seen her before, her face shining with rapture, turning slightly to her right side, turned a little away from the viewer, her arms outstretched from her torso. All around her, surrounding her, outlined in faint, glowing blue, were the outlines of a tesseract, encompassing her, protecting her. It was clear that here, in the vision, she had truly come into her own. She floated in space, inside a translucent tesseract, wearing the ritual robes of a high Perklaren contestant of the Game, the Inner Game, intricate and arcane Game patterns and emblems embroidered vertically down a panel of linen on the front of her robe, and also along the hem of the robe about her pretty, delicate feet, and on the borders of the wide sleeves of the garment. Behind her, almost in the direction she was facing, as if looking over her shoulder, was a background of the patterns of some Game projected upward onto a spherical ceiling and part of a wall, an immense multicolored Game diagram, stopped in midflight.

They felt the Will fading, the image fading with it, not changing, but dimming, losing color contrast, becoming pastelled, becoming empty outlines, fading, fading, graying, darkening, and out. Their optic nerves resumed transmitting the images of a nighttime forest, by a fence, to their visual centers. And Maellenkleth lay relaxed against the fence, as if asleep, the face relaxed, peaceful. Morlenden, his hand still under her slender neck, could feel her cooling. Life had departed this body.

Fellirian hiccuped nervously. "What was she sending?"

Kris answered, "Something about a matrix Mevlannen has. Take it to Sanjirmil. . . . She's dead now."

"I know," said Morlenden. "Had you ever seen her send an image like that before?" He knew very well that somehow she had imposed an image of herself upon a background of the Inner Game. He also knew that none of the rest of the Derens had seen that before.

Krisshantem answered, "No, nothing like that. I could recognize a Game display, but it is in a strange form. Was that Inner Game?"

"Yes. And I don't know what the significance of it is."

The boy said, "I never saw her do anything like that before. I didn't realize she could override like that, even though she taught me override. . . . That pattern on the display she did show me once, but plain and flat, not like that curved screen-ceiling. . . . It is something very special, I know that, something very secret." He sat back on his heels, shaking his head. "That was the old Maellen, there, in the end, the old Maellen and something more. She was sending Truth, then, not playing or concealing, though she had not the time to tell us what it means. I know it not. But it must have been a powerful thing, to have endured through autoforgetting and restructuring; she believed something powerfully."

Fellirian said slowly, "Truth is what we believe; and of course we become what we believe ourselves to be. Unlimited things. Only the lesser are provable. She sent to us what she was to herself."

Morlenden asked, "Do you know what she meant?"

"No."

"Must we, then, do as she asked?"

"I still shake from the force of it; of course we must, we cannot choose at this point, but follow it through to the very end. That is why she sent that image in the end, the very end. She said, there, 'Do this for me, it is my very life.' To have retained it through all she endured, it must have been the central immanent fact of her life, something she lived with daily, ingrained in her at the cellular level, beyond the reach of even autoforgetting. It was that which lent meaning to her life."

Kris added, "It was truly her, this I know. There was much that she did not tell me, but I could sense that we were close to it; she took me as far as she could. And if you will not pursue this, Morlenden, then I will."

"Rest in ease, Krisshantem. I will take it. I think not to the ends of the Earth, either, for Mevlannen I can find."

Fellirian added, "And it must be quickly, too, Olede. There was an urgency in her, something that must be done quickly. And we should do this without informing the Perwathwiy or Sanjirmil. It will be difficult and perilous, a risk, that trip all the way across the continent. They will be watchful, wary, after what was done here tonight. I know some tricks yet, though, and with the watchfulness there may also be much confusion, enough to slip through. . . ." She stopped now, thinking. "And now let us act in reverence toward this poor body that has endured so much, and for what? Yes, let us do it, for they will come, looking for their shock troops."

Kris said, as Fellirian got to her feet, "She said once to me

that she did that which she performed outside because she enjoyed it, the shadow-play, the feints, the skill of passing unseen on many errands; but that overriding all personal likes
and dislikes was a higher reason, that we would all know of
it, within her lifetime. She thought, before fertility, which was
why she was working so hard to instruct me in the Game
basics, and gather support for her proposal to have us declared *shartoorh* Dirklarens. I do not know why, but I know
the meaning of her words and her deeds: this was for us. The
people."

Morlenden said, also getting to his feet, "Then may it have
been a worthy price, for she paid with two lives for it: not
many would go so far as to risk even one."

Kaldherman had been silent through the whole adventure.
Now he spoke. "I have an unraveled thread of my own, you
thinkers and worriers and ponderers; I wish to know how it is
the five of us, with no more than knives, best armed and
trained forerunners?"

Cannialin also asked, "Indeed. Where are the wild-eyed,
merciless humans, who are reputed to shoot and burn without
stint? These were willing enough to shoot one in the back,
but when the scars would be in the front side, they milled
about like geese in the slaughteryard. I admit to no cow-
ardice, but I had not thought myself so fearsome before. Kal-
der, perhaps: he had a look about him just now that would
have wormed a dog, but me?"

Fellirian said, "Ayali, you do not know how strange you
look with knife in hand ... indeed, I fear you myself sometimes at home, when you are slicing a fowl's throat. The only
thing I can say is that they must not be accustomed to
resistance, much less attack upon themselves; but that raises
many questions in my mind, and an answer that makes questions isn't such a good one, is it?"

Morlenden said, "You mean they just have to threaten, not
actually do anything?"

"So it seems. They respond quickly enough. That I have
seen with my own eyes, and the targets always run, and are
gathered. No one resists."

"And what if someone did?"

"Unthinkable."

"Do they have any idea what a foundation they have built
upon, that a dozen determined men could take over the
whole planet?"

No one answered Morlenden's question. And now they all

stood about Maellenkleth, and bent to pick her up. In the background they could still hear the humming and throbbing of the hovercraft, now somewhat nearer. Morlenden was still somewhat stunned, and he felt light-headed, still not quite himself. It had been unthinkable that he had been shot at by an unknown assassin; but to do as he had done here, this night: that was an even more remote conception. Yet he had done it, and as he thought back on it, he felt convinced that it was right, proper. Revenge, and self-survival. And something, some unknown quantity in the unseen underworld, had shifted, changed, and now he was being borne along on the main current of an uncharted stream, flowing to an unknown destination. He shrugged, a gesture that the others missed.

And he said, half to himself, which they also did not notice, lifting the girl up to Kaldherman and Krisshantem, who had climbed the fence, "Watching? Confused? Yes, they will be all those things ... and maybe they will not be watching half so well as they imagine they do. This one moved among them unseen. Now I . . . ?"

And they began the painful process of lifting Maellen's body over the fence. She was of the Water elemental, and would have to be returned to the waters; they would have to carry her a long way.

FIFTEEN

When I write, betimes, in my Journal, I always feel supremely confident I solve all problems, not only with ease, but with style as well, seasoned with considerable wit. . . . We also may note the same condition in men who have been deprived of Oxygen. This is enough to make one wonder.
—*The Vaseline Dreams of Hundifer Soames*

That which had gathered in the office of Klaneth Parleau, Chairman of Seaboard South Region, could only be called a mob, and at the moment, all of its constituent parts were trying to talk at once, to each other, to nobody, to anybody, perhaps even to themselves, all utilizing the maximum in volume to make themselves heard. Nobody managed to hear anything but din and confusion. It was, in a word, chaos. Parleau watched in astounded consternation, striving mightily to capture their attention, but his efforts, normally successful, were useless. In fact, they added measurably to the reigning confusion. The members just talked louder and heard less. At last, in total exasperation, Parleau picked up a heavy paperweight, a large stainless steel cube a handsbreadth on a side, and pounded his appointment book until the noise at least died down enough for him to be heard.

"Damn it to hell!" roared the chairman, uncharacteristically in the full grip of his temper. "Is this a Regional Board of Inquiry, or a panel discussion among anarchists?" The noise level dropped some more. They were offended that the chairman should call them anarchists. It became almost quiet. Parleau did not intend to let them rest there. He roared on, "Is this the office of a Regional Chairman, or is it a bandits' den?"

And at last, true, blessed silence fell. Parleau commanded, "Blantine, read the names of those present!"

A voice, hoarse from bawling at the others, started, from somewhere near the far end of the table, "But, Chairman, we . . ."

"Shut the hell up, Gerlin! Recorder, read the names as instructed—programmed, unprogrammed, and soon to be deprogrammed."

Blantine, the recorder, a junior administrative apprentice, hastily borrowed from the shift currently working days, began in a voice full of uneasiness. "Doctor Mandor Klyten, Department of Alien Affairs; Edner Eykor, S-eighteen, Security; Aseph Plattsman, S-twelve, Control; Thoro Gerlin, M-six, Tactical Units . . ." And continuing through several others, at last finishing and sitting down, trying his best to appear inconspicuous. He had not listed himself as a member. He did not intend to add anything or contribute, save record what they said.

Parleau was still standing. He added, not willing to let the apprentice clerk off the hook, either, "And Cretus Blantine, Recorder." He noted that the reading of names had its desired effect: they were now all quiet and attentive.

Parleau began, "We are here to determine the causes and consequences of a series of incidents that occurred two days ago in this Region, in or near Complex Ten." Parleau observed some fidgeting out of the corner of his eye, and added, "This board is hereby convened by instruction of Continental Secretariat, Denver, Central High Plains Region." Here he paused to let it sink in, with the implications. A Regional Chairman held power in his own region, of course, but impelled by ConSec, he could bring forces to bear from outside the region. He thought, *Argue, would they? We'll see what kind of song they sing for Section Q when they go to explain this*. He said, "Plattsman, review events."

Plattsman, after consulting some logs, began, "At about the sixteenth hour, the girl we had been holding, the vandal identified as one Maellenkleth Srith Perklaren, was released in the custody and responsibility of a party of New Humans who had previously been identified. And immediately the problem commences. Somehow, the transaction, though handled according to instructions and regulational data, was actually performed by a Hando Errat, accompanied by agents under his personal control. We conjecture that there was a plan to abduct the whole party at some other point, before they could return the girl to the reservation. However, at Complex Ten, the New Human party somehow evaded Errat's men and escaped into the Urblex. I may add here that none of this was reported until much later, owing to the substitution of agents. Also, reporting and monitoring was further delayed because somehow the New Humans removed the Commnet Interconnect from the agent who had been carrying it, abandoning it several miles to the west. This unit had not responded to a routine maintenance call-up, so autolocation was initiated. At the same time, our own monitor at the Institute stop reported no contact, and Complex Seven picked up the false agents in the tube terminal, failing exit procedure. Regional Control called for a Tactical Team, but too much time had elapsed, and detailed tracking with chemsensors was deemed unlikely. The TacTeam was deployed into the woods adjacent to the reservation boundary, reporting a live track. They descended, grounded, the carryall standing by. After some time elapsed, the carryall reported no contact, although it observed some action. It returned for reinforcements, onloaded, and returned to the site. The team on the ground did not respond, so a thorough search was made of the area. One member was found near the grounding site, and the rest were located near the fence, in deceased condition."

Parleau said, "Continue."

"Subsequent investigation, necessarily hasty, has established that six New Humans were observed transiting Complex Ten. Of the weapons possessed by the TacTeam, only the wireguide had been discharged. One dart was not located, the other was still attached to the guide. That dart retained blood, which lab has identified as identical with the blood of the girl we were detaining. Nothing else was found. All members were terminated either by knife wounds, or by blows of a blunt instrument, skillfully applied. From appearances, the investigation team concluded that the party crossed the fence into the reservation, taking the girl with them. Her condition is unknown, but from the amount of blood on the scene, her survival is doubtful."

Parleau said, "I wish to emphasize several interesting points about this preliminary report. One, of most pressing interest, is that there was a mix of agents. What was to be a routine exercise went to hell in a handbasket, and fast. We, in short, have been penetrated, but by whom and for what purpose? Item two: all witnesses in Ten say that there were six New Humans. I repeat. Six. How so six? We knew of three, plus one basket-case. But there were six, self-propelled. Item three: the call for TacTeam was requested under signal forty—operative in the field needs assistance, fugitives to be remanded for interrogation—but no description was given, and when Control tried to recontact, the line was dead. Four: six members of a TacTeam, and the best systems money and mind can make, were defeated and heinously slain by unarmed farmers, who disappeared. If you do not have questions out of all this, I certainly do."

Eykor responded, "We have the junior agent. It appears that he knew little of what was going on, being kept deliberately in the dark, by Errat and the other agent. I am ashamed to say that he was one of our own men, recruited under some peculiar circumstances. He was low, and had no access, and so could not verify or disprove what Errat told him. I have recommended retraining and reconditioning, and tentative reestablishment, pending good behavior, of course."

"How did Errat get on that detail? Why weren't your own men on it?"

"They say they were properly relieved by Errat."

"Who the hell is this Errat?"

Plattsman answered, "Both Errat and the other agent have vanished into thin air. All routes have been closed, but I think that will prove nothing. Errat identified himself as an

THE GAMEPLAYERS OF ZAN

operative out of Secretariat. This was formerly true, as we have uncovered. He was assigned to Section Q, Overseas Branch, but at present had been in retired status. I might add, that was Retired Status After Cause. He was last reported residing in Appalachian Region. That was from Section Q. Appalachian officially denied ever having known such a person. We believe that Errat was the one who called the request for TacTeam. He had all the correct codes and authenticators, and the call was made, so we have traced, from Building eight-nine-oh-five. He had never left it, at least until then."

Parleau asked, "Are you sure he isn't there yet?"

Eykor affirmed, "We have screened everybody, body-search. The building has been scoured. He isn't there."

Plattsman continued, "Control Staff, in conjunction with some friends we have at ConSec-Q, think that Errat had two purposes, not one. The first was to prevent at all cost the girl from returning; she would there be turned over to others in the plot with him for unknown uses. The second was more interesting: you see, there is a faction in A.R. that would like very much to gain control of the Institute for their own purposes. As you know, the Region is historically poor. Errat has been identified as a sympathizer with this group by an informant we have planted. The secondary purpose of this mission for him was apparently to embarrass us. He did so, but by then the rest had started to add to it, so it was completely out of control. We think he wanted us to recapture the New Human party. The resulting uproar would make us look bad. . . ."

Parleau asked, sitting down at last, "Could Errat have been working with them, the ler? They did have a supremacist organization way back in the old days. . . ." Parleau had been reading his history.

"We have not found any evidence whatsoever that Errat was working with *any* group of New Humans, present or past. His dossier lists him as being violently anti-ler. Our implant in in A.R. confirms his association with like-minded groups in the Region, and elsewhere."

Parleau sighed deeply. "Well, whoever he was with, had his plan worked, the girl would have been taken and we'd be in the thick of it for sure. We were saved that, at least. But what we're in isn't a whole lot better. . . . And Errat's gone, you say?"

Eykor answered, "Not out of Seaboard South, unless he got out almost immediately, and there is low probability there. We sealed all crossings, everywhere. Nobody in or out without authenticated identification. There is no way he can get out, unless he walks through the reservation, which I doubt. It will take time, but we'll get him."

Plattsman commented, "You may not, so plan for the contingency. What we have been able to get out of Q suggests that he was formerly engaged in some pretty slippery wetwork for ConSec, working Tricontinent and Africa-Sud for them. God only knows what he was doing for them; those people are tough and they play the game hard. I think that if he could survive that as a career, he could probably come and go here pretty much as he pleases."

Eykor exclaimed, "But he was a Controller!"

"Ostensibly, a Controller. In fact, he was the worst sort of spy, and I suspect an assassin. Don't flinch; we still have them, and have good use of them. The Federated Earth Government hasn't been able to eliminate local interests, and right now they're not likely to. As a fact, we encourage it as general policy; the war of spies prevents a war of men, of armies."

Parleau said, "Perhaps, but that's a dangerous game, that substitute. It could lead to worse than skirmishes and riots. And to think that someone turned a wild man like Errat loose among us. . . ."

Plattsman countered, "No, Chairman, they did not turn him loose. He was acting on his own, or with at best a small group. Certain other bodies found it convenient to look the other way. Apparently his friends in A.R. hoped that if the cards fell out right they could make their move. But as things go, they are stumbling more than we are—you'd think it happened there, to hear them deny any connection with Errat."

Parleau exclaimed, "Acted on his own! Nobody acts on his own!"

"Errat did, apparently," Plattsman said blandly.

"No, no, I refuse to believe that, in this day and age. Could he in turn have been manipulated . . . ?"

"Manipulate a manipulator? Now, there's an art form indeed!"

"I'm serious. Klyten, had this worked as planned, could this have benefited anyone in the reservation?"

"Chairman, there was a supremacist faction long ago, but it was largely discredited by the separationists and has not been very noticeable since. The separationists were the ones responsible for helping to consolidate the people and for setting up the reservation. It was heading for a showdown, but segregating the populations cooled things off, and the extremists were replaced by more flexible groups. But back at the height of it, the supremacist faction was in contact with some humans, the most extreme. Were there any left, I suppose that Errat could have made contact."

"Too many loose ends . . . this gets worse and worse, doesn't it? Well, now: what about the six ler? What happened to the girl? We know she had to be one of the six."

Klyten answered, "All we can say is that she recovered. How, in so short a time, is beyond me."

"Recovered! Is that possible?"

"As fast as it must have happened? I have no idea. It must be, but the method is unknown. Also the reason why they would risk an obviously secret method to recover her. I thought that she might have been faking, but no, it couldn't be. I *know* what an autoforgetter looks like, and she was one for sure. This condition has no analog in humans—it is not amnesia. It is in fact a form of bodiless death. The persona ends. Of course, it isn't perfect, but for practical purposes it works as advertised. Now, supposedly, such a person can be retrained, but the result is something similar to severe retardation . . . but what she knew and was protecting, she took with her. They did not retrieve her to interrogate her. Nor did they make her functional by an unknown methodology to do that, either."

"What could Errat have wanted with her?"

"Unknown. I personally think he wanted an incident."

"That's even worse."

"Yes, Chairman, that is so. Oh, and by the way, speaking of things worse, and no human analogs, my research people found out what is wrong with the second girl. You know, the one Plattsman found in the photographs."

"Tell us that one, Klyten; there's no shortage of bad news here, so you may as well add your share."

Klyten ignored the remark, and continued, "They have a psychotic condition, which in the literature is called, for want of a better term, 'Serial Obession.' "

Plattsman asked, "What is the effect of it?"

"Apparently it is occasioned by extreme mental stress, and involves a severe breakdown in the seat of consciousness. It renders the victim incapable of handling reality in a multiplex, simultaneous manner; they then address each simplex component serially, one at a time. Because the rest drift and go astray, they try to compensate by extreme attention to the problem, and then the next one as it comes up. Because they are behind, and know it, they have to be more attentive as they handle the next problem."

Parleau commented, "That certainly doesn't sound like a psychosis to me. It doesn't even sound like a problem."

"Well, Chairman, they say that every psychosis has an analog in a political theory. They also say that psychoses are remnants of earlier attempts at consciousness. According to what I have read, Serial Obsession is a normal condition for humans—it isn't a problem to us, true. But it is a severe one to them. The corrective oscillations become progressively deeper and more violent with time. Very gradually, but certainly. The end-product is continual manic violence applied to everything, rather like a standing temper tantrum."

He paused. "And two things apply here: the first is that it's like other ler psychoses in that the victim knows he's insane, and can compensate for it and seek a cure; the other is that the by-product of the compensation is a state of vigorous well-being that increases with time ... the victim just can't understand why things keep getting worse despite his best attempts. They tend not to seek a cure, and have to be overpowered eventually. Thankfully, this extremely dangerous condition is very rare. We found only enough cases in the records to substantiate an analysis of the condition. But in regard to the second girl, I can imagine no more dangerous an adversary."

Parleau asked, "Why is that important, here?"

"Because, Chairman, this so-called plan of Errat's shows many of the hallmarks of the influence of such a person; the apparent indecision upon a concrete goal, the ambivalence, the confusion. We were confused because, in essense, Errat and his plan were confused. I agree with you in that something as audacious as this would be doubtful, energized by Errat alone. And if he were acting with a group, this aspect of it would have been suppressed by the combined minds of the group—that is how we humans handle the problem. We dampen it by the views of others—we discuss and argue and mutually agree, and then act. Yes, now that I think of it, I am sure of it," Klyten said.

Plattsman said, "Possible, possible. Fits Control Theory well enough. The planner influences the plan. Plain, straightforward. That's how we trace plans back to their source, no matter how obvious the first reading of the source is."

Parleau said, "So it is possible, then, that Errat was working for a ler? That's unreal! What could they gain from it?"

"Rationally, it would seem little. But we are conjecturing a possibly dangerous, shrewd psychotic, too."

Plattsman exclaimed, "The third man in the crowd-scans! Damn! Why didn't we think of it before? I didn't even think to try to match them with the file images of Errat. I'll bet they match."

Klyten said, "Probably will. But it doesn't help us anymore. We still don't know what he wanted, ultimately. Or his contact, if there was one."

Parleau said, "Wait, wait a minute. We are drifting farther and farther away from the central issue. In fact that seems to characterize this whole proceeding, from the time the girl was discovered in Isolation."

Eykor brightened. "A plot, Chairman?"

"No, inattention to the main issue. The committee system doesn't seem to save us from serial obsessions of our own, for which I thank Klyten for reminding me. We have been reacting to the wrong stimuli all along. We may be seeing too much, and becoming bemused with the process. We're looking at details, trying to run an investigation ... and the real events are flowing along and jumping up and biting us on the asses, now almost daily. We are looking bad, may I remind you. We simply have to get on top of this thing, and quickly, too."

Parleau stopped, and looked up at the distant ceiling. He mused, "Now here we have a girl who most probably has something to hide." He shot a quick glare at Eykor, then at Plattsman. "And don't try now to figure what. And by contrast, we have a group of ler who ostensibly have nothing to hide, in fact, one is certified clean by our own Control. But the first, the girl goes passive and loses her mind, and the latter fight like a regiment of devils. Now what in hell are we dealing with? Answer me that."

Klyten said, "The girl knew escape was improbable. The group was close to the fence."

"Hmph. That tells the obvious. It doesn't explain the severity of the response."

Eykor said, "There was a man-loss in that."

Parleau responded, "I hardly need reminders of that, either. What I am after is *why* they were so aggressive."

Klyten said, "Defense, revenge, who knows. We can't even determine who made the first move."

Eykor interrupted, "They made the first move! They fled, they evaded, they . . ."

"They would possibly have done neither had not Errat set a goon-squad on them," commented Parleau. "So now let me summarize where we are. All this time we've been playing it close to find out, to see, to know. And with this we get behind. And so we now find ourselves being put in an increasingly defensive position in regard to Appalachian and Con-Sec. I can well imagine what will be next: Piedmont will start agitating for a piece of the action, on some shabby pretext—they always wait for someone else to stir up the muck, and then they try to scoop up whatever they can."

Eykor asked, "Then what are we to do, different than we've been doing?"

"I have the plan, suggested by this very meeting. First: Control and Security, get Errat, and I don't care how you do it. Alive. I want him interrogated, no restraints, and I want everything out of him. But especially what in the hell was he trying to do and for whom. Second, I want to go back to the original incident, the girl. The instruments. Make up some working models. Eykor and Security do both; the rest of you do what he asks. I'm beginning to think we were right in the beginning. That's what comes of second-thoughts. And now," he said, wagging his index finger pedantically, "I have to leave, for a conference call with ConSec. I hope what I have to say will satisfy them for the moment, buy time, until we can get a basic handle on this. I hope that we all have this reasonably straight. And if you have any further business, feel free to continue. I'm off to the Communications Center."

Parleau stood, as did the others in deference to him. He gathered some notes from his desk, and left the office without ceremony.

The others who were left were silent for a time, but that was only for the moment, and shortly the old free-for-all resumed. The clerk, who had sincerely been trying to keep up with the discussion, now gave up in consternation and elected to sit back and wait until his services were called for. They were not. After an hour, he discreetly left the table, and then the office, and returned to his shift assignment. They didn't even know he was gone.

The members of the Regional Board of Inquiry, occasional though the Board was, were creatures of ingrained habit and products of a unique environment. That this environment included in its capabilities the ability to monitor and observe distant events through electronic relay systems and Controllers was taken for granted by all of them. But the very ease with which they monitored distant events and made decision upon that which they saw, tended to build in them a habit of overconfident insularity, of projecting pseudorealities that possessed the disturbing habit of coming unglued, without existential reference and constant updating.

Thus, in their analysis of the event that occurred near Complex Ten, they were basically correctly oriented to the most pressing problem: Errat. But lacking data, they all too hastily were willing to accept the assumption that he was running. He was not. Or that he knew a lot about what the planner behind him was after. He did not. Errat was content to act, as if alone, on a set of internal directions. He was, in essence, inertially guided, rather than controlled, by Command or exterior reference.

Errat knew these things both from his long association with Controllers and his experiences as an agent for Continental Secretariat; especially that the key personnel of Seaboard South Region would make those assumptions, or something very close to them. He also knew that the successful undergrounder did not so much physically hide or run, as he relied upon flaws in the perceptual field of his opposition. He had not been in the field for some time, but the old skills did not die out, being founded upon universals about behavior, and he found them coming back easily. And his feedback told him that, at least to date, he had been completely correct.

Nor did Errat trouble himself overly with deep self-analysis. He was in the field primarily because he enjoyed his work in that environment. Perhaps it would have been more correct to venture that he was addicted to it, and had been away from it so long now that he had been playing a very minor game in his own right, just to keep the hand fresh, so to speak. Then this had come along and offered a fine opportunity to work on a project, and, as a fine, artistic flourish, betray them all, and vanish, letting both parties go down locked in a death-grip; he felt only contempt for both parties, the secretive contact who had intercepted him, and the Region authorities alike. He thought of an aphorism to cover the situation, as he often did: the conspirator(s) were secretive because they were weak and ineffective; the Region authorities were weak and ineffective because they were secretive.

Hando Errat was not under any illusion that he was secure, however much contempt he had for Seaboard South Region. Indeed, the greater part of his camouflage was based upon constant mobility, lack of fixture and base. This, admittedly, was somewhat a challenge in a society that placed a premium on lack of movement, but that only added spice to it. And wasn't particularly difficult. He had been prepared for it. That, indeed, had been one of his first lessons, one that had enabled him to survive—that a good agent is not necessarily the one who gets quick results and promotions, but the one who survives to come another day. He had reflected on that lesson often, since this contingency had begun. Perhaps they would be interested to learn just how easily one could move around, when one could anticipate. After all—after Al Qahira, Esh-Sham, El Kuds the Holy, Jidda, Aden—Seaboard South had been a piece of cake to penetrate.

Errat had affected the appearance of a maintenance man in this phase of his movements, and it had been a good disguise. He would hate to give it up. The fastidious avoided his grimy coveralls, and the local precinct Controllers and Security men never looked twice; maint-techs were considered the most conservative and habit-bound members of society, stable and fixed, beginning one day, ending it, always in standard time.

He was engaged in moving his location again, but still within Region Central. He had never left it; indeed, he had not properly even left the sight of an observer perched atop 8905 ... had there been such an observer knowing what to look for. They would expect him to make for the northern border of the Region, toward his ostensible home. But there was only a cubicle in the public dormitory there, and he could give that away without a thought. No, he had remained in Region Central. Later, he would drift to the south. They expected him to run, and he was standing still. And why chase him at all? He had left deliberate traces of himself at the last, so they would; he had even used his own programmed name, rather than an alias.

Of course there was real danger; but for now he discounted the possibility that Seaboard South would call in operatives from ConSec, some of whom Errat had first trained himself. No, they wouldn't do that; they were too tied up in their own embarrassment to call them in, and by the time they came in on their own, he would be long gone. Let them look for him! But of all things, he was not worried about what Eykor might think of doing; the man had the imagination of an earwig, and in that hadn't changed since Errat had first seen him as a Security man, way back when, in Alexandria, posted there from somewhere in Europe. His handling of that mutant girl had been typical: doing a halfway job, depending on machines, and then half-covering it up, protecting department hands. Contemptible all across the board! He knew that if he had got hold of her, she would have spoken, indeed would have begged to sing. And when they had got what they wanted out of her, it would have been worth sweeping it under the rug and to hell with the protected people, the Muties and their fine little country farm. What did they have to enforce it with? A pack was only as good as the arms that backed it. . . .

Errat walked through the rainy streets of the night, all in all, not too apprehensive. Alert, but by no means paranoid. Nobody seemed to be following him that he could detect, although a couple of incidents had cast some suspicions that way and sharpened his senses. Nothing he could put his finger on, though, and there were none of the follow-on betrayals of presence. He had highly sophisticated means to spot trackers. No, he had written it off as a symptom of his being out of practice. He felt completely in control of the situation, and being out in the open, on the street, actually gave him a feeling of exhilaration.

In the quarter in which he was now walking, there were fewer lights and less traffic. He could see very well, however, by the sky-glow, the city light reflected from the low clouds. December, Twelvemonth. In this part of Central, the buildings were still the pastel-stained blocks of the newer parts of the city, but this was not a part of the city devoted to plazas and terminals. Rather more like the warehouse quarter, local supply depots and the like, mixed with shabby rooming houses, transdorms, workers' godowns. He listened to the sounds of the city at night: distant machinery sounds, relaxed and unhurried, muted. Water gurgling in drains, splashing from vehicles. The humming of a hovercraft. There would be few out on a wet night like this. He listened carefully, for this was his environment, as some ancient predator might have listened to the sounds of the jungle. The predators were gone, but their example remained for the last predator, Man. The world was City, denser or less dense. The pattern of sounds now completely reassured him; things were normal, and exactly as they should be.

Errat reached his destination, a down-at-the-heels roomer, used mostly by assistance-recips, itennies, retired laborers, and taxmen, all of whom had never made it to secure a family license. He looked it over carefully with his practiced eye, verifying what he had thought of the place earlier. A safe place for a couple of days, from which to put out his sensitive antennae into the grapevines of the neighborhood, time to watch the vidcasts and read between the lines. Then, thus reoriented, to move from once more.

There was a doorman, as he expected, but this one did not seem either alert or zealous in his duties. In fact, he seemed half asleep; perhaps more than half.

Errat approached the doorway, feigning a slight confusion, a hesitation, all the time watching the doorman for signs of betrayal. There were none. The man was becoming aware of him, but there was no alarm in his manner, just a slight annoyance, countered by a desire to interact with someone while at his post. And a sense of superiority, out of the position of doorman, while the stranger in the street, in the rain, had nothing, no place, no peers. He could afford to be haughty, but no so much that the stranger would become angry. A delicate balance of pecking orders. The doorman thought he knew his game well. Errat was a player of the same game who was leagues ahead of him.

Errat greeted him, "Evening."

"Yourself," answered the doorman. "Need in, or just visiting?"

"Like in if I can." Errat sat down his duffel, which looked as if it contained tools, but which in reality contained clothing and makeup.

"Bag?"

"Corrosion-controlman, me. Hell of a job."

"Looks like. Where ya been? In the sewers?"

" 'Bout. Workin' the cableways. You'd think they'd make 'em so's a body cud stand, but no, ya haf'ta crawl." As Errat registered the doorman's speech patterns, he swiftly and subtly aligned his own speech patterns to fit them. Nothing worked so well as a properly reproduced local accent.

" 'Ja see any?"

"See any what?"

"C'rosyun."

"Shee-yit."

"Looks like. Well, what's yur name and number?"

"Tanner, twenty-four-A— Wait a min't, I'll dig those papers out, they're aright here. . . ." Errat fumbled for something in the deep pockets of the coverall, a prolonged process.

The doorman, convinced of his sincerity, watched him fumble for a time, and then said, "Man, there's no need, there. Bugger it! Hold on, the nightmon's out, but I'll get you something. We got empties."

"No, no. I'll need 'um for the ledge."

"Na, na, bugger the ledge, the ledgerkeep, and the 'orse 'e sat 'is arse on. We'll get to it, by and by. How long ya be?"

"Semipermer, me. Working this sector."

"Well, then, all right! No prob, come on." And he lurched off his stool, opening the outer gate for Errat to enter. Now together, they walked down a drafty, damp, poorly lit hallway, arriving at a board beside a small window in the wall. The window was closed. From the board, the night watchman now removed a key, fumbling and deciding, handing it to Errat. There was a tag attached to the key, with a piece of dirty and frayed string.

"Here y'are, two-oh-one. Up the stairs and to the right; ya can't miss it. It's the only one to the right, har, har. Say, want a sip a' caffers?"

"I'd like, but I gotta bag. I mean, the sheets are really barkin'. Been a long un. How 'bout tomorra?"

"Ya off?"

"Can take it."

"Well, all right! Say then, see ya then, um?"

"Will do, there. What was your name?"

"Bork, me. Paulie Bork."

"See ya then, Paulie."

Errat turned to the stairwell and started up, feigning tiredness and an older, hard-worked body. He reflected as he did so that he didn't have to fake too much; he actually was tired. Letdown. He was past the last event of the day. This place was going to be perfect, perfect. Shabby and forgotten, except in the mind of some renewal planner, who would replace it with something no less trashy. How else keep the proles busy? But it was no matter tha'. He found himself slipping unconsciously into the gutter idiom as he climbed the narrow stairs, unable to resist the temptation to fall completely into the character of it. No doubt about it, he was tired, but it was also good to be out in the field once again, out on the killing floor, on the line.

Errat found the room, unlocked the door, and entered, relocking it as he closed it. He let his bag settle to the floor,

quietly. In the dimness he could make out a bed, a wash-
stand. The bed was small, probably too soft and too lumpy.
Where was the chair and desk? There was usually one. Yes,
there it was; by the window he saw an outline of a chair, his
eyes adjusting. He smelled deeply, sifting the odors of the
room, waiting for the expected odor of transient old rooms,
of musty sheets and smoke-abused curtains. Yes, just like he
expected. And Errat's skin crawled.

There was something else in the odors of the room. He
reached for the light switch on the wall behind him by the
door, felt for it, fumbled, fighting panic generated by something he could smell but not see, found it, flipped it. Nothing
happened. He tried to recover quickly, get control of the situation. He admitted to a moment of fear. He cursed the
slowness of night-vision, trying to see into the furry shadows,
backlighted by the window. Yes, the desk. On the desk. It was
between two windows, and the backlighting had obscured it.
Something bulky and body-sized on the desk. He inhaled
deeply and slowly, trying to catch the elusive scent, muttering
under his breath about faulty lights, emitting minor obsceni-
ties, reaching for his throw-knife at the same time. A heavy
plastic, it could not be detected by the finest weapon-detector,
and could even be bent, slowly, to fit. He also had a gun,
made of similar material, but he knew he'd never reach it.
But he knew one thing; he had time. If it was here to kill and
ask no questions, they would have already tried.

He felt the reassuring warm solidity of the throw-knife.
What was that scent? Wet clothing. Somebody had been out
in the light rain, with him, for the rain had only started less
than an hour ago. Ergo, following him. Hmph. Damn skillful
job, that. ConSec, already? No, darkened rooms weren't their
game. And under the wet clothing, a warm body, also damp,
a little sweaty, a little nervous. Still. There was another scent,
an adrenaline odor, and something else, something tense that
made him tense in turn. And there was more, too, female,
perhaps, and something more.

Errat took a chance. "Zandro? Zandro Milar?" That had
been the name of his elusive contact through this whole
thing, the contact who had sought him out, found him. The
one who made payments, advised, called, always by madden-
ingly indirect methods. All Errat had managed to discover
about this contact was that the owner of the name was probably female, and younger than himself. He had further suspicions, but they made no immediate sense, and he needed

additional data. He breathed again, trying to get a bearing on the source of the odor-presence. No luck. Whoever had come in had been in long enough to muddy the air. He watched the bulk on the desk intently, watching for movement. He could not tell. His eyes were still adjusting.

A voice emanated from the desk, much like the one he had heard before. Female, throaty, almost hoarse, but with the betrayals of youth in it, too. "Indeed. Speak quietly, there may be monitors." Yes, the same. And what an odd accent. Errat plumbed his encyclopedic memory, trying to place the accent. He couldn't. It didn't register at all. It continued, "Yes, you were correct. I am Milar. And you certainly have stirred up the anthill."

Errat listened carefully, finding direction. Smell wasn't good enough to find, in a situation like this, or in wind. But sound was, almost as good as seeing. He moved his head slightly from side to side as the figure spoke, getting the range. Yes, he had it. He could do it. Just like the time in Zinder, when he had got his man in total darkness. The fool! He had stopped to gloat, and had paid. This one was the same. They all were. The source of the voice seemed a little off, little low, as if the owner were half reclining. Odd pose for a threat. She probably had a needler on him. No problem, there! Needlers were invariably low-velocity. He could do it, and move, playing the slowness of her reactions and the slowness of the weapon against her. Yes, there. He thought he saw the suggestion of movement, a slight shift. Or had it been?

He said, buying time, "You said that I was to kill the girl and those who came for her, or salt them away, and keep them confused. I did not get the girl, it is true, but much confusion resulted. Seaboard South," he hazarded, "is now discredited."

"You hired reptiles to do primate work." Errat heard, and thought that an odd turn of phrase.

"Couldn't get anyone else." He was stalling now. He edged imperceptibly closer to the figure on the desk. God, but she was careless, talking while he closed in. Send babes to do grown-up's work was just not the word. But he could hear the threat in the voice, accent or not. Yes, this one would be easy.

The voice said, "We are dissatisfied, unfulfilled in our most fervent hopings."

Errat listened, still weight-shifting, creeping immeasurably forward, slowly, closer, closer. Shooting in the dark like this, you had to get as close as possible, reduce the CEP* of a quick-thrown knife. Yes, it was Milar. The odd speech patterns, the accent, the Modanglic of an educated foreigner, one who didn't speak Modanglic as a native. Where could that be? There were few places left where it wasn't spoken, and he thought he knew all those accents. Errat felt some regrets. He would hate to kill this Milar before he found out who she was and who she represented. All the same . . .

He said, "They may have set hopes too high for realization. And the direction I received was not a model of clarity."

"Those are insignificant. Our affair here is with the failure of the prime operative."

Errat now had his knife straightened, in pre-throw position, his muscles relaxed, but set and ready to obey for the one swift stroke. He said, taunting, "Not the operative, but the purveyor of instructions!" On the last word he threw the knife at the target he had picked. It would be the throat. He could not risk the blade being turned by the ribs. The throat. Disable now, and polish off in a moment, after some tactical repair and a quick interrogation. He was expert at that. But even as he released the knife he had the smallest hesitation, as if something weren't right. The feeling had been nagging him all afternoon. Even as it left his hand, he knew there was something wrong, all wrong, and he had made the wrong move. What was it? The knife struck, that he heard, but the sound was not that of a knife penetrating flesh. Instantly, as the fact registered in his mind, he felt a sudden sharp pressure at his back, up and to the left side between the ribs, like a rough shove in a crowd, in a queue, followed by heat and pressure at his heart. Incredible heat! He tried to move, to take a breath. He couldn't. His feet seemed nailed to the floor, his chest bound with iron. The universe contracted to a node of pain, his chest, his back. _So this is what it feels like to be knifed_, the rational part of his mind thought, coolly and idly.

He did manage to start a turn before he completely lost control of his legs. Yes, his assassin had been behind him all the while, waiting by the door, absolutely quiet. He must have almost touched her. How had she projected her voice, been so quiet? These things disturbed Errat greatly, and he

* Circular Error Probable.

thought upon them, as he collapsed to the floor, his consciousness fading. And the last thing he saw was the figure of a woman bending over him, her heavy clothing rustling loudly. And then there was nothing.

The person who had claimed to be the bearer of the programmed name Zandro Milar slipped quietly out of the shadows, the deeper shadows by the door, moving stiffly, awkwardly, to stifle the rustling of clothing. The figure bent over Errat, as if listening, or casting for a scent, a gesture curiously animal-like. It did not touch the body. Apparently satisfied, it straightened and stepped over the body to the desk. There, it removed an object from the bundle on the desk, inserted it in a small carrybag it was carrying. Then it stopped, pausing, not so much looking, as it did not move its head, but reminding itself, reviewing circumstances. It recalled something, and went back to one of the windows, carefully opening it a crack. There was a slight draft, and then the night air started seeping into the room. Then it stepped over the body, reaching the door, where again it paused, an interminable moment, listening. There was no presence in the hall outside. It opened the door a crack. There was a stronger draft. Setting the lock, Zandro Milar stepped outside and closed the door, listening for the click of the lock.

In the hallway, had anyone been there to see, the harsh light would have revealed a slender, smallish woman, dark of complexion, a swarthy olive that suggested a Mediterranean type, sharp-featured, perhaps an Iberian, or an Arab, who might have been attractive had it not been for a predatory cast to her facial structure. She wore the awkward clothing of the day with singular gracelessness.

Milar walked quietly down the hallway to a room at the far end, entered, carefully closing the door behind her. Inside, she seemed to slump, relaxing, and sat on the bed, removing her shoes, which seemed to bother her more than all the rest of the clothing. She leaned back and wriggled her toes, relaxing at last. After a moment, she got up again, and removed all the clothing she had been wearing, and adding the carrybag, placed all of it in a small suitcase. She finished, straightened, and walked across the room to a closet. Passing before the single mirror in the room, she glanced at the reflection, seeing it only very dimly, even in the city light coming in the windows from outside. She smiled. Out of her clothes, her motions were no longer lumpish and crude, but fluid and graceful. She flexed her hands, stretched until joints cracked. She checked the closet, verifying that another set of clothing was there, a man's coverall. Satisfied, she returned to the lumpy bed, lay on it, naked, pulling the covers around her, and fell instantly asleep.

After a time, her breathing became deep and regular, and then she revealed, unknown to her, her only flaw as an operative. She began to mutter, almost inaudibly, in her sleep. Even then, some part of her remembered who and where she was, so that the muttering was very quiet, indeed. It was doubtful if it could have been heard outside the room. Even inside the room, one would have to listen closely to hear it at all. And it would have been valueless to hear it, for the muttering was not in Modanglic. More specifically and strictly, it really wasn't in a language, at least not in the sense of anyone who might have been there to hear it.

When the light from the window had brightened to a certain degree, Milar awoke, as if on some internal timer. She dressed, first donning a tight undergarment that smoothed and obscured the shape of her body, which although undeniably female, was also subtle of curve, wiry, and muscular. Then, over that, the coverall of a hard-laborer. Her hair was short, a deep dull black, a gun-metal blue in the highlights. This she tucked into a tattered flat cap affected by most heavy workmen. She checked a cheap pocket chronometer, nodded to herself. Then, carefully inspecting the room one last time, picked up the suitcase, left the room, and headed down the hallway.

Last night's rain had blown off toward the east, toward the Green Sea; now it was winter-bright outside, and the light was full of blue overtones, which she saw and appreciated. In the building, she could hear others getting up and being about, getting ready for the events of the day. More significantly, which brought her back to reality, the doorman would have been relieved now by a Daysider, or perhaps no relief at all. She looked, as she entered the lower hall. Correct. No one was there. She walked calmly out of the building, fighting an intense urge to run. She fought with herself, knowing she had to get control of herself. It began to pass. The adrenaline she might release could trip stress-monitors all up and down the street. She forced herself to be calm, repeating certain formulas to herself. She paused by the corner, looked back.

Good. Nothing. Now she relaxed in truth, feeling it flood into her.

Not for nothing had she followed Errat carefully, at great risk to herself from him and from others. She had studied him before she had picked him to do the task for her, and now that it had been bungled, she had used that information to predict his movements. It had been interesting, but also too easy. Not half as hard as the one she had him set up. That one had escaped for almost a year before she finally nailed her down. And of course Errat had to be eliminated, for in him was a trace to her. Unlike Errat, she did not enjoy wetwork, as she had heard him call it. But there had been no cure for it; she had to do it herself. And by the time they discovered Errat, she would be long safe. Yes, and maybe more. . . . Perhaps then she would have the hammer in her hand, the power, and then there would be a reordering, a replacing, indeed. But back to affairs. There was one more tiresome loop to close, a painful one, but one that had to be.

She placed the suitcase in a public locker, designed to foil the most determined thief, paying the fee into the credit-box, extracting the identification slip, with its magnetic numbers. This she took to the tube-train terminal and threw in a collecting trashpile, wadded up and unrecognizable. After that, she purchased a ticket for the Institute Halt, and settled in the waiting room, smiling an odd little half-smile to herself. She had taken some extra days, it was true, to do this job herself, but it had been good work. Now, if she could only catch the other in time, she would have all the loose ends tied off for good.

BOOK THREE

Navis et Arx

SIXTEEN

> *When one extracts all the irrational elements
> from love, that which is left is a thing unendur-
> able, unreasonable, and it is most irrational that
> one should care to pursue it.*
>
> *—Ibid*

With assistance and advice from Kaldherman, the aid of a
rascally, squint-eyed elder known as Jaskovbey the Smug-
gler, who lived on the banks of the River Yadh, and an attitude of bored disinterest on the part of officials of Piedmont
Region, across the river to the west, Morlenden—using nothing more elaborate than Manthevdam, an assumed name—
openly boarded a tube in Piedmont Central, and with one
change in Oconee Region, and another on the West Coast,
reached a point close by the reputed location of the house of
Mevlannen Srith Perklaren. In three days.

Morlenden had his directions to get there, gained from
Klervondaf as they walked home from the northeast: west
from the old settlement of Santa Barbara, continuing on the
local transport, now aboveground to Jalama, where the route
turned north, and follow the coast. It was not entirely without hazard; he was walking in the back door of the main
continental spaceflight center, but it was not, by and large,
guarded, reflecting the widespread belief that the main
concern of Man lay not in ways to depart the Earth, but in
ensuring more ways to survive upon it. In fact, the space program had rather languished for the past two centuries, and
aside from timid, careful forays around the inner Solar System, and rarer probes into the outer portions, there was little
activity. Even the telescope project, which to Morlenden's
ears had sounded amazing, was half asleep. Work progressed

at a measured pace. A slow one. And there were no enemies
to guard against. . . .

Morlenden left the transport early in the morning, and
aside from a glance around to get his bearings, did not look
back. He spent the morning negotiating country given over to
pasturage, some desultory farming; but soon the land became
too isolated, too precipitous for even that, and even that
shred of civilization fell behind him. Now he walked along
above the empty cliffs, above a most strange sea in the wan-
ing light of afternoon, plodding on toward a holding hidden
away in one of the last pockets of wilderness on the coasts of
old North America.

Morlenden was not well-traveled, and had never seen salt
water before (Fellirian had seen the Green Sea once, before
their weaving. He had asked, "What did it look like?" And
she had answered, "Just like a big lake; you can't see the
other side. Oh, yes, it smelled funny, and there were waves.")
and now he was walking along the edge of the largest ocean
in the season of storms. He found it fascinating, full of nov-
elty and endless mystery, but also alien and disturbing; this
was the Pacific, and the season was winter. A cold wind blew
off the sea, and though he could remember seeing palm trees
farther back, it was a cold wind that chilled him to the bone.
The sky seemed clear, but there was a milky film in it, an
unsettled unsteadiness, as if, at any moment, a storm might
blow up, or fog, or rain. He had heard as much about the
region. And along the way he had walked, he had seen the
ruined remains of buildings and posts, eroded and abraded by
the constant salt-laden wind.

Mevlannen reportedly spent her days on Earth, when she
was not working, in a cabin perched atop one of the local
mountains. Pico Tranquillon it was named in the older human language of the area. Morlenden thought, looking about
himself as he walked, that the name was most curious: a
tranquil peak above a quiet sea. That was what the name
meant. But the sea was not quiet; the surf grumbled away,
sometimes roared, sometimes growled, and constantly ground
away at shells and rocklings in the shallows. It heaved and
crawled, that quiet sea, like some live thing. Morlenden
avoided looking into the shimmering, pearl-horizoned distances overly long; he sensed some weakness in himself for
this empty place.

And the tranquil peak? The wind whipped at his cloak,
and now it was rising, fretting and fraying the wild grasses,

hissing at the windblown trees, dark cypresses. The sky watched, unstable, ready now to permutate and change on the instant. In the place of the peak of tranquility, there was nothing tranquil at all, unless it was the wavelike repose of the land and its life, its sense of steady enduring, in the midst of flux.

He walked on in the fading afternoon, becoming uncomfortable in the bite of the relentless wind off the cold ocean. He had seen colder weather, even slept out of doors in some of it, back in the reservation. He had seen snow, often, and he knew it was rare here, yet it was still uncomfortable. There was a feeling of unwelcome to it. The wind, the unimaginable sea full of mysteries, the merciless alien surf and its constant grumblings, the iodine reek of the sea close to hand, unescapable. And he was uncomfortable with his role as well—the bearer of bad tidings. And no doubt she would be expecting a younger Tlanhman; she would get a parent phase half-elder long past the change, who moreover was beginning to feel fatigued, snared in cobwebs, enmeshed in a labyrinth of plot within plot. It could be unpleasant. And he could not imagine how the girl lived out here alone.

The path—once upon a time, long ago, a road—had led him inward from the beach cliffs and across some deserted flats where yellow wild grain glistened and rippled in the afternoon light. There were remnants of buildings, sheds; this had been a prosperous farm once. Long ago. They were all gone now. Out on the point, on a headland, west and to his left, he could make out the shapes of another ruin, some building long since fallen in upon itself. There were pilings in the water. Hawks patrolled the air, rattlesnakes guarded the ground. There was something lonely and beautiful beyond bearing directly here; he could see clearly, although he could not frame it in words. Descriptions wouldn't do; what it needed was a legendman to set a terrible drama in these lands, for only in lines of action could the true shape of the place be drawn. Now there was a pervasive melancholy in the air, something in the light. One was impelled to heroic deeds, but also to much brooding. Yes, perhaps the light, an odd, porcelain light, half filtered by the sea air. Or the wind, which was definitely rising, now roaring on its own account from time to time. Morlenden pulled his cloak tighter, raised and fastened the hood, and followed the path upward, stopping occasionally to catch his breath.

He had worked a good part of the way up to the peak when the light began failing, a thickening in the air. The shadows deepened, spread, grew. Clouds began to appear overhead, subtle, close to the earth, vague in exact shape, salmon and rose-colored, tints of an impossible fleeting yellow. He felt more uneasy, although in his life he had walked many a lonely mile; and from somewhere far below him now, he heard, from far away, carried by the wind, a strange howling. Like a dog, but unlike, too, full of idiotic laughter. He shivered, and not from the wind; he had walked there not long before. An eerie place for the girl, full of ghosts and spirits.

He almost walked into the place before he realized that he had attained it. Morlenden had been following switchbacks, one after another, walking up the unending mountain trail, and suddenly there were no more, and he was in a shallow saddle between the peak itself and a lower western shoulder. He could see into the north, across a tumbled, shadowy land of valley and uplands beyond, now filling like a bowl with darkness. The clouds were closer overhead, moving swiftly, rippling and leaping with eagerness.

And before him, sheltered under the shoulder of Pico Tranquillon, was a tiny stone cabin, the yellow light inside it spilling out into the darkening evening and the night. A thin streamer of smoke was being torn from the stone chimney. An odd little place, not at all like anyplace a ler would live in, but for the moment, he thought it was the cheeriest thing he had ever seen. And above, on the peak itself, were more ruins: shells of concrete, the twisted frameworks of some metal apparatus tangled above them. The wind hissed in the metal, hating it, wearing it down only slightly slower than it wore at the rocks. Morlenden hurried to the door, knocked.

He hadn't expected Mevlannen, the insibling of Maellenkleth, to resemble the latter. After all, it had been the *Nerh*, Klervondaf, who had shared an insibling parent with Maellen. This one would be a stranger; they had different parents in the flesh. The person he saw in the opened doorway was a ler girl of the appropriate age, about twenty, but she looked older. She was dark-haired, as much as he could see of her, but pale-skinned and rather light-eyed. She had a sharp, foxy quality of face that contrasted sharply with the rounded softness of Maellen. But none of the predatory in it, as Sanjirmil, either. The sharpness here was one of fineness and delicacy, not of muscles held tensed in opposition.

Her hair was straight, dark brown, very fine in texture,

worn longer than was seemly for a girl her age. . . . Then he recalled where she had been the last five years or so. Her skin was a pale snow-creamy color, lightly spotted with tiny freckles. The nose was straight and narrow, this reminding him most of Taskellan. The winter overshirt she wore concealed most of her body, but from the long, slender neck and the fine, delicate collarbone, he could see that she was thinner than the average, who tended toward a slightly more strong frame.

Behind the girl was a fireplace, and in it a fire was built and brightly burning; not a traditional hearth, but a heavy stonework fireplace, presumably of human style, although Morlenden had never seen one. The fireplace, and a couple of oil lamps, seemed to be the only light. The girl, backlit by the warm glow, looked at him with unconcealed curiosity.

She began, tentatively, as if describing a phenomenon, rather than speaking directly. "I was told by the public message service that a visitor was coming . . . and one stands in my door, in the evening, after the fashion of a traveler, almost as one who would go on the Salt Pilgrimage. Yet there is not salt here."

He answered, "I am Morlenden Deren, and I am your visitor. The name I have used to travel under, and the clothing, only suggest a poor enough disguise."

"I am Mevlannen Srith Perklaren." The voice was, for all its indirection, even and plain, cool and reserved. It was the voice of one who had learned privacy, and who did not offer invitations casually. "Am I the one you seek?"

"You are. May I come into your house? There is much we must say."

She stepped back from the doorway, making a motion with her right hand for him to enter. The motion was in the same underlanguage as had been her words, reserve, skepticism. Yet also within was hunger and loneliness as well. Morlenden saw, and deeply regretted the news that he was to bring. More yet he regretted that he had been born too soon: he deeply appreciated what the graceful, reserved motions offered. What was being displayed here. All for nothing. He stepped inside the door, over the threshold, hearing the door latch behind him.

She held out her hands to him to take his cloak, and he slipped out of it and handed it to her. He proceeded forward bluntly. "The reason I have come is twofold: one, to bring you bad tidings; and the other, to be told something by you, if you will believe that I am indeed the one to carry it."

She hung the cloak on a peg in the wall by the fireplace. "I had thought when the word came it might be something bad," she said quietly, turning back to him. "You know that no one ever comes here. Ever. At first, I would journey home, but as things went forward, lately . . ."

"I understand some of it. I have been to the *yos* of the Perklarens. And I see that you are now a stranger in your own *yos*."

"True. But are we not all thus, one time or another? But never mind that. I have a nice supper. Will you eat here with me, sleep with me tonight?"

"I had hoped to. I have never come so far before."

She turned from her place by the fire. "This is one of the few places where the world as it was of old has been kept. It used to be said, of the lands along this coast, and another place farther north, that here creation still continued. Mael was here . . . and loved it. My fellow workers think it peculiar that I should live alone on top of Pico Tranquillon, but it suits me. They are terrified by the loneliness, but those are my needs. Solitude. I am not bothered here; when I am down, I am free to sit by the window, watch the sea and the sky, and dream. . . . You know that I am an engineer, but were I that and nothing more, I would be a poor one, I think."

Morlenden looked about the tiny cabin. He nodded approvingly. "Yes, I understand. It is a cozy home here. I did not know that it could be thus, here, outside."

"I tried to get a *yos* cast here, but the Revens would not hear of it. . . . So I built this place myself. It is a copy of a human cabin; I learned from places I have seen along this coast. Odd, that, for in the older times, this country, here, was the place where all the newest things were tried. . . . And now it is the only place on the continent where even a trace of the old ways remain."

Morlenden agreed, noting her hands as he did. Built it herself? With those delicate, needleworker hands, pale and slim fingers? There was more to her than met the eye. But he knew that would be the case. Too much ocean, too much deep space, too much an alien society, the society of humans. Mevlannen had undergone a sea-change.

She said, "So. We will have all night to talk about things.

And I read from your face, Morlenden Deren, that I will be unhappy by that which I will hear. So let us eat. Come, sit." She faced him with an arch, coy expression, yet with something wistful in it as well. And as if she sensed his appraisal of her, she said, "I know well enough we could not be even casual lovers, even for a night; but you can, if you will, lend me for a time some small part of that which I have given up. Lost, now. I need talk, the warmth of my own . . . too much have I seen of silence and conspiracy." She finished and moved around the table with a curious floating grace, a slow, flowing, dancelike motion that caused her overskirt to flow, and eddy about her slender body.

Morlenden sat at a rude table that incorporated benches into its form. It looked hand-planed, rough-finished. She had said that she had made this cabin herself. The table too, obviously. She was a capable one, this Mevlannen, for all her delicacy and slenderness of figure. . . .

After supper, which they partook in silence, they sat by the fire on cushions, cross-legged like tailors, and drank steaming cups of coffee, to Morlenden's taste a harsh, bitter drink. Mevlannen had also laced it heavily with brandy. The girl seemed used to it, and as he drank, Morlenden found that it did banish the fatigue and apprehensions he felt.

Mevlannen looked blankly into the fire. She said, suddenly, "Bring me your bad tidings, now."

He began hesitantly, "It is Maellenkleth . . . she had an accident." He stopped. This would lead nowhere. He could circle it all night and never tell her. She needed to know. Bluntness would be best. The cuts of it were deep, but they would heal faster.

"Some months back, Maellenkleth was captured outside by humans. After that, something they did apparently frightened her, and she autoforgot."

Mevlannen continued looking into the fire, giving no sign. She nodded, once, curtly, to acknowledge that she had heard him.

He continued, "We, the Derens, were commissioned by the Perwathwiy Srith to locate her, determine what had happened to her. But they would tell us nothing, none of them. . . . We went to Krisshantem, a *hifzer*, who was her last lover, and with him, we retrieved her from the place where they had kept her. And with Krisshantem leading, performed a restoration. On the way back to the reservation, some agents tried to prevent us from reaching our destination. In escaping them, they pressed the hunt, and on the fence she was shot by a wire-guide. She died soon after that, after we made revenge upon those who would use a proscribed weapon."

Mevlannen nodded again. "Who performed the rites? She was of the Water elemental."

"We knew, and we did it. The Derens. Taskellan witnessed for the Perklarens, or rather for so much as is left of them."

"What has happened to Kler and Tas? Tell me."

"Klervondaf is living with the Braid of Plindestier. We have taken in Taskellan. He was too young; he needed a Braid, a home. Why were your parents not at home? Why did they not come? Your Braid is full of mysteries, but that one is most far from me."

"Didn't they tell you anything? The Perwathwiy? Sanjirmil?"

"They would say nothing. I wormed out some information about Mael from them, as I went, but it was not much, and concerned only her. I have talked with Sanjirmil, but she was more opaque in her words than the others were in their silences."

"I see. Yes, I can imagine that—that they would not have told you. They couldn't. Yes, it is true . . . the parents Perklaren were not at home as they should have been, and they could not do right for Mael. I know why; I understand. They would do it that way . . . there was no choice."

"So you know."

"Yes. All too much. That is why I do not travel. I am, I suppose, in it even thicker than was poor Mael. She was our valiant soldier, she was, all the while we stayed in the back, working, working. . . ."

"I was told, in her last words, by Maellenkleth, to get from you a matrix, to return and transmit it to Sanjirmil. Do you also know the significance of this?"

She started, an abrupt movement, alarm on her face. "The matrix? Now? Are you sure of this thing?"

"Certain as I am of little else. She was dying, and a part of the old persona emerged, just enough to get that out. Will you give it to me, and will you tell me what is so important that a girl should die twice before her time to protect it?"

"Yes . . . I will tell you. Everything. They should have, themselves, from the beginning. You could stumble, and undo the work of generations. You should have known. They should have done it all, initiated you. . . ."

"Krisshantem taught me the Outer Game."

"Not good enough by far, but it will help you understand."

"Then why not more?"

"They probably feared that outside you would trip stressies."

"Stressies?"

"Chemical stress-monitors. They detect anxiety chemically. In your scent, your breath. They are everywhere, but of course more so in the East. They work on us, too. In fact, we usually give stronger readings through them. That is why they would not tell you. You must take oath to autoforget to protect it."

"I would not reveal a secret, no more than Maellen."

"Just so, just so. I do not doubt you. But we simply could not risk sending many into oblivion. And if a centipede loses enough legs, even it will stop walking. And of course, things can be traced."

The girl arose now, refilled the cups, and returned to the place before the fire. She did not evidence any emotion Morlenden could identify, but her eyes were moist, reflecting brightly the light of the fire. She blinked rapidly. A log in the fire collapsed, sending a whirl of sparks up the chimney. Outside, the wind took up a constant moan, and Morlenden could hear rain pelting on the windowpane.

Mevlannen looked up. "I will tell you what I know. Then the matrix. You will understand it then. I will not have you stumbling in the dark anymore. You are far too dangerous that way. But you must oathmake to me, on your name, that you will autoforget to protect it."

Morlenden hesitated, drawn by the mystery, but also repelled by the idea of autoforgetting. He said, "Then so be it. On my name, which no one else has ever carried."

She looked deeply at him, into him, with eyes as bright and piercing as needles of fire. They were a soft, pale-blue color, almost gray, but in the firelight and the intensity of the moment, he did not see the color, so much as he felt that he was being weighed and measured as he had never been before. Apparently she saw what she wished to see. She took a deep breath.

"Very well ... now I don't know how to tell this to you properly, for I am not a tale-teller. I know not where to start it; I have lived with it, as did Mael, all my life. And for some of the recent parts, since I came out here, there will be guessing. They will be accurate enough. You see, Mael was to

come here in person, when the time was ripe, for the matrix.
No other way; her, alone, when the time came. And so by
what you have said, and its truth, I know it is time, but faster
than was expected. After this, you may tell me why this is
so."

Morlenden settled back. "I will do what I can. And now, I
am ready."

SEVENTEEN

> *Every word that we utter must decrease the*
> *ignorance and increase the mystery.*
>
> —*Ibid*

> *The real beginnings of a journey occur long*
> *before the act of physical departure.*
>
> —*Enosis ton Barbaron*

Mevlannen began, "And now will I give you blunt stroke
for blunt stroke, Morlenden Deren. It is thus: we who are the
pampered and protected curios, we who live lives character-
ized by the forerunners as all too agricultural and oversexed,
we who supposedly fear technology . . . *we* possess a true
ship of the deep spaces, ship and ark, ark and weapon, which
was to have carried all of us to a new world beyond the stars,
our own place, our world."

Morlenden listened to her, heard her words clearly, with
no misunderstanding of them, but all the same he wondered
if the news of the death of Maellenkleth had not under-
mined her sanity; that perhaps she was now reliving a vague
legend that had circulated about the reservation for several
hundreds of years. She had taken the news calmly, too
calmly, and now her words were those of romantic bravado. . . . Or was it true? He asked, not concealing his dis-
belief, "You mean a machine, like the humans build and use
to take you to the telescope? And this would take . . . *all of
us* to some other world? Aside from being preposterous,
where is such a large and weighty device located, that no one
has seen it all these years?"

"I will answer your objections, one by one. Our starship is like the forerunner craft only in that it moves in the same medium, it moves living creatures across the void. But end-functions do not determine things, only the manner of their use. The means, not the ends. And the means determine the shape of the tool. But yes, originally, it was for all of us, and yes, it will go to the stars, as far as we have to. And above all, yes, it is hidden now, but soon it will be revealed. And it was to protect that secret that Maellen paid the price, her price, her value. And why you have been told nothing up to now, why you never suspected. It has been a secret since before there was a reservation, indeed it is the *sole reason* that there is such a thing as the reservation, quiet and isolated from the struggles of this world. And there has never been a leak, not when this was just a dream, a theory, nor when it was building, nor when it is almost ready."

"Not completely leak-free. There are legends, common knowledge among the children, though we all called them nonsense sooner or later. Who could imagine such a thing?"

"Legends? *We* nurtured the legend. We, Morlenden; the Perklarens, the Terklarens, the Revens, Dragonfly Lodge, we who are *Kai Hrunon*, the Shadow that Governs. We kept it alive, so that when all was in readiness, need, we would send word in a truth-speaker, and the people would come."

And now Mevlannen stopped, thinking, reaching for some graceful entry into the story she had longed all her life to tell someone, a stranger, but never had. But all her life she had lived in the community of those who knew those whose whole lives consisted of an intricate dance about a point that all acknowledged, an understood, unspoken, implied but invisible keystone of their lives.

She began again, "It was in the beginning, when they started the Braids, the Law, the Way. Before the reservation. You must understand that. The whole thing with us, the entire culture, the way we perceived, everything was engineered to convince all outside observers that there never could be such a thing of the people. A vast prestidigitation that also had to fool the magician as well, or at any rate most of him. And of course it was successful, as you will be the first to admit. So successful that even our own imagine it to be no more than a child's fable; so successful that the disguise has taken root on its own, and now guides the inner long-range plan as well. The values of the disguise have now permeated the real plan. And when we leave Earth, the concepts and the

way of life that we take with us to transplant on strange soil
are not the values of the originators of the plan, but those of
the shadow-play that protected them all these centuries.

". . . But in the beginning, we were not sure it could be
done; it was a hope, a theory, a gamble. But the suspicion
was so strong we could not ignore it; so it was started at the
mountain called Madness. Inside, it was hollowed out, a little
at a time, a handful, a pocket-load, to make a place for the
ark that was to be. And just as gradually, in the smoky meditation halls of Dragonfly Lodge, one pocketful of principle at
a time, it began to come into view, to manifest itself. It was
then we learned that the whole concept of ideas about space
travel we had been laboring under was wrong, full of limits
we would *never* transcend . . . like powering aircraft with
coal-fired steam engines. It would never fly, and should it, by
accident, it would never take us anywhere, or anyone else for
that matter.

"Now spaceflight had been approached by the forerunners,
and some good work they did, work we are still using in the
very program in which I am involved. But it has limits that
any child can see; and to escape them, a whole series of fantasies was concocted, leading nowhere in hard science. What
was the concept? That one moves in space according to Newton and his bloody laws of motion: forced-power, imposition
of will, the Fire elemental, chemical rockets, ion-drives, so-
lar-wind sails. All wrong. It was exactly like when the
forerunners in prehistory first sailed upon seas; they could
only use natural forces—buoyancy, floating ships with sails to
catch the wind, launched by the tides. And we, standing on
the shore of a new and terrible sea, would do the same; we,
too, would tap tides and winds and currents. Only all those
would be analogs, stranger forms of energy-flow in a larger
and more multiplex universe."

Morlenden said, "I have world-knowledge; you mean that
you tap directly into things like gravity, solar wind, things
like that?"

"No." Her sharp, delicate face became focused, intense.
"No. Those things you speak of, the principles, they are nth-
order derivatives of the basic underlying forces we tap. In the
things you know, there are no words for the currents, the
flows, the forces, the concepts. And we have taken care to ensure that this remains so, forever, until we are ready to give
up the secret.

"Now we saw that space was sea, the great sea. And we saw the analogy of ships of one kind of sea comparing to ships of the other sea. Just so, so that even in Singlespeech we still call a container of people that moves according to control in that medium a *ship*. But the flaw in the old concept was that we tried to leapfrog to powered ships, fueled ships, before we even knew the nature of that new sea. Or about the kinds of power we could use. Then we *saw*. And understood. And when we did, we also understood why we could not test it with a model. You will see also. So we pushed the thinkers, the theoreticians; some collapsed from the effort, others retired in disgust and discouragement. But always some stayed, and at last we knew enough to begin. Then the Player Braids were formed: first were the Klarens, who were to become the *Per-Klarens* when the second Player Braid was added, the *Ter-Klarens*. And thus we have been, until this last generation."

"Thus you have been. To do what?" asked Morlenden, with a hint of sarcasm in his voice. "Indeed do *what?* Play a distracting Game for three hundred years?"

She laughed, a light, playful silvery laugh. "No, no. You all have been carefully led to assume that the root *klarh-* was Earth aspect, 'to play.' Hence, in turn, the *Players.* . . . It is not Earth aspect: it is Fire, and that means . . ."

". . . to fly! Not Players, but Flyers!"

"Indeed, to fly, to soar, to float upon the currents. We are not idle, privileged entertainers, Morlenden Deren; we are the pilot-astrogators of the Great Ark, the One Ship. There was no other way to keep the skill and the knowledge alive, save in a public Game that everyone could see and think he knew."

"Very well. What does the Game have to do with piloting? I know the Game, thanks to Krisshantem, but I fail to see . . ."

"The hard question; thus hard answer. Let me build a dynamic identification-series for you: consider vehicles. You make a cart, a wagon, hitch it to a pony, and off you go. Its purpose is to go, but it can be stopped, and it doesn't change, or stop being a cart. Yes? Now consider a bicycle, which must be in balance to go. Yes? Now an aircraft; it can only be stopped when it is finished being a functional airplane, yes? You can't stop it just anywhere, and never in the air, unless you have rotary wings, which is just cheating the system. Yes? Just so the leap to the Ship. It is a quantum leap into a new concept in machines, if indeed that is the proper word. Before, we had machines that could be turned off. The more complex they became, the harder to turn off. With the ship, we enter the concept-world of machines that can't be turned off—at all. They must be *on* to exist. Once you reach a certain stage in the assembly of it, it's *on* and that's all there is to it. And when you build it, you are building something very specific; that is the Law of Multiplexity. The more developed the machine, the more unique it becomes.

"So, then," she continued, "this machine can only operate, be *on*, exist—in one mode only. A spaceship, which can't be turned off. Now, in the true-mode of that existence the laws we limited living creatures perceive about the universe are so distorted that they may as well not apply. One doesn't look out a window to see where one is going! The kind of space that the ship perceives, operates in, is to creatures such as you and I, chaotic, meaningless, and *dangerous*, when perceived directly, if we can at all. To confront it directly is destructive to the primate mind, indeed the whole vertebrate nervous system. At present, Dragonfly Lodge thinks that this underlying reality-universe is destructive to all minds, whatever their configuration, life-form or robotic. Basic to the universe: that its inmost reality *cannot* be perceived. A limit. So we interpose a symbolizer, and that translates the view into something we can perceive, and control. And we must control it, for like the sailing ship our Ship emulates, it cannot exist uncontrolled, and there can be no automaton to do it for us. It is flown *manually*, all the time; even to hold it in place relative to our perceptual field. For at the level of reality we are operating at here, to perceive *is* to manipulate. As you go further down into mystery, they become more and more similar; even the forerunners know that. But at the Ship they converge."

Morlenden thought a moment, then said, "And I see; the symoblizer portrays a Game."

"Just so. That is the Inner Game. And the Outer Game we have played in public is a much simplified form of the kind of thing we see in the Sensorium, which is display screen and control system all in one. Not combined; it *is* both. That we see the functions as separate is a measure of our distance from the Eternal. It is accurate enough, but of course certain configurations cannot be attained in the Outer Game, since they would lead to flight, too, and an open gameboard is no ship to fly in, but only an unmounted sail."

"It . . . flaps away?"

"About that. Yes, very good. And in two-dimensional display, we have the tesselations: triangular, quadrangular, pentagonal, hexagonal, octagonal, although this last leaves holes in the continuum and therein uncontrolled things happen. These symbolize the different kinds of space we can use ... space-three, space-four, space-five, space-six, and space-eight. Each one has a different range and kind of thing it can perceive and control. *Pertrol* equals both. Within limits, we can set distances as we will."

"I see; when one flies the Ship, one actually is playing a more difficult Game, in which space itself plays the role of antagonist."

"Yes. And there is no way we could practice using the Ship's display. There, to simulate is to replace. So we invented the Outer, public Game, to keep us trained in the basics so we would always be ready when the time came."

"You are one of the pilot-astrogators?"

"No. I would have been, had either Maellen or I been born male. It takes four, and no less, to face that which the symbolizer depicts . . . this is why Braids were invented. The real reason. Not the genetic reason we use—that it keeps us all mixed and gene-pooled. That is excuse. You see? There must be four, and the only bond that will hold is the sexual-emotional one. You will not understand now, but I will say and you must believe that the Game in the Ship cannot be approached as a job, a vocation, a career, or recreation. To the contrary, it is Life and Death itself at work there. In the Inner Game, we call the Game *Dhum Welur*, the Mind of God. And that Mind is a terrible mind, that one may not face directly and remain whole. Some of the forerunners guessed it long ago—first the Hebrews far back in time, others along the way, and they wisely left it alone, left the Arcana alone. That is why those who studied the occult arts were either fools or doomed. Fools if they were wrong, and most were; doomed if right. The forerunners *know*, and stay away."

"It's that alien?"

"Yes. More than you can imagine. . . . Consider now, here in this cabin atop this mountain. We will go outside and look at, into the sky. We will see clouds, storm, and through rents in the clouds, stars. Ordinary enough, you can say; yet I have seen the same sky and the same clouds-of-the-world in space-three . . . it is different, full of terrors, of things we cannot understand, save to avoid, other things. . . ."

She stopped for a moment, apparently looking into some interior memory.

Then she continued, "So I suppose that things would have continued thus indefinitely. But the Ship was nearing completion, and it was estimated that the need for two Player Braids and the deception of the public Game were at an end. Thus the Perklaren insiblings, who were yet to wave at that time, and because they were the higher Braid, took a drug that disrupted the normal sexual-selection process of the insiblings* for that generation. They knew that it would make the *Toorhon* turn out to be the same sex, but they did not know which sex it would be."

"They did this by intent?"

"Yes. And it would have been ... was to be ... of no great effect. But that is one of the ironies of the Game, I think. It does not let you go so easily. The Ship can't be turned off; the Game can't be left, just like that. It will have its price. And so here is the essence of it: Sanjirmil was the inheritor of the Game, by the actions taken by the Perklaren insiblings before the birth of my generation. But in the province of the Game, Sanjirmil is actually not suited to it at all. Relative to the Game, and only to the Game, she is uninspired and ... well, stupid. She hasn't the mind for it, although she is capable in other areas. Maellen, on the other hand, had a natural-born talent for it, the best we ever had. She was, by irony or accident, a natural prodigy for the Game, the only one ever so born. A genius. But it was too late, things had gone too far, the momentum was carrying us, perhaps the Game now controlling us and wished to teach us a lesson. I don't know. But as it stood, it would have been cruel enough. But this ties into another problem. . . ."

"Which is?"

"I said that the Ship was a machine that could not be turned off. That there was no way; that at a certain point in its construction it becomes *on*, activated, and assumes some of the responsibility for constructing itself, growing itself, while being guided. And so at that point, it turns itself on; *and flight begins, ready for it or not.* We knew it would be that way—thus the theorists had predicted. After all, it's not a hard prediction—you or I could do as well. But they could

* The first offspring was randomly selected, but thereafter the sex of the children was controlled pheronomically to maintain the fifty-fifty sexual ratio required by the insibling mating pattern.

not tell the time when the event would occur. That is why we had the two Player Braids—to keep us all sharp and prepared for it by means of the artificial rivalry between us. And well it was, too, that the Terklarens had done so well by this generation; but evil, too. An evil star was after our fate. For the event occurred about fifteen years ago."

"About the time of the birth of Taskellan?"

"Yes. Just after. Maellen and I were just five, little children, *hazhon-hazhoun*, children's children. So the Flyers all had to go to work, alternating in the Sensorium, all the hours of the day, the days of the week . . . for fifteen years."

"I don't understand. . . ."

"It must be manually flown to hold it in place!" she exclaimed. "Its position at a specific place upon the Earth is not held there by gravity and momentum, as are the other things; that it stays in that place, it must be flown *there*. As we sit here, we move in many ways, but are held fast in a matrix of local forces. The Earth rotates, revolves in the Earth-moon system, revolves about the sun, follows an orbit about the galaxy, moves with the galaxy in the local galactic group, and participates in the steady-state expansion of the universe . . . those motions and their multiplex sum must be reversed and fed into the Ship so that it stays in its cave. Those motions, and many others that we do not see . . . some of these countermotions are those which may not be seen. There are terrors in the universe, and they are not the ones we imagined. And if we do not compensate, then the Ship would drift off on its own, following the currents as it feels them. . . . Perhaps the word *drift* is inappropriate, for seen by an outsider on the surface, this drift would seem like an explosion; the Ship would explosively depart the immediate area at something close to *c*, the velocity of light, a significant fraction of it, interacting violently with matter in its path and around it. At the value of *c* it possessed, it would have enough mass, once it moved, to disrupt the balance of the whole solar system. It would, of course, be destroyed in the first moment of unguided flight, but no matter; it would destroy everything else."

"I don't understand . . . why doesn't it disrupt things now, if it has that much mass?"

"Speed alone. Relativity. The mass approaches infinity as the speed approaches unity-*c*. Held at rest, it has its own material mass, a few thousand tons. This is damped by the control field, so that it appears massless. Makes it easy to move, short-field. But turned loose, it takes off at almost a full light; so that the mass is approximately equal to two-point-five *suns*. This is above limits within a given volume of space, so the result is a linear supernova as long as it lasts. Those are the limits ... say, from the mass of Jupiter to two-point-five suns. There is some inexactitude in our calculations, but at any rate, at either extreme, the result is doom; so what does it matter? And as if it made any difference, we cannot determine the vector either. It is a heavy responsibility, flying."

"Indeed, to know the Flyers have been sitting on a bomb for fifteen years. They have been flying it *manually*?"

"Manually. While the rest of the Ship was being grown and built. Finished, the life-support systems completed. There have never been enough people to do it, the work that isn't done by the Ship. And by the Canon of the Law of the Flyers, only a formed Braid can fly. That means that only two crews are available, although exceptions are made by executive order of the High Reven, to allow relief so the outside Game can go on, and continue its deception. . . . The last time I was home, I was told that an exemption would be made for Sanjirmil and her Braid, if she could assemble one."

"So that is why the parent Perklarens were never home."

"Yes. And why I am here. But their story first. They were at a holy mountain, the Mountain of Madness, inside the Ship, flying alone in the darkness, in space-three, triangular tessela-tion, hardest of all. Matrix twelve; fine detail work deep inside a gravity well, the solar gravity well. The Ship is spheri-cal in shape and sits in a cradle in the rock, in the cavern; it has only moved about an inch in all that time. You could sit on that very hill and not know it was there, a few score feet under your very fundament."

She said, after a moment, "Klervondaf was initiated but not trained. Taskellan was not initiated. Both Maellen and I were, of course. We did not stop being insiblings. The Inner Game was our heritage and our right. But instead of Player-Flyers, we were to take different roles, so that the last step might be implemented; I would come here, to the Trojan Project, and Maellen would secretly soldier for us in the outer world. I chose loneliness, and Maellenkleth chose dan-ger, and ultimately, death."

"Who decided? How?"

"The Shadow, as in all things. We divided it up, Maellen and I, with no more thought than we would share a piece of cake. There was no particular reason. We were so very young ... and she was good at the Game, and wanted to remain where she could at least study it, pass on her insights. I am only average, like anyone else. Better than Sanjirmil, but nothing like Maellen. And so I am here ... but in many ways I like my work, both the outer and inner portions of it. I like to make things work, and so have done well by my employers, even as I used their instrument to do other things. . . ."

She shook her head, as if still unbelieving. "So I am an astronaut, an engineer. When I would prefer a *yos*, and now, until I weave, an eager circle of lovers."

Morlenden interrupted her musing. "I see that Maellenkleth was to run destructive interference for the rest of you."

"Yes. One last trick."

"And you?"

"Mine was the last part, a small one, but important. I was to see that the telescope was built, and help build it, so I could have a good reason for using it without arousing suspicion."

"And what were you to use it for?"

"You know we have poor night-vision; that is why the telescope. Not for magnification, but for the gathering of light. Otherwise one of us could have done this from the ground. So, then, I was to obtain views, visually, polychromatically, of the space all around Earth, in all directions, and memorize. Then, using all those views from different points along the Earth's orbit about the sun, combine the views together, to make up in my mind a three-dimensional map of interstellar space from eidetic memory. I would have an excellent dimensional view, because I would have a parallax baseline one hundred and eighty-five miles long, the diameter of the orbit. After I had the image, I could convert that into a three-dimensional grid map, using Multispeech space-matrix coordinates, which would then be used in the comparison astrogation base."

"How so?"

"On a clear night, you look at the stars. Can you see any order in their arrangement?"

Morlenden hesitated. ". . . No. I see the brighter constellations, but they are somewhat arbitrary. I cannot tell what is near or far, or in relation to what. Lights in the sky. Jupiter and Mars seem as far, or as near, as Sirius, Vega, Deneb."

For the names of the stars and planets he had used, Morlenden had unconsciously used the words as he had heard them from Fellirian; the old Modanglic names. It was only after he had spoken the words that he realized how alien and strange they sounded. Mevlannen noticed as well. A light smile danced across her face.

"You do not know the names of the stars, for those who name are also those who seek order. It was a slow process, for we had to work in part from ancient maps. We do not see them all from the ground. Painstaking research, thousands of nights of careful watching, care and secrecy lest it be known that we even look at the stars. But we have our own names for the stars, the near ones that we know and feel, and the far ones that we use as reference points. You know the Canon of Names: one syllable for things, two for places, three for people, four for stars, and five for the 'Attributes of God*.' So that Borlinmeldreth is that which the forerunners call Sirius; Kathiarvashien, Sigma Doradus; Skarmethseldir, Deneb. There are many names we have had to learn, recite by rote."

Morlenden said, "Names, yes, but it is still without order."

"So it seems. But there is a great and mighty system of order in space, although it cannot be seen by a creature on the surface, without a matrix in the imagination. It is on too vast a scale for us. And we are talking about visuals, that which we see with our eyes; you cannot begin to imagine what the same volume looks like when seen through the symbolizer in space-four. Or any other. More than chaotic, it is alive with forces and unknown objects whose nature we cannot determine. Eddies and currents are there, and waves and winds and storms whose source and sink we do not know. And as the ancient forerunner Polynesian navigators saw lights in the sea that indicated land over the horizon, the glory of the sea, so do we also see glory in the sea of space, but it is a glory that makes us very afraid as well; it crawls like the Pacific Ocean down there below Pico Tranquillon. And for such a

* Theological terminology. But in this convention was also a tradition that a person's name, proper plus surname, also equated to five syllables, by dropping all numerical prefixes to the surname. (The last syllable of the surname, -en, was a short form of the syllable *ghenh-*, a root meaning "family." By and large, the ler found the guttural—*gh*—distasteful and would drop it whenever they could get away with it.) In this view, then, all persons were theologically considered to be "Attributes of God."

Ship, there can be no anchorage anywhere; for the pilot, no landfall, though a planet be found, and the passengers, the people, disembark. For us, a planetfall is just more work in space-three. . . . And there are other things, too, things we can only dimly perceive in the Game, things which have no visual analog at all. They move, they appear to have volition. Are they forms of life? Perhaps. So however well we think we see space in the display, we have to have a reference set of coordinates from the visual perception. Because some things show in the Game that cannot be seen and we must know where these are. And we must know arbitrary things, too—like which way is Galactic North, G-South, Solar North, S-South. The reference for Galactic Meridian. Translating. Our eyes see geodesic lines to the stars, but in the Ship there is no such thing, and the two must be integrated. That integration has been my real mission, and it is this for which I have been trained."

She paused, then continued, "It is a problem in synesthesia as well; we always assumed sight was sight, period. But it was not to be so: what the symbolizer depicts would be best described as being most like a sense of smell, whose operation we then see through the symbolizer. That is not good, but it will have to do."

Morlenden at first suppressed a smile, but then he laughed aloud. "So you sniff your way along, blind but for the memorized view, eh?" But he laughed uneasily, for he did not like the image that came to his mind—that of a hound blinded, nose to the earth, questing in the air, cautiously sniffing out a trail to a place he never knew before, but which had to smell right. And avoid a universe full of things, whose perceptions he could not verify by sight. Morlenden added, "That is the damndest thing I ever heard in my life."

Mevlannen smiled with him. "I laughed, too, Morlenden, when I was initiated, and so have we all. Except Sanjirmil. She never laughed. But the dangers are real, and there is much confusion. Naturally we do not desire to get lost—only to leave Earth and make planetfall on a world upon which we can live. And so thus was my part in it: to reconcile what we see with our eyes and what we perceive in the symbolizer. This I have done, and my task is finished."

She stopped speaking, her voice at the last becoming hoarse. Now she looked, and she saw that her cup was empty. Morlenden's was as well. Adding his cup to hers in her hand, she arose, refilled them both, and returned to her place by the fire. She seemed dazed, abstracted.

Morlenden also was abstracted, trying to integrate what he had heard here with what else he heard. Mevlannen had explained a lot, the whole background. But, astounding though it was, it did not explain what had happened to Maellenkleth. Or to him. He thought again; he thought he could see the answer on the horizon, but he did not care for the shape of it. There was much yet to comprehend.

He began, "I have many questions, Mevlannen. The Shadow, Maellenkleth, Sanjirmil . . . I hardly know where to begin."

She answered tentatively, "I know the basics; I also know what I have done. But recently, I am out of touch. Remember, I have been out here five years; there is much you will know better than I."

"Well, then. The first part. I understand secrecy. But I feel cheated that a whole way of life was engineered as a deception, rather than a reality, however good it was for us all. . . . There are things we do out of that which do not come easy, after all. I know these things well. What will it all have been for?" he asked.

"That we will be free, to have a world of our own. Is that not enough? And remember the means defining the tool . . . it was thus we were defined."

"Have you considered, you of the Shadow, that the people will become cynical?"

"That was considered in the beginning, but it was hoped that they wouldn't be, that they would graft on those values; 'the grafted tree bears the sweetest fruit,' say the Pomen Braidsmen. And it has been good for us, we have thrived under our increased family structure as we would have under no other model we had at the time. And now we are used to it; I should not wish any other way."

"So we say, here . . . but there is also the idea of the government. Ostensibly there were the Revens and the Derens, and that was it—cheerful, law-abiding light anarchy. But now you tell me that this has not been so, that we were ruled in reality all these years in secret by a government we didn't even know existed, a council calling itself *Kai Hrunon*, 'The Very Shadow.' Was the Reven Braid the real ruler?"

"In a word, yes. In another, no. You would, for example, never have been permitted to challenge an arbitration by Pellandrey or his insibling Devlathdar; that it was never done in the past is a measure of our tact, which is what civilization *is*."

"But it was always otherwise."

"Mostly. Outer: a Braid to settle disputes, and another to confer familial legitimacy; but inside, in the Shadow, it was a majority of elders, and at that, primarily of the Flyer Braid background. And there one rules. The Perwathwiy Srith. And the traditional rote is that the Reven arbitrates only aground. In space, the senior Flyer rules. In the name of the Shadow and the Plan."

"I see a danger here: if the Ship cannot be turned off and is always flying, then what now prevents the most ambitious Flyer from taking power and keeping it, using the argument that since the Ship is flying, his is the power. What prevents this?"

"Necessity for discretion. Tradition. And the fact that as of now, most of the people are still outside the Ship, and would probably ignore orders from within it. Also there is always violence; we are not forbidden it."

"Who is senior Flyer now?"

"When my Perklaren parents took the step to end Perklaren continuity, leadership automatically went to the Braid with continuity. That would of course be the Terklarens."

"Sanjirmil!"

"No, at least, not when I left. She is not yet of age. Her parent generation, the Terklaren insiblings Daeliarnan and Monvargos; such were affairs when I left."

"But it would go to Sanjirmil?"

"Yes, that is so."

"And you said that Maellenkleth was your soldier, your valiant one?"

"Aye, just so. She always demanded to be in the front of everything, since she could not have the Game. She was brave, even foolhardy."

"Did she act alone, by her own will, or was she directed?"

"In matters outside the reservation, Sanjirmil spoke for the Shadow, when she was not flying. A lot of exemptions were made for her. She was to be allowed to make up her Braid co-spouses early. They needed that, for the work of flying is too demanding for just two crews, and each crew must be four."

"This deception and its effects; one of them may have been the unnecessary death of your insibling. Do you understand this from what I have said?"

She looked away from Morlenden, uneasily, her eyes fixed elsewhere, on nothing, anything. After a time she spoke, but it was with a voice quiet and subdued. "We always knew that there was peril in the way we had chosen. Risk and reward, you know. They who risk not, receive not. But we always had to balance those dangers against what would happen if the humans derived the secret of the Ship. We knew that we could not build such a Ship openly, for they would simply take it. How could they not want it? Starships? And once we considered sharing it with them, but that was voted down. Studies and tests indicated that if they ever discovered the Inner Game, the matrix overdrive, they would integrate autopilot devices into it; and therein is horror. What we deal with in the Game no machine can handle, because what we do, every second, is *decide*, and no machine can do that for us. And we use hunch to make those guesses and decisions. We are using resources we do not entirely understand. But under an autopilot, things would start to slip and the corrections would pile up and the machine would just lock up. It is extremely dangerous to manipulate underlying forces in the universe, and one must always do it consciously, never automatically. . . . To observe is to manipulate and once you start you must continue or destroy the device that allows you to do it. But you can't play span-of-attention with it, play with it and then forget it. And robots would get tied up in the nature of transcendental numbers and become bemused by the algorithm, which is endless."

She added, "We were all told, in the most graphic terms imaginable, what the risks were at each stage of the Game, both to the people, and the ones in individual situations. I know Maellenkleth knew the risks, and she took them freely; I cannot question that further. That she paid it is to the honor of her memory."

Morlenden answered, "I cannot find fault with your loyalty, nor with Maellenkleth's. She stood up to the heaviest of responsibilities, and performed as she said she would; she was no oath-breaker. But there has been the suspicion in my mind that such a sacrifice need not have been made, and that there was more to her capture and death than meets the eye. That there are forces at work, right now, in your carefully cultured system that could be destructive to the people and the Ship as well."

"But I cannot imagine . . ."

"Of course you cannot. You have been out of touch for five years. But there is evil afoot in our garden, and I am now trying to find the source of it. What you have told me is valuable, but it does not yet bridge the gap. So let me ask you: *why* was Maellen sent out to destroy instruments?"

"It must be that she was sent, Morlenden. She was not willful in that way. Only in regard to the Game. But destroy instruments? Unusual, that. The outriders were supposed only to observe. What instruments?"

"As I was told, a device to measure magnetism, feel the field strength of the area in which it was. Another measured the field strength of gravity from point to point. Small, portable things, but accurate and discriminatory. Also not presently in use, which we all found curious."

"As I do also. . . . You could detect the Ship with those instruments, but since they were not in use . . ."

"You could detect it? How?"

"If you have a large mass of ferric ore or metal, it distorts the local magnetic field, concentrates the lines, makes the field more intense. The Ship, operating, causes the reverse of this—it weakens the local magnetic field. As for the other, the gravity meter, that could also be used in similar fashion: in essence, the mass of the Ship shows much less than you would expect. This is because the inertia is constantly damped by the matrix overdrive. Surveying a mountain with such an instrument, one would expect a higher reading due to the increased mass, but instead, what you see when the Ship is inside is as if there were a massless hole in the mountain. If the instrument was tuned for fine-detail resolution, you could see that the 'hole' was spherical. . . . If they were going to use them, or could conceivably be expected to, then I could understand destroying them. But of that I cannot speak; I know nothing."

"So we cannot determine if they were to be used or not, here."

"No. Like so much of the wide world, Morlenden, you and I can talk all night, share what we imagine, what we know, but all the same there is much else which we cannot know, of what we share and meld together. Truth takes many, and even then we err. Both true things and provable things as well."

Morlenden said, "Well, then, true or not, I will have to return much as I came . . . but at the least you can return with me, rejoin your family and friends."

"No. I can never come back. That was one of the prices
for this. I have a short tether. I will continue my work."

"We may have taken on the values of the macrodeception,
but that does not mean that you have to do the same in your
part of it. And we need your skill, Engineer. And if nothing
else, we still require the services of a resident star-gazer, if
only to remember the lore of the skies of Old Earth for those
who will have left it forever, and to search out the skies of
the new world, wherever it will be, though I find it strange
and awesome even to speak of it. Or is it that you fear to return?"

"Perceptive and cruel you are, even as you extend your
hand. It is true I fear it. I have lived here long. . . . We here
have become accustomed to one another's strangeness. But
after the manner of the people, I have been contaminated by
many of the concepts I have worked with."

She stopped, fatigue showing along the lines of her face,
her straight, delicate jawline. Fatigue and repressed grief were
beginning to penetrate her defenses, break down the fortress
of her solitude. The pale eyes softened, looked inward. Morlenden could not read the sense of her thoughts: perhaps she
was thinking about space; or of past childhood days with her
insibling, now vanished into the dust and the past. He could
imagine her as a child of the people, but harder it was to
picture her in his mind in a spacesuit, the tender, pale adolescent body encased, indistinguishable from the others, forerunners one and all. It disturbed him, following the idea to its
hermetic conclusion, that only in gentler environments did
creatures allow themselves the differentiation in form between
male and female. The harsher the environment, the less difference showed. Space . . . even that was not the ultimate yet.
There were worse things, he sensed.

Mevlannen began speaking again, now reflective rather
than assertive. It was gentle speech, and her eyes were unfocused, undirected. She spoke of the stars; and Morlenden let
her go uninterruptedly, for she needed this.

As she spoke of the stars and her work, a gentle glow animated her face, a something-inside which had not shown before. Morlenden thought that he knew the stars well enough;
he could see the brighter ones as well as any ler*, but the

* On the whole, from the surface of the Earth, considering also the
generally dusty air of the times, the average ler could, on a clear
night, perhaps see down to the fourth magnitude. Norm most of
the time was only third-magnitude objects.

night sky was no spangled glory to him—it was a furry black emptiness, broken by a number of scattered points. How could he comprehend what Mevlannen Srith Perklaren saw in space, sidereal day after sidereal day in the endless lidless night of space, perched like a bird in her instrument's prime focus, struck dumb, he was sure, by the incredible, unimaginable sight before her, and awed into insignificance by the three-dimensional image she was building up, line by painful line, position by position, via eidetic recall comparison. And she pronounced the resounding four-syllable names of the stars, in itself a wild, haunting poetry of unknown places and distant journeys, that curdled unknown longings in himself as he heard the names for the first time.

Thondalrhenvir, Alpha Crucis; Lothpaellufkresh, Betelgeuse; Norrimveldrith, Great Rigel. On and on went the multisyllabic list, mixed with ancient Latin and Greek and Arabic names and numbers and letters, the recitation, points of light in a sky of darkness, reference points and possible future havens for astrogators and pilots who were going to step off the fixed and safe shore and swim in that ever-moving stream. There were names of distant galaxies, which Morlenden did not know at all: Lethlinverdaerlan, M31 in Andromeda; Vardaindralmerran, Maffei I; Klaflanpurliendor, the Greater Magellanic Cloud. Some equated only to numbers on obscure surveys, most by human sky-watchers, a few numbered by Mevlannen and her predecessor, Thalvillai, a Perklaren of another generation: Avila 3125, Elane 10110. Morlenden wished to be able to visualize it, desperately, but he felt that he was falling short of that inner image that illuminated the eyes and face of the girl, places she would never be closer to than right now, no matter she stayed on Earth or left it. And there were the nearer stars, the neighbor-lights that Man and ler alike had looked at with longing and burning curiosity: Yallov-yardir, Tau Ceti, twelve lights; Diylarmendar, Epsilon Eridani; Thifserminlen, Epsilon Indi; Holdurfarlof, 61 Cygni A; Dharhamnerlaz, Lalande 21185; Melforshamdan, Proxima Centauri; Tandelkvanlin, Barnard's Star; Partherlondrin and Khaliannindos, Alpha Centauri A and B.

And Morlenden thought of his own life, the routines of it, of logbooks and Braid diagrams, of visits and ceremonies and parties, of the security of position and identity in a stable and fixed hereditary society. He thought of foot journeys in the changing forest, all the familiar things he and Fellirian knew. And however restricted the reservation had been, he knew that it had been a good life there and he did not wish to leave it. And which now to lose—the place or the role? He was sure it would be place-lost, for one could always change role; the outsiblings did it every year.

When she stopped for a moment, he gently interrupted her. "Mevlannen? There is another thing I should have told you. Do you know anything about a boy named Krisshantem?"

She looked at him blankly. "Nothing."

"He was Maellen's last lover. I understand that she was planning and working toward petitioning the Revens to allow her, with this Krisshantem, to form a Third-player Braid. They would be *shartoorh*. She taught him the Outer Game, and in fact was apparently receiving some covert support for her plan from Pellandrey Reven, and I think, the Perwathwiy also. Was it possible that this would have any effect on the Ship?"

"I don't know. We could not predict when the Ship would activate, so we could not better predict when it would be ready for flight. When I left, it was felt that the Ship would fly before Mael and I would come of age. Just before. That would have been ten years from now. But as you have doubtless found out, Maellenkleth was always dissatisfied with her change of role, and who could blame her? She was an authentic genius in the Game, and therefore also in the Ship. But of course that plan of hers would be against the decision of the Shadow and the beneficiaries of that decision, the Terklarens, and of course Sanjirmil. Against Maellenkleth at the height of her powers in the Game, Sanjirmil would have been ridiculous as master of the Game, and could not have survived open competition for it. And fear not, Maellenkleth would have forced it. No doubt the intent was resented, especially her bringing an outsider into the Game. The Shadow always carefully selected the outsiblings we wove with."

"So it would have hurt Sanjirmil."

"Indeed, oh, without doubt. Oh, and I see what you think! Hm ... no, she is capable of it. They feared each other greatly, Mael and Sanjir. And we all knew that the way things turned out was largely a matter of accidental timing. But when you are dealing with generational turnover periods of two fourteens and seven years, you have to have the bearing that considers a lot can happen in those years. So it fell to Sanjir, and many of us did not like it, but what could we replace her with? When I left home, nothing. Any way we moved, we were distorting our own canon, which we had always obeyed in our advantage. It would have been cynical indeed to go against it because things did not turn out as some of us might have wanted."

She looked away a moment. Then, "You must understand that in one way, the way most of the Shadow would have seen it, Maellenkleth was wrong. They would say that since the Braid in agenetic, talent doesn't matter when it's low, so it shouldn't when it's high. We all loved her dearly, but almost from the very beginning she read herself out of it. There was no accident with the Players; they took deliberate action. The accident was with Maellenkleth; she was too good, and what an irony that was, how cruel! And she never understood why she had to give up that which she did best of all things. You know she was a prodigy, but what does that mean? I will tell you: she was a full-Player, rated at level fourteen, when she was ten years old. The best we ever had prior to her was the Perwathwiy, and she only attained level eleven at her peak, and by the kind of discipline that breaks minds and bodies before their time. The average is around seven, and you must be a five to be admitted to the Inner Game."

"What is Sanjirmil?"

"Her norm, which is set when one is a child, was always subentry, a three or four. But somehow she made it with a five when she had to. How, I don't know. The numbers are not additive but exponential; there is no way a three could become a five and stay sane; it takes too much."

She stopped, then said, "Now come close to me, for I will give you the numbers. I have not made up my mind yet, and would sleep on it; yet I will give them to you so they will not be lost if I decide to stay here. . . . Now listen close, for these are matrix numbers and they are hard to catch just right."

Morlenden assented and moved closer to the girl, very close, so that their faces were almost touching. He became still, opening his mind and will to Mevlannen. All he could see of her were her eyes, whose exact color was now elusive in the firelight. The eyes were expressionless, but they were reddened in the whites and glittered with moisture. Her breath was heavily scented with the brandy she had been dosing the coffee with, and he could also detect the scent of the oil of her face. There was no preliminary warning, as there had been with Krisshantem, but rather like Sanjirmil, it started immediately, seizing his mind, blanking his vision, and inserting the coordinate matrix at once, easily. He did not understand what he was receiving, but he had no time to think of it, just retain the matrix the way he got it. It came at lightning speed, but, for all its speed, it seemed to go on for a long time, and soon Morlenden became aware of nothing but spatial numbers, sometimes broken into shorter or longer strings. Holistic, like a visual, but also something different. This did not build a picture that he could see. By the time it came to the end, which came without notice or warning, save a little twist that he did not catch, the fire was much dimmer, and he saw again the sad eyes close before him.

He said, "I have it. Are you sure Sanjir will understand?"

Mevlannen unfolded her legs from beneath her and stood, stretching like a cat. She looked closely at Morlenden, as if seeking some reassurance, or looking for a sign, of something. What? She said, "Yes. She will understand, all that I gave, and more. . . . I add a caution; never speak of what you have from me to anyone, never recite it to anyone but Sanjirmil, even to yourself. You must do neither, or you will fail us all. Only Sanjirmil!"

"Why can't you tell her yourself?"

"Because I was not to come back!" She almost wailed. And after a moment, added, "And anyway, knowing what I do now, I will not be permitted to get close to Sanjir. They will think of me, rightly or wrongly, that I carry a vendetta against her."

"I know. I see it, too. I do not know how it came to be, but she is my suspect."

An unpleasant grimace flashed across Mevlannen's face. It creased her mouth upward at the corners for that moment, but it could not be called a smile. She said, "Indeed . . . so remember your oath, and my instructions. Only to her! Do you feel arightly? You look peculiar."

Morlenden did feel odd, and he could not locate the source, which seemed to be fading even as he tried to find the cause of the feeling. There was something . . . no, nothing seemed out of place. "Yes, of course, I'm fine. Very tired."

"Do not feel badly over that; you now have much of what we have carried all our lives. It is a weight. And for you, now, it is fresh. . . . You will pass through the stressies unmarked."

She turned away from him, allowing the loose overshirt to

flow around the contours of her slender, almost fragile body after the manner of all ler girls since the beginning of their time, walking slowly around the room, putting out the lamps and candles that were still burning. She stooped and shook down the fire, at the last, covering the fireplace with a metal screen. The room sank into a deeper darkness, and in the soft, dimensionless dimness, Mevlannen took on an air of expectation, of longing. Morlenden remembered how it had been, and in his mind kicked himself for the circumstances that were. This was indeed a priceless gift, and he was powerless to do more with it than appreciate deeply.

She picked up the last candle, and said softly, "Now you must sleep with me, for there is but one bed."

He started to protest, but she came quietly to him and laid a finger gently over his mouth. The hand was uncharacteristically hard and cool, for all its delicacy a hand of great strength. She said, "I understand all too well what you will say. I know its truth as I know my own. But though I would have that, I wish more.... We are sharers now of a great secret, and are comrades endangered by the world, more than you know. That makes us close, as close as poor Mael and I. The last of our kind who slept with me was her, Maellen who gave up nights with someone much more exciting, to come here and be with me. It was just like when we were little children and all we had to do was play games with what we thought was life, and when we were tired we would tumble into bed and sleep in a pile like cats around the hearthfire, making each other secure against the unknown we had both seen. I have never slept so soundly since."

Morlenden said, "I understand. I will hold you, too."

She said, "There is one thing more . . . I should have thought of it."

"What is it?"

"That in the Outer Game, we always allowed the Terklarens a certain latitude for cheating when they were in the adversary role, the role that equates to the real universe in the Inner Game."

"Cheating? What for?"

"So we prepare for the real thing. That is what the real universe seems to do: cheat. Perhaps it does cheat, although that is a conscious process and that leads to speculations I do not care to make about the nature of things. . . . But it has its own rules and our job as Players is to understand those rules as best we can. We can manipulate the microcosm and the macrocosm through the Game, but we cannot impose our conception of order upon it; we have to play its way. So there are degrees of subtlety, and then further subtleties, and just when we think we've got it fixed and secure for all time, it makes a change on us, some little change, some exception. . . . We all know that this means we must learn more, but it feels like cheating. Not fair! So we had allowed the adversary Player team to cheat a little in the Outer Game, to prepare us for those little shifts in the Inner, which is not a Game at all, but basic life and death."

Morlenden asked, "Wouldn't this tend to make the adversary Players a little dishonest?"

"There is no doubt of this side effect. All things have consequences, paraconsequences. Sometimes we look too hard at the effect we want, and forget that there are others, some of which may be of greater strength."

"Why do you tell me this?"

"So that you may know what you have walked into. We know it and compensate for it. It is so automatic that we do not even think of it, normally. They did not tell you, and I did not until this moment. An oversight. But one that could have crucial ends."

"All of you?"

"Around other Players, we allow for it, but around others we sometimes lose sight of the fact that others do not play by our rules."

"So now that I have at last contacted the Players, I risk being tricked and gulled at every stage of the Game."

There was only a little light by which to see, but in that light he could see that at his last question Mevlannen had turned away from him slightly, an expression of pain on her face. "No," she said. "Not so much that. Or perhaps yes, you may." She straightened. "Be on your guard now, even with me. But especially with Sanjirmil."

Morlenden was tempted, but he did not speak of what else he knew and suspected. "Sanjirmil?"

"Yes. Because she never learned the counterprogram to the cheating. It is an ethical exercise. Somehow, she never got it. They tried to catch up, but you know how those things are. Once out of sequence, and it's gone forever. They tried, but no one knows if it took. . . . She can be dangerous."

Morlenden nodded, an idea forming in his mind. He saw that it was not lack of data which had prevented it from coming earlier, but that he had been suppressing the obvious conclusion all the time. And the knowledge did not cheer him; it told him of a blind side he had carried unknowing, a dirty little secret about almost-forbidden fruits, of sweaty, hard supple bodies and salty kisses, and an image which would never have mattered save for intervening circumstances and an accident. Yes. Now he knew. It remained only to verify it.

He followed Mevlannen into the rear of the cabin. There, in a separate little room, was a hard, Spartan bed, after the human style, piled high with crude but homey quilts.

She blew out the candle she had been carrying to light the way, making a fragile little puff of breath as she did so. Afterward, in the darkness, over the sounds of wind and rain and storm fretting at the cabin walls, and the stunted, slanting junipers sliding against it, he heard the silky sounds of her overshirt, slipping off her body over her head, and falling to the floor. He sensed, rather than seeing or hearing directly, the girl Mevlannen moving across the floor, and then heard the quilts rustling as she slipped her bare body into the bed.

He removed his own overshirt, not without hesitation, and then, feeling the chill of the room, slid into bed beside her, feeling first the hard, rough fabrics against him; she moved close, flowing into a space he had made with his arm, stretching full length against him. Although the intent she had was not particularly erotic, nevertheless it was, and as such was maddening. The change in Morlenden had been years ago; he and Fellirian had lost both the will and the way after Fellirian had completed and delivered her third pregnancy. But they still retained their memories and they never forgot, and the senses still performed their functions. So he knew fully the desirability of this smooth, supple young girl, eager for love; yet at the same time the thing he felt would not proceed further than a thought, a memory. If it had any body-response at all, he felt it only vaguely somewhere in the vicinity of the heart, perhaps the diaphragm, where it diffused into a something for which there was no word Morlenden knew: something ludicrous and incapable of response, feeling like some unnamed intermediate sensation, between extreme tenderness and indigestion.

She lay quietly, breathing evenly, deeply. After a time, the breathing became softer, shallower, and once or twice, her body trembled slightly. Now the combination of fatigue and Mevlannen's amazing revelation began to tell on him, and the warmth of the body next to him relaxed him further, into semiconsciousness. It was in this half-sleep that he thought he heard her say something, but he could not be sure she had said anything at all. It had sounded like, "Forgive me for that which I have done." But when he listened again, there was nothing, and she never repeated it. And so, with a head full of rushing visions and dire suspicions, Morlenden dropped into sleep like a round pebble falling into a quiet pond.

When he awoke in the morning, the rosy light from the east was pressing at the curtains of the tiny window, which he had not seen the night before; he noted immediately that the warm presence that had been next to him was not there, that she was gone, and that the cabin now carried the silence of emptiness. He arose, donned his old clothes. There was no note, nothing. He rummaged around, and eventually found some biscuits in the cupboard which apparently had been left for him to find. He slipped his cloak over the overshirt and left, trying to find a way to lock the door behind him. There was none. Apparently, it could only be barred from inside. He gave up, and started down the path, back the way he had come, along the saddle which would take him down to the cliffs above the blue sea, now smooth and glassy, except for perfect swells breaking in precise patterns along the shore, rippling their crests from left to right, leaving a faint rooster's-tail trailing above and behind them. Old Sun painted a clear, golden light over the ocean, the grassy clifftops.

He negotiated the saddle, and turned through two sharp switchbacks to a lower level, where he found Mevlannen sitting on an ancient juniper stump, dressed in a heavy winter overshirt and cloak that looked as if they had not been worn for some time. She was looking silently down at the sea; now and again a stray puff of breeze would ripple a loose strand of hair that had escaped the hood of the cloak.

He greeted the girl, "Daystar light your way as mine! Are you waiting to say farewell?"

She turned and looked at him blandly, as if he should have already known what her answer would be. "Here is a place I love dearly, and here I gave my part to the plan; but here I will not stay and offer a barren fertility to the forerunners while my kin journey to the stars. I will come with you if you offer me the new family of Taskellan."

Morlenden nodded. "Just so and no more; but you will have to call me now Kadh'olede, not Ser Deren."

"So much will I do gladly. It has been a long time. Will your own Braidschildren not resent us?"

"No. I think not, although our *Nerh*, Pethmirvin, will not approve of your stealing boyfriends from her."

"Oh. I don't know yet if I can."

"Never mind. I have something in mind to keep you busy for a time."

"You will keep secrets?"

"Indeed I will."

"Very well." She stood, shaking herself off. "Can we get back, do you think?"

"I had no difficulty coming here. Their attention seems elsewhere, now. We will ride, and then we will walk a space; what can we do but try? Tell them you have been on the Salt Pilgrimage, if they ask. And of course, use a name other than your own, just as I will do."

Mevlannen nodded. She looked back, up the mountain, just once, at the summit of Pico Tranquillon. She could not see the cabin from where she stood. Then she turned and started down the narrow path to the sea, rippling far below them in the morning light. Morlenden joined her and together they walked down to the sea, and back into the world.

EIGHTEEN

The pathology of the poet says that the unde-
vout astronomer is mad.

—A.E. Waite

Eykor, carrying a sheaf of papers, untidily arranged into a cumbersome bundle, greeted Parleau in the hallway outside the chairman's office. "Chairman, a moment; may I have a word?"

"Certainly, Eykor. It's free, now. Come along." Parleau led the way past the shiftsman administrator who sat impassively and said nothing.

Eykor followed, carrying the unwieldy sheaf of paperwork as if it concealed a very touchy bomb. Once inside the private office, he carefully placed the bundle on the conference end of Parleau's desk, and turned to the chairman. He began, excitedly, "Chairman, over in the department we have been pursuing several aspects of this series of incidents centered on the girl-vandal. We have found more loose ends. Too many. We are now in the embarrassing position of having more clues than crimes or criminals."

"Go on." Parleau knew very well that to one such as Eykor crime flourished everywhere, even in the mind. He would never root them all out, but all the same he would never stop trying, either, heedless of the misery he caused along the way, and the mistakes he made. It was not hatred of crime that made him that way, but rather an excess of zeal to duty, and too narrow a view. Such types were ultimately dangerous to all unless kept under strict supervision; and of course, well-supplied with a variety of real criminal activities to keep them to task, preoccupy their attention; everything was evidence, otherwise.

Eykor said, "We found Errat."

"More specifically, please."

"Errat was discovered in a terminated condition, in a run-down rooming house near the warehouse quarter. Here, in Region Central. It was handled routinely by neighborhood Security, until an alert watchman noted the reports. Then we got the department into it."

"Aha. Continue."

"By the time we got there, of course the body had been removed, but the room had not been too disturbed, so we were able to have the forensic pathologist go over the room microscopically. We did the same with Errat, when we caught up with the body. Errat had been dispatched with a single penetration of a sharp, pointed object in the upper left back; he terminated virtually instantly; there was not a sign of struggle, anywhere. We believe he was taken by surprise."

"Knifing's a common enough cause of murder."

"This was different; it was done without slashing, no side movement at all. We were able to reconstruct the shape of the weapon."

"Errat seemed to be a free agent for persons unknown. This would indicate that one of them got close to him and had time to aim carefully."

"Exactly. And it was an unusual weapon; it was straight, two-edged, about two hands long, but rather thick, for the kinds of knife we are familiar with. It was not metal, but wood, a very hard wood sealed with a coating that was once volatile and which contained many impurities."

"I know of no tool like that."

"Neither did we. At least not in our own community. But with the New Humans, such knives are commonplace. They are used for dress and for the settling of feuds. Moreover, this suggested deduction was confirmed by other traces we were able to derive from objects in the room. You see, the fractions are different, between us and them, the chemical traces. The detector-men went crazy until it occurred to them that their machine was actually correct. I got into the Archives with Klyten and we reconstructed a basic outline to describe the person who was in the room with Errat: it was a ler female, probably adolescent, although there are conflicting indications. Also, the traces were distorted by a very high reading for adrenaline fractions and residuals, and another family of residual fractions that doesn't equate to anything. Whoever was in there was very tense, more or less permanently. And we also checked with Control. The traces we found, the unknown ones, are the same as the unidentified female in the crowd-scans."

"Good God, man! What else could you get on whoever it is?"

"Very little else, Chairman. But at least we were able to make that correlation. Of course we checked out all the inhabitants of the building very carefully. Nothing. And of course no one could recall any ler being in the neighborhood for any period. Never had seen one. But female, allegedly from Inspection Bureau, had been there, but was no longer. The name she used is unimportant; it didn't check anywhere. The stress-monitors in the area were tripped, but they had been that way for years—nobody had checked them, so it would seem. I am sad to say we lost the trail there."

"Nothing? No trace, no track, no description?"

"Nothing that would do us any good. We think that whoever she was, she was also using multiple identities and disguises; it is a ler, all right, but she knows procedures well and moves with impunity."

"A sobering thought, Eykor. The other one, the one we caught, also moved freely among us for years. I wonder how many others are doing the same."

"Plattsman is running a close-order check of all the stress-monitor reports now. Of necessity this degrades current operations, but we have to know."

"Agreed. That we must. And how about travel permits?"

"All accounted for. Nothing this side of the reservation. There is another thing about this ... we don't know the motive for Errat's murder. We think he was silenced. His usefulness was done. He seemed to think he was more important than he was; but he was just a screening pawn, and when his part was over, he was dispensed with."

"Ugh. Cold-blooded, that one. Well, I agree, this largely negates the earlier possibility that he could have been a free agent. He was tied to someone. But who, and for what purpose? There is someone inside. . . ."

"Yes. The operation was professional. Every person either knew nothing and dead-ended there, or was eliminated. We think Errat seriously underestimated his contact. Why, with his noted experience in wetwork, we can't tell."

"That is odd."

"He was known to be violently anti-ler and we do not believe he would have willingly allied himself with them. But this raises more questions, too; what kind of group or organ of the ler would wish such an incident precipitated? Or, perhaps, what was intended to happen failed. That was why they got Errat."

"This sounds worse and worse. Will we ever get to the bottom of it?"

"Perhaps we can find one answer, Chairman. Recall the original incident? Well, we wouldn't have caught her, but for the fact that the patrols in that area had been put on increased alert. Why were they? Who put them on it? Their chief got a call purporting to be from Security Central, but there are no records of the call anywhere, and nobody can make any connection at all. We think the call was made by Errat; we have tentative vocal identification with the man who received the call. Again, how would he know to do that? He must have been instructed to. But why?"

"Eykor, have you considered the possibility that this entire sequence of events has nothing to do per se with us? That would explain why it seems to go nowhere. We are seeing it from the wrong angle, as it were."

"I thought that, too ... but why go to all the trouble, Chairman? We checked with Klyten. The ler can have a feud any time they want. They have no prohibition against murder. Only against certain kinds of weapons."

"Someone wants a vendetta, but doesn't want it known."

"May be that, Chairman. But I have something more, which you should also integrate."

"More? By all means go on."

"The instruments the girl destroyed. We persuaded Research Section to try to rebuild them. They were not able on short notice to reconstruct the originals, but they did something almost as good: they built up replicas. Breadboard jobs, to be sure, but they work. They are crude and delicate and they lack the fine discrimination of the originals, but they tell an interesting story. We tested them out and used them in the gliders."

"What did you get?"

"It's all in the report and the attachments. But here's what is significant: we uncovered a most singular feature." Eykor turned from the chairman to the pile of papers and leafed through them until he located a large semitransparency covered with contour lines. This he displayed to Parleau. "This is the averaged collation from all the runs we made. It depicts the field strength of gravity in the general area of the reservation. And here," he said, withdrawing another sheet of similar size from the pile, "is a carto of the reservation, in the same scale, for comparison; what we should expect to see is a general correlation and co-location of regions of higher density of gravitational strength with areas of hills, ridgelines, and the like. And low-density areas with depressions, valleys."

Parleau looked at the unlabeled masses of contour lines. He said, "I see . . . but what am I supposed to see?"

"The expected correlation is true everywhere on the reservation grounds and surrounding area, except for this one unique area, here." He pointed out a location on the density chart. "In the northwest we found an area that shows a definite negative correlation."

"You are certain it was not instrument error."

"Absolutely. That is why it took so long, so many days, to get this to you. We wanted it to be complete. There were some anomalies, but they occur everywhere, and they shift in time and location, as one would expect in transient malfunctions. But not this place. This one shows perfectly circular every time. And when we tried the Magnetic Anomaly Detector, we got the same thing, in exactly the same place; a circular area of greatly reduced field strength."

"You are certain there is no doubt of these readings?"

"Absolutely none. It's all there in the report. A fine piece of work by the junior Security men, I must say."

"What do you attribute this to?"

"Unknown. We sent the phenomenological description around, but nobody could come up with any probable cause. We thought a hollowed-out cavern, but the readings we have are much too deep for that, on the gravity scans, and a cave would hardly affect the magnetic field at all; if it did, it would be very slight. Also, a cave would have to have an entry, of which photo recon did not find any trace whatsoever. In other words, simple absence of matter isn't enough."

Eykor wasn't finished. He turned again and withdrew still another chart from the pile, which was now becoming scattered and untidy. "There's some more, here. This chart, on the same scale as the other two, is a replica of a sociological chart that was prepared for Vance and Klyten, twenty years ago. What it shows is the location of each family group and elder commune, and their interconnections. Like a market diagram of a primitive society. The colors, if you study it for a while, reveal a certain hierarchy. Now, up to the present, this has lain in the files, collecting dust, an academic curio, nothing more. But transposed in the proper scale, and overlaid on the other charts we already have . . ."

Eykor spread the charts out, and aligned them according to little tickmarks on the sides, so that they were in exact relationship to one another. He said, pointing with his free hand, "Now here is the mountain where we located the anomaly; here, in this ridgeline running northeastward from the river. And here, on the north side, is the home of the Second-player family group, while just opposite, on the south of the ridge, is the home of the First-players. Now east and north—and here, again in the north—is the elder commune, Dragonfly Lodge, and opposite that on the south is the house of the ruling dynasty, the Revens or judges. The locations form a perfect square, with the anomaly at its exact center. The locations are also at the four major points of the compass with regard to the anomaly. We had them run a Fourier analysis of this last chart, using the most elaborate program we could devise, plus trained recon interpreters, and we can say that nowhere else does a configuration like this exist in regard to any feature, natural or otherwise. All the rest are either randomly placed, or located in relation to obvious economic nodes and crossings. There is only one interpretation: that those four groups have access to the anomaly!"

Parleau stood back from the desk, scratching his chin, staring down at the charts. "Plausible, plausible, indeed."

"We cannot dismiss this as not being a weapon. It is assuredly not a natural object; natural objects are neither massless, nor do they depress a magnetic field."

Parleau mused, "Agreed. We can't assume that it's neutral or benign. . . . It has been there for some time, obviously; and were it for the general welfare, I should imagine they would not have hidden it so well. And of course, we see that those groups have been mixed up with it from the beginning."

Eykor continued, "Yes. And this at last explains why the girl, a First-player by family, chose to lose her mind rather than take the chance she might reveal even an innocent association that could lead eventually to this. But we still don't know why she did it; I mean, it's stupid, after all; it just called our attention to it."

"Maybe she was preventing an ongoing project from seeing that by accident."

"We thought of it; and checked the records. There was no such project in view. The instruments would have lain there another thousand years for all I know."

"Come on! Are you certain, Eykor?"

"Absolutely, Chairman. Control ran their collator through it; Research Center also. There was *no plan* to use the instruments in any manner."

"Then she did her work for nothing. Or did she? Is this like the Errat thing, where we can't see the true intent because it isn't aimed at us? But if we hadn't caught her, we'd never have made the connection."

"We might have thought to make up breadboards and use them."

"But against whom? We'd have the whole world as suspect, then."

"Chairman, I believe we agree that Errat was working for someone, on instructions. Someone he didn't know. He called the patrol out, and she was captured . . . what if she was supposed to be captured?"

"God, you're a worse speculator than Plattsman. What would be the purpose of that?"

"I can think of innumerable possibilities. It's expensive, but you've heard of agents provocateurs. We use them. This could be the same thing, only with an event as bait. To get us to do something precipitately. Also, Errat was at the root of the incident in which the girl was wounded or killed."

"Aha! The first time wasn't enough, so they trailed the bait in front of us again, eh?"

"Something like that . . . they seem to be trying to provoke a first strike. But people who invite first strikes usually do so secure in the knowledge that they can weather it and use something worse in return. They want justification to use it. What? Whatever is located in the anomaly!"

"Hm. An exercise in subtle moralities. . . . But all this does not match well with their high regard for life, nor with their ideals of lack of interaction with us."

"Someone wasn't nonviolent with Errat. Someone precipitated some very un-nonviolent behavior to the girl, probably intended. There's no high regard for life, ours or theirs, in that. But they're uninvolved, I should say . . . so uninvolved they don't care how they get our attention."

"There is something in what you say. . . . Does Klyten know these conclusions?"

"No. He saw the questions we had, not the end result."

Parleau depressed a call-button and requested that the administrator call on Mandor Klyten. After a short wait, for Klyten spent considerable time in that very building, and happened to be in, the academician appeared in Parleau's office, arriving slightly flushed. Parleau quickly made a résumé of the case so far as Eykor had presented it, summarizing their opinions. Then he asked, "We've gone so far, but we lack a certain expertise to analyze intentions. I'd like to hear your view of these developments."

Klyten hesitated, looking about randomly, as if trying to build an image in his mind's eye to match that which he had heard. He shook his head.

"I agree completely with Eykor that something is there and that it can't be natural . . . but we can't say what it is, based solely upon what it is *not*. We can prove negatives, until doomsday and we'd still be no closer to it than when we started; the range of negatives is infinite. But I'm hesitant to leap to the conclusion that it is a weapon, just because it isn't natural. They do in fact have an elaborate ethical system that does invite the aggressor to make the first move, and their culture has elaborate structures built into it to reduce and displace the already low level of aggression which is in them. Yet, they know as well as we the kind of things we can bring to bear on them. We still have the old nuclear warheads stashed away, and we have no shortage of people, too. Hell, we could send a million-man army in there, each man armed with a switch, for that matter. And I don't understand the kind of logic that would invite that kind of risk at all. That's too much. So I'll say this: if there is a weapon involved, that's not all it is."

"Not only a weapon . . ." Parleau mused, "then a principle, an invention . . . an artifact, a thing which could have many uses. What might be some of the possibilities?"

"Damnation! Wide open, there. Be imaginative. People don't hide things, or their containers, for generations, unless the thing is very special, a breakthrough in concept. So we can disregard little piddling things like a new aircraft, a new gunsight, a more efficient power source. They do that stuff in the Institute every day and don't care who knows it. Think wildly: matter transmission. A faster-than-light drive-system. Force Fields. Hell's bells, why not a time machine? Who knows?"

"So . . . it's an *it*, truly. Do we want it?"

"Want it? Chairman, of course we want it! We want it all, as the saying goes, and the horse it came on. The question is—can we use it and will it do us any good?"

"Hmph. We get it and then we worry about that."

"No, no. All technology is not an unlimited blessing. Everything has consequences. We pick for the consequence we want, and to hell with the rest; we'll adjust after the fact. But we usually don't stop to ask if the particular consequence we are seeking is even major or minor, and what are *all* the others. For drugs, we do this, and take risks accordingly, giving a man a poison for the chance it will cure before it kills. Consider the bad old days, when we had the old sovereign nations. Some were well-off, some were very badly off. So one chooses, say, to spend money on the ability to build a nuclear weapon, when one should be investing in the most carefully structured management system. Now one has a bomb. Not only does this piss away money for nothing, but it prevents its being spent on something useful. And not only that; now the influence of it allows this state to influence the spread of its incompetence into neighboring areas, eventually blighting the entire region. There was exactly such a case. The entire area just collapsed, taking with it into oblivion a billion lives, half a dozen cultures, and about ten major languages. There's a consequence we don't want," Klyten said.

"It's not the technology—it's the use they put it to," Parleau said.

"Yes. But in their case at least they knew what they were buying. We don't even know that. We might even have to invent a need for it. Remember lasers? History? They invented them, and then worked like dogs to find a use for them. Or noble-gas chemistry; the same. There wasn't any use for stuff like xenon tetrafluoride; still isn't. It could be very dangerous for us even to try to use it."

"We've been dealing with them through the Institute for three hundred years, applying Institute solutions to just about everything that's come along. So far it's helped us greatly—helped us survive, as a fact."

"That's true, Chairman. But you miss one facet of this relationship: the Institute always operates on the basis of strict question-and-answer. Problem-solution thinking. Very specific."

"Explain, please."

"They don't accept a problem to work on unless we ask the question."

"What's so difficult about that?"

"The Institute does not do open-ended research for any group of humans on the planet, or anyone else, for that matter. The Institute works only on conceptual problems that have cleared the Priorities Board; limited stuff, that's all. Ask the question first. Like Columbus—he would ask, 'Which way to America?' They would answer, 'We'll tell you where it is.' But he didn't know it existed. Now he says, 'Is there an America?' and they tell him that it isn't part of the Indies. Not the right question. Now in some of the communes they do pure research, you know, really open-ended speculation, just to see where those roots lead. But the by-products of that are never made available, even for their own people. As for us, those people won't even pass the time of day with us."

Parleau exclaimed, "Well, then, we've been fooled the whole time!"

"No, no, I couldn't say that; they have applied themselves down there, and they've done good work. They produce solutions, tools, programs, plans, and it has always been a high-quality, first-class product. Why, the kind of loosely federated planetary government we have today was invented there. I can name a lot of other things we take for granted, too. Shifter Society is another. They have always given their best."

Parleau was following another track, and did not pursue the values of the Institute, but soundlessly shifted gears into something else that was bothering him. "You say the elders do some pure research?"

"Some elders; some communes. The ones that do so tend

to specialize in one degree or another. One, for example, does genetics, another natural science, another higher mathematics. And of course certain Braids prefer to wind up in certain lodges that are somewhat restricted, while other lodges are no more than what they seem to be—simple communes, resembling the monastic communities of our own history. There is even, so I hear, an analog of the Trappists: silence, meditation, devotion, poverty, humility. Their product is an illuminated devotional text; that, and paintings. From what I have seen, they seem fond of the Dutch Panoramists—Holbein, Bosch, those."

"Do you know Dragonfly Lodge?"

"Only slightly, mostly by reputation. They do Game work; and they are by far the most secretive. . . . Oh, I see. Yes, of course. The girl was a Player."

"Klyten, you haven't seen the half of it; I should well agree they are secretive, since it appears that they have something to hide. Eykor has associated that lodge with the Players Braids and the ruling Braid as well, and tied that to the original incident with the girl. And, in addition, an unusual anomaly that ties in also .. and most probably to Errat."

Klyten, taken somewhat aback, maintained his composure. When Parleau had summarized before, he had done so lightly, without attributing significances. Now it all came together. He replied, noncommittally, "I know them by reputation only, so to speak."

Eykor saw his opportunity to press a point. He asked, pointedly, "Is it true that when they turn the house over to the next generation, the ex-parents then move into various elder lodges?"

Klyten answered absently, "Well, that's not strictly true. Just generally. Some go off alone, others . . ."

"But most go to the lodges?"

"Yes, you could say that, but . . ."

"And do Braids go where they please, or are there trends and standing associations?"

"Oh, definitely, trends and associations. Braids tend to be associated with lodges as a matter of tradition. Not exactly on a one-for-one basis, you understand. There is some mixing. Here you must understand that they don't ever see choice as an Aristotelian dilemma of two options; I should use the word *quadrilemma*, if anything. They would call such a choice situation the consideration of the Fire Path, the Air

Path, the Earth Path, the Water Path. Tradition and habit and precedent also play their parts; what one is expected to do by one's peers, for instance. . . ."

Eykor interrupted the dissertation. "For instance, where do members of the Player Braids go when they reach elder status?"

Klyten knew he was being led, but he seemed powerless to stop it. "Wait a moment, there, let me think. I study the ler, not emulate their mental processes, particularly the one of total recall. . . . It would seem that I've seen something on that; yes, of course. They go to Dragonfly Lodge. Yes, I recall it now. They have the highest correlation of any occupational group with an elder lodge."

Parleau asked, "Correlation?"

"Yes. That's where I saw it. A sociological report written some years ago. The Perklarens have a correlation with Dragonfly Lodge of something near ninety-five percent. The Terklarens are even higher; in some periods they have maintained one hundred percent for several generations running. The next association with that lodge was much lower, less than fifty percent, and all the other elder lodges show even lower correlations, down in the twenties, usually."

"Who else joins Dragonfly Lodge?" asked Parleau.

"Only one other Braid: the Revens. Almost all the insiblings, none of the outsiblings. Or the afterparents. Yes, now that I recall it, I wondered about it at the time, that association of the Revens with Dragonfly. I could see no purpose in it. . . ."

Parleau said quietly, glancing at Eykor, "Then it would be reasonably accurate to aver that, for the most part, Dragonfly Lodge is composed in the main of ex-Players and ex-judges."

"I believe that is accurate. There are some scattered few other individuals, but they are rare . . . something less than five percent of membership. It's a restricted lodge."

"Restricted? How so?"

"There are four kinds of lodges: open, closed, male, female. The male and female lodges are obvious in their member selection; they recruit. The open lodges take in anyone. They welcome all. Closed lodges take in only those they want; word gets around, and few apply who are not wanted."

"Four elementals, again?"

"Exactly. Opens are Water aspect. Male and female are,

respectively, Air and Earth aspects. The closed lodges are Fire aspect."

"What does Fire aspect connote to you?"

"Decision, order, organization, will, discipline. Willpower, planning, that sort of thing."

Parleau asked, following another tangent, "And in what aspect does the root *revh-* mean 'judge'?"

"Fire."

Eykor began pacing back and forth rapidly, saying, "We've got it now, for sure."

Parleau asked, "What do we have? We have little more than what we had from the beginning. Just putting it together better, confirming the connections. We still don't know what the artifact does."

"But, Chairman, we can now confirm that this is no yesterday's plot; it's been going on for generations! Those Braids got together, they made a perfect disguise and refuge, an elder lodge, and set up . . ."

Klyten interrupted, "No, no. Not that way! You've got it ass-backwards. The Braids didn't invent the lodges; it was the other way: the lodges invented the Braids!"

Parleau asked, "What?"

Klyten continued, "That's basic ler history, Chairman. I hadn't brought it up before because I assumed that it was common knowledge. The institution of the lodges predates the first generation of the earliest Braids by about a hundred years."

"Who made the decisions, then? Who was boss?"

"Of the organized lodges in existence today, less than a third can trace their roots to the pre-Braid, pre-reservation period. At first they were mixed all over with us. At that time, I believe the DNA conversions were still going on. The organization now known as Dragonfly Lodge was simply the best-organized group of them. They set the whole thing in motion."

"You say, 'now known as.' What were they then?"

"Hm. I believe they were then working on large-scale synthesis of all that was known in certain areas, you know, catching up and integrating. Mathematics, space flight, power-source technology, nuclear engineering, quantum mechanics. They especially revere Max Planck."

"Planck?"

"Planck, Dirac, Einstein, Fermi. A few others. Also Von Neumann, Conway. They were early games theorists."

Parleau withdrew a little, as if he were studying some deep interior panorama. At last he said, "I had a suspicion about this, always did, about those little bastards. Especially after Eykor showed me the maps and cartos of the area of the anomaly. We always feared that they would turn around on us and produce an advanced human type completely off the scale as far as mind and ability went. And that's what I almost thought it might have been. But now, I think we can narrow it down more than that, for they would fear that more than we would. So, Eykor, I want Plan Two-twelve implemented quietly, no fuss. As soon as we can get it going gracefully."

Eykor was not prepared for what he had won. "Implement it, Chairman?"

"Yes, implement it. Mobilize the assault forces and as soon as we reach readiness phase, go in there and take that hill and whatever is in it. It cannot be ready to use, or else they would already be using it, on us, doubtless. Never mind the occupation of the reservation, that part of the plan. We don't need the whole thing, just that hill. Get us there, and in."

"Chairman, it'll be hard to get it started. It's Twelvemonth, near New Year's. A lot of the troops we could call up are off on otpusk*."

"Well, get them back as best you can and get to it. Don't wait for me, build it up to readiness and go on in. And have your people ready for anything. Anything. They would be fools not to try to defend it, perhaps destroy it. Let's have no more of the business of the TacTeam that went after the girl. They must be ruthless and grab, and shoot. After we get it, we won't need to make apologies for what we did, to them, or to anyone else."

Eykor was still a little behind Parleau. He asked, "But what's in the mountain, Chairman?" He now saw something growing in Parleau's expression, something whose traces had always been there, but which had been subtle, camouflaged, blended, hidden. But with the ultimate before him, in his mind's eye, Parleau was matching those ultimates with some ultimates of his own. He answered Eykor, smiling once again,

---

* Otpusk. A Russianism that had replaced such terms as furlough, leave, vacation.

satisfied that he now knew all he needed to know: "It is either the damndest weapon you ever saw, the key to supreme power, or it's a starship. Nothing else would be worth so much trouble to them. Perhaps both. Either way, it has power. And whatever people say, we were here first, it's our planet. And I think the time has come to terminate the reservation, the Institute, and all the rubbish that goes with it. Their useful life is over, and they've delivered it. Klyten, could you operate what they find in that cavern?"

"You jest, Chairman. Of course I couldn't. And I doubt seriously that if what you say is true, we'd find anyone to operate it, either. Willingly."

"We'll get someone, Klyten. Be assured of that. We will find an operator, one way or another."

Klyten looked away, and pretended to become interested in the untidy pile of documentation brought in by Eykor, turning and hiding his face so that neither Eykor nor Parleau, now earnestly engaged in a discussion of plans, programs, options, could see him clearly and read on his face what was thereon plain. He saw Parleau more clearly than usual, now that Parleau thought he knew what was hidden in the anomaly in the hill. He had always kept his vice in check, playing the system and abiding by its rules, but with even the hopeful hint of raw power close to his hands, he was now throwing off all restraint and betting everything on what he thought he could capture and use. This last made Klyten apprehensive; for while his loyalties were not in question, he too had followed the argument from its inception with the capture of the girl. And from his own knowledge of the ler he felt the leading edge of fear: for if there was anything at all to the conjectures of the chairman, there would be defense for it, even for probing directly at it. And Klyten could not say with assurance that his own people had the resources to pay that price, and all its unforeseen billings. Best to have let this all alone, yet none of them could stop the procedure that was gaining momentum here, leading them here, to this choice-point, this nexus, with all the consequences it could have. They didn't even see them. They didn't even know such things existed. And of course he could see that they were in the act of rendering his own position obsolete; he would end his days in Inventory Management, yet.

It was in that state of mind that he caught a fragment of Parleau's speech, not said in anger, or even excitement, but calmly, as if one would ask an associate to pick up some article of commerce for him. Parleau said, "... And while you're at it, pick up that Vance and bring him up here. He's had far too close an association with those people. His hour's passed."

NINETEEN

*The Times we know are pregnant with the seeds
of Change, that mighty idol of the race
of youth, which seeks in each and every place
to lend new hope to oft-recurring deeds;
we say, the future holds our dearest needs,
but Present holds for us the barest trace
of those who were, with sometime-tortured grace,
the builders of our world, who built with deeds.*

*But now—they've come and gone, and what they made
now fades before our very eyes; and when
it's gone, we'll sing of this—our Golden Age,
forgetting that each age is purest Jade,
while Time, that Eiron to the hearts of men,
will smile at us, and turn another page.*

—*Time the Eiron,* 1964

There were four: Fellirian, Morlenden, Krisshantem, and Mevlannen, all alike now standing on the northern slope of Grozgor, the Mountain of Madness. So it had been, that in the last clear light by which to see, they had reached the end of the narrow pathing under the trees, among the weathered rocks of a dry streambed, and now they stood waiting, listening. Their directions would take them only so far and no farther. They listened for what they might have expected to hear; perhaps the sound of muffled machinery from that which was inside the mountain. But there was nothing; no sign, no presence, no trace. The mountain was silent. Far to the west, near the horizon, the sky was red, while higher up, it was the color of winter, a pale aqua. Overhead it was a hard ultramarine. The shortest day, Winter Solstice; it was a holiday in the calendar of the New People, and they would now all have been home in the *yos*, partying and cooking, singing and drinking homemade beer, while in the yard, the heavy baking oven would have contained a large goose, stuffed with a bread-and-sage pudding. The children would have been into everything, Peth fidgeting to get away to the woods and her latest boy, winter or not.... Solsticeday was older than the ler.

They stood in the cold, shuffling about nervously, cold and acutely uncomfortable. Here was Grozgor, and here came the elders of the house of Dragonfly, as it was said, "to restore their flagging vision." For them, a holy place. For the rest, a place of unknown damnations. Morlenden wondered about the wisdom of coming here, now, when back in the security of their own *yos*, it had seemed straightforward and easy: they would come here and ask for judgment of the Reven. Now ...

Fellirian shyly asked Mevlannen, "Have you ever been inside it?"

She answered, "Many times. But long ago, to be sure. Much will have changed since then. They will be finishing what they have of it."

Fellirian touched the girl's arm lightly. "Sh, now. Someone comes."

They looked in the direction Fellirian had turned; there, in the weak light, was one where none had been before, a pale, still figure, in the place where the dry wash had deeply undercut the banks. The figure, dressed in a simple, light overshirt without decoration or herald, seemed to ignore the cold, which had become intense. They could see that it was probably parent phase, but they could not make out enough of the face under the raised hood to tell who it was.

The figure came a little closer, hesitating, then speaking softly, gravely, as if in reverence of the place in which he stood. "I am Pellandrey Reven. What will you require here?"

Fellirian felt rooted to the cold, stony ground. She said, "Some who have come to seek justice: Fellirian, whom you know, and Morlenden, of the Derens. Also Krisshantem, one who has none to sponsor him, and Mevlannen Srith Perklaren. Those also are known to you."

Pellandrey stepped closer, saying, "Yes, I see. Forgive me for not recognizing you. I came here from bright light." Pellandrey was slightly built, almost thin, with fine, smooth, clas-

sical features on a long, well-defined face. Still, with an inner
calm, Morlenden had never seen before. Pellandrey added,
"Are you well, all of you?"

Fellirian answered quietly, "We are well."

Pellandrey said, "You speak of justice?"

"Yes. And of a message which Morlenden must bear to
Sanjirmil. She is in this place?"

The answer was guarded, cautious. "She is here."

Morlenden said, "And we must speak of things within the
mountain, and of things between exemplars of your Game."

"Is that the issue of judgment?"

"No, there are others."

"So, then. I, Pellandrey, am your servant and your guide
here." He seemed to sense a measure of how much they
knew, and it did not seem to bother him greatly. "But inside?" He continued, "Ah, now, there is a thing . . . you understand that it is not permitted to speak out in the world of
that which is within Grozgor? If it is that you are knowledgeable and have kept the faith, then you may enter within and
become illuminated in truth. And if not, then I cannot permit
you to leave."

Morlenden answered, "There is much that we do not
know, but of what we know we have spoken to no one."

It was dark now, dark enough so that they could not make
out the features of the face of Pellandrey, but they could
sense movement, a gesture—a smile? Morlenden thought not;
such a face as one that went with the words would not smile
. . . and if it did, it would be a smile he did not wish to see.
The Reven said, "Who was told? By whom?"

Morlenden said, "Mostly, by Mevlannen. Much I have suspected from what was told to me by others. I have spoken of
these things only with Fellirian; there are few secrets between
us. Only that which we each did during the *vayyon* remains
private. Krisshantem does not know, save what he has as-
sayed on his own. And no one else."

"Only the *vayyon*, eh? A good thing, that. It is the only
secret an insibling should have. And this other, it is almost
the same, the kind one should keep above all. So it must be;
you will see another sunrise." They all felt a withdrawing, a
fading of an icy regard. Pellandrey turned from them, saying,
"Follow me." He assumed obedience without comment. As
the High Reven, the Arbitrator of the People, he had but one
commandment: preserve the people. He completed the motion and began walking back up the streambed, never looking

back, or even seeming to notice them. The four who waited followed.

The entrance, if that was truly what it was, appeared to be a simple cleft in the rock face, set in an odd little corner where at some time in the past the intermittent stream had undercut the rock in its passage down the mountain. It was not apparent as an opening into anything conceivable from any angle, appearing only as some blind pocket whose deepest corners were filled with shadows, even in the brightness of day.

Here, Pellandrey stopped and again turned to them. He said, "There is not time for proper instruction in the form of the motions, so perform as best you are able according to your lights. Watch the motions I make and perform them exactly the same. Otherwise there is danger. Do you understand? Let Mevlannen go first; she knows. There is an interface at this point between two universes, and great energies are involved. Do this seriously. On your own. No one can do it for you."

He turned back to the cleft in the rock, and stood quietly, facing the darkness. Taking a deep breath, and holding it, he then raised his arms to the side, as if for balance, then bringing them around to the front, as if he were intending to dive into a pool of water. Then he stepped off, a half-stride, half-dance, two steps, and made a short, easy jump, as if leaping gracefully over some unseen obstacle. He moved straight ahead, but as his figure merged with the darkness of the shadowed cleft, it seemed as if he had somehow turned a corner, for they could no longer see him, or even sense his presence. It was as if Pellandrey had never been. No sound accompanied this act, and no sense whatsoever of anything having happened at all. But Pellandrey was gone.

Mevlannen stepped forward, moved to the place where Pellandrey had stood. She looked back once, nodding, adding in a voice that was now very small, "Yes, this is the way of it." She made the motions, took the two steps, and, just as Pellandrey had before her, vanished as soon as her shape merged with the cleft in the rock face.

Morlenden, Fellirian, and Krisshantem looked at one another tentatively, unbelieving. Krisshantem shrugged. "One must believe," he said, and without further words, went to the place, faced the rock, made the motions. And was not there.

Fellirian looked closely at the place, as if not believing her eyes. She slid closer to the cleft, tried to peer inside. She saw nothing. A darkness, an emptiness within a shadow. She listened, cocking her head; there was no sound. In its place there was a stuffy deadness, as if something were absorbing sound. No. No one was there. It was absurd. She shook her head, once, and then went to the place from which the others had already started. From there, she too took the deep breath, made the motions, took the two steps and the little leaping glide, and went straight into the corner that one could not see. There was silence. Fellirian was not there anymore.

Morlenden listened. There was nothing but the silences of the rocks, the out-of-doors. There was no wind in the bare trees over his head. Now he, too, walked to the cleft, peered inside. He thought he could make out the end of it. It was shallow, after all, not a cave. But when he tried to focus on the end he thought was there, his eyes refused to form an image. Too dark, he thought. Although it didn't feel quite like darkness, absence of light, something below a threshold. There was something else. Something he could not see. He shrugged, straightened, looked all around himself, as if for the last time: at the streambed, the mountain, the sky, the trees. Then he, too, went to the place, made the motions—the indrawn breath, the arms, the steps, the leap; he expected to land in a dark cave and stub his toe, but as he left the ground and the darkness met him, he felt an instant of weightless vertigo, a picoinstant of formless churning chaos and blinding energy, a roaring in his ears of disorganized, torn sound, a brightness and a body-wrenching that made his stomach churn. And he was standing.

Morlenden had shut his eyes at the lights, as if from reflex. Now he opened them. He was in a plain, dim chamber, apparently brown in color. The light came from every place, no place. There was no opening anywhere: it was a perfect cube. Sealed. The others were waiting for him. The chamber gave back no sound whatsoever; the silence was the deepest he had ever heard. Yet there was, under the stillness, some subliminal perception of energy, tremendous energies, carefully balanced and held in check. He said, "Where are we?"

Pellandrey said, reluctantly, as if he did not wish to, "No place. Keep as still as you can and make no attempt to touch the walls. Watch me and do as I do again. This is the difficult part; yet, if you make the transition successfully, you will be in the Ship. Feel the resistance and pass through it into reality again. Now attend!"

Pellandrey moved to the exact center of the chamber, stood quietly. With a minimum of preparatory actions, he suddenly jumped straight up; about at the exact spatial center of the cube, he vanished. Silently. Morlenden had tried to see exactly what had happened to him, but it eluded him conceptually; it seemed that the figure *receded*, too fast to follow, yet stayed where it was.

Now Mevlannen followed, now Krisshantem, now Fellirian; all moved, one by one, to the center, leaped upward, vanished. Morlenden stood alone. He looked carefully about the small, bare chamber. There was little enough to see. There was air, but it seemed stale, like cave air. The sound was dead. He had to listen carefully to hear himself breathe. He looked more closely at the walls, which were no more than a body-length away. He could easily step forward and touch them. He approached the nearer wall, looked closely, tried to find a point on it, focus on it. He could not. What he thought was surface was only an illusion of a surface; when he tried to see it directly, he felt disoriented instead. He was unable to define the depth of what he saw. There was no reference point upon which to focus. Morlenden strained, again trying to force an order onto it. And at the furthest extreme of his efforts, he sensed, rather than saw, motion, perhaps the suggestion of motion; a slow boiling or churning, immensely powerful, a Brownian motion that concealed a subtle sense of underlying order beneath the random movements. He looked down at the floor; there, he now saw, at the extremes of vision, the same effect as in the walls, which were all alike of a dull, rich brown that remained a surface only as long as one did not look at it too closely.

Again, he shrugged. They had had faith and made the absurd motions; he would also. From the center, Morlenden also jumped up, straight up, flexing his knees as little as possible.

His first thought was that there was something wrong with the force of gravity, because instead of slowing down as he rose, somehow he was accelerating, and the chamber faded, and in its place there was nothing, no sensation of anything. Where he was, was an imaginary number, a software program with nothing to manipulate, pure abstract process. He hung sensationless, divorced even from feedback from his own body. He did not know if he was breathing or not. He tried to move, but felt nothing. He tried imagining that he moved. He felt a resistance. It gave him an eerie feeling in the pit of his mind. The more he imagined, the more concrete feeling became. Gradually, he felt an opening, but it seemed too small. He embraced it, pulled. He was moving rapidly above a plain, conveyed by forces but not in any vehicle. It was lighted from an unknown source, an absolutely flat surface, littered with shapeless lumps that were the same brownish color as the plain, the same color as the walls of the chamber. He was passing by the lumps, but there were more ... there was a suggestion of shape to them, but he couldn't quite see it. He was moving to an abstract perspective horizon, a child's drawing, the imagination of a madman. He made an effort, the lunge of panic, trying to free himself, and the plain vanished.

Spatial orientation and normal sensation returned. He was alone in a small, bare room, but at least a room made of things he could understand, touch: it was basically metal, but was overlaid mostly with beautiful dark wooden paneling, dark wood and handwoven cloth, familiar as the product of his own people. This air had odor, temperature. It was cool, almost cold. Yes, it was chilly. He shivered. There were odors of machinery, material, distant people. The floor was reassuringly solid and in the right place. He moved from the center, to touch the walls, make sure ... as he did, in quick succession, the rest materialized into the room, displacing air with little puffs as they materialized. Pellandrey came last. When he saw Morlenden to the side, his face took on an expression of amused consternation. Fellirian had come with her eyes tightly closed, standing in a semicrouch, a wrestling posture. She bore on her face an expression of strain, grimacing with effort.

Morlenden reached for Fellirian, touched her shoulder. She opened her eyes, looking quickly around her, straightening. There was a sense of Machine all around them, a presense of controlled, bound energy, of vital, surging power. Faint noises came now to their ears from other parts of the Ship: metallic sounds; muffled voices; something that sounded like very ordinary hammering.

Fellirian asked, "Where are we?"

Pellandrey answered, "On the Ship, of course. You will note that Morlenden arrived before us, although he was last to depart the staging chamber. That is an effect we get sometimes when we go through the gate more than one at a time. Sequence reversal. We do not understand the continuum through which we just passed very well at all. The entry was not a product of design. We would prefer the door-flap of a *yos*, to be frank. But in part, it . . . ah, happened. After we found it, we were able to modify it somewhat. Now we can control it a little, and come and go."

Morlenden said, "I saw a plain, with odd lumps scattered over it. I was moving, flying; there was no end to it."

"The plain? You saw it?"

"Indeed I did, and I did not like what I saw."

Pellendrey shook his head. "We do not know where that place is . . . attempts to explore it, examine it, more closely, have failed, mostly. Most do not experience it at all, and most who do, do not live to tell tales of it. The lumps are, we believe, the remains of those who have failed, over the years. I have been there once, and I will not speak of what I did there, nor what I learned." Here he stopped, as if recalling something distasteful. "I will not return, willingly. There is one among us who does, though."

Morlenden asked, "Who?" But he thought he would know the answer.

Pellendrey said, "Sanjirmil." He would say no more, not of her. He added, "You are lucky to have seen it and lived."

He turned now, and brushed aside an ordinary doorway curtain, as if doing no more than escorting visitors into a *yos* somewhere, motioning them to follow him along a dim hallway that was revealed. "Come along," he said. "We'll go now into the Prime Sensorium; there we may speak of what you will."

He set off along the corridor, making no further remarks. The four followed, equally silently, struck dumb by the contrast between the unreality of the entry and the plain homeliness of the interior furnishings. They moved steadily through a maze; all save Mevlannen. She knew where she was.

They came to an intersecting corridor, turned into it, and immediately began walking down a steep incline. Other corridors ran into it from both sides, leading off into other sections of the Ship. From one they heard the hammering noises they had heard earlier. There was also the odor of sawdust, of iron.

They switched corridors many times, sometimes walking on the level, sometimes down inclines. Some passages were narrow, connecting hallways; others were broad thoroughfares. No section was straight for long, but would jog off, and then back again. Fellirian followed politely, but after a long time of this she could not contain her curiosity any longer, and asked, "And where are the engines, the fuel, the bunkers?"

"None," answered Pellandrey. "This is not a powered ship, a fueled ship, but the analog of a sailing ship; we only take enough power to run life-support, operate the synthesizer. That power comes from batteries which are energized by the flux around the Ship." He added, as an afterthought, "The problem is not that we don't have enough, but that we have too much."

"Then what do you do with it?"

"It must be used within the system from which it was derived; we have been using the excess to regularize the orbit of Pluto, the outermost. It is small in mass as planetary bodies go, but it is sufficient. Understand we do not do anything radical to it. And what we do is not very obvious. Mevlannen can tell you that, I believe."

Mevlannen agreed. "For a year I watched, compared, made calculations; the change we have put into it will not be sensible enough to read for thirty years."

Morlenden started to speak, but the moment passed, and Pellandrey turned again to lead them through the maze of corridors. They went through another series of junctions, nodes, at last a dim nexus of five passages. Pellandrey stopped before a large, metal hatch set into the bulkhead, secured with threaded T-handles about the perimeter. There was no legend on the hatch, but in a place of curtains and easily sliding panels, such a doorway could only have one meaning: *Keep out*. Pellandrey bent and began to unfasten the handles, methodically, one at a time. When he finished, he turned back to them, hand on the hatch, poised to push it inward.

Mevlannen said, "I cannot pass within, if Sanjirmil is now there."

Pellandrey asked, "And why so?"

"We are enemies; long ago we made a pact. I thought that it would not come to a meeting again, so I agreed. Outside, in the forest, alone, one on one, I would take my chances, but here, in the seat of her power, I would fear. I cannot enter; I will be attacked on sight."

"Just so. She is there. But you came for a judgment, so you must enter, else we hear and decide in the place where we stand. To judge is most serious; would you have us settle the matter like conspirators behind the warehouse, skulkers in the alley?"

Morlenden said, "I ask that it be here, if Mevlannen so wishes. I am her sponsor in any event—it is my argument."

Pellandrey shrugged. "Very well. Speak."

Morlenden did not waste time with formalities, saying, "You know the history of the Perklarens, so we need not recite it; you also know whence came Krisshantem, here, and what his course had been, and your own part in it. Thus, and thus. These two are of suitable age, and both possess valuable knowledge that must not perish. I ask that they be declared *shartoorh* here and designated to weave upon maturity in their own Braid."

Pellandrey turned a cold, steady gaze on Morlenden. "You already know too much, Morlenden Deren. And what will be their role? What will they do?"

Morlenden pressed on, not turning at all from what he came for. "I confess that my original intent had been to resurrect the thrust of the course Maellenkleth had been on, but I see now that such would be folly. Therefore I ask that they be called Ṣkazen, lore-masters, those who know and those who remember. Too long have we left that function to elders who will answer to none."

Pellandrey turned a little, avoiding them all with his expressionless eyes. He seemed to look into a distance, weighing imponderables. After a time, he said, "There is much consequence to this. I see, I know; ripples in time across the centuries; there will be the usual objections."

"It is against just such that I strive here, Pellandrey Reven. These two have earned what I ask."

"I know, I know; just as had Maellenkleth. Even as I steered her for my own reasons, I recited arguments to myself upon why I could not do what she asked in the end. And had it come to a Dirklaren Braid . . . I do not know. We cannot spend much time on would-have-been's."

"Very well. This petition, then, on its own weight."

The Reven looked now intently at both, Mevlannen and Krisshantem. He asked, "You two are known to one another? And do you agree to this?" They both nodded agreement, moving closer together instinctively.

"Whose idea was this? Let it speak now."

Morlenden said, "Mine, but only of late."

"There will be a price. Will you two agree to pay it?"

Again they nodded. Pellandrey said, "The ritual is inappropriate for the circumstances. Therefore I do exercise that right which is mine by inheritance. So be the request of Morlenden Deren, let none here forget it until the end of time."

Mevlannen and Krisshantem looked at each other with shining faces. Pellandrey added, grimly, "Do not forget the price among the rejoicing of new-lovers, as I see you have become." They turned back to him. "And my price is thus. Mevlannen, I lay a prohibition upon you for the peace of the people: you and all your descendants hereafter will be forbidden the Game, Outer and Inner. Krisshantem, you and all your descendants hereafter will make your dwelling place in the heart of the most dense habitation among us. When we build cities, there you shall go. And last I invoke a tradition, which may not be contravened, upon both of you. It has been the practice of the past that *shartoorh* do not know one another, or at the least, as little as possible. Thus henceforth you shall live separately until your fertility commences. This means one of you must leave the *yos* of the Derens. Now you know the weight of it. Decide."

Mevlannen spoke before any of them. "It will be me."

"Very well. . . . You were to give the matrix to Maellenkleth. Who has it?"

"Morlenden Deren carries the matrix to Sanjirmil."

"So, then. You two will depart from this place to the common room. Never stand before this door again."

They lingered for a moment, as if trying to think of something to say, but nothing came; and at last they turned together, and, Mevlannen leading the way, made their way into one of the ascending corridors, fading into the dimness.

Again the sound of the Ship returned to them. An odd silence, broken at intervals by distant, faint sounds of continuing construction; faint, unintelligible voices, hammering. Pellandrey waited, until he was sure that Mevlannen and Krisshantem had passed from hearing. Then he turned back to the massive hatch, saying to those remaining, "This is Prime. You might wish to say control room, or bridge, or perhaps quarterdeck, recalling the sailing ships of old. Within here is the Inner Game. Follow me."

He ducked and stepped over the high sill into it; Morlenden and Fellirian followed. Pellandrey closed and dogged down the hatch behind them.

Morlenden and Fellirian stood quite still for a time, trying to relate what they saw to something they knew. They could see immediately that they were in a circular room, roofed by a low, broadly domed ceiling about two hundred feet across. The floor was an inverted, shallow truncated cone, descending to a central pit. They were on a wide ledge that circled the chamber.

Morlenden saw, but he could not assemble it into a meaningful picture. It was too alien. Nothing in the room related to anything he had seen before.

If Morlenden had not known what to expect, Fellirian's problem was that she knew too much. More used to human ways of doing things, she expected a control room to contain dials, screens, banks of instruments, lights, indicators, windows, portholes, levers, knobs. Considered in that light, it was an austere, bare, and enigmatic room.

Above the platform, there was only the ceiling dome, a Game display, made of some dull translucent material that did not reflect any of the light from the floor. And at odd intervals around the sloping walls of the cone leading to the pit, there were small recesses spotted here and there, each fitted with comfortable reclining chairs. Beside each were small panels, containing a few indicator lights, some empty receptacles, a button board. Steps recessed into the material of the sloping sides led to these from the pit floor. There was the actual control; there were four identical consoles, with their operators' chairs, also recliners, tilted back, so the occupants could see the ceiling at all times. The chairs were actually luxurious cradles, surrounded on both sides by massed banks of keyboards, very much like the Game control keyboards of the Outer Game except that there were many more of them, enormous curved banks of keyboard strips and panels of tiny buttons, arranged on both sides of the recliners within arm's reach, not in front or behind.

Above, the dome was dimly lit; only the central portion seemed to be active, about a fifth of its entire area. The only other lighting in the room came from small lamps over each keyboard bank, and panels in the narrow strip between domed ceiling and conical pit. The recesses were all empty; the operators' positions were filled. They did not seem to be overly exerting themselves.

The four in the pit appeared to be late adolescents by appearance, reclining in their operators' cradles, all with both hands moving steadily over the banks of keyboard controls, not hurriedly, but steadily and deliberately, touching here, gliding, pausing there, always moving on; and they never

took their eyes off the ceiling for an instant, always keeping
the living, changing, ceaselessly permutating display above
their heads in sight. At the same time, though serious at their
work, there was also a casual air to it as well, a watchful
casualness, as if they were doing something easy and long-
practiced. Each wore about their heads a light, lacy frame-
work, which supported tiny earplugs and a microphone
before their lips. And if the visitors on the deck above them
watched very closely, they could see, from time to time, their
lips moving ever so slightly; and when one spoke, the others'
eyes would follow to a particular spot in the display above.
The movements of their hands would change in rhythm, in
scale, and somehow, something would change in the display.
Neither Morlenden nor Fellirian could spot what changes
took place—the Inner Game was simply too fast-moving.
Morlenden found his inadvertent indoctrination as an Outer
Player to be of no help at all.

One below nodded, spoke into the microphone. The others
nodded, too, and it seemed that a moment of watchfulness
had passed.

Morlenden whispered to Fellirian, "Yonder lies Sanjirmil.
On the right hand, to the rear. I would recognize her anywhere; her hair has a dusty blue sheen that even this half-
light cannot obscure."

"Indeed. And that must be her Braid, with her."

Pellandrey, overhearing them, agreed. "Yes. The Ter-
klarens-to-be. Tundarstven, her *Toorh*, to her left; in front,
Sunderlai and Leffandel, Srith and Tlanh. Both were *Thes*."

Sanjirmil's *Toorh* wore a gray homespun overshirt, plain
and austere, with a light woolen cloak against the chill air of
the Ship. Sunderlai, a rounded, soft-girl with a childish face,
wore one in pale blues, shadings in shadowed snow. Leffandel
wore brighter colors, with a brown cloak. Sanjirmil wore
black; her overshirt was of the color of night, broken by
short, vertical strokes in curvings of stark white. Her cloak
was of leather, lined inside in dark gray, of a lusterless black.

Pellandrey said softly, "Morlenden, you spoke of judgment; say what you must now."

"Little more than a month ago," he began. "the Perwathwiy Srith came with an offer of gold, that we would find Maellenkleth, determining along the way what became of her.
We have done so, as far as we have been able." And he began to tell what he had laboriously put together, the whole
tale, how there had been enmity and rivalry between Mael-

lenkleth and Sanjirmil, how the younger girl, disenfranchised
by the onrushing weight of consequences, had been driven
from the one thing she did best of all, and how Sanjirmil, a
poor Player at best, had by the same consequences inherited
the Inner Game. He told how Maellenkleth had planned to
challenge her rival, and how an already poor relationship had
deteriorated into open hositility, and how Sanjirmil had inten-
tionally sent Maellenkleth on a fool's errand, knowing she
would be captured. He told Pellandrey how Maellenkleth
died, and what she told him as she did. And he spoke of
other things as well, of veiled threats, of an arrow, of a creature of the forest who haunted his steps. And at last he said,
"And now I am come to this place for judgment against her
for all that I have said. I will stand for the truth of what I
have alleged."

Pellandrey looked at the ceiling dome for a long time, saying nothing. His hands gripped the rail tightly, as he leaned
his weight upon it for support.

At last he turned to Morlenden and Fellirian, saying, "We
already know of the uproar over the instruments. Sanjirmil
herself told us that much after her visit, with Perwathwiy, to
your *yos*. So much we could verify ourselves, and so we
made appropriate plans. I suppose as she knew we would."

"Then you agree that I must have this judgment?"

Pellandrey glanced wearily to the place where lay Sanjirmil, controlling the Inner Game, the Zan. "In principle, I
agree, concur, all the way. But I am not free to act in this,
and I cannot render judgment to you."

"Why not?"

"Because I myself am not entirely without blame in all
this; and as you have accused Sanjirmil, then so must you accuse me, for much of this would have been prevented. Could
have been. It is a most long story; will you stay a while to
hear it?"

"We will," they said.

"Very well. In your tale, you said what Mevlannen told
you, and what you had put together. So you will remember
that the Ship activated on its own fifteen, a fourteen and one,
years ago? Very good. What you do not know and have not
known until now is what happened on that day. Now I will
tell you and you will see."

"The Ship was not active then, so we only maintained a
watch here, not a flying crew. But there were hours in the

day when we used the display, which was completed, for the training of the novices. That it was complete should have warned us, but it did not. We kept our eyes too close to the old plan. And so on that day, there was a student at the controls, with two elders giving her additional instruction; she needed all the extra she could get, for she wasn't good at the Game at all; in fact, we were despairing of ever getting her up even to novice level. But she was a fighter, and she persisted, where others would have given up and accepted their true role. Where others *had* given up in the past history of the Game. So there was an extra session. Perwathwiy and Trethyankov were making her pretend she was flying solo, one of the emergency procedures. She had just taken the controls, was not even properly prepared to control, and the activation commenced. There was no warning, no symptom, nothing. One minute a working board seemingly connected to nothing, the next live. She, the poor girl, thought it was an exercise Perwathwiy had dreamed up, and she was determined not to fail, even though she knew that she would. She could never catch on to the way of it. So she took command and ordered Perwathwiy and Trethyankov to their places. But they knew, already. The ship was starting to move. By a supreme effort of will, the elders managed to get her steered in the right direction. Then Trethyankov died. Of shock, of strain, of fear ... who knows? Then Perwathwiy collapsed of the strain of it, passing out completely. The girl flew on, now much too busy even to notice. She knew she was alone, solo, in the real thing, at last; she knew she couldn't do it, but she had to, for there was no one to call. All she could do was hold on until the changing of the watch, on the hope that some Player would happen by the sensor control and relieve her. She had no hope ... but she had nerve and a fierce will to survive, to win, to prove to the people that she could, when they needed her. And so she did. Alone. Trethyankov, of course, did not revive. Perwathwiy would come back to consciousness, but would be beaten down each time, over and over again, by the combined assault of the living display and the voice of the girl-student, which was by now full Command-override Multispeech.

"And so it continued. We knew what had happened, for when the Ship activated, it sealed itself. Those who were in were in to stay. As it was, it was a full day before anyone thought to look in here. They were immediately struck down, just as had been Perwathwiy. She had built a wall about herself, and no one could enter here to relieve her. At last, a combination of earplugs and iron discipline allowed an emergency crew of four to take it from her, remove her, and start flying properly.

"She had to be physically overpowered with great violence, and after it was done, she, too, collapsed. Three days she had flown solo in a task that takes four people, without food or water. She was raving, hysterical, and quite mad. Utterly insane. For a year she lay as one dead. Perwathwiy took nearly as long to recover. We cared for the girl, for we all were deep in her debt; she had done the impossible. But we could not effect a cure. The wall still stood. Not even a battery of Speakers could break her. She was impervious. And after a long time, a year, she came out of it, of her own, seeming normal, and possessed a great skill in the Game, albeit a heavy-handed skill that none of us liked. And so with care we brought her back to this room in short stages, gradually letting her fly again, with a crew of elders who had been most carefully selected. During that time we also tried, from time to time, to get into her mind by Multispeech, to see if she was sane again. But she would never allow it. In fact, some of those who tried did not return from the attempt."

Morlenden shuddered. "And so the girl was Sanjirmil. . . ."

"Exactly. And we were all wrong to let her back into it, in this place, for we came to depend on her. This, here, is not a thing you can get a replacement for off the path outside. Even among the theorists. And so I was wrong, too, for having been a part of allowing it to happen. When Maellenkleth came along, I sought to bend Sanjirmil to my way by the threat of the return of Maellenkleth. Yes, of course it was Sanjirmil who sent her to capture, disminding, death. I would even suspect her of leaving none of it to chance. She doesn't in anything else."

Fellirian said, "But you cannot let her go unpunished!"

Pellandrey answered. "It is not me who lets her go in any condition. She has solidified her position, of course, and in matters of flying is the sole arbiter, not I. My charter has diminished greatly. And even if I had the power to do as you wish, I would likely not, for she cannot now be replaced. And still there is no one who can use Command-override on her. She has built a defense against it. There are few who could dare her physically, and none who could do both at once and neutralize her. . . . You have only confirmed what our worst fears were, laid on the last line."

Morlenden said, heatedly, "No one will dirty their hands, is that it? Then I will. I'll go down there now and give it to her with a bark still on it."

Pellandrey said, "I would have you do it, but you do not realize what you face. Others have done the very acts you say you will do. They are not among us now; do you understand that? You saw the amber plain. You saw what was on it. That is what happens to those who have tried: cast into limbo. Down deep in her mind she is still reliving the three days when it was Sanjirmil against the living, ongoing pattern of the universe. And won. But the price was her sanity, and unlike all others, she will not permit a cure. If she did, it would be to return to the old self, and the pride that drove her to survive is too fierce for that. Believe me. I know these things. I am a fourteenth-degree master of Multispeech, and of single violence. I tried. Command-override Multispeech with the most skillful assault I could muster. For my pains, I, too, was cast forth like a leaf in the wind. And there I remained for a long time, or so it seemed to me. There I wandered in the silences of a dead place out of space and out of time, still defending myself against an enemy who was not even interested enough to appear. At last I was permitted to return. I knew then what we had on our hands."

Morlenden said, "I saw that place. Why couldn't you just use the Game controls when she is off-shift and block it, or move it away?"

"Because it is not under the control of the Game; out of space and out of time. When you go there, you may exit, if you do at all, before you entered it. Or perhaps the same instant. Or perhaps centuries later. It is not a place in the universe, speaking analytically and strictly; it is a place built by the part of her mind that never sleeps and never stops playing. It is, in short, a place which is under her absolute control. You have the visual reference matrix in your memory; give it to her and make no attempt on her. I have warned you of the consequences."

Fellirian said, "It would seem to me that you have put yourself in a most unpleasant dilemma: you cannot keep her for the poison that is in her, and you cannot throw her away because she has become *Huszan*, the master of the Game. If you persist in this she will undoubtedly lead you into courses not foreseen by those who planned this venture. She will take a vehicle of life and make of it an instrument of death, of conquest. I have seen much of the forerunner world beyond the reservation; I do not care for the way they run it. But even less would I care to see Sanjirmil in her present condition made ruler of it all."

"At present, she remains true to the original program. Part of her is still with us. We use that part to guide the rest of her. But all this has complicated our task immeasurably. For instance, there is the matter of takeoff time. When we found out about the instruments, and saw the increase in investigative activity, we knew we would have to move things up."

Morlenden interjected, "And she told me there was no time to wait, when I said we had the rest of our lives!"

"Exactly. We did not know the cause of the event then, but our response to its consequences was plain enough: takeoff day had to be moved back, or else the confrontation would come here. As it is, we will just make it barely in time, and for that we have paid a terrible price. . . ."

He was interrupted by the hatch, in which fastening bolts were now unscrewing. Presently the hatch swung inward, and four elders, led by Perwathwiy, stepped over the sealing edge and into Control. Pellandrey turned to her and said, "It was as we feared. I was telling them about takeoff day being moved back."

Perwathwiy answered, "Yes, just so. We will all pay for what we allowed to happen. We spent Maellenkleth badly, and for it will receive sorrow. But it goes far beyond us, and into the wider world of the humans."

Fellirian asked, "How so, that?"

"When the plan to leave Earth was devised, it was debated then whether to attempt to rule men by force, or slowly, over the years, build within them, of their own selves, a way that would save them from themselves. It was the latter; after all, we owed our existence to them. This plan, which was to bring their world under control and let it down to a more reasonable level, was to have been complete at about the same time that the Ship was completed. Because, after it activated, the Ship grows itself, and for the estimated population we would have then we would need so much space. Then we would leave and we would have also paid our debt."

Fellirian said, "You say would . . ."

"Just so. Would have been. Not to be, now. We have had to cut it off, to ensure the survival of the people and the values we have nourished."

"But it should be almost complete!" Fellirian said. "Surely

they will have the benefit of that part of it which has been finished!"

"No. Not to be. It was a holistic plan, the only one we could use; they could not be aware of it until it was complete. Absolutely complete, the last step done, in exact sequence. By aborting it as we have done, we have only postponed the reckoning, not put it away. At first nothing will seem amiss. Ten years, fifty, a hundred. More. But from the first, because the weave of the seamless garment was not completed, it will begin to unravel. First a little, then more, then a lot."

Morlenden said, "The result?"

"Ten thousand years of barbarism. Those who come to follow us to space after that, when civilization rises again, will have little, if any, knowledge of these years. They will see the ruins, but they will not understand them."

Morlenden said, haltingly, "Srith Perwathwiy, I am sorry for the news I have brought."

"I knew all along . . . I and the others, we only wished that we might have it proved otherwise. . . . Now you are illuminated, just as we are. And you have come with no better cure than the ones we have already tried and failed. And so now I leave you, to relieve the Terklarens of their shift. I hear that you bring the matrix of Mevlannen. Go ahead and pass it on to her, that we may be the more swiftly on our way." And she turned from them and walked along the ledge until she came to a passage down into the pit, the others silently following her in the dim half-light, like phantoms on a phantom errand. Elders, in overshirts, their hoods pulled up over the heads like cowls . . . they descended into the pit with the motions of familiarity, but with reluctance, too, dragging their steps. They were trapped into an iron sequence of events and were blindly following that track now, though it might lead them all to something unimaginable—doom, unknowable change.

They reached the floor of the pit, joined the Flyers at their keyboards. There was no ceremony, no camaraderie; Perwathwiy went to the main console and spoke briefly with Sanjirmil. Then, taking the headset from her, she slid into the reclining cradle as Sanjirmil slid out of it, both without any wasted motions. It looked easy. But in Morlenden's mind was the knowledge of how many years had gone into those motions.

Now standing, Sanjirmil waited patiently, her head thrown

back, still attentive to the small active section of the Game display being shown in the dome overhead. Perwathwiy from her master's chair now directed the changeover of the rest, minding things carefully while they exchanged places, one at a time. Each slid into place and took up the motions of his predecessor, eyes on the ceiling. Those relieved moved away from their cradles, staring blindly after hours at it. None looked up. And when the new crew was in place and now in control, Perwathwiy's bony, ribbed hands flickered over the master keyboards to either side of her, and in the ceiling over their heads, the full display came on.

A muted white light immediately flooded the entire room, and the ceiling came alive, the whole surface of it, down to the coping along the vertical wall bordering the observation ledge; and the domed ceiling was covered with the same flickering, roiling, permutating endless recursive pattern of a complex and large-scale Game in progress, but moving so fast the untrained eye could not follow it for more than an instant. This array used tiny cells of the triangular tesselation, demarcated by fine black lines, fine as a spider's web. The activity was dense and *busy*: currents of motion flowed through it, forms appeared, coalescing out of others, then dissolving. Others held their existence and their position, but changed in shape constantly. To Fellirian it was a stunning window into hell and chaos, the primal chaos that underlies all appearances of the outer world of trees and rocks and stones and creatures, buildings and power and abstract reasonings. Here was displayed in graphic, visual form, the way things were, at some unknowable and unimaginable microlevel, and there was, to the eye, no meaning to it at all, much less the thought of controlling and manipulating that mighty flow over their heads: it was madness to look at it for more than a second.

Fellirian dropped her head, breathing hard, her breath coming in long sobs that shook her whole body. After a time, she said, simply, "My mind is too small." Morlenden had been staring at it, awestruck, dumb, his mouth hanging open in astonishment, for nothing he had seen during his partial indoctrination into the Game had prepared him for this. At last, he too dropped his head, a dazed expression on his face.

Pellandrey said, "This is the array Mevlannen spoke of, space-three; fine detail-work inside a planetary system. I know you are not Players, so I will not try to point out bodies in the solar system in the display. This display in full is part of changeover; the smaller partial unit is enough to keep the Ship moored, but we must take the larger view every eight hours, just to keep an eye on things."

Morlenden said, "I don't see how you could show me any particular body in that welter—it all looks the same, the same density everywhere."

"It always looks thus. The great Game we tap into in the universe goes on everywhere, source and sink and flow; it is different kinds, different patterns, rather than different densities that determines, in the macrocosm you and I inhabit, just what an object becomes—here, a planet; and there, an unseen flux of energy from a distant galaxy."

"How far can you see in these various display patterns?"

"There is no limit save that which we bring to it—the finite limits of ourselves, imperfect creatures just as all the rest. The greater the area of the display, the more you can do with it. The small partial is sufficient to hold the Ship; we need full to move it out of the planetary system. And of course there are limits to what even a trained mind can handle—it gets too dense. Space-three is only good out to about, say, a parsec. In deep space, with virtual velocities in whole-number multiples of c, we use the higher-order tesselations; space-four, the several fives, the three sixes. Those we use for the most distant viewing."

Fellirian was regaining control of herself once again; she looked to the ceiling display once, then away. The Perwathwiy, down in the pit, sensing that they had seen as much as they could understand at that time, abruptly returned the display program to the reduced section they had first seen when they had come into this place. The light in the control room died back to its previous dimness.

Fellirian said, "And what of time delay? When you look into the distance, do you also see into the far past, as they do with the telescopes?"

"No. The Game has the same time everywhere; everything that we see and everything that we see happening is happening at that instant. That which is here displayed is an absolute universe, not a relativistic one; this is how things are, right now. No matter how far we have pushed it."

She said, "And what of us? What are we to do when Mor's transmission of the matrix to Sanjirmil is complete?"

"We had all hoped that you would rest from your journey here, in the Ship, until the morning. Then we have a decision to make."

"Is time really different in here?"

"Sometimes ... but mostly it's just a manner of speaking. Stay here tonight; there will be time tomorrow."

"Will there be, Pellandrey?"

He hesitated. "Time enough," he said laboriously, "for that which we all must do, painful though it will be. I should have you fresh for that."

TWENTY

In the Game, Symmetry, however and whenever attained, is not lost, nor can it be.
—The Game Texts

And so they all waited along the encircling ledge for the relieved Braid to come up out of the pit to meet them. For a time, Sanjirmil stood close beside the Perwathwiy Srith, by the main console keyboard, apparently answering questions, adding small operator observations. The visitors could not catch the words, nor discern their meaning; the words were inaudible, and accompanied by an odd, but total, lack of bodily gestures; Fellirian inferred from this that Perwathwiy and Sanjirmil were speaking in one or another mode of Multispeech.

And while the leaders conversed, the others began drifting up out of the pit, picking their way along carefully, as if dazed, now that they were free of the strain of flying. They were all visibly fatigued. The younger girl, Sunderlai, in particular, seemed dazed and disoriented by the weight of her past shift at the controls: her attention seemed distracted, her motions as she climbed the stairs almost clumsy. A shame; Sunderlai was a small, delicate girl, of soft, rounded contours, whose skin was the color of whipped honey. The girl was yet just a child, round-faced, pleasant, pretty although not a beauty. But all in all, a healthy, lively young girl. Or would have been. Fellirian could imagine it well enough: selection, unbeknown to the girl herself, then early uprooting from *yos* and homelands, and placement into hard training so that she could fly under the hardest taskmaster of all—Sanjirmil.

The others were not so different. They were all fatigued and distracted. Numb from the long hours at the consoles. In Sanjirmil's insibling, Tundarstven, the effect seemed less pronounced, replaced by something more like a deep indifference. And Sanjirmil turned from her conversation with the Perwathwiy, said something to her insibling that Fellirian did not catch completely, something about the session they had just finished, deep in Inner Game terminology. And the habit of the flying shift was still deep in him, for he turned to her immediately, but his reply, which came after a little pause, was consciously himself and nothing else, accompanied by a little gesture of the hand, signifying indifference. By that little exchange, Fellirian could see the influence Sanjirmil wielded over them; some Daimons could be exorcised only by indifference.

The three others of Sanjirmil's Braid climbed out of the pit, and departed the room immediately through the main hatch. Sanjirmil, last to leave, was now apparently finished with her remarks with the Perwathwiy, and she, too, left the console area, turning away from it, so it seemed, with reluctance and dragging step. She began climbing up to the railed ledge about the pit, shedding as she climbed some but not all of that steely air of control she carried with her when she had been controlling. She, too, was visibly fatigued, but she did not seem disoriented as the others had. Sanjirmil had reserves they had not begun to learn of yet. And as she approached closer, Fellirian noticed the younger girl's eyes in particular; they held a peculiar expression, an almost glassy cast, which upon closer inspection seemed not so much inattention or unfocusing, but an unconscious scanning habit, an almost total reliance on peripheral vision. Of course; she understood: only with trained peripheral vision could they see and respond to the visual field shimmering above them, especially when the full display was on.

Sanjirmil reached the landing, opposite Fellirian. The eerie scanning gaze turned in their direction, took in Pellandrey, Fellirian, Morlenden. She read all their faces instantly, selecting that which she would fix her real attention upon. She knew Pellandrey had nothing new for her. Fellirian she dismissed from the first. A traditional rival Fellirian had been, the loyal insibling, but no more than that.

In the timeless way of all creatures that move about freely, as they faced each other, they took the measure of one another's worth and weight. For her own part, Fellirian felt the

confidence her maturity and parenthood had brought to her—
through the hundreds of decisions she had made therefrom,
the problems solved. She also had her place at the Institute to
support her as well. She knew herself to be a person of consequence. But Sanjirmil possessed an enormously strong will, a
ferocious directional vector, and of course the deception of
her insanity; she was convinced she was right. And here, in
this place, she had the power of her position behind her, for
in effect the Ship was hers. But there was more: Sanjirmil
possessed an almost terrifying power of sexuality. Fellirian
could seense it, could almost feel the waves of it buffeting her,
waves of pure body. Extreme, perverse. Fellirian had never
met a girl before possessed of such a raw force, such a
strength of it.

Sanjirmil approached her slowly. Fellirian watched her
come, powerless to run, or to turn her aside. Seen from the
ledge, when she had been reclining in her control cradle, the
dark clothing Sanjirmil wore had been hardly more than a
distraction, but here, close, on equal level, Fellirian saw the
figure coming toward her, impressively dressed in stone black,
broken only by thin lines of white. Their eyes met, focused,
locked on; the glassy, unfocused look in Sanjirmil's eyes
faded, being replaced by a disturbingly direct gaze of naked
will, corrosive ability, unlimited malice. It was a gaze that
burned. Fellirian instinctively looked away, breaking first,
protecting herself from something she sensed was far beyond
her abilities to subdue.

She spoke, almost involuntarily. "Morlenden has the matrix
from Mevlannen."

Sanjirmil nodded, shifting her gaze back to the scanning
mode, as if it had been no more than what she had been expecting to hear. And now she faced Morlenden, fixing him
with that same disturbing gaze. He saw her much as had Fellirian, but deeper, too, for this fey, dangerous creature, almost out of control of all of them together, this girl in black,
had once been known to him; and had sat not an arm's
length away in a silent room, with him. But now she was at
her time, at her full maturity, at the summit of her powers,
secure in her own place, and he felt the strength of her rather
more acutely than had Fellirian.

Sanjirmil's working overshirt was limp from the hours she
had spent at the console-keyboard in the pit, and through it,
the angular, primitive contours of her body showed easily.
Along her face and neck and forearms, the only exposed

parts, the warm streaky tone was more obvious; a hard, burnished olive along the lines of bone and tendon; soft, dull rose in the softer hollows. Wiry and yet ripe, too, erotic without comment, where others of this color were only lovely, or attractive. He thought that perhaps this effect was due to the shape; for Sanjirmil did not follow the rather undifferentiated unisex shape of the typical ler girl, flat-chested and narrow-hipped, but was closer to the ancient human shape, with its curves, hollows, fullnesses, increased sexual differentiation. And Morlenden was aware that even tired from a full shift at the master console, her body could still evoke responses in himself, even after the great change. He felt intimidated, demanded upon.

He sensed hostility in her, not well concealed, under the drive and power she projected. It was not a hostility of envy now, however it might have been in the beginning; now it was a hostility of arrogance, contempt, hubris, nurtured, for all too long, by too much responsibility piled on by accident, in one by nature not prepared for it. There was no cure for it, he saw as had Pellandrey; circumstances had worked their evil magic upon them all, just as they had with others and their plans, dreams. Morlenden did not doubt whatsoever that whatever strange creatures shared the universe with human and ler, they also had faced the same dilemmas; indeed, just now, somewhere else, some *thing* was facing the problems they faced, or something similar. Morlenden felt a sudden surge of sympathy for the unknown beings; for he did not like the weight of it. He felt it acutely; too acutely. There was something lurking in the back of his mind, something just out of sight, something enlarging this meeting with Sanjirmil into something more than what it was. . . . And what could he say to her in reproof that Pellandrey had already not tried? He searched; there was nothing he thought he could add; yet there was this anticipation growing in him. It was most curious, as an emotion; for he now had no real desire to see Sanjirmil again, certainly not with a lover's zest and zeal; but it felt something like that. But alien, too, as if there were more components to it.

She was before him now; and he could see her as through an enlarging glass, with an immanence and a terror. As with all strong-natured ones, she possessed a roiled, complex, turbulent persona, further stirred by a stormy, disturbed sequence of memories. She might well be insane; Morlenden was certain that her memory would be all the clearer for it.

Empathetic, he reached with his instincts, a gestalt perception of her, projected outward and continually verified by the reality of the ever-present *now*. Yes, he could see it, in the larger-than-life figure before him, coming closer, closer, close enough to reach out and touch, although he knew not if he dared, now. Yes, he could see it: Sanjirmil had been a tomboy, *Dantlanosi*, wiry, strong, aggressive; she had preferred to do it standing up, under a cool bridge in the rain, quick and hard, no quarter asked, none given, a hot and sweaty, piercingly sweet embrace and coupling.

That was her nature; but it has all been taken from her by the accident that had made her a Player, but also a monster. What was left was the intense inwardness of the insibling, but now, of course, greatly magnified out of proportion. Once she had had the same chance at the rude freedoms of the adolescent as the rest of them, the easy and casual promiscuity, the relaxed and lazy affairs that came with time and the twenties. But she had not had them; instead, Sanjirmil had known a terrible stress, and won; but at what price? And somewhere in her was the knowledge, carefully hidden from obvious surfacing, that as with all insanities, the price for return did not stay fixed but slowly and inexorably grew ever larger. He knew that she would not return normally, of her own will, now. Now? Now there remained only the matrix to pass to her, and perhaps a few words, now that he knew. Yes, perhaps that was the sense of apprehension he felt. He would have Sanjirmil in a position of weakness when she was receiving; perhaps then he could . . . deflect her from her course, nudge her aside by a reference to their shared memories, their past?

He spoke first. "I have brought the matrix from Mevlannen, to you as directed. Are you ready to receive?" And as he spoke to her, he felt a wild surge of anticipation, quite out of character, and he did not understand why he should feel so exultant, so . . . wild. What the hell was happening to him? The room began to shrink, to converge, to focus on himself, Sanjirmil. *What was happening?* Whatever it was, he felt increasingly powerless to change the course of things. A wild abandon took him, whispering in his inner ear, *Let it be! Let what will come to pass, so come to pass. You will like it and ride willingly with it into the future!*

Sanjirmil answered simply, softly, with a voice betraying deep fatigue: "So I have waited, knowing the time to have come for the integration of Game and matrix. Speak on, then, messenger. *Deskris* . . . I await you."

Her eyes ceased scanning, found Morlenden's, locked on
them. Morlenden began, and it was easy, for all he had to do
was remember the sequence Mevlannen had inserted in him,
recall it and let it go. There was no composition on his part
at all; just remember and release. Easy. And the wild anticipation in his heart leaped up like a wildfire, exulting. *Almost
there*, it seemed to say, *almost there, and the moment will be
within this scene.* He sang the sequence softly to her, slowly,
feeling, inexpertly, how she as receiver was leaning slowly
into his influence, becoming a part of him, an extension of
himself. All the result of Multispeech, of course; but also a
lot of the relationship went into it, too. She was letting Morlenden take over part of her because she trusted Morlenden
as she trusted no one else in the world. And he saw on the
edge of his perceptions that somehow the feral glow was fading out of her eyes, the tense set of her harsh, angular face,
once loved violently and intensely. There were other, familiar
emotions beginning to show upon it, and something she heard
and recognized, something she could say she truly knew as
no one else did. These new emotions flickered over the harsh
but softening face, like firelight over a raw, new stone wall.
Her thin lips were tensed and white with concentration, as
she reached for the more subtle nuances of the matrix, integrating it as she went.

And the string of matrix numbers suddenly ended, ran out;
there had been no warning, no anticipation, nor was there for
what replaced them: Morlenden found himself speaking,
quite involuntarily, in the strongest Command-override he
had ever heard. Sanjirmil's ego defenses, her will defenses,
against outside control by Multispeech Command-mode were
not down, but they had been relaxed to the point where they
might as well have been. The sudden assault, which took
Morlenden by as much surprise as it did Sanjirmil, battered
down her will, hammered it flat, beat it down, and began
reaching for the central node inside her mind that would
make her sane; yes, sane, as it also killed her from inside. His
voice echoed and boomed in his head like the voice of a god,
probing, tearing, reaching. And an image of Mevlannen, who
was saying, *Sorry about the compulsion, Morlenden. I
warned you that we'd cheat you. I knew who sent Mael to
her death, but I would never get close enough to do it myself.
But you would, and here you are now. And now extract our
revenge! Destroy this thing before you. It can't be cured, it
can only be killed, and from the inside. NOW!*

So here was the source of the anticipation, the exultation, that he had been feeling as the moment approached; not himself at all, but a compulsion Mevlannen had set into him as she had herself passed the matrix to him. Morlenden hesitated, for as much as he wished to avenge Maellenkleth, he had never attained malice toward Sanjirmil. Only anger. And now, that hesitation almost became the end of him, for although Morlenden still had inhibitions, even to the resistance of Mevlannen's compulsion, Sanjirmil had no such inhibitions whatsoever. And he was about to find that where survival was at stake, she could shed fatigue like a pine tree shedding raindrops in a sudden wind.

In the instant he had argued with himself, hesitated, fought the compulsion, his attention had dropped off Sanjirmil. And now she recovered from the Multispeech assault upon her. And he lost belief in the program Mevlannen had set into him, and now the words became just words, falling off Sanjirmil harmlessly. The room winked out in his perceptions, and was replaced with a boundless darkness. He could imagine, but not see, Sanjirmil, gathering herself, recovering, now rising to strike back. He moved hesitantly. He was in great danger, he knew, and began looking for a way he could defend himself against the approaching counterattack.

And a voice shouted at him from all sides: *So it was to be you after all, was it? It was just as I feared the day I came with Perwathwiy: you would unravel the long string and turn against me, too, as have all the rest. Well, then, you have come so far; so witness what others who have tried came to see. Some are there yet. You will join them.*

And instantly the furry darkness was replaced with the abstract plain he had glimpsed before. Only now he was standing on the surface, dazed, disoriented, looking about. There was no one there but him. A brown, flat plain, illuminated by a wan, amber, sourceless light, arrowed off into infinity, a horizon that seemed staggeringly far away. Sanjirmil had dropped Morlenden into her own private limbo.

He forced himself to think, not to panic and run, which he was sure the others had done. Run wildly, as they had done, and he knew death would come from a thousand directions, in unknowable ways. He had to think. Morlenden looked at the "ground." It seemed faintly etched with parallel lines, which he could follow, now that he saw them, off to the horizon. Then there was something regular about this place, after all. And he knew that this limbo was Game-generated, by

Sanjirmil, but part of some Game program still. He forced
himself to remember all that he had learned from Krisshantem, to try to find a way out. He began, hesitantly, vocalizing
short bursts of Game language, in Command-mode. At first,
nothing happened, but with one segment there was a sudden
wavering of the brown horizon. Yes. His heart leaped. Yes!
He could pull this limbo down and walk out of the ruins. He
probed at it again.

Now a spot developed, just off-center in his field of vision,
like a migraine spot, a pulsing, wavering blot of black and
bumblebee-yellow, pulsing, growing, writhing into his field of
vision, taking his attention. He increased his efforts. The
patch of yellow and black increased in intensity, and he began to hear a humming in his ears, becoming louder, and at
the same time he began to feel a will pressing hard against
him, harder, harder. . . . The patch of writhing color grew,
becoming immense, covering a third of the scene, and then
suddenly shrank, taking on form, someone . . . and Sanjirmil
materialized out of the patch, with no warning, with a curious, dancelike motion, her leather cloak swirling about her
and settling as she materialized into this strange world with a
faint *pop* of displaced air. And now she stood only feet away,
dressed in black, her figure set in a posture of dire menace,
slowly approaching him, slightly circling.

"Ho, Morlenden!" she challenged him. "You are more resourceful than I thought. A Player, no less! How did you come
by it?"

He faced her, ceasing for the moment his efforts to break
the walls of limbo. "The same way I came to attack you,
Sanjir. Things have been put into me that I did not ask for."

"I know Mevlannen set a compulsion in you; things like
that leave traces, like the scent of the hunter on his traps."

"Krisshantem set a program of an Outer Player into me.
And I see the light, with it. I'm going to pull down this hell
you've made."

"I don't doubt for a minute you would, if I let you. You
are the first to realize it could be done, although far better
Players have come here . . . and failed. That is why I come in
person. What must be done . . . but you know that. Can you
dissuade me before I . . . ?"

"Dissuade you? I don't intend to. Keep your distance, or I
will reactivate the destruction program of Mevlannen. I know
you are powerful, Sanjir, but you cannot cover both ends."
And without warning, he slipped into Command-override,

trying the instructions of Mevlannen again, but this time with belief and a deep sense of self-preservation behind them as well. Sanjirmil was unprepared for the second attack; she had apparently thought that all she would have to do was enter limbo and dispose of this troublesome stranger. . . . Now she staggered back, her image wavering, the horizon suddenly gone unsteady. She had never caught one like this! He was fighting back! Unthinkable! She exerted a mighty effort that made veins emerge into sharp relief around her forehead, countering in Command-override of her own; and Morlenden again felt himself gripped in the clutches of a monster will. The strange world steadied, as well as her image. And she began circling him, like a wolf, closing slowly. Morlenden also began moving, circling her, keeping up his own song as he went, for he knew that to waver now would be instant termination; he would never return from this place, wherever it was.

He called to her, "Ho, Sanjirmil! I can stalemate you indefinitely! Attack me and I unravel your limbo. Patch up your world-lines and I'll attack *you*."

She replied through a grimace of effort, "Stalemate, you think. There is no time here save my time. I'll wear you down. But know that this is not my heart's desire, Morlen. . . ."

"Speak of heart's desire, then. We have little else to say to one another, it would seem, here, save malice."

"If you will cease fighting me, and join me in my crusade against stupidity, I will share it with you, thus and thus. Share and share alike. You are too good to waste in absurd combat like this."

"Why did you send Maellenkleth out to certain capture?"

"You have said it, therefore you know why. I read the old human story of *Damvidhlan and Baethshevban** and saw my way clear. Maellen fell, of course, to the role of the Great Hurthayyan, or as the forerunners call him, Uriah-the-Hittite. Like him, she was fond, overly fond, of the front of the battle, and like him, she was espoused to a being I coveted, the regard of the rest of the Game community. So I, like Damvidhlan, sent her to the place where it was hottest."

Morlenden interrupted. "It would not be like you to leave a thing like that to chance."

"No," she said sadly. "No chance. I had been cultivating a

*David and Bathsheba

vile agent of the humans, holding him for some extraordinary deed. And there it was. Through him I made sure she was captured. A man named Errat. In the end he became too slippery, and I had to dispose of him. Too dangerous. It is a fearsome thing to deal with humans; they are dangerous ... full of a thousand enmities. Their thoughts subvert one's own, take over, and you become like them. That is why I went out to finish Errat; he was corrupting me."

"Hah!" Morlenden barked. "You corrupted by Errat? I should think it the other way. If you did eliminate him, you did him a favor."

"I shot the arrow at you, to warn you. Do not make me wish to be sorry I missed."

"Not much of a miss, was it? Or do you claim it after the fact? That is a score I must even with you myself: you loosed upon me a weapon that leaves the hand."

"I saw you were coming to it, and would not be deceived by hope. Perwathwiy and the rest I could keep off, for they wanted to believe . . . but I saw the way you were going would lead you to me in the end. I agree it was unwise . . . but you cannot obtain judgment upon me for it, for I have narrowed the field of Players. They need me now, notwithstanding the fact that I am master of the Ship."

"Then you do not need my help." Morlenden turned from her and began unraveling the ends of the strange half-world Sanjirmil had made. She abruptly countered, stabilizing it again, a flush of hot anger radiating from her.

"Stop that! You know not what forces you will release!"

"Since you were caught by the Ship, Sanjir, you have lived by playing upon the unthinkable, that there were things others would not do. I see that. But I will do them, won't I? You have gone too far, and I will stop you."

"Regardless of the cost to the people?"

"Look at what you have cost them already! We were innocent, but evil has entered us, wearing your overshirt, your boots, your leather cape. I do not wish to see this evil carried to the stars, however you will have it."

"Join me, come with me, be my love again as you once were. We fly soon to the new worlds, and I will set you above me when we land, above Pellandrey."

"No."

"You owe him nothing. He stole the heart of your insibling in her *vayyon*, long ago. Yes, I know, though you do not. It was Pellandrey and Fellirian, and it has remained so all these years."

"No. The *vayyon* is the *vayyon*. One can do that. I hold no grudge. Will have none of it. Is it now that you cannot overcome me, so you bring forth these cheap arguments? Indeed you are wavering."

"I do not waver in what must be done. See!" And again Morlenden felt the pressure of her will, beating upon him, relentless as the tide. He felt himself being forced, step by step, move by move, into a crouching posture, an ancient posture of defense. And now she advanced on him, pressing close. Morlenden fought back with all the powers he could muster, defending, picking at the wall that was closing around him, compressing him, closing him in. She stood before him, a figure in dark clothing in the eerie half-light of the amber plain, her hands flexing. "See!" she cried. "It would be so easy to snuff you out. But I am merciful, and something of me still loves you. Desist, oh Morlenden, from your resistance against me; join me. You are worth far more to me as a willing friend than as a vanquished enemy. Anyone can vanquish enemies. It is easy."

In her gloating over her Multispeech powers, and her immense powers as a Player, she had come too close, closed her web of power too closely about Morlenden. He looked at it closely, feeling along its boundaries with his mind, feeling for a line of weakness. She had to have one, somewhere.

She was saying, "My last offer: You have the basic skills, I see. I offer you one half of everything that is mine, the power and the glory. Only say that you will accept me for what I am; for I cannot help that."

"No." Morlenden grimaced, still feeling along her will for a weak point. And he found it. A minuscule crack: her memory of him. It was the one thing that someone else would have easily missed; for she had told no one of their dalliance long ago. Into this crack Morlenden flowed, working his way along the weakened lines of will-force in the web of Multispeech Command-override. And then he was inside her defenses, no longer outside, and he did not hesitate now, for to falter here would mean the end. She wailed, "Nooooo . . ." and he found the node in her mind he was looking for, and turned loose, in all its horrors, the destructive program of Mevlannen, but now under his control. She fought him like a wild beast, and the plain vanished utterly, and he was filled with vertigo, but he did not let go for an instant. She turned

and fied, but Morlenden pursued her like an avenging angel.
He was now pulling himself laboriously through a labyrinth
of insanity, of the whole elaborate network she had built up
over the years. But at last he came to the center, to the central node, the event in her memory that had started it all, the
memory of that time in the Ship, when it had activated and
she had had to face the awful cosmos alone. And Morlenden
saw the basic flaw, reached into it, and repaired it, and
watched the rest, now falling into line after it, readjusting. It
was over. The process was now fixed, unstoppable, and in the
end she would be different. He was sure she would be diminished, though it pained him to reduce her thus.

And they were back in the master Control room, with no
warning, seemingly at the same instant they had left it, only
now he was holding Sanjirmil in his arms, supporting her as
she sank against him, her body heaving with dry sobs that
shook her whole body. Her eyes were closed tightly, and between sobs, she was moving her lips soundlessly, muttering
something. Pellandrey and Fellirian looked at the two of
them, amazed at the change in Sanjirmil, which had seemingly come instantly; one moment she had been master of the
Control room; the next, collapsed in Morlenden's arms.

Pellandrey stepped forward, eyes blazing. "What have you
done to her?"

Morlenden spoke over his shoulder, never taking his eyes
off the girl. "Cured her, that's what. She'll probably never fly
again, but she can remember the basic integration, the matrix
plus the Game-view of the stars, and she can guide you. But
she's disarmed now. I've clipped her wings."

"You fool, do you know what you've done? You've con-
demned us to wait until we can replace her. And we don't
have that much time; the forces she stirred in the human
world will be reaching here within the week, according to our
computations."

Morlenden said, over his shoulder, "If you let this one as
she was lead you to that pass, then you're a fool and deserve
the blame yourself for what happened. She was insane, you
dodo, and she was poisoning all of you, one by one. You let
her get this far; all along the way there were actions you
would not take, and she knew it, read you all perfectly. Until
she had you locked into total dependence on her. God only
knows what she would have done once she lifted the ship off,
in the condition she was in. She'd probably have turned the
whole range of weaponry you have aboard here on Earth and

blighted it. All we want to do is get away clean, not leave a legacy of revenge behind us."

Fellirian agreed with Morlenden. "I follow his argument; if we allowed that to happen, they would never forgive and they would never let it leave their minds. They would reinvent the starship just to hunt us down. I will not have that Daimon pursuing us across space to the ends of the universe."

Morlenden added, "If worse comes, sit in for her yourself. I know she was systematically eliminating potential replacements; but there have to be some left who can take her place. Use them. And make her work for you as an astrogator. You have the leverage now."

Pellandrey answered, after a time, "You are right, of course. I admit the flaw; we have all here been living with it too long, and the rationalizations always come too easy. And so what did you learn from her? What are the crimes of Sanjirmil, in specific?"

Morlenden said, "To punish her further is meaningless. She will flog herself to a shred, now that she has her whole mind back. What more could we do to her that would bring her victims back? What can we add that will strike down other Sanjirmils to come? We can do no more than be ready for them when they come, and stop them then. I will not say what I learned of this one. Let it rest there: you would not judge her and act, because of her position as master of the Game. So I took my case to the Game master, disagreed with her arbitration, and settled the matter with her alone. Proceed with your plan, Pellandrey."

"When I finish telling you what I started to a moment ago, you will not be so kindhearted."

"Pah. I have never been kind in my life. I am being practical."

"Very well, practical. But you will recall that we sensed increased human interest in this site as a result of Sanjirmil's manipulations? That this had interrupted and aborted one timetable, the program we were putting into human society?"

"Yes."

"It interrupted more than that; it also interrupted the orderly growth of the Ship. . . ."

Fellirian put her hands to her mouth, and said, simply, "Oh."

"And the Ship grows only at a certain rate, controlled by the Game. This gives us our basic interior space, which we must then render habitable. We had things tied into our racial birthrate, so that at a certain time, the available space in the Ship would be exactly that required for the whole of the people."

Morlenden said, slowly, "So if the Ship can fly now, it would do so with less room. . . ."

"Exactly. According to what Maellenkleth knew from her own capture, the time was then near. We are actually overdue a departure even now. We must fly next week at the latest, or risk, according to our studies, having to fight our way out. It may be so already, now. And there isn't room for everyone. Do you understand? There isn't room."

"So someone must stay behind?"

"Yes."

"Who?"

"All children and adolescents will go. All elders, except for a handful designated as absolutely essential, will stay behind."

Fellirian said, in a very small voice, "You left out the parent phase."

Pellandrey said, "Some Braids will have to leave two of the parents behind, with the elders."

Morlenden laid Sanjirmil down, very gently, along the floor of the ledge. He straightened, and said, "And who are these Braids? Are they known to you? Better yet, are they known to themselves?"

"Tomorrow we send the runners out, to bring the gathering of the people. We have worked it this way, so the knowledge of role will not be lost: All Braids that carry a number in their surname must cast lots among themselves, or somehow make a decision. And of course, what little government we have will set the example and bite this most bitter bullet."

Fellirian said, "There are only two Braids in the so-called government . . . you and us."

"Yes. Correct. Us, and you. And so now you know, Fellirian Deren; and you are *Klandorh*, so you must decide how you will levy it among yourselves. The Revens have already made their decision. I should have waited until morning to reveal this to you, for morning is a better time for bad news."

Morlenden said, "There is no time for bad news. And you say this will bring the numbers down to what the Ship can carry?"

"Yes. With a little space left over to cover pregnancies that occur along the way. Right now, we do not know how long we will be in space."

Morlenden said, "And what is the decision of the Revens?"

Pellandrey answered, "You do not reveal the crimes of Sanjirmil; neither do I reveal what is already set. You will see which of us leaves the ship grounds, when the Ship leaves. I would have none copy our example, for the sake of copying it; it *is* a hard way, but I have decreed that each so affected must face it themselves. And so you as well."

Fellirian shook her head, as if clearing cobwebs from her eyes. "Then we shall have to return to our *yos*, and there take counsel."

Pellandrey placed his hand on her shoulder. "That is why we asked that you spend the night here, think, and return fresh. It is the kind of thing that we would have none do in a hasty way, for the results will be forever."

Fellirian looked at Pellandrey blankly. "No," she said. And to Morlenden, "I don't know how long, subjectively, you were locked in with Sanjirmil. Can you brave the cold, insibling?"

Morlenden placed his hands together, locked them, and pulled hard on them until his shoulders creaked. Then he straightened, and said, "Tonight it is. Let us return now." And to Pellandrey he said, "When must we be here, and what must we bring?"

"The runners leave tomorrow, and decision must be taken upon the news. Bring your most precious goods, what each can carry with his own hands. And what you can remember, for we will build this world again. That is what will go out with the runners."

She said, "Then we must leave. We will be our own runners. Although I may have to call for help to convince Kaldherman. He will doubtless think it absurd." And she smiled, but it was a weak smile.

Morlenden said, "You may escort us out of this labyrinth, Pellandrey. Although I am sure it will be easier to come and go, now that Sanjirmil's tumor on the body of space-time has vanished back into the no-place from whence she built it."

Pellandrey turned back to the hatch, with heavy step. "Very well. It shall be as you will. Make the choice wisely. There can be no regrets."

And so they left the master Control room. Along the way, Pellandrey met some elders, whom he directed to go to the Control room and care for Sanjirmil. And seemingly in a shorter time than it took them to enter the Ship, they were at the portals of the great Ship, which were now standing open,

as Morlenden had suspected. They walked forth, into the
night, and Fellirian did not look back.

For a time, Pellandrey stood outside, in the cold, clear
night, the stars shining brightly overhead, clear for once
through the haze of the sky of Old Earth.

But when they reached the last point on the trail that they
could look back from, and Morlenden and Fellirian stopped
to look back just once, there was no one to be seen. And they
turned homeward, and began the long walk back, in the dark
and the still cold, breath-steam clouds wreathing their faces.
They were not entirely certain of exactly when the moment
occurred, but after a certain time, they noticed they were
clasping one another's hands tightly as they walked. Morlenden grinned sheepishly at his insibling, and Fellirian looked
back quickly at him, but the expression on her face was not
one which could easily have been read in the chilly darkness.

TWENTY-ONE

Spring, 2610

It was the end of a day that had promised rain, the skies
being filled with ragged, wet-looking clouds, rag-ends of
clouds, all moving by overhead at a fast pace through the
branches which were just now beginning to green out. But
not yet. Not a drop had fallen. The air was heavy,
oppressive, but at the same time filled with promise, for it
had been a dry spring, a late one, too.

Morlenden leaned on his shovel beside a long mound of
fresh earth, and looked off into the distance, as if looking for
a sign. It was darker over in the west than it had been, and it
seemed there was the distant rumble of thunder there, although he couldn't be quite sure; his hearing wasn't quite
what it had been.

For a long time, his thoughts had been quite blank, devoid
of any particular sense of direction; now he let it come again,
reminding him of what else had to be done. Here was Fellirian. Earth aspect; now returned to it, in the spring, under a
hawthorn tree they themselves had planted, how many years

ago. Before Pethmirvin. It didn't matter when, exactly—for the tree had grown to some size, and the branches were drooping with age.

They had not been morbid about the end, when they had talked of it at all; yet under their hopes and fears, somehow they had always assumed that they would be part of some family group, some lodge, when one or the other came to the end. But it was not to have been—in the end, it was just them, living in the same *yos* they had been born in, still marveling they had not tired of each other's company after so many years; she had complained of feeling tired, and had lain down for a nap. And like that, so easily, had sighed, smiled once at Morlenden, and breathed no more. Somehow, he had managed to do what had to be done. There was no one else nearby to help him with it.

Now he remembered it all. How they had returned home, and argued violently through the day, deciding who would go with the children, in the Ship. But there had been no wavering on Fellirian's part, for she had made up her mind on the way home, and would not be budged from it, no matter how Kaldherman had argued, fumed, and stormed about. And so they had agreed that Kaldherman and Cannialin would take the children to the Ship and go with them, and that they would remain behind. And then they had left, and the *yos* had fallen silent.

The insiblings did not go with them, nor did they journey to Grozgor, to see the Ship depart, for it was too painful for them. But they heard it emerge from the hollow place in the mountain, and there were lights in the sky in the northwest, and a distant murmur of sound, and then all was quiet again. The Ship was a full day ahead of the finally mobilized occupation forces, which arrived at the mountain and found only a smoking crater. They had been met there by a small delegation of elders, who politely explained that they were late, and they could do as they liked. Another group had emerged at the Institute, there using what communication facilities were available to spread the word into the forerunner government, explaining exactly, painfully exactly, what had happened. And what must then be done.

It had been a trying period. There had been much change in Seaboard South Region; but there had also been turbulence in other places as well, as the impact of the departure of the Ship and the people had permeated through the levels and bureaus. There had been a great unwillingness to believe that there had been a holistic plan, to pay off the debt to Man for having brought the ler into existence in the beginning. But in the end it had quieted, and the remaining ler and the humans had set out to work together and salvage as much as they could of the original. This had been Fellirian's aim. Vance also returned from the sanctum of 8905, to the Institute, and played a major part as long as he had been able.

Had they been successful? No one could tell, for the momentum of the plan intended for humanity had been so slow and long-ranging that even in a span of sixty years, they could not yet see any sign of change, though they looked constantly. The world had not yet changed in any way they could see. Even those elders most familiar with it could make no predictions, no forecasts. Earth went on much as it had before, only now more cautiously.

Morlenden tried to project in his mind how it must have gone for the children in the sixty-odd intervening years. He could not. Sixty years. In the last meeting with Pellandrey, they had been told that the Ship was expected to be in space less than a year, before they stopped it and began settling a new planet. And then, the resumption of their lives, under strange skies. Or perhaps they might not be so strange. Sixty years. Peth would have woven into another Braid, lived her entire woven period out, and become an elder, living somewhere else. He found it hard to imagine. For him, things remained as they had been in 2550. Morlenden shook his head. He knew these things to be true, but all the same he could not see them.

At last, he straightened, plucking his shovel out of the ground, and started back to the *yos*. Yes, he thought he could hear the mumbling of distant thunder off in the west, which had grown very dark now. He stored the shovel in the tool closet, under the overhang of the back of the *yos*, and made his way around to the front. He climbed the stairs to the entry, pausing to remove his boots before entering the *yos*, an action he had performed so many times it was almost automatic now. He moved slowly. Age was beginning to catch up with him. It was hard to bend over. And as he finished, and was just straightening back to a standing position, one hand on the wooden railing, he felt a very cold and very fat raindrop impact on the back of his neck, sending a little shock wave of shivers through his body. Morlenden smiled in spite of himself. Yes. She'd be pleased. He looked out over the yard. The wind was up, whispering in the trees. There was an odor of ozone in the air, a promise of another season of growth. He understood the symbol: life goes on. Yes. He understood completely. He turned and went into the *yos*, and began laying out a fire for supper.

DAW PRESENTS MARION ZIMMER BRADLEY

"A writer of absolute competency . . ."—Theodore Sturgeon

☐ **THE HERITAGE OF HASTUR**
"A rich and highly colorful tale of politics and magic, courage and pressure . . . Topflight adventure in every way."—Analog. "May well be Bradley's masterpiece."—Newsday. "It is a triumph."—Science Fiction Review.
(#UW1189—$1.50)

☐ **DARKOVER LANDFALL**
"Both literate and exciting, with much of that searching fable quality that made **Lord of the Flies** so provocative."—**New York Times**. The novel of Darkover's origin.
(#UY1256—$1.25)

☐ **HUNTERS OF THE RED MOON**
"May be even more of a treat for devoted Bradley fans than her excellent Darkover series . . . sf adventure in the grand tradition."—Luna. (#UY1230—$1.25)

☐ **THE SHATTERED CHAIN**
"Primarily concerned with the role of women in the Darkover society . . . Bradley's gift is provocative, a top-notch blend of sword-and-sorcery and the finest speculative fiction."—Wilson Library Bulletin.
(#UW1229—$1.50)

DAW BOOKS are represented by the publishers of Signet and Mentor Books, THE NEW AMERICAN LIBRARY, INC.